SPELLBREAKER

Severe dyslexia kept Blake Charlton from reading fluently until he was twelve. Ten years later he graduated summa cum laude from Yale University. He has been an English teacher, a biomedical technical writer and a learning disability tutor and currently attends Stanford University School of Medicine.

By Blake Charlton

Spellwright
Spellbound
Spellbreaker

Spellbreaker

BLAKE CHARLTON

HARPER
Voyager

Harper*Voyager*
An imprint of HarperCollins*Publishers*
1 London Bridge Street,
London SE1 9GF

www.harpercollins.co.uk

This paperback edition 2016
1

First published in Great Britain by
Harper*Voyager* 2016

Map by Rhys Davies

A catalogue record for this book is
available from the British Library

ISBN: 978 0 00 736891 4

Printed and bound in Great Britain by Clays Ltd, St Ives plc

MIX
Paper from
responsible sources
FSC
www.fsc.org FSC® C007454

What would an ocean be without a monster lurking in the dark? It would be like sleep without dreams.

—WERNER HERZOG

Where there is a monster, there is a miracle.

—OGDEN NASH

Every night and every morn
Some to misery are born.
Every morn and every night
Some are born to sweet delight.

—WILLIAM BLAKE

PART 1

To test a spell that predicts the future, try to murder the man selling it; if you can, it can't. That, at least, was Leandra's rationale for poisoning the smuggler's blackrice liqueur.

On a secluded beach, they knelt and faced each other across a seaworn bamboo table. Above, a clear night sky crowded with stars and two half-moons. To Leandra's left, a grove of slender palms, crosshatched moonshadows, short green grass. To her right, an expanse of dark seawater and lush limestone formations known as the Bay of Standing Islands.

Leandra's catamaran rocked between two such limestone formations that rose narrow from the bay but widened into craggy rock, vines, and ferny cycads. "Mountains on stilts," her illustrious father had once called the standing islands.

Across the table, the smuggler cleared his throat. Leandra, using several intermediaries, had agreed to meet him on this beach east of Chandralu. Both parties had asked that names not be used; however, as was the way of such meetings, neither party had asked that homicidal duplicity not be used. So Leandra picked up the smuggler's porcelain bottle of blackrice liqueur. Calmly she poured the ambercolored spirit into his wooden cup.

He was watching her every action, but it was too late. She had already drawn a needle from her sleeve and held it against the bottle's neck so the liqueur poured over its poisoned point. Then she filled her own cup, knowing the toxin had washed off.

The smuggler was a handsome man of middle years—flawless black skin, black goatee chased with silver, wide nose, large eyes. He wore a blue lungi and loose white blouse as if he were of the Lotus People, but his posture was laxer, his speech quicker than was polite in Lotus culture.

Also notable, the smuggler had wrapped a cloth around his head to conceal the spell he was selling. In places, a crimson glow shone through the headwrap. Because Leandra perceived some divine languages as red light, the glow suggested that the man was what he claimed to be—which is to say the kind of man that filled Leandra with hatred so molten hot that it would transform any sensible woman into an eye-gouging, throat-biting whirl of violence. Fortunately, Leandra was not a sensible woman.

She lifted her cup with one hand and flicked the needle away with the other. The smuggler did not hear it strike sand. "To your future," she said.

"To your future," he echoed. Blank expression.

With one draft, Leandra downed her blackrice liqueur. It was a fragrant, gratuitously alcoholic substance. The Lotus People called it mandana and drank it when conducting religious ceremonies or business transactions. Having lived in the Ixonian Archipelago for thirteen years, Leandra had drunk gallons of the stuff without becoming accustomed to it. She wondered if anyone ever did.

The mandana traveled down her throat as liquid and up her sinuses as harsh, flavored vapor. Every inch from her stomach to nosetip burned as if scrubbed with astringent. Taste came last and started sweet like chewed sugarcane but then curdled into something that approximated honeyed monkey vomit.

Throughout the miniature alcoholic ordeal, Leandra kept her expression pleasant. Fortunate that she did; the smuggler was studying her. She wasn't much to see, short and frail, wearing a long-sleeved dress of pale yellow. A black silk headdress tied below her chin hid her dark hair and pale neck.

Leandra was unaccustomed to the gaze of strangers; in daylight, she wore a veil that concealed all but her eyes. Her disease required that she avoid sunlight.

A lover had once remarked that, in certain circumstances, her wide brown eyes seemed misleadingly innocent and vulnerable. Given the smuggler's scrutiny, Leandra hoped that these "certain circumstances" included those in which she was plotting murder.

The smuggler raised his cup to drink, but then his face tensed. He paused and looked past Leandra. Maybe ten feet away stood four-armed Dhrun—Leandra's divine protector, brawler, erstwhile confidant.

"Oh, don't mind my bodyguard," she said while turning to regard Dhrun, who presently was manifesting his youngest incarnation. "He couldn't harm a soul unless he's got something sharp to jam through . . . oh . . . well . . . he does seem to have two rather long swords, doesn't he?"

The smuggler stared at her flatly.

What Leandra had said wasn't strictly true; Dhrun was deadliest bare-handed, but she had liked the way the quip sounded. So she broadened her smile and asked the smuggler, "Not one for levity?"

"Not at the moment."

"Pity. But truly, don't mind my bodyguard. Your men hiding in the grove could reach us before he could." She looked at the silhouettes scattered among the palms. An untrained eye would mistake them for stumps or rocks, but Leandra could see at least six figures. The closest crouched not six feet away and carried all the implements necessary to poke distressingly large holes in a body. She gave the camouflaged assassin a slight nod.

Leandra made sure that she had no bad habits, only full-blown addictions—flirting with danger being one of her favorites.

The smuggler was still studying Dhrun. "He isn't human, is he?"

"What was your first clue, his third or fourth arm?"

The smuggler scowled. "It's hard to know what to expect in the league, especially on Ixos. Your islands are a menagerie of demigods or divinity complexes or whatever you call them. So, this . . . bodyguard . . . is a god?"

"No, he is the complex of three souls: a god of wrestling named Dhrun; his avatar, a young human wrestler who took the name of Dhrunarman after winning last year's championship; and an ancient Cloud Culture goddess of victory named Nika. So a man, a god, and a goddess, not unusual for a divinity complex, some parts of him are divine, some parts are human; he just has to decide which parts."

"What are his choices?"

"Male, female, some of the ports of call lying between the two, if you catch my drift."

"I do not catch it."

"No, I suppose you wouldn't."

The smuggler looked at her catamaran. Its twin hulls and the decks that stretched between them shone in the moonlight.

Leandra's patience thinned. "As agreed, my crew remained aboard. You needn't worry about an attack."

"Something is wrong."

"What do you mean?"

He looked out at the Bay of Standing Islands. "No ship followed you here?"

"None."

"You're certain?"

"My captain and crew are Sea People; they know how to navigate the standing islands unseen."

"But you've heard the rumors?"

"Rumors of what? That the Disjunction has come at last? That after thirty damn years of waiting around, Los and the demons of the Ancient Continent finally found their backsides with both hands and crossed the ocean?"

Thirty-four years ago, Nicodemus Weal and his wife, Francesca DeVega, had defeated the demon Typhon; however, a dragon known as the Savanna Walker had escaped to the Ancient Continent, which should have allowed the demons to cross the ocean to destroy all human language in the War of Disjunction. But the demons had not come. No one knew why. Now after three decades of anticipation, some doubted that the demons would ever come.

The smuggler snorted. "No, no, nothing about the Disjunction. These are rumors of another human war. Reports of crop failures have come from Verdant. Seems the Silent Blight is worsening in the empire, and perhaps Empress Vivian is eying Ixos's rice and taro fields. The shipyards of Abuja are frantic with construction. A new fleet of hierophantic airships flies above Trillinion."

Leandra kept her face impassive.

He continued. "The league is reinforcing Lorn's northern border and sending ships to Ixos. Seems the peace between the empire and the league might spring another of its little leaks. The next year could see the Blockade of Ogun all over again. Or perhaps a second round of the Goldensward War. But you might know more about that?"

Leandra only stared.

The smuggler's full lips peeled back into a smile. White teeth, moonlight. "You're not one to hand out information. Good, good. Then consider how another human war might make our trade . . . particularly lucrative."

"You have a proposal?"

"In Abuja there's talk of a new power in Chandralu. The Cult of the Undivided Society, it's called. They don't worship neodemons like the usual cults; they worship the ancient demons. The empire and the league claim to have hunted down all of the demon worshipers after Typhon's defeat, but maybe they missed a few. The Undivided Society is tired of waiting for the Disjunction and aims to hurry it along a step or two. Have you heard of it?"

"Tall tales from sailors drunk on kava, nothing more. The tellers often follow it with an account of the Floating Island."

"Floating island?"

"Stories of an island of ghosts or neodemons that isn't fixed to the sea floor but floats around the archipelago. Those who make landfall are doomed to damnation or reincarnation as pubic lice or whatever. My point is that sailors are better known for creativity than reliability."

"And you think this Cult of the Undivided Society is just another sea yarn, just another floating island?"

"There's no proof the cult exists."

"But the Empress Vivian is offering a heavy purse for such proof. And she is sure to offer more now that her half-brother is in Ixos."

Leandra stiffened. Twenty days ago Nicodemus Weal, the empress's half-brother, had arrived in Chandralu ostensibly to cast his metaspells, which allowed deities to thrive in the league kingdoms. But in truth, he had come to reinforce the archipelago against possible imperial attack. More distressing, upon arrival, Nicodemus had heard rumors of the Undivided Society and of two neodemons attacking caravans near Chandralu. Therefore, Nicodemus had launched efforts not only to support his daughter, the Lady Warden of Ixos, but also to investigate her competency.

Leandra found this distressing for two reasons. First, she feared the smuggler would flee if he learned that Nicodemus had doubled the ships patrolling the bay. Second, she was, after all, Nicodemus's daughter.

Family isn't a word; it's a sentence.

For three decades Leandra's family had served as the wardens of the league, tasked with converting or destroying neodemons. As the Warden of Ixos, she was responsible for suppressing neodemons in the archipelago. If Nicodemus thought that the two marauding neodemons and the rumors of the Undivided Society signified her incompetence, he might revoke her independence.

Fifteen days ago, Nicodemus and his followers had set out to hunt one of two neodemons. He might return any day. Although Leandra did not dislike her father, there was much she hoped to accomplish before he returned, including closing a deal with this disturbingly well-informed smuggler. She looked at the man. "Should I learn anything about the Undivided Society, you will be the first to know. But I am not inclined to enter into a new agreement until the present one is concluded to my satisfaction."

"Ah, yes, your prophetic spell," the smuggler said and raised his cup to his lips. But then he paused and looked out to the bay. "Your pardon, but . . . I think I might . . . I sense . . . some danger . . ."

Leandra turned and saw nothing but moonlit waves and towering limestone islands. "Look, there is no ship among the islands. No army hiding under the table. No Nicodemus bloody Weal about to fall out of a God-of-god's damned coconut tree. I am here to purchase that prophetic spell, but that text seems to be giving you distressingly little information about the future. What is this danger? Shouldn't your spell foresee what it will be?"

"This spell doesn't work that way. It allows me to feel forward into time."

She frowned. "That sounds . . . rather ungentlemanly."

"I can sense the emotions of all the different men I might become in an hour."

"And how many of these men are there?"

"A near infinite number. I'm not aware of them all, but when many of them experience anxiety, I grow wary."

Leandra studied the smuggler's face. "What could be frightening them?"

"You saw no ships amid the standing islands?"

"No dammed ships. And no other threats."

"Very well . . ." He looked down at his mandana. "Perhaps it's just apprehension." He raised the cup to his lips.

Leandra put her head to one side. Even with a prophetic spell around his head, he was going to drink poison? Feeling forward in time, as wondrous as it sounded, seemed as useful as a boiling pot made of Lornish butter.

But then the smuggler froze. He peered into his liqueur and frowned. He lowered the cup, paused, raised it back toward his lips, lowered it again. He looked at her, eyes narrowed, put the cup down.

Leandra allowed herself a small laugh. "Is there a problem?"

"The closer I bring the mandana to my lips, the more of my future selves are writhing in terror. What in the Creator's name did you put in here?"

She shrugged. "The extract of a puffer fish liver, just a few drops. The hydromancers call it tetrodotoxin; it's an old recipe of the Sea People. Just a bit of local flavor."

"And what flavor would that be?"

"The flavor of nothing," she said airily. "But half an hour from now your mouth would tingle. Then your face and hands would go numb. All your muscles would slacken and you'd stop breathing. As a windfall, you would be perfectly aware as paralysis caused you to suffocate to death."

"Antidote?"

"None."

"You have a very trusting soul."

"I do," she admitted. "One day it'll be the death of someone else. Likely several someone elses. But don't be too upset; I now have evidence that your prophetic spell is genuine."

"You could have tried the text." He picked up a slim leather folio from the ground beside him.

She shook her head. "What's to stop you from selling me a death sentence? I will purchase the text around your head or nothing at all."

"Killing you would not be good business. There is more I would like to sell you and information I hope you will sell to me. On the next trip I could have more substantial texts."

"Then let me increase your profit. I'll double your price if you tell me where you get these spells."

The man studied her but said nothing.

She pointed to his head. "A text that powerful couldn't be written; it had to be part of a deity. I'm guessing you chopped one of the empire's gods into sellable pieces."

"You forget that imperial spellwrights have revolutionized composition. With Vivian's metaspells, they are changing the rules." He nodded toward the folio. "Inscribing brief godspells onto paper for example." Previously, godspells could be imbued only into a deity's ark stone.

Leandra shook her head. "Perhaps you had an imperial spellwright to set that godspell on paper, but no human mind could have composed it. Tell me where and how you are deconstructing deities. In return, I will investigate your Undivided Society. That or I could pay a large sum of jade."

He studied her. "I wonder why you should want such information . . . and how much it is worth to you. Some information isn't for sale to just anyone."

"Then perhaps when our partnership is stronger?"

"Shall we meet again? Perhaps tomorrow . . . in the city?"

Leandra considered. "If this exchange proves satisfactory . . . tomorrow at dusk, my bodyguard will meet you by the Lesser Sacred Pool. You know where that is?"

He nodded.

"Come alone. If there is anyone else with you, you'll never find us again. Understood?"

"Indeed. In the meantime, maybe you could tell me more about yourself?" he asked before seeing her blank expression and quickly adding, "Perhaps not your name or station, but—"

"If you discover my identity, then I will have to dispose of you in several large and bloody pieces deposited almost directly into a shark's belly. I say 'almost directly' because the shark's teeth would have to act as brief but effective intermediaries. And neither of us would want that."

"Neither of us would."

"Good, now for that godspell." She gestured to her guard.

A moment later Dhrun placed two small chests next to the smuggler and opened them. One was filled with rough-cut jade and balls of opium. In the other chest lay plates of Lornish steel and lacquered Dralish wood, each imbued with black market magical language.

The smuggler sorted through the jade and then held his hands over the steel and wood, seemingly able to sense magical text. Only a spellwright using a synesthetic reaction could do so. That made him a rogue wizard perhaps? Or maybe a pyromancer? "It is good," the smuggler said before holding out his folio.

"The godspell around your head," Leandra said coldly.

"They're identical, down to the last rune."

She shook her head.

"How could I sell you this spell? I can't remove this spell from my head."

"My bodyguard will assist."

The smuggler eyed Dhrun's face, which presently was that of youthful Dhrunarman—light brown skin, aquiline nose, densely curled black hair, sparse beard. Dressed in a black lungi and a vest of scale armor, which showed to good advantage all four of his powerfully built arms, Dhrun looked every bit a young Ixonian divinity complex.

The smuggler looked back at Leandra. "Very well, but before I remove my headwrap, I will admit to being in disguise. I am not of the Lotus People."

"You fill me with shock," she said in deadpan before leaning forward. "What do most of your future selves feel an hour from now?"

"Some are satisfied . . . but some are agitated, a few very much so."

"You still must smuggle your payments back into the city or out of the bay."

He seemed to consider this and then removed his headwrap. His forehead was encircled by rubicund prose. Though Leandra was not fluent in the red language, her inheritance from her mother allowed her to visualize the divine text.

Then she realized that the smuggler's hair consisted of silvering dreadlocks. "You're Trillinonish," she said and was struck by a sensation of familiarity. Had she seen this man before? No, it wasn't possible. And yet . . . she couldn't shake the feeling.

Dhrun put his upper hands to the back of the smuggler's head. The radiant godspell slackened from his brow and then fell away. Holding the sentences as if they were a necklace, Dhrun carried the crimson language to Leandra and stood behind her.

As Leandra removed her headdress, she was aware of Dhrun's lower hands resting on her shoulder and his upper hands moving near her ears. She caught glimpses of the godspell's red glow, but she felt nothing press against her forehead or scalp. "Is the godspell around—" she started to ask, but then she perceived . . . what was it?

It was like nothing earthly.

Currents of emotion moved all around her but not through her. She felt them only partially, as if she were watching a poignant shadow play or listening to a touching song. But these sympathetic feelings were sparked not from actors or lyrics, but from the multiplicity of her future selves. There were thousands of her possible selves. Hundreds of thousands? No one could say how many.

Most of herselves felt variations on her present anxieties, but a few were filled with strange emotions changing too fast to identify. Concentrating on one of these improbable futures was like trying to barehandcatch an oiled gecko. And yet . . . Leandra couldn't resist mentally chasing these bright futures.

Dhrun had walked back to the smuggler and was using his upper hands to pull rubicund sentences from the smuggler's folio and tie them around the man's head.

Leandra closed her eyes and concentrated on the alluring futures. Again they flitted away, but not before one gave her a glimpse into an hour hence in which she felt unabashed triumph. Leandra's excitement grew. Perhaps she could learn the smuggler's identity? Discover how he was eviscerating deities?

With even more vigor, Leandra mentally chased after this triumphant future. Within moments she lost it within a sea of banal hours.

Something more was needed.

Leandra peered through slit eyelids. Dhrun was adjusting the godspell tied around the smuggler's head. Neither man was attending to her.

Because of her parentage, Leandra could give herself over to her disease and gain temporary fluency in the magical language she was touching. In this state, she could perfectly understand and misspell any magical text. For a price, she became the universal spellbreaker.

If she used this ability now, she could alter her new godspell; however, this would undoubtedly cause the divine aspects of her body, which she had inherited from her mother, to attack the human aspects she had inherited from her father. The result would be a disease flare, possibly with dire consequences. And yet if she could catch that triumphant future, the rewards might justify the risks.

A change ran through her futures; more and more of them were filled with shock. Some also felt triumph, others raw horror. A different future had become probable, and the more she thought about that future, the more probable it became.

Leandra brought a hand up to her forehead and let her disease consume her. Soon her joints would ache and a rash would unfurl across the bridge of her nose, her forehead, her cheeks. Perhaps this flare would be so bad that Leandra would need to urinate frequently and her hands and face would swell. The God-of-god's willing, the flare would not be so bad as to cause her perception to expand. But now, in this painless moment, she forgot the risks as her mind joined with the godspell.

For an instant, she became the text's progenitor—a minor but ancient Trillinonish goddess of artistry, beauty, dance. The impoverished priests of her temple had sold her ark stone to the smugglers for thirty lengths of gold. The smugglers had bound her in a textual cage and cracked open her skull to pull the living language out of her mind. Her shrieks deafened two men.

In the next instant, Leandra returned to her own skull. Her hands were shaking as she thought of what the smuggler's people had done.

Neither the smuggler nor Dhrun had noticed any change in Leandra. No doubt this was because of a side effect of Leandra's current condition. When her disease flared, Leandra caused those nearby to better understand any language with which she was working. Fortunately an increased awareness of the red language had made the two men more preoccupied with the text around the smuggler's brow.

Leandra wanted to know more about how the godspell around her head had been created. The imperial spellwright who had edited it had shaped the text so that it would project a human mind forward by one hour, but in the flare of her disease Leandra was less human, more textual.

Carefully she misspelled one word in the godspell's first sentence and so increased her perception twenty-four times farther into the future. No other mortal creature but she could have made this misspelling, not even her illustrious father.

Normally Leandra would have been proud of such an achievement, but now she felt nothing but overwhelmed by the newly perceptible future selves. If she had thought the next hour contained a multiplicity of futures, the next day produced a million times as many, a hundred million times as many.

She swayed, struggling to retain her sanity amid the prismatic spray of herselves. In the past her hybrid-mind had been prone to dangerous expansions of perception, but nothing so dangerous as this had ever happened before. Now only one thing saved her from madness. Only one thing allowed her to grab the table with both hands as if she were drunk.

A little less than a third of her future selves were wracked by a specific guilt. Though Leandra had never felt it before, she recognized the dreadful emotion as that belonging to someone who had recently killed a dear friend, a family member, or a lover.

Another third of her future selves were filled with the anxieties of someone fleeing danger and wracked with a devastating guilt about the sudden death of everyone she loved.

But the last third of her future selves felt nothing. Nothing at all. And they felt nothing, because they were all dead.

With her godspell-laced mind working so hotly in the future, Leandra deduced the implications of these emotions into her own, personal prophecy: In one day's time, she had to choose between dying or murdering someone she loved. If she tried to run or avoid the prophecy, everyone she loved would perish.

Leandra misspelled her godspell again so that she could feel only an hour forward. The prism of herselves collapsed enough so that it no longer drove her toward insanity. Her breathing slowed. Her heart calmed. But now she needed to hurry back to Chandralu and solve the mystery of her future murder.

She shuddered as she remembered the emotions of the women she would become. She could not run or everyone she knew would suffer. No way around it. In one day's time, she would have to murder someone she loved or die.

She looked up at Dhrun. He looked back at her with curious, beautifully dark eyes.

Leandra was left with one question.

Who?

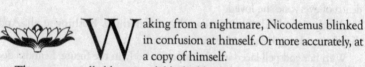aking from a nightmare, Nicodemus blinked in confusion at himself. Or more accurately, at a copy of himself.

The copy, equally blurry-eyed, blinked back.

They were lying in a dark tent. Humid night. Outside, jungle insects whirred and a river lapped.

Nicodemus could not understand where he was or what he was seeing. The man before him was himself: long raven hair streaked with silver, dark olive skin, chest and arms illuminated with indigo tattoos, wearing a white lungi. But unlike Nicodemus, this man was limned by a wan silvery aura.

If an Ixonian deity chose to ignite their aura, it could not be manipulated or extinguished; a godspell prevented this. Not all deities chose to ignite their auras. But for those who did, an aura authenticated a claim of divinity—useful in an archipelago of gods and imposters. Because an aura shone in proportion to its divinity's strength, the sputtering light around Nicodemus's copy indicated that he was a god near deconstruction.

Nicodemus wondered if he was dreaming still. He remembered a nightmare of . . . what? A claustrophobic prison, blinding light. There had been a baby with a woman's face, chains, water around his legs. One of his teeth had fallen out. And . . . and . . . something more to the nightmare, something of fear and sweetness, an intimation of implacability. Nicodemus tried to remember . . .

"You won't," said a low voice, Nicodemus's own voice. "It was a dream of death. That's as far as you will get."

"What?" Nicodemus croaked.

"You can't recall the dream," the copy said. Outside, the whirring jungle insects grew louder, softer. A frog made its creaking song.

The copy spoke again, now in a distracted, singsong whisper. "Dreams fill us with a sleeping amnesia that makes us forget ourselves and our world. It unmoors us so that we can float away to all points fantastic, all points horrific. When we wake, the amnesia flows away, taking with it the dream. Before we forgot ourselves; now we forget the dream. We might run after it, try to cup it in our hands. But though a dream is vast, it is fluid. It leaves only fragmented memory, like the tide leaves shells and spiny sea creatures. Impossibly the dream escapes us. Impossibly the ocean drains into the seabed. We are left awake, drydocked as ourselves in this finite world."

Nicodemus sat up, felt as if he were drunk.

"This has happened before," the copy said. "When we split while asleep, you forget."

Nicodemus could only blink.

"Here," his copy said and laid a hand on Nicodemus's shoulder. His touch, insubstantial as ash, ignited a flare of memories. Nicodemus tried to understand himself.

Perhaps . . . he was the bastard infant of a minor Spirish noble. His ability to spell was being stolen by the demon Typhon into the Emerald of Arahest . . . No, no . . .

Perhaps he was a young wizardly apprentice in Starhaven with a disability called cacography that made every spell he touched misspell. An inhuman creature was loose in the academy, murdering his peers with misspells. Perhaps he was the Halcyon, prophesied to repel the Disjunction. And . . . No . . . that had passed.

Perhaps he was a renegade spellwright hiding in Avel, using tattooed skinspells to wage a clandestine war against the demon Typhon. And maybe he wasn't the Halcyon; maybe that was his half-sister, Vivian. Perhaps he was the Storm Petrel, the demonic champion. But . . . now he was older. Now no one knew who was the Halcyon, Nicodemus or the Vivian. Certainly . . .

And then Nicodemus knew that he was now past sixty, middle-aged for a spellwright. His wife was named Francesca, his daughter Leandra.

Three decades ago, Francesca and he had defeated Typhon but a dragon known as the Savanna Walker had crossed the ocean. That should have started the Disjunction, but now thirty years later, the demons had still not come. Why?

Vivian had united Trillinon, Verdant, and Spires into the Second Neosolar Empire. There she used the Emerald of Arahest to cast metaspells that made magical language more consistent and logical. As a result, the empire's spellwrights were growing stronger, their deities weaker. An era of invention and industry had increased the empire's power with frightening speed. But Vivian's metaspells also inhibited misspelling in Language Prime, decreasing the diversity of animals and plants, making them more liable to crop failure.

Dral, Lorn, and Ixos had formed the League of Starfall with Nicodemus as their champion, their Halcyon. While Nicodemus's cacography prevented him from writing many spells, it improved his ability to write and cast his unique metaspells, which were, in a way, metamisspells—they caused magical language to become more random, more creatively chaotic, more intuitive. This strengthened the league's deities and allowed them to proliferate. The increased divine strength had, so far, allowed the league to match the empire's power. But an increase in deities meant an increase in neodemons, and so Nicodemus's family had become the league's wardens who hunted, converted, or deconstructed neodemons.

Nicodemus's head began to ache as he tried to make sense of his present situation. "I think," he said, "I arrived in Chandralu twenty days ago. That's when I cast my metaspell?"

His copy nodded.

"Since then, I've led a party up the Matrunda River, hunting one of the neodemons that has eluded Leandra?"

Another nod. "You're after a neodemon called the River Thief. Hence all . . . this." He gestured to the tent.

Nicodemus began to understand. Wherever he cast his metaspell, new deities were incarnated in response to prayers. "So after I cast my metaspell, some of the Ixonians began to illegally pray to me?"

"Hence, me," the copy said while looking at his hands. "Enough Ixonians prayed to you that I was incarnated with the requisites of assisting your safety and success. In the thoughts of the prayerful, you were the model of incarnation so—"

Nicodemus finished the thought for him. "So because of my disability, you are a god of cacography? One of your requisites is to increase misspelling?"

The copy laid a hand on Nicodemus's shoulder. "See through my eyes." The god removed a sheet from his legs. A dull crimson light, as from dying coals, filled the tent. Where the copy's feet should have been writhed two masses of red language. The diseased sentences coiled and folded, raising angry blisters in the god's skin. The deconstructing language was working its way up his legs. "I am a text of cacography. I am the incarnation of my own deconstruction."

In the past thirty years, Nicodemus's life—and those of his wife and daughter—had often depended upon the ability to quickly understand new deities, what models they were incarnated upon, and what requisites they were created to satisfy. Nicodemus had become a scholar of divine taxonomy. That is how he recognized his copy as one of the rarer types of deity, one of the least important, one of the saddest. It gave Nicodemus a hollow feeling.

"How long do you have left?"

The dying god looked away.

"Could we save you by fusing you into a divinity complex? Perhaps with a deity of healing?"

The dying god shook his head. "Our requisites would be too much opposed; the conflict would destroy our incarnation."

"When was your last incarnation?"

"A year and a half ago, in Highland, right after you and Francesca brought down that lycanthrope neodemon. You'll recall more clearly after my deconstruction." He smiled sadly. "It was . . . memorable."

Nicodemus touched his own hip and he did remember, vaguely. "Right now I can't remember which was worse, the wolf god's claws when I tricked it into attacking me, or the tongue lashing Fran gave me afterward."

"The tongue lashing. It's not even close. I heard half of her tirade and wondered if you might cry. I don't know how you bear your existence."

Nicodemus sniffed. "And here I thought that between us, you had ended up on the pitiable side of things."

"I might be a dying god doomed to cyclical reincarnation and agonizing death, but I could never withstand the torments of your natural condition."

"You mean the human awareness of mortality?"

"I mean marriage."

Nicodemus snorted and his copy produced a mischievous smile.

"Does laughing at mortals make your fate more bearable?"

"A little," the copy said, his smile faltering. "Especially when you lot do particularly idiotic things."

The keloid scar on Nicodemus's back began to itch. He tried to scratch it. The scar had formed when Typhon had used the Emerald of Arahest to steal his ability to spell. Scar and emerald retained the ability to communicate. Because his half-sister now possessed that gem, Nicodemus had tattooed a matrix of spells around the scar to prevent any such communication.

Nicodemus struggled to remember why he had given the Emerald to his sister, but then he thought of his metaspells and the league kingdoms, rich in divinity and culture. If he had held on to the Emerald, its ability to spell with absolute precision would have stifled the error, the creativity that generated his metaspells.

These thoughts led to vivid memories of the last time he had seen his sister in the city of Avel, their cold farewell.

The dying god flinched. Nicodemus turned his attention back to the present as his copy pulled from his mouth a broken molar. The shattered tooth evaporated into sentence fragments.

The god's aura dimmed even further as he said, "I was reincarnated the day after you cast the metaspell. So long as we both inhabited your body, I shared your thoughts. But when you dreamed, I had a few independent ideas. I've come to believe that deities are only the dreams of mortals. In the moment before waking, it's hard to know who is more real, dreamer or dream. But after we wake . . ." His voice died away as he held up a hand and grimaced as two fingers peeled open into crimson misspells.

"What would mortals be without dreams?"

The dying god nodded. "A fair question. One the empire might soon answer. But no time for politics. I didn't want to split away tonight. I was hoping to live a few more days, but I've discovered two things you must know. The first concerns the neodemon you're hunting, the one they call the River Thief. As we speak, the neodemon's devotees are stealing the cargo from your second boat."

Nicodemus swore and started toward the tent flap.

"Wait," the dying god said, his forearms now dissolving. "Because of my requisite to aid you, I have to tell you . . . something has happened to Leandra."

Nicodemus's chest tightened. "What?"

"Something altered Leandra. Some contact with divinity . . . the exact nature I can't tell . . . But when I try to investigate, I detect only one of her thoughts, a powerful belief."

"And?"

"You're not going to like it."

"I already don't like it."

Slowly the dying god lay on his back. His waist had become a roiling red tumor. "Less than an hour ago, Leandra had the powerful conviction that—" The dying god's face twisted in pain and his wan silvery aura flickered.

Nicodemus realized what was happening. New divinities were incarnated when enough people prayed for resolution of a certain problem. All goals that helped answer those prayers were known as a deity's requisites. Fulfillment of requisite caused the magical text of a prayer to be dispersed from an ark stone to the deity.

One of the dying god's requisites was to aid Nicodemus. Satisfying this requisite by telling him about Leandra was causing prayerful text to be released from arks across the archipelago to his body. However, the dying god's other requisite was to increase misspelling; therefore, the surge of textual power was forcing him to misspell himself.

"What is it? What happened to Leandra?" Nicodemus asked.

"Leandra believes . . ." he said between labored breaths, "that in the next . . . next day . . . she will try to murder her mother." With that, the dying god unraveled into darkness.

"Oh damn it all," Nicodemus groaned, "not again."

CHAPTER THREE

H ow can one investigate a murder that hasn't yet
been committed? And how, exactly, should such
an investigator proceed when she will become the
murderer? Leandra wrestled with these questions while sailing to Keyway
Island.

Navigating the eastern waters of the Bay of Standing Islands required
great skill; the vertical islands were dense enough to obscure the horizon,
tall enough to block many of the stars. Only natives could sail the stone laby-
rinth safely, and Leandra had taught only her most loyal captains the way to
Keyway Island.

Presently on a mile-long stretch of open water, the catamaran was making good speed, but soon the sailors would have to close-reef the sails and
paddle from the catamaran's two hulls.

From her customary spot on the forward center deck, Leandra watched
the moonlit water slide below. Her concentration was periodically broken
by the disease flare she had ignited when misspelling the smuggler's godspell. First had come a dull bellyache. Then her wrists and fingers began to
throb. Fortunately she hadn't developed a rash or needed to pee frequently; if
things got that bad, she might have to start taking the hydromancer's stress
hormone to suppress her body's attack on her textual aspects.

Most importantly, the divine aspects of her mind had not begun to expand her perception; that would threaten both her sanity and her ability to
breathe. She prayed that her body would show her a little mercy, not that
she deserved any. But if her two aspects, divine and human, could refrain
from attacking each other for just a little longer, the present flare would prove
a mild one.

Then Leandra realized that by using the godspell around her head, she
already knew that in an hour's time the majority of her future selves would
still be anxious, achy, fatigued, and cranky. "Rot it all," she muttered before

taking a deep breath and trying to think clearly about the prophecy she had made using the godspell.

Now as before, she had no doubts. If she tried to run from this prophecy, everyone she knew would soon die. But if she did not run, she would have to choose between her own death and committing murder. If she tried again to misspell the godspell so that she saw farther than an hour into the future, the multiplicity of her future selves would drive her insane.

The only thing left to do was to investigate her murders. So . . . whom might she have to kill and why? She fingered a slim leather wallet she kept tied at her waist. Inside she kept enough needles and poison to kill without pain or mess.

When the time came would she kill the loved one or herself? Hard to say. There would be a great deal on the line, and she had never been one to balk at a necessary task. Then again, her body had been trying to kill her for thirty-three years. Maybe, out of pure spite, she'd beat it to its task. The thought made her smirk.

Then she realized that she was being dramatic, a bad habit. And she didn't allow herself bad habits, only addictions, so . . . time to focus on investigation.

But, God-of-gods damn it, how?

As the Warden of Ixos, she had investigated dozens of murders thought to have been committed by neodemons or their devotees. Her parents had taught her how to do so, something of the family trade.

In most of her previous investigations, Leandra had discovered the guilty deities and converted or killed them. Several times the murders had gone unsolved. But she had been able to examine a corpse, gather evidence, interview witnesses. In her present situation, there wouldn't be a corpse until she made one, and there damn well wouldn't be any evidence or witnesses because she wouldn't be so sloppy as to allow any.

There was, however, at least one analogy to her previous investigations. Instead of listing suspected killers, she could list suspected victims. So watching the moonlit waves slide under the catamaran's center deck, Leandra considered everyone she loved.

It didn't take very long.

For one thing, she had to consider only those she loved so much that murdering them would cause her the extreme agony that she had sensed through the prophetic text. For another thing, she didn't love many people.

That realization made her smirk at the dark water and, by extension, at the idiocy of the universe.

So, anyway, her list of loved ones. First was her illustrious father, Lord Nicodemus Weal, Warden of Lorn, and—depending on whom you asked—the righteous Halcyon or the demonic Storm Petrel. If he discovered what she was concealing, Leandra might have a motive for patricide. But she doubted Nicodemus would ever discover her secrets, or if he did that he would react in a way that would require violence.

Second there was her draconic mother, Magistra Francesca DeVega, first Physician of the Clerical Order, Warden of Dral. If the true contents of Leandra's heart were ever made plain, the one most likely to endanger Leandra would be her mother.

Just then Leandra's focus was crowded out by unwelcome memories of fourteen years past. The Goldensward War had brought empire and league to the brink of total war. Leandra and her mother had been in Port Mercy at the time. What had happened next . . . seeing her mother's teeth like that . . . well . . . only by the thinnest of chances had mother and daughter survived each other. Leandra thought of her mother's teeth and tried to shut out those memories.

Then with profound relief, Leandra remembered that her mother was in the South. Two months ago, Leandra had received a report from Dral that Francesca and her followers were in Warth—too far away to murder.

Odd. An hour previous, she had felt through the godspell that some of her future selves were relieved. Sensing an emotion before its experience was like hearing an echo before the shout.

Leandra looked away to the standing islands. At the waterline the bay had worn the limestone to pillars upon which the rocky islands balanced. Atop the larger islands stood jungle-covered ruins—walls and rock piles mostly. These were the remains of the ancient Lotus city of Sukrapor, destroyed by a long-ago war with the Sea People's deities.

Leandra's thoughts returned to her possible victims. There were other names she could add, but none seemed very likely to incite her to murder. There was an ancient woman who had taken care of her when she was a child. And there was Thaddeus, a scholar of the Cloud Culture and her long-ago lover . . . but she had little feeling left for him. In fact, she said a short prayer that, if she had to kill anybody, it would be him.

This thought made her, again, quirk a smile at the dark water and by extension the idiotic universe.

A thought occurred to her: She had been considering people presently in Chandralu, but every night ships from all six human kingdoms sailed into port. "Pass the word for Captain Holokai," she said. Lieutenant Peleki, standing near the mast, echoed her call and the sailors repeated it down the ship. A moment later, Holokai presented himself.

The captain stood six and a half feet tall. Handsome if slightly too angular features, clean shaven head and face. But it was his complexion that was most remarkable; on his chest and face, he had fair skin that never tanned or burned. Yet his limbs and back were dark, almost gray.

Presently Holokai wore a lungi, bright red with a white fern pattern, tied in the style of the Sea People. In his right hand, he held a leimako—a stylized paddle, the blade of which was serrated with mako shark teeth. Among the Sea People, the leimako was a weapon restricted to great warriors and leaders. In Holokai's hands, this particular leimako had unusual properties.

Holokai tried to regard Leandra with his usual casual smile, but his dark eyes betrayed a concern. He knew something strange had happened on the beach with the smuggler.

Leandra felt the fist of her emotions loosen in his presence as she had prophetically felt an hour previous—again an echo-before-the-shout emotion.

Looking at Holokai, Leandra realized that if she were honest with herself, truly honest, she had better add another name to the list of potential victims. "Captain, I have strange questions for you. Come closer."

Frowning, Holokai did so. Privacy aboard a fighting catamaran was rare. Nearly every spoken word would be overheard and repeated by some sailor. Asking for a private conference would sow gossip among the crew. Not a good thing, but not an avoidable one either.

"Old friend . . ." Leandra whispered before trailing off. What, exactly, did one ask of a friend one might soon murder? "Screw it all," she muttered. "Can you think of a reason why I might want to kill you sometime early tomorrow morning?"

Holokai snorted. "Hey, Lea," he said in the rolling accent of the Inner Islands Sea People, "can you think of a reason why you wouldn't want to kill me? Especially if we had another night—"

"Kai, I'm serious. From the smuggler's prophetic text, I learned that tomorrow morning I'll have to choose between killing someone I trust—" no need to say "love" around him "—or dying myself. So, why might I kill you tomorrow morning?"

Holokai's smile fell. "You're not fooling."

"Not fooling."

"Can't you just run away—"

"There's no running, no way to avoid it. It'd be a piss-poor prophecy if I could avoid it by drinking myself stupid. And, before you ask, I can't sense more than an hour into the future again without going insane." Leandra tried to soften her tone. "Look, Kai, something big has started. So, why might I have to kill you? I'm asking."

Holokai looked to see if the lieutenant was listening then turned back to her. "No, Lea, not unless you changed your mind about . . ." He blushed slightly. "You know, my requisite to give the people of my island a son."

"No, I haven't changed my mind. We both know my disease prevents my helping you there. Our agreement stands. But is there a reason I should change my mind? Should I doubt my trust in you?"

"No, Lea." His eyes searched her face. "No."

Leandra frowned. Did he seem just slightly guilty? Or would anyone feel a bit jumpy if so questioned? "Is there something you want to tell me, Kai?"

"Lea . . . no . . ."

She remained silent, which was in her opinion the best way to wring out a confession.

He stared at her a bit longer, the blush growing across his pale cheeks.

"Do you," she asked calmly, "have any reason to be displeased with me?"

"Oh, no. . . . No, no," He said quickly. In daylight, his face would be red as a hibiscus blossom.

At last Leandra took pity. Loud enough for the lieutenant to hear, she asked, "How long would it take you to search for new ships in the bay or ships that will enter the Cerulean Strait by tomorrow morning? I need to know if I might expect anyone new in Chandralu."

He looked westward. "I'd need to cover about a hundred miles or so to be certain. But sixty miles should give us a good enough idea, and I've been feeling strong lately, so . . ." His gaze went soft as his mind became a calculus of winds and tides. "Considering it all, that should give us a pretty good idea of who's gonna tie up to the docks tomorrow. You give me five hours, maybe six, I'll get it done."

"Your speed is always impressive."

He spoke softly. "Maybe I'll impress you with more than speed later, hey?"

Leandra rolled her eyes. "If you can get it done, Captain."

"Lea, there's one more thing?"

"Oh?"

"I wasn't going to say nothing, but since you're telling me all this, maybe it's a night for strange things to happen."

Leandra tapped her index fingers together in the Sea Culture gesture for "Get on with it then."

"So I thought I saw something flying between the standing islands behind us."

"Flying?"

He scratched his chin. "Sounds strange, hey? I'd say it was a pelican but it seemed too big, too fast. Thing is, it's not a deity. I would have sensed that. And I'm not even sure I did see it. Maybe just jumpy, you know?"

Scowling, Leandra looked aft at the standing islands in their wake. She saw only moonlit rock and vegetation. "You're sure there's no ship following us to Keyway? Now would be a very, very bad time to be discovered."

"I'm sure."

"All right. Before you go searching for new ships, double back along our wake to make sure no one's following."

He paused. "Lea, you get us into trouble?"

"No."

"How bad?"

"I said I didn't get us into trouble."

"As bad as when that mercenary elephant god turned neodemon?"

"That was barely a skirmish."

"We only got out of his camp alive because his lieutenant went insane, and they still ambushed me at the shore."

Leandra rolled her eyes. "You recovered from the crushed pelvis the very next day."

"So we're in hotter water now? How hot? As bad as the jellyfish neodemon or the mosquito goddess?"

Leandra suppressed a shudder. "We got out of those scrapes alive," she said, though in truth, many in their party had not. "Kai, you're fretting again. Let me do that. We're not in trouble now, but we will be if you don't follow your orders."

He stared into her eyes a moment longer but turned away. "Hey Peleki, take us in to Keyway Island. I'll meet you there. You got the shark's lei." He tossed the leimako to the lieutenant, who caught the shark toothed oar and nodded. "Yes, Captain."

With that, Holokai flashed a smile at Leandra and dove off the center deck and into the dark water without a splash.

As Leandra watched her old friend swim away, she held a hand over her belly. The pain from the flare was getting worse. Sometimes her disease would double her over with pain, puff up her face and joints like rising bread. Then she'd have to take the disgusting stress hormone the hydromancers made with their aqueous runes. That would stop the human aspects of her body from attacking her textual aspects, but the drug's other effects were horrible. She hated her body for its civil wars, her disease.

Leandra wondered again if, in one day's time, she might kill the human half of herself. That might count as murdering someone she loved. Perhaps the textual half of her would live on. That thought withered her smile. She would hate to become like her mother. And, anyway, to kill only the human half of herself wouldn't be possible.

Leandra turned her thoughts to other people she might have to kill. Having sent Holokai to search for those just coming into the city, she should also consider those just now coming into her affection.

"Huh," Leandra said in surprise as she added another name to the list. "Lieutenant, pass the word for Dhrun."

Lieutenant Peleki sent the command down the ship. While she waited, Leandra considered the white half-moon and its watery reflection amid the standing islands.

When she was six years old, her father had taken her from Lorn to Ixos for the first time. Their first night in Chandralu, looking up from the Floating City, a young Leandra asked her father why all three moons had followed them across the ocean. He laughed and tried to explain about the moons being so far away that they looked the same from anywhere. She hadn't believed him.

"My lady," a voice said behind her.

Leandra turned to see that Dhrun had changed her manifestation; the divinity complex was now a tall, fair-skinned, athletic woman. This was the incarnation of a Cloud Culture goddess of victory. She had been known as Nika before fusing with Dhrun, a male Lotus Culture neodemon of wrestling, and his avatar Dhrunarman, the winner of last year's wrestling tournament. The resulting trinity had taken its most powerful incarnation's name even though it rarely manifested that incarnation.

In her Nika manifestation, Dhrun wore the same black lungi and scale armor vest that she had on the beach; however, these vestments now covered shapely hips, two small breasts, and four muscular but distinctly feminine arms. Her eyes were wide, long lashed, very dark.

When composing her divinity complex, Dhrun had chosen not to light an aura around her body to announce her divinity; her four arms achieved the same feat without increasing her visibility during more covert activities.

Presently Dhrun bowed her head and pressed her hand to her heart in the custom of the Cloud Culture. Absently, Leandra realized that Holokai's crew, all of whom were Sea People, would find Dhrun an excellent sailing companion given that she was of all three cultures and could help the ship fulfill the Trinity Mandate, which required all official Ixonian endeavors to involve at least one member of each of the archipelago's three cultures.

"My friend," Leandra said while pressing her own hand to her heart, "would you step closer?"

Dhrun did so, curiosity plain on her face.

"You have been in my service for a year now?" Leandra asked.

"A little less."

"And how do you find it?"

"It suits me well."

"Is there any reason why you would be dissatisfied?"

Dhrun's smile never wavered. "I should like a little more time in the wrestling arena. A goddess does like to be worshiped, after all. And I am second in your esteem after Holokai. I should like to be first; given my requisites, I am a bit competitive."

"I've already warned you about baiting Holokai."

Dhrun smiled. "I thought you hated how much your parents pun."

"Pun?"

"Baiting Holokai, given his . . . other incarnation. I thought you were punning."

"Oh Creator, no, not intentionally. I mean that I can't have you and Holokai fighting."

"Why do you doubt my satisfaction in your service?"

Leandra considered the goddess's face. "You are the only neodemon I've ever known who converted herself."

Dhrun's smile brightened. "Ah, my conversion. It wasn't easy, you know, breaking into your bedroom chamber like that."

"If it were easy, I suppose you wouldn't have done it."

"I wouldn't have," she agreed before stepping beside Leandra. With her lower arms, Dhrun took Leandra by the elbow and led her to the portside hull, where they could better watch the whitemoon's reflection. Walking made Leandra's knees ache, but now they stood together like two friends. It was a comforting feeling.

Just then Leandra realized that many of her future selves felt almost nothing, or bursts of nonsensical emotion. She tensed, wondering what strange catastrophe would happen in the next hour. Some magical attack? Maybe her disease flare would worsen and expand her perception to a maddening degree? Or maybe . . . Suddenly she laughed.

"What is it, my lady?" Dhrun asked.

"An hour from now, I will likely be asleep and dreaming. I can feel it. It's a strange sensation."

The goddess frowned.

Leandra continued in a more serious tone, "We were talking about your conversion, its suspicious nature."

Dhrun snorted. "You're suspicious only because, when you finally discovered me in your bedroom, you had to admit that I looked better in your blue Lornish dress than you do."

"It does look better on you," Leandra grumbled, enjoying the banter. It was nice having another woman to talk to, even if Dhrun wasn't always a woman. "Won't you tell me why you decided to arrange your own conversion? You were a successful neodemon. You could have avoided detection for years."

Dhrun only smiled. "Didn't we agree that we would never discuss what came before?"

"Your crimes were that great?"

The goddess's smile faltered by a degree. "That would be telling."

Leandra laughed. "I will give you more time in the wrestling arena if you can answer a rather difficult question."

"You know I can't resist a challenge."

"Why would I want to kill you tomorrow morning?"

"Because you realized that the green Spirish dress also looks better on me?"

Leandra smiled but then looked directly into Dhrun's eyes.

"Oh," the goddess said, "you are serious?"

"I am."

Farther aft, the lieutenant called for the sails to be brought down and for all sailors to take up positions along the hulls to paddle into Keyway Island.

Dhrun cleared her throat. "You speak like one who has received a prophecy."

"Through the godspell I bought from the smuggler."

"I don't mean to doubt you, but is it a . . . strong prophecy?"

"I inherited my mother's ability to comprehend the possibilities of the future. I do not have her gift for seeing the landscape of time, but I am a good enough judge. I foresaw that I cannot escape the choice between killing someone I love sometime early tomorrow morning or dying myself. Hence, goddess, my challenge to you."

Dhrun nodded. "Then . . . I suppose you might dispose of me if my death would advance our cause significantly—say by eviscerating me to make one of those godspells you are buying from the smuggler."

"Well played," Leandra said softly. "Here I thought I was interrogating you. You know, for a young divinity, you are impressively shrewd."

"Oh the boys are young, but Nika—like most everything in the Cloud Culture—has been around forever. I was first incarnated when the Cloud People were still a seafaring tribe on the western Spirish coast. I have some hazy memories of the Spirish tribes destroying our cities and exiling us to the sea. There were decades of wandering before we fought the outer islands away from the Lotus People."

"Maybe you should stop playing with the boys so much and write some of it down, for posterity."

"There's no glory in posterity. Victory begets posterity, not the other way around. But to answer your question, my lady, if you were to kill me tomorrow, it would be to deconstruct me and sell some part of my text to that smuggler we just met."

Leandra met the goddess's eyes. "You know I am dealing with the smuggler to discover how to stop his kind."

"My lady, I am two thirds a wrestler," Dhrun said. As she spoke the arm interlaced with Leandra's became thicker, hairier.

When Leandra looked up at Dhrun's face, the divinity had manifested Dhrunarman: dark eyes, strong jaw covered by a scrim of a youthful beard. Dhrun's voice, so suddenly male, was low. "Learning an illegal hold helps one escape it, but it also increases the temptation to use it."

"Dhru, do you think me that ruthless?"

He looked at her with a young man's face but through the eyes of an ancient soul. "Most divinity complexes I've encountered are a fixed mixture of the beings that fused to create them. There are very few who, like me, can shift within the bounds of our incarnations. Would you agree?"

Leandra said that she would.

"When you can change so fast—from male to female, from young to old— you can see how fast everyone else changes but doesn't realize it simply because the color of their hair or skin or what's between their legs is constant. It seems to me that every soul—human or divine—is far more flexible than it ever supposes."

Leandra paused to think about this and looked aft. She was supposed to be watching for whatever Holokai might have seen flying between the Standing Islands. Seeing nothing but moonlit limestone, she turned back to divinity complex.

"So, you think that under the right circumstances—perhaps if deconstructing you would benefit our cause—I could become that ruthless?"

Dhrun took both of her shoulders in his upper hands and looked into her eyes. "I know what our cause means to you. I know how much you have suffered." He paused. "And, given how much I believe in our cause, part of me hopes that, if it would mean victory, you would be that cold and calculating. So if I may, I'll turn the question around: Do you think you could be that ruthless?"

Leandra made her expression as blank as her heart felt.

Slowly, he nodded. "I thought so."

CHAPTER FOUR

There was only one problem with Nicodemus's metaspell: Wherever he cast it, prayers were answered.

Literally.

In league kingdoms, five thousand or so humans praying about a specific need incarnated a deity dedicated to that need's resolution. The goals that helped answer those prayers became a deity's "requisites." Satisfying such requisites caused prayerful text to be cast from ark stones to deities, bestowing power and pleasure.

As a result, Nicodemus's metaspells created disciplined armies led by war goddesses, artisans trained by sly deities of skill, crops protected by jovial— if not always sober—harvest gods, and so on. The "divine mob" or "god mob," as they were called when tongues were in cheeks, had made the league as powerful as the empire. The problem was that some human prayers, and therefore some gods of the mob, were malignant. The problem was the proliferation of neodemons.

And it was one hell of a problem.

Neodemons were far weaker than the true demons of the Ancient Continent, but they could nonetheless manifest all the malicious potentials of the human heart. And thirty years of hunting neodemons had lead Nicodemus to believe that such potentials were nearly infinite in variety and ingenuity.

Nicodemus opened the doorflap and stood amid a dark camp—round tents, a cooking fire gone to ash and embers. On three sides, night-black jungle climbed up to starry groves of sky. Just beyond the camp, a sandy riverbank formed a cove where five river barges had been moored. A gap stood between the first and the third boat like a missing tooth.

Roughly sixty yards out on the mile-wide river floated the stolen barge. Three stranger vessels—a riverboat and two canoes—were lashed to the barge. Several figures moved between them: humans, or at least humanoids, probably piratical devotees of the River Thief.

Nicodemus groaned. After arriving in Chandralu twenty days ago, he had learned that Leandra had failed for a year to dispatch two neodemons—one a monkey goddess of brigands, attacking caravans south and east of the city; the other, a water god known as the River Thief, was stealing cargo from the Matrunda River merchants between Chandralu and the ancient Lotus capital of Matrupor.

None of the merchants had realized they were the River Thief's victims until they docked in Chandralu and discovered their merchandise had been replaced with river stones. The merchants had tried setting guards, changing routes, employing mercenary divinities, but nothing deterred the River Thief. More disconcerting, Leandra had twice led investigations to Matrupor without uncovering a clue as to how the pirate god achieved such spectacular larceny.

Hearing this, Nicodemus had suspected one of Leandra's officers was corrupt and informing the River Thief. So Nicodemus had told both Leandra and the Sacred Regent of Ixos he would hunt the monkey neodemon when, in fact, he had secretly led several barges filled with Lornish steel up river to Matrupor, hoping that the River Thief would mistake him for a merchant and strike.

But the journey had been uneventful. Under the guidance of Magistra Doria Kokalas, his envoy from the hydromancers, Nicodemus had sold his cargo in the ancient Lotus capital for a modest profit and filled his barges with rice, silk, jade. Wondering if the black market would attract the River Thief's attention, Nicodemus had hidden contraband opium in each of his barges.

Four days ago the party had embarked from Matrupor, hopeful of being burgled. But last night Nicodemus had fallen asleep with expectations of failure; they were only a day's journey from the Bay of Standing Islands. And yet here he was, swatting mosquitoes and watching one of his barges being looted.

He studied the river currents and the lapping shoreline waves. The water seemed mundane, but on the sandy bank two of his watchmen lay unmoving. No simple achievement considering that both were master spellwrights. Whatever kind of neodemon the River Thief turned out to be, he clearly was what Nicodemus considered a "subtle" deity.

An ominous sign.

Most young neodemons were blunt minded: fire-breathing attacks on the

village walls, tidal waves hurled against merchant ships, hypnotic songs inducing love, madness, or—given the similarity of the two states—both. That
sort of thing.

A neodemon whose attack hid his nature was either experienced or an
incarnation of guile; a dangerous opponent either way. In fact, the short but
colorful list of neodemonic characteristics Nicodemus considered more dangerous than "subtlety" included such qualities as "sustained by the prayers of
more than fifty thousand," "an incarnation of lightning or pestilence," and
"is presently eating my still-beating heart."

Although subtle neodemons made perilous enemies, they could also be
made into powerful allies. Nicodemus had to try to convert the River Thief
into a god of the league's pantheon.

After a last look at the stolen barge, Nicodemus crawled to the next tent
and pulled back its flap. Before he could whisper, the entryway was filled with
a brutish face—wiry white hair, bulbous nose, horsey teeth. Magister John
of Starhaven, once Nicodemus's childhood companion and now his personal
secretary. The big man's small brown eyes mashed shut, opened wide. "Nico,
what—"

Nicodemus held up a hand. "Who's in there with you?"

"Just . . . Rory."

Rory of Calad was Nicodemus's envoy from the druids of Dral and an excellent choice for an infiltration game; however, on this journey, Rory had
made a rival of Sir Claude DeFral, the new envoy from the highsmiths of
Lorn. Favoring one man might cause trouble. "Where's Sir Claude?"

John blinked. "Next tent over."

"Good. Wake Rory up, quietly."

When John crawled back into the tent, Nicodemus rose just far enough to
see the river. Neither the barge nor the strangers had moved. If the River
Thief fled, Nicodemus could do little more than rouse his party and pursue.
The chances of catching a riparian god on a nocturnal river chase were
minuscule. Nicodemus had to hope that after unloading his present prize,
the River Thief would loot another barge.

"Nico!" John whispered from his tent. "Nico, I can't wake Rory."

"Dead?"

"Still breathing; he pulls his hands back when I pinch his nailbeds. But
there's something . . ." John held a hand to his mouth. "There's something
funny about how I'm thinking. It's like I'm feverish or . . . back in Starhaven."

Nicodemus frowned. "Starhaven?"

"I can't seem to think of . . . some things."

"Dammit," Nicodemus whispered as he realized what the River Thief had done.

When John had been a boy, the demon Typhon had cursed his mind to induce a stereotype of retardation. The demon had then placed John among Starhaven's cacographers to unwittingly spy on Nicodemus. During Nicodemus's initial confrontation with Typhon, John had escaped the curse and regained his natural intellect. However, the struggle had separated John and Nicodemus for a decade.

That John felt as he had in Starhaven suggested he might have a curse locked around his mind. The River Thief might have cast an incapacitating godspell on the whole party. Only he and John would be resistant; Nicodemus because his cacography would misspell the text, John because his childhood spent battling such a spell had given him some inherent immunity. "John, drag Rory to me."

"Why—"

"Just do it quickly and . . . well . . . here, let's free you completely." Nicodemus peeled a tattooed disspell from his neck. The luminous violet sentences folded into a tight cage.

Nicodemus had learned this violet language from the kobolds of the Pinnacle Mountains. It was one of the few magical languages with a structure logical enough to resist his cacography; however, it was sensitive to sunlight and would deconstruct in anything brighter than two moonlight.

With a wrist flick, Nicodemus cast the disspell against John's forehead. The violet prose sprang around John's head before sinking into his skull. The luminous sentences flickered as they deconstructed the River Thief's spell.

The big man's head bobbed backward. He flinched, grimaced, wrinkled his nose, sneezed. "Flaming hells, Nico, it feels like you just filled your mouth with snow and started licking my brain."

"What an expressive image you've come up with," Nicodemus said dryly. John had never lost his puerile fascination with vulgar imagery. As a child, Nicodemus had gotten into many Jejune wordfights with the big man. Now, it was less amusing.

"You could have warned me." John groaned.

"Somehow the River Thief has obtunded our party and is stealing our cargo. That's why you've agreed to haul, with particular care and haste, Rory out here."

Nicodemus could not pull the druid from the tent as his touch misspelled the Language Prime texts in almost any living creature, thereby cursing them with mortal cankers. His wife and daughter, being partially textual, were among the few who could survive his touch. This immunity had been a great comfort to him years ago when his family had still been close together, physically and emotionally.

John disappeared into the tent and after some rustling pulled a limp Rory of Calad into the moonlight.

The druid was maybe six feet tall, dressed in white robes, broad shouldered, in possession of long glossy auburn locks. His freckles and slight chubbiness gave him a disarmingly youthful air that belied his fifty years.

Nicodemus cast a disspell onto the druid's head. As the sentences contracted, Rory's eyes fluttered. Then the violet sentences crushed the godspell around his mind. Rory convulsed once, opened his eyes, rolled over, vomited.

Nicodemus grimaced sympathetically. "John, quietly as you can, haul Sir Claude over here. Stay low. Rory, can you hear me?"

The druid spat. "Yes, but it feels as if—"

"As if a block of frozen mucus is fondling your brain?" John asked helpfully.

Rory looked up at John, frowned. "Yes . . . yes, that's exactly what it feels like."

Nicodemus rolled his eyes. "Shut it you two. John, fetch Sir Claude and one of his metal books. Rory, hold still." Nicodemus began to forge a shadowganger spell on his forearm.

The druid pressed a hand to his stomach. "I promise not to move another muscle unless it involves puking myself inside out."

Nicodemus pulled the shadowganger spell from his arm and cast it on the druid. The violet paragraphs spun around Rory, bending light away from him until he seemed another moonshadow.

John appeared with Sir Claude thrown over his right arm and a massive book pinned to his side by his left. With little ceremony, John let the book drop. It clanged softly on the ground. Then John laid the knight onto his back.

Sir Claude DeFral—highsmith of Lorn, knight of the Order of the Oriflamme, veteran of the Goldensward War, spy, and assassin—was a thin spellwright in his sixties. His skin was dark brown, his head shaved, his goatee silver. Presently his head lolled back and his mouth fell open. The very picture of coma.

Nicodemus cast a disspell onto the highsmith's head. John was muttering something about slime, snow, and brains when Sir Claude calmly opened his eyes and looked with puzzlement at Nicodemus, John, and the human shadow that was Rory. "Let me guess, my lord," Sir Claude said, "last night we drank too much?"

"Everyone's a joker tonight," Nicodemus muttered.

Sir Claude propped himself onto his elbows and looked at Rory. "Druid, such a surprise to meet you here. At least I assume it's you; no one else but you would produce quite such a corpulent shadow."

"Don't you two start," Nicodemus growled. "Listen, we haven't much time. Somehow the River Thief snuffed our watch. He's taking our boats out on the river to loot them one by one. I still don't know what he is—a water god I'll wager—but for all we know he could be a wind neodemon or a ghost from the Floating Island. Whatever he is, he might flee downriver at any moment. So Rory, Sir Claude, and I are going to play a Wounded Bird infiltration game."

John frowned. "What about Doria?"

Magistra Doria Kokalas was Nicodemus's envoy from the hydromancers, a senior clerical physician, and the party's only native Ixonian. Therefore she was—Nicodemus realized too late—the only one who could have judged this plan's feasibility. "There's no time to get Magistra."

"She's not going to like that," Rory said.

"Nor will she like you two bungling our only chance to take down the River Thief," Nicodemus replied as he cast a shadowganger spell first on Sir Claude and then on himself. "Here's the game: The three of us stow away on the third boat. Once they take her out and board her, Sir Claude will play the Wounded Bird to get the River Thief's complete attention. I'll hop in the water and play a Papa to the Rescue. The neodemon will either try to kill me outright—if so, Rory, set the boat on them—or more likely the neodemon will spellbind Sir Claude and me and set off downriver. You two give me an hour to proselytize. If the River Thief converts, great. If not, I play spellbreaker while Rory kills everyone and keeps the boat afloat until Doria catches up with us. Understood?"

"How will Doria know to catch up with you?" John asked.

"You're going to tell her," Nicodemus replied. "As soon as we stow away, disspell the godspell around Doria's mind. Tell her about our infiltration game and that she's to come after us."

Rory coughed. "She's not going to like that."

"You already said that," Nicodemus replied. "Other comments?"

The shadowganger subtext had transformed Sir Claude into a shadow. He picked up the massive book, which John had dropped next to him. This was one of Sir Claude's copies of the Canticle of Iron, a tome of thin metal sheets upon which the Lornish holy texts and many highsmith spells were written.

"My lord," Sir Claude said as he rose to a crouch, "are you sure you want to place your honored life, not to mention my own humble existence, in the hands of a tulip gardener?" He nodded toward Rory. "I am, of course, deeply impressed by the druidic art of cultivating pansies, but forgive me if I'm just a bit queasy about playing Wounded Bird to a hostile river god, in the middle of said god's river, while hoping a spellwright schooled in the deadly art of pruning will protect me."

Rory snorted. "Perhaps we should rely on your deadly art of whining, given that you can only regurgitate the same four spells over and over."

"Oh, you've caught me out, druid," Sir Claude replied with lazy sarcasm. "I am quaking in my boots. Would you hold my hand to help me feel safe?"

"The two of you will shut, the burning hells, up," Nicodemus growled. "You will both do as ordered or I will personally deconstruct the excuse for prose you both call original. Am I understood?"

Sir Claude muttered, "Yes, my lord," and Rory grunted.

"So, yes, Sir Claude, we are going to put our lives in the hands of a gardener because—as I hope you aren't too stupid to appreciate—druids can spellwright in wood and our barges are covered so completely with Rory's subtexts that he alone can keep us safe when there's blood in the water. So, if you want to survive your Wounded Bird act, then you had better make friends with the white robe."

The knight bowed to Rory. "Sir, my words were spoken both in haste and with little thought for your many and various excellent qualities. I am profoundly apologetic." His tone was anything but.

The druid started to reply but Nicodemus cut him off, "We're going." He turned toward the boats.

"But Nico," John interrupted, "if you're going to play Papa to the Rescue by jumping in the river . . . what about your first rule of fighting a water god?"

Nicodemus paused. "We don't know for certain that the River Thief is a water god. It's only the most likely possibility."

"Or for that matter, my lord," Sir Claude added, "what about your second rule of fighting a water god?"

They had a point. "Well . . ." Nicodemus said, "the exception proves the rule."

Sir Claude coughed. "Forgive me, my lord . . . but . . . I believe some excellent scholarship has shown that the modern use of that saying is incorrect."

"What?"

"I think the original sense of 'prove' could mean either 'to establish' or 'to test.' It's something called a contranym: a word that means both one thing and it's oppo—"

"I know what a—" Nicodemus started to snap.

"So if you're going to get in the water while trying to take down a water neodemon," John added helpfully, "you're going to try to prove your rule is a bad one."

"Hey, who here is prophetically connected to the inherent ambiguity and error in language?" Nicodemus asked.

"Technically," John replied, "you."

"Then, technically, I decide what rules we're try to prove and how. Right?" No one spoke.

"Good," he said curtly. "Follow me." He turned and ran for the third riverboat.

As his bare feet padded along the dirt, Nicodemus struggled against the urge to glance back. He had no doubt that Rory—young and thirsty for glory—would follow, but Sir Claude had joined Nicodemus's party only recently.

However Nicodemus did not look back; doing so would show a concern for insubordination, and the past thirty years had taught him that the best way to prevent insubordination was to pretend it was impossible and then land like a lightning bolt on anyone who acted otherwise.

So Nicodemus dashed from tent to tent down the riverbank. Blue and white moonlight wavered on the currents. The stolen boat had turned and the stranger vessels were disengaging. There wasn't much time now. Though the tropical night was humid, a chill ran through Nicodemus.

Beside him sounded footfalls on sand as Rory and Sir Claude caught up. Nicodemus paused and then ran for the third boat. He passed one of the incapacitated watchmen and then waded waist deep into the river to the moored barge. Then he was pulling himself onto the bow and scurrying down the hatch into the cramped hold. His every step seemed to make some board creak. In his imagination the wooden complaints rolled out across the water, clear and loud enough to alarm the River Thief.

The hold was as humid as a dog's mouth. Nicodemus cast a few flamefly spells to shed flickering light over cargo lashed in place. Carefully he climbed over two chests and wedged himself between a barrel and the portside hull.

A moment later he saw Rory's bulky shadow come down the hatch into the hold. Nicodemus cast another flamefly paragraph to let the druid know where he'd hidden himself. The druid found a hiding place in the aft hold.

A creak from the stairs announced Sir Claude's arrival. Again Nicodemus threw out a flamefly spell. A moment later Rory cast some druidic text that briefly burned with blue flame. Sir Claude paused and then disappeared into the shadows near the starboard hull. Nicodemus was impressed. By choosing that spot, Sir Claude had evened the boat's ballast. Now they wouldn't list to one side and raise any suspicions. That Sir Claude would know to do such a thing raised Nicodemus's curiosity.

Per reports from his Lornish allies, Sir Claude had been knighted fourteen years ago during the Goldensward War—a border dispute between Lorn and Spires that rapidly escalated in hostility between league and empire and was resolved only with frantic diplomacy. Afterward Sir Claude had become a royal spy who worked his way into the confidence of a seditious seraph before revealing his treachery to Argent, Lorn's metallic overgod. Nothing in those reports suggested Sir Claude's exposure to matters maritime. It made Nicodemus wonder if there was something more to Sir Claude than he had appreciated.

Had the Lornish crown sent him one of their spies as an emissary to send a message? Or to keep a closer eye on him? Nicodemus couldn't rule out those possibilities. However, the Lornish crown could have chosen Sir Claude because they knew he would make a valuable addition to Nicodemus's entourage: he was deadly in combat, knowledgeable of diplomacy, and had the quick-witted and sarcastic personality that Nicodemus preferred. Nicodemus had often sent back emissaries who were aloof, sycophantic, or humorless. Leandra and Francesca had expressed similar preferences for their emissaries and counselors.

This thought lead Nicodemus to briefly reflect on his family. When Leandra was young, they had been together always and relished one another's sharp wit, ironic humor, and proclivity for wordplay. But then the demands of league and a disastrous disagreement between Francesca and Leandra had scattered the family. Now each of them had re-created their family's culture within their own entourage.

The last of the flamefly paragraphs burned out and returned the hold to darkness. Nicodemus's ruminations about family faded as his leg began to ache where it was jammed against the barrel. Worse, the heat and stale air made him sweat profusely. Time dragged on.

Nicodemus was wondering if he should sneak abovedeck to see what the pirates were doing when he heard an oar's splash. The sound came again and

Nicodemus felt his stomach tighten. Time passed even more slowly. Another splash, a low whisper and then—as much felt as heard—the hush of a keel sliding on sand. Had the river pirates brought in the second boat? Moments later soft footfalls sounded on the deck.

The boat rocked and then glided backward. The splashing oars sounded again. Nicodemus supposed the river pirates were using the canoes to haul the boats out.

Creaking sounded from the stairs. Nicodemus turned to see a dark figure stepping down from the deck. Blue moonlight revealed glimpses of a young woman, bared wet shoulders, hair braided back, a long knife in her right hand, peering into the darkness.

Nicodemus wondered if she were a spellwright and if she would cast a luminescent spell to inspect cargo. If so he'd have to kill her silently. But long moments passed, the River Thief's devotee looked from side to side, but she cast no light. Not a spellwright then. She turned and hurried back up the stairs.

Nicodemus fought the urge to move as water continued to splash against the hull. Finally the sensation of acceleration lessened. The splashing oars changed tempo. Someone called out soft commands. Something thumped against the hull and the deck rang with more footsteps. One of the stranger vessels had closed with their boat.

Suddenly Nicodemus realized that he had not told Sir Claude when to start his Wounded Bird routine. Now—when the raiders were preoccupied with boarding and before they organized themselves to loot the hold—would be perfect. Worried that Sir Claude would miss the opportunity, Nicodemus cast a single flamefly paragraph. The incandescent light it shed revealed a scene that made Nicodemus breathe easier.

The highsmith had crawled from his hiding place and opened his Canticle of Iron. The spellbook's metallic sheets had come alive and were folding themselves into an animated suit of armor around the knight. Each sheet was covered with the highsmith magical language, which functioned only within metal. Like all knights of the Oriflamme, Sir Claude had mastered the variations of a half dozen spells that composed such metallolinguistic armor.

Two razor thin swords grew from Sir Claude's fists. An angular helmet folded around his head, leaving only a thin slit for vision. Thus armored, a Lornish knight was one of the most dangerous combatants in the six human kingdoms.

As Nicodemus's flamefly paragraph burnt out, Sir Claude crept to the base of the stairs and then, as silent as a trained assassin, charged up to the deck. The knight's armor accelerated his steps to inhuman speed.

Not a moment after the knight disappeared from Nicodemus's view, a scream broke the night's quiet. Two blows sounded on the deck and then a splash, which Nicodemus supposed was that of a body striking water. A chorus of voices rose in alarm.

Nicodemus crawled out of his hiding place and made for the stairs. Up through the hatch, he saw a single dark figure clutching a boarding ax. The man raised the weapon and charged toward the bow.

Nicodemus pulled free the first few sentences of a disspell written across his left chest. Pain seared through his skin as the spell spread across his body, covering him in a protective text that would attack any other magical text that touched him. This combined with his cacography would make him briefly impervious to most any godspell. Soon every patch of Nicodemus's skin shone with the disspell's violet light.

Screams and crashes sounded from the bow. There was a sudden crack and the boat lurched. The neodemon had joined the fray. Nicodemus ran up the steps.

After the hold's blackness, the wide and starry sky above the glossy river dazzled. Nicodemus glanced forward and saw a fountain of white light; the glare outlined the metallic Sir Claude as a pirate swung a boarding ax against the knight's armored back. The blade clanged against steel. Sir Claude spun with inhuman quickness and ran his left sword through the pirate's gut.

No one noticed Nicodemus as he sprinted to the stern, planted his foot on the gunnel, and dove out over the water. He had just enough time, suspended above the dark currents, to extend his arms and put his head down. Then the shock of water and deceleration, diving deep. He arched his back and coursed upward, his long hair streaming.

When his head broke surface, Nicodemus turned and began to overhand stroke back toward the stolen boat. The disspells covering his body began to churn faster and their luminosity grew. No doubt the water was laced with the River Thief's godspells. So long as his disspells lasted, Nicodemus would burn through such texts. The River Thief would now be aware of Nicodemus's approach but unable to stop him.

Or so Nicodemus had thought. Not two strokes from the boat, Nicodemus felt his disspells deconstruct. Paragraphs snapped with audible cracks and flaked off like old paint. In moments, he was swimming linguistically naked. He took one more stroke and was reaching for the barge when the currents around him erupted into a fury of force and foam.

The water became gelatinous. Somewhere on the boat sounded three detonations. Something hard locked around Nicodemus's feet and yanked him underwater.

Pulled down through ten feet of limpid river, Nicodemus stretched his arms up toward the vanishing light and wondered if he were, after all, a fool for testing his first rule of fighting with a water god.

Or, for that matter, his second rule.

A geyser of light erupted from somewhere above water. Nicodemus's ears rang with the sound of his own voice. When an envoy first joined his party, he would sometimes test the newcomer about different types of neodemons. "What," he would ask, "is first rule of bringing down any water god?"

When the envoy did not know the answer, John and Doria—who had heard his lectures many times—would reply in monotone, "Don't get in the God-of-god's damned water."

Nicodemus would nod and ask, "And what is the second rule of bringing down any water god?"

His followers would flatly reply, "Don't get into the God-of-god's damned water."

As Nicodemus's world dissolved into blackness, he prayed for an exception to prove his rules.

CHAPTER FIVE

Nicodemus thought he was still drowning in the river when he found himself hanging upside down on his stolen barge. Water dripped into his eyes, blurred his vision, plastered his long hair to his face. A soft green light shone behind him.

Inversion filled Nicodemus's head with pressure while strange texts blunted his thoughts, preventing him from spellwrighting. It seemed the neodemon had cast several censoring spells around his mind—several because Nicodemus's cacography was slowly dispelling the texts in direct contact with him. If he focused on misspelling, he could accelerate their deconstruction. But for the moment, it served his purposes to appear harmless.

"You are censored and bound by the feet," announced a calm female voice. "I wouldn't attempt to free your body or mind unless you'd like to be formally introduced to excruciating pain."

"Thank you, but we're old acquaintances," Nicodemus croaked while spitting the hair away from his mouth. "No need for formalities." He held his arms up, trying to push down on the deck and release the pain in his ankles. But the boards were nearly half a foot out of reach.

"That you are a spellwright is obvious," the calm voice said. "An adept at disspells, nonetheless. What I cannot surmise is in what languages you spellwright. Enlighten me on that subject."

Nicodemus coughed a few more times and gathered his wits. He had to lie as little as possible; it would keep his story straight and make things smoother if the deity converted. "I studied with the kobold skinmages of the Pinnacle Mountains. Touching my skin could be dangerous."

"I have never heard of skinmages. Are there many of you in the South?"

"Not many who are human. I may be the only one." At last Nicodemus cleared the water and hair from his face and discovered a swaying view of the ship's deck, its gunnel, the jungled riverbanks of the Matrunda sliding past. Apparently the River Thief had believed his Papa to the Rescue routine and was fleeing downriver with a new captive.

Gradually Nicodemus's eyes adjusted to the dim green glow shining behind him. Three sailors stood by the gunnel. Their lungi were tied high to keep the garment above the knees. Two had fresh wounds on their bare chests and were looking aft for pursuing ships. The third glared down at what appeared to be a four-foot metallic cocoon that had grown metallic tentacles and jammed them into the ribbing of the boat's hull.

Nicodemus recognized this as the endgame of Sir Claude's Wounded Bird routine. As the spells animating his armor wound down, the crouching knight had edited his metallolinguistic armor into a defensive conformation that insinuated itself into the boat's structure; this to prevent the sailors from tipping him into the river. Presently, an eye slit opened in his helmet to allow Sir Claude to watch Nicodemus attempt a conversion.

"So," the unseen female speaker behind Nicodemus said, "what forces put the world's only human skinmage and a Lornish knight in the company of an Ixonian river merchant smuggling opium?"

Nicodemus turned his head to try to see his interrogator but succeeded only in getting more wet hair in his eyes. "Could I know whom I am addressing?"

"This is not that kind of conversation."

"What kind is it?"

"The kind where you tell me what I want to know or I find out how hard it is to fit a knife blade into your spine."

"I've never been good at those."

"I'll start with your lower back so you get plenty of practice before you die. So, tell me why you and the metal man ended up in the same opium running outfit."

"Ambition, greed, maybe a dash of desperation."

"Go on."

"My past was a bloody one; I had to leave the South. Once I made it to Chandralu, an old associate matched me with smugglers hiring spellwrights willing to protect a new opium buying expedition. Sir Iron Ass over there had similar reasons for leaving Lorn."

While Nicodemus was speaking, the green light shining behind him brightened. "So," his interrogator asked, "some Southern thugs want in on the Matrunda opium run?"

"That would be a safe assumption," Nicodemus replied. "And would it also be safe to assume that I am talking to the River Thief's avatar? Perhaps his high priestess?"

The woman laughed, a light sound with a note of private amusement. This bothered Nicodemus though he could not tell why. "What would make you assume that?" the woman asked.

"Forgive a foreigner's ignorance. I've heard nothing about what the River Thief's requisites might be; however, when you heard there might be more traffic on the Matrunda opium run, the light behind me grew brighter. If one of the River Thief's requisites is theft, then increased smuggling on the Matrunda would offer more chances to fulfill that requisite and make the neodemon more powerful. That might produce a more luminous aura around his avatar."

Two of the sailors looked at Nicodemus, their expressions cold. The unseen woman spoke again. "An impressive bit of deduction, skinmage. You have dealt with neodemons before?"

"The situation I left in the South was complicated. It left me with certain skills that the River Thief might find useful."

"You want to join us? Why should the River Thief trust a mercenary who betrays his former employer?"

"I contracted to protect the ships with my life. I was the only one in the camp who discovered your caper and the only one who risked his life to stop you. In your hands, I'm as good as a dead man. Therefore, my contract is complete."

"An honorable mercenary? I'm sure the world is just crawling with those."

"'Honorable' exceeds my expectations. I was hoping for something as humble as 'not worth killing just now.'"

"If we were to consider your offer, what could you tell us of these Southerners muscling in on the Matrunda run?"

"I can tell you that this expedition had a peculiar buyer in mind for the opium."

"Oh?"

Nicodemus thought fast to concoct a lie that might reveal more about the River Thief's requisites. He chose one his wife was fond of telling to deities of theft. "Perhaps you've heard of Lorn's stringent laws limiting spellwrighting. Recently, their metallic overgod has forbidden clerical physicians from casting any text upon the mind of any Lornish man, woman, or child. In Skydoc there is an infirmary for children. Some of their patients are in continuous pain. Lorn won't allow the physicians to stock the necessary medicines and now they can't cast spells to relieve their pain. So, the physicians hired a group of . . . thugs, as you say . . . to smuggle enough opium into Skydoc to relieve the children's suffering."

As Nicodemus spoke, the green light behind him dimmed. Noting this, Nicodemus laughed out loud. He knew exactly what kind of neodemon the River Thief was.

"That was exceptionally clever," the woman said coldly. "So much so, I might have to test this knife on your spine after all."

"I have an unusually compact spine. Stabbing me might waste a good knife."

"Fortunately I have several to hand."

Nicodemus's heart began to race. "I have skills you can use. No one knows divinity like I do. Consider how quickly I gleaned your River Thief's requisites. Clearly he is a water god, and a subtle one, or he never would have been able to sneak our boats out one by one. Clearly he is a god of thieves, or your aura would not have brightened at the prospect of larceny. But the River Thief's mandate cannot be theft alone or learning that you had just stolen medicine for children would not have weakened your aura. The River Thief's requisites are for equitable theft—steal from the powerful and give to the poor, that sort of thing. That type of neodemon, it's a rare kind of god. I could help him flourish."

Again Nicodemus's interviewer produced laughter that rang with a peculiar note of amusement. "I can't decide if you are the most dangerous captive we've ever abducted or if you're just shockingly full of bullshit."

"Those are not mutually exclusive possibilities."

"Or maybe you're simply God-of-god's damned insane."

"I admit that story about the children was, technically, bullshit. But it is proof of my skills. I could render my knowledge to the River Thief. I could help him steal on a greater order of magnitude. I could help him steal from other deities." The green light flickered.

"And how could the River Thief achieve such amazing feats of equitable theft?"

"Government."

The unseen woman and the three sailors all burst into hearty laughter.

So began the last phase of the infiltration game. Things would be more dangerous now that Nicodemus had to tell the truth. "It sounds like a joke, but trust me I am not here to amuse. No force has greater potential for deprivation of property than a government, and if the River Thief's requisite is for equitable theft, then he could help ensure that they get it right, for once."

The sailors had stopped laughing but were now looking at Nicodemus with expectant grins, as if anticipating a punch line to a joke.

Nicodemus frowned at them. "Say the River Thief has requisites more specific than simple theft. If he must perpetrate extortion or embezzlement, he could become a god of the treasury and steal all the money nobles hide from tax collectors. Or perhaps the River Thief has a requisite for burglary or fraud, then it's espionage for him. Your god could be stealing from Empress Vivian rather than from dingy river merchants. Think, and think hard, about everything the River Thief could do for his worshipers if he could dip into the imperial wealth or if he commanded a fraction of all the taxes in Ixos or the taxes in all three league kingdoms. I'm offering a chance for your god to shape the league's destiny."

The sailors had stopped smiling. One had gone back to playing aft lookout. The other two sailors were again staring at Nicodemus's unseen interrogator. "You suggest that the River Thief should be enslaved in one of the regency's pet divinity complexes?"

Nicodemus had known this question was coming. Usually it was asked just before a neodemon either converted or tried to expose Nicodemus's internal organs to air. "Why would I suggest such a small prize?" he asked. "Joining an existing complex is for the neodemons who need the Sacred Regent's protection. But it's the other way around for the River Thief; the Sacred Regent needs protection from him. With the right go-between—namely me— you could name your terms. Or forget the regency entirely, we could go directly to the Council of Starfall and give your god a jurisdiction greater than this kingdom's."

Someone from the bow called out and one of the sailors hurried away. But what did his interrogator think? She would be the key to the River Thief. A moment passed in which only the creaking of boards and the lapping of water sounded. Then, at last, the interrogator said, "You must have a very high opinion of yourself, that you think you could achieve such a feat."

"I have managed to get one or two things done in my youth. I could catch the right ears for you."

"Skinmage," his interrogator asked, her voice growing tense, "I begin to fear that you have not been completely forthcoming regarding who you are. That or you are a consummate lunatic. To whom am I speaking?"

"This is not that kind of conversation."

"Are you fond of trying to reverse situations in which you are bound and censored with a knife point to your kidneys?"

Something cold and sharp press up against Nicodemus's left flank. "I try not to make a habit out of it," he replied with as much composure as he could muster. "But, truly, I can help the River Thief gain power beyond any previous. Even more importantly, I can offer him protection."

The woman snorted. "No, I'm afraid that won't work. The River Thief has no need to fear the Trimuril or Leandra Weal." Her voice grew louder. "They have never found us, and they never will."

Nicodemus waited a moment before speaking softly. "Your crew is listening, so perhaps you would let me whisper something to you."

Nicodemus felt pressure on his sides and then heard his interrogator speaking close behind his head. "You have exactly one breath to convince me that I shouldn't cut you into pieces small enough for the river fish to swallow."

"It's too late," Nicodemus whispered. "You've swallowed poison bait."

She was silent for a moment. "What do you mean?"

"Think about what I just offered so loudly. Who could make such an offer?"

"No one."

"No one except Nicodemus Weal," he said before belatedly adding, "Or his wife. If you do convert, don't tell Francesca I forgot that part."

"You're mad as a monkey in heat."

"You are the River Thief's avatar, yes?" he asked.

Rather than answer him, she said, "You can't be the Halcyon; we've had reports that Nicodemus Weal went after a brigand goddess to the east of Chandralu nearly thirty days ago. There's been no word that he came back."

"Where do you get such information?" Nicodemus asked. "Tell me and I could make things even easier for you."

His interrogator said nothing.

"Do you have an informant among my daughter's officers? Is one of them in your purse? Is that how you have been avoiding Leandra?"

"Lies," the woman said faintly.

Nicodemus continued. "I needed you and your men to hear what I had to say. It was my only chance of saving the River Thief. Unless he converts, you and your crew will die. Then I will find your god and deconstruct him into stray punctuation. You are his avatar, yes? You need to let me speak to him."

His interrogator sniffed and muttered "him" under her breath. Suddenly Nicodemus recognized in her voice a peculiar kind of annoyance. Nicodemus's gut clenched. "Oh . . . bloody burning hell!"

"What?"

"I've been a complete . . . ass."

"Just when I begin to believe I should take you seriously, you say something completely insane."

"I just realized why you are not taking me seriously."

"Because you keep saying completely insane things?"

"Because the reports I received in Chandralu described the River Thief as a water god, and I believed them."

The interrogator was silent.

"You are not an avatar?"

"What makes you say that?"

"The River Thief isn't a water god. She's a water goddess. You are the River Thief."

There was a short pause. "At least you are not the stupidest man I have ever met. But I can't say that's much of a compliment."

"Goddess, please forgive me. You are clearly a subtle deity, one that would be a great boon to the league. But if you remain a neodemon, I have no choice but to bring you down."

"Try to bring me down."

"I wouldn't let you capture me if I couldn't ensure my safety. What's more you're not a fighting deity; you've gotten by all these years by concealment."

She didn't reply.

"And you're brave," Nicodemus added. "When confronted with their possible death, most deities bluster. It's one of the downsides of immortality, I think."

"Downsides, mortal? I am the one who has you upside down and censored."

"Do you think that will help you survive?"

A long pause. "Not if you're telling me the truth, Nicodemus Weal."

"I am. Now, help me to save you. What are your requisites? How can I help you thrive in the league?"

The goddess's voice sounded slightly sad. "There can be no place for me in the league, or anywhere where humans rule."

Nicodemus snorted. "Don't be dramatic. Any deity can live within the league, especially here on Ixos." He paused. "Though I suppose any deity incarnated on this continent could live free. But you are a neodemon, not a demon."

There was no reply.

"Goddess, you do not seriously mean to tell me that you crossed the great ocean, that you're a demon of the Ancient Continent?"

Still no reply.

"You're bluffing," Nicodemus insisted, though he felt a twinge of fear. "You can't expect me to believe that after waiting thirty years for the Disjunction, the dread god Los would send over a single steal-from-the-rich-to-do-good demoness."

"No one believes the Disjunction is coming. Not even your daughter."

"What?"

"Listen to me, I am in fact a divinity complex of three goddesses—one of them quite old. My requisites are complicated. What you are offering, equitable theft without being bound by the Sacred Regent, could you accommodate the requisites for all three of us?"

"Unless there is a truly outrageous requisite, human pain or sacrifice or something like that."

"No, no. Nothing barbaric."

"Then I can bring you into the league's pantheon."

"Then . . . we shall talk." Something moved behind Nicodemus. "Raise your hands. I'll cut you down."

Nicodemus obeyed and felt something jerk at his legs. He fell a half foot before landing on his hands and rolling easily up to a crouch. Being rightside up after so long was strange. The blood flowed out of his head and he felt as if he could think more clearly.

Grateful, he turned to regard the River Thief and discovered a lithe female figure, wrapped in a white cloth that floated around all six of her graceful arms—one pair of arms from each of the goddesses that had fused to form her complex. The sight made him think of a different river goddess, one he had known long ago.

In each of her six hands, the River Thief held a different kind of knife: a narrow dirk, a throwing dagger, a wavering kris, and so forth. Around her silhouette glowed an aura of blue-green light. Nicodemus was about to bow to the neodemon he hoped to convert, but then he saw her face and he froze.

For the second time that night, Nicodemus could not make sense of what he was seeing. The neodemon's face . . . it filled his mind with confusion and fear. A single, absurd question pressed itself into his every thought with undeniable urgency. Before he realized what he was doing, Nicodemus asked, "Goddess, why do you have my daughter's face?"

CHAPTER SIX

From the catamaran's forward center deck, Leandra regarded the broad limestone formation that was Keyway Island.

Roughly circular and a mile in diameter, Keyway looked from the outside like the bay's other large standing islands. However, wind and tide had hollowed out Keyway's center, leaving a wide pool enclosed by a fortresslike formation and accessible only through a breach in the limestone on the island's southern face. During high tide, the breach seemed nothing more than a sliver in the stone. Low tide, however, exposed a tunnel thirty feet wide and fifty feet long that led into Keyway Pool. At low tide, expert sailors could maneuver into Keyway Pool something as large as, say, a fifty-foot war catamaran. With Lieutenant Peleki bellowing orders, Leandra's crew did just such a thing.

During the careful maneuvering, Leandra again looked aft at the standing islands. As before, she saw tall moonlit limestone, but this time she glimpsed something dark disappearing behind one of the islands. It made her breath catch. Was this what Holokai had seen? It had happened so fast and seemed so small. The next moment something took flight from a nearby island, and Leandra let out a brief laugh. Some kind of seabird. Nothing more.

Relieved, Leandra turned back as the catamaran coasted into Keyway Pool and looked up in satisfaction at her secret village.

Scattered across the Bay of Standing Islands were several famous "sea villages"—small settlements carved into the limestone islands and adorned with bamboo decks, bridges, and palisades. The inhabitants were mostly fisherman, a few merchants. They were remarkable places.

The sea village of Azure Strait had been built below the ruins of Sukrapor. On the island's top stood ruined temples crowded with strangler fig trees— their grasping roots patiently tightened around temple facades and statues of the Lotus gods who had been killed in their war with the Sea gods.

Another example of a sea village was Feather Island, the southernmost and largest of its kind. The houses there climbed two limestone formations that stood so close that they were linked by several rope bridges, which swung in a slight breeze. Leandra had no great fear of heights, but once she had crossed such a bridge and found that the disconcerting sway of the blue world—tropical sky above, churning tides below—had made her stomach lurch.

Most every sea village was an exquisite sight at evening, when the inhabitants lit kakui nut lamps and the vertical villages lit up the rock faces like something from a dream.

Keyway Pool, the secret sea village built by Leandra and her followers, was nothing so picturesque. There were no buildings on the outer island walls, nothing that would identify it as an inhabited island.

But inside the island, the pool was nearly a quarter mile in diameter and surprisingly transparent. When sunlight fell onto the water, one could often look down through forty feet or so to see the bottom's bright marine life. Near the high-water mark, carved into the limestone, were the docks and stores. Above this, in a nearly complete circle, was a row of deeply cut rooms covered with wooden fronts and connected by a sturdy boardwalk, protected from sun and rain by roofs of palm frond thatch. Two more levels were built above the first and connected by rope ladders with bamboo rungs.

Farther up the walls, where they met the island's top, the limestone had been carved into expanding terraces. With divine assistance, earth had been brought from the big island and placed onto each terrace so that each grew a particular crop: rice for the Lotus Culture, taro for the Sea Culture, chickpeas or lentils for Cloud Culture. A smaller terrace, directly below Leandra's spacious quarters, held a young plumeria tree, which was slowly snowing pale blossoms onto the pool.

Presently forty souls—most human, all refugees—called the secret village home. But work was underway on another level, and given that the limestone walls ascended nearly a hundred feet farther up to the island's top. One day there could be as many as a hundred souls living in Keyway Pool. That is, if Leandra could keep her people and their cause secret and safe.

As the crew docked the catamaran, kukui lamps flickered into brightness along the second and third levels, and one of the dockworkers lit two torches, the reflections of which danced on the water and attracted the sleek, dark silhouettes of fish.

According to Sea Culture custom, Lieutenant Peleki accompanied Leandra onto the dock while brandishing the leimako to signify her status as the village's chieftain. Dhrun, manifesting Dhrunarman, followed close behind.

They were met by Master Alo, a sun-wrinkled old man with a long plait of white hair.

Until twenty years ago, he had been the high priest of a Verdantine goddess of wildfire. Then the empire had deconstructed his deity and seized all of his order's lands and holdings. A few co-religionists had helped him escape to Ixos. Ever since, he had served as steward of Keyway Pool.

"Master Alo," she said with a nod. "It is always a pleasure to return to your sunny countenance."

The old priest regarded her with an expression that was about as emotive as a bucket.

"I trust nothing urgent happened while I was away," she said with a hopeful note.

"News came in from Chandralu by sea canoe last night. It seems a royal messenger appeared at your family complex yesterday evening. The Sacred Regent has summoned you to his court and was distressed that you could not be found."

Leandra winced. "What did his sacred majesty want?"

"The messenger did not say."

"Has my father returned to the city?"

"No report of that. But there is civil unrest. Apparently a fishing boat came back to the docks yesterday after going missing for three days. Half the crew lay dead and rotting on deck and the survivors were raving about sea ghosts or the Floating Island having come into the bay."

Leandra frowned. "That fairy tale again?"

"That's what some rumors say. The crew was mostly Sea People. Some of their relatives blamed the event on a new neodemon from the Lornish immigrants in the Naukaa District. A brawl broke out in one of the Cowry Street winehouses."

"Any other evidence that the Lornish immigrants have formed a cult or a neodemon?"

"Just more whispers about the Cult of the Undivided Society trying to speed the day of Disjunction."

Dhrun cleared his throat. "Ten days or so ago, I heard a rumor in the wrestling arena. A story that a young Lotus fisherman had gone kayak fishing in the Standing Islands and come back having lost his wits and raving about finding a whirlpool that sucked everything down to the underworld while a plume of smoke appeared out of nowhere sixty feet above the sea. Apparently the fisherman became feverish and died a few days later. I thought it was all a fiction."

Leandra straightened. "Well, I always do love these creative little bits of unsubstantiated rumor and hearsay that will be a complete waste of time to investigate, but I'll add a possible neodemon in the bay to my list of concerns. Are there any other lovely rumors I should know about?"

Alo shrugged. "There's talk of crop failures in Verdant. The rice merchants are already racing each other to be the first to profit from it."

"Typical," Leandra muttered. Her father had discovered that the Silent Blight had started when the demon Typhon had first landed on the New Continent. The demon's metaspells prevented misspelling in Language Prime; this reduced the ability of life to diversify itself. However, Nicodemus's metaspells, which made language more intuitive and chaotic, had reversed the Silent Blight in the league kingdoms. The empress's metaspells, on the other hand, decreased error in language and so exacerbated the Silent Blight. The past fifteen years had seen three crop failures in the empire. "Is there anything else, Alo?"

"The matter of our funds."

"Matter?" Leandra asked, more shrilly than intended. "At last reckoning, we had nearly three thousand rupees worth of uncut jade in our treasury."

"Perhaps you recall taking half of that for your little rendezvous with the smuggler. If I ask how much jade you have brought back, will I receive an answer other than petulance?"

"Certainly, how about peevishness?"

"My lady, the going rates of peevishness are quite low."

"Sullenness then?"

"In even less demand than surliness this year," Alo said with a sigh. "So, you spent all of that jade?"

"Okay, now you're just begging me to go back to petulance," she said petulantly.

"Thus swings the great pendulum of our cause," Alo said dryly, "from great riches to near ruination. As I have previously mentioned, in three days we must pay for provisions for Keyway Island, maintenance of the catamaran, and wages for your crew. Then there are the bribes to the city watch, the bay admiral, and the treasury officers."

"Oh," Leandra said with a start, "and there's something else to add to your pendulum."

"Another expense?"

"A large one."

"My Lady Warden, may I now offer *you* petulance?"

"No, I have the market cornered."

"How about irritability then?"

"Recently devalued from over-production. I am sorry, Alo, but I'll need the rest of the jade when I meet with the smuggler again tomorrow night."

"Perhaps I can better explain what a precarious state we are in. We can't afford another such godspell unless it magically produces rupees from my earwax."

"Given how much earwax you produce, that would be wondrous. But in the meantime have we any incomes? Are we expecting a payment from our allies?"

The old man shook his head. "We have had no news from the Society of the Eastern Road; perhaps your father has undone them. Vashrama's gang is again late on their protection fees. Captain Tupo's catamarans are still at sea. The shipment from the Matrupor is now ten days late, and we don't expect to hear from our allies on the Outer Islands for at least another season."

She looked at Dhrun. "What about the wrestling arena? Our connections with the gambling houses?"

The divinity complex shook his head. "No tournament until after the Night of Bright Souls. Back when I was a neodemon, I could have arranged a back-alley match. But now that I'm officially in the pantheon . . ." He shrugged all four shoulders.

"Lovely," Leandra muttered before raising her voice for those still working on the catamaran. "Lieutenant, leave a torch burning for Captain Holokai, and wake me when he returns. The rest of you, to bed. We will have an early start. Alo and Dhrun, please follow me." She headed off of the docks and onto the village's boardwalk.

Her knees ached and there was still pain in her belly, but it wasn't as bad as before. With luck, her disease flare would burn itself out. It was time she was due a little luck. Just a little.

"Perhaps," Alo said from behind her, "I should approach one of the banking houses—"

She stopped. "No credit. If we must, I'll use my family's funds. But credit would draw a line of inquiry and that will lead the wrong people here."

"So you have said, but—"

"How much silver do we need?"

Without pause the old man said, "Two thousand five hundred thirty-two rupees."

Leandra tried to keep her face impassive. "When?"

"In three days, if you want to keep the officials happily bribed and everyone on this island eating."

"Right. I'll see to it." For all she knew she might die in one day's time. Or maybe the royal summons would at last uncover her cause, the little game she had been playing with the universe. Maybe everything would go to one of the burning hells when she killed someone she loved. Really, there was no reason to worry about the money. Not yet there wasn't.

Alo was looking at her dubiously.

She nodded at him. "Thank you Master Alo. Sorry to wake you from your bed. Before you retire, will you see that the catamaran is fully supplied? I will be setting off for Chandralu at next low tide."

He bowed and withdrew.

Dhrun bowed as well. "Shall I—"

"No, I need someone to talk to right now, but not anyone with . . . all of"—she made fluttery hands at his scruffy beard—"that."

The divinity complex smiled as his beard fell to his feet like dirty snow. His skin smoothed, his chin receded, eyes widened; his body slipped into that of the athletic goddess of victory. "Better?" Dhrun asked once she fully manifested Nika.

Leandra nodded. "Better." She turned and climbed up a rope ladder that lay before her quarters. These were the widest rooms in Keyway Pool, but still they were as cramped as a cabin in a Lornish galley. Leandra could see why some who had taken refuge in Keyway felt as if it were a prison.

Leandra lit a stick of incense and then stepped behind her bathing screen. Someone had set up an urn of fresh water, a bamboo ladle, and a bar of soap. Leandra carefully unbound her wallet of poisoner's needles and her throwing knives. She laid them carefully on the stool next to the screen.

"Since we've established that you are so very old and wise, and I should emphasize old," she said to Dhrun while undressing, "perhaps you could advise me about investigating the murder I might commit sometime early tomorrow morning." Using the ladle, she poured the cool water over her head.

"Well, you've already interrogated me and, I assume, Holokai."

Leandra shivered as the sweat and seawater washed off of her. "Indeed."

"So who's left to interview?"

"My father if he returns, which would be troublesome. My mother would be but she is on the other side of the ocean. Then there's my old lover—"

"The handsome lapsed wizard you mentioned that night we drank too much kava?"

"That would be Thaddeus."

"The one who was so smart and so interested in how text can alter a mind?"

"The one and only."

"Didn't you tell me how wonderful things were in the bedroom with him?"

"Let's say the kava was doing the speaking."

"He was the one who would spellwright after smoking opium?"

"You have the damnedest memory for embarrassing things I mention in passing."

"Drunkenly mention in passing."

"Right."

"And didn't he break your heart with that other woman?"

"Three other women."

"Well, I hope you have to kill him."

"Me too." Leandra sighed as she ladled more water on herself. With the soap, she began to lather herself starting with her swollen knees. "Dhru, that smuggler who sold us this godspell, did you notice anything . . . familiar about him?"

"What do you mean?"

"I can't shake the sensation that I've seen him somewhere else before, but it doesn't seem possible. Perhaps I have heard him described to me. Did he seem familiar to you at all?"

"He did not," Dhrun said before pausing. "But I must say again that I don't trust him."

"Of course we can't trust him; he's a smuggler."

"No, no. I mean it just seems too implausible that his contacts find us and offer to sell us prophetic texts just when our cause is in its most dire time."

"And what of his story of the empire preparing for conflict with the league?"

"It sounds a little much to me," Dhrun said. "Though I suppose it's possible there could be another incident like the Ogun Blockade." Twenty-two years ago, the empire had placed heavy tariffs on Ixonian traders, and the airships off of the Isles of Ogun had failed to protect the merchants from pirates.

When Ixonian spies discovered that a corrupt air marshal was protecting a small clan of pirates in exchange for half their plunder, the league invaded the Ogun Isles on the pretext of ridding the islands of piracy. The empire took this as a violation of their sovereignty and a yearlong, bloody war was fought over the islands. Eventually the Ixonian fleet and Tagrana, a powerful war goddess capable of transforming unarmed men and women into tiger-like warriors, captured all of the Ogun Isles and blockaded the city, forcing concessions from the empire.

Leandra considered the possibility that some new tension was arising between Ixos and Trillinon. "But ever since the blockade, the empire has tried to avoid all conflict with Ixos. The empress would far rather play her politics on the Spirish boarder with Lorn."

"Every woman can change her mind, even an empress."

"True," Leandra said as she ladled more water over herself.

"To back up for a second," Dhrun asked, "you are absolutely sure your prophecy about having to kill someone is strong?"

"Yes. If I run, everyone I love will die."

"But perhaps if you were simply to forget about the whole thing?"

"I doubt it would work, wouldn't be much different from running. Anyway, how could one forget that one is going to become a murderer?"

"Lots of wine?"

Leandra laughed but then asked, "Is there any out there?"

She could hear Dhrun walking about the small rooms. Leandra washed the last of the soap from her body. "No," Dhrun said at last. "Let me see if there's any in the provisions room."

"That is kind of you."

"It would be kind if I didn't plan to drink most of it myself."

Leandra smiled.

She heard the creaking of the goddess descending the rope ladder. Leandra poured another ladleful of water over her head and then toweled off before slipping into the robes draped over the screen.

Leandra walked onto her deck and saw that most of the kukui lamps were snuffed. Only a single torch burned on the docks. In the pool below the torch, several fish swam languid circles.

Leandra was starting to wonder if her belly pain was subsiding when she heard the rope creak behind her. She turned and saw Dhrun climbing with her two upper arms and holding in her lower right hand a small porcelain bottle, in her lower left two porcelain cups. Leandra smiled. "I really should not drink during a disease flare."

"You really shouldn't," Dhrun agreed. "I'll sacrifice myself and drink it all for you." The goddess held one cup in each lower hand and poured rice wine into them both with her upper right hand. She offered one.

Leandra accepted. "Well, I wouldn't want you to sacrifice too much. And besides, I can't have any bad habits—"

"Only full-blown addictions," Dhrun finished for her in mock boredom. "Now, I can assure you that I haven't put any tetrodotoxin in here." She raised her cup.

"To friends who never need to poison each other," Leandra said. They clinked cups in the Southern fashion. Leandra sipped the rice wine. It was a touch oversweet, but still enjoyable. "I'm surprised Alo spends the rupees for provision room wine."

"Oh, he doesn't," Dhrun said. "He hides a personal cache in the back of his bookshelf. Sometimes he even has a bottle of mandana. In any case, I saw he was still on the docks and so liberated this from his quarters."

Leandra laughed. "Remind me to get something nice for that dear man when we return to the city."

"I would suggest a gift of two thousand five hundred thirty-two rupees, or he may well burst a blood vessel."

"Right," Leandra said with a sigh and turned back to her deck. "Tomorrow is going to be busy." They drank silently and watched the torchlight reflected on the pool water. The fish carved their erratic circuits near the dock torch.

At last Leandra announced that she would sleep. Dhrun shifted back into his Dhrunarman incarnation and took up guard near the ladder.

Almost the instant Leandra put her head to the pillow, she fell into a dream of a dark seascape with a rolling deck beneath her. The ocean was filled with a whirlpool. A hundred feet above her, a billowing plume of smoke formed from nothing. Holokai and Thaddeus were there, both very angry. Then she was in a Dralish forest, everything so cool and green and the high oak boughs arching above her. Wind in the leaves. She was a child and her father's voice was calling . . . calling . . .

Leandra woke and the memory of the dream twisted into nothing. She tried to recall but her gut was filled with a sickening, queasy feeling, as if she were terribly worried. The more she tried to remember the dream, the faster it slipped away.

Leandra sat up. The sky above the pool was filled with dappled clouds just barely illuminated with early dawn.

Then Leandra realized that her gut didn't hurt; rather, in an hour, most of her future selves would be frantically worried. It was the prophetic godspell.

Something this morning was going to distress her. Scowling, Leandra rubbed her forehead where she supposed her godspell to be. She might not have bought the text if she had known that it would wake her an hour early every morning.

Dhrun was standing guard, all four arms folded. He hadn't moved since she fell asleep. She wondered what the deity thought about when he became so still.

Leandra flopped back into bed, still irritated at her godspell, hoping to fall back asleep. But after a minute she realized her bladder was uncomfortably full. So, she hauled herself over to the chamber pot and then back to the sheets. But when she was lying still, she found she could not stop wondering about what was going to fill her with such apprehension in less than an hour's time. She tossed and turned for a while longer and then gave up on sleep and walked out to her deck.

The morning was darkening as a fat cloud occluded the sky above the pool. She looked down into the water, a few scattered rain drops were falling. A light, warm tropical rain.

It was high tide now and the torch left on the dock was still burning. Leandra looked down into the pellucid water and was shocked to see a massive, nightmarelike figure slip through the now submarine opening that admitted her catamaran. The creature swam a powerful circle around the pool, causing the surface to churn into small whirlpools and eddies.

Leandra hurried to the rope ladder. "Should I follow—" Dhrun asked before Leandra interrupted. "No, stay here. I'll send for you in a moment."

She hurried down the ladder and across the boardwalk. By the time she reached the dock, Holokai was already sitting at its edge, wet, humanoid, naked. He was breathing hard but grinning. "Fast, huh?" he said with a grin. "I told you I was feeling strong. I think even more people have been praying for me lately. But, I could eat for three days straight."

"Poor hunting on the way back?" she asked. Usually Holokai returned from a long swim with a belly full of harbor seal.

He shook his head. "No time. About five miles outside the Cerulean Strait, I circled a few times below an inbound Southern ship. But when I came near the surface, I woke something up. Never felt a presence like that before. Hey, Lea, why don't you tell me next time you send me to surf a tidal wave, huh?" He laughed.

Leandra's belly began to hurt. "What do you mean?"

"You know . . . you know how it is. My kind, in my element, I can feel another like me. I don't like getting too close, especially in open water. But maybe that's just me, you know?"

"Holokai," Leandra interrupted, her patience thinning, "what did you sense out there? Another god?"

His face became thoughtful. "Yeah, like another god. But not another god, I don't think. It's funny, Lea, the presence . . . it was like . . . like . . ."

Leandra's belly began to ache with anxiety. "Did you breech?"

"Very briefly, just got one eye above the water. Some of those Southern sailor boys like to get brave with harpoons and I'm hungry, yeah, but I'm not that hungry." He grimaced, maybe remembering the last time he had eaten a sailor.

"But the ship's name, Kai, the thing written in gold leaf on the side of the ship, what did it read?"

Holokai frowned. Reading was not his strong point when his eyes were all black. At last he said, *"The High Queen's Lance."*

Leandra groaned. Her parents had fallen in love during the political intrigue in the Spirish city of Avel that involved a Spirish airship named the *Queen's Lance.*

"Lea, you know what I think the presence was that I felt. It was like . . . well . . . from what you told me I think it was like . . ."

"Like a dragon?" Lea asked.

"Hey, how'd you know?"

Leandra growled a word in two clipped syllables as only an irate adult child can: "Moth-er."

CHAPTER SEVEN

Nicodemus and the neodemon wearing his daughter's face stared at each other with incomprehension. "Your daughter's face?" the River Thief asked.

"You're . . ." Nicodemus stuttered. "You're impersonating her?"

"Leandra Weal? The Warden of Ixos?" the River Thief asked. "She has my face?"

"You have hers."

The River Thief's eyes narrowed with sudden comprehension. "So . . ." All six of her hands tightened around their knives.

Nicodemus dodged just as the neodemon's right uppermost arm flicked back and then forward. Her throwing dagger passed within an inch of his shoulder as he misspelled the last of censoring texts from his mind. The River Thief leapt forward with a three-arm knife thrust. Nicodemus danced back but not before her lowermost knife cut into his hip.

"Stop!" Nicodemus cried and pulled a blasting spell from his stomach. He flicked it at the neodemon's feet with his right hand while using his left to cast a shielding spell on the deck before him.

A wall of protective indigo words shot up to Nicodemus's waist. The River Thief lunged again, this time leading with the kris in her mid-left hand. But Nicodemus ducked below his shielding spell just as his blasting spell detonated. A shockwave momentarily knocked every thought from Nicodemus's mind and set his ears ringing.

In the next instant, he found himself staggering to his feet. Two sailors were charging, knives raised. "Rory!" Nicodemus called as he reached to his hip and pulled free a coruscation of paragraphs that leapt from his skin to form a two-handed textual sword. "Rory, now!"

To Nicodemus's relief and horror, the deck before the charging sailors exploded into an array of razor-thin spikes each five or six feet in length. The giant splinters punched straight into the sailors' legs and bellies.

The night erupted into screams. Nicodemus looked around and saw that every one of the River Thief's sailors had been similarly impaled by a nightmare blossoming of splinters.

A booming crash turned Nicodemus's eyes starboard. His blasting text had knocked the River Thief into the gunnel; there, Rory had made the wood come alive with spikes, one or two of which had pierced the neodemon's side but most had broken harmlessly. Large barklike growths had emerged from the gunnel to envelop three of the neodemon's arms. But the blue-green aura surrounding the River Thief ignited into flames and burned her restraints.

Suddenly, the barge lurched and Nicodemus nearly lost his balance. A fountain of water erupted from the river behind the neodemon as she tore herself free of the barklike bindings.

"Goddess, wait!" Nicodemus yelled. "It doesn't have to be like this!"

The neodemon turned toward him. Her eyes burned with a merciless white light. She advanced, more carefully now. The barge shook again and Nicodemus stumbled. The River Thief danced forward, slashing with first her left middle arm then all of her right arms. Nicodemus met the first slash with his textual sword then jumped back to avoid the other blades. With a yell and downward slash, he severed her right uppermost arm at the elbow.

Shrieking, the neodemon lurched backward. Nicodemus pressed his attack and knocked free another of her knives. He was about to thrust into her gut when she jumped away and fell. A roar of thrashing water erupted from somewhere behind Nicodemus. The barge lurched again.

"Goddess, yield! It doesn't have to be like this!" Nicodemus yelled again.

"There's no safe place!" She raised two of her hands in clenched fists and suddenly the deck bucked. Nicodemus fell forward.

"The hull's cracking!" yelled a muffled voice that Nicodemus recognized as Rory's. He glimpsed the druid's white robes as the man pulled himself up from the hatch. "Nico, she's using her godspell to batter the ship. If we go under, we all die!"

The River Goddess hissed. With one of her arms she grabbed Nicodemus's foot and with the other she started to drive a dirk into his calf. But where she touched him, the blue-green fire of her aura vanished as his cacography misspelled her godspell.

She shrieked and pulled her hand back. Her knife had not sunk more than an inch into Nicodemus's calf.

Nicodemus had lost the sword text, but he was close enough now that it did not matter. He lurched forward and caught one of the River Thief's wrists. Her cyan aura winked out where he touched and she screamed.

"Goddess, you have to yield!" Again the boat heaved. Nicodemus and the neodemon slid across a deck to slam into the gunnel.

"We're taking on water!" Rory yelled.

"Goddess!" Nicodemus yelled. "Yield!"

"I cannot," the River Thief gasped while trying to free her arm from Nicodemus's grasp. With two of her other arms, she grabbed the top of the gunnel.

"Don't let her into the water!" Rory cried just as the neodemon shrieked, "Let me go!"

"Yield!" Nicodemus bellowed.

She continued to struggle, all her arms flailing. Something sharp cut into Nicodemus's shoulder. "There can be peace no more!" the neodemon yelled. "I see her now. She will end this world!"

Nicodemus caught another of her hands. Their faces were now inches apart; her blank white eyes stared into his green ones. "Peace no more," she whispered, and then, instead of trying to escape, she wrapped all her arms and her legs around Nicodemus. The air around them crackled as his cacography misspelled her.

"Wait," Nicodemus cried. "Wait, you—" He needed to know why she was wearing his daughter's face and if she truly was a demon of the Ancient Continent. But the River Thief grasped him tighter. In a blaze of blue and green scintilla, she dissolved into light and air.

Nicodemus found himself lying in darkness, bleeding onto the deck.

CHAPTER EIGHT

Francesca DeVega watched the sailors race about the deck and swarm over the rigging. To the east, dawn limned the Ixonian headlands with sunlight. The new day was dappled with seaborne clouds.

The sight made Francesca's chest tighten, a familiar sensation since leaving Starfall Island a month ago. The news she was bringing Nicodemus could not be trusted to a messenger or colaboris spell, so she had been forced to leave the Dralish pantheon to the chaos it called self-governance. If the Council had been successful, warships were even now sailing toward Chandralu. Compounding Francesca's political worries was the anticipation of reunion with her husband and daughter. So, a lovely jaunt through the tropics this would not be. Pity. She could use one.

Last night Francesca had woken in her cabin with the knowledge that an unknown sea deity was circling below their ship. It was a strong divine presence; one that made Francesca's textual mind flare into prophetic calculation. As had happened only briefly since her confrontation with Typhon thirty years ago, Francesca had perceived the future as a landscape into which she was traveling.

It had been a fleeting glimpse, and she had gained only three insights. First, the deity swimming below her might, in the coming days, kill her. Second, most of her futures and the sea deity's futures intersected at Chandralu's infirmary. How, she couldn't say. And third, the coming events in Chandralu had the potential for vast and permanent consequences in all six human kingdoms.

This last insight was a confirmation of what she had already suspected, the news she was bringing to Nicodemus being what it was. She prayed again to the Creator that the Council had been successful and that the forces of Dral and Lorn had been marshaled and dispatched to Ixos.

After sensing the sea deity, Francesca had risen from her bunk, unintentionally waking her student and cabin mate. She had hurried on deck to peer down into the starlit waters in hopes of spotting her future opponent. A kraken god perhaps? A whale goddess? Some divinity complex of human and marine animal? She wanted to glimpse at least some part of it. Maybe just a tentacle? But the divinity circled the boat only once more and swam with shocking speed north toward Chandralu.

Her student, the physician Ellen D'Valin, had followed her on deck and was soon joined by the twin druids, Tam and Kenna, both of Thorntree. Ellen had worn the haggard but alert expression of a physician called from her bed. The twin druids—their pale faces always so similar—blinked in the lingering confusion of sleep. The four of them comprised the entirety of Francesca's party—the smallest she had traveled with in years.

If Francesca had better control over her ability to transform into a dragon, she would have left them all behind and flown to Chandralu. But her incarnations were what they were, and so she had been forced to suffer another sea voyage. At least that had the advantage of keeping her in good company.

She had tried to send her party back to bed, but after hearing about the sea deity circling below, they insisted on staying with her.

She wondered what, exactly, they thought they could do for a dragon that she could not do for herself. For surely an attacking sea deity would induce her draconic incarnation. But there was no use pointing this out to her followers as it would only make them feel small and insignificant. Then, the next time she tried to send them out on a small and insignificant task, they would object on the grounds of smallness and insignificance.

Many years ago, remaining quiet had been a perennial problem for Francesca, but years of leadership had taught her the importance of shutting up. Well, mostly they had. Mostly.

So Francesca had stood with her party until the ship's bell had rung and the watch changed. She perceived the bell's sound as a lovely vivid red cloud to her right that faded into a quieter, quavering scintilla and then dissolved into silence.

Thirty-four years ago, when she and Nicodemus had been embroiled in the demon Typhon's usurpation of Avel, a half-dragon named the Savanna Walker had attacked her and permanently restructured her mind. The Savanna Walker was in fact the distorted remains of an ancient cacographer named James Berr. His touch had caused her ears to report their sensation to the part of her mind that perceived vision.

Initially this synesthetic perception of sound had made Francesca effectively deaf. But over time she had adapted to the peculiarities of her mind, learned to interpret sound as vision. Words were recognizable by their geometry and color, individual voices by their particular hues and shapes. Music, initially overwhelming almost hallucinogenic, had become a stream of color and light through time—sometimes pulsatile, sometimes free flowing—which was entirely indescribable to those with typical hearing. As a result, her tastes in poetry and song changed away from classical structure toward the novel and spontaneous. It had taken her decades, but Francesca had transformed what had been a debilitating difference into a unique way of apprehending and appreciating the universe.

Presently, Francesca's adaptation to her synesthetic hearing had become so expert that she experienced no anxiety about interpreting sound or communicating.

So after perceiving the ship's vivid red bell toll, Francesca had tried to keep her party out of the sailor's way. But when the first mate invited them to return to their cabins with less than perfect politeness, Francesca finally convinced the young people to sleep while they could.

They had left her alone with the night sky to think about the sea deity. That it had been subtle enough to hide its identity suggested it was not some newly incarnated neodemon. But no legitimate member of the Ixonian pantheon would have come so close without declaring itself. The realization had darkened her mood and left her grimacing into the wind.

Francesca contemplated how quickly the world was changing. Less than fifty years ago, all the magical societies from wizards to pyromancers were still meeting in convocations to ensure that no magical society would, at least overtly, participate in the wars between kingdoms. Now the empire openly filled its ranks with the hierophants, pyromancers, shamans, and the wizards of Astrophell. Meanwhile, the wizards of Starfall Keep, the druids, and the highsmiths were committed to fighting in any conflict that threatened a league kingdom.

These reflections further darkened Francesca's mood until the sun crested the eastern headlands. Then the tropical wind blew just cool enough to be pleasant. After a month of rolling decks and salt beef and hardtack, there was the promise of solid land underfoot and Ixonian curry in the belly. It was enough to lift her mood.

She turned toward the sunrise and felt the wind tossing her long brown hair. She looked north and saw the Cerulean Strait—a narrow stretch of water between the Chandralu peninsula and the northern headlands that connected the ocean with the Bay of Standing Islands. She could not yet make out any of the famous limestone islands as they were found only in the bay's eastern waters.

Decades ago Francesca had been written by the ancient demon Typhon and placed in the city of Avel in an attempt to convert Nicodemus. Together, she and Nico had escaped the demon's control and defeated him.

In creating Francesca, Typhon had given her memories of a physician who had studied in the clerical academy in Port Mercy and then practiced in the famous infirmary of Chandralu. As a result, Francesca had a wealth of personal and historical memories of the archipelago.

It had been a long time since she'd last visited. Ixos was now her daughter's domain—for better or worse—and her memories of the archipelago and its history had become intermingled with the guilt, longing, and anger that she felt whenever she thought of Leandra.

In fact, Francesca had lately come to see how well Ixos fit Leandra. For example, the Ixonian histories reported that the ancient Lotus People had built Sukrapor, their first and greatest city, on a wide limestone mantle where the Bay of Standing Islands now stood. Back then, there was no bay, only a narrow estuary where the Matrunda River met the sea. Sukrapor had thrived until the Sea People had ventured out of the inner island chain on voyaging canoes and catamarans. The wars between the two cultures had been savage.

The fiercest battles had been fought in the estuary; the Sea People's ancient gods had again and again smashed themselves into the rock mantle below Sukrapor, dissolving limestone from beneath the city into the hundreds of tall standing islands that lined the eastern aspect of the bay.

The Sea People would have been victorious if the ancient Lotus gods had not made a desperate alliance with the Cloud People of the outer island chain. Though few in number, the Cloud People possessed the earliest form of the hydromancer's magical language. When the first water temple was built and the nascent order of hydromancers had formed, the balance of power in the archipelago had evened.

The wars had raged for decades, weakening all combatants, and ended only when the First Neosolar Empire expanded out of Trillinion to subjugate the entire archipelago. Under imperial rule, the Lotus People had retreated up the Matrunda River to build Matrundapor. An age later, when the First Neosolar Empire had crumbled, one deity from each of the archipelago's cultures had fused themselves together to form the Trimuril, the first divinity complex. United under this deity, the three Ixonian peoples won independence as the kingdom of Ixos and founded Chandralu as their capital.

However, as was so often the case in history, strife among the cultures had continued. The ancient prejudices remained. Skirmishes and even small wars between Sea and Lotus, Cloud and Sea, Lotus and Cloud continued to the present day.

Francesca wondered again if this history wasn't the reason Leandra had chosen to dedicate her short life to the archipelago. The Lotus Culture, the Sea Culture, the Cloud Culture, all composed the body of Ixos. Each was now dependent on the others, and yet periodically at war with one another.

Ixos, the archipelago, was vibrantly alive and yet at war with itself, just as Leandra's body was intensely alive and yet at war with itself.

Thinking of her daughter's disease felt like a taste of ash to Francesca. She thought of all the patients she had cured. Francesca would have forsaken them all if it had allowed her to cure her daughter. Instead, she had only managed to turn her daughter's childhood into an endless series of examinations and experiments. During all those years, they had made only one discovery: During a disease flare, high doses of stress hormones could calm her body's attack on her textual aspects.

Until this discovery, Francesca had not thought that Leandra would live past her tenth year. Now, even though she took the stress hormones during her disease flares, it did not seem that Leandra would live past forty years, a very young age to die for someone of her heritage. So it was that Leandra was Francesca's most beautiful creation, her greatest failure.

Francesca thought about her other mistakes as a mother. At the time, there had seemed to be so little choice. So little choice, especially fourteen years ago in Port Mercy. Perhaps it was that night, that exact night, when she had lost her daughter.

"Magistra?"

Francesca turned to see that Ellen had come back up on deck. She was a petite woman, dark skin, deep-set brown eyes, short glossy black hair, wearing a grand wizard's black robes. It was good to see her. "Ellen, were you able to sleep at all?"

Ellen stepped beside her. "Slept like the dead, which always makes me happy."

"Am I not letting you sleep enough?"

"No," Ellen said while looking at the sea. "But since I enjoy sleeping like the dead, I assume it's evidence that I won't mind actually being dead."

"There's a cheerful morning greeting for you."

Ellen smiled. "I forgot that Magistra is an immortal before she is a physician, so gallows humor will be lost on her."

"I'm afraid, my brilliant student, that your humor is lost on almost everyone."

"Better to have a lost sense of humor than none at all."

Francesca scowled. "You laugh at my jokes."

"A junior physician is required to laugh with her senior physicians when they are present. It helps make up for how much she laughs at them in their absence."

Francesca looked at her sideways. "You are reminding me why I chose you as my Lornish envoy."

"Because you respect my judgment and enjoy my dry wit?"

"No, because you're short."

"Well, they say brevity is the soul of wit . . ." Ellen looked over at Francesca's collarbone and then, exaggeratedly, looked up at her six feet of height. "Oh my, Magistra, I think I may have discovered why you're not funny."

Francesca sighed. "So you don't have any bright ideas about who that sea deity was either?"

"None," Ellen mumbled. The young physician always took failure at any task, even the impossible ones, as a personal insult. Maybe that was why Francesca liked her.

They stood together and listened to the sailors call to each other. Finally Ellen broke their reverie. "Magistra, you don't seem that nervous about meeting your daughter."

"That's nice to hear, because I feel like I might puke."

"Dragon's vomit?"

"Crack another pun and you might make this one do so."

"Don't you think that is mildly hypocritical of you?"

"There's nothing mild about my hypocrisy. I too am guilty of puns."

"So," Ellen said and then sighed, "you couldn't think of a reason why that sea deity showed up either?"

"Nope."

They fell silent again. The sun, now fully up, was illuminating the bright clouds and the dark Ixonian jungles. Through the Cerulean Strait, Francesca could make out the first of the Standing Islands.

"Magistra, this is apropos of nothing, but given what you've told me of your past, can I ask a rather personal question?"

"If I say 'no,' would that stop you from doing so?"

"Previous experience suggests not."

"Better get it over with then."

"When we take our news to Lord Nicodemus, do you really think your daughter might try to kill you?"

"Yes," Francesca said, "and I wouldn't blame her."

CHAPTER NINE

L eandra was brushing her hair when she heard the rope outside her quarters creak. It made her smile.

Again she ran her tortoiseshell comb through her hair, glossy raven black like her father's. Her wrists ached and her stomach still felt uncomfortable, but it seemed her disease flare was cooling despite the rice wine with Dhrun last night.

Behind her, the floorboards creaked. "Come in, Kai. Close the curtains."

"How'd you know it was me?"

She tapped her temples. "An hour ago, I felt a few of my future selves were experiencing moments of . . . unsustainable pleasure. The more I thought of returning to my bedroom the more of my future selves began to feel such unsustainable pleasure."

"Come on now, you know that sustainable problem only happened to me that one night." He laughed. "I had an excuse; it was Bright Souls' Night on Mokumako and my devotees drank too much kava and forgot about my requisites." His firm hands landed lightly on her back and begin to massage her shoulder muscles.

She sighed as her muscles unknotted. Mokumako was Holokai's home island, rimmed by cliffs and covered with jungle and cloud forest. She had met him there years ago, and his cult was still centered on that island.

"Did you want to talk about any of your requisites in particular?" she asked.

Holokai's cult was a throwback to the golden age of the Sea People, when they had raided across the archipelago. His cult believed that, when the Disjunction came, he would defend the island from the demons. His requisites were to destroy any divinity posing a threat to his island. His cult also prayed that Holokai would one day father a demigod who would lead them to glory.

As a result, particularly in the morning when his worshipers were their most fervent, Holokai developed the powerful desire to sire that demigod. Long ago he and Leandra had discovered that her condition had left her infertile, but she did not mind helping her captain practice for such an important task. In fact, for the past few days he had received an unexpectedly large amount of prayerful energy. He wasn't sure why his followers had become more devout, but because it made him particularly vigorous during certain actives, he wasn't questioning it.

"Is the catamaran ready?" Leandra whispered.

"You know her captain wouldn't rest if there was anything more to do for her. I thought there was another lady who might want help getting shipshape."

She leaned back against his chest and smiled.

"You feeling better about the news that your mother might be in the bay?"

"I wouldn't say better, but at least I can prepare myself."

"You truly haven't seen her since Port Mercy fourteen years ago?"

"Truly."

"You ever gonna tell me what happened that drove you apart?"

"Sure, how about just before the seas boil?"

Holokai stopped massaging her shoulders. "So this thing with prophecy and you needing to kill someone and your mother's coming into the bay . . . do you think it has to do with the Disjunction? How bad do you think it is?"

Leandra rolled her eyes. She'd forgotten how touchy he could get about prophecy. "Not bad enough to interrupt a back massage."

He started working his hands again. "Hey, Lea, I'm serious."

"I don't see how this could be connected to the Disjunction. There's no evidence of demons crossing the ocean. I just caught a glimpse of what's coming for me."

"But the possibility of war between empire and league—"

"Politics. The empire is cannibalizing deities to become stronger than the league, and the league is pumping out deities to keep up with the empire. Maybe they'll fight another small war to see who's got the upper hand lately. Whatever happens, neither civilization is going to give half a damn that they are torturing their own to crush the other one. Our job is to be different. That and stay alive."

Holokai grunted agreement. "And about staying alive . . . is what we're dealing with like that incident with the mercenary elephant god?"

"You keep harping on that."

"He did crush half the bones in my body."

"Do you even have bones when you're a shark? I thought you were all cartilage."

"Not the point. I want to know what we're facing. How hot is the water we've landed in?"

"In terms of tight scrapes we have been in before?"

"That'll do."

Leandra considered. Since becoming Warden of Ixos, she had placed herself and her crew in mortal danger only three times. The first was the attempt to take down an elephant mercenary god who had gone neodemon and was trying to pressure the Sacred Regent to let him enter the Trimuril's divinity complex. Leandra was trying to convert him back into the pantheon when things turned violent. If one of the neodemon's lieutenants hadn't gone mad, they never would have escaped.

Leandra's second mistake had involved a jellyfish neodemon who had made his bloodthirsty devotees immune to the sting of his twenty-mile-long tentacles, which he wrapped around a fleet of their pirate ships.

Leandra had attacked with a full squadron and lost two ships and half her crew. She had been forced to flee and survived only because the sea became unusually hazy that evening and they lost their pursuer in the gathering dark. The remains of her squadron had just limped back into harbor. Blessedly, a powerful storm had struck and washed the neodemon onto shore where he died.

More recently, there had been the discovery of a mosquito goddess on the northern coast of the big island. She had been sucking blood from neighboring villagers and divine language from rival deities. When trying to escape after a failed conversion, Leandra and her party had gotten lost in a mangrove swamp. They heard the mosquito goddess's swarm filling the air miles away. The neodemon's insectoid manifestations were truly nightmarish. They had watched her swarm over a man. The bugs covered every inch of exposed skin and wriggled under chain mail. They sucked him dry of blood in moments. Leandra's party would have suffered the same gruesome fate if a nearby volcano hadn't erupted and filled the air with smoke that confused the swarm.

The more she thought about her three failures, the more Leandra realized that she still lived only because luck—the lieutenant's madness, the sea storm, the volcanic eruption—had averted disaster. But then again, who could claim differently in such a precarious world? Every soul in Chandralu was alive only because fortune had spared them from war, disease, disaster. And, she reminded herself, only three of her expeditions had failed while her successes numbered in the hundreds.

She looked up at Holokai. "I'd say it's a dangerous situation we're in, maybe as bad as that botched conversion of the elephant god, but nowhere near as bad as the jellyfish or the mosquitoes."

A bit of the tension went out of his eyes. He didn't like thinking much for himself. Sharks, as a rule, are not being overly thoughtful. "Okay then."

She leaned back against his chest. "Now, wasn't there . . . something else you were concerned about?"

He laughed softly as his hands slipped down her back, tracing along her skin, to hang around her waist. Then she could feel his fingers working as they gathered in the cloth of her robes. Slowly, slowly her hemline rose up to her knees. "Maybe one thing."

She reached back to press her palm against his hips. "What's that?"

Softly he kissed her neck. "You're sure no one will disturb us?"

"I gave everyone chores to keep them busy for an hour."

He kept gathering in her robes, drawing the hemline up her thighs. "And Dhrun?"

"Him too." He began to kiss her neck.

"You're sure?"

His hands stopped working and pressed against her hips. "You worry too much about four-arms. I took care of him." He turned her and she looked up into his handsome face. His deep brown eyes looked into hers. "I mean it now. You think about him too much."

She smiled at him. "Your dimples don't show when you're jealous." She reached up and ran a hand along his cheek. "There's no need."

He pulled her close. "I'm not jealous. But he's an odd one. He converted himself. What kind of neodemon converts himself?"

"One who has requisites for glory and can pick a leader to get him there. And we agreed that he never had to talk about his past before conversion."

Kai frowned. "He gets out of line. He's too competitive when the whole crew has to paddle together."

"I'll talk to him—"

"No, no . . . We got something more important to worry about now." He kissed her again, even more gently than before, but she could feel the almost limitless strength in his arms.

"Oh?"

His fingers started working again and slowly drew the hem of her robes up her thighs, over her hips.

A board his first barge, Nicodemus watched Rory direct repairs to the barge that the River Thief had tried to steal.

After Nicodemus had dispelled the neodemon, Rory had edited the druidic text in the ship to keep it afloat. Sir Claude had emerged from his metallic cocoon and—though careful never to touch his patient—treated Nicodemus's minor wounds.

As dawn began to hide stars behind vivid sky, the rest of Nicodemus's party appeared on the river. John had had difficulty rousing Doria from the River Thief's godspell. It was only with the neodemon's death, after which her godspells rapidly decayed, that John woke Doria and the rest of the party.

Rory was barking commands to the pilot of the fourth barge as he and a dozen sailors lashed the two barges together. Rory wanted to transfer some text from one boat to another to complete the repairs. Nicodemus tightened the blanket he had wrapped around his shoulders even though the tropical morning was warm and the coming day promised to be hot.

"I haven't blackmailed you yet," a woman said behind him, "only because I haven't decided what I want to extort from you."

Nicodemus turned to see Magistra Doria Kokalas, his envoy from the hydromancers of Ixos. At one hundred ten years old, Doria was the most senior spellwright in Nicodemus's court. Born of the Cloud People in Chandralu, Doria had trained first in her native city as a hydromancer then as a clerical physician in Port Mercy.

Despite her age, Doria stood straight at nearly five feet ten inches and possessed brown eyes that were only just beginning to cloud over. Her long white hair was tied back into a ponytail and she absently bothered the sleeves of her long blue robes.

Nicodemus smiled. "Magistra, it is good to see you on this fine Ixonian morning."

"Don't change the subject; when I tell your wife about the risks you took attempting to convert a minor neodemon, her head will explode."

"Not until after she made sure mine exploded first."

"What did you expect? You married a dragon."

"Doria, I'm sorry I didn't wake you up. By the time I thought of it, it was too late."

"Oh, it's nothing that I can't forgive after a little blackmail."

"What are you hoping to extort from me? A large estate? A position on the league's council?"

"I was thinking more along the lines of five to six handsome young men to cook for me, carry me about on a palanquin, give the occasional foot massage." She shrugged.

Nicodemus laughed. Of all the envoys and personal advisors he had known, Doria was the one he liked and trusted most. Likely that was because she had been twenty-five years in his service; the other envoys had had the bad habit of getting killed.

"Five to six handsome servants sounds a bit much. How about two?"

The water mage smiled at him. "Didn't you have a 'First rule of fighting a water goddess' or something to that effect?"

"The River Thief had requisites for equitable theft; you know how useful she could have been to us."

"But you didn't know that when you got into the God-of-god's damned water, did you?"

"Three handsome young servants," Nicodemus replied. "Final offer." Just then a cry from the barge turned their eyes to the repairs. Something had gone wrong and the two boats nudged each other and began rocking. With a yawp, Rory dove off the bow and splashed into the river.

Doria sighed. "At least you managed to keep your druid and highsmith envoys alive this time around. Maybe these two will last longer than a season."

"They both did rather well."

"Which brings me to why I sought you out on this oh-so-lonely perch of yours." She paused and then nodded aft where Sir Claude was leaning on the gunnel and studying Rory. The druid now swam alongside the barge and periodically reached up to touch its hull to edit the druidic text written within its wood.

"Sir Iron Pants over there," Doria said, "just told me how the River Thief claimed one of the divinities in her goddess complex might have come from the Old Continent. Sir Steel also reports that the neodemon wore your daughter's face."

"It's not a tall tale. I asked Sir Claude to inform you when no one would overhear."

"So he did."

"Can you think of any way we might find out if the River Thief was from the Old Continent?"

"Given that Freckles down there"—she gestured to Rory's red head bobbing in the river—"killed all of the River Thief's crew before we could question them . . . no, nothing comes to mind."

"It's my fault. I should have ordered Rory to restrain them if possible."

"You should have. And you should have woken me."

"Agreed."

"As for why the neodemon should be wearing Leandra's face . . . other than the fact that it's a young and lovely face . . . no, I can't think of any earthly reason the goddess would do such a thing."

Nicodemus nodded and changed the subject. "What's your opinion of Sir Claude? Can we trust him?"

Doria looked the knight up and down. "Well, he's sarcastic enough to fit in with our crew. I think we can trust him to do his duty, especially if that duty involves picking a fight with Freckles. Those two have it out for each other in a way that I can't figure out. Did they know each other before?"

"No."

"Did one of them kill the other's brother or something during one of the skirmishes between Lorn and Dral?"

"They deny it and there was no mention of such in the reports I read. In fact, Sir Claude was a veteran of the Goldensward War in the north of Lorn, and Rory a veteran of the Whiteforest Wars in southern Dral. I don't think they've come within a hundred miles of each other until they joined my service."

Doria made a thoughtful sound. "I wonder what it is then. Maybe just personal dislike. Anyway, my Lord Warden, what are we to do about preventing the River Thief from reincarnating?"

"Magistra, you are my advisor. Aren't you supposed to be advising me?"

"I'm too old to do my own work. That's why I went into politics."

"Very well, given the River Thief's requisites, I am wagering her cult will be mostly in the river villages."

"Because of the requisite for equability?"

"The urban deities of theft are a more ruthless lot."

Doria waggled her head from side to side as she did when weighing evidence. "That she was a complex of three makes it harder to say. Could be a city thief goddess fused with an ancient river goddess of the poor."

Nicodemus raised an eyebrow. "Five thousand thieves praying near a single ark? Only place that could happen would be Chandralu. Lea might be having some trouble bringing down these rural neodemons; she hasn't had any trouble in the city. If there had been a newly incarnated goddess of theft she would have known."

Doria chewed her lip. "So, you'd argue that it's more likely that five thousand souls along this river began to pray to steal a bit of the wealth that flows between Matrupor and Chandralu? It isn't the worst idea I ever heard. "

"High praise from you, Magistra."

"So we float back to Chandralu and tell the prince regent he's got to find a way to let the villages in on the trade wealth? Let them charge tolls maybe? Or maybe have the crown build temples and schools to share the wealth?"

"Fiery heaven, I'm not suggesting a thing. Leandra is Warden of Ixos. Keeping the discontents from reincarnating the River Thief is her problem."

Doria sniffed. "Typical. That's just typical of the father."

"What? I would be respecting the sovereignty of her office."

"Look, you know she's doing something wrong. You know things are out of hand in rural Ixos. So she's going to have to change; would you agree?"

"I have this feeling that if I agree, you're going to find some way of making me feel like an ass."

"You don't have to do anything in particular for me to make you feel like an ass."

"Such a comfort you are, Magistra. All right, so, yes, I know Lea will have to change."

"So you can't just solve the problems and tell her she has to change."

"I can't?" Nicodemus asked. He had thought Doria was going to applaud his respect for his daughter's independence.

"Of course not. You have to help her to change."

"Oh, yes, of course," Nicodemus muttered, though he had no idea how exactly he was supposed to do such a thing.

"You would have done better with a son."

"I would?"

"There's a saying among the Cloud People—"

"You never quoted Cloud People sayings when we were in the South."

"Being home makes me nostalgic. Now, do you want a gem of invaluable wisdom from my people or not?"

"I do."

"So the saying is 'to be a good father to a son, a man merely has to be kind, wise, or clever.'"

"I don't get it. What does a man need to be a good father to a daughter?"

"But that's the point! There's nothing specific that can make you good at it. It's just a"—She waved one hand in the air—"you know, a certain"—more vigorous hand waving, perhaps indicating the complexity of the sought-after attributes—"a certain combination."

"Truly, a gem of invaluable wisdom."

"Stop. You're ruining the effect."

"Doria, you've never had a daughter. You've never even had children."

"But I've been a daughter. And that, don't you think, better qualifies me to know what a daughter needs than would, oh I don't know, screwing up the raising of one, hmm?"

"Lea is thirty-three years old now, the Warden of a whole kingdom. It's hardly like I'm still raising her."

"A son is a son until he finds a wife; a daughter is a daughter for life."

"Another saying of the Cloud People?"

"Oh, please, no. You think we'd rhyme so sentimentally like that? The Cloud People are nothing if not practical. I heard that in Dral."

"It sounds Dralish, but that doesn't mean it's not stupid," Nicodemus replied. "And while I appreciate that raising daughters is a difficult task, I don't know if your generalities apply to Lea. She is after all half-human and half-textual, the daughter of a dragon, too damn clever by half, fond of getting into trouble, and continuously fighting a disease that will—everyone agrees—kill her far too soon." An unintended note of hurt had entered Nicodemus's voice.

Doria waited a moment before saying, "Yes. Yes, you're right. Leandra's situation is unique." She waited another moment. "So, raising a daughter is difficult. But for your daughter, that's especially so."

Nicodemus took a long breath. He needed to hurry back to his daughter. Away to the east, one of the big-bellied clouds was dropping a curtain of rain onto the jungle.

CHAPTER TEN

Beneath cloud-dappled skies, the catamaran caught the wind with a bulging expanse of white sail and seemed to fly over the bay water. Even Leandra's limited nautical sensibilities appreciated a rightness to the ship's angles of wind to sail and water to hull. The resulting speed exhilarated.

The sailors shared her sensation or perhaps generated it as they hurried to their tasks, hollering to one another. Even Dhrun was content enough that he did not balk when Holokai bellowed orders.

Standing on the forward deck, Leandra smiled as she thought about what she and Holokai had done back on Keyway Island. Her reminiscence was disturbed only when a strong wind required that she readjust her headdress and veil. Her disease made her painfully sensitive to sunlight: a few moments of exposure induced a rash, prolonged exposure, the full horror of a flare.

Just then the catamaran passed under a cloud's shadow and the blue water lost its dazzle. The change turned Leandra's thoughts to Chandralu and what lay before them. She wondered when Francesca would arrive in the city.

A sailor let out a laughing yawp. Leandra turned and saw a man leaning over the catamaran's starboard hull. A dribbling between his legs gained force to become an arc of urine into the ocean. His mates, Dhrun among them, called approval or criticism.

Leandra tried to be charitable as she considered the sailor. He was, after all, subject to several of the sea's intoxicants: impending payment, fine sailing, a port where he could exchange his rupees for kava or women. Leandra had spent her childhood on expeditions to take down neodemons: long caravans snaking across Lornish plains, wild mounted hunts dashing through Dralish forests, sea canoes voyaging across Ixonian waves. In her experience, men who dedicated their lives to going elsewhere—despite their colorful diversities of appearance—were cut from similarly rough but gaudy cloth. She appreciated the joy they took from risks and reward. And yet the sailor's arc of urine aggravated her present dissatisfaction with humanity and its abortive sorrows.

So she turned to stare dispassionately at the showboating sailor. It wasn't very impressive, his piss or penis. Another crewman was making for the starboard hull, lifting up his lungi and boasting that he could do better. Then he noticed Leandra's stare.

The crewman dropped his lungi and turned back to some detail of the rigging. Noticing the silence, the rest of the crew turned to look at him, then at her. In a few moments, all hands were tending to ropes or sails.

Leandra looked to the bow and the lush, rolling hills of the Chandralu peninsula. About four miles ahead stood Mount Jalavata, the extinct volcano on which Chandralu was built.

Mount Jalavata rose to a great height until its tip touched the underbelly of a cloud that, more days than not, hung above the mountain and churned in the sea winds. Presently hidden among the clouds was the Pavilion of the Sky, where her father cast his metaspell to spread out across the archipelago.

Inside the volcano, the crater was filled with chill lake water that sank to depths known only to the gods—for on those placid waters was the Floating City, the home of the Ixonian pantheon.

At various points along the eastern slope, tunnels had been carved into the volcano. Through a series of baffles and floodgates, the crater's water flowed out and down the volcano's slope, which had been cut into terraces for the cultivation of taro and rice.

Amid these paddy fields, enclosed by twenty-foot-high walls, was bright Chandralu. The city, like the mountainside, was cut into terraces; sixteen terraces, to be precise, each nearly twenty feet tall and eighty deep. Lying as they did between two tall ridges, most of the terraces ran a convex course and so appeared like the rows of a giant amphitheater.

Nearly all of the architecture was that of the Cloud Culture: cylindrical pavilions surrounded by close-packed, two-story rectangular houses with slanted roofs and verdigris copper gutters. Nearly every wall was whitewashed. At noon the city became almost painfully bright.

As Holokai brought them into the harbor, Leandra could make out the city's detail. Not all the whitewashed houses were the same white: Some were drab, some dirty, some faintly hued with tan or brown, a few so white they seemed solar. In the finer districts the buildings sported doors, shutters, railings painted in competitively vivid color: violet, crimson, yellow. On the higher and wealthier terraces, beautiful trees—palm, jacaranda, plumeria, banyan—lined the streets, and the shady green of gardens interrupted the white buildings.

The only architectural exceptions were the three limestone temple-mountains, built in the intricate Lotus style, standing dark and cool over the rest of the blazing city.

After they docked, Holokai reported to the port authorities while Leandra talked with Dhrun. The divinity complex had stowed his swords and stood on the deck wearing only a short lungi. Bare-chested, he cut a conspicuous picture. Several dockworkers stared at the young god of wrestling. Dhrun smiled at them, enjoying the attention and anticipating their future prayers at the next wrestling tournament.

"You're such a peacock," Leandra casually accused.

"The male or the female of the species? They're very different."

"Don't be difficult. Whenever someone refers to peacocks they're talking about the males with their fancy plumage." She gestured to his bare chest.

He smiled. "Maybe they shouldn't."

"You're not going to carry a sword in the city?"

He gave her a four-shouldered shrug. "Everyone knows I'm deadlier with my bare hands. It's only outside the city when the weapons stop fools from attacking me."

"There are fools in the city too, you know."

Just then Holokai returned and began to pay the crew.

Leandra had noticed with relief that there was no sign of her mother's ship in the harbor. A few minutes later, flanked by Holokai and Dhrun, she left the docks to find a way through the bustling Bay Market Plaza. It was a chaotic, beautiful market day. All around her fishmongers hawked every type of food from the ocean: seaweed, tuna, dolphinfish, amberjack, grouper, snapper—all neatly decapitated, gutted, and arranged in circular displays. Octopus tentacles were hung to dry in the sun like laundry on a clothesline.

Atop some of the stalls and nearby roofs peered troops of Chandralu's infamous macaque monkeys, who could be as merciless as the city's thugs. The long-tailed, wide-faced, furry little brutes had learned every conceivable ploy to steal food. The larger troops would execute brutal smash-and-grab-style raids on food stalls left guarded by children or the elderly. Or a monkey might play a Wounded Bird game or a mother might offer her adorable babies to be petted by a softhearted human while other members of the troop quick-fingered any morsel left inadequately guarded.

On the Bay Market's western edge stood a tiny open-air temple, no more than twenty feet in diameter. Inside, a four-man gamelan ensemble struck small hammers upon their many brass instruments in a style of gamelan unique to Chandralu. Each musician played through a cycle upon his instruments, and the different musical cycles went into and fell out of sync with the other. It produced a bright, clanging, circular music, at times almost cacophonous.

As a child, Leandra had thought gamelan music exotic, harsh. Now it was a small pleasure, an example of Lotus Culture, a reminder that she was home. A priest, dressed in multicolored robes, was accompanying the gamelan music in song that exhorted the crowd to pray to the Trimuril and the other official deities of the Ixonian pantheon.

Past the pavilion stood the bottom of the Jacaranda Steps, which climbed the mountainside to the Water Temple at the city's upper limit.

The Jacaranda Steps themselves were built of gray stone, broad and long enough to allow for the tread of elephants, which were used to carry goods and materials across the city. Starting about a third of the way to the city's top, the Jacaranda Steps were lined with shops and stalls that grew more opulent as the steps rose higher until they were replaced by the largest and most beautiful family compounds. The jacaranda trees that gave the stairway its name flanked the steps every ten feet. At this time of year their branches were in full purple bloom.

The Jacaranda Steps would have been a charming scene except for the lower terraces. Here they were lined by the poor—some selling brass baubles spread out on blankets, others rattling beggar's bowls or calling out pleading songs. Here was the vast and horrible variety of suffering. Here were men who had lost an arm or a leg. Here were starving mothers with hollow eyes. They cradled their infants, who wailed or lay slack as flies buzzed around their faces.

Leandra, like all denizens of the Chandralu, had learned to look at such commonplace misery without reaction. It was only when she thought of the fact that there were no spellwrights among the miserable that Leandra could feel anything. Then the emotion that came was anger. Throughout history, spellwrights were exempt from destitution. The longer she thought about it, the hotter Leandra's anger burned.

Whether a child would become a spellwright or not was a chance event; however, the chances were improved by education. In the empire, where Leandra's aunt had invested in grammar schools and printing presses, a larger number of children were become spellwrights and more of them from the poorer classes. That was an admirable improvement, certainly, but it still didn't change the fact those born magically illiterate were vulnerable.

It was the capriciousness of the universe that angered Leandra. That some were born able to become spellwrights, others born poor, and others—like her—born to suffer lifelong disease. The unfairness of it all boiled in her like childish rage.

As she eyed the grubby crowd, Leandra tried to push down her anger and focus. Getting past the lower steps could be difficult. Among the poor would be some of the miserable deities: gods and goddesses who had been abandoned by their devotees or who had suffered injury or deprivation at the hands of other deities or powerful humans. Often these destitute divinities fused into large complexes to pool their meager strengths.

In fact, as Leandra picked her way through the crowds, she glimpsed the eight-armed, many-headed Baruvalman, sometimes called Baru. A sallow aura shone around him.

Leandra's heart sank. Baru was a complex of so many pitiful divinities that his speech was often nonsensical and his actions—driven by so many different requisites—often led him into danger. But somehow, most likely through bribery, Baru had managed to place an ark stone in the Floating City and become an official member of the Ixonian pantheon and therefore was entitled to Leandra's protection.

Of the several interactions Leandra had had with Baru, all had been unpleasant and one had been disastrous. Presently Baru was doing the only thing most miserable deities could do, beg for prayers.

"Walk fast," Leandra said while glancing over her shoulder at Dhrun and Holokai.

Holokai eyed the ragged crowd and tightened his grip on his leimako. The shark's teeth shone opalescent in the sunlight. Dhrun on the other hand was peering up into jacaranda boughs, smiling serenely, almost stupidly, at a blue-feathered songbird that was making a chortling song not dissimilar to the gamelan music.

Dhrun and Holokai, quite the pair Leandra had found. She began to march up the steps trying to keep her eyes on the step in front of her. When passing Baruvalman she adjusted her headdress to hide her face. But just as she feared, the pitiful deity began calling louder.

"Blessed is the Halcyon, who will protect us from the demons crossing the ocean!" Baru said in a resonant male voice. "Blessed is his daughter," he called, this time a shrill child's voice, "who protects the humblest citizens of Chandralu from the neodemons." His voice was now that of a quavering old crone's. "Blessed is that bane of neodemons, that maker of circles. Blessed is that generous, that pious, that virtuous woman!"

Well, Leandra thought, at least I know he isn't talking about me.

She walked faster, but from the corner of her eye she saw the pitiful divinity complex was struggling to his feet. He was naked as usual, his flabby body androgynous. One of his eight arms had been amputated below the elbow and his sallow aura sputtered. That was new and troubling. His head was an ever-rotating cylinder from which projected the faces of his most dominant incarnations. Presently, he was looking at Leandra with the face of an old woman, but she could also see the head of a praying mantis, a child, a scarred warrior.

"And more blessed by the Creator would be the Warden of Ixos if she prayed, ever so briefly, to the humblest of deities, to the deity who knows the city!" he said in the buzzing voice of the praying mantis.

Holokai stepped toward the pitiful complex, who shambled back, two of his hands brought up to shield his rotating face, two pressed palms together in supplication.

"My apologies, Baru," Leandra said while marching faster up the steps, "we are on urgent business."

"Of course, of course," Baru said from a child's face. The effect was eerie. "Of course such a mighty woman, a maker of circles could not spare any consideration for the humble Baruvalman. She bears on her shoulders the weight of all society . . . and undivided society."

Leandra turned to look at the divinity complex, who was now on his knees, all possible hands pressed together in supplication. Leandra spoke with a lowered voice. "Baru, my time is short. What is your meaning?"

He bowed. "Oh, nothing, nothing. If only I could assist the mighty lady, for surely she shall be called upon to investigate last night's unfortunate violence on Cowry Street. And surely, she will want to know about how all the humblest denizens of the city, divine and human, are living in fear."

"Baru, what do you know of what happened last night?"

"The simple Baruvalman wishes he could help the great circle maker, but he is so weak. There are so few prayerful in this city. If only he had enough prayers to look after the starving children and the disabled old men."

More like opium addicts and petty thugs, Leandra thought; there were already official patron deities for both destitute children and elderly.

"Tell me something useful," Leandra said, "and I will have one of my servants pray for you tonight." She would have prayed herself, but doing so might worsen her disease flare.

"Oh, Baruvalman wishes he could, honored warden, honored circle maker. But he is so weak . . . so weak . . ." he bowed his head, now that of a crone, and pressed it to the step.

Leandra grimaced. "Get up. Why are you calling me a circle maker? And what are you alluding to? Are people talking about the Cult of the Undivided Society again?"

"So weak . . . so weak . . ." Baru muttered and bumped his forehead against the stone step.

Leandra sighed. "What requisite must I pray for?"

Baru sat up and spoke in a rush. "For the making better of the discomfort of the poor, sickly, and constantly itching in the lower eastern docks, second terrace."

Leandra sighed. Baru had to make the prayer so specific to ensure that an ark stone would not divert it to another deity with requisites better suited to the resolution of the prayer.

Leandra supposed that it wouldn't be such a bad thing if one miserable soul received succor, no matter how small, from Baru. So she pressed her palms together and brought them to her forehead, in the style of the Lotus Culture, and she prayed for what she had been asked for.

She felt a fraction of the strength in her muscles being converted into divine text by one of the city's ark stones. That prayer would now sit in that ark until a deity satisfied its requisite, at which point it would be distributed to that deity.

When Leandra looked, she saw Baruvalman scrabbling away from her; no doubt making for a known beggar in the lower eastern docks who had a rash Baru could scratch and so gain the prayer.

"Kai," Leandra said, "please remind our divine friend here of his promise." But even as she spoke, Holokai had blocked Baruvalman's retreat.

The pitiful divinity complex looked back and up at Leandra, now with the child's face and an addict's expression of need. "People say there's a Lornish neodemon in the Bay of Standing Islands. That is it, isn't it?"

"We knew that already."

"Some say also that the neodemon is killing off the weaker deities in the city. Other people say it's the Cult of the Undivided Society, that they are taking divinity complexes apart and feeding them to their new neodemon. But everyone agrees, oh yes, that humble souls like me need to be safe. Someone might snap us up."

Leandra thought about this for a moment. For the past ten years there had been wild rumors about the Cult of the Undivided Society trying to instigate the Disjunction or to serve the demons once they crossed the ocean. Normally Leandra would have ignored such nonsense. But last night the smuggler from Trillinon had inquired about the cult. "Any more rumors?" she asked.

Baru shook a praying mantis head. "Oh no! No, no. Well, yes. There is talk that the Silent Blight is worse in the empire. Crop failures. The rich merchants are very much excited about becoming rich when they—"

"I've heard," Leandra interrupted. "But, tell me, why did you call me a maker of circles?"

Baru looked at her with confusion. "Everyone is calling the great lady that. And her father."

"No one calls my family that. Are you sure? Or are you just making all this up?"

"Oh, yes, great lady. I mean, no, no. I would never make anything up? May humble Baruvalman go now, great lady? I can tell you whatever you like. May he go, humble Baru?"

Leandra studied him for a moment longer and then nodded to Holokai, who stepped aside. Baruvalman scurried off into a narrow alley between two whitewashed walls.

"Damned waste," Leandra grumbled as she turned back up the steps.

"Hey Lea, you sure that prayer won't make your flare worse?" Holokai asked beside her. "You said it could do that."

"I don't think so," she said while pressing her hand to her belly. "Though according to the godspell about my head, I'll have more belly pain in an hour. And now that I think about it, about an hour ago there were a few future selves who were confused and distressed about something."

"Baruvalman always makes me feel confused and distressed," Dhrun said. He was smiling as if it were amusing.

They continued up the steps and Leandra adjusted her headwrap. The sun was rising high. Then Leandra glanced back toward the bay, intending to check if her mother's ship had sailed into view. By chance, she glanced down a muddy alleyway in the Naukaa district. Lines of laundry were hung between two buildings, and the ragged forms of two sleeping beggars were huddled under an eave. But what caught her eye was an image of what Chandralu most precisely meant to her.

Lying maybe five feet from her, at the opening of the alleyway, was a discarded mango rind. Suddenly Leandra's ability to perceive the world around her expanded. The mango rind, it was perfectly concave, almost a geometric idealization of curved space. The inner surface retained only shreds of glistening yellow-orange flesh. The lip of the outer skin was a deep green, mottled with black flecks, toward its rim blushing deeply red. Alone, the rind would not have meant much of anything to Leandra. But this rind, she could not help but notice, lay motionless in a small pool of liquid feces.

It was a trifling detail—a distasteful smudge compared to the bright day, the beautiful city. Most would have ignored it, but Leandra could not look away.

Spurred on by the godspell around her head, the divine aspects of Leandra's mind leapt forward. Her body, weakened by her recent prayer, flared into its disease. With her textual mind working so hotly, Leandra's perception continued to widen.

Leandra could sense every fiber of her robes, her headdress, the leather of her sandals. Then she sensed Holokai and Dhrun, their every divine sentence.

Out and out her divine perception stretched. Now it included the buildings around her, the mud in the alley, the mango rind, the shit. Her perception included more and more of the city until the limits of herself began to dissolve.

Now she not only sensed the city's whitewashed walls, but felt the hot sunlight shining upon them. Now she not only sensed the distant temple-mountains but also became their cool stone hallways. She became the docks. She was the wooden planks groaning under cargo and foot. She was the stalls up in the Hanging Market filled with bags of dark coffee, plates of ground taro root, tiny piles of sugar, larger piles of salt; pyramids of jackfruit, mountain apples, lychee; folded bolts of silk, arrays of hammered bronze amulets, jade necklaces, cheap baubles.

In the Water Temple, she was the marigolds on a young bride's flower necklaces. In the Lower Banyan District, she was a bougainvillea vine trying to swallow a kitchen wall. She was the smoke coming from a cooking fire, the wooden ring of a man striking his wife, the lone brass rupee in a beggar's bowl. She was a hovel in the Naukaa District, stinking and empty after a cholera outbreak. She was a squat plumeria tree dropping white petals on an old black dog.

"Lea!"

She discovered that Holokai was gripping her right arm. She was falling. Her vision dimmed. . . . Grab his arm. . . . Hold on. . . . Dhrun loomed over her, his dark face a mask of concern.

"You stopped breathing!" Holokai's voice boomed in her ear. He shook her. "I can't even look away from you for a second, hey? You start breathing now, okay? No fooling. Start breathing."

He slapped her, hard. Everything shifted. Her cheek stung. At last, Leandra's perception began to consolidate.

"You start breathing, Lea!" Holokai shouted. "No fooling now!"

What he was saying . . . it seemed absurd . . . until . . . until . . .

He drew his hand back as if to slap her again, but now air rushed out of her lungs.

"No!" she squeaked between gasps of air. "I'm . . . breathing . . ."

She felt a tangle of emotions: terror, giddiness, a distance from the world as if she were intoxicated. She was clinging to Holokai's arm, panting.

They waited.

When her breathing finally slowed, Holokai asked, "It happen again? You becoming the city?"

"Yes."

"Huh. You know how I could tell? You said that your disease flares make other people near you fluent in the magical languages you're near, right? Well, this time, I was looking over at four-arms over there"—he nodded at Dhrun—"and I could understand some of his prose. Pretty clever, hey?"

Leandra only nodded. Suddenly her vision blurred with tears. She stood up straight. She tried to rub the tears from her eyes. She thought of the beautiful things she had been, the disgusting ones: the shit and the wooden ring worn by a man beating his wife. The tears seemed to grow hotter in her eyes. "Creator damn it all, I hate this disgusting city!" she swore even as her heart ached for the beautiful city, her city.

She kept rubbing at her tears until they stopped. Hopefully this wouldn't rekindle her disease flare. Hopefully she wouldn't need to take the stress hormones again.

Holokai and Dhrun waited until Leandra could stand on her own. "It was that prayer to Baruvalman," she said, "and this new spell around my head. That's what tipped me over."

Holokai nodded. "Well then, no more tipping, hey?"

Dhrun gingerly touched her shoulder with his lower right arm.

"Are we ready to go?" she asked.

Dhrun answered. "We are, but there is no need to rush to your family compound if it's going to kill you."

"Right," she said and took a few deep breaths. "Right." At last she turned toward the Jacaranda Steps. "I'm fine. Let's go."

"Lea, you sure you're all right?" Holokai whispered, so softly that not even Dhrun could hear it. "If you do that again when I'm not around, that might be the end."

"It's okay," she said while gingerly feeling her tender belly. "There are worse ways to die. So come on, let's go find one."

CHAPTER ELEVEN

The ghost ship listed. A sailor was rowing Nicode-mus from the first barge to the smoldering ship, the bay water blue around them.

The pilot of the lead barge had seen a column of smoke as their convoy left the Matrunda River and entered the Bay of Standing Islands. The captain had wanted to avoid any trouble, but Nicodemus ordered him to investigate.

Over the horizon had come a small junk. What was left of her rigging smoldered. Not a stitch of sail remained. Scorch marks raked her bow. No one moved on her deck and not even the loudest of hails raised a soul from belowdecks.

Nicodemus had sent Doria, Sir Claude, and three armed sailors to investigate. When Doria had shouted for him to follow, he knew they had found something important. The swells were minimal, so Nicodemus made it to the ghost ship's deck without taking an embarrassing dip into the bay.

First Nicodemus noticed the bodies. Four men. Or, Nicodemus corrected himself, very likely four men. Two were burnt beyond recognition of sex. The other two wore drab, bloodstained lungi and were sprawled on deck.

Then Nicodemus noticed the smell. Burnt flesh and . . . something else . . . Doria was standing by the mast, frowning at a book in her hands. "There's a smell like . . ." he said and paused to sniff. "Maybe like . . . hot metal maybe . . . or like sulfur?"

"It smells like vog," she said without looking up from her book.

"Vog?"

"Pollution from active volcanoes or from lava flows meeting the sea. It can get pretty bad north of the big island and near the active volcanoes on the outer island chain."

Nicodemus sniffed again. "But there's no active volcano near here, is there?"

"Not for hundreds of miles."

"Then why should this boat smell like vog?"

"I'm not sure, but it's hardly her most pressing mystery." She held up the book. "According to the captain's journal, she's a merchant sailing out of Feather Island, makes a run to Chandralu once every three days or so. Sometimes she takes commissions to ship cargo to the other sea villages. Three days ago she was in Chandralu. The last entry put her in Feather Island yesterday. There's no entry about departure. The hold has been half emptied. The ballast is off. She's tilted back."

Nicodemus looked at the bodies. "You think she had to leave her home port in a hurry?"

Doria clapped the book shut. "I do. Even a half competent crew would have redistributed her cargo. If she was attacked on the water, the pirates would have taken her as prize or sunk her."

"So what attacked her in the harbor? Never known raiders to burn someone that badly." He nodded to one of the blackened bodies. "Not in combat at least. A fire neodemon?"

"I'd say lava neodemon, given the scent of vog. But given what's in the cabin, it's got to be more than your commonplace lava neodemon."

"What's in the cabin?"

Doria took a deep breath. "There are some things in my life I wish I could unsee and unremember. What is in the cabin, it's one of those things."

"That bad?"

"That bad."

Nicodemus raised his eyebrows. Doria wasn't one to exaggerate. He followed her aft. The moment he set foot in the cabin he regretted it. Three bodies were huddled in the corner, all badly burned, all of them children. The oldest couldn't have been more than six.

"Seeing how they're huddled, I'm guessing the crew was trying to get them off the island, away from whatever was attacking," Doria said beside him. "The children's burns are bad, but not bad enough to kill. It's mysterious. Those two however . . ." she gestured behind Nicodemus.

He turned to find two adult bodies sitting against the wall, their heads lolling at odd angles. Below the neck, each man was painted with blackening blood. In each hand, each man held a curved knife. "Opened each other's throats?" he asked.

"Too far apart. Slit their own."

"Madness then. Something drove them mad."

"Something on Feather Island," someone said from behind them. Nicodemus looked back to see a pale Rory and a thin-lipped Sir Claude standing in the doorway. Their expressions were tense. Apparently the present situation was enough to quell their feud.

Nicodemus nodded. "Or something that was on Feather Island a few hours ago."

Doria sighed. "Should we continue on to Chandralu?"

Nicodemus rolled his neck as he thought. His keloid scar was itching again. Distracted, he wondered if he should rewrite the tattooed spells around it. But then he forced himself to focus. Head to the city or investigate? "If we did find trouble on Feather Island, we'd be in river barges, which are hardly ideal for fighting. And except for Doria, none of us is suited for combat afloat."

Doria shrugged. "Leandra on her catamaran and with her shark god in tow wouldn't be a bad idea . . . but, Nico, what if this neodemon gets away?"

"My Lord Warden," Sir Claude added, "the neodemon who did this must have very, very malicious requisites. Burning his victims, driving them to . . ."

Nicodemus nodded. "One of the deadliest creatures I have ever faced was the Savanna Walker of Avel. He had been born with the same capabilities that I have, but by distorting his Language Prime and his magical language, he learned how to wound the minds around him, causing insanity."

Doria made a thoughtful sound. "You never told me the Savanna Walker produced carnage like this."

Nicodemus shook his head. "It was different. The Savanna Walker could induce blindness, deafness, aphasia, that sort of thing. When he completely corrupted a mind, he made men his homicidal slaves. But he never made men suicidal and he had no power of flame. The lava neodemon that did this may be as dangerous or even more so. Sir Claude, I take your point. We can't let this monster roam the bay."

The knight bowed his head.

Nicodemus turned to look at the three children. He tried not to shudder. "It seems I had better figure how much we will have to bribe the captain to change course for Feather Island."

Whatever trouble Leandra had gotten herself into, she was going to have to manage it alone for a bit longer. And whatever had made Leandra think she might murder her mother . . . well . . . he would just have to trust his wife and daughter to find some way to avoid killing each other.

CHAPTER TWELVE

Empress Vivian Niyol, the Blessed Halcyon, the Creator's Champion of Humanity, the Future Vanquisher of Los and his Demonic Invasion, the Sovereign of all the Kingdoms of the Second Neosolar Empire—whose exalted person had been raised above every menial task—had to line edit.

And it was glorious.

Vivian had to line edit every waking moment without pause, rest, reservation. She wrote in Numinous. Its golden spun-glass sentences coursed into her room from every direction and wove themselves into an incandescent halo suspended a few inches above her head. Down from this halo a hundred thousand sentences dropped like lightning bolts to pierce her brain.

This was her master spell.

Maintenance of this glorious text required all of her attention, all of her strength. The text was of staggering length and spread out from her in all directions for several miles, coordinating several thousand subspells of many different languages.

The task of constantly casting, recasting, editing, rewriting the master spell required so much of Vivian's mind that it intoxicated her. Literally, wonderfully. Her existence had become trancelike. The intricacy of the world had been replaced by innumerable concatenating paragraphs, the brightness of the sky by a luminosity of prose.

In this exalted state, Vivian could not remember or understand things which previously had been elementary. She knew that she sat on a wide comfortable wooden throne. The room around her was small, but furnished with thickly woven rugs and white cushions. She remembered, vaguely, that along one wall ran a gallery of windows looking out onto blue sky and swirling clouds. But the brilliance of her Numinous text outshone the daylight and illuminated the dark. Vivian had lost track of time shortly after she had first cast this master spell twenty days . . . or had it been thirty . . . or even forty . . . days ago. She couldn't tell.

And as for the spell's function . . . it was for . . . for . . . She could re-member only that it was designed to fool her half-brother Nicodemus.

Older memories were clearer. For example, around her neck she wore a simple silver necklace, which held the Emerald of Arahest against her chest. She remembered that it was only through this magical artifact that she could cast and recast the master spell.

She remembered that the Emerald held her half-brother's ability to spell. The demon Typhon had stolen this ability into the Emerald when Nicode-mus was an infant. Vivian had been born with an identical ability; however, years ago, during the intrigue in Avel, the creature known as the Savanna Walker had destroyed that portion of Vivian's mind.

After Typhon had been defeated, Nicodemus had given her the Emerald. At first she had not understood it. His explanation at the time—that his cacography had made him a champion for creativity and intuitiveness in language—had seemed weak.

However, once Nicodemus had begun to cast his metaspells and new divinities swarmed across the league kingdoms, she had seen how shrewd her half-brother had been to give up the Emerald. Nicodemus was infinitely more dangerous without it. He and his demonically written wife had cre-ated a new, dangerous civilization through exploitation of religion and su-perstition.

Vivian's more recent memories were nebulous things; they seemed to have shape until she reached for them, and then they dissolved. Nicodemus had recently committed . . . some transgression. What . . . she couldn't remember.

The wizardly prophecies described the Halcyon as the protector of hu-manity during the Disjunction, but they also described the Storm Petrel, who would betray humanity. She had hoped Nicodemus would not be involved in prophecy. But perhaps Vivian's previous self had discovered that Nicode-mus was in fact the Storm Petrel.

Vivian tried harder to recall, but the halo's sentences began to strike her head more frequently. Tension gathered in the Numinous matrix. She put aside everything but the master spell. She had to keep casting and recasting.

Before she had begun this spell, she had decided on a course of action. Vivian could remember her feelings of absolute certainty, but now she couldn't recall the reason for her actions. Whatever they had been, they had been good enough to convince her former self; therefore, her present self had to trust in the unknown Vivian who had made those decisions. Trust at least until the master spell had served its purpose and the return of her memories would build a bridge between her past and present.

So she edited and it was glorious. Time passed, she could not tell how much. She found herself musing about time and emotion. Usually, she decided what she wanted to feel in the future and then acted to bring that future into being.

She wondered if it was better to be guided by the person she had been or by the person she wanted to be? Perhaps there was no difference. In both cases one was subject to the urgencies and uncertainties of now.

As more and more of the gloriously intricate sentences flowed through Vivian's mind, she felt more detached, more suffused with the beauty of language.

In a way, she decided, believing that one's past or future could guide the present was a necessary fantasy. The truth of the future or past was unknowable. Every soul existed and acted within the eternal and pressing instant of now, and then—to make existence bearable—wrote a story to connect past, present, and future.

The thought filled her with tranquility. At some point, she would need to leave the spell, attend to her body. But before that time came, she had to build up enough reserve text and governing subspells for the master spell to function for the five or six hours she would need to eat and sleep.

It was an act of war, she remembered briefly. That was what Nicodemus had done. A covert act of war he must have thought she would not discover. But the truth had come to light, and now there was an end to the thirty years of tenuous peace.

Now humanity needed one leader to fight the coming demonic horde, the Pandemonium. Vivian would be that leader. Again, the tension gathered in the sentences that pierced her mind.

So she refocused on line editing. The text became the universe. It was cold, intricate, uncaring, beautiful. There was no past and no future. Every moment struck the universe and sent beauty running through it like vibrations through a temple bell.

Gradually Vivian became aware of someone else moving through her room, picking his way through the matrix of golden sentences. He edited with skill, moving the filamentous prose without deconstructing a single word. Only one imperial spellwright would be so gifted.

Vivian judged that she had given the master spell enough reserve that she could take the time to greet her old friend. He wouldn't have disturbed her spellwrighting for anything other than important news.

Vivian cast the governing subspells into action and felt several sentences withdraw from her brain. The miniature lightning sentences ceased to strike. When only a few words connected her to the master spell, she reached up and lifted the halo of text a few inches above her head.

Bodily sensation—exhaustion, hunger, fatigue—returned, and her mind cleared a little.

Before her stood her oldest friend, her most trusted advisor, Dean Lotannu Akomma. Age had coarsened his dark features, but he was still handsome if no longer strikingly so. The silver in his goatee and dreadlocks, the wrinkles around his eyes made him look distinguished, pleasingly worn-in by the world. He was dressed in the black robes of his office. An eight-pointed silver star on a field of red had been sewn into his sleeves, indicating his rank as a Dean of Astrophell, one of the most powerful spellwrights alive.

"Empress," he said with a bow.

She smiled, feeling both her fatigue and the anamnestic fog that had covered her recent memories. "There's no need for ceremony, old friend, is there? No one else is here?"

"No one else," he said with a smile, perfect white teeth. Then he studied her face. "How are you, Vivian?"

She rolled her shoulders. "It's hardest when I pause." Her mind and eyes wandered up to the halo of text. "I can only spare a few moments. I should get back to it so that there will be enough reserve text for me to sleep." She looked back down at him. "How do I look?"

"Surprisingly well considering the feat you're attempting, or . . . achieving I should say. Perhaps you've lost a pound or two that you shouldn't have. I can have the servants bring up a second dessert each night."

She smiled. "Thank you, but I can't finish what they bring now. I haven't much appetite." She stretched her back, found it sore. "So, what's so important that I am lucky enough to see you?" A thought occurred to her. "Has the master spell served its purpose? Am I to stop?" She felt a little dismay about that prospect.

"Not yet," Lotannu said with a bow. "I've disturbed you because a report has just come in from Chandralu. Our agent in that city confirms that Leandra Weal has returned with a godspell that augments her cognition. Our agent speculates that Leandra acquired the text from a godspell smuggler." He smiled knowingly.

A dull pain sprouted behind Vivian's eyes, threatened to bloom into a headache. Trying to remember hurt. "Apologies, Lotannu, I know we want to stop such smuggling, but I can't remember what. . . . Didn't we decide that it was in our best interest if she gained independence?"

"Correct. This is both expected and a beneficial turn of events; however, there is an unforeseen development. It seems that Leandra is able to modify the godspell to briefly give her stronger-than-predicted prophecies."

"With what consequences?"

"Likely none; however, there is a possibility that she might become too powerful for us to contain. If that were to happen . . . well . . . we have talked about the need to remove her, but I never thought it might come when you were writing the master spell."

"Ah," Vivian said, remembering snatches of conversation, "you worry that you might need to assassinate her in the next few days and you want my permission."

"She is your relation."

"She is. All other things being equal—though they never are—I'd rather she was safe. But given that the world is what it is, you still have my permission to use the force you deem necessary." She paused. "But, old friend, if she has such powerful prophecy won't that make her hard to assassinate?"

"I might have contrived something."

"You brought me out of my reverie so you could brag?"

He turned his palms upward in a comical gesture of helplessness in the face of his own brilliance. "Leandra's godspell allows her to feel the emotions of her possible future selves. I happen to have a counterpart spell—derived from the same deconstructed goddess—that will prevent Leandra from feeling any of the future selves directly affected by the caster."

"You've created a subtext in time?" Vivian asked. "It blinds Leandra to the possible futures you create?"

"It should make Leandra more vulnerable. She will learn to trust the godspell, making her more vulnerable to ambush from whatever agent I confer the counterpart spell upon."

"Let us hope it doesn't come to that."

"Indeed."

"Was there anything else you needed from me?"

"No, Empress."

She looked up to her halo of prose, felt both elated and exhausted by the prospect of venturing back into the master spell. "Before I go . . ." She looked back down at Lotannu. "How are things going, generally?"

"I could tell you specifics."

She shook her head. "Trying to remember the present circumstances makes it hard to keep up with the master spell. It's easier if you tell me generally how we are doing."

He bowed. "We are doing well."

"Does Nicodemus suspect?"

"Not as far as I can tell. No one but our agents in Ixos knows what is headed their way."

"Good," she said and reached up to her halo. "Very good." She pulled the halo down and the golden sentences descended. "You may leave me now, old friend."

And so the empress began to edit again, line by line. She cast and recast her master spell. Its intricacy was just as cold and beautiful as the world.

Soon, confined in the expanse of her spell, Vivian discovered that infinity stretched only from one sentence to its close and that eternity was well contained within an hour.

CHAPTER THIRTEEN

L eandra was continually being surprised by the stupidity of men. Not that she hadn't done a few stupid things herself. Not that she didn't have regrets, some of them powerful. But if she were a man, she'd never be so idiotic as to threaten a woman guarded by two gods.

Even if she hadn't recognized the gods—in this case, Holokai and Dhrun—she would have at the very least trod lightly around a man brandishing a paddle studded with shark teeth and accompanied by a four-armed wrestler.

No matter how she looked at it, two pairs of muscular arms on one body seemed like one very compelling reason—or four very compelling reasons, depending on how one looked at it—for any and everyone contemplating mischief to piss off now and forever.

This was why she was so surprised when the beggar came at her with a knife.

They had been walking north into the Jacaranda District via the Utrana Way, about a quarter the way up the city. Beyond the walls, the terraces became mirrorlike flooded rice or taro paddies. To the east, the bay stretched out and the many dappled clouds cast a giant checkerboard pattern upon it. At the bay's edge the Standing Islands serrated the horizon.

It was a beautiful and tranquil morning, casual in its tropical brilliance, and of a kind that reminded Leandra of why she had fallen in love with the city.

Utrana Way itself was nothing grand, but nothing dingy either. It ran along the fifth of the city's sixteen terraces. On the bayside stood a waist-high wall; volcanoside, houses and pavilions. A lone monkey had been perched on a gutter, scanning the street with larcenous intent.

Leandra's party had passed light traffic: young women carrying baskets of fruit, an elephant hauling timber for some new building, a rice merchant pushing a cart laden with heavy sacks. Then they had passed the beggar.

He was a squat man, with a dirty lungi and a single wooden bowl. He had been singing. They'd heard it a long way off. "A ruuu-pee. A rupee please. A rupee for a simple man and his starving children." At the end of this refrain, he would shake his wooden bowel causing the few coins inside to jingle. Then he'd start again. "A ruuu-pee. A rupee please."

As Leandra had walked past, he had shaken his bowl three times rapidly and then flung his arm out. In the next instant, he was on his feet lunging at her with a knife.

Leandra jumped back, cried out in alarm. Before a thought could form in her mind, Dhrun's lower right hand clamped down on the attacker's wrist. He diverted the man's thrust away from her and pulled along the axis of the thrust, making the attacker yelp as he fell forward.

There was a slap and then a twittering sound. Dhrun's right upper arm snapped up and, as if performing a conjuring trick, held the shaft of a small vibrating arrow. A moment later Leandra realized that a few steps down the street, another beggar was pointing a crossbow at her. As she realized that Dhrun had caught the crossbow bolt, the god of wrestling wrapped his upper right arm around the forehead of the man who had lunged at her and then twisted. There was a crack.

Behind Leandra someone bellowed. She spun around and began fumbling for the knives in her belt, but then she saw that Holokai was standing over a third attacker, a big man dressed in a fine lungi. He lay sprawled out, his mouth working as if he were trying to speak. A ragged wound ran down the man's left collarbone, his chest, and then opened up into his belly. At the end of the wound lay Holokai's long-handled leimako, its shark's teeth glistening with blood.

"Wait!" Leandra screamed. "We need to question—"

But Holokai's eyes had gone black. The skin on his face and belly were white as paper. His arms and back were dark gray. He crouched and with a powerful jump leapt at the man who had been holding the crossbow.

The would-be assassin turned to run. But Holokai flew nearly eight feet into the air and closed the distance between them in moments. With a vicious overhand slash, he brought the leimako down on the man's back. When the weapon made contact, the shark's teeth sprang out, becoming twice their size, digging into the crossbowman.

"No!" Leandra found herself yelling. "Alive. We need them alive." But she turned to Dhrun and saw that he had thrown the knifeman to the ground. The thug's head tilted at an angle that was not possible with an intact spine. "We need . . . to question them," she finished lamely.

Dhrun turned around, looking up and down the street, up to the roof-tops. Suddenly Leandra realized with relief that Dhrun had held his human incarnation, the one called Dhrunarman. If he had assumed his most power-ful incarnation, the neodemon named Dhrun, there would be potential for massacre. "Keep your incarnation," Leandra heard herself say stupidly.

"Of course," Dhrun growled.

Meanwhile Holokai was pacing around them both, his overly long face fixed into a rictus, his teeth large and serrated.

An eerie moment passed, silent save for the slap of sandals on paving stones. Then someone distantly began shouting an alarm.

Leandra lowered her hands, tried to make herself breathe calmly. She looked around for more attackers but saw none. Foolish though, she realized, for her to expect to see a threat if Dhrun and Holokai had not yet spotted any.

"Creator damn it!" she swore while looking down at their three assail-ants. Those that Holokai had sawed in half were filling the street with pools of red. She would have to get Holokai away from them.

"Who in the God-of-god's name is that bloody stupid?" Leandra asked with a calmness that belied her racing heart. "How amazingly, incredibly, mind-blisteringly dumb do three humans have to be to attack us?"

"At least one of them was a spellwright," Dhrun said beside her. He showed her his upper left forearm, which was stained with blood weeping from a long smooth wound. Thanks to Dhrun's divinity, the gash was already closing. The would-be assassin had cast some wartext against Dhrun.

From farther down in the city, shrill whistles began to sound. Leandra heard faint footfalls of running. Someone had alerted the red cloaks, the city watch.

"Lovely," Leandra growled. "Just lovely. I'm a quarter mile from home and now we're going to be interrogated."

"There's no evidence you were here," Dhrun said. "I can tell the watch it was just me and Captain Crazy Fish." He nodded over at Holokai, who was still circling.

"No, someone might have seen us," Leandra grumbled before raising her voice. "Kai!" He kept circling but turned his black eyes toward her. "Kai! Stop pacing, for pity's sake, and stand farther away from the blood." She made a shooing motion.

Holokai's face remained as blank as stone, but he made one more circuit around them and then stalked away down the street. The whistles and foot-falls grew louder. Leandra turned and saw two men with thin red cloaks and short spears trot up the Jacaranda Steps and toward them.

"Do we have a story?" Dhrun asked as the red cloaks approached.

"No, the truth. But let me do the talking," she said while moving into the shade of a building and undoing her headdress. She hoped one of the red cloaks would recognize her.

"Sacred ocean, damn it all," one of the watchmen muttered while looking down at the bodies. "Another one."

Both of the red cloaks were lean, lanky men, wearing short lungi under their cloaks of office. The shorter and older of the two had black skin and a beard chased with silver. His face seemed familiar, and Leandra cursed her poor memory for names. A little familiarity could go a long way in situations like this.

Fortunately he seemed to recognize her. After taking in the three bodies he turned to her and nodded. "My Lady Warden, I am sorry to meet you again like this. Are you hurt?"

"No . . . no . . ." she paused unsure how to address him. Captain of the watch, wasn't he? She had a vague feeling she had met him when investigating a neodemon of forbidden erotic love who had taken to inducing amnesia in certain young woman and men before others took advantage of them. A truly disgusting business. Leandra hadn't been at all sorry when she had caught the neodemon and dispelled him into a thousand agonizing pieces.

But now she needed to remember the captain's name. Something that started with a K? Damn. She put a hand to her chest as if steadying herself. "No, Captain. I'm not hurt."

The silver-bearded watchman turned to Dhrun. "That your changeling wrestler?"

"He is."

"Oh yeah?" The younger man looked at Dhrun with a sudden smile. "Been going to the arena since I was a little fry, with my dad of course. He'd always have us pray for the wrestler that he'd put money on, so I guess that made me a devotee of you back when you was a neodemon, hey?"

Dhrun pressed his palms together; the upper pair he brought to his forehead, the lower pair he brought to his heart. The most formal of greetings. "It is always a pleasure to meet a devotee of the arena."

The younger watchman was grinning like an idiot as he bowed in the style of the Sea People. "Honor's all mine, my lord. I made a bundle last year when I bet on Dhrunarman. Was overjoyed when he won and joined your divinity complex." Then he lowered his voice to conspiratorial volume. "Don't suppose you could give me any divine tips on who's the smart bet for this year's championship, hey?"

The older watchman cleared his throat loudly.

"Oh, right, Captain Kekoa," the younger man said. "Sorry, my lord"—this to Dhrun—"investigation and all." Dhrun nodded as the younger man bent to examine the body at his feet.

Now Lea remembered: Captain Pika Kekoa, very competent and respected, originally of the Sea Culture, who then disavowed all cultures when he became a captain of the city's watch and therefore a high priest of Dhamma, the high goddess of law and justice.

Captain Kekoa was looking at Holokai twenty paces down the street. He was still prowling in circles, but his coloring looked more human. Leandra hoped his eyes and teeth were also. The captain started to ask, "Is that your sh—"

"Sea god," Leandra interrupted. "Best not to say what he is. Makes it harder for him to come back to his human incarnation. That's why I have him pacing away from the meat. His leimako did for those two." She nodded to the two men who'd been half chewed open by Holokai's blows. The pool of blood under each body was now growing sticky dark in the tropical sunlight.

Leandra preemptively offered her story. "My officers and I came in this morning from patrolling the bay. I was returning to my family compound, when we passed that man." She nodded to the body that the younger watchman was inspecting. "Seems he was a spellwright of some kind. He cast a wartext against Dhrun and came at me with a knife. The other two appeared out of nowhere. One attacked Holokai and the other loosed a crossbow at me."

Dhrun held out the bolt.

"Nice catch," Captain Kekoa grunted.

"Captain," the young watchman said while examining the side of the knife man. "It's another one."

Captain Kekoa stood behind his partner. Whatever he saw there made him swear. "Where are they all coming from?"

Leandra refitted her headdress and went to the captain's side. By pulling the lungi slightly down, the younger watchman had revealed on the dead man's hip a tattoo of a circle contained within a square. It looked too exact to have been made by human hands.

"What is it?" she asked.

"Well . . . I suppose it is safe to tell you, my Lady Warden, since it's likely it's you and your officers who are going to have to figure this mess out. But that tattoo is what the street folk are calling the Perfect Circle. Supposedly it's a symbol of the Cult of the Undivided Society."

Leandra snorted. "Rubbish." Suddenly her stomach tensed. Hadn't Baruvalman called her a circle maker? "I've heard rumors of the Undivided Society for years and never heard of such a tattoo."

"Me either," the captain agreed. "But last night was full of changes. Maybe you heard about that brawl on Cowry Street? That left two bodies on the street, one of them with a Perfect Circle tattoo. Then the nightwatch were kept busy with attacks on minor deities. What I heard was that two miserable deities—one the goddess of a village cleared out by plague last year and another a god of lepers—were killed."

"Killed?" Leandra asked.

"Surprised me too. Dhamma has manifested herself in the city to investigate and doubled the watch. That's why we could be here so quickly. Reports say the attackers were in groups of three or four, some disguised as beggars, some as red cloaks. There was an attack on the god of the Banyan Districts that failed; he killed two men, both with Perfect Circle tattoos." The captain nodded toward the corpse at his feet. "Though, if you're right about this one being a spellwright, that's a first."

The younger watchman had finished examining the man that Dhrun had killed and moved on to the other two bodies.

"Any idea who they are?" Leandra asked.

The captain shrugged. "At this point my best guess, crazy as it sounds, would be that the Cult of the Undivided Society is real after all. Maybe they're tired of waiting for the demons to come across the ocean and decided to raise a little hell of their own."

Leandra had to work to keep her expression neutral. Meanwhile, the younger watchmen had collected the weapons of the attackers. "All three have the tattoo," he reported to the captain. "Nothing special about the weapons. The crossbow's of a Dralish design, but that's the most common found on the archipelago. The crossbowman only had three other bolts on him. The knives are steel push daggers, nothing fancy. They could have been forged anywhere in the northern three kingdoms. No coins."

"No other weapons? No spellbooks?" Leandra asked.

"None, my Lady Warden."

Leandra thought for a moment. "Lightly armed, so they weren't expecting much of a fight. In fact, given what you told me, there were four attacks and only two succeeded."

"That we know of," the watchman added.

Leandra nodded. "Fair enough. But still, attacking my party or the Banyan god with those ticklers"—she nodded to the weapons in the watchman's hands—"means the attackers don't know how to size up their targets."

"You don't think it's the Cult of the Undivided Society?"

"I don't think it's any cult. If a neodemon is subtle enough to keep itself hidden during an attack, it's subtle enough to avoid attacking any deity who might be a danger to them."

"But this isn't a neodemon attacking," the younger watchmen said. "It's the devotees. Devotees who want to bring the true demons across the ocean."

"True, devotees can get carried away. But four different attacks across the city, two on poorly chosen targets? The cult would have to be coordinated enough to arm their kill teams but ignorant enough to attack gods far too powerful for them."

"So, you think it's what, an incompetent cult?" the young watchman asked.

Leandra shook her head. "More likely it's some organization pretending to be a cult. An organization that doesn't know much about Ixos or divinities."

The captain of the watch frowned. "What sort of organization would be like that?"

"I don't know," Leandra said, though there was a certain Trillinonish smuggler whom she wanted to question on the subject. Come to think of it, she also wanted to ask some questions of that miserable Baruvalman. He had called her a circle maker. Did Baru think she had killed those miserable deities? Not likely. If he had, he should have run from her instead of pestering her. Baru likely knew more than he let on, or knew more than he was aware of.

Leandra cleared her throat. "Who would want to pretend to be a cult? That would be an excellent mystery for a captain of the watch to solve."

Captain Kekoa smiled weakly. "And I'll be wishing to fish up a whale while I'm at it. But I will tell my goddess of what you said, though I suspect you might be seeing her before I will."

"I think I might indeed," she grumbled while motioning to Dhrun. "Captain, is there anything else you require of me? I have a royal summons I have to attend to, and I now suspect that it might be related to the ill news you have brought me."

"No, my Lady Warden. Please pray to Dhamma for justice to find whoever is behind this." He bowed.

She and Dhrun returned the gesture and then set off for her family compound. Holokai fell in beside her. She saw with relief that his eyes and teeth were humanoid. His expression was one of pained restraint. This was the trouble with gods of violence: a taste always made them want more.

"Hungry?" she asked. In truth, she was impressed that he had avoided touching any of the bodies.

"Enough to eat a whole pig," he groaned through tensed jaw.

"Can you wait until your afternoon prayers reach you?"

"Not if you bring me anywhere near a pig," Holokai grunted and then began to glare at Dhrun with eyes going all black. "Something amusing, four-arms?"

Leandra turned to see that Dhrun was looking at the other god with a smirk. "No, Captain Holokai," he said in a calm tone. His hands were pressed together in supplication at his heart and his belly. "I am impressed that you're able to suppress such instincts."

Holokai brought his leimako up, grasping its long handle with both hands. "You'd be even more impressed if I stopped suppressing the instinct to saw off a few of your extra limbs, insect."

"I have never wrestled a fish before," Dhrun said thoughtfully. "Slippery, I guess you'd be. Might be a challenge, if you can control your tiny fish brain."

"What makes you think you can talk back to me, bug? You hiding some reason to think you're so important?"

"Kai," Leandra said in a warning tone.

The shark god continued. "I mean it, four-arms, what are you hiding? Why did you convert yourself? What were you as a neodemon?"

The smirk fell from Dhrun's face. All four of his arms flexed.

Leandra stepped between them. "Stop it, both of you, and start using the withered organs you call brains."

The two gods stared at each other for a long moment. Then, slowly, Dhrun took a step back. "Ten thousand apologies."

Holokai showed his serrated teeth for a moment but then looked at Lea and bowed his head.

The party continued their march in silence save for Leandra's occasional grumbling about gods of violence and the stupidity of men.

CHAPTER FOURTEEN

F eather Island smoldered.

The mile-wide limestone island had been eroded at its southern end creating a shelf of land, which at its extremity erupted into one of two plateaued towers of rock. The tower that stood at the edge of the shelf was called the Near Tower; its twin, which erupted straight from the sea, was known as the Far Tower.

Nicodemus had visited Feather Island twice before. Then every flat surface had been covered with rectangular whitewashed houses. Into every vertical surface had been carved rooms adorned with boardwalks and palm-thatch awnings. There had been bright hyacinth flowers and bougainvillea vines. Between the two rock towers, rope bridges had stretched at three different levels.

But now the houses on the Shelf had been burnt, many to the ground. The charred trail of fire climbed its way up the southern face of the Near Tower. The bottom and top rope bridges dangled in the wind. The middle bridge had somehow remained hanging but had lost some of its support lines. Crowds of gulls were flapping about the docks, red strips hanging from some of their beaks. Nicodemus had a queasy feeling about what the gulls were eating.

"You have to stay aboard," Doria grumbled beside him on the barge's deck. "I realize we don't have the time to wait until dark. But in this much sunlight, you're barely even a spellwright."

"I am the only one who could naturally disspell whatever godspell the neodemon used to drive the sailors into insanity."

"The boys and I have cast enough wards on our minds to keep out anything but the library of Astrophell. If we run into trouble, you'll hear about it and come ashore."

"First thing I'd hear might be your screams as you cut your own throats," Nicodemus said before giving Doria a level stare. "So thank you for your concern, Magistra, but I will be leading the exploration of Feather Island."

Doria was still dressed in her blue hydromancer robes, but she had hung twin bandoleers over her chest to hold several small glass vials. They were filled with liquids ranging in color from rusty red to a nacreous white. Within these vials were the concentrated aqueous spells hydromancers cast to turn plain water into a variety of other extraordinary substances. Doria had also slung a large water skin around one shoulder.

Nicodemus had changed into tan trousers, a white shirt, a leather longvest. The tropical heat made him sweat, but all the cloth would prevent him from accidently giving one of his friends a canker curse if their skin touched. Nicodemus looked away from the island and out to the horizon. The line where sky met sea wasn't as sharp as usual. "Does it seem hazier near the island?"

"Not haze, vog," Doria said shortly. "You can smell it."

Nicodemus sniffed. "Only faintly. But why should there be vog near Feather Island? Lava neodemon?"

"Lava neodemon."

Nicodemus grunted. "This might be interesting."

"Which is why, you have to stay—"

Nicodemus held up his hand.

"Oh!" Doria said in exasperation. "Fine. Have it your way. But when you're burning to a crisp . . ."

Thankfully, she let her invective die off when she noticed Rory and Sir Claude coming up from belowdecks. The knight was once again covered in his metallolinguistic armor, though he had left his head bare. Rory had strapped brightly lacquered, spell-encrusted wooden plates around his chest, back, arms, legs. The druid also hefted a quarterstaff, as thick as a man's wrist.

The two men had taken so long belowdecks preparing that Nicodemus had worried they were exchanging violent words, verbally or magically. But now they stood stiffly side by side. A moment later, John, dressed in his usual wizardly black, joined them.

"A simple sweep of the village in two teams of two," Nicodemus said. "Rory and I will search the Near Tower. Sir Claude and Magistra, the Shelf. At the first sign of a neodemon, call for the others. John, you stay aboard and make sure the crew doesn't lose their nerve and sail off without us. Understand?"

When everyone nodded, they went over the side and took their seats on a bobbing rowboat. When Sir Claude got in and the weight of his armor made the small craft tip, Rory made the predictably snide remark about the knight being too fat to fight, which led to Sir Claude's predictably snide suggestion that the druid put on enough weight to threaten something other than a bed of violets, which in turn led to Nicodemus's predictably firm command for them both to shut, the flaming hells, up.

In a way, Nicodemus found the squabbling calming; this was normal for the party. Rory and Sir Claude were at their game again. Maybe they hadn't been as rattled by the sight of those dead children as he had been. He hoped so. They needed to keep their wits about them.

As a sailor rowed them to Feather Island's docks, they all fell into an uneasy silence. The wind brought acrid smells: burning wood, something sulfurous like rotten eggs, the far more disturbing odor of cooked meat. As they climbed from the rowboat to the dock, a nearby scrum of seagulls took flight, uncovering a mutilated body. Once the rowboat was empty save for the sailor, he quickly shoved off and began beating back to the barge.

"Rory," Nicodemus said while gesturing to the Near Tower. "You have the lead."

"Try not to get yourself killed, white robe," Sir Claude muttered as the metal plates around his shoulders folded into a helmet. "Or we'll have to find some grandmother gardener to take your place."

"What was that?" Rory replied. "I couldn't hear that over the sound of your gigantic opinion of yourself being crammed into that tiny metal box of unoriginal prose."

But rather than respond, the knight only saluted Rory and then Nicodemus. "Shall I take the lead, Magistra?" he asked of Doria with a bow.

She waved her hand. "Yes, yes."

There sounded a loud bang and then screeching chaos of gulls. Nicodemus turned to see a flock of the white birds exploding from a terrace halfway up the Near Tower. For a moment, he thought he could hear a wailing voice. It reminded him of something he had heard elsewhere. Something familiar . . . But then there came a second bang and a second burst of seagulls exploded from higher up on the tower.

"I think the boardwalks are collapsing," Rory said. "The fire's weakened the wood. I can cast texts into the wood to keep us safe."

"I'm not worried so much about the unstable boardwalks, Rory," Nicodemus answered as they started off down the dock and toward the base of the tower. "I'm worried about what might have made it unstable."

Rory stopped and pointed down. Nicodemus followed his finger to see a long fluid run of stone in the layered shapes of wax drippings..

"Lava flow?" Nicodemus asked.

"Well it sure doesn't look like it's made out of Lornish cheese."

They continued to pick their way through the ruined buildings at ground level. Rory took the lead, his quarterstaff leveled in front of him as they entered each new building.

Nothing moved but the seagulls as they picked at the bodies strewn among the rubble. The dead were men and women, villagers, none of them armed. Most of the dead were burned, but some others had wounds made by blades.

The stony remains of lava flows ran between and into some houses. Curiously, some buildings had been ransacked while others seemed untouched. Particularly odd was a storehouse filled with casks of rice, wholesome and untouched. In one small house, they found a man dangling from the rafters by a noose. "The madness that killed the sailors?" Rory asked.

"So it seems." Over the years Nicodemus had seen many destroyed villages. He had learned how to interpret ruins. Towns sacked by humans left telltale signs of looting: guards killed by blade or arrow, women violated and murdered, houses broken apart in search of anything valuable.

Villages destroyed by a neodemon might have similar signs, especially in the case of brigand gods, but more often the valuables were untouched. More often strewn across the town would be gruesome findings: evidence of torture, enslavement, sacrifice, or whatever else might satisfy a neodemon's malicious requisites.

Rory made a thoughtful sound. "Half of it seems to suggest the town was sacked, the other half that some lava neodemon with requisites for horror and insanity tore through the place."

"Could be the neodemon drove the villagers mad enough that they started to sack their own houses," Nicodemus muttered. "Let's go up a level."

Carved into the Near Tower was a spiral staircase that, after a rotation within the stone, opened onto the level above. Just as Nicodemus came out of the staircase, Rory pointed to a plateau ahead of them that was covered by rubble. Something had blasted the limestone above causing a small landslide. Amid the rocks lay a motionless male leg, naked to the hip. The rest of the body was hidden under the rubble. A curved blade had been tucked into the belt, the first weapon they had seen.

Carefully Rory approached, his quarterstaff out in front of him. Nothing moved and there was no sound but the roar of waves and the squabbling of gulls. Rory jabbed the leg. It remained motionless. Carefully he pressed his palm against the thigh, then shook it. "Cold but not yet stiff." Dead less than half a day then. Rory pulled the dead man's knife free of its sheath—a steel blade, the hilt and pommel tapering to teardrop points.

Nicodemus frowned. "That's a Spirish knife. Let me see it." After the druid handed it over, Nicodemus looked the weapon over until there was no doubt left in him. "Perhaps he bought it from a merchant in Chandralu. Perhaps. But I've never known a man in a fishing village to carry such a fine weapon."

"Nico," Rory said in a tone that made the other man look up.

Rory was pointing toward a mark on the man's hip. Nicodemus leaned closer to see that it was a tattoo, a circle contained within a square. It looked like a diagram from a mathematics text. "What is it?"

Rory shook his head. "I've never seen—" the druid's words were cut off by a crash from somewhere above them. The floorboards shook, and for a moment Nicodemus again thought he could hear a wailing that was strangely familiar. But then came the crying of gulls and he decided he had imagined the human voice.

Rory was on his feet, pressing his hand against a wooden beam that supported the boardwalk above them. "Something is moving two levels up and to the west."

Nicodemus felt a faint heat move across his cheeks. This was his synesthetic reaction, how his body sensed unknown magical language moving near him. "Anything else you can learn through your wood spells?"

The druid shook his head. "Not without giving away our presence, and we might want the advantage of surprise, no?"

"Advantage of surprise, yes," Nicodemus muttered and looked out at the houses on the village's shelf. Doria and Sir Claude happened to be standing before a ruined building looking at something above Nicodemus. Perhaps whatever had caused the bang? Nicodemus waved his arm and was relieved to see Doria look at him. He motioned for them to come to him and then pointed up to where the mysterious thing was. Doria nodded, and the two of them began to trot toward the tower.

"Whatever it is, it's moving," Rory said. "It's farther around the tower now. I think it saw Sir Claude and Magistra coming."

"Can you tell if there's a way out of the tower over there?"

The druid screwed his eyes together. "I think . . . yes . . . I think so."

"We can't chance it getting away. Come on. We go after it and hope Doria and Claude reach us in time." He headed back toward the spiral staircase but then stopped for Rory to pass him. "Take the lead. If you can, get it into someplace dark and I'll do the rest."

The druid ran forward and up the spiral steps. Around and around they went and came out onto a boardwalk that was twenty or thirty feet above the island's shelf. To their right, the walkway wrapped around the island to run into a covered tunnel. To the left the boardwalk had been burned into blacked stumps that stuck out of the limestone, leaving a gap of about ten feet of airy nothing before the walkway resumed its course and met up with the remaining rope bridge that connected with the Far Tower. "This way!" Rory pointed.

"I was afraid you were going to say that." Nicodemus said eying the gap.

"Not a problem." Rory thumped the bottom of his quarterstaff against the nearest of the burned stumps. Blue light shone from the burnt stump and then it grew a shoot of tender green wood which unfolded broad oak leaves. An instant later, the wood grew straight out from the stump to form a branch as thick as a man's thumb. Roots spread from the new growth to form identical branches from the charred stump two spaces over. On and on the roots went, until the row of thin branches reached the far edge of the walkway.

Nicodemus peered through the thin branches to the sharp rocks far below. Rory picked up his staff and quickstepped over them as easily as if he were hurrying across a creek.

Muttering about having to look foolish in his last moments before death, Nicodemus took a deep breath and quickstepped across the gap, slipping only at the end when Rory caught his sleeve.

"That was—" Rory started to say.

"Don't compliment me," Nicodemus grumbled. "And why under heaven are you holding my arm? If you had touched my skin, you'd have canker curses floating through your blood right now."

The druid looked down at his hand where it was locked around Nicodemus's wrist and then let go.

They continued along the boardwalk, peering into the dwellings that had been cut into the rock. Mostly they found the same horrors as they had on the lower levels: villagers killed, some of the dwellings looted, some relatively untouched. It made no sense, and something else about the village was bothering Nicodemus. The sensation struck him most strongly when he was looking at a sleeping cot that had no sheets or mosquito net. He was trying to remember if mosquito nets were needed in sea villages when, from the next room over, there sounded a choked cry and a thunderclap loud enough to leave Nicodemus's ears ringing.

Rory rushed out onto the boardwalk and then, raising his quarterstaff, into the next dwelling. Nicodemus followed after. It took a moment for his eyes to adjust to the dimness; he had thought that when they did, he would be staring at a sadistic lava neodemon casting spells to drive them both insane.

Instead, and to his complete incomprehension, he discovered three young men, all dressed in drab lungi and standing over a large spread of cloth. They were working their hands frantically. Toward one end the sheets were blood-stained. Just beyond this lay a villager's burnt corpse.

On the other side of the sheet, a young woman squatted. Her left arm was filled with a wide codex and her right arm moved frantically upon the pages.

Suddenly things clicked into place for Nicodemus. "Rory!" he blurted. "Get back! The town wasn't attacked by a neodemon."

Rory looked at him in confusion and had just enough time to say "It wasn't?" before the sheet below him leapt up and, with an edge as sharp as any razor, lunged for his throat.

CHAPTER FIFTEEN

In Chandralu, the definitive metric of civic power was the compound. Guilds, temples, powerful families, merchant cartels, the army, the navy, the judiciary, or any other organization desiring legitimacy had to maintain a compound to conduct daily affairs and house those pledged to its success. Only the poorest families maintained independent households.

The heart of any compound was its pavilion—a round central building containing a shrine to the Trimuril and abutting smaller, usually residential, buildings.

The humblest compounds consisted of a single-story pavilion and a lone house. Larger compounds included multistory pavilions and labyrinthine buildings that spanned several terraces and boasted lily gardens, small orchards, private bathing pools of blue crater water. The grandest compounds had their own carpenters, blacksmiths, weavers, and even small markets.

The Sacred Regent had granted Leandra a modest compound in the outer Utrana district. A two-story pavilion connected to residential buildings spanning two terraces.

When a still grumbling Leandra led Dhrun and Holokai up to her compound's only gatehouse on Utrana Way, she found a single guard was sitting just inside the iron bars. The other servants called him Old Mykos even though he wasn't much over forty and still possessed a full head of shaggy black hair and the muscular thick arms of the wrestler he had once been.

"Did you keep the place safe while I was gone, Mykos?" Leandra asked as the guard unlocked the gate.

Shrugging, Mykos pressed his palms together and then split them apart—a common Cloud Culture gesture to lament the world's shortcomings. "What can I say, my Lady Warden, the compound was beset by a troop of monkeys. It was left to poor Old Mykos to fight them off. You'd think the other guards would have helped . . ." Another shrug. "What can you do?"

Leandra smiled as she walked through the guardhouse into the pavilion. "However did you fight them off?"

"I threatened to go get my wife."

"Harsh."

"Ten of them dropped dead of fright," Mykos said as he followed the party. "Shall I inform Vhivek that you are returned?" As chamberlain, Vhivek—an exceedingly polite old Lotus man—supervised the compound's daily operation.

"Please don't or Vhivek will try to serve me some extravagant meal," Leandra said. "We won't be staying long. Oh, and Mykos, have my lord father or my lady mother arrived?"

The guard raised a bushy eyebrow. "No and no. I did not know we were expecting the Lady Warden of Dral."

"It seems that we are, joyously. Do you know if Roslyn is in the compound?"

"Yes, my lady. Where else would the dear be?"

"Thank you, Mykos. Please don't admit anyone while I am in the compound."

He nodded and turned back to the gatehouse.

Though not grand, Leandra's pavilion was a pleasant space. Twenty feet above, an unadorned dome opened at regular intervals to form skylights that let rectangular beams of sunlight stream down among wooden pillars. A walkway made a circuit around the second story and provided access to the various houses connected to the pavilion. In the center of the pavilion's ground floor lay a small reflecting pool. Behind it stood a stylized painting of a red lotus below a bulging white cloud, both limned with gold leaf. Here was the obligatory shrine to the Trimuril, the high divinity complex of the Kingdom of Ixos. It was also a representation of the Trinity Mandate: the oldest and most fundamental law of Ixos, which required every official building and endeavor to have a representation—and ideally a representative—of all three cultures.

Tradition required a prayer to the Trimuril after returning from a sea journey. However, given her recent disease flare, Leandra excused herself. "Kai, you may go to the kitchens, but don't gorge yourself," Leandra said while mounting the wooden stairway that spiraled around the pavilion walls and led up to the second story.

Wordlessly Holokai headed off toward the kitchen, his expression one of pained concentration. "And don't pester the cooks!" she called after him.

"May I visit the arena?" Dhrun asked from her side.

"Only if you can be back in half an hour," Leandra answered more sharply than she intended. They had reached the top of the stairs and were making their way around the walkway, the beams groaning under the divinity complex's considerable weight.

Dhrun did not answer, but Leandra would have bet her last rupee that he was making his infuriatingly half smile that might signify obedient contentment or silently amused judgment.

"Wait here," she said and turned down a hallway and then climbed another flight of stairs to a building that stood on the terrace above. She stopped at the last door on the right. After a deep breath, Leandra took down her headdress, pushed the door open, and stepped into a small but bright room. There was a small four-poster bed in one corner, draped with a thin mosquito net. A wide window opened east, looking out at the bright city descending to the azure bay. A cloud was passing overhead putting the Lower Banyan Districts into shadow. A few drops of rain landed on the windowsill.

Before the window, wrapped in a shawl despite the tropical heat, was thin Roslyn. A small table stood beside her chair, a plate of mostly untouched rice and curry sitting upon it.

"Rosie?" Leandra asked.

Roslyn of the Amber Wood blinked. She had always been a small woman, barely over five feet and as slender as a young palm. But age had stooped her a few inches and stolen away pounds she could barely afford to lose.

"Rosie?" Leandra said loudly. The elderly woman blinked then looked up at Leandra. It was hard to believe that this skeletal face was the same that had given her the vivid smiles and the reprimanding frowns of a childhood nurse.

"Lady Francesca," Rosyln said. "You've come to visit."

"It's Leandra, Rosie," she said loudly. "Not Francesca."

"What?" Her watery blue eyes were searching Leandra's face.

"I'm your little Lea, Rosie," Leandra nearly shouted. "I've played a trick on you and grew up."

"You did?"

"I did." Leandra had forgotten how hard it was to continue talking this loudly.

"Why . . . so you did. That's wonderful. How old are you, dear?"

"Thirty-three."

"Thirty-three! Sacred Mother Forest! Why that's wonderful. Everyone said you wouldn't see fifteen."

"I always hated doing what others told me."

"You certainly did. Do you remember when I told you to finish your reading in your room . . . and you snuck out the window and your father found you with the handsome merchant's son? Do you remember?"

"I try not to."

"What?"

"Rosie, they have lunch for you here." She picked up the plate of curry. She looked at the food in surprise. "Oh, I'm not hungry."

Leandra lifted a forkful of rice. "But you'll have a bite for me, won't you?"

Roslyn eyed the fork uneasily. "Maybe later. Lea, my dear, are you married?"

"You know I wouldn't want to torture some poor man by marrying him."

Roselyn chuckled. "No, no. Just waiting for a man that deserves you, and my, but it will take a long string of winters to find him."

When Leandra was sixteen years old, her mother had somehow talked her into enrolling in the academy of Port Mercy, where she had started a physician's training. Well, one might call it "training," if skipping her lectures and shirking infirmary duty could be called training. Nevertheless, in those two years, Leandra had seen enough senility to know that it came in a spectrum ranging from confusion to inconsolable sadness to delirious anger. Though she hated herself just a little bit more for it, Leandra was grateful that time was going to kill Roslyn by flattening her mind into child-like pleasantness rather than by any of its other, crueler methods.

The Creator knew that Leandra's disease was going to make her own death far more horrible than the one that was sitting before her, blinking rheumy eyes out a sunlit window.

Regardless, Leandra had the answer she had come for; there could be no reason why she should have to murder this old woman whose mind and spirit had all but passed out of this life.

"I love you, Rosie," she said at normal volume, knowing that the old woman couldn't hear her. It was a cowardly thing. She should yell it. But instead she kissed the old woman on the cheek and said her goodbyes.

CHAPTER SIXTEEN

R ory, get back!" Nicodemus bellowed.

Ahead of him, the druid stood above a sheet lunging for his throat. On the other side of the cloth, three young men worked their hands in complex patterns.

Suddenly, Nicodemus understood the ruins of Feather Island. Not a stitch of cloth remained in the village, and the hierophants' magical language was written upon cloth. The slash wounds on the villagers might come from spell-stiffened cloth rather than steel. The villagers hadn't been attacked by neodemons; they had been attacked by, "Wind mages!" Nicodemus yelled.

Rory danced back and brought up his quarterstaff. Where druidic wood met hierophantic cloth, white light blazed. Heat burned across Nicodemus's face and the cloth went slack. Two more strips of cloth billowed up and lunged for the druid.

Nicodemus jumped forward and grabbed one of the cloth spells. Sending a jolt of cacographic force down the sheet, he misspelled the text within. Beyond the sheets, the hierophants yelled. Beside them, the young woman with the book worked her hands more frantically across the pages.

Questions blazed into Nicodemus's mind. Hierophants were the spell-wrights of Spires. They created the empire's airships and provided their fleets with sails that could generate their own wind. Many hierophants came to Ixos as members of imperial trading missions. But why should they have ransacked and destroyed a poor sea village? It didn't make any sense.

A strip of white cloth shot across the room and thrust a sharpened point into Nicodemus's left side. He felt something sharp punch through his leather longvest and into his skin. With a cry he stumbled back and grabbed hold of the eel-ike cloth, dispelling it. But apparently the hierophants had learned; this sheet wasn't connected to the rest of the cloth and so he could not misspell any more of their texts.

Rory let out a war cry. His quarterstaff had elongated and shaped itself into smooth wooden blades. With expert dexterity, he spun the staff around, slashing apart the strips of magical cloth snaking around him. The druid's lacquered armor had come alive to cover every aspect of his body. The plates about his shoulders had folded around his head and formed a stag's antlers.

The druid ran into the fray, slashing through cloth and trying to reach the hierophants.

"Rory, fall back!" Nicodemus shouted. "Wait for the others!" Nicodemus took another step toward the door, but then remembered that not all of the villagers had suffered cutting wounds. Most of them had been burned.

Nicodemus looked at the woman flipping through the large book. If the others were imperial hierophants, than she might just be an imperial "Pyromancer!" Nicodemus yelled just as the woman reached into a page and pulled back an arc of dazzling white light.

Nicodemus sprinted out of the room. Behind him, he caught a glimpse of Rory rewriting his staff and armor into liquid wood that formed a blast shield. Nicodemus threw himself onto the boardwalk, landing painfully on one side. He had just enough time to grab one of the boards before the shockwave hit. A brain-rattling force jolted through him. Scalding heat ran along his exposed arms.

Nicodemus opened his eyes, half expecting to find that the blast had knocked him off the walkway to his death on the rocks below. But, thank the Creator, he saw his raw knuckles still tightened around the boards. To his right, he could see that the boardwalk had been scorched by the heat, a small flame dancing from the wood.

"Rory?" Nicodemus yelled. He rolled over, tried to stand, and to his nearly overpowering relief, found Doria and Sir Claude standing above him. Both were breathing hard from the run.

"It's the empire!" he croaked. "Three hierophants and a pyromancer. I don't know how much text they have left. Rory's in there."

Sir Claude stepped forward. "Rory?"

Doria caught his shoulder. "Wait!" she barked with undeniable authority as she unslung the water skin from her back. She tossed the water skin through the doorway from which the flames had come. A moment later there was a loud pop and then a fine mist rolled out of the doorway. These droplets would contain potent amounts of the hydromancer's disspells. There were few spellwrights better able to neutralize hostile text than hydromancers. In a moment the mist fell. "Now, Sir Claude!" Doria yelled and gave the knight a shove.

Swords of fluid metal grew from both of the knight's hands as he charged into the room.

"We need one of them alive," Nicodemus said. "At least one for questioning."

Doria pulled a vial filled with rusty red liquid from her bandoleer and made for the doorway. There was another bang. Shouting. Carefully, Nicodemus struggled to his feet. Inside he found Rory on his knees, alive and trying to regain his feet. One the hierophants lay next to him, impaled by what seemed to be Rory's quarterstaff made into a spear.

Sir Claude hacked a serpentine cloth in half. The cloth whipped around, slashing into his chest but made only a dull clang against his armor.

Doria kicked the spellbook out of the pyromancer's hands and then spiked a glass vial on the floor beneath the woman. The pyromancer staggered backward. With another vial, Doria splashed some colorless liquid into her face.

Suddenly wind buffeted through the room and sent Nicodemus's long hair flying. An expansive sheet billowed up and flew toward the door. Ropes extended from the cloth to form a harness around one of the hierophants. "He's escaping on a lofting kite!" Nicodemus yelled, as a blast of wind knocked him over.

Sir Claude leapt forward with a backhand slash but missed as the hierophant shot away. His lofting kite hit the door with a thump. Nicodemus's ears popped. Then the lofting kite was through and pulling the wind mage up into the sky. Sir Claude threw something that glinted metallic in the sunlight before it struck the fleeing wind mage in the calf. The hierophant rose up and out of sight.

Nicodemus scrambled to his feet and ran to the door. The hierophant was flying over bay water, gaining altitude and flying north. A moment later he passed over a standing island and out of view. "Fiery heaven!" Nicodemus swore. "Now whoever sent those wind mages will know we're on to them."

He turned back to the room. Rory was on his knees, holding his head. His wooden plate armor had fallen off. Meanwhile, Doria and Sir Claude were facing the pyromancer. She had backed against the wall, stumbling as if drunk. A few gouts of flame leapt from her hands as she extemporized sentences of the pyromancer's incendiary language.

Sir Claude was pointing his two swords at her. But Doria held both her empty hands up. "Peace, Magistra," she said. "Peace. There's nothing you can do now except get yourself hurt. I cast a hydromantic spell onto you when I dashed that water into your face. You're feeling a bit funny now. You're going to go to sleep soon."

For the first time, Nicodemus got a good look at the pyromancer. She had dark olive skin and long black hair. Her brown eyes were full of hatred and her lips pulled back in a sneer. She stumbled and steadied herself against the wall. Her head swung around and she seemed to focus on Nicodemus. Her eyes narrowed as if in recognition.

Nicodemus held his hands up to show that he had no weapon.

"Peace, Magistra," Doria said again. "It's over."

The young pyromancer screamed and charged at Nicodemus. At first he stood his ground, thinking to block her exit. But the moment before she reached him, Nicodemus realized that if their skin touched, the resulting canker curse would kill her in a matter of hours. So much for questioning her then. Clumsily he jumped out of the way, stumbled, fell on his back.

In the next instant she was on him. Tiny flames danced along her knuckles as she punched him in the cheek. Suddenly, metal-clad arms wrapped around the pyromancer and pulled her off of Nicodemus. "Her hand!" he said. "Doria, where she hit me. The canker curse."

He struggled to his feet and saw that Sir Claude had the pyromancer pinned to the floor. Her eyes were fluttering and she struggled weakly, clearly altered by whatever spell Doria had cast into her face. Meanwhile Doria was examining her hand. Three black tumors already grew from the woman's knuckles. The dark tissue spread down her fingers and onto the back of her hand.

"This hand comes off right now," Doria commanded. "Rory, pin her down. Sir Claude, you'll amputate."

The druid took the knight's place holding the pyromancer down. Sir Claude hurried to stand behind Doria.

"She has only moments before this canker spreads into her blood. Then she's dead." She spread the woman's hand open and pulled hard on her index finger and pinky. "That spell I cast on her mind, she's as anesthetized as I dare make her. She should also be amnestic. It's going to hurt like hell, but at least she won't remember it. I need your blade to be as sharp and as hot as possible. It's got to be hot enough to cauterize the wound, to burn it, so she won't bleed out afterward. Can you do this?" She looked up at the knight.

Sir Claude's helmet had peeled back to reveal his grim expression. Nicodemus understood. Killing a violent enemy was one thing, chopping off a restrained woman's hand quite another. But with steady hands the knight brought both his swords together. They became liquid, began moving up and down against each other. It created a horrible screeching sound. Within moments the friction and whatever spells the knight was casting in the metal made the blade glow orange.

Doria pulled harder on the pyromancer's index finger and pinky, stretching the arm taut. "Cut just along the palm. Try to save her thumb."

She pulled back harder. Sir Claude raised his sword, and Nicodemus fought the urge to look away. With a grunt, Sir Claude brought his sword down. The blade crashed into the floor and Doria fell back onto her bottom. In her lap, smoking slightly and stinking, were all four of the pyromancer's fingers.

There was a moment of unearthly silence. "Creator," Nicodemus whispered to himself, "be merciful."

Then the pyromancer began to scream.

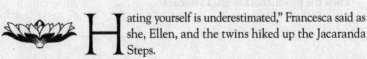"H ating yourself is underestimated," Francesca said as she, Ellen, and the twins hiked up the Jacaranda Steps.

Returning to Chandralu was a strange experience for Francesca. She had been written from the memories of a physician who had trained in the city's infirmary three hundred years ago. The resulting clash of her recollections with present realities was making Francesca maudlin and philosophical; that, she supposed, was not a good combination for any woman, but it was especially not so for a semi-draconic one, in whom the two emotions might result not only in pessimistic musings but also in a bodily transformation, much wailing, gnashing of foot-long teeth, and generalized dragon-based chaos among the citizenry.

The party had stepped ashore not half an hour before and had been met by a lesser wizard from Chandralu's colaboris station. He carried a cyphered message from the Counsel of Starfall to Francesca. She had eagerly pulled several luminous Numinous paragraphs from the envelope. But after translating the magical text, she found nothing encouraging.

The message reported that nothing new had been learned regarding her "recent grave discovery," which she had come to Chandralu to deliver to Nicodemus. The message went on to explain that the Council had attempted but failed to establish a diplomatic connection with the empress's court.

Francesca was disappointed, scared, and brooding on what she could have done to avoid the present political situation, hence her present and dangerous self-critical and philosophical mood.

"No one can hate you as much as you can hate yourself because no one knows you as well as you know yourself," she said to her party. "In fact, loathing of similarities is underestimated in general. Think of all the attention we give to differences. We act as if all prejudice or injustice or war is caused by hating things or people who are different from us. I hate that woman because she wears different clothes. Or we fought that war because they worship different gods. We always say that sort of thing. We pretend that we could enter a golden age of peace if we could learn not to distrust foreign things and people."

"We couldn't?" Ellen asked, deadpan. The twins, as usual, were silent.

"No, the distrust of difference isn't everything," Francesca continued, warming to her argument. "Who can upset you more than someone who is similar to you?"

"But Magistra, you upset me all the time."

"Exactly my point. I chose you as a student because you reminded me of myself when I was younger."

"I find that very upsetting."

"You see!" Francesca said, playing up her passionate voice against Ellen's flatness.

"Magistra, I am astounded by your rhetoric."

"What kind of hatred is worse than self-hatred?"

"Hatred of menstrual cramps?"

"Isn't that usually a punch line from one of my jokes?"

"That's why I thought it'd make you laugh. But given your present argument, maybe I should have guessed you'd dislike your own punch lines more than anyone else's."

"Well, regardless, isn't that a form of self-hatred? Are you not hating your own uterus at that moment?"

"It is such a surprise," Ellen said in a tone that indicated that it was anything but, "to find that you have turned my attempt at humor into substance for your argument."

"And in medicine, Ellen, in medicine what disease is worse for a body than a disease perpetrated by one's own body? Consider how the body's inflammatory response to infection can cause septic shock? Or how our own tissue can turn against us to become a lethal tumor?"

"Yes, Magistra," Ellen answered, her tone suddenly soft. "And there is the torment your daughter suffers as the different aspects of her nature attack each other."

Francesca looked at the younger woman, surprised by her frankness and perspicacity.

Ellen squeezed Francesca's shoulder. A natural gesture, reassuring for a moment, and then painful, as Francesca realized that Leandra would never have done the same. Francesca's anger melted into guilt and misery.

"Yes, you're right," Francesca said, wondering how she had screwed things up so royally that she was closer to her student than to her daughter.

The party continued up the Jacaranda Steps. On either side of the steps the poor called out for money or prayers, depending on whether they were human or divine. Looking at them rekindled Francesca's exasperation. It was a good feeling; one that helped her stop thinking about her daughter.

"Another example of my argument," Francesca said, resuming her impassioned tone. "There never have been so many poor on the Jacaranda Steps. It used to be that anyone half able to work had enough to eat. The regency made arrangements for the sick and destitute. But the past thirty years have produced crowds of poor in every kingdom and they are growing every day. Because of the god mob, more children are surviving infancy, the elderly are living longer. But we haven't figured out how to care for them. The rich are getting richer, the poor poorer. All in the name of matching our strength to the empire's."

"Magistra?" Tam said. Prompting both Francesca and Ellen to look back at the twin druids.

The twins had been together since birth. Early in puberty they had been born to magic at exactly the same time. As sometimes happens with twins, Tam and Kenna had developed their own unique dialect; however, whereas most twins developed unique spoken communication, Tam and Kenna had developed a unique communication in the druidic magical languages. This is what gave them both their special abilities and their uncanny reticence.

In fact, Tam and Kenna spoke so infrequently that others often mistook them for mutes or forgot that they were nearby.

Tam had lowered his eyebrows. At least Francesca thought that he had. Both of the twins had hair so blond and skin so fair that sometimes she could not make out their eyebrows. "I fail to see what relevance the poor have to do with your argument about hatred and similarity."

"Ah!" Francesca said with a nod. "Because this world changed, this glorious burgeoning of our kingdoms, has been caused by creatures like me." She tapped her chest. "It's the mixing of divine and human language that's created the god mob and because of the benefits the mob brings, a burgeoning population that outstrips our ability to care for it. Then there are the neodemons, who are not all that different from me, who terrorize the weak and empower the wicked. And why do we do it all? Why do we keep populating our lands with divinities? Simply to try to keep up with the empire. If we gave half as much thought to caring for our own as we do to matching the empire's might, we wouldn't have any poor lining these steps."

Tam nodded and then glanced at Kenna. Both of their faces became blank as stone. They began walking in perfect step with each other.

Francesca and Ellen turned back to the steps. Above them one of the billowing clouds had covered the sun and had begun to drop a light tropical rain. The merchants retreated farther into their stalls. The poor huddled closer to the jacaranda trees or each other.

"You know Plumeria Way used to be where the upper city walls stood? What are now the Upper Banyan and Plumeria Districts were just rice paddies," Francesca explained as they passed Utrana Way. She could have turned right and sought out their family's compound. Likely that would have helped her find Leandra. But she wanted to investigate one thing first. They continued up the steps.

"No, Magistra, I didn't know that," Ellen said.

"Granted, that was three centuries ago, but there's no doubt that now the city is growing too fast," Leandra complained. "Look at all this poverty. Far too fast. It's enough to make a woman mad."

"Of course, Magistra," Ellen said.

"I sound like a sour old woman who complains all the time, don't I?"

"Of course not, Magistra."

"Ellen, I have always admired how well you are able to lie."

"The feeling is mutual, Magistra."

Francesca cracked a smile and then let the party fall into silence. They continued up the steps. The crowds of poor slowly dwindled as they rose higher in the city. They passed an elephant hauling produce down to the Bay Market. The massive animal's ears displayed stylized lotus flowers drawn in red-and-white chalk. The rain was making the design run. The mahout riding on the elephant's back called out a singsong warning to the traffic ahead of him.

At last, Francesca turned left onto Plumeria Way, which ran the length of the city's eighth terrace. Being the only wide and well-paved street that connected all four major stairways, Plumeria Way was nearly always thick with traffic: pedestrians, palanquin crews, elephants, hand-pushed carts, all in a variety of colors, styles, and wealth that ranged from resplendent to tattered.

Although the light rain seemed to have kept some pedestrians at home, there was enough traffic to require Francesca and her followers to weave their way through a crowd.

Francesca and Ellen had donned lightweight black robes to signify that they were wizards and their red stoles to signify that they were clerical physicians. Behind them Tam and Kenna were dressed in their stark druidic white and carrying thick wooden quarterstaffs. Some recognized their robes and steered clear of them. The rest of the traffic—most troubling among them being the two-ton pachyderms—either did not recognize or did not care that they were about to run over a pack of spellwrights.

"Magistra, we could commission a palanquin for you," Ellen suggested.

"Don't be ridiculous." After all that time cooped up on a boat, Francesca would be damned if they'd stuff her into some wooden box.

"It's just that those in palanquins seem so much less likely to suffer a horrible crushing death beneath an elephant's foot."

"If you're having trouble keeping up, Ellen, I'll give you a piggyback ride."

"I'd like that very much, Magistra."

The traffic increased as the Plumeria Way led them onto Sacred Regent Plaza: a broad square of bare dark red earth at the center of which stood the Banyan of Ages.

Long before Francesca's predecessor set foot in Chandralu, the first trunk of this ancient tree grew in this square and represented the city's heart. Over the centuries, the tree had sent up massive, arching boughs in all directions. From these boughs dangled the aerial roots that made banyan trees so distinctive. Over time these roots had become so thick as to become new, buttresslike trunks.

In the memory of Francesca's predecessor, the Banyan of Ages had been one tree—almost a miniature forest unto itself. Now after three centuries of growth, the ancient central tree had decayed back to red earth. The result was a ring tree, not dissimilar from the "fairy rings" of redwood trees she had seen in the Auburn Hills outside Avel.

In the banyan's ring stood a small pool of salt water around a massive standing stone, upon which stylized lotuses and clouds were painted in tints of gold and silver. This was one of the city's many divine arks, which transformed the prayers of the citizens into divine language. When Nicodemus had begun to cast his metaspells, these new stone arks began to grow wherever enough of the prayerful gathered.

Before Nicodemus had cast his metaspells, all arks held the soul of only one divinity or divinity complex and could convert the strength of the prayerful into magical text for only one particular divinity. However, Nicodemus's metaspell had made magical language more intuitive. Therefore, all of the new arks stored the souls of any newly incarnated deity, and they could create prayerful magical language for any divinity within a network of ark stones. Though no one had foreseen this as a result of Nicodemus's metaspell, it had provided the driving mechanism of the proliferation of divinities.

Presently, Francesca could see three priests of the Trimuril calling in shrill yellow voices for prayers to the patron divinity complex of the kingdom. Perhaps thirty citizens stood with palms pressed together and held over their hearts, praying away a small amount of their strength to the Trimuril.

Francesca hurried through the Banyan of Ages to the far side of Sacred Regent Plaza, where Plumeria Way continued. On the volcano side of the eighth terrace stood the three-story pavilion of Chandralu's famous infirmary.

The infirmary, like every other civic organization, had a compound. In this case the attached buildings consisted of patient wards, operating theaters, apothecaries.

The wide doors to the infirmary's pavilion were open to the street, where a crowd gathered in a sedate riot. Given how much pushing and cajoling took place in the pavilion's queues, waiting for a physician was something of an athletic event. The sick often came with their families and servants to help reach the triage clerk. Ellen and Francesca confidently stepped into the madness. Many saw their red stoles and stepped aside.

The twins did not fare so well. Francesca looked back and saw the two white robes being baffled by elbows and shoulders. So she took Tam by his hand. He in turn grabbed his sister's hand. Like a mother leading her children, Francesca hauled them through the crowd.

When at last they reached the guard in front of the physicians' entrance, Francesca was sweating so much that her robes stuck uncomfortably to her back. The guard, a young man with light brown skin and a pubescent attempt at a goatee, eyed Francesca's red stole. A small baton hung from the sash above his lungi.

"Physicians," he said in a tone that didn't so much border on politeness as violate its sovereignty, "I don't recognize you."

Ellen stepped forward and with a bow said, "May I present Magistra Francesca DeVega, Lady Warden of Dral and erstwhile dragon, who I would say has eaten insolent little men for breakfast if I weren't afraid that you would fail to take it literally. We're here to see the dean."

Confusion washed across the guard's face. "You a-are the Lady . . ." he stammered before turning to whisper something urgent into a nearby doorway. Francesca perceived the whisper as thin streams of white light unfurling into the doorway. The sound was too dim for her to make out the shape of any words.

A moment later, an older guard with a captain's gold chain around his neck appeared. "Magistra," he said and pressed both palms together over his heart before bowing. "Please follow me."

They followed the captain through a hallway and then up a steep set of stairs to another, narrower hallway. Francesca realized that she was already disoriented. The infirmary had grown so much. They took another set of stairs before the guard led them into what looked like a small lecture hall.

"Please wait here," he said with a bow and then hurried away. The twins walked to the window and stared out at the city. They were holding hands as they must have done as children. Francesca could never decide if it was charming or creepy when they did that. Maybe both.

Ellen stood next to Francesca. "Magister Sarvna is going to have an ulcer when he hears that you're here unannounced."

Francesca frowned. "Magister Sarvna, Dean of the Chandralu infirmary. Now there's another example of similarity causing annoyance."

Ellen shrugged. "Sarvna is nice enough, maybe a bit slippery and talks too much. How do you think you two are similar?"

"You don't think I talk too much?"

"Well, you got me there."

"Magistra DeVega, it has been too long since you visited us!" a booming burgundy-hued voice announced.

Francesca turned to see Magister Sarvna hurrying into the lecture hall, followed by a train of junior physicians. Sarvna was a short man with thin white hair receding behind a long, pale forehead. His plump face was pleasant and beardless. His short arms and thick fingers were habitually clasped together above his potbelly. He wore the blue robes of a hydromancer and an elaborately decorated physician's stole.

The crowd behind him consisted of maybe twenty spellwrights. Their robes ranged from the bright orange of pyromancers to the green of heirophants to the gray of common mages. Each wore a red stole with various designs indicating specialty.

Francesca nodded. "Magister Sarvna, I am sorry to show up unannounced."

"Not at all. It is an honor to have you grace our infirmary."

The dean's rosy tone gave Francesca pause. He should have been irritated. Perhaps he saw an opportunity to earn a political favor. "I won't take up much of your time. When approaching the Cerulean Strait last night, an unknown sea god or goddess circled under my ship and sparked my meager ability to prophesize. I foresaw that something in this infirmary intertwined our futures. Perhaps you can help me discover what the something is."

Francesca had expected the dean to frown at her outlandish request. Certainly she saw faces behind his expressing disbelief. In fact two physicians seemed to have started an argument. But, strangely, the dean's pleasant smile became brighter.

"Why don't I have the provost form a committee to investigate the matter? They can start by interviewing the senior physicians on each ward and reviewing the possible sea deities who might be involved."

Inwardly Francesca flinched. She had forgotten how slowly the gears of academia turned. But having asked, she could do nothing more than nod and say, "Thank you kindly, Magister."

"While this committee is being convened, perhaps you will tour our facilities. I believe you will be most impressed by how much we have accomplished with the funds that the League of Starfall has allotted to our order."

So Sarvna wanted to get around the Ixonian Crown and appeal directly to the Council of Starfall for funding. She should have seen it coming. Not that Francesca was against the funding of public infirmaries, quite the opposite, but she had far more pressing concerns.

"Magister you are too kind," Francesca said. "As you no doubt remember, my predecessor trained at this institution many . . . many . . . years ago. Be assured of my full support." The argument at the back of Sarvna's cadre continued. This made Francesca pause before she continued, "However, there is an urgent political matter to which I must attend with my husband and daughter . . ." Her voice died as the argument at the back of the crowd intensified.

Francesca's textual mind churned, glimpsing the landscape of likely futures. This argument became a valley in time; one she might follow down into an intersection with the unknown sea deity. "Your pardon," she said while approaching the argument. "Magister and Magistra, would you mind sharing the substance of your discussion."

The two argumenteurs—a young woman with dark skin and darker freckles, and an older man with pale heavy jowls—looked up and froze under the crowd's scrutiny.

"My lady, forgive us," the bejowled old man said. "My student and I were just discussing an unusual case." He glared at the young woman who returned the expression.

"Of course—" Sarvna started to say.

"Magistra," Francesca said to the younger physician, "what case were you discussing?"

The young physician looked at Francesca, plainly embarrassed, but then she glanced at the older physician, who shook his head slightly. That was enough to cure her stage fright. Her mouth set in a hard line, she turned back to Francesca. "A case of postpartum mortality that may be connected to your mysterious sea deity."

"Of course there are unfortunate events in this infirmary," Sarvna quickly interjected, "as there are at every infirmary—"

Francesca held up her hand. "Magister, I don't doubt your institution. But I should like to hear the rest of this case." She gestured to the young physician. "Magistra, you must introduce yourself."

The young physician blushed. "I am Magistra Nneka Ubo, originally of Ibadan. I earned my wizard's hood in Astrophell and completed clerical training at Port Mercy before coming here for my first year of obstetric training."

A wave of memories then for Francesca: the roughness of an infant's hair as it crowned; the laboring mother's cries; her two hands on the baby's head, guiding it down toward the ground to deliver the upper shoulder out of the vagina; then pulling up to the sky and the lower shoulder delivers; suddenly in your arms the whole, hot, slippery baby making its stereotypical cries; the mother crying still perhaps but now with joy; maybe the previously stoic father going teary-eyed. Congratulations, she had thought so many times, congratulations on somehow making another human and passed it though your pelvis without killing it or yourself. Always had felt like a victory. Except when it wasn't. Then it had been bitter, a dead infant, a dead mother. Dangerous business, creating or being created; funny that it should be so. She remembered then becoming a mother herself. Leandra's delivery had gone perfectly, only five hours of labor. The trouble had started . . . much later.

Francesca came out of her reverie. She smiled at the young obstetrician. "Well, Magistra Ubo, your first year of training must be nearing an end. How many babies have you brought into the world?"

"One hundred seventeen vaginal deliveries: five breech deliveries and two sets of twins; fifty-six deliveries via surgical section of the uterus."

Francesca nodded. "I cringe to think how little you must sleep. But now, tell me why I should want to hear about a case of postpartum mortality?"

Magistra Ubo glanced at the other physicians but then continued. "Two nights ago I was woken with a message that there was a woman in New Village, only thirty weeks pregnant by report, who had gone into premature labor. I packed my things and headed down toward the village. But I found that the Low Gates were still closed. Just on the other side, a woman had been wrapped up in blankets and left on the ground. She reported that a group of men had carried her to the gate. She claimed she had delivered only moments before. Then they just left her. When I finally got through the gate, I found a pale young woman with copious vaginal bleeding. I sent for a stretcher, I conducted a bimanual exam hoping to find some amount of retained placenta responsible for the bleed. I also began uterine massage. It was at this point . . ." She paused, a flicker of doubt. ". . . at that point when I sustained a laceration."

"I'm sorry," Francesca interrupted.

"On my probing hand."

"Her uterus cut you?"

"The stretcher arrived and we began to carry her back to the infirmary. While walking with her, she reported that she had given birth to a full-term and healthy baby boy not five hours ago. However, she was confused. She did not know what had happened to the child and became tearful. When I asked where she lived and if she had family who would support her, she grew agitated. She begged me not to ask any more questions. At this point, I noticed that under her blankets she wore one of the loose dresses commonly worn by the devotees of the Pillow House."

"Pillow House?" Francesca asked.

Magister Sarvna coughed, a gray sound. "The Mithuna divinity complex is the patron divinity of erotic love and there is a . . . temple . . . dedicated to her in New Village."

"I see. Go on."

The young physician nodded. "Unfortunately, neither my maneuvers nor the subsequent assistance of more senior physicians could slow the patient's bleeding. She passed into the next life shortly after midnight."

"I am sorry to hear it," Francesca said.

"An autopsy . . ." Magistra Ubo continued but then looked Dean Sarvna. He, however, kept his eyes on Francesca. So Magistra Ubo continued, "An autopsy revealed . . . pathology not consistent with any known disease of pregnancy. In fact, the findings support a divinopathophysiology." This being physician's jargon for "a divine process that causes disease."

"Do they now?" Francesca asked.

"Describing the findings . . ." Magistra Ubo struggled to find the words.

"Perhaps," Dean Sarvna suggested, "Magistra DeVega would like to see the findings for herself?"

Francesca looked at the chubby man and discovered, much to her surprise, that she liked him. "Yes, I would. How far is your morgue?"

"Not far," Magistra Ubo replied. "But I must say that the findings are . . . unusually disturbing, even to the physicians who perform autopsies daily."

"Ah," Francesca answered with a smile, "that is one perk of having been semi-draconic for the past thirty years. Unless a process involves a neodemon trying to introduce pathology into my own internal organs with fangs, tentacles, or more disturbing appendages, I am not going to be disturbed."

"With all respect, my Lady Warden," Magistra Ubo said, "in this case, you may be wrong."

"To the morgue then," Francesca said with a challenging smile. "The burning hells will freeze before I am wrong about this."

So Magistra Ubo led Francesca and Dean Sarvna down a narrow stairway. The rest of Francesca's party and the dean's followed close behind. As they went, Dean Sarvna expressed his dismay that the imperial kingdoms were no longer sending their young spellwrights to Port Mercy to be trained as physicians. In fact, he reported, Empress Vivian had opened an Imperial College of Physicians in Trillinon, which even accepted magically illiterate students.

Clearly the dean was most troubled by the idea of non-spellwrights becoming physicians. Francesca, on the other hand, saw the empress's refusal to send physicians to Port Mercy as an ominous political sign of imperial ambition.

When the party reached the morgue, Magistra Ubo spoke to one of the attendants who led Francesca to a body covered with stained brown cloth. When Magistra Ubo pulled a sheet back, Francesca involuntarily stopped her breath.

Her whole body tensed as she tried to avoid losing her composure . . . or vomiting. It took Francesca a moment to realize her mistake. She had trained as a physician in an era when disease caused by divinity had been so rare that she had seen virtually none of it. Worse, she had never before seen divinopathophysiology after the birth of her daughter, who had endured a lifetime of pain caused by divinopathology.

Therefore, Francesca's revulsion was intensified by the revulsion and loathing she had felt a thousand times before for herself and what her own linguistic nature had done to her daughter. Here it was again: proof that similarities, and not differences, caused the strongest loathing.

There is no hatred like self-hatred.

"Well, Magistra," she said, still unable to look away from the nightmare uterus, "the burning hells might have just gotten a bit chilly."

CHAPTER EIGHTEEN

Every city is divisible by its vices; or so Leandra had concluded after a decade hunting the incarnations of malicious prayers from every district of every city in the league.

What was a banking district but a temple of greed? What were noble palaces if not monuments of vanity? Sanctimony bred in a city's sacred places; prejudice in its courts; malice in its strongholds.

Not that Leandra was a model of virtue. Not that she didn't occasionally indulge in all the above vices. Not that her life's driving force wasn't a particular flavor of sanctimonious arrogance. But at least she was mindful of her potential for hypocrisy. The average-fine-upstanding-citizens, on the other hand, found no place more sacred than his city's shrines, no place more noble than the wealthy neighborhoods. The only district in which the fine-upstandings found vice was the slum, where they saw every human failing from laziness to lust to stupidity to whatever transgression the given fine-upstandings felt they were not personally perpetrating on the world at large. That is probably why the Naukaa District—Chandralu's slum—made Lea so unreasonably angry and violent.

"Aren't we supposed to go up to the Floating City?" Holokai asked as Leandra lead her party down the Jacaranda Steps. "Don't you have to respond to that royal summons?"

"There's someone we need to talk to in the Naukaa."

"Doesn't that place make you unreasonably angry and violent?"

"Shut up before I punch you in the face, Kai."

"Oh, hey, yeah, that's the place."

"Captain Holokai, what an excellent rapport you are developing with the Lady Warden," Dhrun remarked.

"Would be a lot more excellent if I could get her to punch you in the face instead of me."

Ignoring them, Leandra continued down the steps. She had hoped to find

Baruvalman and ask him some pointed questions about why he had called her a "circle maker," but the pitiful divinity complex was not among the miserables lining the steps.

Though faint, Leandra heard the booming voice of the Bay Market's crier. She looked toward the harbor and saw two new ships at anchor, one of them a Dralish galley. "Kai, is that *The High Queen's Lance?*"

Holokai squinted. "Always hard when I've seen the ship only from below, but . . . yeah, that's her."

"You're sure."

"Yeah. Sure."

Leandra swore. Her mother would soon hike up to their family compound or the Floating City. Time to get off the Jacaranda Steps. "Kai, hurry down to hear the crier's news, then find us on the Naukaa's second terrace."

The shark god nodded and trotted off. The traffic going the other way was quick to step out of the way of his leimako.

Leandra led Dhrun south onto the fifth terrace road. This was part of the Lower Banyan District, populated mostly by Cloud People and their fine pavilions. Leandra walked along the paved street until she found a narrow alley between two compounds. They hurried down the alley to the terrace's edge. The path ended but some of stones in the terrace wall below protruded to make a staircase. There were no handrails and the stone steps were far apart.

Leandra carefully descended to the fourth terrace, then hurried across its street and down another protruding-stones-staircase to the third terrace. Here they entered the Naukaa, the lowest of all of Chandralu's neighborhoods, metaphorically and literally. There were no compounds here, only wobbly shacks. The walls were dirty, the roofs palm frond thatch, the streets muddy.

While leading Dhrun down to the second terrace, Leandra noticed the usual swarms of thin children playing between the shacks. Gaunt mothers watched from low doorways. On the second terrace road, they found Holokai waiting for them. "What's the news?" Leandra asked.

"A bunch of refugee boats came in from Feather Island. The village there was attacked this morning, attacked bad."

Leandra grunted. "Like we need anything else to go wrong. Who attacked the village?" She started southward along the road.

"Sounds like a lava neodemon," Holokai said, falling in step behind her. "But there are other rumors."

"Let me guess," she interrupted. "The rumors mostly accuse the Cult of the Undivided Society of attacking the village, or of worshiping the demons of the Ancient Continent, or of somehow inciting the War of Disjunction?"

"Well, yeah, those rumors and the one about the Floating Island wandering into the bay."

"Lovely," Leandra grumbled. "More dirt in muddy waters."

Dhrun said, "An attack on Feather Island, same time there are attacks on city deities. Connected?"

"Likely so. We just have to figure out how." Leandra touched her forehead. Through her godspell, she felt that most of her hour-from-now selves were filled with a particular type of frustration that only her father could inspire. Her mood darkened further. Apparently, Nicodemus would soon return to Chandralu.

The party continued along the street. Now in addition to the wobbly shacks and gaunt children, there were a few winehouses with women lolling about on second-story patios and sneering men standing around the doorways.

Leandra looked about the district and muttered, "Skinny mothers, skinny fathers, skinny whores and pimps and children. This stupid world. Dhrun, what's the only difference between that building"—she nodded to a whorehouse—"and a bank?"

"When you pay the bank to screw you, you don't enjoy it."

She frowned back at Dhrun. "I told you that one already?"

Dhrun only bowed his head, but Holokai laughed and said, "Sunny mood you're in today, Lea."

"Any sunnier and we should shade our eyes," Dhrun added with a conspiratorial smile.

"Don't you two start grinning at each other."

"I thought you wanted us to get along," Holokai complained.

"I want you to not tear each other's throats out, not get along."

The two divinities looked at each other. Holokai shrugged and Dhrun smiled.

Leandra exhaled in exasperation. Here the second terrace curved left toward the bay. Several terraces above them to their right towered the massive structure of the Sea Temple. The many spires crowning its temple-mountain were a cool gray against the vivid blue sky.

They crossed a small stone footbridge, a small civic stream running quickly below. A sudden whiff of feces made Leandra's nose crinkle.

From the temple at the city's top, water from the volcano's crater bubbled clean and clear. A system of channels divided the flow and ran it down and through the city, providing running water to all. As a result wealthy Chandralu was cleaner than any other city in the world. But in the city's lowest and poorest terraces, the civic streams often ran dark with sewage.

In Lorn there was a colorful, if also disgusting, saying that "Shit rolls downhill," which Leandra took to mean that generally all bad things were sent down from the powerful to the weak. However, in beautiful Chandralu, shit ran downhill literally.

So did cholera.

The most powerful deity in the Naukaa was Eka, whose sole requisite was the curing of cholera. A recent outbreak of the horrible disease—which caused diarrhea severe enough to kill by dehydration—had inspired so many fervent prayers that Eka's incarnation had gained an intense luminosity. At night, her aura could be seen winking fireflylike as she walked among Naukaa's shacks.

As Leandra led the two divinities over the footbridge, she frowned at the stream and wondered if the disease was coursing through the water. Then she glanced up at the dark volcano and thought about the Floating City, the massive amount of political, textual, and divine power concentrated there. So much power at the heights, so little down here.

At the end of the terrace stood a winehouse larger and sturdier than its neighbors. The second-story patios were empty save for two monkeys perched on the railing, one grooming the other.

"You two," she said to Dhrun and Holokai, "if someone tries to free me from the burden of existence, do the favor to them first. Otherwise don't do or say anything unless I tell you to."

Inside she found a dark room filled with benches and low tables. It hadn't changed much. Three men sat near the window, studying some paper spread between them. Leandra had heard a family of Cloud People had recently bought the place. Likely these were the new owners.

They wore the loose longvests and pants of the Cloud Culture and kept their hair plaited. Two were young men, thick black hair, wiry of build. The third had more silver than black in his hair but a broad chest and thick arms. A curved knife was tucked into his belt. "We don't start serving until—" he started to say before looking up.

"Thaddeus" was all Leandra said in response.

"Maybe he doesn't want to see you," the old man said. As the younger men turned, light glinted from knives at their belts as well.

"If I don't see him, a paddle serrated with sharks teeth will be wielded in anger, and a four-armed god of wrestling will practice his time-honored craft of removing limbs from their sockets." Leandra paused. "He wants to see me."

The two younger men flicked their eyes at silver hair, who studied her a moment before agreeing, "I think he wants to see you too." He nodded to a doorway covered with a ratty curtain. "Up the stairs, second door on your right. I doubt he's awake or that you can wake him."

"Typical," Leandra snorted while climbing the steps. "Same winehouse, same room. Typical." When she reached Thad's door, Leandra didn't bother to knock but nodded to Dhrun. With a four-handed shove, Dhrun broke the door into splinters and twisted metal.

Leandra was about to step through when she groaned and raised a hand to her forehead.

"What is it?" Holokai asked with apprehension.

"I just had the distinct impression that in an hour, I'll likely go from being frustrated with my father to feeling very grateful for him."

"What does that mean?" Dhrun asked.

"I haven't a clue. Never mind. Let's go." She stepped inside and found Thaddeus's small room almost unchanged. The walls were lined with bookshelves and scroll racks. In the far corner, beneath the window and a tattered mosquito net, lay a middle-aged man sprawled on a sleeping pallet.

Thaddeus's handsome features were relaxed and almost angelic in sleep. His skin was light brown, his wild hair salt-and-pepper, matching the four-day stubble on his face. He wore a wrinkled tan longvest.

A squat table beside the sleeping pallet held an ornate tray of opium paraphernalia. Leandra frowned at the slender pipe and the squat lamp. Strong memories then—tropical nights under a mosquito net, she and Thaddeus entwined, humid darkness, vivid dreams.

"You want me to wake him?" Holokai asked.

Leandra shook her head. "You won't be able to. He's a wizard. Well, used to be one. Before sleeping he likes to cast Numinous spells onto his brain to give himself quaternary cognition and intensify his opium dreams. He'll have cast some rather viscous protective texts about himself."

She walked to his bedside. "Given how fast he's breathing, I'd guess opium's mostly worn off." Beside the opium tray she found a folded piece of paper. In his familiar looping scrawl, Thaddeus had written "In Emergency, tear above my head."

Leandra moved the mosquito net and then picked up the sheet and unceremoniously tore it in half over Thaddeus's forehead. She hoped whatever spell was written on the paper was unlocking his brain from its far wandering dreams. After a few moments, his lids began to flutter.

So she poked him in the ribs, hard. "Good morning, Sunshine."

Clumsily, Thaddeus tried to push her away. She poked him again. "Time to rise and commune with the mysteries of the universe."

Thaddeus groaned. His eyelids opened slowly, revealing pinpoint pupils. He seemed to focus. Then he snapped awake and jerked away from Leandra as if she were a cobra. "Gah! Ah, ah," he spluttered. "Gah! Lea?"

"Probably not. Probably you're hallucinating." Using her foot, she tilted his bedside table until his opium paraphernalia crashed to the floor. Pretending at primness, she sat on the low table and then with false cheeriness asked, "So, how are things?"

Thaddeus was still breathing hard. He looked from her to Dhrun to his four arms back to her again. "When you said you wanted a man who would always lend you a hand, I thought you just meant two of them." He paused for a laugh that was not forthcoming. "No wonder it didn't work out between us."

"That wasn't the only way you were physically disappointing."

"If he physically surpasses me in some other way," Thaddeus added, "I don't want to see it."

"Not to worry. Unlike you, his most remarkable physical feats don't involve scratching himself in public."

Thaddeus hauled himself into a sitting position. "I'm not hallucinating then; only you could be so caustic."

Leandra bowed if he had just complimented her.

"Well," Thaddeus said, "maybe your mother could have done better."

Leandra frowned. "You always know how to say the exact wrong thing."

"Call it a gift."

"I called it everything else already, guess we'll go with gift."

"So why do I have the, ahem, pleasure of your sudden and ominous company? Not to mention the sudden and ominous company of your—" He looked from Dhrun to Holokai. "Would you say goons?"

"I would say goons."

He cracked a lopsided smile. Still handsome, she had to give him that. Bastard. "Very well, why have I been graced with the company of the Warden of Ixos and her goons?"

"Before I answer, tell me what you know of the fight on Cowry Street last night or of the recent attacks on city deities."

"There was violence?"

"A brawl on Cowry Street. Since then small groups of men, some of them spellwrights, have been attacking minor deities throughout the city. What are people saying about this?"

"Lea . . . last night I was . . ."

"Oblivious to the world because you were smoking opium with halfhearted intentions of unlocking the secrets of your mind that then predictably devolved into satisfying the pathetic wants of your addiction?"

"You make it sound so negative."

"Last night I got my hands on a godspell from the empire."

"You don't say."

"At the cost of a disease flare, I had a particularly strong bit of prophecy."

"Were you able to perceive time as a landscape?" During their years of experimentation, Thaddeus had tried to write for her a Numinous spell that would give her the same glimpses into prophecy that her mother had. Most of his experiments had done nothing, a few had made her spectacularly intoxicated, and one caused her to vomit—violently but not without satisfaction—into Thaddeus's lap.

"No," Leandra said patiently. "Nothing like that. The godspell allows me to feel forward into time. I have enough experience with it now to know that it's accurate. Normally, it allows me to feel only an hour forward. But during a disease flare, it allowed me to feel a day forward. I felt beyond any doubt that sometime in the dark hours of this coming morning I will have to choose between murdering someone I love and dying."

Thaddeus was leaning forward, all slackness of sleep and intoxication gone from his expression. "Fascinating."

"So now I have to ask you, Thad, why might I need to murder you?"

He only blinked. "But you don't lov—"

"Don't," she interrupted firmly, "make stupid observations or I will have Holokai jam a few shark's teeth into your ass."

He looked confused. "But after that, ahem, trouble with that other woman—"

"Three other women."

"Three other women, you couldn't lov—"

"Holokai." She gestured. "His ass and the shark's teeth, if you would be so kind."

"No, no, wait!" Thaddeus blurted. "I'm sorry. I'm sorry. Yes, well . . . I am sorry about that. Truly contrite."

"I don't doubt it," she said in a voice that communicated just how much she doubted it. "However, you haven't answered the question. Why might I need to kill you in just a few hours?"

"Other than the three other women?"

"Wanting to kill you, Thad, and needing to kill you are different things. Why might I need to kill you?"

He blinked. "I can't think of anything."

"Neither can I." Leandra sighed. "Which is too bad, because if I have to kill anyone on my list of possible victims, I would choose you."

"What happens if you just run away from the city?"

"The prophecy assures me that everyone I know and love will die. So I can't just run or hide or smoke enough opium to fog my brain into oblivion."

"I see," he was absently biting his thumbnail, as he often did when thinking.

"It is too bad I can't stop myself from loving."

"I'll say it is. That would solve everything."

"It is too bad that you can't cast a spell on my mind that would stop me from loving."

"You mean like that time I tried to write a spell that could stop someone from feeling hatred? The one we talked about—" He looked at her. "Oh."

"So we come to the second reason for my little visit," she said. "Do you still have the drafts?"

He looked past her to the bookshelves. "Somewhere. But I never got past casting it on monkeys and then dunking them in water."

"It wasn't your most compassionate moment, but if I remember, none of the monkeys died."

"No and they didn't bite me afterward either. But, you can't mean you want me to . . ."

"I want you to."

A sudden wide smile broke across his handsome face. "No one's ever done anything like that before."

She raised an eyebrow. "Ever?"

"Two famous linguists have written about the theory behind such a text. The first was Magister Agwu Shannon, your father's former teacher. And the second was Magister Lotannu Akomma, your aunt's confidant and the current Dean of Astrophell. I met him when I was training at Astrophell, you know."

Leandra frowned as an idea tickled her brain. Something about the name bothered her. "What does Akomma look like?"

"Tall, very dark skin, long dreadlocks going to gray. Doesn't talk much. Well, doesn't talk much for an academic. Why?"

Leandra shook her head. "Never mind. You were saying?"

"Maybe Lotannu Akomma could write a spell that could stop someone from loving, or someone like him, but I couldn't. I'm . . ." He gestured to the opium paraphernalia now scattered on the floor. "I'm me."

"It is quite the handicap," she said. "But I want your best effort and I want it tonight."

"But—"

"You owe me," she said in a voice suddenly low and vicious.

Thaddeus held still for a moment but then nodded. "All right, tonight I'll try to stop you from being able to love."

"You tried to do that to me years ago without magic and failed." Leandra stood. "So this time, you'd better succeed."

elowdecks, Nicodemus stepped into the cabin and found the pyromancer asleep in her hammock. Sir Claude had bound her ankles and wrists with metal. Doria had bandaged her amputated right palm.

Nicodemus sat on a stool and pulled a brown vial from his belt purse. In his other hand, he held a small cloth bundle he hoped he would not have to unwrap.

The years had given him occasion to interrogate prisoners. At times he had been harsh, even cruel, but never yet a torturer—not because he was a good man, but because he was a lucky one. There had always been alternative methods of motivating prisoners. Maybe one day his luck would wear out. Maybe that day was today.

Nicodemus looked up from the brown vial and saw that the pyromancer had opened her eyes and was studying him. Though her expression was neutral, the tension around her mouth betrayed her pain. She hid it well.

"You know who I am?" he asked.

She nodded.

"Magistra Doria Kokalas has explained about your hand? We cut out the canker curse in time to save your life. You understand about my touch and the canker curse?"

Again, a nod.

"I told Magistra to withhold pain medication until after we talked. I need clearheaded answers. So I propose a trade." He held up the brown vial. "The alcoholic tincture of opium."

The pyromancer's eyes fixed on the vial.

"My wife tells me that physicians who fail to give the proper pain medication after surgery are guilty of torture."

"How convenient for you," the pyromancer said between stiff lips.

"It's good that you have a quick wit. This will go faster. So then, perhaps you can start by telling me your name."

She only glared at him.

Nicodemus looked at the brown vile. "It is a bit of a strange thought, to torture by withholding. Say the word 'torture' and the mind jumps to the clichés—thumbscrews, hot irons, that sort of thing. But if you think about it, this leaves fewer scars, less mess on the floor. It's perfectly justifiable until you've given clear answers."

"Whatever your justification, you know it's monstrous," the pyromancer blurted. "You know you, your wife, and the league are all monsters. Your intermingling of humanity and divinity is an abomination to the Creator."

"So we get down to business. We in the league worship the Creator as well, you know."

"You place your petty gods before the Creator."

"That's the new teaching in the empire? Your rivals are inhuman, so it's permissible or maybe even necessary to destroy them? Hardly original thinking. But then what—other than something monstrous—is original?"

"You'll not get another word from me."

"Not even your name?"

She looked away.

The barge rocked and set her hammock swaying. "Torture by withholding," Nicodemus said slowly. "Maybe it shouldn't be all that surprising; after all, what is more painful than kindness or love withheld? What's more harmful than a lie by omission?"

She said nothing.

"Very well, perhaps not your name. But perhaps you can tell me why imperial spellwrights are brutalizing small villages on the Bay of Standing Islands? Why kill all those innocent villagers?"

Her face twisted with hatred. "We d-din't—" she stuttered in rage but then pursed her lips.

"Go on."

She closed her eyes.

"Let me guess: You were ordered not to talk if you were captured."

"Ordered not to be captured," she growled. "It was only because that bitch cast that hydromancer spell on me and I was confused. If I had been clearheaded, I wouldn't have attacked you. I would have cut my own throat."

"That's your preferred method? Is that why you drove the villagers into a madness in which they did the same?"

"We didn't cause that madness."

"You really shouldn't tease me like this. We've only an hour more until we reach Chandralu." He paused to consider the vial. "You will be taken, under guard of course, to the infirmary. Magistra Kokalas explained to me that amputations are more complicated than one might think. Taking off a limb is not so simple as sawing off a heel of bread. They will have to revise our crude field operation, take out some of the bones and meat in your palm so that there will be enough slack in the skin so they can sew the skin together. Does that make sense?"

She didn't move or speak.

"I would like to tell them that you have been cooperative and to be generous with the pain medication. I would hate to say that you have yet to explain the imperial presence in Ixos and that therefore they would have to use . . . what was it Doria said . . . the minimum necessary anesthetic, I believe."

The pyromancer was pressing her lips together so tightly they blanched.

Nicodemus sighed. "Talking to you like this . . . It makes me think back to when I was a disabled boy—always afraid of others, of punishment, of powerlessness. Sometimes I wonder how I became so ruthless. Sometimes I wonder if I could have been anything but ruthless. Sometimes I wish I could go back to being that disabled boy again. He would have pitied you. But being who I am now and knowing the part you played in brutalizing the village of Feather Island, I don't feel much pity."

"You should have been permanently censored as a child, like all the cacographic children," she snarled. "That would have stopped you from worshiping misspelling and error and the unholy union of human and divine language. You turned your back on the Creator."

"Your sincerity is impressive," Nicodemus said. "Having spent the last thirty years proselytizing neodemons into gods and goddesses, I can appreciate what you are attempting."

"You know in your heart that you and the league are idolaters. You should be teaching the people to worship the Creator and to be thinking for themselves, rather than cowering before your idols."

Nicodemus nodded. "I had heard that there was a new age dawning in the empire. My half-sister's metaspells making language more logical have enabled new wonders. I read a report about the cannons of Trillinon. If it's true, it is most impressive. But now you are telling me that along with your great learning and achievements you are developing the madness of war? That your young authors hope to destroy our kingdoms; when in fact, both league and empire should come together so that we might survive the Disjunction?"

She laughed. "There are some that say you're a fool, that you're the biggest fool in the league. I never thought it possible, but listening to you . . .

Well, maybe I am doing you a favor. You're a fool if you don't already know that your petty gods and the idolaters who worship them are working to bring the Disjunction sooner. The empress has evidence that they are doing so through the Cult of the Undivided Society."

"Who told you these things?"

"That's what you should already know. That's what any fool in your place would know."

"Why did imperial spellwrights attack Feather Island?" Nicodemus raised his voice for the first time. "Why did you kill innocent villagers?"

"We didn't start any violence."

"Do you know how we found you? There was a ghost ship floating out in the bay. All the men aboard were horribly burned. And so were the children. The children that you murdered. How could you?"

"We didn't harm any childr—" The pyromancer cut herself off midsentence. "We didn't."

"Then tell me who did."

She shook her head.

Nicodemus put the vial back into his belt purse and held his cloth bundle in both hands. "You are an intelligent woman. You know what I am capable of. You know that I believe you were responsible for what happened to those children. So know then that I will carry through with what I am about to threaten."

She said nothing.

He held up the cloth bundle between them. "You're brave enough that maybe you could bear the pain of your hand without opium. But take a long look at this." He unwound the cloth bundle to reveal a chunk of nightmare. In places the skin was still intact, but mostly it was a motley of ulcerations, pus, boney growths. It formed four ropes of flesh at the end of which—nearly pushed off by the force of the tumors—were four human fingernails. "These," Nicodemus said, "are your fingers."

The pyromancer's eyes were locked on the nightmare of flesh ravaged by the canker curses. She began breathing fast.

"This will be simple as anything," Nicodemus said calmly. "I touch the stump of your right hand. Just a tap. I'll tell Doria that it looks like the canker is back. She'll cut off your whole hand this time. But you and I will have another one of these chats. I'll tap whatever stump they give you. Then that will need to come off. You get the picture. Or maybe I won't tell the physicians at all. Maybe I'll just let the disease rot you inside out. It's a fate I wouldn't wish on anyone but a murderer of innocents."

The pyromancer shook her head.

"Why did you slaughter everyone on Feather Island?"

"We didn't!" She still shook her head, a film of tears made her eyes bright.

"Who did then? Tell me!"

"We didn't! We didn't!"

Nicodemus stood. "Why did you murder those children?" He threw her nightmare fingers onto the pyromancer's stomach.

"GET IT OFF! GET IT OFF OF ME!" she shrieked as her nightmare fingers rolled down to her lap.

"Why did you kill those children?"

"We didn't do it! We didn't! Oh Creator, get it off of me!"

"Who did?"

"CREATOR HELP ME! GET IT OFF OF ME!" she screamed. "Get it off! Get it off!"

Nicodemus plucked up the nightmare fingers without touching her. "Who killed the children?"

"It was one of your neodemons," she said between sobs. "I swear on the Creator's name! We were attacked in the morning."

"What neodemon?"

"I don't know. My regiment was hidden in Feather Village. We had bribed the locals to hide us, and early this morning we received orders to leave. I don't know where to. I don't know what we were meant to do. But when we were getting ready, a neodemon attacked us. I never got to see it. There was fire everywhere and smoke. It smelled like sulfur from the burning hells. When the smoke got into the villagers, they attacked us. They had sold us out to some neodemon that they were worshiping. Our captain ordered a counterattack. We tried to get what we could from the village before escaping."

She paused to catch her breath. "More and more of the villagers started to attack us, but some killed themselves. There was lava and smoke everywhere. A few of us hid in the Near Tower. We could feel the ground shake as the neodemon walked about on the village's Shelf. It was hell." She began sobbing.

Nicodemus sat down, his mind working hotly. If she were telling the truth then the ruins would make more sense: half of the buildings looted, half of them untouched.

"It was either one of your neodemons, or your cults have finally helped the ancient demons cross the ocean," the pyromancer said. "The worst was the children. They just began to scream and scream until suddenly they just died. Just dead." Another sob.

Nicodemus had never encountered a neodemon powerful enough to do what was described. He had a sinking feeling in his gut.

The pyromancer continued. "Those of us in the Near Tower gathered all the cloth we could so that the hierophants could write lofting kites to get us off the island. The neodemon seemed to leave the island. All we had to do was fend off the occasional surviving villager who would attack us. But then you came and killed everyone."

"Everyone but that one hierophant who escaped," Nicodemus said calmly. "Where was he going?"

She shook her head, mucus glistening on her upper lip. "To the rest of the imperial expedition. I don't know where it is. Only the wind mages know."

"How many are in the expedition?"

"They didn't tell us anything else. We're just scouts."

"And who is leading the expedition?"

"Magister Lotannu Akomma."

"Of course," Nicodemus grumbled. "Of course Vivian would send him." He cleared his throat. "Why send scouts to the bay?"

"The empress found some evidence that the Cult of the Undivided Society is trying to bring on the Disjunction. That's all I know. Creator help me. Creator forgive me but that's all I know. It was one of your demons who attacked. This is all your fault! You have to stop worshiping the demons and trust in the Creator and the empress. You have to." She began sobbing again.

"Was your expedition scouting in preparation for an invasion?"

"I don't know."

Nicodemus took in a long breath. An imperial expedition was somewhere close enough for a hierophant to reach via lofting kite. Whether the empire intended an invasion or some smaller action, this would mean bloodshed. No two ways around it.

"What else should I know?" Nicodemus asked in a softer voice.

"I've told you everything. Creator forgive me but I did." More tears.

Nicodemus took the vial from his belt purse. "You did the right thing, Magistra." She shook her head and began sobbing harder. Nicodemus waited patiently. "You have been through hell. I am sorry for that."

Her breathing finally slowed.

Nicodemus stepped closer. "You need this for the shock as much as for the pain in your hand." He held up the tincture of opium. "Here, Magistra."

"I don't care if it's poison," she said in the pitiful voice of one who has been sobbing and now has a stuffed nose. "I hope it is poison so that I don't have to live with these memories anymore."

"It is not poison, Magistra. It will make you sleep. I am sorry I had to be so rough with you; I needed to know the truth. No one will hurt you now."

He offered the vial again, and this time the pyromancer leaned her head forward and greedily drank down its contents. Nicodemus did not blame her.

She made a scrunched up face. "It's bitter."

For a moment Nicodemus felt a pang of nostalgia; her expression reminded him of Leandra's when she had been a girl and he had forced her to take medicine. He fetched a water skin from the wall and squirted some of it into her mouth. She swallowed and continued to cry.

Nicodemus sat on the stool again. Gradually, his prisoner began to breathe slower and slower until he was sure she was asleep. He picked up the horror that was her remaining fingers and wrapped them in cloth. Just outside the cabin, he found Doria staring at him with hard eyes.

"You heard?" he asked.

"Did you have to be so cruel?"

"You heard what attacked Feather Island?"

Doria's expression softened slightly. "The results don't always justify the methods."

"What if Feather Island was attacked, not by a neodemon, but by a demon from the Ancient Continent? What if the River Thief wasn't lying?"

Doria only frowned.

"Not to mention the imperial forces somewhere in the bay? Still think I was too cruel?"

"You weren't actually going to give her the canker curse, were you?"

"I hope not, my old friend. I hope not." He shook his head. "But I just don't know." He started down the hall. "See that the prisoner is not in any pain, but do not forget to keep her bound and censored."

"Yes, my Lord Warden," Doria said coldly to his back.

Nicodemus pressed a hand to his face and blew out a long breath. War. It was going to be war. Either with the empire or with the demons of the Ancient Continent. He didn't know which was worse.

His train of thought stopped when he heard a sudden exhalation. Then a wooden thump. He looked up and saw that he was passing by Rory's cabin. There came a muffled groan as if in pain. Farther down the hall stood two sailors, both looking at the cabin with a mixture of curiosity and fear.

"What is it?" Nicodemus asked.

"We saw the Lornishman heading this way," one of them whispered.

"Fiery heaven," Nicodemus swore. This was the last thing he needed. Couldn't Rory and Sir Claude put their damned stupid feud aside for one bloody moment? Nicodemus kicked the door open ready to break up the fight and deliver a blistering tirade. "CREATOR DAMN IT ALL," he began to bellow.

He was therefore shocked to discover that the two men with arms locked around each other were not trying to kill each other. They were kissing.

Passionately.

The tirade froze in Nicodemus's throat. Rory's eyes turned to Nicodemus and bulged. He leapt away from Sir Claude, tripped over his hammock, and avoided falling only when the knight caught him by the waist.

Sir Claude looked at Nicodemus with a calm expression of challenge. But Rory's face became a mask of shame. In fact, the druid was looking past Nicodemus and into the hallway to see if anyone else was there.

Suddenly the events of the past months reshuffled themselves in Nicodemus's mind: the rivalry between Rory and Sir Claude, the words seemingly spoken in anger, Sir Claude's insistent renewal of the conflict, the few times both men had been missing together, and now Rory's obvious desire to keep what had just happened secret. The reshuffle completed. Nicodemus understood. Both of them wanted it, but only one of them wanted it hidden.

Nicodemus cursed himself as a fool for not seeing it earlier and then became acutely aware of the sailors in the hallway. Reflexively, he stepped into the cabin and slammed the door to keep anyone from seeing.

He looked at Rory. Rory looked back at him with fear. They both looked at Sir Claude, who only shrugged. Then Rory looked at the door behind Nicodemus, obviously thinking of the sailors who would be listening on the other side.

Nicodemus doubted the sailors would care if they found out about the two men; Ixonians were accepting in that regard. But Rory was Dralish, and in the South such relations were illicit. Rory, like most in his culture, would want to keep such affections private. So Nicodemus didn't want to reveal . . . But now he had to . . . How could he . . .

Suddenly it came to him. Nicodemus raised his voice. "CREATOR DAMN IT ALL," he bellowed. "HOW IN THE NAME OF ALL THINGS DIVINE CAN YOU TWO KEEP UP A GOD-OF-GOD'S DAMNED CHILDISH FEUD AT A TIME LIKE THIS?"

But of course this was the best time to be together. When better than after the trauma of battle to seek comfort in a lover's arms?

Nicodemus continued to yell. "I HAVE HAD IT UP TO MY EYEBALLS WITH YOUR FIGHTING!" Nicodemus paused, unsure what to say next.

Rory nodded vigorously. "Keep going," he mouthed. "Keep going."

Sir Claude rolled his eyes.

"THIS IS THE LAST GOD-OF-GOD'S DAMN TIME I AM GOING TO CATCH YOU TWO KIS—" Nicodemus stopped himself. "KICKING EACH OTHER WHEN YOU'RE DOWN." He improvised.

Rory kept nodding vigorously. Sir Claude shook his head.

"SO . . ." Nicodemus yelled, "I AM ORDERING YOU TWO TO STOP FIGHTING. AND . . . uhh . . . BY MY COMMAND THE TWO OF YOU ARE CONFINED TO THIS CABIN. YOU'RE GOING TO WORK THIS OUT LIKE CIVILIZED MEN. AND WHEN YOU COME ON DECK IN CHANDRALU, WE WILL HAVE PEACE. IF YOU DON'T I WILL PERSONALLY . . . um . . . WRING YOUR GOD-OF-GOD'S DAMNED NECKS UNTIL YOU COUGH UP BLOOD."

Sir Claude made a wry face and mouthed, "Cough up blood?"

Nicodemus shrugged. "AM I UNDERSTOOD?" he yelled.

"Yes, Nicodemus!" Rory answered quickly.

Sir Claude was rolling his eyes again, but Rory jabbed an elbow into his ribs.

"Ouff!" Sir Claude said before, "Yes, my lord."

Nicodemus looked at the two men. "What now?" he mouthed.

"Go out," Rory whispered. "Slam the door. Throw your hands in the air. Act annoyed."

Sir Claude looked at Rory with an expression of disbelief that mellowed into a begrudging smile.

So Nicodemus stormed out of the cabin, slammed the door, and threw his hands in the air. "Damn Lornish and Dralish men and their damn stupid rivalry!" he announced for the now more sizable audience of eavesdropping sailors. Really, he was going to have to convince Rory that no one aboard would care if they knew. But for now Nicodemus put on his most annoyed expression and marched up onto the deck.

Once out in the open, looking out on blue tropical waters, Nicodemus smiled. How had he not seen it? He couldn't wait to tell Doria. But then his smile wilted. Could he tell Doria if Rory didn't want anyone to know? Could he even tell Francesca?

Nicodemus looked astern and saw John leaning on the railing and looking down into the water. He had a sudden urge to join his old friend and reminisce about years ago, when they had both been so young, boys at play in Starhaven.

He couldn't do that. He had to focus on the present situation. So he took a long breath. What kind of a man had he become? One moment he was contemplating torturing a woman; the next he was worrying about helping his comrades hide an affair.

With a start Nicodemus realized that he was still holding the cloth-wrapped remains of his prisoner's fingers. He flinched as he thought of what he had threatened to do. After a moment longer, he dropped the fingers into the bay.

As the nightmarish remains sank below the waves, Nicodemus wondered if he had a bit of a demon inside of him. Maybe all men did. But at least, amid chaos and blood, there was the potential for something better. Rory and Claude had found that potential, or so he hoped.

He looked off toward the bright city of Chandralu, the extinct volcano beyond. About twenty days ago, he had been atop that volcano, in the Pavilion of the Sky to cast his metaspell. He had thought then that his visit to the islands would be unremarkable, the usual politics, the usual intrigues that somehow kept the peace between league and empire.

But now . . . now it seemed the rules were changing. War would come to this bright city. Perhaps he would need to cast his metaspell again far sooner than he expected.

The keloid scar on Nicodemus's back began to itch, likely because he was thinking of the Emerald. Idly, he scratched the scar and wondered once again at the prophecies. Both empire and league claimed that their champion was the Halcyon and that of the other was the Storm Petrel. He had anguished for so long about what he might truly be. But now he began to wonder if perhaps neither he nor his half-sister were inherently savior or destroyer. If war were coming, then surely the survivor would claim to be the Halcyon and bend history to suit.

Just then a white seabird flew overhead. Nicodemus sighed. Turned his thoughts back to his family and his friends—Rory and Sir Claude.

Yes, bloody times were coming, chaos was coming, a test of character and prophecy. But within all that was coming would be the most important struggle: the fight to protect the best of human potentials.

CHAPTER TWENTY

In the infirmary's morgue, Francesca tried to keep her composure as she stared at the horror of the dead woman's uterus.

For reasons unknown, medical custom dictated that among physicians confronting a medical mystery, the most senior among them must interrogate her juniors about said mystery so as to maximize their education. Sadly, most senior physicians only maximized their juniors' embarrassment.

Although Francesca had learned much—especially regarding romance and parenthood—from educational embarrassment, she thought the ritual interrogation of junior physicians was a God-of-gods damned stupid custom. However, the sudden stillness in the morgue announced the crowd's expectation that she execute said God-of-gods damned stupid custom upon some poor soul regarding the dead woman.

"Magistra D'Valin," Francesca asked Ellen, because interrogating a physician not in her service would be impolite, "what is a teratoma?"

"A teratoma is a rare tumor of the ovaries," Ellen replied in a voice steadier than Francesca had expected. "They are encapsulated and sometimes contain hair, skin, teeth, nerves, or bone. There are few reports of teratomata containing complete eyeballs or miniature limbs."

"Correct," Francesca said. "Magistra Ubo raised the possibility that this disease is divine in origin. Before we accept that, we must rule out mundane disease. So, are these findings consistent with a teratoma?"

"No, Magistra."

"Please describe the relevant findings."

"This was a young female, appearing approximately twenty years of age, well developed, well nourished, very pale. A Y-shaped incision has been cut, starting at both shoulders and meeting below the sternum before traveling down to the pelvis. The abdominal wall has been reflected to reveal a gravid uterus, larger than expected for a full-term pregnancy. The uterus has been dissected along its lateral aspects and reflected superiorly to reveal that the muscular wall of the uterus contains successive rows of large, well-formed, and serrated teeth."

Francesca cleared her throat again. "I am impressed by the levelness of your tone, Magistra. I admitted to Magistra Ubo that the findings disturb me. You are unimpressed?"

"On the contrary, Magistra, if the soul were capable of regurgitation, I would be projectile vomiting spiritual mess."

"It is strangely reassuring to hear that even you are affected, Ellen. Is there anything about the findings you find particularly striking?"

"The serrated teeth embedded in the uterus are far too large to be human."

"An interesting observation, Magistra. Is that why you believe these findings are not consistent with a teratoma?"

"One among several reasons. Teratomas are tumors of the ovaries, whereas these findings are within the uterus. Moreover, teratomas are classically described as encapsulated, which these teeth are not, horrifyingly so. And while there have been many reports of teratomas containing human teeth, I am not aware of any report of a teratoma growing non-human teeth or non-human tissue of any kind."

"Magistra, I find no flaws in your logic." Francesca turned to Dean Sarvna. Idiotically and paradoxically, medical custom dictated that an interrogation end by inviting other senior physicians to continue it. "Magister, is there anything you should like to add?"

"No, I am most impressed by your student. Clearly, she had an excellent teacher. I would agree that this is a most troubling case of divinopathophysiology."

Grateful that Sarvna had not prolonged the interrogation, Francesca gestured to Magistra Ubo, who mercifully covered the nightmare of muscle and teeth with a sheet. Francesca looked at the young physician. "You said that the mother did not know what happened to her child?"

Magistra Ubo nodded.

"What has been done to locate the child?"

The young physician glanced at Dean Sarvna. "Nothing, Magistra."

"Does the infirmary still provide the city's orphanages with a physician?"

"We do, Magistra," an older physician in blue robes said from behind the dean. "I oversee that service."

She nodded to the man. "Do you know if any of the city's orphanages have, in the past two days, received a male infant? Perhaps one who seemed semi-divine or sustained unusual lacerations during delivery?"

The man shook his head. "The orphanages have not taken in any new infants."

"None?"

"Our only new ward is a boy judged to be of about four years. He was abandoned at the royal orphanage of New Village yesterday morning."

Francesca turned to Magistra Ubo. "You said the woman likely came from the Pillow House, which is in New Village?"

The young physician nodded.

"The child seems too old. It is not much of a connection, but it is all we have." Francesca paused before nodding first to Ubo then Sarvna. "Magistra, Magister, thank you both for this potentially vital discovery. I must investigate immediately; however, you can be assured that I am grateful and will do everything I can to champion your cause to the Council of Starfall."

Sarvna, his pudgy face brightening, prattled away about his plans for the infirmary. He repeated his offer to provide her with a tour of the grounds, but Francesca was already retreating toward the exit. After more rounds of bowing and formalities, Francesca and her followers escaped onto Plumeria Way.

After the morgue's dim and quiet horror, the city street presented to her synesthetic mind a blaze of color and sound: the sunbright whitewashed houses, two girls arguing in shrill sallow voices, the distant shimmering sapphire bay, the rich brown rhythmic thudding of an elephant plodding past. Life in its every hue. Francesca paused to take in a long breath and then asked her followers, "So, what have we learned?"

Tam opened his mouth but Kenna shook her head slightly. He started to frown but she raised her hand. They looked at each other and then a Francesca. With synchronized movements, they shrugged.

Ellen spoke. "Regarding what is happening politically in Chandralu, we're still clueless. But perhaps we could conclude that there's an entanglement between your mysterious sea deity and the prostitutes of Chandralu? Perhaps." She paused, frowned. "But personally the only thing I learned was that I'm never ever getting into bed with a divinity."

"Ever the astute student, Ellen."

Ellen studied her. "Thinking about your daughter?"

"Always," Francesca said as she watched a thin old man push a cart of taro root down the street.

"Magistra, perhaps you are being too hard on yourself."

"There's no loathing like self-loathing."

"Does Leandra know you torture yourself like this?"

Francesca sucked in a long breath. "I hope not; she's got enough problems of her own. Come on." She led them back through Sacred Regent Plaza and then down the Lily Steps. The cloud which had been raining on the city had floated off over the bay and presently was dropping a curtain of rain onto the water.

The Lily Steps were narrower than the Jacaranda Steps and less crowded. To their right stretched the Lotus District, which was veined with civic streams and tranquil pools. To their left stood the Brightside District, where the most powerful families of the Sea People had built their expansive compounds. The three terraces of Brightside curved away to end on a tall sea cliff, atop which stood the temple-mountain of the Sea Temple. Far below that beautiful structure would be the rotting streets of the Naukaa.

Francesca took long slow breaths and tried to focus on the sky, the steps before her, anything to get the nightmare uterus out of her mind.

She found herself staring at the Sea Temple, dark and cool in the morning's gathering heat. She had always admired temple-mountains, which were uniquely Ixonian architectural achievements. They consisted of a wide central, octagonal tower that rose nearly one hundred and fifty feet before tapering into a series of spires. Each temple-mountain was a stylistic representation of Mount Ixram, the massive volcano on the island's north side. It had been the Ixonian pantheon's first home when the Trimuril fused the three cultures together to fight off the crumbling First Neosolar Empire.

At the bottom of the Lily Steps they turned right and continued on to Lily Way, which occasionally rose into gentle bridges as it crossed many civic streams. When Francesca's predecessor had trained in Chandralu, the street had been a spacious place where the wealthiest Lotus families built long compounds around tranquil lily ponds. But about a hundred years ago, the Lower Gate had been built that provided direct access to the New Village, which stood directly below the city walls. As a result, shops and merchant stalls proliferated along Lily Way. Buildings independent of any compound had sprung up to loom over the street. At points, the way grew so narrow that Francesca could have stretched out her arms and touched either side of the street.

The Lower Gate had once been a fortified sluice through which the district's water flowed down a few tumbling waterfalls to the bay. A narrow land gate had been built next to the sluice. Francesca watched as Ellen shouted bright green and blue words over the white roar of water to one of the guards, asking for directions to the royal orphanage. He shouted back, bright orange words, and pointed.

The party set off down the steps. New Village lay below them as a loose collection of buildings centered round a small wharf. Only three of the houses had more than one story. There were no whitewashed walls, no roofing other than palm thatch, and nothing but red mud in the streets; nevertheless, the village was cleaner and less crowded than anything in the Naukaa district.

"Ellen," Francesca asked as they turned onto a street, "have you heard of this Pillow House or the Mithuna divinity complex? I don't remember it being mentioned on my previous visits."

"I heard a lot about it when I was training at the infirmary. They are not the sort of things one mentions to visiting dignitaries in my assessment."

"Oh? So then, what is your assessment of Mithuna?"

"Do you want my overly optimistic or my overly simplistic assessment?"

"I want you to tell me what you actually think. What are the chances I can hear that?"

"Slim to none."

"Fine. Then let's start with your overly optimistic assessment of Mithuna."

"Very well," Ellen answered in her rapid, dispassionate physician tone, "Mithuna is an often misunderstood divinity complex with the requisite of illuminating the erotic aspects of human affection, which despite being demonized by some cultures are both natural and potentially enriching to the mind and soul; and whom—considering my personal frustrations in such matters for a depressing number of years—I should probably spend more time contemplating, but whom I probably won't contemplate secondary to my belief that all men are either too dumb, obnoxious, or self-centered to make any of it worthwhile."

"Whatever happened to that druidic scholar you used to visit in Thorntree?"

"Turned out to be too dumb, obnoxious, and self-centered to be worthwhile."

"All three? An overachiever."

"Certainly that's how he saw himself."

"But returning to Mithuna: What is your overly simplistic assessment?"

She shrugged. "Goddess of prostitution."

"Ah," Francesca said. "You know, I've always thought it strange how the three different kingdoms react to such divinities. In Lorn, they label them all neodemons and my husband is obliged to deconstruct them, which I think is a little obtuse as prostitution continues with or without them. In Dral, we tend to ignore them or leave them to local custom. And now you're telling me that Ixos has brought their erotic divinities within their pantheon. I suppose that would make the whole affair easier to govern."

They were nearing the village's edge. Only a few buildings stood ahead; beyond them the terrace became a taro paddy.

"Well," Ellen said, "I wouldn't say that the Ixonians have completely accepted Mithuna. She is forbidden within the city walls, so she built her Pillow House out here. There is still prostitution in the Naukaa, especially on the second terrace. There it's illegal and of a cheaper sort, run by local thugs and mixed up with opium running. So the men with money and reputations have to hike out to the New Village. It can make for quite a lot of male foot traffic out the Lower Gate."

Francesca snorted. "Men, sometimes they won't pray to a god of healing during a plague, but they are always willing to pray to the erotic deities. Do we know where this Pillow House is anyway?" She gestured to the rickety wooden structures lining the street. "If we can't find the child, I suppose that would be the next logical place to investigate."

"I don't, but we could always wait until dusk and follow the line of furtive rich men. Meantime, I believe that is the orphanage." She pointed to a wide complex of buildings.

Francesca frowned. It seemed too quiet. When she knocked on the doorway, a tired-looking woman with deep-set eyes appeared and reported that all of the children had been taken down to the beach.

So Francesca walked down narrow stone steps placed between two taro paddies and discovered a small white-sand beach. The sandy bottom shone beneath the gentle waves and extended maybe ten feet from the shore.

A small chaos of children stretched across the beach. The eldest splashed about in the water. The youngest tottered in the shade of a plumeria tree. Several minders moved among them. All were women, young, exhausted, even when smiling at their charges.

Francesca saw only one man—tall, thin, bushy black hair, wearing the flowing robes of a priest of the Trimuril. Noticing the spellwrights, he walked over and introduced himself as Brother Palakan.

Ellen introduced Francesca and explained their search for a newly adopted ward of the regency. The priest looked dubious, so Ellen produced from her belt purse a writ from the Starfall Council. If anything, the writ increased Brother Palakan's skepticism; however, he eventually gestured to a group of children sprinting up and down the beach.

"The one you're after is the tall boy with dark hair. The one who's hanging back from the others. So far, he never seems to be in the middle of things, but always a few steps away."

"And what is his name?" Francesca asked.

Brother Palakan laughed. "I was hoping you knew. He refuses to tell us his name or where he comes from. The children have taken to calling him Lolo since an older boy tried to push him around and he fought back. Lolo is slang among the Sea People for a crazy person. I'm hoping it doesn't stick."

"How did he became a ward of the regency?" Francesca asked. "There are many destitute children in Chandralu. The regency isn't in the habit of adopting them all."

Brother Palakan shook his head. "Sadly it is so. But Lolo is something of a mystery. Two days ago, I received a letter ordering me to expect a new ward and describing him. It was written on Floating City parchment and delivered by an acolyte. But it was unsigned. I thought more information would come with the boy. But that evening at dinner, Lolo simply showed up in the doorway. The next morning, I sent a messenger to the Floating City but no one knew who wrote the letter about Lolo. So when I saw your party, I thought you had come to tell me about him."

Francesca frowned. "Could the letter you received have been faked?"

The priest thought about it. "Unlikely. But perhaps you could tell me why you are looking for Lolo?"

Francesca shook her head. "I dare not, for your sake and for his. I should like to talk to him though."

Brother Palakan studied her for a long time before nodding. "Very well, Magistra. But do take care; Lolo is not the easiest child to approach, and I would guess that he has already been through a great deal."

Francesca nodded and then walked past the priest.

Centuries ago, Francesca's predecessor had noted that there is a unique sense of embarrassment felt by someone who walks onto a warm beach fully clothed; this sense is accentuated when others are splashing about in less or no clothing.

Surrounded by children dressed in lungi or—in the case of the youngest—nothing at all, Francesca became acutely aware of her preposterous full-length black robes. Some children cast curious looks at the party.

"Ellen," Francesca said in a soft voice, "it occurs to me now that I don't know how you are around children."

"Because I avoid them, religiously."

"What did you do when you had a child for a patient?"

"I made sure to cry before and louder than the child."

"How did that work out for you?"

"Pretty well, actually. Some of the toddlers would try to comfort me."

Just then the party came within fifteen paces of Lolo's knot of boys, who were now roughhousing. He stood away from the tumbling bodies, on the beach just above the water, neither included nor excluded.

The other boys noticed the newcomers and—with the easy acceptance of children who are cared for by many different adults—ignored them. One boy yelled something about getting another boy in trouble. Suddenly the whole pack of brats began to joyfully shriek before sprinting away down the beach. In moments they were halfway across the cove from Francesca and Ellen.

"Can't we just find a neodemon to attack us?" Ellen complained. "It would be so much easier to bear."

"But I'm good with children," Francesca said.

"Good at making them run away?"

"Remind me to halve your allowance."

"But, Magistra, you don't pay me any allowance."

"That doesn't seem right. All right, tell you what, figure out how we can talk to that boy and I'll start paying you an allowance."

"I sense a trap."

The boys had resumed their play, this time where a small cool stream ran down the beach into the bay. The water from the volcano's crater was icy cold, so the boys kicked it at each other and yelped when splashed.

Francesca wondered if she should hike up her robes and go wading in after them. Maybe splash a few boys? How had playing with children become so strange to her?

"Magistra," Ellen began to suggest, "what if I pay you to . . ." A sudden chorus of childish wonder interrupted her.

Both women turned to see that Tam and Kenna had stripped themselves down to small clothes and waded out into the waves with the children. Both the twins were thin and wiry. Their pale skin shone in the sunlight like the city's whitewashed walls.

Together the twins had planted one of their quarterstaffs into the sand beneath the waves, where it had grown roots and a thick-trunked broad-leafed tree that looked something like a mangrove. One bough grew to about thirty feet before it dropped a single aerial root that had woven itself into a rope swing.

As Francesca watched, the twins climbed up the trunk of their creation. Tam fetched the root for his sister and then, after she had taken hold, pushed her out of the tree.

With a shrill yip, a bright green sound, Kenna swung far out over the small waves. Her toes cut a line in the aquamarine salt water before she swung up to the top of her arc. She released the root-rope and with an exalted yawp tucked herself into a ball. Her mane of blond hair became an upward flume, and she splashed, butt-first, into the water.

As one, every child on the beach made that particular, strained sound that all parents recognizes as meaning, "Me next!"

There followed a miniature stampede of children from all over the beach toward the tree. Lolo's pack of boys shot past Francesca. In moments the boys were wading out toward the tree. But Lolo remained on the beach, watching.

"I'm taking back every mean thought I have ever had about the twins being weird," Ellen said.

"Or creepy," Francesca added.

"Or creepy. Definitely taking those back too."

Kenna had stayed in the water so that after Tam helped a child swing out from the tree to plop into the water, she could direct the young one back to the shore. Some of the children's minders had waded out, at first seemingly concerned the children were going to hurt themselves, but then curious. Francesca saw one young woman climbing up the tree for her own chance to swing.

"Ellen," Francesca said, "since I don't pay you enough—"

"Or anything."

"—since I don't pay you anything, why don't you try out the swing—"

"I'd sooner chew twenty cotton balls for an hour."

"—or walk along the beach, while I try talking to young Lolo?"

"Yes, Magistra. Right away, Magistra. It's amazing how well you read my mind, Magistra," Ellen said flatly as she walked in the opposite direction of the children.

Francesca studied Lolo as she approached. He did indeed seem to be about four to five years old. The skin on his back seemed darker than his belly. Two lines of linear dark brown scars, very much like bite marks, ran down his back, just along the outer aspect of his shoulder blade. So then, the boy had either been attacked by a shark, or maybe during his birth he had been cut by . . .

"Lolo?" Francesca said.

The boy calmly looked up at her. His face was indeed paler than his back. "You're not a woman," he said with a child's frankness.

"Oh?" she said squatting next to him.

"I can see it hanging around you. It looks like a cloud that is sometimes dark and sometimes light."

"You're very clever. I am not like other women. My name is Francesca."

The boy only nodded and went back to watching the other children on the tree.

"Do you want a turn on the rope swing?" she asked.

He only shook his head.

"Doesn't it look like fun?"

He frowned and—in that peculiar way some little boys can—looked as if he were an old man. "It looks fun," he admitted. "But not in the salt water. No salt water."

"And why is that?"

"The other day, Brother Palakan told us three stories of how humans were made on the Old Continent."

"Three stories?"

The boy nodded his head solemnly. "He said that because we are Ixonians, we have to be able to believe in three different stories at the same time. One story for each of the three Peoples."

"Did he now?"

"The Sea People have a story about how the humans were once fish in the sacred ocean, and it was only the bravest and cleverest fish that learned to worship the gods and walk on land to become our ancestors on the Ancient Continent. The Lotus People have a story about how the first man and first woman were born in a lotus blossom in a garden of the gods. And the Cloud People have a story about the first humans being made out of light by a god who lives beyond the sky. But you know what, Francesca?"

"What, Lolo?"

"I know I was a fish."

"You were a fish?"

He nodded gravely. "Can I tell you a secret?"

When she nodded, he leaned forward, put two small hands on her shoulders and then put his mouth to her ear before whispering dim gray words: "When I was a fish I did a bad thing." He looked down at his right big toe, which he was absently driving into the sand.

Francesca put her head to one side. "What did you do?"

The boy only shook his head.

"Lolo, do you have another name?"

Again he shook his head.

"Do you know who your father is? Or your mother?"

For a moment Francesca feared he was about to cry, but then his expression set. "No, I don't know."

"Lolo, how old are you?"

"Two and a half days old."

Well, Francesca thought, he could be right. Some deities were incarnated fully grown. So what would be so strange about a demigod growing two years a day? "Lolo, I would like to take you to a very special place, where gods and goddess and people like you and me live. I would like to take you to a city on a lake that sits inside that volcano." She pointed up to Mount Jalavata.

"You mean the Floating City?" he asked. "Brother Palakan told us about it."

"Yes, the Floating City. We might be able to find your father there. Would you like that?"

The boy looked back down at his foot. "Maybe."

"What wouldn't you like about that?"

He continued to drill his toe into the sand. Francesca waited but he still did not respond. It was then that she remembered that sometimes with children and elderly patients, one had to wait for prolonged periods of time. One of her mentors would start counting in his head after he asked a patient a question and would only break the silence if he reached one hundred and twenty-three. She hadn't asked why that number, though she guessed it was as good as any other.

She got to fifty-six when the boy quietly said, "Because of the water."

"The water below the Floating City?"

The boy nodded without looking up from his foot.

"That is fresh water. Not salt water."

"You're sure?"

She nodded. "It's the same water that flows down the channels and that everyone in this city drinks every day. You can't drink salt water."

"But I can," he said softly.

Just then Francesca noticed the sound of soft footfalls on the beach. She looked up to see Ellen approaching. With a flick of her hand, Ellen cast a dull green sentence between then. Francesca caught it and translated the script into "*The priest wants to take the children back to the orphanage. Should I stall?*"

"Who's that?" Lolo asked.

"This is Ellen," Francesca she explained. "She's a friend of mine."

"She's not like you. She's a normal woman," Lolo proclaimed in his solemn voice.

"You know," Francesca answered, "I think that is the single nicest thing anyone has ever said about Ellen." She cracked a smile at her student and then cast a reply spell. *"No need to stall. This is the boy. Tell the priest we will take custody of him."*

Ellen caught the sentence, nodded, and replied. *"What kind of deity is our mysterious sea deity?"*

Francesca replied. *"Give me a moment and I might find out. But whatever he is, holding his son hostage should give us some leverage."*

Ellen translated the text and nodded again. "It was nice to meet you, Lolo."

The little boy just stared at her.

With uncharacteristic discomfort, Ellen turned and walked up the beach. Francesca turned back to Lolo. "So we'll take you up to the Floating City, okay?"

"Okay," he said softly.

"You know, Lolo, since I'm not a normal woman, since I'm more like you, I can help you with your salt water problem."

"How?"

"First I have to know what kind of problem it is. Would you let me carry you into the water?"

He shook his head vigorously.

"I promise you; I can stop any bad thing from happening. Then, maybe, we can take you out on that swing."

They both turned to watch as Tam launched a girl from the tree trunk. She swung down, laughing, lost her grip at the bottom of the arc and toppled into the water, much to the amusement of her peers. A moment later, the girl came up spluttering and laughing.

Lolo was looking up at her. "I want to go."

Francesca held out her arms. "Then let's go."

He studied her arms with obvious suspicion for a moment. "You promise?"

"I promise."

He took a few tentative steps toward Francesca. Gently she slid one arm behind his back and the other under his legs. She grunted while straightening; he was heavier than she had expected. He clung to her shoulders.

"It's going to be fine," she said as she waded out into the bay away from the other children. She waded until the water was about waist deep and then sank down, submerging Lolo's feet.

Nothing happened.

She lowered herself farther, submerging his legs, hips, shoulders. Nothing. He was staring at her with dark eyes.

"Everything is going to be just fine," she said and dunked him under the water. A sudden shockwave ripped through her body and the water around her erupted. The boy in her arms was gone and in his place was an inhuman back, covered with tiny gray scales and incredibly muscular. It thrashed against her. All around her shot vectors of force and need. Before her appeared a snapping maw, teeth wide and serrated. Teeth that Francesca had seen growing from a womb.

The young demigod fought harder in her arms. She could feel his hunger, how he longed to speed away from her and toward the warm bodies splashing nearby. Such easy feeding.

But Francesca held tight. The nightmare maw clamped down on her arm, trying to punch serrated teeth into her flesh. Her own textual nature reacted. The resulting detonation sent the demigod flying up through the air to land with a heavy black slap on the beach.

There was a moment of unearthly silence. Francesca calmly jogged up the shore and took the distraught five-year-old into her arms. He clung to her and sobbed.

Everyone else on the beach stared at Francesca. She smiled at them to show that nothing was amiss. You know, just your standard, everyday clash between two creatures half made of flesh and half of magical language. Nothing to get excited about. Lovely beach weather, isn't it?

Now she could make out the little boy's whimpering: "I killed her. I killed her."

Francesca made cooing sounds.

"I killed her when I was a fish swimming in her belly. I killed her."

Francesca let out a long sigh. So that was it. He didn't know his mother's name, didn't know his own name, but he knew that his creation had been his mother's end. Those teeth his creation had created in her uterus had cut into his back.

Wasn't a safe business at all, creating or being created. Francesca held the boy tighter as he let out long, despondently blue howls. The poor child, not two days old and he'd discovered the terrifying, hateful part of himself. There was no hatred like self-hatred.

In the empire, there were some that said that the proliferation of deities in the league was bringing back the Age of Wonders, which had taken place uncounted millennia ago on the Ancient Continent. It had been an age of gods, goddesses, heroes, epic wars, heavenly cities, marvels beyond imagination. But Francesca knew now that it must have also been an age of great horror and sorrow.

The boy was still sobbing in her arms. "Hush now," she whispered in his ear while carrying him up the beach. "Hush. Hush. It's all going to be all right. It's going to be all right. We just need to teach you how to control yourself once you're in the salt water. We just need to teach you when to bite and when not to. Hush hush. It'll be okay. We'll take you up to the Floating City." She patted him on the back until he began to calm down.

When Lolo was at last quiet, she leaned back a little to look at his tear-stained face, his small nose slick with mucus. "It's all going to be okay," she said.

"It'll be okay?"

"It will. Just remember today's lesson: Even though you're a shark god, it's still a really, really bad idea to bite a dragon."

CHAPTER TWENTY-ONE

By midlife a man should learn to avoid both tasks beyond his capabilities and forces beyond his comprehension. Or put another way, by midlife a man should know to avoid a fight between his wife and daughter. That, at least, was Nicodemus's conclusion fourteen years ago in Port Mercy when he had attempted to mend the rift between Leandra and Francesca. Since then neither woman had seen the other, but now they were about to meet—or perhaps already had met—under alarming circumstances.

Walking up the Jacaranda Steps and into the Water Temple, Nicodemus struggled to keep his expression calm.

Ahead of him strode Sir Claude, confident as ever. Doria walked silently at his right, her expression blank. Rory, figuratively and literally on the other hand, wore a scrunched expression of anxiety so obviously uncomfortable that Nicodemus felt both sorry for him and better about his own disquietude.

John was taking news of their return to the family compound and would rejoin the party in the Floating City.

After passing through the Water Temple's rounded marble gate, Nicodemus proceeded onto an arched wooden bridge that crossed a small moat. The water was bright with lily pads, lotus flowers. Drifting about the moat were small pavilions atop pontoons. Each one carried a pair of blue-robed hydromancers lying on cushions and dangling bare legs or arms into the water. To Nicodemus, such hydromancers seemed languorous, but Doria had assured him that all such watermages were rigorously spellwrighting in the water.

Across the moat stretched many whitewashed buildings of the temple compound. At their center stood the massive Water temple-mountain, which, unique among its kind, boasted small fountains bubbling out of the limestone at various levels. The resulting streams fell down the temple-mountain by small baffled steps to the civic canals.

Normal limestone would have eroded under this constant flow. But centuries of hydromancers had built the Watertemple with many and ingenious aqueous spells. The textually infused limestone was impervious to erosion and so perfectly preserved the temple's unique and ornate architectural flourishes.

First-time pilgrims were often impressed by the myriad waterfalls; however, closer inspection revealed that the water flowed over intricate stone carvings: smoking volcanos, elephants crashing through bamboo forests, a man and woman in improbably flexible sexual congress, a mighty storm, a sunburst, a procession of monkeys in a ruined city, stylized waves above blocky sharks. Different carvings had been deemed sacred to various deities and knots of devotees gathered around them, their palms pressed together over their hearts.

At the temple-mountain's base stood a wide tunnel guarded by eight red cloaks. When Nicodemus approached, a watch captain commanded the guards to part. Inside the tunnel, two hydromancer acolytes joined the party; each held a staff tipped with a long thin glass vial.

When the party had walked far enough that the tunnel's mouth became a pinpoint of light, the older of the acolytes touched the glass on their staffs. Churning luminous tendrils climbed up the vials until they radiated soft blue light.

The party began to climb the first set of stairs. Nicodemus eyed Doria; it would be a hard trek through Mount Jalavata to the Floating City.

"What?" Doria asked without looking over. "You're expecting the old lady to curl up with a heart attack?"

"Only trying to be thoughtful."

"Then I wish your thoughts were less full of my falling off the perch."

"They're much less full of those now. You're not breathing half so hard as Rory. But maybe he's out of shape."

"What was that?" Rory asked distractedly.

"I just noticed that Magistra looks like she could run circles around you."

"She could run circles around all of us."

Doria made a satisfied sound and they continued in silence until Nicodemus said, "Sir Claude, are you feeling ill?"

"No, my lord. Why do you ask?"

"You missed a chance to quip with Rory, so either you are suffering an uncharacteristic bout of charity or we should turn around and march down to the infirmary."

"It must be charity then, my lord. I hear it's contagious."

Rory's posture seemed to relax.

Nicodemus smiled. "What do you think, Druid? Sir Claude given to charity?"

"Indeed, I believe he is."

"Well, well, everyone seems to be trying out getting along for a change."

"My lord warden is chatty this afternoon," Doria observed.

"Just trying to keep up morale," he replied.

"Or trying to distract yourself from thinking about your wife and daughter?" Doria asked.

"Is it that obvious?"

No one spoke.

"Oh come on," Nicodemus said, "you're all exaggerating."

Sir Claude coughed, pointedly.

"So what, exactly," Doria asked, "are we supposed to do if your wife and daughter try to kill each other?"

"Stop them."

"Funny," Doria replied, "you've never ordered us to commit suicide before."

Nicodemus sighed. "All right, stay out of their way. See if you can keep anyone else from getting hurt. I should turn the question around: If they go at it again, what should I do?"

"You're the only one who might stop them," Doria said with a shrug.

"Still," Sir Claude said, "would be a shame to watch you die, my lord."

Nicodemus snorted. "Remind me why I chose you lot for my advisors?"

"Our good looks," Doria offered.

"And sage wisdom," Sir Claude chimed in.

"And bravery in combat," Rory added.

"But mostly our good looks," Doria insisted. "Especially mine."

That got a laugh out of everyone. They continued up the steps in silence. Their breathing grew heavier, and their legs ached.

Hot dread began to brew in Nicodemus's stomach once again. He could not keep out thoughts of imperial forces bearing down on the bay, of some neodemonic plot conspiring against Leandra, of his daughter and his wife glaring at each other. Likely everything would go straight to one of the burning hells in a handcart; it seemed part of the general trend.

A circle of light appeared at the tunnel's end and drew Nicodemus out of his ruminations. The hydromantic acolytes touched their glowing vials and their blue lights dimmed.

The party emerged onto Crater Landing—a wide stone plaza cut into the volcano's inner slopes. Behind them stood the monastery of the Trimuril, where two hundred or so priests and priestesses slept and ate.

Behind the monastery, a stone staircase zigzagged up the crater wall to the volcano's rim, which stood so high above them as to occlude much of the sky. A single cloud hung above the crater, churning with such speed and fluidity as to seem dreamlike.

Ahead of Nicodemus stretched the steep green bowl of the crater. From the plaza, wide stone steps ran down to a slate gray lake. Upon the dark water floated a disorder of small vessels—rafts, canoes, kayaks, boats, any and every type of floating thing. There were long stretches of pontoon bridges that connected different parts of the lake and presently bore the steady foot traffic of brightly robed priests and blue-robed hydromancers as they moved about the Floating City performing their duties. The crater valley echoed with discordant voices—some of them singing, some chanting depending on which of the floating craft they were near.

Each of the small vessels contained at least one divine ark stone. To become a member of the Ixonian pantheon, a divinity had to make the pilgrimage to the Floating City at least once and then bind a large portion of their textual soul into one such ark stone. These divine receptacles were then kept upon the lake as hostages. If a divinity were found to be betraying Ixos, the priests would sink whatever craft held the offending deity's ark and the hydromancers would cast powerful spells to dissolve the ark and the soul contained within.

Nicodemus remembered the first time he had brought Leandra to the Floating City. She had been only six years old. The new order of the world had just begun forming. In Dral the rule of the forest prevailed, and the structure of clan and tribe that had shaped the divinities continued to govern them. The strong hunted the weak and a new divinity might be labeled a neodemon for nothing more than attracting the disapproval of a more powerful divinity. A phenomenal amount of divine text was destroyed.

In Lorn too, much divinity was wasted. Worship of any divinity but Argent, the kingdom's metallic oversoul, was forbidden unless the divinity had fused its soul into Argent's divinity complex. All deities with requisites falling outside conservative Lornish sensibilities were destroyed. Even more wasteful, to maintain his domination of the complex, Argent forbade any divinity to approach his power. Therefore, any seraph that attracted too many prayers was labeled a neodemon.

In contrast, Ixonian laws and customs were tolerant even though the trickster Trimuril's authority was unequivocal. By creating the Floating City, the Ixonians allowed an array of divinities to coexist while focusing their power. As a result the archipelago could call upon as much divine power as the other two league kingdoms combined.

When Nicodemus explained this in simpler terms to little Leandra, she stared at the Floating City and asked if that meant that Ixos would be less afraid of the empire. Nicodemus had known his daughter was precocious, but still the observation surprised him. And, indeed, four years later the Wars of the Ogun Blockade were won decisively by the Ixonians against the Trillinonish, whereas the Goldensward War that pitted Lorn against Spires was a disaster for the league.

His little girl had seen all that when she had frowned at the Floating City. Back then no one had thought Leandra would outlive her first decade. Thinking about the little girl he had known—her dark fierce eyes, the force with which she would scream when her disease flared up—filled Nicodemus again with dread.

At the end of the plaza stood six of the Trimuril's priests. Wordlessly, they surrounded Nicodemus's party and began the short walk down the steps to the crater lake.

Nicodemus tried to empty his mind and looked up toward their destination.

At the lake's center, amid the chaos of small craft, the Floating Palace twisted slowly around its anchor. As large as any compound in Chandralu, the Floating Palace consisted of three stories, each decorated with wooden beams lacquered bright red and upturned awnings trimmed with gold leaf.

When Nicodemus's entourage reached the water, they discovered that several priests had maneuvered four rafts into proximity so that his party could walk over one raft after another to a stretch of floating bridge that was currently connected to the palace.

Once on the floating bridge, the party resumed its formation. "You know . . ." Doria said while peering into the black depths of the crater lake, "we hydromancers cast enough text in this lake that if Lea and Fran do get to violence, we might be able to break any of their spells by just pushing them into the water."

Above them the sky darkened as a cloud blew in from the sea. A sheet of warm rain swept across the lake. As one, the party picked up their pace. The hurrying worsened the confusion of Nicodemus's thoughts. He wondered what life would have been like if he were not a cacographic spellwright caught up in prophecy. What if he were a cattle herder or a cobbler or master of some other mundane profession in northern Spires where he had been born?

Maybe it wouldn't matter. Maybe he'd make the same mistakes of ambition and desperation. Maybe his wife and daughter would still quarrel.

The rain intensified, and again the party sped up. The rain became hard, weighing down on them and spurring the party into a jog.

Nicodemus's thoughts coiled in on themselves. Did it matter that Leandra and Francesca had placed kingdoms between each other? Wouldn't it be just as painful if they had placed counties or villages between each other? So long as there was ill will, what did space matter?

He wondered if the doom hovering over his family came not from demons or empire or anything far away, but from within himself. He had the strange sensation that he had changed who he was so many times—cripple, killer, lover, husband, father, warden—and yet this doom had changed with him. Maybe this doom had been part of him, had been separated from him when he was young and was now inexorably making its way back to him.

As a younger man, Nicodemus had thought of life as a presence, like a candle flame that had been lit and would eventually burn out. But with every passing year, he developed a stronger premonition that life was a separation. Before he was born, he had been a complete void; then something had happened that split his birth from his death and flung them far apart; now they were slowly drawing closer together, and though he could twist and turn, baffle their fall toward each other, one day his demise would reunite with his conception, a circle would add a degree to the three hundred fifty-nine already drawn, and he would return to void. Nothing sad about it.

The rain intensified yet again as the party reached the eaves of the Floating Palace. One by one they jumped from the floating bridge to the palace steps. Two priests waited for them at the palace's wide doors. Nicodemus climbed the steps while the others tried to dry their clothes.

"My Lord Warden," one of the priests said while pressing his palms together over his heart. "The Sacred Regent is expecting you. There should be a reception within the hour. We are preparing quarters for you in case you should spend the night. In the meantime, would you like to dry off and change your clothes?"

When Nicodemus said that he would, the priest led him up a flight of stairs to a small room on the second story. Diaphanous curtains covered wide windows looking onto the lake. The clouds had darkened the day and Nicodemus could see that the rain was driving another party to rush along the floating bridge toward the palace. He heard a screen door sliding behind him and turned to see a young priest bringing in dry clothes and a towel. Nico-demus found he was shivering slightly, though from the wet or his nerves he could not say.

He thanked the priest, who put the clothes and towel down before with-drawing. From the floor below sounded the racket of the new party arriving in the palace. Nicodemus gratefully peeled off his longvest and shirt and then picked up the dry towel and pressed it to his face. It was cotton, likely from Trillinion, rough against his skin but with the smell of clean laundry. Look-ing over the clothes, Nicodemus saw that the priest had brought him a Spirish-style white silk blouse, linen pants, and a beautiful deep green longvest. It pleased him that the palace servants had remembered his preferences.

Nicodemus was just about to finish undressing when he heard the door move. "I'm not—" he started to say but the screen slid away to reveal a tall, lithe woman, her long brown hair wet and plastered against her face and shoulders. She wore a wizard's black robes and a red physician's stole. The rain made the cloth cling to her hips, her slight breasts. She hadn't aged a day since he first saw her, could not age a day. The tropical sun had dark-ened the spray of freckles across her fair cheeks. Her mouth was parted slightly and her very dark brown eyes stared at him with what he was sure was a mir-ror of his own desire. It had been almost a year.

"Francesca," he breathed and dropped the towel.

A few steps from the door, he caught her up in his arms and spun her around as she pressed her lips hard into his. She was the heat in his blood, a drug that evaporated all his solid thoughts of death into vapor.

He spun her around again and her feet struck the screen and sent him tottering back. She laughed as he landed her on her feet.

They were fumbling with her clothes now, tossing her stole to the ground and working with clumsy fingers at her collar fastenings.

"But the regent," he said. "We can't—"

"I have to get out of these wet clothes anyway."

"Good point."

"Nico," she whispered as they continued to work at the fastenings, "I'm bringing horrible news from Dral."

"Later," he whispered before pressing in for another urgent kiss and then, "The door."

She turned and with a flick of a wrist sent a silvery paragraph across the room to push the screen door shut. The loud clap made Nicodemus aware that he could hear more people moving around on the floor below. He thought perhaps he heard footsteps and turned to the door.

But then Francesca undid the ties around her collar, drew her robes up over her head and tossed them aside.

"Fran," he said, "someone—"

"Later," she whispered while pressing herself against his chest. Her warmth scattered his wits. He wrapped his arms around her and saw how his dark skin made hers seem fairer. They kissed again and—

Someone walked in the hallway with deliberately heavy tread. Reflexively, Nicodemus put himself between the door and his wife.

A woman cleared her throat. "Magistra, I hope you'll pardon the most regretted interruption."

"Yes, Ellen?" Fran asked.

"Another party has come to the palace. It's your daughter."

CHAPTER TWENTY-TWO

Kneeling in the throne room, Nicodemus looked up at a hundred-ton whale floating an inch above his head. Or he listened to a spider whisper in his ear. Or he straddled the muscular, musky back of an elephant marching rhythmically around the Floating Palace. Or, and more likely, he did none of these things.

Trickster deities always gave Nicodemus a headache.

"Divine Trimuril," Nicodemus said, hiding the annoyance, "might I have a moment? Your godspells are . . ." His perceptions flickered. The whale thrashed. The spider nattered. "A moment . . ." The elephant reared. Groaning, Nicodemus placed both his hands on the floorboards to steady himself.

Leandra had just finished reporting that thugs were attacking minor city deities. Now the Trimuril was trying to communicate directly with Nicodemus and so was unintentionally baffling his perceptions. To almost any other soul, the Trimuril projected herself as one aspect of her trinity. However, Nicodemus's cacography partially misspelled the Trimuril's texts, and so her godspells had an imprecise and often prismatic effect upon him.

Most people thought of tricksters as mischief-makers: clever pranksters, rapacious thieves, clownish dupes. Most would say tricksters were rule-breakers. But in Nicodemus's experience tricksters did not break rules so much as they showed rules to be broken.

Often humans prayed to tricksters for help escaping from dire situations, laws, customs. Tricksters facilitated such escapes by altering perceptions. They might, for example, play the idiot who commits misdeeds to demonstrate the folly of such misdeeds and so—reinforced with perception-altering godspells—reshape the values of a village, city, kingdom. Or they might humiliate another god to change how the god was worshiped. Tricksters were the deities of altered moral perception.

Nicodemus felt his perceptions reel again through the Trimuril's incarnations. He tried to glean unaltered reality by concentrating on what he knew about the Trimuril.

Centuries ago, when the archipelago sought to escape the First Neosolar Empire, each island culture incarnated a different trickster. Oka'pahui, a blue whale navigator goddess, helped Sea People smugglers befuddle the imperial fleets. Elephantine Ghajal had built secret jungle roads for Lotus Culture warriors. Araxa, the Ancestor Spider, taught the Cloud People how to forge and spy. The first Ixonian king had negotiated the fusion of these deities, and the resulting complex had tricked all of the archipelago's pantheons into uniting against the empire.

By focusing on these thoughts, Nicodemus's perceptions consolidated. Gone were the whale, spider, elephant. He knelt in a wide wooden throne room, a row of arched windows behind the dais. To his right knelt his wife, to his left his daughter. They were both looking at him with concerned expressions so similar it made his heart ache. Neither mother nor daughter had looked at or spoken to the other.

Behind Nicodemus sat Doria, Sir Claude, and Rory. To their left sat Leandra's divinities; to their right, Francesca's student Ellen. Presently Rory cocked his head, whispering to Ellen. At the back of the room sat a small crowd of Ixonian dignitaries and deities. Notable in the crowd was Tagrana, the archipelago's most powerful war deity. Her tiger-eyes studied Nicodemus, and a brilliant aura leapt about her muscular body like flames.

In front of Nicodemus stood a dais and a simple wooden throne. Upon it sat the Sacred Regent, who ruled Ixos in the name of an ancient royal family, long ago made figureheads and confined to a temple city on Mount Ixram. The present Sacred Regent was a thin, dark-skinned man well past his first century with lank white hair and blank white eyes. Nicodemus had never learned his given name—which was taboo to mention—but knew that before his elevation, the Sacred Regent had been the head of the hydromantic order. Presently, the regent wore sumptuous robes of yellow silk and an expression of grave consideration.

Beside him stood a short androgynous figure with limestone skin, a slight potbelly, six arms, a shaved head, wide stone eyes, and a slight smile indicating an emotion beyond human conjecture. This was the Trimuril's true incarnation.

"My apologies, Divine Trimuril," Nicodemus said. "I am ready."

The stony incarnation waved one of six hands to dismiss the comment. The divinity moved with irregular, insectlike jerks. "There is no need to apologize." The Trimuril's lips did not move; rather the words came from a thin, screechy voice as if Ancestor Spider's incarnation were sitting on Nicodemus's shoulder and whining in his ear. "I wondered if we might play a game. It would be fun."

With twitchy movements, the Trimuril flatted all six of her palms toward the sky in a gesture of offering. To govern her diverse pantheon, the Trimuril constantly sent her soul into various ark stones to cause her incarnation to appear to the deities she judged to need guidance. She did this with incomprehensible speed. The small pauses in her twitching movement indicated those brief moments when she would send her soul somewhere else on the lake. The fact that she had manifested her soul in her physical incarnation for so long indicated how important she felt the present audience was.

Nicodemus blinked and had to fight down his annoyance. Imperial scouts and an unknown deity stalked the bay and the Trimuril wanted to play? "What game, goddess?" Nicodemus asked levelly.

The Trimuril's enigmatic smile grew. "A game of imitation."

"How do you mean, goddess?"

"I challenge you to do something that I cannot imitate perfectly. The only limitations will be that it must be performed in this room and cannot involve Language Prime. Other than that, your challenge could be anything: a feat of spellwrighting or singing or storytelling or dancing." The statue smiled and the spider voice tittered in his ear. "Anything really. It will be fun."

Nicodemus frowned and then glanced at Francesca and Leandra. They wore reflections of his own confusion and had tilted their heads to one side; apparently the spider was speaking in their ears as well.

Nicodemus turned back to the Trimuril. She had always been his reliable ally, and he could think of no reason why that should have changed. It seemed unlikely that she was trying to punish or humiliate him. "When might we play this game, goddess?"

"Whenever you like, Nicodemus. You simply need to speak your challenge and we will play. You may have as many attempts as you like until you admit defeat. Doesn't that sound like fun?"

No, it bloody didn't. Nicodemus could think of nothing he could do—outside of altering Language Prime texts—that the divinity complex couldn't. "What stakes shall we play for?"

"Ahh," Ancestor Spider said into his ear as the statue pressed her three pairs of palms together. "I would like to play for your daughter."

Nicodemus made a surprised choking sound while Francesca blurted out, "What?"

The Trimuril's expression did not change. "I am a very old divinity, and

I should like to have a child. Did you know I never had? Hearing how your daughter so cleverly discovered these thugs with the perfect circle tattoo—oh, and I agree with her assessment that they are an organization, likely criminal, impersonating a cult—makes me think she would be a good daughter for me, if she and her mother also consent to our game."

"But I don't understand why we should play such a game," Nicodemus said.

"If you should win," Ancestor Spider creaked in Nicodemus's ear, "I will grant any request you might have of me so long as it doesn't harm another soul."

Nicodemus's confusion worsened. He had no requests of the Trimuril and couldn't think of any that he might soon have.

"However," Ancestor Spider continued, "if you should admit that I win, then I will adopt Lady Warden Leandra as my daughter and you will cease all familiar relationships with her."

Nicodemus wondered why either Leandra or he would want such a thing.

Apparently anticipating his confusion, the Sacred Regent spoke, "There is an obscure law that pertains to this game. As the daughter of the Trimuril, Lady Warden Leandra would have a guaranteed seat on the Regency Council."

Francesca started to speak with heated words. "But—"

Leandra interrupted, "I consent."

Nicodemus and Francesca looked over at their daughter in surprised silence.

Ignoring her parents, Leandra kept her eyes on the goddess. "I trust in the Trimuril's wisdom."

"What fun," the spider creaked in Nicodemus's ear. "And Lady Warden Francesca?"

Nicodemus looked over at his wife, who was staring openmouthed. If Nicodemus were not so distressed, he would have been amused to see his unflappable wife at such a loss.

"Consider," said the Trimuril, "that Nicodemus need never invoke the challenge if he doesn't want to."

Francesca closed her mouth. "Goddess, I think perhaps we have more pressing—"

"The divine Trimuril is able to decide what is pressing in her own kingdom," Leandra interrupted.

Nicodemus looked back at his daughter and then to the Trimuril. Were they conspiring? To what purpose?

"Then . . ." Francesca spoke hesitantly, ". . . then I would defer to my husband."

"You'll what?" Nicodemus asked. This was a first.

Francesca looked at him with a flabbergasted expression.

Nicodemus turned back to the Trimuril. The divinity complex regarded him with an enigmatic smile. Impatience overwhelmed Nicodemus. This was ridiculous; they needed to get on with pressing business. "Very well, Goddess, we accept but I can't imagine a situation in which I would challenge you."

"Wonderful fun!" Ancestor Spider creaked in Nicodemus's ear as the statue clapped each of her three pairs of hands, from lowest to highest. "Well then, pardon my interruption. Please continue with your reports. I believe Lady Warden Leandra had just finished telling us about the thugs with the tattoos."

There followed a silence in which Nicodemus waited for the goddess to say more. When she didn't, he looked at Francesca. She looked back at him. They both looked at Leandra, who ignored them both.

"Lord Warden Nicodemus," the Sacred Regent said in his raspy voice, "would you describe your recent expedition in pursuit of the monkey neodemon of brigands to the east who has evaded us for so long?"

"Yes, your excellency," Nicodemus replied and then reported about how he had falsely claimed to pursue the brigand neodemon when he had sought to entrap the River Thief on the Matrunda River. He explained that he had done so because he believed someone in the Regency or in Leandra's service was informing the neodemons. On hearing this, Leandra stiffened.

Nicodemus described his encounter with the River Thief, what he had surmised about her cult, and his recommendations about preventing her reincarnation.

The only thing that Nicodemus withheld was mention that the River Thief had been wearing Leandra's face; he wanted to discuss this with his family before making it public knowledge.

"Most distressing," the Sacred Regent said when he finished. "My Lady Warden Leandra, have you any idea who in your service might have been leaking information to the River Thief?"

"No, your excellency."

The old man frowned as if waiting for the Trimuril to speak. When she did not, he nodded. "We shall investigate immediately."

Nicodemus glanced over at his daughter and could almost feel the coldness radiating off of her. He didn't blame her. It had been an infringement on her independence to take down the River Thief as he did, but still he could not see any other way he could have brought the neodemon down.

"Lord Warden," the regent said. "I hope you do not have any more distressing findings?"

Nicodemus turned back to the dais. "I'm afraid I do, your excellency." He described the carnage at Feather Island and what he had learned from the pyromancer, who was now under guard in the city's infirmary.

As he spoke, the regent's expression grew more and more puckered until the man looked as if he were sucking on a lemon. "Imperial scouts? What can the meaning of this be?"

To Nicodemus's surprise, Francesca spoke. "I'm afraid, your excellency, I have the answer." All eyes turned to his wife. She paused, a little dramatically. "When my husband and I first learned that the empire was strengthening its air and sea fleets, we decided that he would travel to Ixos both to cast his metaspell and also to help deter any thoughts the empress might have had about a misadventure on the archipelago. At the same time, I set my agents in Dral to discover what might be causing the empress's actions. Roughly ten days after Nicodemus set sail, I made a horrible discovery, the news of which I could not trust to a colaboris spell or a messenger."

Leandra clenched her hands so tightly her knuckles blanched. Nicodemus felt the same anxiety.

Francesca continued. "For decades now I have suspected several men and women in Dral of selling information to the empire. Our investigation started by examining their recent activities. Surprisingly, we learned that half of them had disappeared. More distressing, perhaps forty days prior to our investigation, all three of the suspected imperial spies in the city of Cree had met unexpected deaths."

The Sacred Regent made a low, thoughtful sound. Beside him, the Trimuril wore her usual enigmatic smile.

"Further investigation revealed that all the suspected spies had either fallen ill or were the victims of violent accidents during the same time a powerful shape-shifting neodemon was discovered in the city. The exact nature of the neodemon was never discovered because the local deities deconstructed it before my agents or I received word of the events. I sent the druids Kenna and Tam, both of Thorntree, to discover the shape-shifting neodemon's potential worshipers and requisites; however, they found no evidence of his cult in Cree. In fact, they found no evidence of any new worship at all. Given this finding and the neodemon's great power, we suspected that the divinity had migrated from elsewhere. When looking into this possibility, the twins discovered a devotee of the shape-shifter, one of his priestesses no less. She had fled Cree and was trying to make it to Warth. Without her god's protection, she was dispirited and near starvation. After an offer of protection, she confessed that her god was, in fact, an old god of the kingdom of Verdant."

The room was filled with involuntary sounds of surprise. Everyone had heard the rumors that the empire was deconstructing their weakest deities in order to empower their texts and spellwrights, but if deities were fleeing the imperial kingdoms, then the situation was far worse than suspected.

The Sacred Regent cleared his throat. "It was my understanding that it is impossible for a divinity to escape the empire."

"That is the most distressing thing of all," Francesca replied. "The priestess reported that her god was smuggled out of Verdant by spies of the league."

"Impossible," Nicodemus said. "None of our allies would be so foolish."

Behind him, the room filled with murmuring. For the league to smuggle deities out of the empire would be to violate their sovereignty, no different from kidnapping their citizens or stealing from their treasuries. To smuggle imperial deities would be to incite war.

Francesca's expression was calm. "It might sound impossible, but in this case it seems to be the truth. We found witnesses in Calad who had helped the priestess and her god enter Dral. Worse, we believe we have found strong evidence that several other neodemons discovered in Dral and Ixos originated in the empire and were somehow smuggled in."

The surprised murmuring grew louder. The Sacred Regent raised his hands. "There will be silence." When the room quieted again, he motioned for Francesca to continue.

She nodded. "Now I come to the gravest part of my news. The empire has long suspected that their deities are being smuggled into the league. Three years ago, they launched their own investigation, which eventually led them to Cree. It seems that all of the imperial spies in Cree had been seeking the refugee shape-shifter. When they were close to discovering their target, the shape-shifter killed them all. However, one of the spies managed to send a message to his handler in Warth, who has successfully left Dral and has made his way to Trillinon."

Behind Nicodemus, the murmuring rose again.

"It is our belief," Francesca continued over the din, "that this spy has already told the empress that the league is stealing imperial deities. As I am sure everyone in this room realizes, such news will incite the empress to immediate and violent action. For this reason, I met urgently with the Council of Starfall. It was agreed that immediate action was needed. The Council sent all available mundane and spellwright forces to the Spirish border in case of attack there. However, at that time, the Council received news that the Silent Blight caused crops to fail again in Verdant. Unless the empress can quickly secure surplus supplies of food, she will be facing a famine. So now, the empress has both political justification and a powerful incentive to invade Ixos. So the Council decided to send all available Southern deities of war to Ixos."

Francesca paused to draw breath. "I set sail immediately, and I fervently hope that several ships filled with the Southern war deities are even now sailing toward Chandralu. That my husband has discovered imperial scouts in the bay does not surprise me. It is my great fear that the empress will soon launch, if she hasn't already, an attack on the kingdom of Ixos with the full force of the empire's power."

Vivian's glorious golden-prose world tilted.

Her hands, clutching the arms of her throne, told her that she was upright. Yet all around her, the master spell reeled. Then a vertiginous discovery: A subtle textual pressure had been cast against her master spell. Only a deity could write such a complex spell, and the only purpose of such a spell could be to find Vivian.

Using the Emerald, Vivian adjusted her sentences to avoid the strange spell. A moment later her master spell righted itself. Nothing had been damaged. The interfering spell could not have detected her. The satisfaction of a puzzle solved bubbled through Vivian.

But what deity was looking for her? And, for that matter, where was she? Vivian searched her mind for the name of a city and found nothing. She couldn't even recall which kingdom she was in.

Tension was building in her master spell, so she returned to editing. Casting and recasting, such intricate prose . . . Hours passed. Days passed, maybe . . .

Vivian felt movement in the Numinous matrix. Lotannu had returned, so it seemed. She had not talked to Lotannu in . . . She could not recall. In fact, when Vivian tried to remember why she was casting the master spell, dull pain spread behind her eyes and tension gathered in the Numinous matrix.

So she returned to editing. Surprisingly, the spell had little textual reserve, so Vivian redoubled her editing efforts as Lotannu approached. It felt as if she kept him waiting for another hour, but when she raised her hands and lifted her halo, Lotannu stood without sign of impatience. "Empress." He bowed.

"Hello again, old friend. Has the time come to end my master spell?"

"Sadly, no. In fact only a few hours have passed since we spoke last."

"But . . ." Vivian struggled with the fog covering her recent memories but soon gave up. "Is something the matter?"

"There has been an unexpected attack on our expeditionary forces. A dozen of our agents were hidden on Feather Island. All but one has been killed in a . . . puzzling . . . attack."

"Puzzling?"

"The entire village was destroyed by a divinity. From the reports, it sounds like a volcanic god of madness."

"An Ixonian god? Has Nicodemus discovered us?"

"I doubt the god was of the Ixonian pantheon. If he had been, he wouldn't have indiscriminately attacked the village even if we had bribed the leaders. At the very least, he should have tried to take prisoners to interrogate."

"A neodemon then?"

"Too powerful to be a young neodemon. Perhaps if the Ixonians were failing to contain their neodemons for several years we might see something this powerful."

"You don't think . . ."

"I do think."

"Well . . . then we would have either very good or very bad timing."

"I agree. Very bad if the volcanic god truly is an ancient demon and we attack Chandralu; in that case, we might be destroying our strongest ally right before the War of Disjunction."

She nodded, trying and failing to remember the specifics of their present situation. "Go on."

"But it could be very good timing if we stay our hand and the volcanic god is revealed to be the first demon. We might even catch Los unawares."

"Are there disadvantages to delaying?"

"It increases the chances that Nicodemus might discover our purpose. And there's the effect it has on you."

Vivian smiled and her thoughts and eyes wandered again up to her halo. "I don't mind."

He bowed. "Empress, we must have you at full strength once the battle is joined, no matter who we are fighting."

"True. So, act now and incur unknown risks, or delay and do the same."

"It's a dangerous situation."

"I want everything possible done to find this volcanic deity."

Lotannu bowed. "The orders have already been given."

"Of course they have, excellent as always, old friend. There is something you should know . . . I can't tell you how long ago, but since we talked last there was some diffuse text, likely a godspell, that interacted with my master spell. I think it was a seek-and-find spell. I made the necessary adjustments to keep the master spell hidden."

"So if it is an ancient demon, he might be searching for us as we search for him?"

"That or someone in Ixos is more suspicious than we previously thought."

"There is perhaps one action that might save us from the need to decide immediately."

"Well, don't keep your empress in suspense."

"Leandra."

"If she became independent?"

"It would reshuffle power in Chandralu without much weakening them. It would distract the Ixonians and your half-brother, reducing the likelihood they would discover us. All without impeding their ability to fight off an ancient demon."

"You can accelerate Leandra's development?"

He nodded. "But not without risks."

"Such as."

"The resulting redistribution of power might cause a regrettable clash within the family."

A headache was now throbbing through Vivian's temples and she was starting to worry about the master spell. "Lotannu, I need to get back to spellwrighting. Speak plainly."

"If we empower her, Leandra might kill one of her parents. Or . . ."

"Or?"

"We might kill her."

Vivian took in a long breath, thought about what she owed to a niece she had never met, and what she owed to humanity.

It didn't take long.

She reached for her halo and said, "Do it."

CHAPTER TWENTY-THREE

Francesca's news left the throne room silent, made Nicodemus's heart flutter. The Trimuril froze as she spread the dire news through her pantheon by projecting herself into the consciousness of her most trusted divinities.

"We must take immediate action," the Sacred Regent announced and looked at the Trimuril, who gave him a twitching nod. "Before I issue orders to the fleet and army, how would the wardens counsel me?"

Francesca bowed her head. "I have received a colaboris message from the Council of Starfall. They have failed to establish a correspondence with the empress, but if your excellency summoned the imperial ambassador, there might still be time for diplomacy."

The Sacred Regent nodded. "Done. What other counsel?"

Nicodemus could think of nothing and looked to Leandra. For the first time, she glanced at him. In the flash of her wide brown eyes, he saw the little girl he had once known. But then her expression hardened and she turned back to the dais. "Your excellency, given that the perfect circle tattoo was found on the thugs in Chandralu and on Feather Island, I would like to resume my investigation."

"Your dedication is appreciated," the Sacred Regent said; "however, the wardens will remain in the Floating City until a war council can be formed."

"But your excellency, I have avenues of investigation that must be pursued immediately."

"Then Dhamma will pursue them for you."

"I welcome the help of the goddess of justice, but I insist on the importance of my immediate return to Chandralu."

The Sacred Regent frowned. "I do not doubt their importance, but my decision stands."

"Your excellency, my loyalty to the Ixonian peoples prompts me to remark that my authority as a warden comes, not from the regency, but from the Council of Starfall."

Nicodemus started. The wardens did answer to an authority higher than any individual kingdom to reduce political manipulation. However, none of them had yet invoked this authority. Doing so now would test the Sacred Regent's dedication to the league during a time of crisis. Nicodemus glanced at Francesca. Her expression fluctuated between surprise and anger.

"Your excellency," Nicodemus said, his mind racing, "perhaps I might—"

"The Warden of Lorn," Leandra interrupted, "obviously has great experience; however, he is not aware of the current situation in Chandralu."

Nicodemus stared at his daughter as she kept her gaze fixed on the Sacred Regent. Lea, what under heaven are you doing?

"And what is the situation in Chandralu?" a thin spider voice asked in Nicodemus's ear, and apparently Leandra's ear as well. His daughter's expression tensed as the Trimuril pressed all her hands together and bowed.

"The situation is . . . fluid," Leandra replied. "I require one more day's investigation before reporting."

"Perhaps, this is something better discussed in private," the Trimuril said, stepping forward with a fluid motion. The lack of jerkiness indicated that she was maintaining her soul continuously in her body. The Trimuril gestured with her uppermost two hands at Leandra.

Nicodemus's cheeks grew hot in a synesthetic reaction to unknown magical language. On the dais, the Trimuril's smile wilted. She gestured again at Leandra, and the heat on Nicodemus's cheeks doubled.

Then Nicodemus understood what was happening: The Trimuril was attempting to communicate directly with Leandra through her godspells, but Leandra was protecting herself from the trickster's manipulation by inducing a disease flare to misspell the godspells.

"Divine Trimuril," Francesca said, "perhaps I could help resolve this misunderstanding."

But the Trimuril made another gesture toward Leandra. Faint red flashes circled Leandra's head. Nicodemus's stomach clenched. Leandra's dramatic disease flares caused those nearby to become fluent in whatever language she was working. Now Nicodemus was gaining the ability to see the goddess's crimson language.

"Sacred Regent, please intercede," Nicodemus said, but the old man raised a hand in a gesture for silence. Beside him, the Trimuril again gestured toward Leandra.

"Sacred Regent!" Nicodemus repeated. The crimson glow around his daughter's head brightened. How long could Leandra keep this up? The flare would kill her.

Nicodemus found himself on his feet. "Trimuril!" He stepped toward the dais, vaguely aware of forces shifting around him. Another step and a swarm of hydromancers and deities might descend upon him. The first to reach him would likely be tigerlike Tagrana.

"Lea!" Francesca whispered. "Lea, stop this!"

Nicodemus's mind came alive with terrifying images of a draconic transformation. "Lea," he pleaded. But when he looked at her, the crimson luminosity above her head dazzled his vision. "Trimuril," he growled. The goddess's stony lips had pressed into a frown of concentration.

Nicodemus had always assumed that though his daughter's ability to misspell was great, her disease limited what she could disspell. He had assumed that in a contest with the Trimuril, Lea would be overpowered. But now the goddess seemed unsure she could win.

An unexpected twinge of pride moved through Nicodemus, but this twinge was soon lost in the realization that Leandra might get them all killed. "Lea, please," he said in a softer tone and stepped toward her.

He heard Francesca stand. "Trimuril," she said in a threatening tone, "you will stop."

Nicodemus crouched beside his daughter. It was painful to look at the crimson light. "Lea, this is dangerous," he whispered. "Baby, please . . ."

"Trimuril!" Francesca barked.

Nicodemus turned and through his spell-dazzled vision saw his wife moving toward the dais. If she reached it, there would be no going back. She would transform and the Creator alone knew who would survive that. Impossibly, the blaze of light from Leandra intensified. Francesca pointed at the Trimuril. This was it. If Nicodemus didn't do something—

"Game!"

To Nicodemus's surprise, the voice that had yelled that word was his own. "Game!" he repeated and faced the dais. "Trimuril, I'll play your game!"

The crimson blaze around Leandra winked out. Nicodemus found himself blinking at the potbellied Trimuril, who was still bowing slightly, but now her head was tilted with childlike surprise. "What was that?"

"Your imitation game," Nicodemus said. "I make my challenge."

Again each pair of the Trimuril's hands clapped once, lowest to highest, happiness apparent on her face.

Beside him Leandra swayed and put a hand on the ground. The god of wrestling went to her, and with three of his arms, steadied her.

Francesca took Nicodemus's arm and he felt a flush of gratitude for the support. He turned to her and saw that she was looking past Leandra to another one of their daughter's followers: the muscular male deity with a shaved head. A shark god, if Nicodemus remembered correctly. "What is it?" Nicodemus asked faintly.

Francesca seemed to come out of some deep thought. "Nothing. We . . . we just have to get out of this mess. What are you . . ." Her voice trailed off as she turned to realize that the Trimuril was now standing before them, leaning slightly to one side with her lowest arm bent as if it were being held by someone else. She was copying Nicodemus's posture.

"Good, good," she said. "Now remember, you may make as many challenges as you like until you're satisfied that I can perfectly imitate anything that you do."

Nicodemus looked at Francesca, but she only shook her head. So he turned back to the Trimuril. The goddess met his eyes right as he looked at her face. A strange mirror.

His mind racing, Nicodemus stood up straighter and slowly removed his arm from Francesca's. The Trimuril repeated his actions. What could he do that a trickster could not? He was the only living Language Prime spellwright, but the Trimuril had forbidden use of that language. There was nothing else unique about Nicodemus as a spellwright, unless . . .

Nicodemus looked around and noticed a row of windows behind the dais that let in the bright tropical sunlight. Above each hung a tightly rolled curtain of dark blue silk. "Drop the curtains," Nicodemus ordered. "This challenge will be played in darkness."

The Trimuril gave no indication that she had heard, but on the dais the Sacred Regent nodded. An attendant pulled a cord and the curtains fell, dropping the room into near darkness that was broken only by the bright orange aura of the goddess Tagrana. The regent asked the war goddess to withdraw.

As the tigerlike deity left the room, Nicodemus undid his longvest and, reaching inside of it, pulled a tattooed shadowganger spell from his hip. The violet sentences wrapped around him. "Goddess, I don't suppose you can hide in the dark as well as I can." When the shadowganger enveloped Nicodemus in shadow, surprised murmuring filled the room.

The Trimuril's smile grew. "Let us see who can find whom." The goddess sprang up as if to jump into the air but instead vanished.

Nicodemus pulled several sentences from his belly and edited them into his shadowganger spell, reinforcing its sound-deadening paragraphs. His heart thundered as he worked and a wave of fatigue made his legs feel weak. So with extra care he stole away to the crowd of Ixonian dignitaries.

For thirty years, Nicodemus had sharpened his skills at catching neodemons unaware. None had been as powerful as the Trimuril; however, if his prose were inspired, his reflexes sharp, and his luck strong, he would stand a chance.

Nicodemus peeled paragraphs from his shoulder that covered his body with textual mesh to contain his body heat. He had learned the hard way that some deities—particularly those molded upon snakes, insects, and fish—could see heat.

Next he pulled a text from his forearm that coiled into a wide breathing tube. The spell carried his breath down to his feet and then broke out into a wide alluvial fan that spread his exhalations out, making the heat and composition of his breath harder for deities to detect.

Slowly, he stole among the crowd of kneeling dignitaries. Among their murmurings, he had a better chance of hiding. Again his legs ached with fatigue.

Around him, the Ixonian dignitaries whispered. Heads were turning as they tried to discern where Nicodemus or the Trimuril had gone. Nicodemus bent his tired legs and put the weight on the balls of his feet. He had to be ready to jump away from anyone who might accidently bump into him.

Time to wait. Slowly the murmuring subsided. Anticipation grew. The floating palace creaked. Water lapped against wood. Distant voices chanted.

Nicodemus began to wonder how the contest would be decided. He had thought the Trimuril would try to find him. But he had not challenged the goddess to find him; he had challenged her to a game of concealment.

The dignitaries began to shift, their anxiety lessening, boredom threatening. Nicodemus was becoming uncomfortably hot inside his spells. Slowly he stood up straight to relieve the ache in his thighs. So, how could he win? Discover the Trimuril, he supposed.

Carefully he cast a fine spray of indigo sentence fragments written to attach themselves to unknown language. With luck the linguistic spray would be thin enough to avoid whatever textual detection the Trimuril had and yet could adhere to any concealing godspells.

With each gesture, Nicodemus cast a wave of dim indigo that rolled away from him like heavy mist. The linguistic tide rolled out among the audience. The runes formed faint nimbuses around two men wearing blue hydromancer robes. But the spaces between the members of the audience remained clear. The Trimuril did not seem to be near Nicodemus.

Nicodemus stole back toward the dais, casting faint waves of indigo text as he went. Again Nicodemus's spells rolled out but found no purchase.

In the gloom, Nicodemus could now see the rash blooming across Leandra's cheeks. He stepped toward her but then stopped for fear that he might step on some spell the Trimuril had cast as a pressure-sensitive trap.

Again Nicodemus cast out waves of the indigo sentence fragments. The runes formed nimbuses around the shark and the wrestling god. But there was no sign of a concealed deity near them. Then he cast the spells through his wife's party. A nimbus formed around Francesca and her student but revealed nothing else. So Nicodemus cast his spells onto the dais. His texts adhered to the Sacred Regent, but still no sign of the Trimuril.

Running out of ideas, Nicodemus cast his spells into the room's corners but found nothing. So he cast again into the audience of dignitaries. Again, nothing. Now Nicodemus was sweating inside his spells.

He was just about to return to the dais when a creaky voice asked, "Isn't this great fun?"

Nicodemus froze.

"Where are you going to look next?" Ancestor Spider whispered in his ear as she had done for centuries, causing the rise of heroes, the downfall of villains.

Nicodemus did not know if he had been discovered or if the Trimuril was trying to fool him into thinking so. How could he tell?

"Maybe you should look up," the spider said.

Nicodemus did not dare to breathe.

"Really, I think you should look up."

At last Nicodemus had to exhale and did so as slowly as possible.

"Everyone is waiting."

Unsure of what else to do, Nicodemus slowly, very slowly looked up and saw . . . nothing. There was only the ceiling's ornate wooden rafters painted in reds, blues, and gold leaf. Nicodemus's stomach sank. Had had just fallen into a trap?

"Over here," the spider said to his left so suddenly that Nicodemus reflexively looked. What he saw in the darkness looked nothing so much as two slender legs, not an inch from his nose. He flinched, danced a few steps to one side, but somehow the legs followed. Now he could see that the leg connected to two delicate feet perched on the shoulder of his longvest.

Suddenly a disspell struck Nicodemus and his subtext broke into a coruscating chaos of violet and indigo prose that burned into nothing. Nicodemus looked up and saw that, impossibly, the Trimuril's stone incarnation was standing on his shoulder. Her lower two arms were pressed together in prayer, but the uppermost pair reached out and tore down one of the curtains.

Tropical sunlight poured down on Nicodemus, and the goddess on his shoulder.

The room broke into excited murmuring. Someone even started clapping. Nicodemus stood, flushed with embarrassment and confused about how he had lost.

The Trimuril jumped down to the floor, all six of her hands moving in different directions to maintain her balance. As she did so, her movements became fluid but then returned to the usual jerkiness.

"You fell onto my shoulder when I walked over here?"

"Oh no," Ancestor Spider said as the stone incarnation bowed. "Right after you disappeared, I hopped onto your shoulder. You see my bodily incarnation does not weigh more than a spider." She smiled and then conducted a quick dance, moving softly from one foot to another to demonstrate her lightness. "Most people assume all this stone is heavy." She danced a circle. "In fact, I am quite insubstantial." She stopped and looked at him with a smile.

"You were always on my shoulder?"

The Trimuril bowed with slight twitches.

Nicodemus realized the others in the room—Francesca, Leandra, their followers, the dignitaries—had shifted themselves to face the pool of light in which he now stood. It struck him how well positioned they were to be seen, as if on a stage.

Cold anger rolled through Nicodemus. He tried to hold on to the feeling, to feed it. He focused on the ridiculousness of this contest. What would the Trimuril gain by publically besting him? The cold anger gave Nicodemus a sudden idea. If he couldn't best the Trimuril by spellwrighting, then maybe . . . maybe he could best her by doing the opposite. Clenching his jaw, he stepped toward the Trimuril and held out his hand, palms up.

The goddess put her head to one side and regarded him. "We shall go another round? What fun. How do we play?"

"Give me your hands."

The Trimuril hesitated, regarding him with her infuriating smile. For a moment, Nicodemus thought she would refuse or would question what he would do next, either of which would be at least a small victory. But then the goddess reached out with her middle pair of hands to press her palms atop his.

Nicodemus closed his fingers around the goddess's and sent a shock of cacographic force up her arms, dispelling whatever godspells she had in those limbs. It was a risk, he knew; if the goddess treated it as an attack, several hundred furious deities might soon descend upon him. But the Trimuril only stepped backward, her movements again becoming fluid.

Nicodemus glared into the goddess's face, hoping to see shock or anger. But she was quite calm.

Stripped of their godspells, the Trimuril's middle arms had frozen. "The challenge then," Ancestor Spider said into his ear, "is to misspell my arms?"

Without hesitation, the goddess rotated her upper arms downward and her lower arms upward, so that they reached around the frozen middle pair. With fine twitches, she touched the palms of her upper and lower hands. Heat flushed across Nicodemus's face as the lower set of the goddess's arms went rigid.

Nicodemus felt his own back stiffen as he realized that he had lost again. Judging by the increase of whispering in the crowd, the audience had apprehended—perhaps by his posture or expression—that the goddess had prevailed. "Shall we play again?"

Nicodemus glared at the Trimuril, hating her. For the last thirty years, he had never met a neodemon that was his match, but they were all young deities. The Trimuril had a hundred times more devotees and experience than the most powerful neodemon he had ever defeated. Why had he ever agreed to this absurd contest?

The Trimuril gave another of her twitchy bows.

Nicodemus's frustration doubled watching her tiny lurches as she projected her soul elsewhere in the Floating City. Not only was she defeating him handily, she was doing so while governing an entire pantheon.

Suddenly a peculiar idea bloomed in Nicodemus's imagination. He had been reaching for challenges that involved his unique skills. Perhaps he should have been searching for challenges that involved how ordinary he could be. Anger drained out of Nicodemus and he let his posture and his expression relax.

Sensing a change, the Trimuril looked him up and down. "Another game?"

Nicodemus bowed and then got down onto his knees. The floor pressed against his ankles and knees, but he forced himself to focus.

"Is this another game you won't tell me about until the play has begun?" the Trimuril asked. All six of her arms again moved without hindrance. She had repaired all the damage his cacography had done.

"Goddess, I make a simple challenge," Nicodemus said. "I do not think you can imitate the following sequence of gestures."

"Ah, like a challenge of dance." The Trimuril nodded and then knelt into a pose identical to Nicodemus's.

Carefully, slowly, Nicodemus raised his right hand and held it out in front of him. A moment afterward, the Trimuril did the same with her lowermost right hand, her movements fluid.

Slowly Nicodemus brought up his other hand. So did the Trimuril. Nicodemus fought down a sudden flush of self-consciousness. But it didn't matter what he did so long as he kept at it. So he used his left hand to touch his elbow and then his wrist, the gestures meaningless. The Trimuril imitated him. He raised his right hand slightly and repeated the gesture. The Trimuril mirrored him.

The room had grown quiet but now there came the sound of shuffling. Nicodemus ignored this and repeated the nonsense gestures on his opposite side. Again, the goddess copied him. But now her enigmatic smile had changed; something about its character seemed harder.

Nicodemus held out his right hand, this time with his palm facing up and began the process over again. The Trimuril followed suit, but then the spider spoke in his ear, "How much longer will this particular game last? The pantheon is agitated."

Nicodemus did not respond but continued his meaningless gestures.

"Warden," Ancestor Spider said, "there are matters I must see to during this game for our mutual protection."

Nicodemus wondered if the Trimuril were causing these words in any other ears. He doubted it, so he said, "If the divine Trimuril must attend to her pantheon, I will humbly accept an annulment of this challenge."

The Trimuril's expression tensed and then relaxed into understanding. She tilted her head back to silently laugh. "Oh, oh!" the spider wheezed in his ear with great enjoyment. "Oh, I am beaten. What great fun!" The statue was still for a moment and then turned to the audience. "I concede defeat to the Lord Warden," the spider announced in his ear, and apparently in everyone else's for there rose a sudden confusion of voices.

"As the victor," the spider said, "the Warden of Lorn may now ask a favor. What would you like?"

"That my daughter be able to resume her investigation in the city immediately, that all the wardens be allowed to return to Chandralu if it would help assist her."

The Trimuril bowed again. "So it shall be. Now, let us return to the matters at hand." She gestured toward the dais.

Together Nicodemus and the Trimuril walked toward the throne. Around them the curtains were being drawn back and the throne room flooded with tropical sunlight.

Nicodemus saw Francesca and Ellen flicking green sentences to each other. Leandra looked steadier, but her facial rash had spread across the bridge of her nose.

"Why did you do it?" Nicodemus growled under his breath.

"For your daughter of course," Ancestor Spider replied.

"Why should you want to adopt her? It makes no sense."

"Oh, my friend, I have no desire to adopt her. But anyone can see that she's gotten herself into trouble. She's going to need help getting herself—and the rest of us—out of whatever she's gotten into. She's showed us how unwilling she was to accept help. So I need her indebted to someone—namely you or me—who could make her accept help. If I helped Leandra escape her mother, she would have accepted help from me. But now you have saved her from me, so she is in your debt."

When they reached the dais, the Trimuril leapt onto the stage and stood next to the throne.

"Don't you think," Nicodemus grumbled under his breath as he went to his previous seat, "that you could have tried talking to Lea first? Or at least warned me?"

"I could have," Ancestor Spider said nonchalantly, "but that wouldn't have been in the trickster style."

As Nicodemus knelt again, he saw Doria, Sir Claude, and Rory looking at him with concern. He held out a hand to them in what he hoped was a reassuring gesture.

"Besides," Ancestor Spider continued, "I think we both learned something today."

"What do you mean?"

"About her power, of course," Ancestor Spider whispered in his ear. "Who knew she could misspell any text I threw at her. It is troubling."

Nicodemus looked over at Leandra. She was again ignoring him and staring straight ahead.

The Sacred Regent held up his hands. "As our divine Trimuril has determined, the Warden of Ixos shall return to Chandralu as she sees fit. And now, I will call an end to this wardens' council and call for the formation of an immediate war council. All present are to await orders in the front hall." The old man made a gesture and some unseen priests began to beat loud, resonant drums.

The throne room came alive with chatter and movement. Nicodemus rose to his feet, still watching his daughter. Again Leandra glanced at him. But this time he saw not his little girl but a dangerous woman. For the first time, Nicodemus felt guilty relief that his daughter's ability to misspell was tied to her disease. If it were not so, she could break the world's every spell, human or divine.

CHAPTER TWENTY-FOUR

Francesca peered through the crowd, looking for Leandra.

Dignitaries and officials were milling about the front hall. Francesca perceived their indistinct chatter as a muddy colored sound. Some had formed cliques to discuss the political developments. Others were calling for servants to carry messages back to Chandralu. Nicodemus was in private conversation with the Sacred Regent. But Francesca didn't mind; there was someone she wanted to see without her husband.

"Shall I ask if the twins need help with Lolo?" Ellen asked.

"No, I need you to make our offer as discussed." Francesca looked over at her student. "Besides, if the twins couldn't handle Lolo, would you want to help?"

"Only if I could complain about it so bitterly that you would regret sending me."

"Such a great help you are, Ellen."

"It's not my fault that Lolo is a strange child. He gives me the shivers."

"I bet you were a strange child."

"Are you saying I'm not a strange adult?"

"If I lie to you, will it make you feel better?"

"Probably. By the way, who is the druid in your husband's service?"

"Rory of Calad? He's been with Nico a little over a year. Veteran of the White Forest Wars." She looked at the other woman. "Why?"

"No particular reason. He made a few interesting remarks to me in the throne room. I should like to take his measure since we're likely to be working with him in the coming days."

Francesca frowned at her for a moment, but then glimpsed Leandra's four-armed wrestling god . . . or goddess, rather. The divinity had changed genders between throne room and hall. On her daughter's other side stood the sea god who had to be Lolo's father.

Francesca held up a finger to silence Ellen. "Time for you to make our offer," she muttered and then strode through the crowd and bumped into a man who had accidently stepped back into her way. The unwitting dignitary turned, angry words perched on his lips, but on recognizing Francesca jumped into anxious apologies.

When Francesca planted herself before her daughter's party, the wrestling goddess and the sea god eyed her with apprehension. Leandra was leaning heavily on the wrestler's arm. There was a tightness around her eyes and mouth that hinted at the agony of a disease flare. A florid rash now covered her cheeks, nose, eyelids. The sight formed something tight and painful in Francesca's chest. Her suffering daughter . . .

Time seemed to slow. Those around them became unusually still. Then Francesca said, "Leandra," because despite having rehearsed a small speech about putting the past in the past, that was what came out.

"Francesca," Leandra replied in the same tone.

Francesca felt a sudden pang that her daughter had not called her "mother," but in the next instant she decided that she was being unfair. Hadn't she greeted her by name? Francesca cleared her throat. "You need to start taking the highest dose of the stress hormones."

During Leandra's childhood, Francesca had desperately sought a treatment. After much research, Francesca had deduced that her daughter's symptoms were similar to rheumatologic diseases in humans.

One of the few pieces of medical knowledge that had survived from the civilization on the Ancient Continent was that such diseases were caused by certain aspects of a body attacking others. Francesca had discovered that women who had mild forms of rheumatologic disease might experience relief from their symptoms toward the end of pregnancy. Curiously, other patients with rheumatologic disease who sustained traumatic injury experienced brief resolution of their symptoms when recovering.

Extensive experimentation in Port Mercy revealed that a stress hormone produced by the adrenal glands caused reduced rheumatologic symptoms. Francesca had used her influence on the Council of Starfall and in Port Mercy to assign several hydromancers to research how to re-create this specific stress hormone with the hydromancer's aqueous spells.

The results had been immediate and encouraging. By giving Leandra high doses of the medication, she could stop a disease flare; however, they also caused increased risk of infection, muscle wasting, weight gain. It was both a vital and a horrible drug. Unsurprisingly, deciding when and how much to give Leandra had led to some of the fiercest clashes between mother and daughter.

That is why, as soon as Francesca mentioned the drug, she knew it had been the wrong thing to say. To Francesca, the stress hormone symbolized everything she had done for her daughter. But to Leandra, the drug symbolized a childhood of misery. "Thank you, Francesca, I am well aware of how to treat my disease."

"Yes, of course," Francesca said automatically even though she had the powerful urge to remind her daughter to taper the dosage over several days to prevent withdrawal. "Of course. I am sorry."

Leandra's expression did not change.

Francesca noticed that Ellen now stood next to the sea god. Ellen flicked her wrist at the god and a golden sentence arced between them. The sea god looked at Ellen, his eyes narrowing.

Leandra had not noticed the exchange, but even so Francesca cleared her throat more loudly than before. "Is there anything I can do to help with your investigation in Chandralu?"

"No, thank you."

"You're sure?"

"Quite sure."

Ellen and the sea god were now whispering. Francesca kept her eyes on her daughter. "Maybe you will think of something later. I can check in on your party in a few hours."

"That won't be necessary."

"But perhaps you would reconsider that . . ." Francesca paused as her frustration rose. She had imagined this reunion so many times, and now she was spoiling it. "Lea . . . I'm sorry."

Her daughter's face remained stony.

"Lea, everything that happened . . . all those years ago in Port Mercy . . . I'm sorry."

"There's no need to revisit the matter."

"I just wanted . . . to say that I am sorry."

Leandra let another moment stretch out before she nodded. "The Sacred Regent has given me quarters in the Floating Palace, and I need to rest before returning to the city." She paused again. "But perhaps we'll talk tomorrow."

Frustration grew hot in Francesca. She had apologized, hadn't she? But with great will, she kept her face neutral and nodded. "I hope we do."

Then Leandra nodded to her wrestling goddess and they made for the other end of the hall. The crowd cleared a path for them as they went.

"Well?" Francesca asked.

Ellen held out a dim green sentence. Francesca took it and translated it into "*He's a shark god named Holokai from a large island in the Inner Chain. His requisites are to destroy—and by that I assume he means "eat"—divinities that might threaten his island and to produce a son who will lead the islanders to glory.*"

Francesca chewed her lip for a moment and then handed back a reply. "*Lea must have refitted his requisite to her purposes as Warden. But how could the Trimuril allow a deity who does such horrible things to women to exist? Forces should have been exerted on his cult to change that requisite. Is Lea aware of his requisite for a son?*"

Ellen replied. "*He claimed that she is, but neither he nor Leandra seem to know about Lolo. He had apparently been trying for a very long time to produce a child . . . with Lea.*"

Francesca shuddered as she remembered the teeth within the uterus. What was Lea thinking? "*And a meeting on the balcony?*"

Ellen took the question and flicked back the answer: "*He agreed but demanded that we give him Lolo right away.*"

Francesca snorted and was about to reply when someone approached. She looked up to see Rory of Calad. "Lady Warden," the redheaded man said with a bow, "the Lord Warden has just emerged from the throne room and asks you to join him."

Francesca nodded. "Lead the way, Druid."

They found Nicodemus on the throne room steps with his hydromancer, Magistra Doria Kokalas, and his Lornish highsmith, whom Francesca had not yet met. She took a moment to examine her husband. Their previous reunion had been so brief, so urgent. He was standing straight, his expression controlled, and yet something had changed.

He was still beautiful. His skin was still a smooth dark olive, his eyes still bright green, his longvest still outlined his muscular arms and shoulders. There was more silver in his long black hair. And his still beardless face had become more careworn. But there was something else—around his eyes perhaps—that suggested a deep weariness. Francesca felt a thrill of fear for her mortal husband. How much longer did she have with him?

On seeing her, the tension around Nicodemus's eyes lessened. He walked down the steps and when she held out her hands he took them and kissed her cheeks. They began walking toward the end of the hall, arm in arm, as they would have at a reception in the Southern kingdoms. It was only after a few steps that Francesca realized it would have been more in keeping with Ixonian custom to bow to each other and walk side by side.

"Have you talked to Lea?"

"I did. It could have gone . . . better. She is in a bad flare. I tried to talk to her about her medications, but . . ."

"It could have gone better?" Nicodemus finished.

"You could say that."

He sighed. "Did you make things worse?"

Francesca tightened her jaw. "I did not . . . You know, it is not entirely my fault that things are rocky between us. She is not the most reasonable daughter."

"Yes, of course," Nicodemus replied wearily.

"And it is not as if you are always able to make her see sense."

"I'm sorry, my love; I misspoke. I should have asked if the two of you were on better or worse terms."

Francesca balled her hands into fists and then relaxed them. "She did say that we might speak again. Once she gets settled in, I'll see if she'll let me talk to her about the stress hormones and—"

"Don't you think it would be better if I went?"

"Oh, so you want to manage her medication?"

"She's been managing her own medications for ten years now. If you think it's important that she see a physician, I can take Doria."

Francesca glanced back at the old hydromancer, who bowed. Frustration again boiled through Francesca even though Nicodemus's idea was a good one. Doria was an excellent physician and a hydromancer besides; using her aqueous spells, she could forge more of the stress hormone or change its potency. And yet . . . and yet . . . "How are Lea and I supposed to make peace if you keep us from seeing each other?"

"I'm not keeping you from seeing each other," Nicodemus said as they came to the bottom of a stairway and stopped. "I just think that when she is dealing with a disease flare, it might be hard for her to have a productive conversation with you given . . . given your history."

"Without that 'history,' as you put it, Lea would have died."

"I don't doubt it."

"You don't doubt it, but you never took part in it. If I had been as nonchalant about Leandra's disease as you were, she'd be dead."

"I'm not a physician; I couldn't have done what you did. I am fortunate to have you. I was just trying to support both my wife and my daughter."

You mean you wanted to be liked, Francesca thought. You wanted to be the lenient parent. You left the bitter task of treating her disease to me. And when the moment of crisis came in Port Mercy, I was the one who had to make the hard decision and now our daughter hates me but not you.

Somehow Francesca managed to keep silent, in part because she had already made these complaints to her husband. Also she knew that Nicodemus had been telling the truth, that he was doing his best for wife and daughter.

"Let me go to her," Nicodemus said. "Please. You can see her afterward."

She looked at his haggard expression and then felt a confusion of emotions. There was again a premonition of the grief his mortality would bring. There was her continued frustration and bitterness. But now there was also regret for something lost. Not an hour ago, at their reunion, he had looked at her and seen the beautiful, dangerous creature with whom he had fallen in love. His face had been alive with desire. Now he stared at her with exhaustion. Now he saw only an angry, unreasonable mother. She had been meaning to tell him about Lolo, but now she changed her mind. She was sure that he would object to her plan or insist that he join it.

Slowly she exhaled. "Very well, you can go see her. And now that I think of it, perhaps you should let her rest for a bit beforehand."

"That sounds wise."

Francesca nodded. "I have to meet with my two druids and tell them what has happened. I'll see you in our quarters afterward."

He gave her a slight smile and squeezed her hand. "Thank you, my love."

She felt something loosen in her chest.

"There is something else . . ." Nicodemus said hesitantly and then glanced about. "Lea is in some kind of trouble we don't know about. That's why the Trimuril played that little game; she wanted Lea to be indebted to someone so that she would accept help."

"That was clever. Lea's too proud to ever have accepted help otherwise."

"Maybe, but there is something I didn't tell the Trimuril. When I took down the River Thief, she was wearing Leandra's face?"

"Her what?"

"Her face. The neodemon was wearing Leandra's face."

"But why would she do that?"

"I don't know, and we need to find out. That's another reason you should let me talk to her first."

Francesca looked into her husband's green eyes. "Very well, talk to her and I'll tend to my business." She let go of his hand and started up the stairs, but as she went she noticed that beside her Ellen was talking to Rory.

"My Lady Warden," Ellen said casually, "the druid here and I were just discussing some of the techniques the Lord Warden's party has used to convert neodemons. They might be of use to us. May I finish our conversation before joining you?"

At first, Francesca thought this was a ploy to get out of having to deal with Lolo. But then Francesca realized Ellen had spoken with unusual warmth. She was also standing uncharacteristically close to the druid.

Francesca looked at the man, who bowed his head respectfully. The red hair and freckles looked good on his boyish face.

Then Francesca understood. She was mildly surprised. But what was the harm? "Yes, that is a good idea, Magistra. In fact, would you and the druid please write up a brief comparison of our methods so that we might give them to the rest of our party?"

Ellen smiled conspiratorially. "Of course, Lady Warden."

Francesca was about to say more but then she looked past Ellen and Rory to Nicodemus. He was looking up at her with the most peculiar expression, his mouth flat with something like fear. As she watched, he pointedly looked at Rory, then Ellen, then back to her. Very slightly, he shook his head.

Francesca fought the urge to frown. Whatever on earth was Nicodemus trying to tell her? Behind her husband, his Lornish highsmith was staring with great amusement at Rory and Ellen. Did the druid have some other woman? Francesca doubted it; she would have remembered Nicodemus mentioning that.

She looked back at Ellen and Rory, who both seemed happy in each other's company. Surely there was no harm in letting them flirt. "Yes, Magistra," Francesca said, "please do come find me after you have a thorough discussion."

Ellen nodded but farther down the stairs Nicodemus shook his head, now with pronounced vehemence. Beside him, the Lornish highsmith looked as if he might start laughing. How strange they both were being.

"I will see you soon, husband," she said and then walked up the rest of the stairs, all the time wondering what Nicodemus could possibly have against Rory flirting with an intelligent and pretty woman.

CHAPTER TWENTY-FIVE

rancesca waited on the balcony as the shark god circled. Holokai, she reminded herself, that was his name. In his human incarnation, he was pretending to inspect the rooms below her daughter's quarters for possible threats. He moved closer with each pass, circling.

Ignoring him, Francesca put aside her anxieties about Leandra. She studied the blue tropical sky. The balcony, which was on the second floor of the Floating Palace, presently faced the tunnel to Chandralu and the blocky monastery. The dark staircase cut switchbacks as it climbed the crater's inner slope to the volcano's peak.

Behind her, bare feet slapped against wooden planks. Francesca turned to see that Holokai had finally stepped out onto the balcony. Staring with dark eyes, he stopped five feet away from her. He was about to speak when she held up a warning finger. From her belt purse she pulled a single sheet of paper and peeled from it a subrosa spell. With a wrist flick, she cast the spell above them where it bloomed into a wide cage of sound-deadening petals of silvery Magnus prose. When it completed, Francesca nodded. "You can speak now. Not even the Trimuril can overhear us."

The shark god was glaring at her. "Where's my son?"

Francesca smiled politely. "Are you addressing me?"

His dark eyes widened. "You see anyone else out here, hey?"

Francesca looked him up and down.

"Where's my son?"

She turned away. "Leave," she said flatly. "I don't deal with petty gods who don't know their place."

A spasm of fury scurried across his face. "Don't you—" His voice died as she stepped toward him.

"Listen carefully, you oversized mackerel, maybe you never came across anything in the ocean to frighten you, maybe hunting neodemons with my daughter never challenged you, but now you are trifling with forces that will chew you into chum. You felt it when you swam under my boat last night. At sea, you knew how much danger you were in. That's why you swam away then and why you will scurry away now."

He blinked at her, taken aback. Away from his element, the shark god was no match for her. That was true. But she was exaggerating. At sea, she had foreseen that Holokai was one of the few souls who could kill her in the coming days. Of course, he didn't need to know that.

The shark god blinked again, pulled his lips back slightly. "You wanted this meeting. And if you have my—"

"I invited you here," Francesca interrupted to make sure he never felt in control, "to discuss the future of your son. That was before I knew you couldn't match wits against a brain-damaged goat. So you're going to walk away from me before I tear you a fresh set of gills, and you're going to forget that you ever had a son because you're clearly too God-of-god's damned stupid to raise one." She took another step forward.

The shark god reflexively stepped back, but again his lips pulled back. "Bit hypocritical for you to lecture anyone about bringing up a child, hey Francesca? Maybe I'll go ask Lea what she thinks—"

Francesca laughed. "Excellent idea, tell Leandra. How do you think she'll react to learning you came to talk to me without her knowledge?"

Another spasm of fury moved across the shark god's face.

"Maybe I should tell her you slipped away to meet me?"

Holokai's eyes started to blacken.

Francesca knew better than to back down. She showed her own teeth and stepped forward again. "That's right, guppy. You want to solve it that way, you just go right ahead."

Again the shark god blinked, took another step back. His eyes whitened.

Francesca nodded. "Good. Do you want to try this again?"

He stared at her for a long moment, and then said, "For the sake of my son."

She only watched him coldly.

At last, and with some difficulty, he said, "Lady Warden, I am here because of your . . . invitation."

"Yes, thank you for coming, honored sea god. I wish to discuss the issue of your son."

"I didn't know I was a father. Are you sure you have my son?"

Francesca gestured down to the lake. The shark god turned and saw a small floating pavilion, on the edges of which sat Kenna, her white druid robes hiked up to her knees and her pale legs dangling in the water. She was looking up toward the balcony. A few feet away, her brother was dogpaddling next to Lolo. The childish god was smiling and then began to splash Tam, who pretended to be shocked. This precipitated more smiling, splashing.

The shark god shifted his feet but did not change his expression. "He's mine? Are we sure?"

Francesca recognized the desire in the question. "He's happy in this lake's fresh water, but when I dropped him into ocean, he grew fins and serrated teeth. And perhaps you will want to see this." She raised her hand.

Down on the floating pavilion, Kenna returned the gesture and then touched the wooden plank beside her. A blue glow grew where her finger touched wood. A small part of the pavilion broke off to float on its own. The raft sprouted lily pads across the water and then grew a bud that opened into a lotus blossom.

Lolo pointed at the druidic bloom, his eyes wide. With his chubby arms he paddled over to the druidic construct. With difficulty he tried to haul himself up onto it. Tam swam behind him, and gave him a slight push. As Lolo climbed onto the lotus spell, the sun shone on his back and the rows of scars that formed a shark bite. They had had come from the uterus of the child's poor mother. Holokai drew in a sharp breath.

"His mother was a devotee in the Pillow House," Francesca said.

"But that was only a few days ago."

"These things happen with demigods. Some are born old and grow young. Some start life with adult minds. In Lolo's case—"

"Lolo? You named my son 'crazy?'"

"It is what the children of the orphanage named him. The orphanage you abandoned him to."

"I didn't abandon him; I didn't even know about him! I didn't . . ." His eyes narrowed and he seemed to become thoughtful. "He must be why I was feeling so strong a few days before Lea took us to see the smuggler. I thought those in my cult had become more prayerful . . . but actually I had fulfilled the requisite of providing the son they had been praying for."

Leandra didn't know what he was talking about and didn't care. "Lolo's gestation was particularly rapid," she said sternly to get his attention. "His nature filled his mother's uterus with shark's teeth that cut into his back. She bled to death after giving birth to him. He knows this, on some level, and it terrifies him."

Holokai's mouth bent downward in pain. "Not his fault."

"No, it's yours."

The shark god glared at her but said nothing.

"Lolo has been aging two years a day. You've abandoned him for the first six years of his life. Vital years. Thank the God-of-gods someone on the Floating City arranged for him to be placed into the orphanage."

"That would be one of the priests my devotees have paid off to watch out for any possible child of mine," Holokai growled. "Seems he never counted on things developing so quickly. But still, he'll have to answer to me why he didn't get a message to me faster."

"You have done this to other woman?"

The shark god looked back to Lolo and did not answer.

"Disgusting," Leandra sneered. "You were going to do that to my daughter."

He shook his head. "She said she wasn't in any danger of having a baby."

"But you knew about the danger to the other women?"

He flared his nostrils. "It's happened very rarely before. Most often, no child is produced or the pregnancy stops on its own."

"And you hid from Lea the few women whose bodies were filled with shark teeth?"

"It's in my requisites. It's nothing I can help."

"No, I don't suppose you can. How is it the Trimuril hasn't found a way to stop your devotees from praying for such a gruesome thing?"

He didn't respond.

"So that's how you're written: The demigod son your devotees pray for over anything else?"

Again he glared at her.

"This time silence won't get you out of answering. Before we can talk about Lolo's future, I need to know if you will put him before Leandra."

"She knows I must."

"But she doesn't yet know you have a son. And we will keep it that way until I am satisfied that you can be trusted with Lolo."

"You have no right."

"That child has known me for what is a year of his life. My officers and I are already more of a family to him than anyone else. Creator in heaven, in five days he's going to be an adolescent shark god. Do you have even the slightest idea of the trouble he could get himself into?"

"You still have no right!"

"I have a right to protect my daughter."

Holokai narrowed his eyes. "She can protect herself."

"If that's so, then you'll have your son on your island before you know it."

The shark god rolled his shoulders, let out a breath as if he were considering something.

"This will be easier for everyone, including you and your son, if you real-ize you've been broken to my will. You're a god of blood. You know when you've lost a fight. You're mine now."

Silence.

"You say it or I send you back to my daughter and I keep your son."

"Then I'm yours."

"Good. So, I need to know what Leandra was hiding in the throne room today."

"What she was hiding?"

"Don't make me think you're any dumber because I already think you'd need instructions on how to drool. Lea *needed* to get back to the city tonight. She induced a disease flare to keep the Trimuril from finding out why. It can't be simply to investigate the thugs attacking petty deities."

"It's not."

"Well then, why?"

"If I am going to do this for you, I need to know what I'm getting into. There're things I need to know before I go back to Lea."

"Such as?"

"Such as what happened fourteen years ago in Port Mercy? Why does Lea hate you so much?"

"Fair enough. You should know how to keep things from getting worse between Lea and me. But first, tell me why does she need to go back to Chan-dralu today? Does she know who's behind the attacks on petty deities? Is it the empire or the Cult of the Undivided Society? Or is it some criminal organization?"

Holokai was silent for a moment. Then he looked back toward Lolo. The boyish god was standing on the raft and periodically dodging Tam, who was trying to tickle him. At last, Holokai said, "She knows it's not the Undivided Society."

Francesca frowned. "How?"

"Because," Holokai said with a sigh, "the Cult of the Undivided Society worships Leandra."

CHAPTER TWENTY-SIX

Leandra looked with trepidation into the chamber pot. Her gut clenched when she saw that her urine was tea-dark and foamy.

This flare was going to be a horror.

Her joints ached, a rash bloomed across her cheeks, fatigue weighed on her like a wet blanket, and now any deep breath flashed pain through her chest. This last symptom frightened her most. When she was eleven, a severe flare had produced the same pain. For hours, her mother had listened to her chest and thumped her back before deciding that her heart was surrounded by dangerous amounts of fluid. So Francesca had written a six-inch needlelike spell and then inserted it just below Leandra's sternum and pushed it up to her heart. After Francesca had drained the fluid, Leandra felt a weight removed from her chest. She had drawn in long, hungry breaths.

Ever since, Leandra had remembered her mother's tense expression as she had pressed the needle up into her chest. Leandra had associated that cold, focused expression with the unfairness of childhood disease. But now, she wondered what it had been like to be her mother. How horrible it must have been to hold that needle.

And yet . . . there was always something implacable about her mother's love. Fourteen years ago in Port Mercy . . .

Leandra forced her thoughts elsewhere. She washed up and went back to the common room of her quarters. Outside, late-afternoon sunlight was pouring down on the Floating City.

Dhrun stood looking out the window, her back to Lea. The goddess's upper arms were absently brushing back her short black hair and her lower arms were resting on the windowsill. She turned around. "Are you all right?"

"I will be," she said while gingerly sitting on her daybed. She took another deep breath and thought that the resulting pain was less than before.

Dhrun sat beside her. "Should we get a physician?"

"I've already taken a high dose of the stress hormone. There's nothing else a physician might do." Except, she did not say, stick a needle in my heart. But if things got worse . . . well . . . there should still be enough time to call for her mother.

"Maybe you should let me go in your place to meet with the smuggler."

"Not you too." Before Holokai had gone to search the surrounding rooms for threats, he had tried to argue Leandra into letting him do the same thing.

"Lea," Dhrun said gently, "things are in a bad way. Your father took down the River Thief."

Leandra pressed a hand to her head and then laid herself down onto the daybed. "He did, the bastard. Clever of him to lie and say he was going after the other neodemon."

"Maybe it's time we approached your father? Maybe your mother as well?"

"That'd be disastrous."

"Do we have another choice? The empire is threatening and there's some unknown deity in the bay. Not to mention our lack of funds. Maybe your father would be able to limit the damage."

Leandra shook her head again. "He's too committed to maintaining peace between empire and league. Everything we've worked for would fall apart. You're a goddess of victory, would you ever want to concede defeat?"

Dhrun paused. "There's a difference between losing a point and losing a match."

"Besides, from what I know of my future, I am more likely to murder my father than seek his help."

"Why should that be?"

"I think my father knows more about our cause than he was letting on. It might be a matter of choosing between him and our cause."

"Well then, at least things are getting better with your mother."

"Don't underestimate her ability to drive me insane. Which reminds me . . . Sometimes high doses of the stress hormone can drive people mad. Literally, they can become psychotic. If I lose it, I'm counting on you to talk me back to normal."

"I can try, but you were never that normal to begin with," Dhrun said, patting Leandra's hand. It was a friendly, protective gesture. Leandra felt a tightness in her chest that had nothing to do with her disease. She took Dhrun's hand, their fingers interlacing. "You've become a good friend."

Dhrun only gave her hand a squeeze. Leandra closed her eyes. If only she could sleep then maybe the world wouldn't weigh so heavily. Dhrun's gentle touch on her hand, the distant chanting on the lake, they washed over Leandra. She felt uncomfortably hot. A flute seemed to be playing far away, the same four notes over and over. She wondered why Holokai had not yet returned. She wondered if she was dreaming.

Then there came a sound, what she could not tell, and Dhrun's hand left hers. A screen door slid open. "Lea," Dhrun's gentle voice spoke again.

A hand gently ran across her face. Leandra groaned as she came more completely awake and aware of the pain in her gut and her joints.

"Lea, your father is here. He wants to see you. Should I ask him to come back?"

Groaning again, Leandra opened her eyes and saw that light was slanting into the window at a different angle. She'd fallen asleep. "No, no," she said and tried to sit up. Dhrun helped her up. She took a deep breath and found that the chest pain was still there but less. It was a good sign. "Help me back to the chamber pot."

Once in private, Leandra discovered that her urine was still dark and frothy. Her ankles were beginning to swell.

After washing up, she tottered back to her daybed and told Dhrun to bring her father in.

As the goddess pulled back the screen door, Leandra tried to straighten out her hair.

Her father stepped into the room, trailed by the hydromancer who had advised him for so long. He approached Leandra as if he might embrace her, but seeing her flat expression, stopped a few feet away. "Hello, Lea," he said with a slight smile. That was brave of him, she thought, the rash on her face must look frightening.

She nodded. "Father."

"How are you feeling?"

"Oh, you know," she said with faked nonchalance and shrugged her shoulders, "peachy."

"I'm sorry I lied to you about going after the River Thief."

"Nothing that I wouldn't have done to you."

"Are you sure you're well enough to go back to Chandralu tonight?"

Leandra clenched her jaw. Her father only ever worried about the problem before him and what role he should fill to resolve it. He could change his personality almost instantly. Leandra had seen him shift from a placid bureaucrat to a bloodthirsty warrior, from a coldhearted assassin to a pacifistic diplomat. Now he was playing the worried father. Leandra was never sure if he had any solid aspect to his personality. It infuriated her mostly because she was so like her father.

Leandra was about to tell Nicodemus that she was capable of making her own decisions when he added, "I brought my physician along in case you'd like to see her instead of your mother."

The heat building inside Leandra cooled. It was a thoughtful gesture. She looked at the physician in the blue robes. The old woman's eyes were beginning to cloud. "You trained in Port Mercy?"

"I did, my Lady Warden."

"Did you know my mother?"

"No, my Lady Warden."

There followed a silence. "I do have one question I would ask you . . . alone."

"I'll step out into the hall," Nicodemus said and retreated.

The hydromancer waited for him to go before saying, "My title is Magistra Doria Kokalas, but if you prefer, call me Doria."

"You know about my condition?"

She nodded.

"Once, as a girl, a disease flare put fluid around my heart? I'm worried that might be happening again."

"What makes you worried about that?"

"When I take a deep breath, I have this pain in my chest."

The hydromancer's eyes tensed. "Might I examine you?" When Leandra nodded, the physician listened to her chest. She thumped her back, pressed on her belly, and then spent what seemed an absurdly long time staring at her neck while Leandra took deep breaths.

Next Doria removed a vial of water that when poured on Leandra's right bicep formed a wide band that contracted to an uncomfortable tightness and then slowly relaxed. Mysteriously a stream of water connected itself to one of the physician's ears.

When Leandra had dressed again, Doria said, "You might have some fluid around your heart or your lungs, but I don't hear the rubbing sound that commonly accompanies such inflammation. I don't appreciate a paradoxical pulse or other concerning signs." She gestured to Leandra's neck as if that would make the things obvious. "If there is fluid around your heart, it doesn't seem to be enough to interfere with your heart's function."

With great relief, Leandra thanked the physician. "I've already taken the high dose of the stress hormone. Is there anything else I should do?"

"Not right now. But I would want you to be near a physician in case the swelling around the heart were to worsen."

Leandra nodded. "Thank you, Doria."

The old woman nodded. "I am happy to be of service. Would you like me to call on you again?"

"If possible. But for now, would you send in my father?"

The hydromancer bowed and left the room. There followed the sliding of the screen door and Nicodemus returned. "Is everything all right?"

"Better than I had feared," she said. "Thank you."

He sat beside her. "What else can I do for you?"

"You've already done too much, including playing whatever foolish game the Trimuril dragged you into."

"Lea, why did you induce this flare?"

"I need to get back to Chandralu."

"Why?"

Her gut went cold. "I'm investigating those who have been attacking petty deities in the city. If they are tied to either the imperial threat or your neodemon of Feather Island, we must know about it soon."

"You're sure you're well enough?"

"After speaking to your physician, I am."

"All right, Lea, I trust you. But . . . there's something else."

Leandra's heart began to strike. "Yes?"

"When I took down the River Thief—"

"Dad," she interrupted, her fear of what he might say next and what she might have to do rising, "could you fetch me a cup of water." She motioned to a pitcher across the room.

He paused as if confused before walking over to the pitcher.

Creator, Leandra prayed, don't let him say it. Don't let him know. Please, anyone but him. Don't make me kill him.

"Here," he said.

When she accepted the cup, Leandra allowed the pain to show in her expression.

He watched her for a moment and then said, "Lea, when I took down the River Thief, she was wearing your face."

Leandra's heart hammered. She was going to have to kill him. There was no way out . . . unless . . . "Oh?" she asked in a voice that by some miracle she kept calm. "Was she?"

Nicodemus's green eyes searched her face. "You don't seem surprised."

"Something similar happened about five years ago," she lied. "In a village on the Matrunda . . . I deconstructed a rival village's alligator neodemon, who had been terrorizing their fisherman. The local village goddess assumed my features to fool the villagers into thinking that it was she who had taken the neodemon down. I think she did it unconsciously. The villagers prayed more fervently to her and her cult grew. That is until my officers heard about what she'd done. After we applied a little pressure on her, she decided not to wear my face again."

Nicodemus was looking into her eyes. "You think the River Thief was impersonating you?"

"I can't think of any other reason why she should have looked like me. Can you?"

"No . . . no. But Lea, why was the River Thief surprised when I said that she had your face?"

"I'm sure she wasn't aware that she had taken on my likeness. Crafty deities alter their manifestations without realizing it. When the worshipers see the changes, they incorporate it into the god's mythologies. And you know how deities believe in their own mythologies. If she's been using my face for a while, the River Thief probably thought it was the other way around— that I had her face."

Nicodemus frowned. "She did say that . . ."

Leandra knew that she was right because she had watched the River Thief slowly and unknowingly take on her likeness.

Nicodemus was still frowning. "But, Lea, aren't you worried that . . . something else is happening?"

"Like what?"

"Well, I suppose I can't think of anything. But, Lea, have you gotten into any kind of trouble?"

"No more than the rest of us."

"And is there anything else you know that would help us?"

"No, Dad, I wish I did," she lied, hopeful for the first time that she wouldn't have to kill her father after all. For that reason, she put her hand down on the bed between them.

He looked down at her hand.

Because of his fluency in Language Prime and his cacography, there were few living things her father could touch without giving them deadly cancer curses. Her mother was one. She was another.

Slowly she took his hand. The pain in his face, which she had not previously noticed, fell away.

It was the wrong thing to do. Leandra knew that. She had done worse— lied, cheated, stolen, killed—but she didn't have many regrets. But now, she regretted how easily she manipulated him.

He gave her a smile, mundane, paternal. She could see the wrinkles around his eyes, the silver in his hair. After everything that had happened to him, he was still just a man in middle age, a man looking at his daughter whom he had greatly underestimated and whom he did not in the least understand. Hollowness opened up in Leandra's chest. Even so she said, "Thank you again for bringing your physician. I didn't want to see mother."

"She does love you."

"I don't want to discuss that now."

"I know I don't understand what it's like to have your condition, but . . . but well, I spent a lot of my childhood feeling like I was broken. It made it hard for me to accept help . . ."

Irritation flashed through the tenderness she had been feeling. "It's not the same. A disability and a disease are different things."

"I know they are, sweetheart, but we do have some things in common. You inherited my misspelling but in you it caused a disease."

"And that's the point, Dad, your cacography isn't going to kill you," she said with more heat than she intended. "You and I don't have that in common at all. My disease is going to kill me and there's nothing either of us or anyone else can do about it."

"I'm sorry that . . . I am not saying it right. It's just . . . that I worry on some level you won't accept help from me because you blame me. I wouldn't fault you. I wanted better for you."

"Dad, that's not it."

He studied her face again and then nodded. "Okay . . . Okay . . . You know the Trimuril played that stupid game today because she wanted you to be indebted to her or to me so that you would accept help from one of us."

Leandra rolled her eyes. "Sounds like her."

"Would you accept help from me?"

She looked into his green eyes, saw the uncertainty. "Yes, Dad," she lied. "When I need help, I will come to you."

The wrinkles around his eyes seemed to lessen.

Leandra was amazed that she could so completely fool her father. Part of her was grateful that she could do so. Part of her was frightened. And, if she was brutally honest with herself, part of her was just a little bit angry that her father should be so clueless. As infuriating as Francesca could be, she would never let her get away with any of this shit.

"Can I check on you later?" Nicodemus asked.

"I'm going into Chandralu. I won't be back in the Floating City tonight,"

Leandra said, hoping that she wouldn't return until the prophecy of murdering someone she loved was resolved.

"Fran and I have to attend the war council, but I doubt it'll run much past sundown. I can likely return to the family compound. You could see me there."

Leandra tried not to flinch. That would be close enough to her that she might still have to kill him. "What do you plan to do other than check on me?"

Nicodemus's gaze became unfocused. "I might need to prepare another metaspell."

"In case Aunt Vivian casts one of her metaspells?"

"It's horrible to imagine things getting as bad as that, but . . . better to have it and not need it than the other way around." He returned from a distant thought and put both of his hands on hers. "Heaven willing, I'll finish up the councils on the Floating City and then see you again in the family compound?"

God-of-gods let's hope not. "Maybe."

"If you need me sooner, you'll come find me in the compound?"

"I will, Dad." She kissed him on the cheek, hating herself for manipulating him so easily.

He squeezed her hand again and then got up to leave. "Keep yourself safe, okay?"

"I will."

He nodded back and went out.

Leandra waited for as long as she could stand before calling for Dhrun.

The screen door slid and the four-armed goddess stepped back into the room.

"We're going straight to Thaddeus as soon as Holokai gets back. Where is that stupid fish?"

"I'll get everything ready." Dhrun bowed. "I don't know about Holokai . . . How was the conversation with your father?"

"I fooled him this time, but mother isn't going to be satisfied with his report. She'll keep pushing. That's why . . ." She paused. "That's why we have to get to Thaddeus immediately. If his spell to stop me from loving doesn't work, then I'm sure . . ." Suddenly she had to blink rapidly. "Then I'm sure I'll have to kill my father."

CHAPTER TWENTY-SEVEN

The Cult of the Undivided Society worships Leandra?" Francesca repeated in confusion. "My daughter, Leandra? How?"

Below them, Tam and Lolo were still splashing around, at play in the lake.

Holokai said, "It started after Port Mercy, when you and she fought. Problem is I don't know what exactly happened between the two of you. You'll have to tell me."

Francesca frowned. "You want me to tell you a private family matter?"

He shrugged and then smirked. "Doesn't matter to me. You were the one asking how the Cult came to worship Lea. I can't tell you how unless I know exactly what happened at Port Mercy."

Francesca's frown deepened as she thought it over. She had Holokai well enough under her control and there was nothing dangerous about his knowing the truth. She nodded. "So, sixteen or seventeen years ago, Lea and I were arguing so much about how to treat her disease that she let me talk her into enrolling in the academy for physicians at Port Mercy. I think mostly she wanted to learn enough to prove me wrong about something, maybe anything. She's not a spellwright, but the academy makes exceptions for those with influence. She was there only two years and a miserable student. But she was away from me and living on her own. We were all a little relieved."

Francesca watched Lolo try to pull Tam underwater. With a laugh the druid obliged and pretended to be dragged underwater. Moments later they both came up sputtering and laughing.

Francesca continued her story. "Leandra met a young man named Tenili. Very handsome, very wealthy. A merchant prince from Besh-Lo, he said. He had connections in Port Mercy and in Verdant. They became lovers and, of course, Lea told her father and me nothing. Tenili told her he wanted to marry her and take her back to Verdant. What Lea didn't know was that he was in truth a minor but ancient Verdantine god of wind. He had cast some clever subtexts about himself to prevent her from seeing the red glow of his divine texts."

Francesca looked back at Holokai. "He was primarily a messenger for the Verdantine pantheon, the kingdom's priestly caste, and the more powerful orders of shamanistic spellwrights. But Vivian's metaspells changed Verdantine society. The deities weakened while the spellwrights grew in power. In particular the wizards gained more and more power in that kingdom. They wanted to weaken the Verdantine pantheon and any shamans who supported them. So the wizards politically isolated Tenili. They planned to attack and deconstruct him. Shortly before they did so, Tenili and his devotees snuck away to Port Mercy, where they were living in exile."

Holokai was frowning. "Did Lea know?"

Francesca shook her head. "Tenili was running a legitimate trading house, but my agents discovered he was in communication with the empress's court. At that time, Nicodemus and I were trading off the duty of Warden of Ixos. It was my year to do so, so I sailed to Port Mercy to investigate. When I landed, things were more strained than usual with Lea. I had no idea why. But then I began to close in on Tenili. Secretly he had agreed to deliver Leandra to the empress in return for an end to his exile."

Holokai grimaced. "This explains . . . a few things about Lea."

"It gets worse. The game between Tenili and me heated up. Two of my officers discovered his identity, but he killed them both before they could report to me. He finally convinced Leandra to run away with him to the empire, though how she could be so stupid still escapes me. In any case, the morning they were to sail, he took her to his trading house. Remember, she's only sixteen. She had iron in her soul even then, but she wasn't yet as wise or cynical as she is now."

The shark god nodded.

"After I discovered my dead agents and figured out who Tenili was and what he intended to do with my daughter, I rashly stormed his trading house. A shaman in Tenili's service, a skinwalker and the guardian of the house, killed my only surviving officer. Unfortunately for him, his attack also induced my draconic transformation."

Francesca paused to draw in a thoughtful breath. "It's never a good idea to separate a dragon from her daughter. So, I killed the skinwalker and began tearing the trading house apart. Inside, Tenili figured out what was happening and so confessed to Leandra. He begged for her forgiveness and promised he would convert for her and join the Ixonian pantheon. She was young and in love; she believed him. But as an avenging dragon, I couldn't be stopped. I kept after him. He was a god of the air, very nimble, and kept hiding behind Lea. She kept pleading his case. When I finally caught him . . . I ate him."

Holokai laughed humorlessly. "Not much else you could do. If there's anybody who'd understand about having to eat somebody, it's a shark god, hey?" He shook his head and looked down to Lolo. "You sorry for eating him?"

"I should be, but truly I'm only sorry I did it in front of Lea. He tried to sell my daughter to the empress; I couldn't let him live."

"You see why I will do anything for my boy?"

"Maybe you're not such a dumb fish after all. Why do you think I knew it would work to meet you like this?"

"You still have no right."

"We both want to make things better for our children. We can help each other."

"You're just telling a pretty story about the ugly thing you're doing."

"Fine, you want the ugly story? Cross me, and I'll raise Lolo as my own personal hostage."

He glared at her again, his eyes darkening by a shade. But when she held his gaze for a long moment, he looked away. "Don't leave much room for choice, do you?"

"None."

"Lea said that about you."

"I don't doubt it. Now, I believe you have something to tell me. How is it that my daughter has a cult?"

"So, my conversion, that's when I found out. I was incarnated twenty years ago by a village of Sea People on Mokumako Island. They prayed to me to consume their enemies, to defend them against the demons when the Disjunction comes, and to provide a son who would lead them to glory. At first, attacking the enemies meant attacking the rival factions on Mokumako Island. I was a young neodemon then, fearless, stupid. For five years, I destroyed other tribes of Sea People and wrecked merchant ships not owned by my devotees. It wasn't long before my cult controlled the island."

"That's when Lea came to take you down?"

"One night I found a young woman swimming alone in my sacred lagoon, which is taboo. I attacked her and of course it was Lea. She flared her disease and nearly killed me. One minute I was a fifteen-foot, two-ton shark, the next she dispelled me down to a scrawny fifteen-year-old boy. She left me with just enough strength to swim back to shore. Next night, she was again swimming in my lagoon. My high priests saw this and were afraid that I was too weak to enforce my own taboos. Their fear stopped them from praying to me. I'd been tangling with her for only a day, and she had me more helpless than an amberjack with a fishing hook through the gills."

Francesca smiled. "That's my girl."

"You ain't kidding. I had been incarnated long enough to know I was a pirate god and that sooner or later the Trimuril would try to either deconstruct me or take my ark hostage and enslave me in some divinity complex. I figured Lea was there to convert me and couldn't see any way to fight it. So I swam out to her in my human incarnation, expecting never to be free again."

His gaze became vague. "It was a moonless night. The two of us out there in the swells. She was nineteen years old then and this was one of her first commands. She hadn't yet been named a warden and feared that she wouldn't be and that you or her father would keep the title. So, she told me I had three choices. I could resist, and she'd deconstruct me and bring the royal fleet down on my island. I could convert and become a war god for the Trimuril. Or I could help her maintain her independence and stay free. If I went with that last choice, there'd be no turning back after she told me how."

"So you went with the third option."

"How could I resist? We swam ashore together, and she told my priests that the Creator had given her a special calling. She said that the world was a corrupt one in which the strong preyed upon the weak. She scorned the priests for using the power of prayer against their brother Ixonians. But it wasn't their fault that the world was so corrupt; the spellwrights had made it that way. She said that the league was no better than the empire. The only difference was that in the empire, cruelty was practiced by the spellwrights on the deities."

"She can't have meant that."

Holokai's forehead creased in surprise. "But she did. And, you know, she's convinced me."

"That the Creator has given her special purpose? That she's some kind of prophet?"

"Oh, no. That part's just for show. She's not got any more contact with the Creator than the rest of us. But she was serious about there being no difference between league and the empire. I have seen countless times what the empire does to their deities. It's horrific, torturing them, pulling them apart so their wizards can figure out how they work."

"And how have you seen this?"

"So that's the thing. What Leandra told the priests, she said that it was right that the wardens hunt down neodemons in the league. But, she said, just as the wardens struggled to save humans in the league from neodemons, they should also save the deities in the empire from the spellwrights."

Francesca pressed a hand to her mouth. "Leandra is the one smuggling the deities out of the empire?"

"She told my priests then that she had been sent to them by the Creator as punishment for what they had done to the island, that she would destroy their god and bring the royal fleet down upon them. But because their god had humbly sacrificed for them and agreed to swear allegiance to her, their cult was going to become one of the many that made up an undivided society of humanity and divinity. They were not to pray to her, but to continue to pray to me as I fought for an undivided society."

Holokai shrugged. "So they did. Lea has brought many other cults into the Undivided Society this way."

"How many?"

"Maybe two dozen. All of them small and well hidden, from all over the archipelago. She makes sure that her deities are free from Trimuril's influence. If the kingdom ever discovered the true Cult of the Undivided Society—" He paused then looked quizzically at Francesca. "By the way, you have figured out that all those rumors that go around about the Cult of the Undivided Society worshiping demons and all that are total nonsense."

"I had hoped you'd say so."

"I do say so. Anyway, to make sure the Trimuril wouldn't hold power over me, Lea directed my priests to pray for a trickster god who could fool the Trimuril into thinking that he was me. They incarnated him within a few days. He's my double, much weaker than I am, and it's his ark that floats somewhere on this lake. My ark is still back on my home island."

Francesca began to understand. "So that is how you can still have a requisite that allows you to kill women."

"I don't kill them. I have told them all what I am and what we are hoping to accomplish. They knew the risks."

Francesca ignored this weak justification. Her mind was busy reinterpreting the last few days. "So . . . when Lea takes a new neodemon into her cult and hides them from the pantheon, it isn't always so neat is it? Sometimes the neodemon's devotees pray to her and that makes the neodemons more like her. And that is why, when Nicodemus fooled the River Thief into attacking him and he saw her . . ."

"She was wearing Leandra's face," Holokai finished. "The River Thief was a member of the Undivided Society. Her cult resides mostly in the river villages, and they prayed to her for equitable theft from all the trade that flows down their river. So she stole from the merchants and smugglers alike. Some of her takeaway she gave to the river villages, but most she gave to the Undivided Society."

Francesca nodded. "And the River Thief knew Leandra would never come after her because she was in Lea's service. It was only because Nicodemus lied to Lea that she made the mistake of attacking him."

"That's it. With the River Thief taken down, it will be a season or more until she's reincarnated. It's a big problem because she brought in so much of our coin. We need the funds now that we're using so many more godspells from the smugglers."

"Godspells?"

"Lea can't smuggle deities out of the empire without circumventing imperial spellwrights. The only way to do that was to use the same spells that they were using. I don't know how that fancy spellwrighting works. But she started buying godspells from special smugglers from the empire. Recently she's bought a spell from a smuggler who's still in Chandralu. The spell lets her know things about an hour into the future. That's how she knew her father would rescue her in the throne room. She sensed that she would be intensely irritated and then grateful for him."

Francesca frowned. "And what of the attackers wearing the Perfect Circle tattoo? How's that connected to Lea?"

"It isn't. They're not connected to us. Hell, a pack of the bloody fools, attacked us on Utrana Way earlier today. Lea thinks they're a bunch of thugs trying to scare people by pretending to be the Undivided Society."

Francesca pressed three fingers against the bridge of her nose as she thought. "Whoever they are, if the empress knew half of what Lea's done, she'd attack the league with everything she has. It'd be a war to destroy all of humanity before the Disjunction even began. How could Leandra do this? How could she risk weakening us before the demons from the Ancient Continent cross the ocean?"

"What's the point in saving a corrupt society? Empire or league, they're both unjust."

"You can't be serious."

"Hey, Francesca, does it look like I'm joking?"

"No. No it does not. God-of-gods damn it all! How are we going to get out of this?" She paused. "How was Lea planning on getting out of this?"

"Can't say that I know her plans, especially as she's just learned what you just said in the throne room, that the shape-shifter we smuggled into Dral has been caught by the empress. But I can say that her plans were to meet again with the smuggler from the empire. She was thinking of buying another godspell from him, maybe she still is, but I think she's now planning to try to pump him for information about what's going on with the attacks on the deities and how soon we might expect an imperial attack."

Francesca drew in a sharp breath. Reliable information from that smuggler that would be invaluable. Francesca had thought to end Leandra's independence, but that might scare away an informant who could help them survive a war with the empire. Francesca focused on Holokai again. "Where is she going to meet this smuggler?"

"The Lesser Sacred Pool at dusk. Four-arms and I will patrol the place before and after."

Francesca nodded, thinking rapidly. "If she and the smuggler have an arrangement, I had better not interfere or I might spoil the exchange. And . . . as I told you . . . I was too heavy-handed with her before. This time, let's see if she can't get out of her own trouble. You won't mention this conversation to her. I will position myself to observe her exchange with the smuggler, so that I can protect her if necessary. No, don't worry. I can take precautions to make sure that neither the smuggler nor Lea notice me."

"There's something else you need to know."

She raised an eyebrow.

"When she first put on the prophetic godspell, she saw a day forward into the future. She foresaw that sometime early in the coming morning, she is going to have to choose between dying and murdering someone she loves. And so far, her primary suspect—"

"Me."

Holokai grunted. "Not hard to guess, yeah?"

"Not hard."

"Any way to avoid the prophecy?"

"She foresaw that if she runs, everyone she knows will die. She talked to a rogue wizard down in the upper Naukaa about a spell that could stop her from loving as a way to escape those possibilities, but I don't think anyone's suspecting that will work."

"Can't imagine it would." Francesca nodded absently and then reaffirmed her decision. "All right. We'll see what Leandra can learn from this smuggler. Where will Lea go after meeting with him?"

"I imagine to the family compound."

"Good, I will be there as well. After she's met with the smuggler, you are to slip away. Just get outside of the compound and I'll find you. Depending on what she discovers, I may talk to her then or see if she can, by some miracle, pull this off on her own. If something unexpected happens and you have to leave the city, I'll post a messenger on the city docks. He'll be the one holding a plumeria branch in one hand. Be sure to get news back to me before morning or I'll assume you've broken trust with me. Understood?"

"Yes, but what about my son?"

Francesca looked down at the water. Both Lolo and Tam had returned to the floating pavilion. The boy had lain down in the shade, his head on Kenna's lap. He seemed to be sleeping while the twins talked. "I will take him to the compound. Keep me informed and my daughter alive until the imperial threat has past and I will return him to you. I will start teaching him now that your duties have kept you away but that you love him and want to take him to his native island." She smiled. "You see, this doesn't have to end poorly. I can't say I was perfect, but I learned a thing or two about raising a child with particular potential."

The shark god looked her up and down. "Just make sure you're not kidding yourself, Francesca. That sounds like a pretty story to hide an ugly thing."

"Then you do the same for yourself, Holokai, when you think about what happened to your son's mother."

He rolled his muscular shoulders. "I won't break trust with you. But I want you to think about all the stories you ever heard about dragons. Every story you ever heard from when you were a little girl to now. You ever hear a story about a dragon who wasn't destructive or greedy? Because I never have. Maybe you ought to rethink how good your plans are."

Anger flushed through Francesca. "It turns out that when you are the most powerful dragon around, you don't have to worry about the past stories because you get to write your own God-of-gods damned story. Now get away from me before I decide to rewrite your ending."

He stared at her, his face suddenly alive with hatred, eyes darkening. She didn't move a muscle. Any sign of weakness would be an invitation to him to break their agreement.

At last he scowled and went away.

Her legs feeling weak, Francesca turned back to the lake and put her hands on the railing. "Lea, how are we all going to get out of this alive?"

Most likely, not all of them would.

The door to Thaddeus's room had been hastily repaired. When Leandra knocked upon the freshly cut wooden planks, the door swung slightly ajar. Outside the winehouse, the volcano's shadow was stretching across the city as evening approached.

There was no answer from Thaddeus's room, so Leandra knocked harder. Her gut still ached and deep breaths still produced chest pain, though less intensely so. Embarrassingly, fatigue had forced her to hire a palanquin to carry her from the Floating Palace to the Naukaa.

She had discovered one consolation: Roughly half an hour previous, she had felt many of her future selves experience surprise and confusion followed by strange euphoria. There were shades of relief and satisfaction in this odd future emotion. Leandra hoped that it heralded a success from Thaddeus.

Ever since she had first sensed this strange euphoria, other possible future emotions had become harder to sense. Perhaps these possible moods were becoming unlikely. Or perhaps something would alter her ability to experience mood in general. Given their goal of casting a spell to prevent her from loving long enough to escape the prophecy, she guessed the latter.

At last Thaddeus called, "Enter."

Leandra pushed the door the rest of the way open and then stepped inside. Thaddeus had never been neat; during periods of intellectual fascination, he had lived in personal disarray. But the sight before Leandra was a new height in scholastic squalor. Opened books and scrolls flopped across his desk, bed, floor. Reams of paper lay over many books and a half-eaten plate of curry. Even the drawer where he kept his opium paraphernalia was stacked with books.

Sitting at his desk, Thad didn't bother to look up but gestured. "Give me a moment to finish checking . . ."

"Thad, I have come—" Leandra started to say.

"Wait, wait."

Surprised, Leandra closed her mouth. Behind her, Dhrun picked her way among the clutter. Holokai stood by the door.

"Okay . . . and . . ." Thad mumbled while running a finger down a blank page.

Suddenly Dhrun froze. The action made Leandra look at her. The goddess pointed to a small codex opened to its back cover. Something was smudged across it. Squinting, Leandra realized that the smudge had come from a boot heel. No one in her party wore boots. She looked to Dhrun, who gave her a four-shrugged shrug.

"Done!" Thaddeus pronounced and stood. His chair scraped against the floor, displacing several books. His expression shone with confident excitement. His collar was open and Leandra saw that he had a new dark patch of skin near his collarbone. A bruise? Thad's smile fell as he took in the rash on her face. "Lea?"

"I'm fine. Were you able to do it?"

He blinked.

"Thad, your spell?"

"Right . . . well, I can't promise anything." He looked at his papers. "But revisiting the text I saw all the mistakes that I must have gone over a hundred times before." His smile filled Leandra with memories. She had loved his passion for his work even though she had hated how it made him a single-minded, inconsiderate ass. But that was the past. "So it will work?"

"I think so. At least I'm certain it's safe. I've added several subspells to disengage if anything goes amiss."

"It's not like you to be certain about safety, Thad. You love the danger of experimentation."

"So I do." He winked. "I don't have any bad habits, only—"

"Full-blown addictions," Leandra finished for him. "But this spell is different? It's safe?"

"I might be reckless with my own head, but I never endanger anyone else. You know that."

What he said was true.

Thad touched his right hand to his heart and his left to his forehead in a Cloud Culture gesture of prayer. "I swear on my mother's grave that this spell is safe."

"Swear on something you care about."

"All right, I'll swear on a week's worth of opium."

Leandra grunted. "Will it stop me from being able to love?"

"Only one way to find out." He flashed his handsome grin, dimples pronounced. He looked at the books strewn around his room as if noticing them for the first time. "Why don't you lie down on the bed?" He began to shift the clutter from his bed to the floor.

When his back was turned, Leandra caught Dhrun's eye. Quickly she pointed to Thaddeus and then to the spot on his collarbone where he had the discoloration. Holokai noticed the exchange and quietly pushed the door shut behind him.

Thaddeus motioned to the bed, and Leandra again glimpsed the discoloration on his collarbone. It seemed to extend down his chest.

"All right," Leandra said as she made for the bed. "It was surprisingly humid today." This was the secret expression for her officers.

"You thought so? I didn't notice," Thaddeus murmured while turning back to his desk. Leandra watched as he reached for one particular sheet.

Seeing this sent a thrill through Leandra. She made up her mind. Quickly she held up her hand, balled it into a fist and then splayed out all her fingers—the prearranged gesture for "Begin an infiltration game." Then she waggled her pinky as if it were injured and pointed to herself in the gesture for "Play a Wounded Bird game. I'm the bird."

Both of her divinities balled their right hands into fists and then splayed out their fingers to indicate that they understood.

Thaddeus moved his hands in a complex pattern over his desk, pulling a spell from the paper and helping it fold. "I will need you to hold very still. In fact, why don't you lie down?"

Leandra put her head back on a pillow, which smelled of Thaddeus and pipe smoke. Her heart was racing.

Thaddeus leaned over her, began to extend his hands. Suddenly four muscular female arms spread out behind him. The lower two snaked under his armpits to wrap around his head in a double shoulder lock. The left upper arm held both of Thad's hands to one side. The right upper hand grasped his throat and squeezed.

Thaddeus's eyes widened the instant before Dhrun twisted into a hip throw. He struck the floor with a crash.

Leandra sat up fast enough to see Holokai kick the door into the hallway. Outside there were three men. The door struck one, knocked him back. Another raised his hands, and something flashed between them. Holokai thrust his leimako through this blaze and into the man's chest. There was a gurgled cry and then a crash. A second flash came from farther down the hall. Holokai grunted and a spray of blood erupted from his shoulder. He lunged out of Leandra's vision. Another flash, a scream.

Leandra struggled onto her feet. There came two more crashes from the hallway. Her knees ached as she hurried across the room.

In the hallway, she found Holokai standing over three bodies, blood spreading around them. He began stalking down the hall, looking for the next threat. The winehouse fell silent for a moment. Then came hushed voices and footsteps from below. A door slammed. Another silent moment. Only Holokai moved.

A simple ambush then. Thaddeus was to knock her out and the three spellwrights would take Holokai and Dhrun unaware. An underpowered attack. By now anyone else connected with the ambush must have fled the winehouse.

Leandra went back into Thaddeus's room. Dhrun had her former lover pinned, both shoulders locked, facedown, on his bed. So long as she had hold of him, Dhrun's divine touch could disspell any text he might extemporize.

Leandra drew a knife from her belt. "Turn him so I can see his right hip."

"They didn't give me a choice! Lea—"

Dhrun turned him with her lower arms; with her upper right, she landed an overhand punch on his jaw. His head rocked back and he moaned.

"Who?" Leandra asked as she pulled aside his longvest and used her knife to cut off his belt.

"They wouldn't tell me," Thaddeus moaned. "They were going to kill me. They cast a Death Sentence on me."

A death sentence was a spell that wrapped itself around the arteries that supplied the heart with blood. Unless it received continuous signal spells, the Death Sentence would contract, deprive the heart of blood, and kill its victim. Dhrun's touch would have dispelled that text, but there was no need to tell Thaddeus that.

"Lea! I swear I wasn't going to cast that spell on y—" Dhrun struck him again in the face.

"Move him more into the window's light," Leandra ordered while exposing his hip. A moment later, Dhrun rolled him toward the window. "Fire and hell," Leandra swore.

On Thaddeus's hip, the skin red and swollen under the ink, was the Perfect Circle tattoo.

CHAPTER TWENTY-EIGHT

Francesca thought it both ironic and fitting that a goddess of justice should have been incarnated first as a deity of death. Ancient Dhamma—willowy, gray skin, lank white hair, all-white eyes—was just one such goddess.

Justice and death, Francesca thought as she and Nicodemus bowed to Dhamma, wouldn't it be nice if the two were related? Certainly something worth praying for. In the state the Creator had left the universe, death and justice weren't simply unrelated, they had never taken tea together. The bastards.

Why should Francesca's innocent daughter have been burdened with terminal disease, and her noble husband bound to mortality, while she—of demonic origin, angry, fractious, often destructive—had been given such a large dose of immortality?

But no matter, no matter, not right now. That was all philosophy. And Dhamma was not the Creator. She was only the goddess that the ancient Ixonians had prayed to for the wicked to die young, the righteous not at all.

Francesca and Nicodemus finished their bows and straightened. He looked more relaxed since talking to Leandra. The poor fool. Lea must have woven him up in some story. Knowing what her daughter was truly up to weighed on Francesca's heart.

Dhamma returned their bow. They were all kneeling in a private tearoom at the top of the Floating Palace. Outside, evening shadows had painted the lake water nearly black.

The Trimuril had asked that Francesca and Nicodemus remain for an emergency war council. Surprisingly the whole affair had taken only a few hours. Call the Trimuril whatever you like—and Francesca had several choice names in mind—but you also had to call her an efficient ruler.

"My Lord and Lady Warden," Dhamma said, "thank you for meeting with me. I will not keep you long. There is not much to do until Lady Warden Leandra returns to us tomorrow."

"We are happy to assist however we can," Francesca said with a nod. Nicodemus had already agreed that she should do most of the talking. "Has your investigation into the attacks on lesser deities revealed anything more?"

"I'm afraid the god of the Banyan Districts, who was attacked earlier, has gone missing."

"Was he attacked again?"

"Possibly, but it might be that he is taking protective measures. I don't want to jump to conclusions. I informed the Lady Warden Leandra of this before she departed."

"Very wise," Francesca said. "Was this the reason you wished to meet with us?"

"No," the goddess said with a slight bow. "As perhaps you both appreciate, the Trimuril is currently preoccupied with governing the pantheon. The present threats provide many opportunities for divine infighting. Preventing such will occupy nearly all of the Trimuril's consciousness for days. So she has charged your daughter and me with maintaining law in Chandralu. Before Leandra departed, we agreed that tonight she would keep the peace in the Lower Banyan, the Naukaa, Jacaranda Slope, and Utra Ridge. I should be responsible for the rest of the city. I offered her the assistance of the night watch, which I had intended to double tonight. However, Leandra declined because her investigations will prevent her from governing the watch. She also feared that they would interfere with her investigation."

Dhamma paused. "Lady Warden Leandra was adamant about her stance. So I briefly discussed the issue with the Trimuril, who suggested that I ask one of you to coordinate the watch in your daughter's portion of the city since she is so preoccupied."

Francesca resisted the urge to sigh. The wheels of politics turn, they always must. Leandra was keeping the city from interfering with her meeting with the smuggler, but the Trimuril was trying to provide Nicodemus with the means to interfere if anything got out of hand. It was a shrewd move; Leandra couldn't protest the oversight if it came through her father.

Nicodemus frowned. "Goddess, we should be happy to assist. But I am not sure I could direct the watch so they would not interfere with my daughter's plans."

Francesca shifted her weight. "Perhaps, husband, I could assist you in that regard?"

The goddess nodded. "We would be most grateful."

"Before we agree, Goddess," Francesca said, "we should discuss how we might govern the watch."

"Either one of you would command the watch in any of the guard stations."

"That would be kind; however, given the need for delicate control, I wonder if we might move command of the watch to our family compound."

Both Nicodemus and the goddess looked at her. Nicodemus was doing a fairly good job of keeping his expression unreadable, but Francesca could tell he was annoyed that she was making such a political bid without first discussing it with him.

"In fact," Francesca continued, "the Wardens might be called upon to keep the peace again. Perhaps we should establish a permanent division of the watch in our family compound."

"And I suppose," Dhamma asked, "you should like to appoint and maintain these guards yourself."

To Francesca's surprise, Nicodemus replied: "To be effective, a commander must be sure of his officers. To better serve the Sacred Regent, the captain of our guards might have a seat on the Outer Council. Perhaps you would agree?"

Pleased that he was playing into her maneuvering, Francesca repressed a smile.

Dhamma put her head to one side and froze in brief consultation with the Trimuril. At last she nodded. "The terms are agreeable."

Nicodemus raised an eyebrow at Francesca to ask if she was satisfied. She showed him her most winning smile and nodded.

Nicodemus grunted. "Very well. One of us will report immediately to our family compound to assume command." He bowed.

The goddess returned the gesture. "That concludes my concerns. Please don't hesitate to consult me should you require assistance."

"Thank you, Goddess. Might we use this room before we set off?"

"Of course, take as long as you need."

They bowed again and the goddess rose and left the room.

"Subrosa?" Nicodemus asked.

Francesca pulled from her belt purse a sheet of paper and cast from it a subrosa spell. In moments, they were surrounded by the sound-deadening paragraphs.

Nicodemus sighed. "All right, Fran, out with it."

"Out with what?"

He crossed his arms.

"What?"

"You know something."

"One or two things."

"Fran."

"You're the one who spoke to Leandra. You haven't even told me what you learned."

"Nothing helpful. She believes that the River Thief was wearing her face as a ploy to win devotees who were mistakenly worshiping her."

"Do you believe that?"

"I can't come up with another explanation. Can you?"

She reached out and took his hand. It wasn't really fair. Nicodemus could touch so few people that he was unduly swayed by physical touch. "Nico, I just want what's best for our family."

He looked down at her hand. "The two of you are so similar it's frightening."

"What do you mean?"

"Lea also took my hand when she wanted to blow smoke in my eyes. I let her do it so she wouldn't shut me out."

"Nico, you shouldn't let her get away with that."

"Why? So that she could be alienated from both of her parents?"

"She doesn't respect you when you let her get away with things like that."

"I'm not trying to win her respect, Fran. I'm trying to get her to accept my bloody help before something disastrous happens."

"And how's that working out for you?"

Nicodemus let go of her hand and pressed his hands to his face. "At least the door is still open." He dropped his hand and reached for hers, but she withdrew it. He looked up into her eyes. "Fran, please, what do you know?"

"I know enough to keep the city watch from interfering with Lea's investigation."

"Will you share?"

"We have to keep the watch away from the Lesser Sacred Pool at dusk, but we should keep them close enough in case help is needed."

"And why must we do this?"

She studied his face but said nothing.

"Fran, why are you withholding this information from me?"

She paused. "I believe that we shouldn't interfere or we might prevent her from gaining some precious information. And . . . the last time I interfered . . . well, we both know how that ended up."

"You don't trust me not to interfere?"

"I don't trust myself."

That admission shut him up for a moment. "The only reason I played along with your idea of running the nightwatch from our compound is that I told Lea I would try to spend the night there. I'm hoping that she'll come to me with her trouble."

"Were you going to have her followed so you could know if she gets into trouble?"

"I am considering it, but I haven't yet."

She smiled. "Perhaps we should have someone near her in case her plans go awry."

"You're already up to something?"

She changed the subject. "But what are you going to do in the compound other than wait around for Lea to come to you?"

"Well, now there's the nightwatch to command, but I was thinking that I should start writing another metaspell—"

"Nico, that's an excellent idea; I was just thinking earlier about how you should in case Vivian tries something."

He nodded slowly. "I'm glad you agree. But you're avoiding my question."

"We should trust our daughter, right?"

"We have trained her well. She's been an excellent Warden so far. Well perhaps not excellent, letting the River Thief escape her for so long. But very good."

Oh Nico, Francesca thought, how wrong you are there. But should I tell you before I know more?

Nicodemus continued. "Do you know of a reason why we shouldn't trust her?"

Francesca did, but she said, "Give me until tomorrow to tell you everything. I will say that I've discovered Lea has had dealings with a smuggler from the empire. I am not sure of their relationship, but I wanted to give her the chance to meet with him at the Lesser Sacred Pool to see what she might learn. If we interfere, even if we simply make Lea tell us everything, that might spook her and scare off the smuggler. We can't risk that."

Nicodemus thought about that before nodding. "All right. What are you planning?"

"I won't follow her, but I'll hide near the Lesser Sacred Pool in case something goes wrong."

"Fran, how do you know that's she's meeting a smuggler?"

"Give me until tomorrow morning? Let's just trust her for tonight."

He again pressed his hands to his face. "Well . . . I suppose we can give her tonight at least." He started to say something more but then stopped.

She squeezed his hand. "Give me until morning."

"Then I had better leave for Chandralu."

She kissed his hand. "Thank you, Nico. I'll place my followers in the compound as well. Oh, I have picked up a young demigod. His name is Lolo and the twins will be looking after him. Nothing for you to worry about."

He frowned at her.

"I'll explain in the morning. Meantime, you have the metaspell to worry about. By the way, what was wrong with you down in the front hall?"

"What do you mean?"

"When I asked Ellen and Rory to work together, you looked like someone poured ice down your pants. Does Rory have some other girl?"

"Not exactly." He was fidgeting with his sleeve.

"You're hiding a secret for your man, aren't you?"

"If I were I wouldn't tell you."

"Oh come on, Nico," she said playfully, "there shouldn't be any secrets between us."

"Then you're going to tell me what you learned about Lea?"

"Well, you have me there," she said quickly before reverting to her playful tone. "Don't look so serious, Nico, this is only gossip."

"Committing gossip would be serious indeed."

Francesca rolled her eyes. "You're so stuffy all of a sudden. I wonder what it could be about Rory . . ."

"Fran, don't we have enough things to worry about? The empire, our daughter's disease, the volcanic deity on the bay who might be Los himself?"

This sobered Francesca enough to erase her smile. "Do you think it's possible whatever is out in the bay is an ancient demon?"

"Whatever destroyed Feather Island was more powerful than any neodemon I have ever seen."

"But if it truly were an ancient demon, why would it hide? Why attack a tiny fishing village?"

"Could be the first demon to cross? Perhaps the harbinger of the Pandemonium?"

Recognizing the concern in her husband's voice, Francesca made her expression as serious as possible. "Husband, in such a difficult time, I have to ask you a grave question."

He looked at her, his green eyes concerned.

"Will you promise to consider what I ask carefully before you respond?"

"Yes, of course."

"You promise?"

"Yes, I promise. Fran, what is it?"

She looked him in the eye, waited a moment, and then asked in her most serious tone, "Rory prefers men?"

Nicodemus looked away.

She laughed. "Oh, it's so cute how you're trying to hide it!"

"Fran, I . . . This is . . ."

"Oh, and your Lornish knight, who was standing behind you and looked like he wanted to laugh, but then looked at Rory, it's the two of them then?"

"Fran, there's no reason for you to think Sir Claude—"

"Sir Claude!" she sung out. "How perfect! That is just so cute. It's like something in one of your knightly romances."

"Fran, in the knightly romances, two men don't—"

"Well they should!" she interrupted. "So, Rory and . . . Sir Claude . . . found each other in your service? Hunting neodemons?" She sighed, remembering how she had fallen in love with Nicodemus during the intrigue that surrounded the events of Avel. Now it seemed romantic, but at the time it seemed terrifying and Nicodemus thick-headed.

Well, at least that last part hadn't changed. Much. She sighed again.

"Fran, now let's get this straight—"

"They're not?" she interrupted.

He paused, confused, but then he caught her wordplay and blew out an exasperated breath.

She laughed again, smiled again, once more let herself dip into old memories. "Good for them. Good for them. Oh, but poor Ellen, just when she thought she found a man who was worth the while." She looked at Nicodemus. "But what's got you all flustered. You don't disapprove, do you?"

"No, no. Of course not. It's only that . . . I never said . . . Hypothetically speaking, if a knight and a druid from very traditional Southern cultures were to . . ." He waved his hand vaguely in a gesture that couldn't possibly have meant "are homosexual" even though that was what he should have been brave enough to say. ". . . well, they might not want everyone to know about it."

"Well, that would be true, especially if we were in the South." She shrugged. "But we're in Ixos."

He looked exhausted. "Fran, I didn't say anything."

She suppressed another smile. "Of course you didn't, my love. I am sorry that I pried. You're trying to be a good friend. Age is turning me into a gossiping old crone. I'll stop. I don't know a thing." But she couldn't stop herself from sighing. "Well then, we had better get ready. I have to get to the Lesser Sacred Pool before Lea or her officers do." She kissed Nicodemus's hand, but then she had a new thought. "Should we have had someone follow Lea until she gets to the Lesser Sacred Pool?"

"It's only a few hours," he said. "Until then I'm sure Lea can keep herself out of anything too bloody."

Blood splattered across Thaddeus's sheets and onto Leandra's legs. Dhrun struck another punch across Thaddeus's jaw, another spray of blood.

"That's enough, Dhru," Leandra said. "Sit him up."

Dhrun hoisted Thaddeus up and kicked his legs over the edge of the bed. Her four arms became a blur as she released the double shoulder lock and twisted both of Thaddeus's hands behind his back in a double arm lock. This forced Thaddeus to lean forward and cry out in pain. Dhrun looked to Leandra, who shook her head. Reluctantly, the goddess relaxed her grip. He stopped yelling and his face went slack.

Leandra pulled the chair over to him. During the fight, she had forgotten her fatigue and pain. Now they flooded back.

From the hallway came sound of wetly tearing flesh. Leandra looked up and saw that the hallway had dimmed into a net of red light that undulated across the walls. "Damn it, Kai," Leandra swore and then shuddered. She had wanted to search the bodies. Again she heard the sound of serrated teeth tearing through flesh. He couldn't resist feeding, not now. Nightmarishly, blood trickled across the floor.

With another shudder, Leandra turned back to Thaddeus. He stopped panting long enough to spit. None of his teeth had come out. Yet. "Thad," she said. "Start talking."

Dhrun tightened one of her arm locks. "Okay!" he yelled. "I'll talk. I'll talk!" When Dhrun relaxed, he panted a few more times and then raggedly said, "They came a few hours after you did. I didn't hear them. I . . . I was working on the loveless spell. Then there was a flash. Next thing I was cen- sored and bound. There was a man with a black beard, pale skin, and blue eyes. He made me tell him everything."

Tears streamed down his face, blood from his nose. "Then he cast the death sentence on my heart. He told me that when you came back, I had to cast a stunning spell on you and that his men would take care of anyone else you brought with you."

"Did he tell you why?"

Thaddeus shook his head and spat again.

"He was a wizard?"

"Yes, I saw him spellwright Magnus and Numinous."

"He was from Astrophell, from the empire?"

"Could have been. But he could have been from Starfall."

"Accent?"

"Nothing distinct."

"Clothes?"

"A plain blouse and longvest. He looked like a merchant of the Cloud Culture."

Leandra chewed on her lip. An hour ago she felt through her godspell a spike of confusion and surprise. That had come to pass. But afterward she had felt a great lifting of emotion. There was something here. She just had to find it.

"What else happened?"

Thaddeus shook his head. "Nothing. He said that they'd be watching me. I was to work on your spell like my life depended on getting it done. Then he punched me in the stomach and left."

"So maybe that's what you needed to become an adequate spellwright."

"A deadline with grave repercussions?"

"A punch in the stomach."

"Lea, believe me, I wasn't going to cast the stunning spell on you."

"Don't, Thad."

"But Lea, I would never—"

"I saw you reach over your research spell for another one. I know you sold me out."

"No, no—"

"They gave you the choice of selling me out or dying. I would have done the same to you. I'm not angry."

"You're not?"

She shook her head. "I have no idea how they found you, whoever they are. I should have anticipated that, or at least warned you."

She caught her old lover's gaze. His left eye was already swelling. It made him look frail, mortal. But the important thing was the eye contact.

"I'm sorry," he murmured, looking down.

"Thad, look at me."

At first he glanced up at her. Then he held her gaze. "I'm sorry." Then his face collapsed like a child's. "Don't kill me."

If he had been stronger, he would have died rather than sell her out. Not that she would have had the strength to do that. Not for him. But she hadn't been given that choice and he had. So went injustice.

"Thad, were you telling the truth about the loveless spell?"

He nodded vigorously. "Maybe it was the death threat, maybe it was the punch in the gut, but I've never produced finer Numinous prose. It will work, or if it doesn't I'm sure it won't hurt you."

Leandra considered this and then looked up to Dhrun. The goddess only shrugged. Leandra wondered what Holokai would think, but when she looked to the hallway she saw only blood pooled on the floor.

Quickly she looked back at Thaddeus. Through her godspell she felt that in an hour, most of her future selves were filled with an expansive, uplifting emotion. In fact, the more she thought about it, the more of her future selves felt that victorious emotion and freedom from pain. The more she thought about it, the more this possible future became the only possible future. "Could you still cast that spell on me?"

"I . . . I could . . . but I don't know why you would trust me."

She tapped her temple. "Through my prophetic spell, I can feel that you will not betray me again and that your spell will succeed."

He looked at her, his face tense.

She nodded. "You're going to cast the loveless spell on me now. If anything goes wrong, Dhrun breaks your neck."

"B-but . . ."

"Is something the matter?"

"No, no . . . I can cast the loveless spell, if that's what you want."

Leandra gestured to Dhrun, who released Thad. With a lurch and a groan her old lover hugged himself. Leandra gave him a moment before she reached out for him. At first he flinched but then let her take his hands. "From what I have sensed through the godspell, your loveless spell may offer me my only escape from a horrible prophecy. So I'm going to tell you once more, very sincerely, don't let me down."

His hands were trembling, but his gaze was firm. "I won't."

"Then let's get to it. Dhrun, watch him. I believe that he is sincere, but if anything happens to me, don't feel any responsibility to make his death quick or painless."

Dhrun grunted.

Tentatively, Thaddeus stood and walked toward his desk. Leandra sat on his bed and pressed a hand to her aching belly. Her knees groaned with pain. But she could still feel the brave new future. Something in her nature cried out for what the loveless spell would bring. For the first time, she felt the touch of what she would call destiny.

Thaddeus was again moving his hands above his desk, but this time with greater care and more intricate motions.

Again Leandra felt as if she were approaching something fated. But then Thaddeus turned toward her with an invisible spell pinched between his fingers, and she wondered if she had lost her mind. Had the stress hormones deranged her thoughts? She hadn't felt this strange future emotion until she had started the steroids. And this sensation of destiny . . .

"Wait, Thad, am I sounding sane?"

"I-I . . . I think so."

Leandra exhaled, annoyed. What else would he say after being beaten half to death? She looked to Dhrun. The goddess seemed to think something over before saying, "You don't seem affected by that medicine, if that's your concern."

Leandra balled her hands into fists, again felt the pain in her gut. Once more she thought about the glorious uplifting future, then nodded to Thaddeus.

"Please," he said, "lie down."

Obeying, Leandra took a deep breath to steady her nerves. Pain squirmed in her chest. The disease flare rekindling? She closed her eyes as Thaddeus leaned over her.

"Hold very still. Very still."

She felt his hands stir the air above her face, heard him shifting weight. In the hallway, Holokai was biting, biting.

Nothing happened.

Long moments passed. Leandra felt Thad's hands move away, heard him step over to the desk. She took another deep breath and noticed that the pain was still there, but no worse. "How much longer?"

"Not long," Thad replied. "Well, not long for such a complicated spell."

Leandra chewed her lip and tried to relax. At last Holokai stopped making the horrible noise in the hallway. Leandra heard the irregular, heavy thud of his feet. The door creaked and the shark god asked, in a blood-drunk voice, what had happened. Dhrun explained. Then silence fell again. Lea tried to count to one hundred but only made it to eighty before again asking, "How much longer?"

"Just . . . a moment."

Thad's hands returned to her face. She started counting again. Around forty her irritation grew. By sixty she wondered if she should ask again. But then she realized that she was counting more and more slowly. Was it sixty she had reached or eighty? Or was she still on forty? Intoxication washed over her.

The room had gone silent. She tried to ask what was happening but could not seem to make her mouth work. She was not breathing, but she did not want for air. Now that she listened for it, she realized that her heart was no longer beating.

A thrill of fear then. Had Thaddeus killed her? She remembered her mother's stories of how the Savanna Walker had deprived her of all sensation, the horror of a mind in isolation, of how Francesca had raged against the Creator at that time. Was that what had happened to Leandra now?

But then Leandra felt the air slowly flowing into her chest, a sudden two-noted thud. Her heart beat, impossibly slow. A vision of tattered curtains pierced through the sliver that she had cracked between her upper and lower eyelid. The motion of her human blood was suspended; she saw in perfect detail the fiber of the tattered curtains, stars just starting to shine through the dimming sky. The brightest star was being circled by a small, pockmarked moon.

As her eyes opened, nature's light spilled into her brain. The universe in both fine and gross detail was dissected for her, demonstrating all of its hot beauty, all its cold indifference.

Then time snapped like the film of a soap bubble. Leandra's lungs expanded. Crying out, she sat up with terrific speed. Her thundering heart seemed to be filling with light, her mind with an elevated emotion that brought her up and up and up, toward ecstasy. All pain had left her gut and joints. Fatigue evaporated like raindrops falling on fire.

Bruised Thaddeus stood beside her, both hands raised as if the moment before he had been holding something delicate. Behind him Dhrun had both sets of arms crossed, her expression tight. Holokai had become taller, more muscular, his eyes all black.

"I . . ." Leandra started to say.

"Did it work?" Thaddeus asked.

She looked at him. His bruised lips and swollen eye were already beginning to darken. And yet his expression shone with curiosity and excitement. She studied him, took in everything from the grease under his nails to the tiny broken blood vessels in the white of his eye. She could see his bruised skin was hotter than the rest of his face. She did not know how she could see heat. But she could.

"Yes. Yes, it worked."

"And the other godspell, did I leave it intact?"

"Yes," she said with some hesitation. She could still feel into the future; however, all future selves felt the similar elevating, expansive mood that she now knew. All choices in the future maintained her present state of lightness.

Leandra drew a deep breath and felt no chest pain. She stood without difficulty.

"And the prophecy?" Dhrun asked. "Are you still bound to murder someone you love in the early morning? Can you tell?"

Leandra frowned, answered with a question: "The rash on my face, how is it looking?"

"Much better. Still there, but better."

Leandra nodded. She needed to test a theory. Closing her eyes she induced a small flare of her disease and misspelled the prophetic godspell around her head so she could feel farther into the future.

"It's . . . different," she said then paused. "I will not murder someone I love. I cannot. It's impossible for me to use the word 'love' as I did. Now I might escape that prophecy. I might not. It doesn't matter because I have been falling toward this night all of my life, the way a rock falls through water."

"Huh?" Holokai asked with slack incomprehension.

Leandra again induced a flare of her disease and returned the godspell's range to an hour before the present so the prismatic futures would not challenge her sanity. She could not say how she knew—perhaps it was the resolution of her pain—but she could tell that invoking her particular talent, invoking her disease, would no longer hurt her. "Thaddeus, you have cured me."

"I have?"

"Misspelling no longer induces a flare. My two natures have ceased warring with each other."

"They have?"

A smile tugged at the corners of her mouth. "They have."

Thaddeus looked at the deities, who looked dumbly back at him. "Well," he said, "that is unexpected."

Leandra's mind raced with new opportunities, new dangers. "Thad, this loveless spell, how might it be removed?"

"If you sit still, any Numinous spellwright could disspell it. But I also wrote a few passages to sense a particular Numinous signaling spell so I can deconstruct it in an emergency."

"I suspected you might have taken such steps. A wise choice. Problem is someone could force you to teach them the deconstruction spell."

He blinked. "Well, yes. I hadn't thought of that. But why should they want to do such a thing?"

"Your loveless has begun a transformation they might want to reverse. I'm afraid that means that we cannot risk your falling into their control."

Thaddeus glanced between her and Dhrun. "Then . . . I'll go with you?"

She shook her head. "You're no good in a fight. And the Creator knows when you might go into withdrawal from whatever you've been using. So, please, sit down." She gestured to his bed.

He stepped back defensively.

"It's all right. We only need to keep your secret safe for the night."

With a look at Dhrun, Thaddeus hesitantly sat.

"Might we take him to your family compound?" Dhrun asked.

"No, if my mother discovered this secret she would use it against our case."

"Keyway Island?" Dhrun suggested.

"No way to get him there safely."

"Hide him somewhere?" Dhrun asked.

"Not possible," Leandra replied, "we have to assume we're being watched. Trust me, with this loveless spell upon my mind and my ability to feel forward by an hour, I have considered every possible future and can tell you there is only one way for us to be entirely safe." She stood and went to the shelf where Thaddeus kept his opium and paraphernalia. "But this won't be difficult. Thad is like me: He keeps no bad habits—"

"Only full blown addictions," Thaddeus said.

"Precisely so." She moved his smoking paraphernalia to examine the bottles behind them. Mostly he had kava, the traditional drink of the Sea People. It was derived from the roots of a particular pepper plant and caused a state of relaxation without dramatically clouding thoughts. She reached passed these to a small porcelain bottle of rice wine and a small vile of dark brown liquid.

"Thad, how much tincture of opium would you need to sleep until sunrise? The drugs will keep us safe. We need a high enough dose that even if the thugs come back and try to wake you, you won't be able to divulge the signal spell. If I remember correctly, that would be about thirty drops?"

"Fifty now," he said with relief. He went on to justify the dose by comparing himself to others in the winehouse who required much more to sleep. So it went with addiction and self-justification. So it went.

Keeping her back to Thad, Leandra prepared two small pewter cups. When she turned around, he had made his bed and was lying back. He had several paper sheets on the bed and was moving his hands between them and his forehead as he cast the Numinous spells that would intensify his intoxication.

Dhrun stepped next to Leandra. "My Lady Warden, did you tell me that the hydroma—"

"Thank you, goddess," Leandra interrupted and handed Thaddeus the first cup. He drank it with apparent expectation. She started to hand him the second, but then paused. "Thad . . . I am sorry. I should have thought about the thugs trying to use you to get to me."

He was pinching something that seemed to be floating before his eyes, likely an intoxicating Numinous sentence that needed to be tucked into place. His expression was one of fixed concentration and he went a little cross-eyed as he worked. "Well, Lea, I haven't always been exactly gentle with you."

"You haven't. But I'm still not sure you deserved what you're getting."

He pressed his thumb to his forehead in an action beyond Leandra's conjecture. "Who gets what they deserve?" he asked with a note of wry Cloud Culture philosophy. "The Creator made this world so that we're all confined within our minds. We have to dream and live and die alone. Even the worst man deserves better than that." The tension around his eyes softened. "I always wonder," he said, and gestured to his head, "if I do all this to get away from life, or into it." He closed his eyes and pushed his head back into his pillow. A smile tugged at his lips.

A dull ache formed in Leandra's chest. Before her transformation, she would have called it pity. His eyes saw only the surface of nature, and yet he had opened the universe to her.

She studied her old lover for a while. His face seemed content despite the bruises. Behind her Dhrun shifted. After maybe a third of an hour had passed, and Leandra was certain the opium had reached its tendrils into Thaddeus's brain, she pushed him gently on the shoulder. "Thad?"

Dreamily, he opened his eyes and smiled. "Lea?"

"Thad," she asked on impulse, "do you remember the first time you saw me?"

"How could I forget?" He paused, eyes floated shut. "That neodemon had its teeth in me . . . neodemon of addiction . . . and the teeth . . . felt so good . . . I would have died . . . and . . ." His eyes floated open. "What man wouldn't want to be saved by a pretty woman?" He held out his hand. Leandra took it. "You saved me, Lea." He squeezed her hand and his eyes fluttered shut again. He smiled. "It is too bad I couldn't save you."

"Maybe you have," she said and wondered at the clarity with which she saw things. "Thad, there's more."

His eyes fluttered open. "More what now?"

"I split up your dose of opium." She held up the second pewter cup.

He took it with an unsteady hand and so she helped him bring it to his mouth and swallow it. "Bitter," he mumbled but then smiled.

She took the cup away from him and set it gently on the desk. "Goodbye, Thad," she said and stood. Holokai and Dhrun were studying her. She motioned for them to follow and went out into the blood-covered hallway. There was no sign of the bodies. "Creator, Kai, even the shoes?" she asked.

The shark god burped.

She didn't look back to see the contented smile she knew was creasing Holokai's face.

Downstairs they found the winehouse empty. Walking out onto the evening street made a few city dwellers scatter. Well, at least the human city dwellers. Two macaque monkeys perched upon a nearby roof stared down at Leandra's party with dark eyes. Leandra could see the lice crawling through their fur, the larcenous thoughts written on their simian expressions.

The palanquin crew that had carried her from the Floating City was gone. She couldn't blame them. Fortunately, with the pain gone from her knees, she could walk on her own.

To the east, the volcano's shadow was stretching out across the bay and the distant Standing Islands were growing bright with the light of the falling sun. "Well," Leandra said, "that took longer than expected. We had better hurry if we're going to make our meeting." She headed east along the terrace road and then the Lesser Sacred Pool. She looked up at the volcano and thought about all of the textual energy stored in the crater lake. She wondered if there were some way to harness that energy to make things right. "Dhrun, I want you to stop by the compound to pick up the chest with the smuggler's possible payment."

"Yes, my Lady Warden," Dhrun said at her side but then added, "Apologies for starting to bring this up in front of Thaddeus, but didn't you once tell me that the hydromancers have a spell that can bring someone out of an opium stupor?"

Leandra nodded. "They do. They cast it directly into the veins and it instantly counteracts the drug. It's amazing to watch. The person comes welling up out of their intoxication like a drowning man comes swimming up to the surface. Instantaneous withdrawal."

They walked in silence down an abandoned street. When the Jacaranda Steps came into view, Dhrun said, "Forgive me, but if the hydromancers can bring someone out of an opium stupor, then didn't we just leave Thaddeus vulnerable again?"

"We would have if I hadn't dropped tetrodotoxin in his second dose."

"But doesn't that mean . . ." Holokai said slowly.

"By now . . ." Leandra said, her thoughts moving faster into the future, making the possibilities clear, orderly, almost crystalline. "By now, he's dead."

PART 2

When Nicodemus's party reached the compound, exhausted from the hike from the Floating City, they were greeted by John. Doria embraced the big man as did Rory and Sir Claude. Nicodemus took this as evidence that ever since facing the horrors of Feather Island, the party had grown closer.

John reported that the compound was in chaos. The house guards were maneuvering a long table onto the pavilion, while the servants hurried the finest plates and bowls out of storage. The kitchens were hotly engaged. When Vhivek, the pavilion's chamberlain, had learned Nicodemus's party was returning, he and the chef had embarked upon an ill-conceived three-course banquet. John had advised against it but had been overruled.

Once inside the pavilion, Nicodemus discovered the promised chaos of guards and servants. Out from the crowd came Vhivek, a gray-haired old man of the Lotus culture, who went into an apoplexy of apologies about his failure to impress. Nicodemus remembered enough of Ixonian protocol to realize that he could not simply call off the banquet without insulting Vhivek. So he claimed a fatigue that would make a banquet impossible. He begged for the personal favor of being allowed to eat simple fare with his party in the kitchen.

Vhivek agreed and boasted that he could serve the team in the Southern fashion. So while Vhivek reversed some of the chaos, the others retreated to their chambers to change before dinner. Nicodemus was about to do likewise when Francesca's twin druids arrived, each one holding the hand of a young boy with a pale face, dark hair, dark eyes. This had to be Lolo.

As they walked, Lolo would stop his feet forcing the druids to pull on his hands and allowing him to swing forward like a pendulum. Nicodemus had seen many parents doing the same, but he couldn't remember if he and Francesca had ever done so for Leandra. He guessed not.

Nicodemus led the druids up to Francesca's quarters. When he asked if they needed anything else, the druids shook their heads, but Lolo walked over to Nicodemus and looked up at him with wide dark eyes. "You're the man who married the dragon?"

Nicodemus took a step back so that he wouldn't accidentally touch and misspell the boy and then squatted down to his eye level. "I am."

Lolo nodded, suddenly solemn beyond his age. "Don't bite her."

"I try not to."

"Very bad things happen if you bite her. And she doesn't like it."

"Thank you for the advice," Nicodemus said while suppressing a smile. "I hope you like it here, Lolo. I'm sure we'll find a wonderful place for you in the Ixonian pantheon."

The boy nodded solemnly again.

Nicodemus stood and looked with curiosity at the druids. Tam explained about how Francesca had dunked the boy in the bay to provoke his transformation. The druid seemed ready to say more, but with a sigh Nicodemus told him to wait. He would need Francesca to explain her thinking. In the meantime he had enough to do, start another metaspell for example. He invited the druids to join him for dinner but they requested a tray be brought up so they could better look after Lolo.

Nicodemus left the room and was about to head back to the pavilion when, for no reason that he could fathom, he thought of Roslyn. Quietly he stole through the hallways to her room. He tapped gently on the door but got no response. He thought he could hear faint snoring so he slid the door back to peer in.

The old nurse, who had cared so diligently for Leandra, was lying on her bed. Nicodemus was again surprised to see how skeletal her face had become, how her lips clung to the teeth she had left. A plate of untouched curry sat on a side table. Despite snoring with a volume surprising for such a small woman, Roslyn seemed peaceful.

Nostalgia and regret churned in Nicodemus as he marveled that time should pass with deliberation in the moment but then speed itself faster and faster into memory. It seemed only days ago that a sickly young Leandra had been sitting in a younger Roslyn's lap. Now there wasn't much time left for Nurse Roslyn before whatever came after life came after her.

Nicodemus slid the door closed and to his surprise found John waiting in the hall. "I came to see if there was anything I could do for the druids." He looked at the door behind Nicodemus. "She okay?"

"I think so. At least she's sleeping well. Thank you, old friend. Maybe you could see if Doria could use any help."

"You know she hates it when you have people check in on her because you think she's a little old lady."

Nicodemus absently scratched the keloid on his back. "I know, but she is a little old lady. Humor me."

John gave him a doubtful look before nodding. "How about you, Nico? You all right?"

"As right as I can expect to be." He chewed his lip. "There is a lot riding on tonight, and all I can do is wait."

"Francesca or Leandra?"

"Both."

"Of course it's both." John smiled. "Did you ever think that we'd be having these problems?"

"Never in a hundred thousand years. So, will you check on Doria?"

John said that he would and that they'd both come down to the kitchen soon. So Nicodemus went back down to the pavilion and happily found the banquet table put away and every face shining with relief. One of the servants showed him to a small room that abutted the kitchen. Somewhere they had found a Southern-style table and chairs. Rory and Sir Claude sat side by side. Their backs were to the door and they hadn't noticed him.

Rory was leaning forward, his right elbow propped at a right angle on the table so that he could rest his forehead upon his hand. His expression was slack with fatigue. Sir Claude sat next to him. The knight's posture was, as usual, dignified, but he was leaning slightly forward so that he could comfortably reach out and hold Rory's other hand. Sir Claude was staring at a space somewhere above Rory's head. Together they became an icon of exhaustion finding comfort in company.

Nicodemus paused for a moment, the sight both accentuating and relieving his own fatigue. It made him think of the past thirty years, of the others who had joined his service. There had been Neha, the fiery hydromancer who had preceded Doria. A rebellious angel of lightning had killed her during the Tonatus Uprising. Then there had been old Sir Robert, the highsmith assassinated by a neodemon of darkness in Bearsleton. Others had died in his service, too many others, and Nicodemus was ashamed that he couldn't recall all of their names.

Nicodemus was not aware of making any sound, but Sir Claude withdrew his hand from Rory's and calmly said, "Good evening, my lord." Rory sat up straight and looked at Nicodemus.

They both started to stand but Nicodemus waved them down. "No, no, please don't mind me." He sat at the head of the table.

As ever, Sir Claude seemed composed and a little distant, but Rory looked first at Nicodemus then at Sir Claude with a haggard expression.

"Please," Nicodemus said, "don't be any different than you were."

After a short silence, Sir Claude said, "This, apparently, is how we were. Which . . ." He looked at Rory and gave him a brief smile. "Which will do for now."

Rory's expression relaxed.

Nicodemus was searching for something else to say when a flash of blue silk appeared in the doorway. "Everyone breathe easy," Doria announced as she walked into the room, "the old bat hasn't died yet. Thank you, Lord Warden, for sending the hospitality squad to go get her." She nodded back at John who was standing in the doorway and giving Nicodemus his best I-told-you-so smile.

Nicodemus and the two other men stood. "Doria," he said, "I'm sorry for setting John on you; I didn't want you to miss dinner."

"No chance of that while my heart still has blood in it," the old hydromancer said as she pulled up a chair. John moved beside her.

When Nicodemus motioned for them to do so, they all sat. A few moments later, the cook and his assistant entered with a steaming tureen. The party fell silent in expectation as the soup was ladled out. They drank it from the bowl in Ixonian fashion. It was rich with chicken and coconut milk, flavored with ginger and lemongrass. Nicodemus could feel its warmth fill him.

When the cook took the soup away, hunger's spell of silence broke and they lapsed into easy conversation, directed mostly by Doria. Nicodemus tried not to study Rory and Sir Claude, but on the few occasions he glanced over they seemed at ease. In fact, they even managed to stir up one of their usual teasing matches.

An air of relaxation came over the party, seemed to come welling up out of them. They had after all brought down the River Thief. The omens of war and Disjunction, they were problems for another day.

This was, Nicodemus reasoned, how every mortal lived: The certainty of death put aside for the comfort of a hot bowl of soup, a vivid blue sky, a friend's laugh. So it was that when the chef returned with rice and curry, the party was filling the small room with laughter and raucous conversation.

Even so Nicodemus found himself lapsing into silence and memories of dinners past, companions now dead. Then he remembered the young pyromancer he had captured on Feather Island. She would be in the infirmary now. He wondered if the physicians had operated on her hand yet to close the skin. He wondered if she were, at that precise moment, in pain or a drugged stupor. She had lost her fingers just that morning. Had there been a way he could have prevented that? Any way?

Suddenly Nicodemus realized that the chef was standing beside him, asking if he should like a shot of kava or rice wine. Nicodemus chose the kava and then waited until everyone else had been served before raising his voice. "A toast." He lifted his cup. "To victory and confusion to the Disjunction." These were his usual words and they sponsored the usual sincere cheers.

But after they drank, he raised his cup again. "These are unusual times—"

"Even more so than usually," Doria interrupted.

"Yes, more than usually," Nicodemus agreed, "and there are darker days ahead, but I cannot imagine finer spellwrights with whom to face them. So here is to you: my companions, my friends." They cheered just as loudly for this but drank deeper.

When Nicodemus sat back down, they followed and the conversation and laughter resumed. He motioned for the cook to take away the wine and kava. A few toasts would keep up morale, but hangovers tomorrow would tempt disaster.

After saying a quick prayer to the Creator that his wife and daughter were safe, Nicodemus turned his attention back to his friends. John and Doria, Rory and Sir Claude, their faces were bright with happiness and what youthful vitality was left to them. Their world was a beautiful one, and he hoped that they would all find enough of it.

CHAPTER THIRTY-ONE

"So Thaddeus was the one?" Dhrun asked as they walked toward the Jacaranda Steps. "He was the loved one you had to murder?"

Leandra glanced back. Dhrun was looking at her with concern, Holokai with incomprehension. "I could have kept Thaddeus alive," Leandra said. "But that would have required unacceptable risk."

Dhrun was silent for a moment and then asked, "Meaning, you might still have to murder someone you love?"

"Loved," she corrected.

"Someone you loved?"

"I might."

Dhrun's expression did not change. "That is a pity."

"It is. Is something wrong, Dhrun?"

"The tetrodotoxin kills because the victim can't breathe, but sailors give rescue breaths to men rescued from drowning. What if someone breaths for Thaddeus?"

"They would have had to discover him already and would have to breathe for him for ten hours."

"Then we're safe?"

"Very safe. Even if his heart still beats as we speak, he's dead."

"It's funny to think about. But I guess I'm not mortal."

"Part of you is."

"Yes, but it's a very cocky part."

"I suppose the common thinking is to assume that death is a state. Some place you are put. But really, death is any state from which someone cannot return . . . Oh!" A sudden half-grasped realization flashed through Leandra's mind. She stopped.

"What is it?" Holokai asked, lowering his leimako.

"Nothing dangerous," she said and started walking. "Just an idea about how to escape . . ." Her voice trailed off as her stream of thoughts flowed backward and forward in time. She realized that an hour ago she had sensed through the prophetic godspell a flush of surprise and danger. At the time, she had attributed it to her encounter with Thaddeus. But now she knew an opportunity to alter her futures was approaching.

A faint sound then, low then high and keening. Leandra held her hand up for Holokai and Dhrun. "There's . . . something . . ."

Dhrun pointed down the street. Out from between two houses shambled something human in shape but with a massive rotating head. A sallow aura lined his silhouette. On the evening breeze came a low, haunting wail. The figure lurched toward them. Holokai stepped in front of Leandra while Dhrun prowled to the right.

Leandra studied the stranger. Though the loveless spell had dramatically sharpened her vision in Thaddeus's room, that effect had lessened. Though still superhuman, her vision was no longer the wonder she had previously known. As such, at their present distance, Leandra distinguished only a few of the newcomer's features as he hobbled toward them. He had seven arms— one of them a stump above the elbow, the uppermost left entirely missing as if the limb had been plucked off.

The figure lurched, seemed to slip, fell. His arms went flailing and there came a howl. When he struggled back to his feet, Leandra saw that one of its lower left arms had snapped off like a twig. He was carrying the lost stump in one hand. The face on his cylindrical head was that of a praying mantis. "It's all right," Leandra said. "It's only Baruvalman."

Holokai relaxed. "Baru don't look good."

Baru lurched toward them with his head spinning, now an infant's, now a scared warrior's. His wailing changed from an infantile shriek to an adult moan. "Lady," he was crying, "lady, help me!"

Leandra looked around, saw nothing but the muddy streets and dilapidated buildings of the Naukaa. No ambush. Even so she said, "Be alert."

As Baru limped toward them, the arm he had been holding broke apart. The fingers fell to the ground and then burned with crimson light. By the time the pitiful divinity complex stood before Leandra, the fractured limb had crumbled into nothing. Surprise swirled through Leandra. She had never seen a deity deconstruct on its own.

Baruvalman was looking at her with the face of a wrinkled crone, eyes wide, slack mouth, few teeth. "Great lady, help me. They say you were doing battle on this terrace. I knew I had to come to you. I knew. You must help me. There has been a mistake." The divinity reached out two hands toward Leandra, but in the next instant Holokai stepped between them.

Baru stumbled backward, his head swiveling around to show the old warrior's. He fell to his knees, all remaining hands pressed together in supplication. "Please, great circle maker, take pity! Your agents have mistaken poor Baruvalman, but this humble god is your servant. He is worth saving from the godly sickness. Cure me!" Tears ran down his cheeks.

Leandra frowned. "Baru, what are you talking about?"

"It was your people. They said they were going to pray for me. They did say that. They very much did say that. I was begging and they said they would, but when I showed them . . ." His head spun to the child's and he pressed his forehead to ground while blubbering.

"Come now, Baru, it can't be as bad as that," Leandra said. He was a divinity complex and should heal quickly. "Whoever approached you, they were no officers of mine."

He began wailing louder.

"Pull it together, Baru. I'll do what I can. Who was it that approached you?"

"A man and a woman, both in new longvests. They said they had just come in from the Outer Island Chain and needed a divine guide. They said they would pray for me if I would show them around. I agreed and led them to a warehouse they said they wanted to see. Yes, very faithfully I did. But behind the warehouse, something happened. They were spellwrights of some kind." He sat up and his head began to spin, all his faces wide-eyed as if searching the street.

"Go on," Leandra said.

Still on his knees, Baru settled on the scared warrior's face. "They wanted to know about the demon in the bay. They said they would hurt me if I left anything out."

Again Leandra looked around the street for possible threats. Nothing. "And what did you tell them?"

"Only what Baruvalman knows, which is what everyone on the street knows, what everyone is saying."

"Which is what?"

"There is a lava demon on the bay."

"Neodemon."

"No, no, no. Great Lady, don't you know this? This is a demon from the Old Continent. The War of Disjunction is here. No doubting it now. Your Cult of the Undivided Society has finally brought a demon of the Ancient World across the ocean, and now he is stalking the bay."

"My cult? I belong to no cult." Which was technically true; the cult belonged to her rather than the other way around.

"B-but great lady, it is said that after the lava demon burned Feather Island you converted the demon and made your own cult. That is why they are calling you 'circle maker,' because you will turn the demons all the way around and use them against themselves, turn them around in a complete circle."

Leandra sighed in relief. She had feared that somehow her secrets had leaked. "Wild rumors, Baru, nothing more. I've found no demon."

"Then . . . you have not usurped the Cult of the Undivided Society who worship the ancient demons?"

"There is no such thing as the Cult of the Undivided Society," she lied.

The pitiful god began wailing again. "Then I am doomed. There is no hope for poor Baruvalman. Poor poor Baruvalman, who was a humble god of this city. Now I have the lava demon's sickness in me and now I will die of the divine disease!"

"Divine disease?"

Baru only wailed.

"Baru! I can't help you if I don't know what is going on."

The pitiful deity quieted enough to look at her with the old crone's face.

"What do you mean by 'divine disease'?"

"Truly, the great circle maker does not know?"

"Truly, you're making this circle maker feel not so great. No, I don't know or I wouldn't have asked."

"But . . . then . . ." He looked up at her and his head rotated to that of the baby, his mouth pulled back with fear and confusion.

"Baru!"

His head swiveled back to the warrior's. "The disease is like leprosy of the gods. The first struck down was the god of the Banyan districts. After he was attacked, his incarnation began rotting. His limbs fell off, so did his nose, right off his face. Yes, yes, it's true. I have heard it from everyone. He deconstructed this afternoon."

"Dhamma told me only that the Banyan god was missing."

"That is only what the red cloaks are saying because they are not knowing. They are saying the street is full of rumors, but this is no rumor. Too many are saying so. And more humble gods have gone vanished. The red cloaks are saying that it is they are being safe, but no, no. The street has it that they have the demon's disease, that they are coming apart. And now

I have the disease." He gestured to his recently lost limbs. "You must help your faithful servant Baruvalman. Please, please, you must."

A dull headache pressing down on Leandra's temples. The pitiful god's story was all mixed up. "Baru, I need you to stay calm and tell me what you know. You were telling me about the two spellwrights who attacked you behind the warehouse. They wanted to know about the lava demon out on the bay. You told them about the rumors . . . and then what?"

He shuddered. "Then they infected me with the divine sickness. And that was when Baruvalman thought that they were your agents, great lady. And Baru cried and yelled and begged for them to let him go because he was a friend. But they would not listen and grabbed his arm."

He shuddered again and all of his remaining hands went to the socket where the uppermost left arm and shoulder had been. "But brave Baruvalman pulled and pulled and then the arm came off in their hands. And Baru ran as fast as he could and hid behind some crates outside another warehouse. Behind him, the spellwrights said that there was nothing good or useful in Baru's arm and there was no use chasing after him."

His head swiveled back to the warrior. "So then, once the spellwrights had gone, Baru asked around where you might be, great lady. When they told me to come here, I came here. But I am brittle now because of the divine sickness. You saw, you saw." He gestured to the forearm that moments ago had snapped when he had fallen.

Leandra drew in a breath and tried to piece together what Baru had told her. Long experience had told her that wild street rumors sometimes grew from seeds of truth. "You thought the spellwrights that attacked you were my officers?"

"They gave me the sickness, so they had to be of the lava demon."

"You're jumping to a conclusion."

"But great lady, where else would the sickness come from?"

Leandra was not even sure the divine sickness was real, but she had never seen anything like what had happened to Baru. "I am not sure, and I suppose it is entirely possible that whatever is stalking the bay is an ancient demon. I must investigate further before making any conclusions. Baru, I am afraid there is nothing I can do for you at this moment, and I cannot be late for—"

"No!" Baruvalman wailed, his head spinning. "No, no, no, you must help. You must!"

"Baru, we can keep you safe by—"

"No, no, no!" He lurched toward her, arms outstretched. Instantly

Dhrun was beside him, two of her muscular arms grasping Baru's to restrain him. There followed two loud cracks and a dull flash. An astounded Dhrun stood holding two of Baruvalman's arms—one broken off at the elbow, the other at the shoulder.

With an unearthly scream, Baruvalman stumbled the other way. Holokai jumped back to keep the pitiful god from crashing into him. Baru slipped, fell. All his remaining arms went flailing, but his chest struck the muddy ground. With a sharp crack, a long fracture of red light ran across his torso. Slowly the two halves of his body slid apart, revealing what seemed to be cables of red light and darkness, linguistic viscera.

With a baby's face, Baruvalman looked down with horror. He was trying to scream, but the shrill cries had become rasps.

Filled with horror and pity, Leandra knelt beside the broken god. He reached out to her. But the instant her skin touched his, the world shifted and Leandra felt as if she might stumble. But then the ground steadied and Baruvalman vanished. Or, more accurately, Leandra could no longer perceive Baru as she had. Rather than the flabby, many-headed body, she saw only a miniature cathedral of crimson prose.

To her surprise, Leandra discovered she was fluent in his red language. The god's linguistic structure was as apparent to her as the segments of an orange are to anyone who removes its peel.

The spell that was Baruvalman was broken, she saw that now. Too many of his essential passages had been corrupted. Leandra knew how, with only a few casual actions, she could break the god into subspells that she then might preserve for her own use.

Shocked, Leandra drew her hand back. The world again spun around her, and then she regained her prior perception of Baruvalman: an agonized, broken god screaming with mortal terror on the ground. Above him stood Dhrun and Holokai, both of their expressions taut.

Leandra's heart was racing. She did not understand what had happened, but she did understand the broken god's suffering and fear. Maybe he could be saved. But likely not. With sudden clarity she saw what she had to do.

"It's going to be all right," she said as soothingly as she could. "Baru, listen to me. The pain will stop soon."

The wide, terrified eyes of Baru's old warrior face found hers.

"It's all right, Baru. I'm here."

His expression relaxed. He stopped trying to scream.

"It's going to be all right. We're here."

"Baruvalman," he mouthed, "is a humble god, a good god."

"Yes, you are. Now . . . here . . . give me your hand."

He reached out for her.

Wearing her most reassuring smile, she reached into him and, as gently as she could, shattered him.

It didn't take long, and once his bright sentences melted into nothing, she set off again down the street. They couldn't be late.

F rancesca checked her subtexts again and avoided Ellen's eyes. They were standing before a third-story window overlooking the Lesser Sacred Pool. Presently the plaza was adopting the evening sky's crimson and deep blues. Beyond the pool, the Palm Steps descended before a panoramic view of terraced Chandralu. If Francesca leaned out of the window, she could have seen—to her left and through the green thorns and crinkle-paper flowers of a bougainvillea vine—the dark heights of the Cloud Temple.

The room belonged to a wealthy rice merchant from the northern part of the main island. The owner had departed for his estates several days ago and left behind only a few servants; who, while dedicated to their employer, had not been above accepting a stack of Francesca's silver rupees for the use of the room.

Francesca had written several subtexts onto the window that made it appear empty even when she was standing in it. A Numinous spellwright searching for a subtext might glean her deception, but to anyone else she would be perfectly hidden.

Francesca had considered hiding places close enough to the pool to cast an eavesdropping subtext on Leandra and the smuggler, but the two of them would take precautions to prevent spellcasting in their vicinity. If either detected a subtext, the encounter would shed more blood than information. So Francesca had played it safe.

"In summary," Ellen said while proofreading the tricky paragraphs in the subtext, "your husband uses more entrapment games than we do to bring down neodemons. Likely it's not terribly useful to us. Rory explained that the situation in Lorn has become complicated since Argent began to reform the inquisition; it's forced many neodemons into more clandestine worship. Rory thinks that Nicodemus will be able to convince Argent to dissolve the inquisition again."

"He'd better," Francesca grumbled. "Their last inquisition touched off two skirmishes with Dral and killed the God-of-gods knows how many innocent Lornish."

Ellen paused but then spoke with more animation than usual. "Funny thing about all this, when Rory and I were comparing notes about Lornish neodemons, the Lornish knight just sat there quietly, stared off in the distance and then smiled at the oddest moments."

"How peculiar," Francesca mumbled.

"I couldn't figure out what he was about. Every other Lornish knight I've known has been rather stuffy." She turned a golden Numinous sentence this way and that in her hand. "You don't think he came to certain . . . conclusions about my intentions?"

"I can't imagine why he would," Francesca said as she finished checking the subtext on the window and then went to the screen door to examine the spells she had cast about it. They were mostly barriers to entry.

Ellen did not reply. In the ensuing silence, Francesca was, for the first time, embarrassed around her student.

"Magistra?" Ellen asked.

"Mmm?" When Francesca looked back she saw that her student was still twisting the Numinous sentence this way and that. Francesca went to her. "Is everything all right?"

Ellen sighed and then edited the sentence she was holding back into the subtext. "Do you think I'm very foolish for having such a sudden . . . interest in Rory."

"No, not at all."

"But there's something you're not telling me."

"There might be," Francesca said, a flush of guilt.

"I've made a fool of myself?"

"Not in the least."

"Rory's made a fool of himself?"

"No . . ."

"Your husband is uncomfortable with the idea?"

"Well, not uncomfortable exactly."

"There's another woman?"

"Well, not another woman exactly."

"Then there's another woman inexactly?"

"Not exactly a woman."

"But . . ." Ellen blinked. "Oh."

Francesca walked over to her.

Ellen let out a dry laugh. "That would be my luck, wouldn't it?" She nodded. "The Lornish knight?"

"I'm not supposed to know."

"Wrangled it out of Lord Nicodemus?"

"He's no good at secrets."

"Well . . ." Ellen sighed. "The knight was more courteous than I would have been. If someone had fawned over my man, I would have scratched her eyes out."

"Didn't you once? Back in Thorntree?"

"In my defense, she was a neodemon of revenge. And it was more her skull I was opening. The eyes just happened to be in the way."

"Understandable. Ellen, would you like a hug?"

"You've never hugged me before, Magistra."

"Your stoicism in the face of disappointment is stoking my maternal instincts."

"Don't those usually involve someone being gruesomely and draconically devoured?"

"Age softens all of us; hugging becomes an acceptable substitute." She opened her arms.

Ellen pretended to shudder. "If you really must. But I have to warn you, it'll be like hugging a post."

Francesca stepped in and wrapped her arms around her student, gently patted her on the back. Ellen, as promised, became postlike.

"See, it's not that bad."

"I'd rather be gruesomely devoured."

"Oh, honey, that can still be arranged."

Ellen snorted with amusement.

Smiling, Francesca released her and in the corner of her eye saw a lone figure dressed in brown robes reach the top of the Palm Steps. She recognized Holokai's bald head. "It looks like Lea's crew is showing up. You had better get back to the compound."

Ellen turned to look out at the shark god. "You're sure I shouldn't stay?"

"You're not going to escape helping the twins with Lolo that easily."

"Can't blame a girl for trying."

"I don't."

Francesca disarmed the barrier spells on the door and slid it back so that Ellen could walk out into the narrow hallway. "And, Ellen, don't worry about Rory."

Ellen nodded and continued down the hall. But just before she reached the stairway she said, "Magistra," and looked back. "Thank you."

Francesca smiled despite another twinge of guilt that she should be so much closer to her student than her daughter. She turned back to the window.

eandra surveyed the Lesser Sacred Pool as the day darkened into dusk. Chanted evening prayers echoed out from the temple behind her. A reflection of sunset-bright clouds quavered on the water.

The Lesser Sacred Pool was more of a wide, slow-moving stream than a proper pool. Several underground channels that carried water from the crater lake to the city filled the pool. An elegant pavilion floated on the glassy surface. Several hydromancers were performing evening ablutions. During the night they kept vigil and continued to strain water for the hydromantic texts that had come from the crater lake.

Every civic stream in Chandralu began in a similar pool where hydromancers could extract both impurities and spells. The recovered aqueous texts were then concentrated and stored in vials or carried back to the lake.

Leandra had always thought it inefficient that the hydromancers should spend so much time casting their spells in the crater lake and then collecting them again in the streams. Several hydromancers had told her that during the cycling from lake to city and back again, many of the hydromantic spells reacted with each other to form more powerful texts. To Leandra that sounded like throwing grapes into the ocean to make them into wine. But however they did it, there was no arguing with the hydromancers' results; every day, they churned out gallons of bizarre and wonderful textual fluids ranging from explosives to medicines to the world's most powerful disspells.

And the hydromantic disspells were the reason for meeting the smuggler at the Lesser Sacred Pool; if things got hot, with either steel or text, the hydromancers would dampen the situation.

Sparse foot traffic flowed around the pool. Most headed down the Palm Steps to see the shadow plays performed in the Bay Market.

Leandra glanced back and saw the Cloud temple-mountain looming high. The faithful were gathered before the temple, some chanting, others praying silently. All wore the flowing gray or brown robes of penitents. It was traditional to pray for forgiveness at the Cloud Temple at dusk, but this crowd seemed unusually large. Leandra supposed the day's ominous news had inflamed religious sentiments. Just then she spotted Holokai, disguised in the crowd by gray robes, walking toward her.

Leandra waited while he stood beside her, as if casually observing the pool. "Searched the whole place twice," he murmured. "No sign of the smuggler. Maybe he won't show, hey?"

"That would be unfortunate. What about the payment? The catamaran?"

She had sent Dhrun to the family compound to fetch their remaining jade. Additionally, she had dispatched Holokai to ready the catamaran.

"I gave Lieutenant Peleki his orders. As to the payment, I saw Dhrun. She said she's got it secure and nearby. She'll be patrolling the top of the Palm Steps."

"So then," Leandra said, "nothing left but waiting."

"Lea, can I ask you a question?"

She looked at the shark god, hearing in his voice a note of anxiety. Or, was it guilt? "Yes?"

"You don't think . . . you don't think that divine sickness that killed Baru is catching?"

Not guilt, then; fear. "I don't know. Have you felt different?"

"No . . . it's just . . . never saw a god come apart like wet paper."

"Poor, simple Baru."

"What do you think it means, the divine sickness? Do you think it really could be from an ancient demon?"

"It could be. But we don't know for a fact that a sickness caused Baru's condition. I could get a firmer grasp on a thrashing dolphinfish than he ever got on reality."

"And then you just . . . took him apart?"

"I'm not sure if that happened because of something inside Baru or because of Thad's loveless spell. Maybe it's both."

Holokai eyed her. "Hey, Lea, you okay with what happened to Thad?"

She looked at him and tried to show him how much she had wished things could be different. "I am, Kai. Are you?"

He studied her for a moment longer and then nodded. "If you are, then, yeah." He nodded again.

"Good. Now, you had better get back into the crowd."

Holokai looked at the pool and the bay beyond. Then he walked back into the crowd around the Cloud Temple.

Leandra examined the Palm Steps and admired the view of the city dropping steeply away. She could see the Sea Temple in shadow, the hazy blue of the bay beyond. Through the prophetic godspell, she had sensed that most of her future selves felt varying degrees of stress, determination, satisfaction. It was a good sign. There was little in her immediate future that might cause fear or pain.

Just then a man walked up the steep Palm Steps. He had a dark hand-some face, a white headwrap and blouse, red lungi. He was carrying two small leather folios, and when he saw Leandra, his smile showed perfect white teeth. The smuggler.

As she had on the beach, Leandra had the sense she had seen him before though she knew that was impossible. She nodded to the smuggler as he walked around the pool to stand next to her.

Flatly he asked, "No blackrice liqueur this time?"

"Nor tetrodotoxin."

"But hopefully as much mutual benefit? Are you satisfied with your god-spell?"

"It's come in handy now and then."

"Then I expect we should do more business."

"You came alone?"

"Alone but I can summon enough help to make you regret any treachery."

Leandra looked around the empty pool and saw only the hydromancers on the pavilion, a few pedestrians on the Palm Steps. She didn't doubt the smuggler but wondered where his support was hiding. "You have something new to sell?"

He glanced at the folios in his hands. "I might. Perhaps you have something you could sell to me in return?"

"I might."

"Information about the Cult of the Undivided Society?"

She nodded.

"Information I would find valuable?" he asked.

"Perhaps we can trade in kind. Perhaps you know something of why thugs are attacking weak deities in Chandralu and claiming to be members of the Undivided Society?"

"They're not?"

"So you know nothing more about the Undivided Society?"

"Nothing more than the empress is offering gold for information about them."

"Pity. So then, what might you have to offer me?"

"A godspell that will allow you to sense all deities within ten miles and, with a little effort, manipulate their attention. You can make yourself invisible to the Ixonian Pantheon, or you could focus a neodemon's attention on your enemy."

"A godspell of misdirection?"

"Precisely."

"That would have been useful a few years ago, but I am afraid the situation has changed."

He snorted. "You aren't good at hiding your interest." He gestured around him. "These islands crawl with divinity. Manipulating what they can see would be raw power."

She bobbed her head from side to side as if weighing the evidence for and against. Bartering, whether for lychee fruit or godspells, was always the same.

The smuggler nodded. "Perhaps you'll tell me what you want these godspells for? I could fetch texts suited to your purpose."

"As I mentioned, if you ever discover my identity, I would be forced to destroy you. And, as you can no doubt understand, you are more valuable to me breathing."

"Then I propose that I sell you this godspell"—he held one of the folios—"and we become partners on your information about the Cult of the Undivided Society. I will give you four tenths of the reward for selling the information to the empire."

"Why, what generous terms you're offering."

"I would be taking the bulk of the risk."

"Spoken like a true merchant. But I repeat myself: You're not fully aware of the environment we are trading in."

"Oh?"

"Once I tell you about the cult, you won't want to sell the information to the empress. You will want to take what profits you can and run from Chandralu while your neck still connects your head to your shoulders."

"And why should you become so worried about my neck?"

"A war with the empire is coming, as you have surmised. Should you survive, I could make you rich by buying information from you."

"Make me a spy?"

She nodded.

"For whom?" he asked.

"Like you give a damn."

He studied her face then laughed. "I guess I don't. But knowing my employer would help my political position."

"My concern for your political position rivals my concern for your toe jam in terms of its smallness. What I am concerned about is making us both wealthy."

While he thought about this, Leandra felt through her godspell. More clearly than before, she sensed that while most of her future selves were dealing with some shade of anxiety, nearly all of them felt the elevating satisfaction of her new loveless state. But, oddly, it seemed as if there were fewer possible futures she could perceive. Was this another side effect of the loveless? Or was she in a situation that was likely to produce only satisfying futures?

"Very well," the smuggler said, breaking her concentration. "This godspell for the agreed-upon price, and your information about the cult in exchange for three-quarters of the earnings you make from any secrets I smuggle to you from the empire."

Leandra shook her head. "The godspell for half the previous price. Remember, you have to flee the city. You won't have time to try to sell it elsewhere. And one-third of the profits from your future secrets."

"At those rates, I might as well throw this book in the sea and ride out the war safely on land."

"You're welcome to." She gestured to the bay.

"You need to make my risk at sea more profitable."

"I can always find another god smuggler, but you cannot find anyone else with my information."

"Why do I need the information if know I should sail on the next tide for home?"

"Then have at it," Leandra said as she repeated her gesture to the bay.

He frowned and looked at the bay, brooded. "This godspell for three-quarters the price, and half the profits for future secrets."

She looked him up and down. When she got to his handsome, care-worn face, goatee chased with silver, he met her eyes. Again she had the sensation that she had met him long ago. At last she said, "It's a deal." She held a fist above her head, then extended first three, then four fingers, the prearranged signal to Dhrun that they had settled for three-fourths the price.

A moment later, she saw the four-armed goddess carrying a chest up the Palm Steps. "I will have my goddess cast your godspell on you first to make sure it isn't a death sentence. You can review the payment. If everything is satisfactory, we can make arrangements for communicating during the war."

The smuggler grunted. "And I suppose you will now tell me what you know about what that war will be?"

Leandra drew a long breath in through her nose. "There is no Cult of the

Undivided Society. At least not as you imagined. No one is worshiping the ancient demons. However, the empress had discovered that some element within the league has been smuggling living deities out of the empire and into the league. No one within the Ixonian pantheon or regency knows who exactly has done this."

"But you do?" he interrupted, quickly grasping the situation.

"That's information with a different price. What you need to know now is that the Council of Starfall has failed to establish diplomatic relations with the empress's court. That, and the buildup of her air and sea fleets, can mean only one thing."

"Invasion of the archipelago."

Leandra frowned. He understood the situation surprisingly fast. Again Leandra searched the godspell to feel her futures; they were again reassuring. And yet, as before, there were far fewer futures that she could perceive. A sudden thrill ran up Leandra's body. What if her godspell was wrong?

Dhrun placed the small chest on the ground before the smuggler. Then the goddess looked out on the pool as if to join their contemplative gazing.

The smuggler glanced at Leandra. "That's your bodyguard? He changed?"

"That's her. She's the same."

"But he's a she."

"She's a she. Don't be dense."

The smuggler looked over a Dhrun and then, with a shrug, held out one of his folios. Dhrun accepted it with her lower hands. The smuggler then bent to peek into the chest while the goddess flipped through the book.

Meanwhile Leandra's mind worked hotly, trying to figure out what had changed her perception of the future. Why could she now feel so few of her future selves?

On the pool, the hydromancers continued their ablutions. Not being fluent in the divine language written in the smuggler's book, the water mages wouldn't take note of the group unless violence broke out.

When the smuggler stood up, Dhrun gestured to his head with the book. The smuggler bent forward and undid his head wrap revealing his silvering dreadlocks. Leandra saw among them a rubicund godspell. She remembered that on the beach, he had claimed to have a godspell identical to the one he had sold her. He must have found some divinity to cast that spell onto him.

Just as she had, the smuggler must have felt an hour forward to their meeting. He must have felt reassured or he would not have come. He would have known she had a similar sense of the future. Therefore, he would know he could not get the better of her unless . . . unless . . .

Leandra's heart began to kick.

The smuggler must have known he could not get the better of Leandra unless he could hide certain futures from the godspell he had sold to her. In fact, if he were to hide the dangerous futures, she would sense only the positive ones. She would take inappropriate risks. Another, stronger thrill of fear ran through Leandra. Was this why she sensed fewer possible futures?

Dhrun had pulled a crimson sentence from the folio and had stepped toward the smuggler's bowed head. Leandra brought her hand to her mouth and, as casually as she could manage, said, "It was surprisingly humid today."

Hearing the coded expression, Dhrun looked up. She balled her hand into a fist and then splayed out her fingers.

"Humid?" the smuggler asked.

"Didn't you think so?" Leandra touched her neck in the gesture for "kill" and then pointed to the smuggler.

Dhrun hesitated only for a moment, but just then the smuggler brought his head up, tossing back his dreadlocks. His face was alive with shock as he felt new futures evolving. Then his expression hardened into grim determination. Dhrun lunged for him, but the smuggler opened the folio in is hand.

A white flash blinded Leandra just before a shockwave knocked her off her feet. She heard a voice crying out. It sounded like her mother calling out a name. A Trillinonish name. A name she had often heard in her childhood. A name that Thaddeus had recently mentioned.

Faintly, Leandra felt her body striking ground. The world spun. Finally she understood the name. She saw how the fracture lines of the past cut jagged paths to intersect in the present.

That was why, just before the world dissolved, Leandra realized who the smuggler truly was.

Francesca's voice cried again.

Mother. Too late.

CHAPTER THIRTY-THREE

Francesca had watched her daughter with growing apprehension. When the smuggler's expression had changed from greed to annoyance, Francesca thought Leandra's bargaining had outmaneuvered his. Maybe it had, but there was something else, something out of place.

A deal had been reached, and the smuggler removed his head wrap while Dhrun prepared to place some text on his head. With growing horror, Francesca watched Leandra flash hand signals to Dhrun. The four-armed goddess hesitated, and the smuggler looked up. It was then that Francesca recognized him. She had never thought to see his face again.

Dhrun reached for the smuggler. Too late. The smuggler opened his folio and a blast of silvery Magnus enveloped them all. Francesca belted out the smuggler's name, "Lotannu!" She planted one foot on the windowsill and leapt out of the window and herself. Time slowed. Her wings stretched out and above, filling with wind. Auburn scales gleaming in the twilight, she dove.

Lotannu's silvery spell had swarmed around Leandra and Dhrun, pinning them to the ground. The goddess struggled, but Leandra lay still. Something erupted from the crowd of robed penitents near the Wind Temple. But Francesca focused on Lotannu, extended her claws and mind toward him to resolve the puzzle of his appearance.

Nicodemus had learned that Lotannu was commanding the imperial expedition. Apparently, Lotannu had established a clandestine connection with Leandra. But why sell such powerful language to Leandra? To win her over to the empire? That seemed an unlikely motive given how revolted Leandra was by the imperial deconstruction of deities.

As Francesca plummeted toward Lotannu, time crawled. Her mind worked furiously. Lotannu looked up. When his eyes landed on Francesca, they widened. A man, even a spellwright, he could not have fully perceived Francesca's draconic form, but Lotannu was expert in how spells and mind interacted. He had some text about his brain allowing him to perceive her. He opened his folio to reveal a page bright with Magnus weaponry.

Now only ten feet above Lotannu, Francesca pushed down hard with her wings and brought her hind legs around, claws spread. Like a hawk, she reached for the man. But his hand closed around a brilliant Magnus paragraph and pulled. Silvery prose erupted from the page. Francesca's talons were seven feet from his chest. He pulled the warspell free of the folio. Luminous sentences spun around his chest. Two feet. Lotannu's spells wove themselves into a shield. One foot. A sudden flash of prophecy then, and Francesca saw the landscape of time disarrayed. Somehow the future had become more fluid than ever before. Her claws splashed into Lotannu's warspell.

Time lurched forward. The air became fluid again, and Francesca crashed down through the prose and her claws dug into the cobblestones, sending up a spray of stone and red dirt. Long silver lashes of Magnus whipped out from where Lotannu had stood to strike her chest and neck. But the sentences shattered on her scales. She grasped her claws around what she hoped was Lotannu's crumpled remains and brought her forelegs around to crush him. But as she smashed her foreclaws into the stone, she saw that she had caught only dirt and stone.

Everywhere people were screaming. Francesca perceived the panic voices as varicolored flairs of light. She strained to pick out one among them that was Leandra's but could not. There was suddenly too much wind, rushing white and gray.

Bellowing rage Francesca swung her head around, searching for her quarry. That was when she saw that the twilight air had filled with what she first thought were massive birds but then realized were hierophantic lofting kites. There had to be more than a dozen of them, the jumpchutes blasting the plaza with torrents of air. They swarmed above her, unable to fully perceive her but aware a powerful force was attacking their leader. Francesca wondered where they had come from but then remembered the unexpectedly large crowd of robed penitents before the Wind Temple.

Just then, one of the hierophants dove at her. The cloth of his jumpchute split into a dozen warkites. Francesca leapt high and then lunged with her long neck between the warkites to the hierophant behind them. He had no time to react. Her jaws closed around him, her teeth punching through the text in his robes, pierced the delicate body beneath. The warkites around her fluttered toward the ground.

Francesca rose, intent on killing another hierophant. But just then pain raked down her back. She turned and saw three warkites raking her wings.

In places the spell-sharped cloth cut through her scales. The brave pilot who had attacked her had constructed a small jumpchute and was trying to escape, but with a quick swat of her foreclaws, she tore him open.

It was then that she saw Lotannu, splashing his way out of the Lesser Sacred Pool on the opposite bank. She dove after him.

Dhrun, now male, had somehow escaped his Magnus bonds and was carrying an unconscious Leandra toward the Palm Steps. Beside him ran Holokai, brandishing his leimako. A hierophant swooped upon them; part of his jumpchute cut itself free and snaked down to encircle the trio, but Holokai slashed through the cloth.

Francesca tried to turn back to Lotannu, but a jumpchute appeared before her, its seams forming razor edges. Nimbly she twisted to fly around it. However, the ploy had given Lotannu enough time to see her attack and leap back into the water.

Francesca splashed down into the pool, trying to crush the wizards. She sent water flying in every direction. Then she realized her mistake. The water burned like acid. The hydromancers had filled it with disspells, which were now eating into her draconic texts. With a tooth-rattling scream, she leapt back into the air, working her wings frantically.

Her spray of dispelling water had at least cleared the air of hierophants; two of them, their jumpchutes disspelled, fell to injury or death. A flair of pain ripped across Francesca's belly. She turned and saw that the hydromancers on the pavilion were throwing glass vials. At the top of their arcs, the vials exploded into blue starbursts.

Roaring, Francesca rose higher. Lotannu ran north toward the Cloud Temple. The urge to attack filled Francesca, but as another hydromancer vial burst, she mastered her instincts and turned toward the Palm Steps to find and protect Leandra.

Below her, Lotannu escaped into the streets behind the temple. Francesca could see two hierophants flying after the wizard, trying to gather him up and escape.

With a few wingbeats, she was above the range of the hydromancers' vials. The city stretched out before her and she became aware of the pedestrians fleeing down alleys and stairs. Pairs of red cloaks were running in the opposite direction. Francesca could not see Leandra. She hoped that Dhrun and Holokai had been smart enough to hide away. With luck, Holokai would take them back to the family compound.

Just then Francesca realized that she was not alone in the twilight sky.

A stranger airship was diving out of the darker eastern sky. No doubt, she was the empire's support for Lotannu's hierophants. Someone aboard her must have a textually augmented mind capable of perceiving Francesca. The airship's white foresails projected forward like curved blades. Her stiff aft sails made reflexive adjustments to keep her on course and in so doing caught glimpses of the sunset's rubicund light. It was one such flash that had caught Francesca's eye. Otherwise, Francesca would have been unaware of the ship until the foresails pierced her like a skewer. A moment later, the ship passed into the volcano's shadow, becoming nearly invisible.

Rage fueled Francesca's heart. She banked down toward the Palm Steps, forcing the airship to increase her angle of attack and so the danger of striking ground. In another moment, Francesca was winging her way down the broad Palm Steps, her wing tips brushing the whitewashed walls on either side, her body snapping clotheslines strung between pavilions.

On the steps below, pedestrians shrieked in bright violet voices as a dimly sensed creature passed overhead. Before her, fluttering kukui lamps illuminated the cityscape, folding down the volcano's slope to the glassy black harbor water.

Francesca saw that her tactic had forced the airship to abort her attack dive. The stranger now flew behind and above Francesca, waiting for her to rise out of the corridor of the Palm Steps. It wasn't going to work; Francesca could follow the steps down to the Bay Market. The airship would either have to pass over her or hover, but an airship without speed was defenseless, unlike a hovering dragon with her teeth, claws, tail.

So Francesca tucked in her wings and dove faster along the steps. As the buildings flashed past, she turned to examine her opponent. It was a lovely airship—long graceful lines, a delicate hexagonal hull, many aft and side sails to allow for maneuverability.

Most times Francesca struggled to distinguish an airship transport from a destroyer, but now the one ship she could identify was flying above. The hierophants had revised her, adding twenty more feet to her length and an additional foresail that ran along the inferior aspect of her bow. Nevertheless, Francesca saw plain as day that she was the *Queen's Lance*.

But who was her captain?

Francesca could make out five green robes in the delicate hexagonal hull. These would be the hierophantic crew. Unexpectedly there were also two bright yellow-and-orange robes. Pyromancers. Francesca had known the empire fostered collaboration among its magical societies, but she had never heard of the wind and fire mages sailing together. The two orange robes began moving their hands rapidly. Abruptly the twilight was broken by a hellish blast. The sound was a burst of fiery orange and red to Francesca's mind. Black smoke billowed down and out of the airship and was swept back over her sails.

A horrible screaming sound, bright green, shot over and ahead of Francesca and then a wide pavilion exploded into fire and rubble. A shockwave smashed into Francesca, pushing her off course and pressing her wing against a building. Frantically she flapped upward through the nightmarish smoke.

So the empire now had pyromantic cannon on hierophantic airships, which they had no qualms about firing into a peaceful city. Wasn't that just God-of-god's damned lovely?

Francesca guessed that the airship's captain would expect his opponent to use the same tactics as a fixed-wing craft. Fortunately for her, dragon wings were anything but fixed.

Hoping the airship had lost sight of her in the smoke, Francesca climbed straight up with heaving wingbeats. A moment later and now directly below her, the Queen's Lance shot through the smoke, dragging tiny black tornadoes in her wake.

Francesca lunged with both her foreclaws; even so, she nearly missed the ship, so great was its speed. She caught only one side sail with her left claw. In the next instant she was yanked forward with unbelievable force. For a moment she thought the ship would tear her claws off. The thrust from the aft sails thrashed against her hind legs and tail. Her hold began to loosen.

Instinctively she pulled her way forward. Her weight brought the stern down and the bow up. Together ship and dragon rose quickly into the air.

The roaring wind, bright white, drowned out most other sounds. But faintly Francesca sensed shouting and suddenly the hull's cloth split to reveal a veiled hierophant. The green-robe was working his hands across the hull's cloth. All around Francesca, the silk formed finlike blades meant to repel her. But with a quick snap of the jaws and head flick, she flung the hierophant into the churning air. She managed to get her hind legs onto the wing. They were flying over the harbor and as high as the volcano's summit.

Bellowing, she raked her front claws across the hull, tearing it open to reveal a hierophant and two pyromancers. With a quick backhand swipe, she knocked one of the fire mages out of the sky. She tried to bite the second, but he cast a blast of fire into her maw.

When she recovered, Francesca found the spellwrights had been enveloped in protective sheets of cloth. She pulled back a foreclaw to strike, but then the world began to spin into a vertiginous whirl of dark water, incandescent sunset, starry sky. The ship had entered a tight barrel roll. She sank her claws into the wings and held on.

Their climb slowed. Soon they would stall. Francesca intended to keep her claws in the airship until the instant before it struck water.

Then she saw another airship diving out of the eastern sky. Though the newcomer stretched three times longer, she was clearly written in homage to the *Queen's Lance*: a slender hull, a baffling array of aft and foresails. There was one frightening difference. Whereas the foresails of the *Queen's Lance* were spell-stiffed silk, the long curving foresails of this ship crackled with what seemed to be lightning.

Francesca craned her neck to get a better look. Her grip loosened as their barrel rolls slowed.

"Francesca!" Someone shouted over the wind. A strained voice. Something familiar about it.

Francesca tightened her claws and brought her head back. Standing atop the airship's hull, his green robes interwoven with the ship's fabric, stood a lone hierophant pulling off his veil. Francesca tensed to strike.

The man pulled off his veil to reveal a handsome face, short gray beard. His turban came free and his curly hair tossed in the breeze. "Francesca!"

Snarling, Francesca leaned forward until her snout was only feet away from the man. The *Queen's Lance* stalled and for a moment, they hung still and silent in the air.

The man glared at her with fierce, light brown eyes. The sun and wind had written their passage in wrinkles around his eyes. He was older now, more careworn. Cyrus Alarcon had been Air Warden of Avel, and Francesca's lover, when she had escaped from and then destroyed the demon Typhon.

They began to fall.

"You can't win," Cyrus yelled and pointed off toward the approaching airship. "That's the *Empress*, Vivian's flagship. She's made from fifty miles of silk and five deconstructed deities of storm and lightning. She was written to hunt air demons during the War of Disjunction. When the war's over, she'll hunt dragons."

They were falling faster now, the wind rushing past. Francesca's draconic heart filled with the hot need to attack. It would be so easy. A quick snap of the jaws . . .

But memories of intimacy checked her.

Cyrus met her gaze. "Give up; it's the only way you'll survive."

Francesca looked at the massive airship, now only a mile away and falling fast toward her. Jagged lightning leapt between her foresails where a sphere of white light was gathering. Francesca snarled at Cyrus.

The Queen's Lance began to spin as they fell. The wind blew Cyrus's hair back and away. The hardness around his eyes had softened. He was watching her now with pity, a hunter's sudden sadness for the beautiful beast he will destroy. This expression, more than she would have thought possible, filled Francesca with fear. "Please, Fran. Save yourself."

A jagged vein of light tore through the air not ten feet above her head. Reticular veins of lightning branched off and struck Francesca's wingtips and tail. Pain coursed through her. The instantaneous thunderclap seemed to shatter the world. To Francesca's mind it was a blast of jagged blue-and-black sound. Her foreclaws lost their grip and her wings slackened.

The *Empress* drew closer. Lightning crackled along her foresails.

After recovering, Francesca kicked with her hind legs, pushing herself away from the *Queen's Lance*. But as when a man jumps off a raft, the lighter airship flew backward and she remained almost stationary. So she flew hard toward the city.

Francesca saw that she had no visible wounds, but years of fighting storm neodemons had taught her that lightning left a trail of burned tissue as it coursed through flesh. Francesca's draconic body, though textual, was in grave danger.

Another bolt of dazzling energy filled the air, this time below Francesca. An instant later came the blue-black sound of the thunderclap. Francesca worked her wings harder. She was only two hundred feet from the harbor. She hazarded a look back and saw that the *Queen's Lance* was climbing into formation on the *Empress's* wing.

The implications of the situation flashed through Francesca's mind. If Lotannu had brought the empress's flagship to Ixos, he would have a plan to ensure the empress's safety. That indicated a massive imperial force. But how could such a force have reached the archipelago unnoticed by the Ixonian pantheon? The war deities alone should have been sent into fits by warships flying over their islands.

For that matter where were the God-of-gods damned war deities of Chandralu? Shouldn't there be hordes of gods spitting fire or hurling boulders at the imperial airships?

A bolt of lightning shot over Francesca's head. This time, one of the branches of energy struck her wingtip and sent agony racing down her body. The world dissolved into blindness, pain, a thunderclap.

An instant later, she found herself falling toward the bay and only with great effort managed to regain her wings. Now she was certain, the light-ning burns had damaged her draconic body so badly it would soon decon-struct itself and return her to her human form. In most circumstances, such a transformation would save her life; however, flying half a mile above the bay was not one such circumstance.

Francesca worked her wings harder. Chandralu had come alive. A con-flagration lit up the Palm Steps where the *Queen's Lance's* cannon fire had landed. She hoped Nicodemus and Leandra were safe. The smoke above the fire was forming a tight dome. Some civic god was weaving a net of air around the flames, trying to suffocate them before they spread.

Red cloaks ran up and down the Palm Steps, across the terraces near the Wind Temple, and across the docks. Among them were figures that shone with light of different hues. Here were Chandralu's war deities, marshaling the city's forces but confused as to what was attacking them. Perhaps they were not even sure if they were under attack. Then Francesca knew there would be no help from the Ixonian pantheon. At least not soon enough. They had no idea of her danger. Indeed, many of the weaker deities would not even perceive her draconic body. The next lightning strike would kill her.

Francesca's heart rebelled. She couldn't die, not while there was so much left to do, not while her husband was so vulnerable, not while her daughter still hated her.

Another searing bolt arched overhead. Another blue-black thunderclap. Francesca dove and then banked hard left, then down again and right, hoping to avoid her death for just a few moments longer. The *Empress* was almost on top of her. The pain in Francesca's wings confused her thoughts, blunted her will. Not long now and she would become a woman naked, weak, falling through liquid sky.

A lightning bolt shot down to her right and hit a galley in the harbor. The thunderclap followed moments after. Francesca was gasping now. Her confused thoughts turned to the first dragon. Nearly forty years ago, Typhon had written that creature and Fellwroth had set it to attack Trillinon. Wounded by the city's spellwrights, the first dragon had dashed itself into the city and set it aflame. Francesca wondered if now she, the third dragon on the New Continent, was racing toward a city that would soon burn.

She craned her neck and saw the sphere of light burning between the *Empress's* foresails. This was it then. At this range the airship could not miss. The killing bolt blazed, dropped.

But as the forked bolt fell, it seemed to strike something, or rather some-thing seemed to strike it. The lightning arced away and into the city. In the next instant, the bolt shot back from the city to the *Empress*. A double thunderclap hit Francesca with percussive force.

With a few wingbeats more, Francesca flew over the docks. That she still drew breath seemed incredible. From below came the shouts of sailors, soldiers, gods as they assembled on the quay.

Forcing her agonized wings to fly her up along the Jacaranda Steps, Francesca looked back to see to her amazement that one of the *Empress*'s foresails had gone slack. The whole airship had entered into a slow downward spiral. As she watched, the array of aft sails reconfigured, righting the ship and pointing her bow upward, breaking the spiral to fly over the harbor.

The sphere of light blazed from the airship's remaining foresails and an instant later an arc of lightning leapt from the ship out and down into the city. But as the lightning branched, Francesca saw defined against the sky an identical but opposite forked bolt leap up from the city to strike the ship. However, this was not an arc of light but one of complete blackness. It was inverse lightning, black lightning.

An instant after the white lightning struck the city, it reversed course and flew back along the path cut by the black lightning until it struck the *Empress*. A yellow sunburst erupted from the airship's bow and she spun downward.

Francesca realized that the black lightning had originated from the Jacaranda Slope district, about halfway down the Utra Way, where her family compound stood. Curiosity overpowered Francesca's pain and exhaustion. Who or what could have cast the black lightning? Some storm god of war? A goddess of lightning?

Though she could feel her draconic body beginning to deconstruct, Francesca forced herself to stay aloft. Every wingbeat was agony, but she flew up the Jacaranda Steps and along the Utra Way. To the east, the *Empress* was retreating toward the bay.

Francesca's wings gave out a hundred yards away from the compound. Her body shaking, she touched her hind legs down on the cobblestones and landed awkwardly on her foreclaws. But she was too weak. She flopped forward, her shoulder breaking cobblestones and digging a gash into the red earth.

The world faded away. There followed brief, vivid dreams of thunderheads over blue waters and memories of the rolling yellow foothills of her Verdantine childhood home. That had been centuries ago, but it felt . . . it felt . . .

Pain returned as pulses through a body that was so much smaller, so much weaker. Groaning, she moved her thin arms and legs, pathetic compared to the glory she had been. The ground beneath her was warm, muddy. Someone was saying her name.

At last Francesca opened her eyes. A man was crouching beside her. Of course it was him. "Nico?" she croaked.

He took her hand. "You're safe. The airships haven't returned."

She was still lying in the gash her draconic body had made in Utra Way. She was naked but someone had laid a blanket over her. Now more self-conscious, she realized a crowd had gathered around Nicodemus. His followers stood close, as did Ellen and the twins.

"Who was it?" Francesca asked. "Who turned the airship? A lightning god? A storm goddess?"

"No . . ." Nicodemus said softly and then looked up to someone standing at Francesca's feet. At first she couldn't make the woman out, her vision was still blurry. Francesca sat up and squinted. "Who are you?"

"I am not so sure that I know anymore."

"Lea?"

"I wouldn't swear to it just now."

"But how did you do it?"

"Dhrun kept the godspell that the smuggler sold us. It manipulates the attention of a deity. When I woke on the way to the pavilion and he explained what was happening, I had him cast the spell on me." She looked up at the sky again. "That airship was written from deconstructed parts of deities. The spells that aimed the ship's lightning were drawn from the part of a goddess's mind that directed her attention. So it was susceptible to misdirection. I confused the ship into throwing the lightning so that it returned from me to strike the ship. It isn't a mistake they will make twice."

"I'm grateful they made it once," Nicodemus said as he more securely wrapped the blanket around Francesca and helped her stand. "Let's get inside."

Francesca's human legs felt weak but she did not seem to be wounded. In fact, other than fatigue and nausea, her strength seemed to be returning. The contact with Nicodemus was helping; Typhon had written her to draw strength from his cacographic abilities. Their first touch had enabled her to achieve her draconic form.

As they started toward the compound, Francesca looked over at her daughter. Leandra looked back with a peculiar expression. Her mouth was pursed slightly, her eyes hooded.

"You saved me from the airship," Francesca said.

"You saved me from the smuggler's ambush."

"I guess . . ." Francesca struggled for the words, resisted the urge to reach out and touch her daughter. "All this time I thought that if anyone was going to kill me . . ."

"You shouldn't have doubted it, Mother. I might have tried to kill you before. I might even try again. But I'll be damned before I let anyone else get away with it."

icodemus waited impatiently as Captain Kekoa of the red cloaks explained his strategy for preventing imperial spies from causing more bloodshed that night.

Nicodemus had trouble listening. The empire had already made its covert play and failed. Their next attack would be massive and beyond the ability of a few hundred red cloaks to prevent. Nevertheless, the city needed policing and Nicodemus needed Kekoa's good regard. So he tried to look attentive as the captain rattled off patrol schedules.

When the man fell silent, Nicodemus said, "Very good, Captain. I agree wholeheartedly. Now, if you could excuse me, I must see to my lady wife and daughter." He turned and climbed the pavilion's stairs. Rory and Sir Claude fell in beside him and they hurried through dark hallways. Servants and guards stepped quickly out of their way.

They came to the compound's tearoom, the windows of which looked out on a nighttime city illuminated with torches. Martial law had been declared and additional fortifications were being built on the docks and city walls.

In the middle of the room stood a long, low table. Darkness seemed to lean in on the few, flickering kukui lamps. Somehow the cook had found time to lay out a traditional Ixonian tea service: a steaming brass teapot, glass bottles of rice wine and kava, porcelain cups.

Leandra and Francesca knelt at the table and stared out at the city. Even in the room's dim light, Nicodemus was struck by how similar they looked: fair skin, pretty faces, freckles, wide brown eyes. Mother and daughter. Behind each woman stood her followers. The lamplight shone on the eyes of Leandra's four-armed wrestling god, who was staring at his daughter with protective concern. Nicodemus allowed himself a moment of pride that she inspired such loyalty.

Nicodemus took a place at the table and looked from his daughter to his wife. Francesca was composed, tension around her eyes. Leandra, on the other hand, was at ease. Her gaze wandered, as if she were distracted.

"So," Nicodemus said, "what happened?"

Oddly Francesca looked to Leandra and then flicked her gaze to Holokai, who seemed to return a knowing look.

Leandra spoke plainly. "I had been cultivating a relationship with a smuggler of imperial godspells. I met with him tonight to try to make him my spy. Instead he nearly killed me. It turns out that he himself was an imperial spy."

"Not just a spy," Francesca said. "But Lotannu Akomma." She described Lotannu's narrow escaped from her attack and the subsequent appearance of the airships. "Since then, my officers have reported that the wind mages killed near the Lesser Sacred Pool all have the perfect circle tattoo on their hips."

"The same tattoo that we found on the bodies on Feather Island?" he asked.

It was Leandra who answered. "The tattoo was also on those who have been attacking minor deities. Now it makes sense why those who attacked the minor deities were so often unsuccessful. We thought the thugs were underestimating the strength of the deities, but it was the other way around. They are imperials. In the empire, under Aunt Vivian's metaspells, spellwrights are much more powerful. Their initial attacks were too weak because they hadn't yet adjusted to how weak they would be within your metaspell."

"But why attack minor deities at all?" Francesca asked. "It doesn't weaken the league significantly and it made them liable to discovery."

"There are rumors of a divine sickness spreading through the minor deities," Leandra replied. "Supposedly the Banyan god was deconstructed by it, and I witnessed the pitiful god Baruvalman suffer from it. When I touched Baru, he nearly came apart. The street rumor is that the divine sickness is from a demon who is out on the bay, but I see Aunt Vivian's hand in it."

Nicodemus understood. "You think the imperial spellwrights have brought to Ixos whatever spell it is they use to deconstruct their own deities?"

Leandra nodded. "I think Lotannu was mining godspells from our deities before attacking us. It would empower his authors and provide godspells to sell to me while he pretended to be a smuggler."

"And why, under the fiery heaven," Nicodemus asked, "were you trying to buy godspells you thought were smuggled out of the empire?"

"To better fulfill my role as a Warden of Ixos."

Francesca shifted in her seat. "Was there another role you were also trying to fulfill?"

For the first time, something like surprise moved across Leandra's expression. She narrowed her eyes at her mother. "What do you mean?"

Francesca didn't reply.

Nicodemus frowned. "Tell me what is going on."

After a tense moment, Francesca spoke. "It was only a question. I agree with Lea. If the empire could prey upon weaker deities, it would cause many to lose faith. Without prayer, our pantheon cannot protect us. There is also the matter of why Lotannu should be willing to sell godspells to Lea."

Leandra grimaced. "He was setting me up. I did not realize, but he had manipulated a prophetic godspell that he sold me. He edited the spell so that it would blind me to certain futures. I stepped into his trap. If not for Mother, I would be bound and censored on some imperial airship right now."

"Without you, Lea, I would now be skewered on the foresails of the empress's flagship. We saved each other."

Leandra pursed her lips and sat a little straighter.

Francesca continued. "I wonder if Lotannu wasn't also trying to undermine the league by empowering you with the godspells."

"What do you mean?" Leandra asked flatly.

"It's no secret that we don't get along. If Lotannu strengthened you when there is something about which we disagree . . .".

"Mother, you sound as if you have something specific in mind."

Nicodemus looked at the two of them. "Creator damn it, you two. What is going on?"

The two women stared at each other for a long moment. But then, at last, Leandra looked away. "It's complicated, but I hope you both appreciate that I am the Warden of Ixos and it is my duty—"

Francesca interrupted. "What we are dealing with goes beyond Ixos."

"Yes, Mother, I see that far better than you imagine. I don't want us to work against each other. If you would let me finish?" She raised her eyebrows.

Francesca took in a sharp breath but then let it out slowly. "Yes, of course."

Nicodemus had never known his wife to back down so easily. Maybe there was hope after all.

Leandra too seemed affected. "Thank you. In fact . . ." She paused as if deciding something. "In fact, after everything that's happening, I could use some wine. Maybe you could too?" She stood and went to the tea service.

Francesca started to speak but again checked herself.

"Don't worry, Mother," Leandra said with a sigh. "My disease flare has resolved."

Nicodemus frowned as he realized that Leandra's rash had disappeared.

Leandra added, "I will explain how that happened, but first may I serve you two?" She adjusted the tray and looked at Nicodemus. "Dad, tea or wine?"

"Both?"

Leandra smiled. "Let's start you on tea then." She set out three cups and picked up the brass teapot. While she poured, she looked at Francesca. "Mom, tea or wine?"

It was the first time in sixteen years that Nicodemus had heard his daughter use that word. It didn't seem to be lost on Francesca. "God-of-gods, wine," she said with the slightest quaver. "I could definitely use a glass of wine."

Leandra poured wine for her mother and herself before distributing the cups. Nicodemus wrapped his hands around the cup, felt its heat.

"To survival," Leandra said and started to raise her cup but bumped the teapot's handle with her elbow and had to quickly correct her motion.

Nicodemus reflexively leaned forward to try to catch the pot if it fell but then remembered how hot it would be. Fortunately the ornate brass thing only wobbled. He saw what he thought was a silver wire below the pot and wondered if it had fallen off. But before he could remark on it, Leandra repeated her toast, "To survival."

So the three of them clinked their cups and sipped.

Leandra said, "I'm leaving the city."

"Oh, God-of-god's damn it, Lea!" Francesca groaned. "I thought you were serious about working together."

"I am serious."

"No, you're not. There's no way you can leave the city. And why would you even want to?"

"Calm down—" Nicodemus started to say.

"I am calm!" Francesca snapped before turning to Leandra. "Why?"

"My people are out on the bay. They aren't safe. It's my duty to protect them."

Nicodemus frowned. "Your people?"

"Dad, I am the one who has been smuggling gods and goddesses out of the empire."

Nicodemus started to laugh but then saw that his daughter's flat expression was not changing. "You're not serious. Lea, that's impossible . . ."

"It is not. For more than a decade, I've run a secret society that has helped about a hundred deities escape the empire. Mostly I've brought them here to Ixos, but maybe thirty have gone to Dral. The shape shifter that the empress discovered was one of mine."

"But . . . Lea . . . that's insane. It's tantamount to declaring war on the empire."

"Maybe."

"But . . ." Nicodemus felt as if his heart were beating behind his eyes. He took another sip of tea to preserve his nerves. "But . . . you can't have done this. It's our duty to preserve peace so we can fight the War of Disjunction."

"What's the point of saving humanity if we're corrupt?"

"God-of-god's damned survival is the point! That thing you just had us toast to. We have to survive."

"You never understood that, Dad. That's what I could never make you understand. All those talks about disability and disease, you never understood. All your life your disability has made you focus on survival. If you had a disease like mine you would know that there's no point to survival if it means doing the wrong thing."

"The wrong thing? What in the burning hells are we doing that's so wrong?"

"We've built a civilization in which the strong prey on the weak. We create divinities to answer our prayers even though many of those prayers are malicious. Our neodemons abuse and kill the weak. And why do we do it? So we can keep up with the empire. And what's the empire do? Cannibalize their deities so they can keep up with us. There's no point to trying to survive the Disjunction if we are no better than the demons."

Nicodemus shook his head. "So you're fixing things by starting a war?"

"I wasn't trying to start a war. I was trying to do the right thing."

"The right thing?" Nicodemus squawked.

"You raised me to defend vulnerable humans from the neodemons in the league. Then why shouldn't I defend vulnerable deities from the spellwrights in the empire?"

"Because it's going to get us all killed!" Nicodemus thumped his hand down on the table and felt his fingers tingling. He was breathing too fast. He turned on Francesca. "This is all about what happened in Port Mercy, isn't it? That god that seduced her was a refugee from the empire and you ate him, so now she has to save every deity in the empire?"

"Nico," Francesca said flatly, "you need to calm down." She looked at Leandra. "He will calm down."

"Calm?" Nicodemus asked. "Our daughter just started a war that will critically weaken humanity before the demons come, and you want me to be calm?" He paused. "Fran, why under a fiery heaven are you so calm."

"There's nothing to gain by being upset."

"Wise advice," Nicodemus said, "which you have taken exactly never!" Then something occurred to him. "Creator help me, Fran, you knew. Why is it I'm always the last one to know anything in this family?"

Judging by a momentary widening of her eyes, Leandra also seemed to be surprised by Francesca's knowledge.

Nicodemus took a long breath, pressed both his hands against the table and felt his fingers tingling. He tried to breathe more slowly. Then he became aware of the tension in the rest of the room. He could hear his followers shifting and saw his wife's spellwrights staring at Leandra's two gods.

Nicodemus blew out a long breath. Francesca was right. He needed to calm down. "All right, so, what do we do about it?"

Leandra replied. "I have a hidden village in the Standing Islands. There are refugees there I must protect."

Francesca leaned forward. "Send Holokai to fetch them back. We don't know where the imperial forces are. And there is still the matter of the lava neodemon loose on the bay. There's no need to risk yourself, Lea."

Leandra shook her head. "These godspells have changed me. You saw when I turned the lightning back on that airship. I will be fine."

Francesca started to talk but paused for a moment before saying, "But as you pointed out, the empire won't let you get away with it again."

Again Leandra shook her head. "I have acquired other talents. Another of my spells has decoupled my ability to misspell from my disease."

"It what?" Nicodemus asked, remembering how Leandra had misspelled every text that the Trimuril had cast at her.

"It's a tertiary cognition spell that stops me from being able to love. And it prevents me from suffering a disease flare when I use my talent. And . . ." Her face became thoughtful. "One other thing . . . these godspells make it seem that there is something more . . . to who I am . . ." Leandra's voice trailed off and her gaze became vague for a long moment before she looked at Nicodemus. "I must separate myself from the league. I will find a way to contact Empress Vivian. I will explain that I acted on my own and that I have since broken from my family. I will let her know her attack against the league is unfounded. All you two have to do is survive until then."

"Lea, that's crazy," Nicodemus said. "If Vivian's launched an invasion of Ixos, there's no turning back."

Leandra gave him a mischievous smile, as if she were still a little girl. "I don't know, Dad, I can be very persuasive."

He stared at her in disbelief. "Lea, the spells on your brain are preventing you from thinking straight."

Francesca cleared her throat. "Lea, we can't let you leave Chandralu."

"You won't be able to stop me."

Francesca cleared her throat. "Lea, in my draconic form I was wounded, but I have been back in contact with your father. If you tried to leave, I'd fly after you." Francesca reached out and took Nicodemus's hand.

Oddly, his fingers felt numb against her touch. He frowned at his hand.

"You could do that, Mom, if you didn't have a patient to tend to."

Both Nicodemus and Francesca stared at her dumbly. At last Francesca said, "Lea, you are sounding very far out of your head. What patient?"

"Yesterday, early in the morning, I acquired a weakly prophetic godspell from Lotannu Akomma. Though it usually gives me limited insight an hour into the future, I temporarily misspelled it so that I could learn what would happen a day in the future. During that time, I discovered that I would have to choose between killing someone I loved and dying myself. If I ran or tried to avoid this fate, everyone I loved would die. Now I know that if I had run, the empire would have destroyed Chandralu. Now something is stopping their attack. I'm not sure what it is yet, but I have to discover what is staying their hand. That is how I will reach the empress."

Francesca tightened her grip of Nicodemus's hand. "Lea this is madness. You don't have to kill anyone."

Leandra looked between her parents, her large brown eyes studying them. "I have been trying to find some way to escape killing one of you. I can't tell you how much I have agonized over it. Even though this spell keeps me from loving, I still feel worry and guilt and the hundred other horrors that it would bring on. That's why I had to try this."

"Try what?" Nicodemus asked more breathlessly than he intended. His lips were tingling.

Leandra looked at her mother. "What is death now in this age of wonders? If a heart stopped, and you were nearby you might be able to restart it. You might say that man died and you brought him back."

Francesca shook her head. "It's more complicated than that, Lea. If a heart were in an arrhythmia I could . . ." She shook her head, spoke again in a firmer voice, "Lea, what are you thinking?"

"Death is a state from which no one has yet come back. And until someone is brought back from one such state, it is death. But what if I put one of you in a state that, for all I know, is death and yet the other one of you were able to bring the other back. Then I would have killed one of you and yet not."

"Lea," Francesca said in disbelief, "are you trying to get into a semantic argument with prophecy?"

Nicodemus's hands and feet felt numb. His lips tingled and it seemed an effort just to breath. "Lea, what are you saying?"

Leandra reached out and took Nicodemus's hand and to his horror he found that he couldn't move his fingers.

Leandra looked at her mother. "I think your first problem will be his mind. If I understand, being aware during what follows would drive him mad. After that, you'll have to write some text that breathes for him. Maybe some spell to pump his blood. I don't know. Maybe it's impossible. If I did know, this wouldn't have a chance of cheating prophecy."

And then Nicodemus understood. His body felt insubstantial. He tried to stand but his legs only flopped beneath the table. He looked at the brass teapot and saw what he had thought had been a bit of silver wire which in fact was a needle.

"Lea," he mumbled with clumsy lips, "what have you . . ."

She looked at him with haunted eyes. "I'm sorry, Daddy. I have to go." She stood.

Francesca screamed something. Nicodemus wanted to stand but flopped backward. Then he was aware that Francesca's arms were around him, laying him on the ground.

His body no longer seemed a body. He could move no limb, could feel no sensation. The visible world blurred, but he could still see his wife hovering over him, pressing her fingers to his neck to find a pulse. Doria and Ellen stood beside his wife, wanting to help but unable to touch him for fear of contracting a canker curse.

Nicodemus could see on his wife's face how fast she was thinking, how desperately she was trying to make a diagnosis. Within the muscles of her forearm, she extemporized a censoring spell to render him unconscious. Frantically she tilted his head back pressed her mouth to his and blew a breath into him. His chest inflated as if it were a bellows or some other lifeless and mechanical thing.

Then Francesca sat up and pulled the censoring spell from her forearm. He tried to push the air from his lungs, to form the sounds to tell her what she needed to know to save his life. But the air came too slowly "T . . ." he said. Tried again. "T . . ." But she cast the spell, and sent him down into unconsciousness before he could speak the name of the poison.

CHAPTER THIRTY-FIVE

The nauseating guilt and fear of a murderer churned through Leandra. It was the same emotion she had felt when her prophetic godspell first projected her mind forward twenty-four hours. Hopefully she had just cheated prophecy.

Dhrun began to lead her out of the tearoom, but Francesca managed to jam a breathing spell down Nicodemus's throat, pass the spell to Ellen, and then run after her daughter. "Lea, don't!"

Leandra wondered if she had misjudged her mother, if draconic jaws were about to close around her. Holokai stepped in front of Francesca. Mother and daughter locked eyes. "Lea, don't do this."

"It's already done," she answered coolly, sadly.

"My lady," Doria said from behind Francesca. "My lady, only one side of his chest is moving. The breathing tube is in too far or maybe he's misspelled your text."

When Francesca looked back, Leandra knew she would get away. Her father's cacography would slowly misspell any therapeutic spell, requiring the physicians to continuously edit their texts. Moreover Francesca was the only one who could tend to Nicodemus without contracting a deadly canker curse.

Leandra straightened. "Go to him, Mother."

Francesca turned back to her daughter. Holokai put out a hand to stop her, but Francesca grabbed the shark god's arm and pulled him close and snarled before pushing him back. "What did you give him, Lea? Tetrodotoxin?"

"My lady," Doria said, "he needs you!"

After glaring for another moment, Francesca went to Nicodemus. As Leandra turned to go, her mother shouted, "Stop her!"

Dhrun stepped out of the tearoom and into the hallway. Leandra followed and saw Mykos with two of his guards all leveling knives at Dhrun. Each man carried a spear, but in close quarters they were useless.

Dhrun crouched. His four arms circled in a wrestler's anticipation. "Step aside, Mykos," Leandra said calmly. "There'd be no point to killing you and your men."

The old guard looked from her to Dhrun. Slowly he lowered his dagger and then nodded to his men, who followed suit with apparent relief. They stepped aside and Dhrun led the party through the dark hallways.

On the wide balcony atop the pavilion's staircase they found her father's spellwrights, Rory and Sir Claude. The druid brandished a large wooden staff, and the knight was covered with fluid metal armor. Two thin blades protruded from the basket hilts around his hands. Behind the spellwrights stood five red cloaks with spears and the space to wield them.

Leandra looked behind her and saw that they had been followed by her mother's twin druids, Mykos, and the two guards.

"My lady warden," Sir Claude said, "you seem lost. Let us conduct you back to your ailing father."

"Very amusing, sir, but stand down and spare us all bloodshed."

"You know we cannot," Sir Claude said. "Please, my lady, for the sake of your father."

Leandra murmured to her gods, "Can we manage it?"

"Not without killing," Dhrun replied. "And maybe not at all if the spellwrights are good."

She nodded. "Leave the spellwrights to me. Take the guards down as fast as you can. Kai, protect our backs."

The shark god grunted in the affirmative.

Leandra walked toward her father's spellwrights. "I appeal to your loyalty to my father. He will need you by his side." She stopped before the knight. Rory's knuckles tightened around his staff and the red cloaks shifted. But Sir Claude did not so much as blink.

"Sir," she said, "there is no point fighting a tidal wave."

"You are not a wave, my lady. You are a woman."

"Betting on what I am would be reckless. Last warning."

"My lady, for your father's sake, turn back."

"For my father's sake, step aside."

"I cannot," he said softly. He paused. His eyes softened. He spoke in a near-whisper. "We've all seen enough death."

Leandra saw the resolve in his dark eyes. He was twice her age, the veteran of a horrible war. She wondered if she would ever know as much of life as he had.

"Very well," she said with a sigh, "take my hand and then lead me back to my father." She held out her empty palm.

Rory and Sir Claude looked at her hand.

"Sir, take my hand and lead us back in peace. Or do you doubt my honor?"

Sir Claude studied her face for a moment. Then the blade and basket hilt on his right hand retracted. He laid his hand in hers and said, "I trust your honor."

"You shouldn't have." She sent a shock of cacographic force through Sir Claude's armor, breaking every spell in his steel and freezing him in place. She lunged for the druid even as blue light burst from his staff. She grasped the wooden weapon and dispelled the text within it. A small explosion knocked her to the ground.

Above her a red cloak thrust a spear at Dhrun. He caught the shaft with his two lower hands while striking the red cloak's face his upper hands. Dhrun pulled the spear from the red cloak's hands and spun it around his waist while shoving the man into the red cloak behind him. Instantly Dhrun lunged at another red cloak, turning the other man's spear with his upper hands and driving his own spear into the man's gut with his lower.

Leandra fought to her feet. Sir Claude would be frozen in his armor until he extemporized enough text to restore its fluidity. But Rory had pulled a wooden button from his sleeves. Blue flames danced from his fist. Leandra leapt upon him, dispelling his every text. So long as she held on to him, he was not a spellwright but only a man.

Nevertheless he was a man with nearly a foot of height and a hundred pounds on her. He slammed his elbow into her jaw. Light flashed across her vision and the world spun. Then she was on her back and looking up at Rory who had pulled another button from his robes. The blue flames again erupted from his fist. He made to strike Leandra, but a spear struck a glancing blow against his hip and he staggered back.

Ten feet away, Dhrun recovered from his spear throw and ran at Rory. Somehow Sir Claude freed himself enough to step in front of the god. With a bellow, Dhrun slammed all his hands into the knight's breastplate.

Sir Claude went tottering backward until his lower back struck the staircase's banister. His momentum tipped him back. With his upper body still immobilized within steel, he could not bend or grasp the railing. He flipped over the rail and fell.

A horrible scream filled the pavilion as Rory fell on Dhrun. Both the druid's fists blazed with blue flames that spread down Dhrun's body whenever a blow landed. But as Rory brought another roundhouse punch down, Dhrun turned to catch the blow with his upper hands and with his lower hands he grasped the man, pivoted his hips, and threw him to the ground. The floorboards buckled. The druid moved his legs weakly but did not get up.

"Go!" Leandra shouted and turned to see how Holokai was faring. Immediately she regretted it. The hall was strewn with bodies and blood. The twin druids were fleeing down the hallway as Holokai crouched over one of the bodies. His eyes were black and cold, his face a mask of blood, his leimako covered in gore.

"Kai, not now!" she yelled. "Come on!"

The shark god looked up. His mouth was all blood and teeth.

Leandra turned around. Rory lay on the ground, groaning. Dhrun stood over him, leveling a spear at this neck. The bodies of red cloaks lay all around. Leandra grabbed Dhrun's arm and ran down the stairs.

The pavilion's ground floor seemed empty. She led her gods out onto a nighttime street lit by torches and three-moonlight. After making sure that Dhrun and Holokai were beside her and unharmed, she looked back at her home of sixteen years. She might never come back.

Through the open door, she saw Rory stumbling down the staircase. Blood flowed from one eyebrow and his face was a contortion of terror. For an instant, Leandra feared that they would have to kill him too. But then he ran toward a crumpled body on the pavilion floor.

As she started off down the dark street, Leandra watched Rory kneel beside the body and try to turn it over. Steel glinted on arms still frozen. When the knight had struck ground head first, the weight of his armor had snapped his neck.

It was a pity.

She had rather liked Sir Claude.

F rancesca jerked awake, stumbled backward. Her hands flailed, pulled taut a silver sentence connected to Nicodemus's breathing apparatus. The runes strained, snapped. A rush of air escaped the bellows, air that should have gone into Nicodemus's lungs.

Beside Francesca, Ellen cried out and with quick fingers extemporized a few sentences to fit the spell back together.

"But I can . . ." Francesca started to say, but Ellen had already repaired the bellows. It contracted and Nicodemus's chest rose.

"My lady, that is twice now," Doria said behind her. "You won't do your husband any good by falling asleep on another spell."

"I'm fine," she insisted. "I haven't been up that long. In training I stayed up for days in a row."

"In training you didn't take on a dragon's form and survive several lightning strikes."

"You have me on that one." Her eyes stung.

Doria's expression softened. "Magistra, you need to sleep."

"But Nicodemus—"

"Will be fine. Besides, Magistra, your patient will need a well-rested physician if anything goes wrong."

Feeling defeated, Francesca turned to the windows. All three moons had set. Three hours until dawn and the city was dark. She looked from Ellen working on Nicodemus's breathing spells to Doria's stern expression.

Nicodemus lay still as death. His heart continued to beat without sign of arrhythmia. That at least was a mercy. She had bound his brain up with censoring spells. Regaining consciousness while paralyzed would surely drive him mad.

With Doria and Ellen's help, Francesca had written three copies of every text needed. Nicodemus gradually dispelled all texts in contact with him. Though the other women could not touch Nicodemus, they could replace the decaying spells. "You're sure you'll be okay?" Francesca asked.

"No," Ellen answered flatly as she worked the bellows, "but if we're not okay, we'll scream loud enough for you to hear."

Doria rolled her eyes. "My lady, go lie down. We'll fetch you at the first sign of trouble."

Francesca looked at her husband's slack face and then nodded. She felt the familiar combination of hunger and the nausea of sleep deprivation. She took a lamp and made her way to the hall.

She found two men sitting vigil. Both stood. In the lamplight she could make out John's large face, anxiety written in his eyes. Beside him stood Rory, looking more like a ghost than a man. His red eyes filled with tears upon seeing Francesca.

John started to ask something but then noticed the other man's expression and placed a large hand on his shoulder.

Francesca, numb with exhaustion, waited while Rory cried. The poor soul, to lose a lover just when they were setting out on life together.

The sight filled Francesca with selfish fear. She prayed that Nicodemus would not leave her in such a state.

Rory was angrily wiping his eyes and muttering apologies.

"No apologies, Rory," she said levelly. She felt more composed now that there was someone who needed her to feel composed. "This is a night of sorrows; we'll get through it together."

The weeping man nodded, sniffed, looked at her with eyes that reflected the lamplight.

"How is . . ." John asked. "How is Nico?"

"He seems stable but we don't know how much longer he will be paralyzed . . . or what he will be like if he recovers. I'm sure now Lea used tetrodotoxin. No known antidotes. There's nothing to do but wait for it to wear off."

John nodded. "Can we help?"

She shook her head. "Sleep if you can." She looked at Rory, who nodded as his face went slack.

For most of the night, Francesca had focused on Nicodemus, breaking only to confer with the Trimuril in her spider incarnation. However, as she had worked, Francesca had overheard the others talking about how Rory had gone into rages, swearing to revenge himself on Dhrun and then collapsing into sorrow. Francesca couldn't blame him. She hoped he could cry himself into enough exhaustion to sleep. "I'm going to lie down."

After John and Rory said their good nights, Francesca walked toward the nearest bedroom. A tangle of emotions washed through her. She had been so worried about Leandra trying to kill her that she never considered what it would be like if she killed Nicodemus. For the thousandth time, she wished Leandra had poisoned her rather than Nicodemus.

She had to stop Leandra from going to the empress. Vivian wouldn't hesitate to kill her. The Trimuril had agreed with her on this point. Francesca didn't know how it could be done, but she needed to bring her daughter back to Chandralu.

When Francesca reached the bedroom, she slid back the screen door. It was a small room with a neatly made cot, the sight of which sent a wave of exhaustion over her.

"Going to bed are we?" a dim gray voice, as that of a spider, squeaked in her ear.

Francesca took a deep breath. "Goddess, I am."

"And how is your husband?"

"Nothing has changed. Nothing to do but wait and see. And, Goddess, have you found any sign of Leandra?"

"She and her gods got their catamaran out of the harbor before news of what happened reached me. None of the sea or sky deities have seen her. We shall continue to look."

"And no sign of the imperial forces?"

"None. It's as if the airship evaporated."

Francesca nodded.

"Nicodemus should have let me win that game back in the Floating City and let me become Leandra's mother."

"I'm beginning to agree with you. And now, if you will excuse me, Goddess, I must sleep."

"Very well. We will confer again in the morning. Good night."

Francesca wished the goddess a good night and then waited long enough for the deity to turn her attention elsewhere. Then she blew out her kukui lamp and set it down. As she undressed, she did allow herself one small hope.

During Leandra's exit from the tearoom, Francesca had managed to get ahold of Holokai. She had leaned in close enough to whisper to the shark god that if he didn't return to Chandralu by sunrise with information of what Leandra was doing, she would kill Lolo.

CHAPTER THIRTY-SIX

Leandra stood on the catamaran's forward deck, guilt and fear flowing like blood through her heart. Again she marveled at how precisely her emotions matched what she had felt through the godspell a day before. Surely this misery would persist until she learned if her gambit had saved her father or murdered him.

It was astounding that she could feel so horrible when the loveless spell was about her mind. She supposed that if she could feel love, the resulting heartache might kill her.

But what else could she have done? Tetrodotoxin had given her father a chance. And, miraculously, she had not tried to kill her mother; although now she might soon have the opposite concern.

The moons had set and left a lonely host of stars. To the east were the first hints of dawn. Not long until Keyway Island. Once her people were safe, Leandra could seek out the empress. She had been foolish to get involved with league and empire. Her destiny was to escape the conflict, to change how the world worked, not who ruled it. Such a task might be impossible. But if she weren't trying to change the world, what was the point of living in it?

"Lea?"

A softly spoken voice broke her reverie. She turned to find Dhrun, still male but now wearing his scale armor vest and two swords. "Yes? What is it?"

He held up a long object wrapped in cloth.

Though they stood in dim starlight, Leandra could see Dhrun's face in detail. His skin had no pores, his iris no pigmented irregularities, his youthful beard no asymmetry. In a way, he was ideal because he was the incarnation of ideas. In a way, he was imperfect because of his flawlessness. But perfect or not, he was one of hers. That, she supposed, was what mattered.

As if sensing this sentiment, Dhrun smiled—a flash of perfect white teeth, a dark handsome face.

It made Leandra laugh at his peculiarity. "Dhrun, what's the matter?"

"I was just wondering if you were doing all right."

"I'm doing all right."

"But now I realize that I have missed your laugh; clearly, I must have come back here to hear your laugh."

"Clearly. So, now have you heard it clearly enough?"

He only stared at her, but now he wore his old inscrutable smile.

She rolled her eyes. "Oh, not this shit again."

"Do you know why they named me Dhrun?"

"I'm willing to bet it has something to do with masculine wrestling idiocy."

"Women wrestle too, you know."

"Ah, but are they as idiotic as the men?"

"Probably not." He smiled.

"So what does Dhrun mean? 'Blazing-fist'? Or 'Steel-muscles'? Or maybe 'Balls-made-out-of-iron'?"

"I think I might adopt that last name, at least when I have them."

"So what does Dhrun mean and what oh-so-opaque reason do you have for bringing it up?"

"It's an ancient Lotus Culture word for the North Star. Not bad for a wrestling god who cannot be thrown or contorted by others to have a name that means 'constant' or 'immovable.'"

"And ironic for someone who is constantly moving"—she gestured to Dhrun's beard to demonstrate his present himselfness—"from one sex to another?" She waved her hand away in a gesture to his notional and future herselfness.

"Maybe ironic, maybe paradoxical, but it's saved me. If all of my incarnations were about consistency and strength and wrestling . . . well, I doubt you would find me interesting."

"Who says I find you interesting?"

"You do with your protestations of friendship. Do you remember, in the Floating City, after your disease flare?"

Leandra sighed. "Yes, sometimes I am such a bitch."

He shrugged, conceding the point.

She continued. "And, yes, Dhrun, you are a good friend. And if you were all muscle and aggression, you'd be flat. I've had such gods in my entourage before, gods of war. They got carried away with the killing and the power. Too many martial requisites and too many destructive abilities. But you, my friend, have been a balanced and flexible asset."

Dhrun pressed his lower palms together over his heart. "I was not aware that my lady had been appreciating my . . . assets."

"You are showing them off lately. So, my constantly changing North Star, why are you bringing all this up?"

"We already established it was clearly to hear you laugh."

"Clearly. But there's clearly something else."

His smile wilted. "What would my lady say the effects of the loveless spell have been?"

"That's what this is about? You think the loveless is making me ruthless?"

"Making you? You were born ruthless enough to make a starving crocodile seem compassionate."

"Oh, Dhrun, there's clearly no need to resort to flattery."

"Clearly."

"So you think the loveless is making me more than ruthless? Cold-blooded?"

"Since the sun went down, we've murdered your old lover, paralyzed your father, and killed his knight."

Leandra look up at the swaths of starry sky. "Busy night."

When Dhrun spoke again, he did so in a softer voice. "I can tell that you clearly find all this . . . regrettable."

"Clearly."

"I wonder if you haven't lost something."

"I've lost the ability to love."

"Something more than that."

"My disease has been cured. Clearly, you don't object to that."

"Who could object to such a thing?"

"It's unclear. I wonder if you could."

The wind ruffled Dhrun's short curly black hair. "I never could, clearly."

"But?"

"Is there something your disease taught you?"

She frowned. It wasn't a question she had considered. "It made me look for something to fight. Maybe I wouldn't care so much about the world's unfairness otherwise."

"You are different from others in power, different from your parents. I devoted myself to you because of how little you care for convention."

"That's not going to change because my disease is cured."

"I am glad to hear it."

"Dhrun, stop screwing around, why did you come?"

"I've learned something I wish to tell you without the loveless spell on your mind." He lifted the cloth-wrapped object he held in his lower two hands.

"What is it?"

"Will you not consider taking the loveless off?"

"There's no Numinous author among us. I can't take it off."

"Your ability to misspell has only strengthened. You could misspell it."

"But then I'd lose it forever."

"So you won't take it off?"

"Why do you want it off?"

"It has to do with . . . has to do with Holokai."

"Look, I can't have you two scrapping right now . . ." Her voice trailed off as his expression tightened. "What is it?"

"It's not that. I wish it were. What I'm about to tell you . . . well . . . I don't want to win this way."

"Win what?"

"Your esteem."

"I already hold you in esteem."

"You hold him higher."

She studied his face again, saw the tension around his mouth. "What happened?"

The god studied her, and she could see in him the youth who had become a champion wrestler. The way he was leaning toward her, the nervous movements of his eyes, it changed how she perceived him. For a moment she saw through the idealized divinity complex to a young man, struggling with complexities of character he had not known he possessed.

Dhrun reached out and took her hand. A resulting shock of information flooded through Leandra's mind. He was no longer a young god, but an elegant body of living prose. He was a masterpiece, an epic.

More shocking was the realization that with a few casual thoughts, Leandra could disperse his central text, expand and then remove his subspells, take them for her own. Then she realized that Dhrun had said something. "What?" she asked, a little breathlessly.

"You're sure you won't take the loveless off?"

She blinked, rapidly adjusting to her double perception of the young god. "Dhru, tell me."

He took another breath and looked up to the sky. "Have you wondered why your mother wasn't surprised when you explained about our society and what we do for refugee deities?"

"I did find it curious."

"Did you notice that your mother grabbed hold of Holokai after you paralyzed your father?"

"Briefly."

"She was close enough to whisper something to Holokai."

"Not a very long something."

"Just now I overheard Holokai ordering Lieutenant Peleki to take the ship into Keyway while he swims a patrol to see if they're being followed."

"A reasonable precaution."

"So it seemed until he told Peleki that he didn't want to burden you with the knowledge that he would be gone. Peleki is to keep you distracted so that you might not notice his absence. Holokai ordered him to admit that he had left the boat only under extreme pressure."

Leandra tensed, thinking back an hour to remember if she had felt anything particularly different about her most likely futures. She had sensed nothing dramatic. Perhaps she had felt a worsening of her present misery compounded by guilt and anxiety. "What did Peleki say?"

"He agreed, of course. He worships Holokai."

"Is Kai still onboard? Has he snuck off already?"

"Not yet."

"Why not?"

"He's looking for this." Using an upper hand, Dhrun unwrapped the cloth-covered object he was holding in his lower hands. At first Leandra thought it was a simple oar. Then she saw the shark's teeth. "I spirited it away. Holokai won't leave the ship until making sure Peleki has it. Without it, the lieutenant can't properly take command of the ship."

Cold apprehension gripped Leandra. She had never known Holokai to hide anything. "You think he . . ." She stopped herself. Whatever doubts she had about her predatory captain, they were not for her changeling and erstwhile confidant to hear. "Thank you, Dhrun." She squeezed his hand. "Thank you. It is clear where your loyalties lie. I am fortunate to have you."

His dark brown eyes were studying her with particular intensity, and suddenly Leandra became aware that they were standing no more than an inch apart. She could feel the heat radiating off of his body. She suffered a twinge of guilt that she should be talking so intimately with one of her crew while entertaining suspicions of another.

She let go of his hand and her double perception of Dhrun as persona and text simplified to only the former. She straightened. "Please tell Captain Holokai that I should like a word in my cabin."

"And shall I accompany the captain?"

"Thank you but that will not be necessary."

Dhrun bowed and headed aft. Leandra went belowdecks into her cabin. It was a small space, low-ceilinged. The forward wall boasted a slim horizontal window that during the day provided a slice of the aquamarine world sliding between the ship's two hulls. Now the window was a bar of night.

Her sleeping pallet had been laid out, so she stowed it and set up her low table. It was a good piece of sea furniture: bamboo legs, polished hardwood tabletop, a few gashes scored during rough weather. She lit a single kukui lamp on the table before kneeling on the cushion behind it.

As the ship rocked, Leandra put her hand on the table and stared at it as if it were someone else's hand. She was changing so fast—texts modified her thoughts, emotions, position in time. And yet she was still herself, wasn't she?

She decided to trust Holokai. Perhaps he had a reasonable explanation, maybe even an obvious one. So she laid the leimako down on the table.

Water rushed below while sailors called. Then heavy footfalls and a scratching on her door.

"Come in, Kai."

The screen door slid back revealing Holokai's broad silhouette. He crouched to step into the cabin. "Hey, Lea, four-arms said you wanted to . . ." His voice trailed off as he saw the leimako. He became perfectly still, ceasing even to breathe. His eyes flicked up to hers. And then she knew. Oh creator, she knew.

His posture was too tense, his mouth too tightly pursed. She knew. It was both a horror and a relief. "Kai, I believe you were looking for this."

He didn't move.

"Dhrun brought it to me."

"If that little bug is playing one of his games—"

"Then you can chew him into foamy pulp," she interrupted with a light tone. "I'll watch." She was amazed that she felt no new strong emotion, only the same mixture of horrors that had filled her since she had paralyzed her father.

"You can't trust that four-armed bug. Think about it, Lea. We don't really know who he is. We don't know what kind of a neodemon he was before he converted himself. Neodemons don't convert themselves. There's something wrong with him."

"All right, Kai, I will look into it. But can you tell me why were you looking for your leimako?"

"I wanted to give command to Peleki while I swam a patrol, see if anyone's following or if something's waiting ahead."

"Why not tell me?"

"You've been through a lot tonight. I didn't think you needed more to worry about."

"All these years sailing together, I have insisted on knowing when you go swimming."

"Tonight was different."

"Different how?"

"You've been through a lot."

"Anything else?"

"No, Lea. I'm sorry if you don't like it. I won't do it again."

"Nothing else you want to tell me?"

"Nothing else."

More than anything else, Leandra felt disappointment. "All right, then. You can take it."

He paused as if misunderstanding. Then he stepped forward and picked up the weapon. "All right then, Lea. Unless I run into trouble, I'll see you in Keyway."

"See you in Keyway," she agreed and waited for him to start to leave before she stopped him. "Kai. Before you go, will you take my hand just for a moment? Just as a precaution."

He turned and looked at her hand. "Precaution how?"

"With the loveless on, I can see how deities are put together. I will know if you're telling the truth."

He looked up at her face. The world seemed perfectly still. Two kinds of future hours lay before Leandra, both alike in fear and guilt, one lonelier than the other. She had given Holokai the choice between the two. But, in either hour, she would continue to fall like a stone through water toward some vaguely sensed discovery that was her destiny.

So she waited for Holokai, who had navigated her through so much in life, to choose their course. She waited with her hand outstretched and her gaze fixed on his face.

He stared back at her, silent, predatory. Then his eyes went black.

Only moments left now.

CHAPTER THIRTY-SEVEN

Francesca woke to a dark room and bright green screaming. For a scattered moment, she thought she was a young physician in an infirmary. The patient sounded like a child. She sat up in bed, pressed her hands to her face, tried to remember the child's diagnosis. But then the horror of her present situation returned: Nicodemus, Leandra.

The child screamed again. To Francesca's synesthetic hearing, the sound was a shrill green flare, burning bright before quavering toward silence only to be renewed with another shrill flare.

She splashed water on her face and hurried out into the dark hallway. There she found Tam holding a kukui lamp. "It's Lolo," he said. "He seems to be having a nightmare, but we can't wake him up."

"Night terrors?" Francesca wondered aloud. Between two and twelve, some children developed episodes of sleep disturbance characterized by thrashing and screaming. The child would be inconsolable, difficult to wake, and if wakened would not recall any nightmare or distress. Lolo's mother had been human, so he might be subject to human pathology. And judging by his rate of growth, he should be about six by now.

Doria appeared in the doorway of the tearoom, where Nicodemus was being treated. "He's doing better," she said before Francesca could ask. "He's starting to breathe on his own. Ellen is with him."

Another shrill green scream. "Tam," Francesca said, "take me to Lolo."

The druid led them to the suite where he and Kenna had been looking after Lolo. Inside they found the wide suite suffused with early dawn's blue light. On the bed, Lolo's small dark figure thrashed next to the stillness of Kenna in her pale druidic robes.

As Francesca approached the bed, she saw that the boy was tossing, curling his knees up then extending them. Though it was dark, Francesca could make out the boy's sudden, spasmodic grimaces followed by expressions of slack-face dreaming. Kenna gently stroked his black hair and made reassuring noises.

"When did it—" Francesca started to ask but was interrupted by Lolo's shrill scream. Kenna increased her reassurance, to no effect.

Francesca sat beside Kenna and laid a hand on the boy's forehead to see if he were feverish, but the instant her hand touched his skin a shock of prophetic understanding ripped through her mind.

Lolo sat bolt upright and yelled "Father!" with such childish longing and fear it made Francesca's heart ache.

Francesca's awareness leapt away from the compound and out onto the Bay of Standing Island. She saw a dark catamaran slipping between the tall limestone islands. She felt the conflict in the ship's cabin. Her daughter and the shark god had come to a crossroads.

Only two potential futures were now probable, and they were diverging fast, becoming better defined. In both futures Leandra gained great strength and the potential of escaping Francesca's life forever. Francesca saw that unless she found a way to reestablish physical contact with her daughter, she would never see her again. The realization closed around her heart. In only one of the probable futures was the shark god still alive.

Into this dreamlike awareness, Francesca saw Lolo's mind shine down onto the catamaran, through its planks to his unknown father held within. She felt the boy's blistering desire to know the one who had created him. She felt Holokai's desperate reciprocation, his need to know who he had created.

And yet between her daughter and herself, Francesca felt nothing. Mother and daughter, estranged. Francesca pressed her mind harder into her prophetic awareness, trying to establish some bond with Leandra. But she could come up with nothing more than the certainty that unless she were physically near Leandra, she would lose her.

Then Francesca's prophecy broke. She was just a woman, sitting on a bed and staring down at a dawn-lit child. Lolo stared up at her with frightened eyes—an expression, she supposed, that must reflect her own.

She felt pity for the boy and his estrangement from his father. She prayed it was not too late for her and Leandra.

Lolo continued to stare at Francesca, but when Kenna gently patted his back, he flopped onto the druid's lap and hugged her leg.

Francesca stood and felt her draconic nature awakening. Waves of heat and strength began to wash through her.

"Lady Warden," Tam said behind her, "what was it? What's wrong with Lolo?"

"The boy misses his father," she said faintly. Such a dangerous thing, to create or be created. "Keep comforting him; he'll be all right. Doria, come with me."

She led the other woman through the hallways back to the tearoom. Inside she found Ellen attending to Nicodemus. He lay supine and almost skewered by a matrix of luminous silver prose. As she watched, he drew a slow breath through the tube she'd slipped into his trachea. The textual bellows contracted, providing pressure to help him take a deeper breath than he could on his own.

"He's doing much better," Ellen reported. "I've been able to reduce the pressure support again. I don't think it will take too much longer to wean him back to breathing on his own. Really, Magistra, you can go back to bed—"

"Can you manage without me?" Francesca interrupted.

"Y-yes. For how long?"

"A day. Maybe longer."

Ellen looked at Doria. "We . . . We can replace the texts as fast as he is deconstructing them. So . . . once we're sure the paralysis has completely worn off, we could deconstruct the censoring spells to wake him up."

Stronger waves of heat washed through Francesca; her draconic nature wouldn't give her much longer before it forced a change. She went to Nicodemus's side and carefully reached between the lines of silver text to take his hand. "Nico," she said, "I'm going to get our girl back."

He lay slack amid the medicinal language. His long glossy hair splayed out into a black halo. He drew another breath; the spells contracted.

Francesca squeezed his hand. "Keep him alive," she said and made for the door. "It's not a good idea to let a dragon's husband die while she is away."

Ellen muttered something about how she tried to keep all of her patients alive whether or not they had been stupid enough to marry a flying lizard. But Francesca ignored her. The need to find her daughter could be denied no longer.

She jogged down the hallways and up the steep stairs. At last she threw open the screen door that led onto the pavilion's roof. She was running now, her feet taking longer and longer strides until she reached the building's edge and leapt out into the churning air.

A band of monkeys, who had been perched on the roof just below, chattered in fear as her dark figure flew overhead.

Now with her auburn wings wide, Francesca climbed above a dawn-lit city. She flew out over the glassy bay to find her daughter.

tepping into Holokai's leimako swing, Leandra grabbed his bicep just before it smashed into her nose. Sharkteeth raked across her back but did not bite deeply. She stumbled but did not fall. This wasn't the blow that would kill her. Holokai's intentions were of escape, not slaughter. He might have managed it too, if she didn't have the loveless spell.

Leandra quick-stepped, kept her balance. Holokai snarled and made ready to strike again, but it was too late. First touch was all she needed. She transformed his fingers into interlocking crimson paragraphs, his palms into subspells. She incorporated them into her own hands, felt their strength.

The leimako clattered on the floor. Holokai staggered back, looked with emotionless fish eyes at the stumps that had been his hands.

Leandra felt only blunted sadness. She had known him as well as it was possible to know another soul, or so she had thought. "How?" she asked softly. "How did she get to you?"

His lips pulled back in a predatory rictus, displaying serrated teeth.

"How did Mother turn you against me?" Leandra said with more passion than intended. "How?" Her eyes stung and she wondered if she were going to cry. In a way, that would be a relief.

Holokai's lips slowly lowered, his eyes lightened by a shade.

"How?"

"My son. She has my son."

"You have a son? After all this time?"

He did not move.

"Creator damn it all. Who had your son? How long ago?

"A pillow house prostitute. Maybe three days ago."

"What happened to her?"

"She died."

"How?"

He only snarled.

"How, damn it?"

"The sickness they get when the baby god starts growing."

"They? Kai, how many have there been?"

Holokai didn't answer.

"Why didn't you tell me?"

"I didn't learn about it until Francesca already had him. There was nothing I could do. If I don't return to Chandralu tonight and tell her where you are going, she'll kill him."

Leandra understood and her stomach lurched. Holokai's worshipers prayed for the birth of his son. Holokai could no more resist the one who controlled his son than a broken wave could resist falling back down the beach.

Leandra understood now the conflict that had raged, was raging, behind his all-black eyes. The pain left Leandra's heart. She wasn't going to cry. There remained only a detached clarity about what needed to be done. She said a prayer of thanks to Thaddeus's departed soul for his loveless spell.

Holokai continued to glare. "I have to go to Francesca. If I don't, she'll kill my boy."

"She made you choose between him and me? You chose him. Was it difficult?"

"Painful. It was very painful. But difficult? How could I abandon my boy?"

How could he, indeed? What was she to him: a commander, a friend, a sometimes lover? How could that tilt the scales against his creation?

"Let me go?" Holokai asked, his eyes human again and pleading. "I can lie to Francesca. You know I'll stay loyal to you. I can be your spy in her court."

"What do you think will happen when my mother discovers you've lied?"

"I can handle myself."

"I'm not worried about you, fish brain."

"My son?"

"Remarkable skills of deduction you have, Kai."

"There has to be a way."

Leandra's sadness became heavier. Strategy had never been Holokai's strength. So she stayed silent, gave him a chance to think it out.

But he only stared at her.

Irritated, she asked, "Do you think my mother will ever give your son to you?"

"Why wouldn't she?"

"Why would she? So long as she keeps him as a ward, she can bend you in any direction she likes. As the boy's warden, she would become the virtual ruler of your island and your people."

"But no, Lea . . . she said . . ."

"Why would she ever surrender such a valuable ward?"

"I . . . don't . . ."

"You can't go to her. She'd use you to drag me back into the league."

"But there has to be a way."

"There is one way."

Holokai's wide-eyed fear relaxed before his eyes narrowed in suspicion. "What way?"

"Abandon this son. You can always try ag—"

Holokai turned to flee. The kukui candle winked out and the cabin became as black as the seafloor. She heard three heavy footsteps and then the cabin door slide back. She reached out with the godspell that redirected divine attention. She focused all of Holokai's attention on herself. There were no more footsteps.

She redoubled her efforts, made it impossible for Holokai to perceive anything but her body. The door rattled, as if the limb touching it were trembling.

It was more than he could resist. She knew. She made him focus on her beating heart, the heat of her flesh. Blood in the water. Then the footsteps sounded again, coming at her.

Unseen teeth closed around Leandra's shoulder, punched through her robes, into her skin.

But contact transformed Holokai from a monster in the dark to glorious text, a billowing sea storm of rubicund prose. She bored into him like a parasite, consuming those passages that could fit into her body and snapping those that barred her way.

Her hands closed around the luminous red prose of his mind, and she saw into his memory: sunlight streaming down through forests of coral; the torchlit jungle of his home island; a taste of blood growing stronger in the water; his admiration for her; his all-encompassing desire for his son. Holokai would be a slave to his son's safety. Her mother would never release the boyish god. There was only one possible future.

With a thought, she scattered his mind and for an instant she became a two-ton shark, thrashing as spears and harpoons punctured her side. She was vomiting blood into the water. So much blood she thought she would turn all the oceans red and herald the world's end as the Sea priests had foreseen.

In the next instant, she was just a woman standing on a ship. Boards creaked, water splashed. There was no blood, no shark. She had gutted him and then absorbed all of his prose. The only thing left of Holokai was his lungi, lying slack on the floor next to his leimako.

Leandra bent down and picked up the weapon. When she stood, she found that her head nearly bumped against the cabin's ceiling. She had grown taller. Her arms and legs coursed with vitality and strength. She felt no pain or blood running down her back. The leimako wounds had closed.

It was a nauseating, cannibalistic feeling to know what had changed her, whom she had consumed. The sadness grew worse in her heart. But after a long breath, she put her sadness aside. There had been no other way. An image of her paralyzed father falling back in his chair flashed before her and she prayed that her mother had found a way to save him.

Then she wondered again who she was that she could do such things as paralyze her father and take apart gods. She wondered again at the dimly perceived destiny she could sense drawing closer. When she focused on that, the pain went away. The world seemed crystalline in its clarity.

She stepped out of her cabin and went on deck. Dhrun waited for her. His expression darkened as he pressed his palms together, both pairs over his heart. When he straightened, she handed him the leimako. "Give this to Peleki and tell him that I saw Holokai off. We are to go to Keyway with all haste. After you speak to Peleki, join me."

Afterward Leandra walked to her usual spot on the forward deck and stared down at the bay water, which was presently reflecting the growing blue of a dawn sky. She knew then that if she dove overboard and into the water, she would take a long and pale shape, teeth and scales and fins. There she would experience Holokai's deep ocean memories, the glory of the hunt, the intoxication of blood in the water.

"Lea?"

She turned and saw Dhrun.

"Peleki says we're almost to Keyway."

Nodding, she leaned on the railing. "These are strange days. Strange and bloody."

Dhrun stepped beside her and placed all four of his hands on the railing. "Captain Holokai?"

"My mother got hold of his son."

"He had a son?"

"Born a few days ago, apparently. Poor Kai, it compromised him. He couldn't do otherwise."

"I see. How soon until his reincarnation?"

"I retained a majority of his prose." She stood taller to emphasize her new height. "Most of the prayers meant for him will come to me. But with enough prayer, there will be another version of Kai swimming around his island. Maybe he'll remember that he's supposed to be serving me, but little more than that."

They stood in silence for a while. "How do you feel?"

"Heavyhearted. But the loveless helps me understand clearly."

"How clearly."

"Crystalline."

He did not reply, so they watched the standing islands. A brisk wind was blowing. Peleki brought the ship around a wide limestone formation and through the maze they saw Keyway Island.

The tide was low enough that they should be able to sail into the island as soon as they reached it. Though Leandra was not physically tired, her heart would welcome the familiar quarters of her hidden sea village. Most particularly she looked forward to seeing Master Alo and hearing his sour but somehow endearing complaints.

Well, maybe she wasn't entirely excited about seeing the old man. She would have to explain their many new hardships and dangers . . . not to mention that she had failed to secure any new funds. But never mind that for now.

As they sailed, Leandra discovered that she found Dhrun's proximity comforting. Suddenly, and to her own surprise, she asked, "Dhru, would you do me a favor?"

"Gladly."

"Tell me why you converted yourself into the Ixonian pantheon. Why break into my bedroom and reveal yourself as a neodemon?"

"Ah, but one of the conditions of my conversion is that we would not talk about what came before it. I was promised amnesty."

"Of course," Leandra said. "I was only curious."

"Why do you ask?"

"I'm not sure. Something about what happened with Kai."

"Then I'll make you a trade."

"What kind of trade?"

"I will tell you why I converted myself, if you take the loveless off."

"Why would I do that?"

"To humor a friend," he said.

"I don't have any humorous friends."

"But you have at least one humorless friend who should be humored. Do it for pity's sake."

"Pity?" She looked at him. His brown eyes met hers. She couldn't say what it was she saw in them, but she found herself saying, "All right, if we can find a way to take the loveless off so that it can be preserved until we put it back on, I'll do so."

"For a whole day," Dhrun added. "At the least."

"Are you a god of wrestling or bargaining?"

"In some ways they're not all that different."

Leandra frowned at him but said nothing.

"Do you want me to take my Nika incarnation?" he asked. "Would you rather talk to a woman?"

"No no," she said faintly and looked back at Keyway Island. "I don't mind you staying like this." She paused. "All right, a whole day if, and only if, it's possible to put it back on. So, tell me how you ended up in my bedroom."

Dhrun took a deep breath. "Where to start . . . well . . . Nika was always the one who had the ideas. Likely you guessed that. She was the only one of us with any legitimacy. Her cult is ancient, coming from a Cloud Culture religion that predates the union of Ixos. The cults of the Cloud People are always small, and because of her origin she always had trouble recruiting followers from the Sea and Lotus Peoples. But somehow she managed to scrape by in a tiny Upper Banyan temple. But for the past century, her cult has become less fashionable even among the Cloud People. Then one day, she realized that her only remaining devotees were three old priestesses."

Dhrun stood up straighter. "So Nika went looking for possible allies to form a divinity complex. Someone who could make her cult more relevant and powerful, but no one in the pantheon wanted to fuse their soul with a dusty old goddess. So, eventually, she started searching for . . . alternatives."

"And by alternatives, you mean neodemons?" Leandra suggested.

"I mean neodemons."

"Go on."

"This was maybe five years ago, just when wrestling was becoming so popular. They built the arena right after that rainy season. Before that we'd wrestle in the yards of winehouses, in rings at festivals, that sort of thing. But after the arena was built, we'd wrestle before thousands. All those men and women, praying for their favorite to win."

"And those prayers incarnated the god Dhrun."

"Incarnated him with some . . . dark requisites."

Leandra had been watching Keyway Island as they drew closer. Now she looked with interest at her companion. "Dark requisites?"

"People in an arena pray for some horrible things; the mildest of which would be for their less favorite wrestlers to be injured. The darkest prayers—especially after a favorite loses a match and all the money bet on him—were for blood."

"Before you formed the divinity complex, Dhrun would sacrifice his own wrestlers?" Leandra asked in surprise.

"Neodemons don't choose their prerequisites."

"Of course," Leandra said weakly.

"And there were worse things than sacrifice, at least I've come to see it that way. Dhrun's cult arranged death matches. The blood sport produced the strongest prayers."

"But there were no rumors of such a cult. We were completely unaware."

"The cult was well organized, very secretive. And that is where the third member of our trinity comes in, the one you know as Dhrunarman."

"The young wrestler who won the tournament last year?"

"He was that too. But before he was renamed as a championship wrestler, he was named Tonoki."

Leandra had to remind herself that her Dhrun was the product of these three different people—Nika, Dhrun, and Dhrunarman. And though her Dhrun had inherited the experiences of all three of these souls, the resulting divinity complex was entirely unique from his predecessors. Or her predecessors, depending on the moment.

Dhrun continued. "Nika discovered the blood sport and the sacrifices. She saw that the cult was on the cusp of discovery. She knew that you would have deconstructed Dhrun rather than try to convert him. So through a long negotiation, she convinced Dhrun and his young devotee that we three needed to form a complex. Dhrun brought raw strength and his powerful cult. Nika brought her mandates for honor, which helped negate the mandates for blood." He paused, his expression troubled.

Leandra frowned. "And Dhrunarman?"

"He was chosen to become a popular champion, someone the citizens saw as one of their own. His celebrity was meant to popularize the sport and win a larger number of prayers to compensate for the lost blood sport prayers."

"But how did you know he would become a celebrity?"

Dhrun sighed. "We decided that he would become the champion of an especially exciting and popular tournament."

"Especially exciting and popular because it was rigged?"

"So . . . how would you feel if you learned that your deity is not only a murderer but also a fraud?"

"Nobody's perfect."

"You're too kind."

"No, no, I am anything but kind." She flexed her hands and felt the powerful prose that had once been Holokai's moving through her. "Anything but kind."

Dhrun didn't reply. They watched the water. Then Dhrun said, "I wonder if you remember . . . During that tournament, you and Holokai brought down a neodemon of theft."

Leandra frowned at her companion as she searched her memory. Then at last it came to her. "Yes, that young air goddess who came in from the Outer Island chain. She picked pockets at the arena and gave the coins to the beggars in exchange for prayers." Leandra laughed. "I had nearly forgotten."

Peleki was belting out orders. It seemed that the tide was indeed low enough for them to sail into the island's pool.

"Perhaps you don't remember," Dhrun continued, "but you took down that air neodemon during one of the matches in which Dhrunarman was wrestling. You made a rather . . . spectacular impression on him."

Leandra laughed. "Your wrestler fancied me?"

"Something like that. And Nika was perhaps a bit envious. She was, after all, an ancient goddess and you were only a mortal. In any case, the confused mixture of admiration and competitiveness led us to break into your bedroom one night and, in our Nika incarnation, see if we didn't look better in some of your dresses." He laughed. "When we did, Nika's jealousy eased a bit. Then you caught me in the bedroom, and the Dhrunarman admiration was overwhelming. There was nothing left to do but convert to you and the pantheon. It has worked out rather well since then, wouldn't you say?"

"I would." Leandra nodded and looked back toward the arch in the stone of Keyway Island. With all hands but her own and Dhrun's rowing, they were speeding through the tunnel.

Leandra could see the pool at the village's center ahead. There were no lights burning in the village. That seemed odd. Usually Master Alo was industrious in the early hours, which usually meant that the rest of the village had to be industrious as well.

"Lea," Dhrun asked gently, "why did you ask me about my past?"

"I've always been curious."

"But why now . . . why after Holokai?"

She pursed her lips and stood up straighter. "It's hard to say. What happened with Kai . . ."

But whatever reason she was going to give flew away from her mind as the catamaran cleared the Keyway tunnel and slipped into the pool. It was then that Leandra first saw the bodies.

There were only two of them lying on the dock, but their arms and legs were splayed at such angles that they could only be dead. Involuntarily, Leandra shouted and pointed at the corpses.

At first Dhrun seemed confused but then he sucked in a sharp breath.

Leandra noticed that in several places the railings around the walkways had been burned out. It seemed all of her followers in Keyway were dead. She yelled, "Peleki! Turn the boat. Turn, we have to get out of here!"

Her mind raced with fear. How could anyone have found Keyway? And why, an hour ago, had she not felt the possibility of her present fear? Then, with horror, she remembered that one man could blind her to certain futures.

"Lotannu!" she whispered. Right after she had bought the first godspell from Lotannu disguised as a smuggler, she had sailed back to Keyway and thought she had spotted something large flying from island to island, following her.

Icy terror closed its fingers around her heart. "Lotannu, if you did this to my people, I swear . . ."

But once again, she could not finish her words.

Above her, the circle of dawn sky visible from the pool was darkened by the shape of something massive. At first she thought it was some new kind of neodemon.

But then she saw, arcing across its foresail, a jagged blaze of lightning.

A thunderclap rolled through Keyway Island. Leandra barked orders but could not hear her own words. Fortunately neither Peleki nor the sailors needed orders to know they had to back-paddle for their lives. With painful slowness, the sailors halted the catamaran's progress, reversed her course back toward the tunnel.

Using her godspell of misdirection, Leandra mentally reached out for the airship. As before, she sensed the remnants of a divine mind that had aimed the airship's lightning, but now the mind had been stripped down to its basic subspells, not enough of an intellect left to misdirect. Hopefully this meant the airship's aim would be impaired.

As if to oblige her curiosity, lightning fell from the ship and struck the highest point of the island. The flash dazzled, the thunderclap deafened. A corona of blasted rock rose from the lightning strike and then rained upon the catamaran. The larger stones punched holes into the deck.

On the starboard hull, a sailor screamed and went down grabbing his shoulder. A bloody limestone shard clattered onto the deck beside him.

Another line of white energy arced down from the airship and struck one of the village staircases, transforming it into a chaos of splinters. Another shower of debris.

Leandra turned, intending to bellow orders to the crew, but found herself lifted into muscular arms. A confusion of crimson text exploded around her. Another flash and thunderclap. For a moment she thought she had been struck by lightning, but then she realized Dhrun had picked her up and was running for the starboard hull.

Indignation jolted through Leandra, and she struggled with the impulse to scold Dhrun or at least deconstruct one of his limbs. But just then a rafter from some blasted village structure crashed onto the forward deck where she had been standing.

Before she could fully appreciate her gratitude, Dhrun hurried them both down a hatch and below the deck of the starboard hull. Above them, Peleki screamed orders and the crew replied with war cries. There followed a double thunderclap, a wail of pain, more war cries.

Through the hatch a square of dawn sky was visible with no sign of the airship. Then came another flash, another thunderclap. Then strange quiet.

Leandra invoked her prophetic godspell, but felt nothing. Lotannu must be in the airship and blinding her to futures his influence created, and there were no longer future hours free of his influence. "What do we do?" Leandra yelled.

"Stay down here!" Dhurn replied.

Leandra looked back up at the hatch and saw that the view of sky had been replaced by dark stone. They had passed into the tunnel. "Put me down!" she yelled. When Dhrun didn't, she hammered her fist against his chest. "Put me down or I'll break you down into loose punctuation, you lumbering heap of paragraphs!"

Dhrun started as if noticing an insect bite and put her down.

Another thunderclap rocked through the ship. Leandra hurried up the hatch. The deck was a mess of stone and wood. Fortunately little rigging had been damaged and the sails were mostly intact. The air felt strange, too warm and wet. There was a strange scent—something of seawater and smoke, something vaguely rotten.

The crew, divided between the two hulls, were stationed with their paddles. Peleki was on the aft center deck, waving his leimako and yelling.

As Leandra made her way toward the lieutenant, a flash came from the tunnel's mouth and was followed by a thunderclap, then debris splashing into water. She had taken only a few more steps when another blast tore through the tunnel. Then another. She clapped her hands over her ears but the sound seemed to pass right through them.

Twenty feet behind them, a large chunk of the tunnel roof gave way. What must have been two tons of rock came crashing down into the water. A forceful spray soaked the deck and the resulting wave pushed the catamaran toward the tunnel's opening. The crew did not have to be told to back-paddle to stop the ship from floating out from under its protection.

At last Leandra reached Peleki and put a hand on his shoulder. The man spun around, nearly stuck her with the leimako. "Hey!" she yelled, dancing away.

The lieutenant's face was tense with fear. "My lady—" was all he could get out before another thunderclap deafened them.

"We can't stay here," Leandra yelled. "They're going to bring the roof down."

"But they'll catch us with the lightning if we try to—" Another thunderclap. He continued to yell but Leandra could not understand what he was saying until, "—to wait for Holokai to save us."

Leandra cursed herself. She might have killed their savior. "How could he save us?"

"He will!"

Another flash and thunderclap. Another ton of rock fell from the tunnel behind them into the water.

"How?" Leandra yelled. "How could Holokai save us?"

The lieutenant blinked at her. "He could . . . he . . . could pull us." He gestured forward. "We could run lines from each bow and create a harness below the forward center deck. Other shark gods have done it."

Leandra felt a flush of relief. It was true that shark and whale deities had pulled their worshipers about on catamarans while they undertook various maritime quests—although, it probably happened more often in tall sea tales than true life. "Rig the harness," Leandra yelled. "Holokai will save us."

Peleki nodded and started to reply but was drowned out by another thunderclap. There was something different about this thunderclap. Leandra looked at the ceiling and frowned. The pause that followed was longer than any previous.

Another thunderclap tore through the tunnel and made her jump, but she had seen no flash of lightning and was now certain that the thunderclap was softer. The airship had pulled back. But why should the empire change position when she was so completely trapped?

Leandra turned around and nearly ran her nose into Dhrun's chest. "Burning hells, watch where you're standing," she said while making her way to the forward center deck. On the prows, the men worked to set up the harness. Another thunderclap echoed through the tunnel. But this time farther away.

"Dhru, I'm going for a swim," she said while untying her lungi. "Help Peleki keep them calm and busy."

"This doesn't seem like the best time . . ." His voice trailed off as she stepped out of her lungi, peeled off her blouse.

She looked back at him in time to find his eyes looking up to meet hers. A blush made his youthful face darker.

She laughed at him. "Here? Now?"

He gave her a four-armed shrug. "Especially here and now. Might be the last thing I see."

She looked down at her naked body and then up at him. "Well, then I'd better give you something else to see." She dove, arms outstretched. The blue water was at first bracing and then transformative. The crimson passages that had been Holokai sprang into motion, covering her with textual construction. She became a creature of long muscle, black eyes, white teeth.

On a faraway island, Holokai's devotees were making the dawn devotions, praying for their shark god to destroy the archipelago's enemies. So, as Leandra swam down into the blue, she felt the divine language wrought by such prayers pour into her new body.

The falling rocks had kicked up debris, clouded the water. Leandra saw only a few bright yellow fish flitting along the underwater tunnel walls. With a whip of her tail, she dove with such speed that at first she found it alarming. Water rushed through her mouth and into her gills. Light faded in the depths. A moment later she passed out of the tunnel and into the bay.

She whipped her tail a few times, propelling herself with an exhilarating lurch of speed. When she was far enough away from the island, she rose in wide circles until she was just below the glassy surface of the swells. Here she discovered that though her shark's eyes were sharp enough in dim waters, the bright morning above the waves presented a blurry confusion. With concentrated effort, she discerned Keyway Island and the massive airship flying above it. Surprisingly, lightning arced up from the ship into the sky, at what she could not tell.

She slowed down to better inspect the airship but discovered that she needed to maintain a minimum speed to keep water moving through her gills. She rose up and breached. The sudden, shocking difference between water and air overwhelmed her and prevented her from concentrating on the ship; however, she could tell that she was now almost two miles away from Keyway Island.

Suddenly Leandra realized that she could swim away, out of the Cerulean Strait and into the open ocean. She swam another circle, turned the idea of fleeing over and then discarded it. Her crew was still on the catamaran. What was the point of escaping the empire if it made her as soulless as they were? Or was she soulless already?

She breached again. This time she discerned that the airship was now hovering over the island and slowly rising. Strangely, half of the aft sails seemed to be in disarray. Lightning again arced up into the sky. For a moment, Leandra saw something dark flying nimbly about in the pale blue sky.

Leandra dared to swim closer, her anxiety building. She had a strong suspicion about what was flying over the airship. If correct, Leandra would have to swim as fast as she could back to the catamaran and pray the crew had finished rigging the harness; the airship might not be distracted for long.

When she was as close as she dared go before diving, Leandra breached again and discovered that the airship had risen to a point nearly half a mile above Keyway Island. Far above the ship gamboled a distant dark shape, her auburn scales glinting in the sunlight. A blaze of lightning shot up from the airship toward the figure. The dragon flitted away.

Leandra had been right.

Fiery heaven, Mother, what are you doing?

Leandra's heart filled with guilt and fear. Was Nicodemus dead now? Or in some state worse than death? He had always feared disability, and now he might have awakened from paralysis crippled. Why had Francesca come for her?

Leandra breached one last time to watch her mother dance around lightning. Creator help her avoid it a bit longer. If the lightning struck true, Leandra did not think she could survive the guilt, loveless spell or no.

So Leandra dove deep through the water as her mother swam through the air.

CHAPTER THIRTY-NINE

Francesca banked hard right and felt as much as saw the lightning bolt tear through the air where, moments before, she had been flying.

As she dove, Francesca sensed a threat that had nothing to do with the airship throwing lightning at her. The sun now hung above the eastern headlands but shone with a crimson glow more characteristic of dusk than dawn. The horizon seemed too hazy. Even the wind felt strange—too warm and smelling of sulfur.

Francesca rode the wind down until an updraft coming off a large standing island made the air turbulent. Then she worked her wings hard, rising away from the *Empress* as lightning arced from the airship into the sky. Whatever Lotannu had done to protect the airship from Leandra's influence had also made the ship a miserable shot.

Francesca had been sweeping the bay for signs of her daughter when the flash and report of lightning drew her here. She had clawed half the ship's aft sails into rags before anti-boarding subspells had repelled her with sharp-edged cloth.

Now Francesca had to maintain a position high enough above the *Empress* to avoid the lightning while threatening a dive attack. She had hoped the *Empress* would soon exhaust her lightning spells and be forced to retreat. However, the ship's captain had directed most of the side sails downward, causing the ship to slowly rise. If he could climb above Francesca, he could ignore her and resume his bombardment. Then there was the matter of support. There was no saying how close the other imperial forces might be.

Light flashed from the *Empress*'s bow and Francesca dropped out of her climb and spiraled away. To her surprise, the airship's bolt shot, not upward at her, but downward.

Then Francesca spotted it. A catamaran was speeding away from the island. Curiously, the sails were reefed and the ship was moving far too fast to be powered by oars. Francesca tucked her wings and dropped. The *Empress* began a shallow dive after the catamaran; so Francesca placed herself directly aft of the ship, reasoning that if the lightning originated from the bow, the ship could not loose a bolt directly behind her without obliterating her own hull. This would be what sea captains call a stern chase—the attacker racing behind its prey, trying to catch its stern.

As Francesca closed in, another lightning bolt shot down from the *Empress* but again struck the island. To her surprise, Francesca got within a half mile of the *Empress* before the airship started to come about. Francesca flapped hard, trying to stay on her stern. But the airship turned too fast. Just as the bow came into view, Francesca dove hard and then pulled up. The air below her crackled with lightning, shook with thunder.

She continued to fly hard toward the *Empress*'s stern. Below her she could see Leandra's catamaran speeding toward a narrow opening between two standing islands. Lightning struck one of the limestone formations, sending a blast of stone flying.

Francesca's excitement rose as she closed the distance with the *Empress*. It seemed that the captain wanted Leandra so badly that he would chance a level stern chase with a dragon.

At five hundred yards, Francesca flexed her foreclaws in anticipation. Leandra's catamaran slipped between the two standing islands, and the *Empress* began to climb over the obstacles. This adjustment would slow the airship and—because Francesca had higher altitude—make her easier to catch. A twinge of doubt moved through Francesca. The ship's captain could not be so stupid as to start climbing during this stern chase unless . . .

Francesca pulled up out of her attack and began to scan the sky. The *Empress*'s captain should give up the stern chase only if he knew he had protection. At last Francesca saw her, hiding in the low crimson sun, another airship.

As Francesca climbed, she saw her stalker adjust her course to stand off. In that moment, Francesca caught the ship's silhouette and knew her for the *Queen's Lance*. She had no doubt that Cyrus was captaining his old ship, watching and waiting for Francesca to close with *Empress* so that he could run his foresails through her back. Francesca glared back at her old lover, hating him.

Ahead of her the *Empress* cleared the standing islands. Impulsively Francesca dove to pick up speed, pulling up only just above the water. It was the same trick she had pulled in Chandralu; now Cyrus wouldn't be able to dive at her with abandon. More importantly, she might lose him among the limestone pillars.

When she reached the twin islands, Francesca tucked her wings together and, like a sparrow flitting through a chink in a barn wall, passed between the islands to spread her wings and glide above the water. Ahead, a corridor of open water stretched for nearly a mile before the standing islands reconstituted their maze.

Leandra's catamaran was halfway across the corridor and veering left to hide among the limestone formations. The *Empress* flew behind her. A bolt of lightning arced down, overshot the catamaran and struck a standing island ahead of her.

As the thunderclap echoed across the bay, Francesca flew left to where she supposed Leandra was headed and then sprinted into the labyrinthine standing islands. Here the limestone formations were spaced far enough apart for easy navigation. She glanced back. The haze seemed to have increased in the last few moments, and the smell of sulfur had grown stronger. It was as if a nearby volcano were spewing out vog.

But all thoughts of the atmosphere vanished when she caught a glimpse of the *Queen's Lance*. Along the inferior aspect of her foresails shone two figures in bright orange-and-yellow robes.

Francesca veered left, nearly smashed her snout into a standing island, flapped hard to rise high enough to clear it. The dark boom of the pyromantic cannon made her dive toward the bay. Some screaming thing shot overhead, and then the base of a standing island ahead of her erupted into molten fire. Slowly the standing island began to fall.

Francesca flew harder and slipped under the island before it crashed into the bay.

A glance back through the spray and smoke told her that the *Queen's Lance* was still right on top of her. So she ducked into a thicket of islands. Here she could hide, but now she had to frantically dart right and left to avoid slamming up against the standing islands.

When enough space opened between the limestone pillars, she spread her wings wide to slow down, felt them scrape against rock and ferny cycads.

Through the array of stones, she glimpsed Lea's catamaran speeding between two standing islands. Above her, looming like a thundercloud, the *Empress* cast out lightning bolt after lightning bolt.

Francesca made a quick calculation about where Leandra was headed and began darting between the standing islands to intercept. The world became a blur of limestone and vines confined by blue water below and hazy sky above. The thunder was booming louder.

When she came to a place where the standing islands were more widely spaced, she hovered near an island's peak and then, with all four of her claws, grasped hold of a rocky outcropping. She flapped her wings twice for balance, then pressed them flat against the stone.

She craned her long neck and spotted the Queen's Lance patrolling an area of dense standing islands about a quarter mile to the east. Francesca clung tighter to the limestone and tried to shuffle sideways along the cliff face to put more of the island between her and the airship, but this disturbed a small flock of white-feathered red-tailed seabirds that rose into the air with screeching scorn.

Francesca froze, afraid that she had attracted an airship's attention. She held her breath and waited, but the Queen's Lance continued to fly slowly, patrolling loops around the dense ticket of islands. Meanwhile the boom of thunder, a dark purple sound, grew louder.

Francesca peered over the standing island and saw Leandra's catamaran come into view, moving fast between standing islands. Before the ship swam a dark shape. Holokai? Surprising. Francesca had guessed the shark god would betray Leandra and run back to Chandralu to save his child.

Francesca clung to the standing island and watched her daughter's ship slide into the maze of standing islands.

The thundering grew louder. The sky began to darken. At first Francesca thought it was the Empress overhead, but when she looked up she saw that it was, almost unbelievably, the haze. The air was taking on a grayish color and smelled not only of sulfur but also of hot metal.

The sky continued to darken but now she saw that the Empress was indeed flying directly overhead. Lightning arced away from the Empress's bow and struck somewhere that Francesca could not see. Francesca pressed her face against the limestone and waited for what seemed an eternity. She would get only one chance.

When at last the aft sails were directly overhead, Francesca leapt and rose with powerful wingbeats toward the flagship's underbelly. At fifty yards away, she roared out a savage attack. She closed the final few feet and threw herself into a clawing attack and caught . . . nothing but air.

Francesca's first sensation was one of unreality. Somehow she was hovering in turbulent air a hundred feet behind the Empress.

It seemed impossible, but the flagship had somehow sensed her surprise attack and nearly tripled its upward thrust. From somewhere behind her there came a boom and then a scream. She turned to see the *Queen's Lance* hovering above her. Then the air next to her burst into a spiny, black star of smoke.

A shockwave swatted Francesca out of the air.

CHAPTER FORTY

Nicodemus blinked rapidly, felt his eyes sting and tear, squeezed them shut. He tried to rub them but could not raise his hand up much farther than his chest. He was still lying flat in his compound's tearoom, slowly reclaiming his body from the tetrodotoxin.

Doria's teasing voice spoke above him. "The result of struggling against paresis is paresis with aggravation."

"What in the burning hells is paresis?" Nicodemus croaked, his voice raw from the breathing tube spell.

"A word my Lord Warden doesn't know?"

"You're enjoying this too much."

"Not technically possible."

"So what does paresis technically mean?"

"So you don't know what it means?"

"Is your practice to aggravate all of the patients you save from certain death?"

"Just those I care about."

Nicodemus smiled at his old friend. "Well, that's reassuring."

"Paresis means partial paralysis, what you're going through as the tetrodotoxin wears off. Don't struggle against it."

"Doesn't Fran have a saying like your paresis saying?"

"The result of surgery to relieve pain is pain with a hole in it," Doria provided. "It's popular among more conservative physicians."

Nicodemus opened his eyes. For a moment, he could focus on Doria's smiling face, wreathed by silvery hair. Behind her, Ellen stood and frowned at them both. The world became blurry again.

"You should be feeling good about your progress," Doria said. "You're clearing the tetrodotoxin faster than I thought possible. Being a Language Prime spellwright must have changed your physiology."

"Can I have some water?"

"Not on your life, literally," Ellen said in her usual flat tone. "Until you're strong enough to protect your airway, nothing but air is going through your mouth."

Nicodemus groaned.

Doria snorted. "I am always so surprised by how much the future savior of humanity whines."

"I'd whine a lot less if I had a less cynical physician. Or if I weren't such a phenomenal disaster as a father that I touched off the war that will doom humanity. At this point, I'm more likely to be the Storm Petrel than the Halcyon."

Ellen made a disgusted noise. "Lord Nicodemus, will you forgive me for speaking frankly?"

"I want to say yes, but that might be a lie."

"Leandra has done something far worse than anything that can be explained by parenting."

Nicodemus said nothing, suffered a sudden and vivid memory of falling backward into paralysis. Fear flushed across him. His daughter . . . How could she . . .

"There are more immediate matters—" Doria started to say in a diplomatic tone.

"Indeed there are," Ellen interrupted. "But eventually we will all have to face who Leandra has chosen to become. Fiery heaven, the woman had a spell cast on her mind to prevent her from being able to love. Who would do such a thing? I hope that when my Lady Warden returns, we can consider if we aren't better off without her."

"Thank you, Magistra," Doria said coldly. "We all know the situation, and our patient has a great deal on his mind. There will be plenty of time to discuss such matters."

Nicodemus still had his eyes closed but if he were to open them he had no doubt he would find the two physicians glaring at each other.

The keloid scar on his back was itching again. Maybe that was a good thing, a sign that he was recovering sensation.

"Forgive me, my Lord Warden, I am worried about your wife." Ellen replied in a tone that, though flat, held a modicum of contrition.

Still struggling to free himself from memories of falling into paralysis, Nicodemus found that he was breathing faster, fighting the urge to sit up. But if he were to try, his weakness would only increase his rising panic. With effort, he slowed his breathing.

"There was a message from the Floating City," Doria said with the tone of someone deliberately changing the subject. "The Trimuril has declared a state of martial prayer. All Ixonians are to worship war deities a minimum of three times a day."

"Seems reasonable," Nicodemus said. He opened his eyes and found he could focus longer. That helped. Ellen had turned to frown out the window. Blurriness returned. Nicodemus blinked rapidly, tears.

Doria cleared her throat. "There's more news. Just before dawn, the Sacred Regent delivered a speech in the Floating Palace, a diatribe from what I heard. He warned that Ixos was under attack by a tyrannical empress who wanted to take away their gods and goddesses. He claimed that the empress wanted to destroy the metaspell written by the Halcyon—that's you, by the way—which allows every human soul to shape the destiny of the archipelago by praying to whatever deity they see fit. The regent claimed that the empress wanted to destroy the gods and create a ruling class of the wizards. He asked if the audience would rather be enslaved by foreign spell-wrights or stand together as equals before the host of divinity."

Nicodemus pursed his lips, was relieved they no longer tingled. "A bit exaggerated, but not too far off the mark."

Ellen sniffed. "If Leandra were here, she'd say there's no difference between empire and league. She'd say that the deities were just as tyrannical as the wizards would be."

"Perhaps," Doria said coldly, "we should let the Lady Warden of Ixos speak for herself."

Nicodemus tried to preempt any further argument. "And how was the Sacred Regent's speech received?"

"Well," Doria answered. "The whole city is in a fervor of prayer."

"I hope it will be enough." Nicodemus tried to scratch his nose, but his clumsy hand only flopped first onto his chest and then his face. But by shaking his head, he managed to find relief.

Over by the window, Ellen drew in a sharp breath. A moment later she murmured "Fiery heaven . . ."

"What is it?" Doria asked.

"Out on the bay, there's—"

But then her words were interrupted by shouting and heavy footsteps. Nicodemus opened his eyes and with effort turned his head toward the door. The footsteps grew loud and John's voice sounded. "Nico! Nico!" The screen door flew back. John stood in the hall, Rory just behind him. "Nico, come up to the roof."

"John," Doria scolded, "the Lord Warden is hardly in a state to dash up several steps. What is it? What's happened?"

"I don't know. No one does."

"But what is it?" she asked.

"I can't say. He needs to come see."

"He can't—" Doria started to say when Nicodemus managed to prop himself up on his elbows.

"He can try," Nicodemus finished. "Someone get me a walking cane or find some way to support me."

In the end, they constructed an impromptu stretcher out of spear shafts and a rug stitched together by Magnus spells. Rory and John carried him up to the roof.

They set him down on the complex's eastern edge. Slowly, laboriously, Nicodemus sat himself up and dangled his legs over the roof's edge. He had to blink his eyes repeatedly, knuckle tears out of them.

"No one knows when it appeared," John said beside Nicodemus. "It seems it was just sort of . . . there . . . when the sun came up. You can see it directly in front of you. And that eruption. That's new. It wasn't doing that when I came to get you."

Nicodemus finished rubbing his eyes. When he opened them, he saw the familiar terraced city falling away to the bay. The blue water ran out to standing islands. A gray haze hung above the horizon, which Nicodemus had sometimes seen above a wildfire on the Lornish plains. The sun had risen above the eastern headlands and now shone hauntingly crimson.

But what commanded the eye's attention, what filled Nicodemus's heart with confusion and fear, was what rose up from the gray islands. He needed to make sure what he had seen was real.

Far out on the bay, rising from the water and above the standing islands, was a dark mountain that, from its peak, was spewing clouds of blackness.

Nicodemus whispered the first word that came to his mind, "Los."

CHAPTER FORTY-ONE

As Francesca fell, shards of pain bore into her body. Her thoughts spun. At last instinct took over. She twisted to right herself. Shrapnel from the pyromantic cannon had torn holes through her wings. Frantically she slowed her descent enough to land gracelessly on an uneven standing island. She slid and had to scramble for purchase.

A barrage of thunderclaps along with the darker boom of cannon fire rolled across the bay. Francesca looked up and saw that the *Queen's Lance* had formed on the *Empress*'s wing. Both airships were discharging what seemed to be their full ordinance into the bay.

Panic raced through Francesca's heart. The airships had caught her daughter and were bombarding her with so much force that, in a few moments, not even underwater Holokai would survive. This was it then. This was how her daughter died, how Francesca's hope was extinguished. She launched herself at the airships. But no sooner had she taken wing than a wave of hot wind slammed into her, sent her tumbling. It took all her strength to keep from dashing into the standing islands. The air reeked of sulfur.

Francesca found herself flying up into wan, ruby sunlight. The wide tropical sun, still not far above the horizon, had become a blurry crimson disk. Francesca's mind filled with images of the world's end: The seas boiling with blood, the sky blotted out by smoke, the sun dying.

Then she realized that the blast of sulfurous wind had also blown the *Empress* and the *Queen's Lance* off their course. In fact, the *Queen's Lance* had struck one of the standing islands. Her aft sails were in disarray and several lofting kites were blooming from her wings as the hierophantic crew abandoned ship. The *Empress* had fared better, rising high enough to clear the limestone pillars. Francesca could just make out the *Empress*'s crew, who were pointing eastward.

She turned, and at first she could not understand what she was seeing. It felt as if she had flown into a nightmare.

Three miles away, above the gray limestone islands, jutted a slender mountain of blackness. From its peak spewed a cloud of what she would have called smoke if it were not contorting so unnaturally. Within the black air writhed arms and hands, human mouths filled with dragon's teeth, long twisting tentacular appendages.

Several memories turned inside Francesca's mind unlocking the nightmarish vision. Nicodemus had said that the bay near Feather Island had been hazy, the air sulfurous as if covered with vog. On Feather Island, Nicodemus found hardened lava flows of a lava demon attack. The captured pyromancer described smoke that had gotten inside the villagers and driven them mad.

In Chandralu there had been rumors of a Sea People fishing boat found with half the crew dead and the other half insane. Other rumors said the fabled Floating Island had wandered into the bay. Francesca had dismissed the reports of whirlpools and black smoke billowing from nothingness into the sky. But now she understood. The black mountain and phantasmagoric smoke were manifestations of a lava divinity too powerful to be a neodemon. This must be demon from the Ancient Continent.

As she watched, the smoke billowed up with unbelievable speed and then down onto the bay, over which it rolled like a river of air. The phantasmagoric shapes—bones and eyes and entrails—rolled along within the smoke, all squirming over each other, reaching for where the airships had attacked Leandra's catamaran.

Leandra! Francesca's fear for her daughter overcame her horror. With new strength, she flew toward where she supposed her daughter had been. The captain of the *Empress* was thinking along similar lines; the massive airship dove toward the previous point of bombardment. Again the *Empress* moved with a speed that Francesca would have thought impossible.

Francesca flew over two standing islands while eying the airship and the nightmare smoke to see who would get to Leandra first. She strained against her own exhaustion. But both the airship and the smoke were too fast. The *Empress* dove down into an opening in the standing islands.

A moment later, Francesca flew over a row of limestone formations and saw what was left of Leandra's catamaran. The starboard hull was missing and the crew were cutting off what was left of the central decks from the portside hull. Around and below the crippled ship swam Holokai's black silhouette.

Not five hundred yards above the ship, the *Empress* was diving fast. Lightning leapt from the airship and struck a limestone formation behind the catamaran. Francesca strained her wings but felt herself weaken. The *Empress* was four hundred yards away from the catamaran. On the other side of the catamaran, the black smoke wrapped its fingers around the standing islands and disgorged itself across the water.

The catamaran's crew pointed and gestured. Two of them dove overboard and began swimming away from the smoke.

The *Empress* was three hundred yards away.

The smoke flung out tendrils that raced around the catamaran to enclose it in a wall of writhing shapes.

Francesca's wings faltered.

The *Empress* was two hundred feet away. Lightning jumped out from the airship, arcing for the catamaran. But tentacles of smoke shot up and wrapped around the lightning. The billowing segments of the smoke flashed like a thundercloud. A chain of lightning ran around the circle of smoke before dying out. A second arc of lightning shot out from the *Empress*, and again the smoke intercepted and dissipated the bolt.

Confused, Francesca pulled out of her dive and flew a slow circle. In her flight from the *Empress*, Leandra seemed to have stumbled upon the lava demon's stronghold. But that would be too coincidental. Now that the nightmare smoke was protecting the catamaran, Francesca suspected that what was unfolding before her was more than coincidence.

The *Empress* swung all her side sails down and forward. The resulting blast of air flattened the swells on the bay but passed through the black air without effect. It would have scattered mundane smoke into a thousand turbulent spirals.

The *Empress* came to a halt so quickly that a hierophant slipped and fell into the air. His green robes billowed into a jumpchute. Black ropes erupted from the smoke and reached out to snare him. Over the white roaring of the wind, Francesca could just recognize his shrieks, frantic yellow sounds.

In the next instant, three plumes of smoke struck the underside of the *Empress*'s foresails. Three bolts of lightning leapt away from the ship to strike either standing islands or aspects of the black smoke.

The *Empress*'s crew burst into panicked action. Many tore strips of sailcloth from the ship and cast them as warkites toward the smoke. But the dark air consumed the constructs as implacably as the sea consumes the drowned. Then the smoke enveloped the airship's entire bow.

Francesca spotted a black-robed figure moving about the hull, waving his hands. Arcs of gold and silver flashed from his hands and began cutting away the ship's foresails. This had to be Lotannu Akomma. Soon the green robes joined him. In moments the *Empress*'s bow fell away and vanished into the churning smoke. As if freed from a tether, the *Empress* leapt back.

Francesca flew another circle and looked down at the catamaran. Maybe ten surviving sailors sat on the remaining hull. Most of the center deck had been cut away. Francesca could make out Dhrun and her daughter, who for some reason was dripping wet and pulling on a blouse and lungi. Holokai had disappeared, likely fled.

Though the smoke continued to swirl around the catamaran, it drew no closer. However, one of the sailors who had jumped overboard was caught by a tendril of the black stuff. It seemed to wrap around his head, burrow into his face.

For a moment, the sailor sank below the surface. When he resurfaced and began swimming toward the catamaran, Leandra pointed and the wrestling god removed both his swords and went to the railing. The swimmer pulled himself up on deck and charged the god. Dhrun sidestepped him and with a wrestler's grace threw the man hard onto the deck. Without pause, the attacker rose and again and threw himself at the god.

Again Dhrun dodged away from the charge, but this time he flipped the swimmer back into the water. A moment later the sailor's head reappeared. But then, for no reason that Francesca could tell, the maniac dove down and did not come up.

Francesca glanced at the *Empress*. She was hovering as her crew swarmed around her, trying to reconfigure her after the damage. So Francesca flew another circle and saw a body floating by the catamaran. It was the sailor who had been tainted by the smoke. He had drowned himself. Nausea churned in Francesca's gut as she realized that this was the fate that had befallen the villagers of Feather Island.

The *Empress*'s crew had stabilized the ship, but she had lost a third of her length. Her capacity to generate lightning seemed to have been lost with her bow. Still she circled.

Francesca studied the smoke, wondering if she could somehow lift her daughter out of the wreckage. At that moment, the smoke parted to the east, forming a corridor of open water to the black volcano from which it had come. It seemed that the lava demon wanted a word with Leandra.

Francesca flew down toward the boat, but as she did the smoke rose in threatening plumes and spikes. She climbed again and continued to circle. The *Empress* kept her distance.

On the water, Leandra seemed to come to the same conclusion that her mother had about the smoke. She made some gestures and her crew began to row. Slowly, the remains of the catamaran made its way down the corridor of smoke toward the volcano.

Exhausted Francesca could not risk an attack on the *Empress*, which did not look in any shape for battle either. So both dragon and airship trailed after Leandra's ship. The sun had risen higher in the sky and lost some of its crimson hue.

After a half hour, they reached the volcano. It seemed to be made of obsidian and was almost perfectly symmetrical. As its steep central spire descended, the black glass mountain expanded until it became horizontal in all directions for several hundred yards before meeting the lapping bay water. The island appeared to be empty. No buildings, no openings or caves, no plants or birds, not even sand or pebbles.

As Leandra's ship neared the shore, the black smoke evaporated. At first, Francesca thought she had hallucinated its disappearance, but then Leandra's crew called out in surprise. Judging by the gestures, some sailors wanted to escape. Leandra, on the other hand, was shaking her head.

Francesca wondered what could possibly be going through her daughter's mind. Though it was unlikely that the deity who had brought Leandra to this island would let her go, she could at least try. But Leandra continued to shake her head and then gestured to the island. With a four-armed god by her side, the sailors did not seem to have much chance for negotiation.

So the crew paddled the battered vessel onto the strange shore. Francesca dove and circled close. There was no eruption, no return of the black smoke. Above her, a swath of white cloth broke away from the *Empress* and formed a lofting kite that held three figures in its dangling harness. Two wore green robes, the other black: Lotannu and two hierophantic pilots for escorts.

Francesca watched as Lotannu's jumpchute landed the three imperials on the island. Leandra's sailors formed a protective knot around her, but Lotannu and his wind mages kept their distance.

With a few wingbeats, Francesca landed on the volcanic island. The shore felt disturbingly warm under her feet, and her claws slid across the glassy rock. Francesca stared down at the black substance and bared her draconic teeth at it.

"Mother."

With a start, Francesca brought her head up and discovered Leandra standing in front of her. Dhrun and her crew stood beside her. The sailors looked up at Francesca with awe, but Leandra regarded her mother as coolly as she might over breakfast. It was hard for Francesca to tell, perspective being so different in draconic form, but it seemed as if her daughter had grown taller.

"Mother," Leandra said, "what do we do next?"

With a draconic throat, Francesca could not make human speech. She could have written a spell, but Leandra could only deconstruct text. So, she only shook her draconic head.

"Is Dad still alive?" Leandra asked, her voice softer.

Francesca nodded.

"Good," Leandra said and nodded at her mother. "As to what we should do next . . ." She let her voice trail away and then looked over at Lotannu and his hierophants. The three of them were about a hundred yards away. Francesca bared her teeth at the imperials. They watched impassively.

"Forget them," Leandra said. "Something has been drawing me here for a long time. Something like destiny."

Now Francesca bared her teeth. What was Leandra talking about? Had she gone completely mad?

Leandra looked up at her mother. "What did you see in the smoke?"

Francesca blinked. Yes, completely mad.

"Every one of my crew saw something different. In the smoke, I saw the faces of all those who have followed me and died. I saw Dad's face too. It frightened me. But the sailors saw writhing snakes or insects or demons."

Confused, Francesca could only put her head to one side.

Leandra sighed. "No, I don't suppose you could tell me." She looked up to the volcano's peak. "So then . . . as soon as we figure out where he is, and before he gets started on destroying humanity, I suppose we should introduce ourselves to the first demon of the invasion. Who knows, we might even meet Los himself."

"No one so grand," said a rasping voice.

Francesca whirled around but saw only the island's black expanse. Behind her Leandra made a thoughtful sound. Francesca whipped her head around and discovered an old man standing ahead of her daughter.

The stranger was thin and bent over by age. A few wiry hairs erupted from his blotchy scalp. His clothes were a confusion of rags and bright silks wrapped about him without regard for function or fashion. He had turned his sunken face to Leandra and was studying her with bright green eyes. "Sorry to disappoint, but the great Los you have already met."

Francesca bared her teeth and started to defensively curl her tail and wings around her daughter. But Leandra held out her hand. "No, Mother." She never took her eyes from the stranger. "We've already met Los? Are you the dread god then?"

The old man smiled, revealing snaggled teeth. "No one so grand. A mere slave, your slave, that is all I am." He bowed far lower than Francesca would have thought possible for his arthritic frame.

"Are you a demon?" Leandra asked. "The lava demon of this island?"

Lotannu and his two hierophants had crept closer. Now they stood well within earshot. Leandra paid them no mind.

The old man straightened. "Not a demon, only a human who was made diamond-minded." He turned his bright green eyes on Francesca. His mouth moved into a slack, geriatric smile. "I would tell you more about myself, but I might bore your mother. She and I met long ago, long before you sent me to find you."

Francesca narrowed her eyes. She had never seen the man before.

Apparently her thoughts were clear on her draconic face, for Leandra said, "I don't think she recognizes you."

"Oh no?" the old man asked. His smile widening but then becoming melancholy. "She and I fought once when I had a different mind. We fought in the sanctuary in Avel, amid pillars and arches of the Hall of Ambassadors. We fought under the open sky and in a redwood forest. I only just escaped her."

A horrible suspicion grew in Francesca's heart. She wanted to leap away from the old man, to spread her wings and be away.

The old man took a wheezing breath, turned his green eyes on Francesca. "There have been days, many days, since then that I wish I had not escaped, that she had killed me in that beautiful room or that beautiful forest. Her husband, your father, could have killed me on the rolling green savanna, under the stars. Often I wonder why he didn't . . . The thoughts that come when a mind is enslaved, they are hard to explain."

Leandra laughed. "You will have to try harder. Nothing you say makes any sense. Who are you, really? And why have you brought me here?"

He turned the horrible green eyes away from Francesca and toward Leandra. "I brought you here at your command."

Leandra blinked. "We've never met before."

"Not in this life. I am your father's old enemy, your distant cousin, your slave." He bowed again. "I have had many names, but many years ago I was called the Savanna Walker."

Francesca's heart began to race. She never saw the Savanna Walker's human body, only his opalescent draconic form.

The old man bowed again to Leandra, sank to his knees. "And you too have had many names. Far from here, you commanded me to cross the ocean again so that you might know who you truly are."

Leandra's eyes focused on something far beyond the old man. "And who am I, truly?"

"You are the engine of the world. You are the change come to destroy the world and remake it." He looked up at her with his green eyes, so like Nicodemus's, and said, "You are the reincarnation of Los."

CHAPTER FORTY-TWO

No one spoke.

Leandra became aware of the wind, lapping waves, birds crying far away. The sky had cleared, the sulfurous odor dissipated. Her heart filled with strange elation even as her thoughts snarled. She cleared her throat and said, "What you say, old man, is impossible."

The ancient creature looked at her with his sunken face, smiled. Black smoke poured from his mouth, nose, eyes. The oily air wrapped around his head, coiled down his body. Faces danced across the smoke—Holokai's, Thaddeus's, her father's. Then the smoke puffed into gossamers that twisted, evaporated. Again a thin pathetic man stood before her, his smile disturbing and sympathetic.

Francesca spread her claws, coiled her tail protectively around her daughter. Dhrun stepped away from the tail while surprised cries came from Lotannu's pilots. Her mother snarled at Lotannu, but a wall of black smoke rose between them. "They will stay," the old man said. "They must hear what I have to say. I will not permit you to harm them."

Francesca turned her snarl on the old man, and for a moment Leandra feared her mother was going to scoop her up and fly away. But then Leandra leaned over and laid a hand on her mother's tail; she seemed to relax.

Leandra looked back into the old man's eyes. She kept her voice flat. "The smoke—cute trick—doesn't change that your claim is impossible."

His smile brightened. "Mortals look back as if the past could have been different. But reweaving the past is the only impossibility. You taught me so when you showed me how to perceive forward into time. The past is alive only within ourselves."

"When did I teach you anything?"

"Thirty-four years ago."

The specificity surprised Leandra. She looked up at her mother, whose draconic eyes studied the stranger with a quickness suggestive of fear. In the coming winter, Leandra would be thirty-four years old. "Thirty-four years?"

"Almost precisely."

"Explain."

The old man's face grew smoother, his motions quicker. "Once I was a wild, wonderful thing on the savanna. You might have heard of me; I had the fecund mind. But Typhon enslaved me, made me a diamond-minded dragon. That is why I now talk . . . this way." He made a sour face. "Typhon set me against your father and later your mother. She wanted to kill me for reasons that she might not be completely aware." He looked up at Francesca.

The dragon growled at him.

The old man nodded as if greeting an old friend. "Typhon sacrificed himself so that I might fly to the Ancient Continent. Often I have wished your mother had killed me then. But I escaped and flew over the rolling savanna of Spires, over the arid plains and farmlands of Verdant, over the twisting sands of the Desert of Oso, past the Burning Rock. There I rested several days, fattening myself on katabeasts and the leonine children of Chimera who hunt them."

As the old man spoke, smoke rose from the ground behind him and formed the shapes of his narration. A slender dragon flew over plains and dunes. He swooped down to sink claws into a massive katabeast. He defended the carcass from a tribe of spear-wielding creatures with human torsos growing from lion bodies.

"I fought the urge to fly north. I thought it would be my death. Who could have said how wide the ocean was? But Typhon had enslaved me, and when my belly grew fat, I took wing with the compulsion." The smoke became a wide-winged dragon flying over undulating waves. "I flew over bright schools of fish and leviathans as large as swimming mountains. I flew through wind and fog and sunlight that seemed bright enough to shine through my soul. Then, on the fourth day, a wind storm struck and blew me west."

The miniature smoke dragon frantically worked his wings as a storm tore wisps from his body and tail. The dragon faltered, fell toward the sea. But then it turned to fly with the wind, gliding unsteadily. Ahead the smoke formed a long coastline of sheer cliffs. Waves dashed themselves into wisps along the shore. "On the sixth day, I reached land." The miniature dragon landed gracelessly atop one of the cliffs and collapsed, breathing heavily.

"But I did not know if the land was the Ancient Continent. Perhaps the storm had blown me into another world." The perspective of the smokeplay expanded to reveal a rolling land covered with pine forests and sharp peaks. A deerlike creature ventured out of the wood to experimentally sniff the sleeping dragon. "But soon I regained my strength." With blurring speed, the miniature dragon pinned the deerlike creature under foreclaws, tore out its throat. The dragon ate and then took wing.

"I explored the vast new land—one filled with the bones of ancient civilizations." Land rolled underneath the dragon until it became a ruined city of strange architecture, all square buildings and crumbling arenas amid trees and shrubs. "But nowhere did I find humanity. Animals, wilderness, that was all. More surprising, nowhere did I find demons."

Leandra blinked. "So it wasn't the Ancient Continent?"

"So I thought, for if there was one thing we know of the Ancient Continent it is that it swarms with demons." He looked from Leandra to Francesca to Lotannu. "How could it not? The human kingdoms built themselves believing that the demons will come for them. So I told myself that I had not found the Ancient Continent for I had not found the ancient demons. And yet as I continued to explore, I found more and more ruins. And such ruins! They fit perfectly the cities of ancient legends—the towers of Berulan, the domes of Ursha'al—that I could not escape the feeling that this was indeed the Ancient Continent."

The smoke showed the landscape rising into mountains which held a ruined city of spires. Then the landscape fell to a wide jungle, punctuated by massive mountainlike pyramids. There followed sand dunes and a ruined city of domes built around an oasis.

The old man continued. "I did not realize then that the past is dead everywhere except within us, where it is vibrantly horrifyingly alive." The smoke dragon pawed through the crumbling temples and collapsing tombs. Then the dragon took wing, and the land stretched into a snowfield below. The dragon flew until the plain grew into a steep volcano beside a wide river. Here there were ruins, but only the tops of the buildings and towers protruded from the mountain. The rest of the city seemed to have been covered by lava flow.

"At last, in the snowy north, I discovered Mount Calax."

The smoke dragon landed amid the ruins and discovered a statue of immense proportions submerged to the waist in ancient lava flow. "I found your stone remains where the Last Emperor and his guardians sacrificed themselves to bind you in stone so humanity might escape across the ocean." A shudder moved through the old man. The tiny dragon approached the statue and then fell into a seizure.

As abruptly as it had formed, the smoke evaporated. Again the old man shuddered. "A godspell placed in me by Typhon wormed its way from me and into your frozen statue. It used my imperial heritage to free you from your prison. Your eyes became smoke, your mouth a conflagration. Your body melted and covered mine. There was only pain. Such great pain."

Leandra pressed her hand to her chest. Just as nightmares enfold the sleeper in horrible inevitability—the monster that cannot be escaped, the fall that cannot be avoided—Leandra felt destiny take hold of her.

The Savanna Walker stood straighter. "That was when I ceased to be Typhon's slave and became yours."

"I have no slaves."

"You have two."

"You're straining my credulity."

"Your present life, it is one of bondage to your human body, to the disease that is wracking it."

"I have been cured of my disease."

"Cured? By the loveless spell?"

Discomfited, she said nothing.

"The loveless spell did not cure you; it only masks your humanity, bringing your divine nature to the surface. That is why you have heightened senses and can deconstruct gods."

Again the nightmarish inevitability filled Leandra. "Not cured?"

The Savanna Walker's expression darkened. "That day nearly thirty-four years ago, I brought you news of Nicodemus Weal and Francesca DeVega and how Typhon had brought them together in hopes of starting a new version of the Disjunction in which the divine language and Language Prime intermingled. I told you how your mother had destroyed Typhon and eaten his remains. In return, you showed me how time truly is, how the future stretches out before us like a landscape, but the past is as confining as a prison cell. You showed me the truth of the past."

"And what is the truth?"

"When our ancestors fled the Ancient Continent, the demons languished. Without human prayer to refresh their divine language, they weakened. Without Los to govern, they fell to fighting. Over the millennia they perished until there were only a few dozen patrolling the southern coast, longing to cross the ocean to seek revenge on humanity. Without sustaining prayer, and with the constant fighting, their minds degenerated into brutishness. Typhon was the only surviving demon who retained his intellect. Then, when he discovered the half-finished golem named Fellwroth on Mount Calax, he transformed the creature into his ark and together they crossed the ocean."

Leandra shook her head. "But Fellwroth reported to my father that demons still stalked the Ancient Continent. Typhon was trying to create a dragon to fly over them to revive Los."

"So they did when Typhon left, but he sailed from the Ancient Continent centuries ago. And his presence on the Ancient Continent stabilized the Pandemonium. Many of the demons had formed a loose alliance against him, agreeing to protect each other should Typhon attack any one of them. Once Typhon left, they destroyed each other."

Suddenly Leandra understood. "That is why the Disjunction hasn't come. Humanity has been wondering why the Pandemonium has not crossed the ocean for the past thirty years. It's because there are no demons left?"

When the Savanna Walker nodded, excited murmuring sounded from Lotannu's hierophants.

Leandra ignored them. "Leaving only you, old man? Are you the invasion?"

He shook his head. "The invasion began thirty years ago. That is why I want those men"—he gestured to Lotannu's party—"to hear what I have to say. If they don't, I will have to find someone similar. You gave specific orders about whom I had to inform to complete the demonic invasion."

Leandra looked around. "You'll forgive me if I'm skeptical about this demonic invasion. There is an acute lack of destroyed civilizations at hand."

"Your goal was never to destroy human civilization, but replace it with something purer, something better. That is your fundamental passion."

The words chilled Leandra. She would have traded empire and league for a less degenerate civilization in a heartbeat.

The Savanna Walker nodded at Leandra. "I see it in your eyes; you are the same in this life. You strengthened me so that I could protect you while you were still young and mortal."

She could only blink at him.

"After commanding me, you gave me your old and massive body. I used it to make this island. With it I can make the fire burn, the lava flow. You showed me how to enhance my talents. Before I could block perception, cause blindness or deafness or aphasia; you showed me how to drive any man or woman into madness. The smoke you believe you see, for example, is nothing. You see in it your projected fears. What happened on Feather Island will give you evidence for all that I say."

Remembering her father's reports of madness and lava flows, Leandra nodded. "But why attack Feather Island?"

"The imperial forces there were tracking you. They were also about to discover your father sailing into the bay from the Matrunda River. To ensure your safety, I destroyed them."

"And the innocent villagers."

The Savanna Walker produced a toothy grin. "I wasn't trying to show off."

"You disgust me."

"With pleasure."

Anger flared in Leandra.

The old man continued. "After empowering me on the Ancient Continent, you told me to return to the human kingdoms and await your reincarnation. You decided that you would be the child of Nicodemus and Francesca. Francesca had eaten the body of Typhon, so her union with Nicodemus became a conduit for your soul into this life as a creature of both divine language and Language Prime."

Francesca flexed her claws.

The Savanna Walker looked up at her. "That was when I first began to wish that you, Francesca, had killed me in that redwood forest. I had been enslaved for nearly a decade already, but all during the quest for Los, I hoped that the dread god would reward my service with freedom. But as his spirit sped away south to be reborn, I knew that I would never be free again."

The old man looked down at his slender frame, his knobby feet. "My true body might not impress. But with the stone and fire of your old incarnation wrapped around me, I became a great dragon. With wings as wide as a city, I flew back to the human lands. It wasn't hard to find you. Your mother and father were then on Starfall Island, as the league was taking its shape. So I became a creature of the sea, floating across the waves just over the horizon. Human eyes could not perceive me, though a few encounters with sailors led to increased rumors about the fabled floating island. Deities straying closer were more troublesome. I had to hunt them down and eat them. Later that year, you were born. Though I was over the blue horizon, I recognized your reincarnation the way a blind man feels the sunshine."

"But . . . why?" was all Leandra could think to ask.

"Your command was to stay close to you and to protect you from any harm. To reveal myself only if you should be in mortal danger. And, not a half an hour ago, that happened when the airships bombarded you. A moment longer, and you would have died. I had no choice but to reveal myself. Your commands were quite clear: Once I revealed myself, I was to reveal to you and your opponents the nature of the struggle you all had unknowingly entered. Conveniently, I've caught all of you together."

Leandra shook her head, trying to keep up. "But . . . you could not have followed me my whole life. I would have noticed something."

"Ah, but you did."

"I did?"

"When you were young, your parents protected you admirably well. I had no cause to come within a hundred miles. But when you became warden of Ixos, especially early on, you would take on neodemons too powerful. I tried to hide my influence as—"

"The mosquito goddess," Leandra said, suddenly understanding. "When we were in the mangrove swamp, hiding from her swarms."

The old man nodded. "I filled the air with smoke that confused the mosquitoes."

"We assumed it was a volcanic eruption," she said numbly, then looked into his eyes. "And when we were fleeing the giant jellyfish neodemon?"

"I made the sea hazy, as if covered with vog, so that you could escape in the night. And as soon as you were in the harbor, I attacked it during a storm and left it dead on the shore."

"And when I botched that conversion of the elephant mercenary god, you drove one of his lieutenants to insanity?"

He nodded and his smile took on an almost avuncular quality. "Only those three times." His gaze became indistinct. "There is little I have enjoyed since Typhon enslaved me, but those three times, when I could move against those gods . . . the sharp taste they had in my gullet." He closed his eyes again.

"But why protect me? Why would I order that?"

"Because early in this life, you were vulnerable and weak. So you ordered me to help you become as strong as possible before I revealed the past and the possible futures to you and your opponents." He nodded to Lotannu's party.

Leandra turned to see the wizard and his two hierophants staring at them with stony expressions.

"I suppose that brings us," Leandra asked, "to the possible futures."

The Savanna Walker was nodding. "As Typhon once explained to your parents, there are two visions of the Disjunction. And although no more demons remain on the Ancient Continent, both visions are coming to pass."

Leandra tapped her index fingers together in the Sea People gesture for "get on with it."

The old man continued. "Life is living language. Your goal was always to escape the brutishness of Language Prime. You started the war that ended civilization on the Ancient Continent by creating a metaspell that began to stop language misspelling. Your plan then was to sterilize all language and create a species more virtuous than humanity. The golem Fellwroth was to be the first such creature, but you were frozen in stone before he was completed. Typhon brought Fellwroth to this land, but being incomplete he failed. However, Typhon also began casting your metaspell to end misspelling in Language Prime, this resulted in the Silent Blight."

The Savanna Walker nodded to himself. "Though Typhon is dead, the Empress Vivian has continued to cast his metaspell. If the empress is victorious in the coming conflict, her metaspells will eventually make the world so sterile as to cause the collapse of civilization. In the resulting chaos, the few remaining divinities will easily enslave humanity."

Leandra looked at Lotannu. "Take that message to my aunt, won't you? Especially the terrifying collapse of civilization and the enslavement of humanity part. He phrased it so well."

The wizard only narrowed his eyes.

"The other vision of the Disjunction was devised by Typhon," the old man continued. "In it, there is hybridization of divinity and humanity. You are the direct result of all this. And through Nicodemus's metaspells, the demonic horde has been re-created in the myriad league deities. True, your deities don't want to destroy all of humanity, only half of humanity, the half living in the empire."

"Lovely world we've built for ourselves," Leandra muttered.

The old man didn't seem to hear. "The result of this conflict will hinge upon you and how you choose to manifest yourself in this life."

"There are choices?"

"The two parts of your nature—divine and mortal—cannot tolerate each other for long. If you can avoid physical harm for ten or maybe twenty years, your divine nature will complete its maturation and kill your mortal body. You will arise then as Los Reborn. You will rally the league's divine host and crush the empire. A new civilization conjoining humanity and divinity will arise and rule for millennia as mortality is slowly weeded out and divinity finds a way to propagate on its own. There will be no more death or disease. The world then is as unimaginable to us as the ocean is to an ant."

Leandra grumbled, "An ant doesn't need to understand the ocean to have strong feelings about being thrown in it."

"However," the Savanna Walker said, "should you die before your life runs its natural course—either by mismanagement of your disease or by violence—then the empire will prevail and—"

"And my aunt will screw everything up in the other direction; I get it. But is there any way we could avoid destroying the underpinning principles of life as we know it?"

The Savanna Walker produced another toothy grin. "Certainly, you just need to find two civilized and powerful people on opposite sides of the current political and religious divide to cooperate with each other and—"

"No, stop. I knew we were all screwed when you got to 'and powerful.'" She turned to Lotannu. "Do you think we could cooperate—"

Two jumpchutes leapt up from the hierophants by Lotannu's side. An instant later, the rigging had pulled all three men two hundred feet into the air and toward the circling *Empress*.

Francesca crouched, ready to leap after prey. But pillars of black smoke erupted from the island, barring Francesca's flight.

Mother and daughter, dragon and woman, rounded on the Savanna Walker. He glared back at them with a leering smile.

"Why?" Leandra growled.

"The wizard must tell the empress what was said here. You commanded a war between the two forms of the Disjunction. Now it is so."

"Then I now command it to be God-of-gods damned not so," she replied.

"You commanded me to prevent you from altering previous orders," the Savanna Walker said through a growing smile. She could see he enjoyed hurting his captor by enacting his captor's orders.

"Why would I command such a stupid thing?"

"You are the dread god, remember? You want the War of Disjunction to happen."

"Tell me what possible future takes place if I command you to be free of slavery and then tear your face off. What happens then?"

His smile stayed wide as he shrugged thin shoulders. "The empress would prevail. I have become the most powerful dragon in the world, and I'm dedicated to protecting you."

A blast of wind washed over them as the *Empress* engaged all her sails and flew off to wherever the imperial forces were concealed.

"I don't own slaves—" Leandra started to say.

"You do now," the Savanna Walker interrupted, still leering.

"What happens if I set you free?"

He closed his eyes and seemed to shudder with pleasure. "You can't, and if you could I would fly as far from humanity as I could and find a part of the world populated by large and very dumb animals that taste good."

"So . . ." Leandra said while narrowing her eyes at the man. "So I have a slave."

He smirked. "Perhaps, when we go to Chandralu, your father will finish what he started so long ago and kill me."

The mention of her father sent a spasm of pain through Leandra's heart. She looked up at her mother, who looked down at her.

"Well, old man," Leandra said without looking away from her mother's inscrutable draconic eyes, "if my father is still alive, he just might do that. Of course, he might also kill me."

CHAPTER FORTY-THREE

With Lotannu holding her arm, Vivian walked the war galley's deck with a queasiness she associated with a recently broken fever. She had spent too long in her master spell, become frail. More upsetting had been the recovered memories and the revelation that Nicodemus had not been smuggling gods out of the empire, Los had.

A bracing wind blew across the deck. All around, the standing islands stretched up to a tropical sky. Slowly the galley sailed between stone formations toward the bay's open water. Other imperial ships—of sea and air—were taking similar courses.

"How long until both fleets are in formation?" she asked.

"No more than an hour."

Vivian brushed her long black hair out of her eyes. This was taking too long. Deconstructing the master spell had proven more difficult than anticipated. During their casting, Vivian had improved many of the subspells, but she had not known how to write them to be quickly stored in spellbooks. As a result, once Lotannu had explained the situation, she had needed several hours to reverse her previous edits. She had wanted to move against Los with speed, but now it was nearly midday and the fleets were just emerging from the standing islands.

They had missed the chance to catch the dread god Los . . . no . . . the dread goddess Los when she was most vulnerable.

But Vivian did have one consolation: Belowdecks several hundred spellbooks now preserved her master spell. If needed, she could reconstitute the spell. Gingerly she touched the Emerald that hung around her neck. All her life she had been training for this moment. "When should we expect the scouts to report back?" she asked.

"Any moment now," Lotannu answered. They both looked up at the sky but saw no lofting kites. "But I would be shocked to hear any report other than Leandra's retreat—"

"Los's retreat," she corrected.

". . . Los's retreat into a Chandralu now bristling with defenses."

"We let our chance escape."

Lotannu bowed his head.

"Not your fault, old friend. Any blame is mine."

They made another lap around the deck. From the railing, her commanders watched. They were of every rank and training in the empire: Spirish admirals, Verdantine nobles, wizards, pyromancers, and on and on. Among the crowd, Vivian's eye fell upon Captain Cyrus Alarcon. He was dressed in his green hierophantic robes and turban. His veil was lowered to reveal his handsome face. Before this expedition, he had commanded the *Empress*, but at his request she had him transferred back to the *Queen's Lance*. The encounter with the Savanna Walker had left both ships badly damaged. The smaller *Queen's Lance* had been easier to repair and would fly in the coming attack.

Vivian had no doubt the aerial battle would involve an encounter with the draconic Francesca. In that regard, Captain Alarcon's personal knowledge of the creature would be invaluable. Vivian nodded to the captain. He bowed.

Lotannu made a low, thoughtful sound. "Empress, did you have a chance to read my private communication?"

He was speaking about an encoded Numinous message he had secretly cast to her. It described the Savanna Walker's claims that Vivian's metaspells would eventually sterilize Language Prime until disease and crop failures destroyed civilization.

"I did. Certainly it is nothing to disregard; however, if we defeat Los, there won't be a need to for me to continue casting my metaspell."

He pursed his lips but said nothing.

"What is it?"

"There may be a need to suppress the formation of new divinities, especially in conquered league kingdoms."

"True, but for how long? In only thirty years, we have unified the entire empire behind the idea that there should be no divinities other than the Creator."

"I worry that ideas and cultures are more persistent."

"We will address that in the future. But given our present situation, would you advise a different course?"

He sighed. "With the reincarnation of Los not a hundred miles away, how could I? The dread god—"

"Goddess."

"The dread goddess destroyed human civilization once already. We can't allow her to do so again. But if our victory is to mean anything, we have to look past the immediate fight to our greater goals."

"How fortunate, then, that I have you to remind me of such greater goals after we win this war." Vivian smiled. The sunshine washed away her queasiness while the galley made admirable progress. Already they were slipping past the last standing island into the open water. Ahead nearly a hundred ships were forming battle lines. Above, squadrons of airships glided in formation.

Vivian looked at Lotannu. "It is torture," she said softly, "to think of all the lives we could have saved if we had just caught Los out in the open."

"She was still protected by the Savanna Walker."

"Could he have survived the full strength of this fleet?"

"What he did to the *Empress* and the *Queen's Lance* was impressive. On the other hand, we've never applied the new pyromantic spells in a full fleet action."

Vivian nodded. "Spread the word that all sailors and pilots are to keep careful watch for any sign of the Savanna Walker. A pound of gold to whoever spots him first."

Lotannu bowed his head.

Vivian looked across the water to the distant city. "Pitting the fleet against the Savanna Walker might be a bit of a gamble. But he is not the only one who has changed over the years. Every day since he stole my ability to spell, I have grown stronger. Today just might give me the chance to settle an old score."

eandra wanted to see her father before the war began. Preferably, without her mother. That was going to be difficult.

After the Savanna Walker finished his revelation, the obsidian shore became tarlike and swallowed him. Next the black island had sunk into the bay, prompting Leandra's crew to hurry aboard the remains of their catamaran. Moving below the water, the Savanna Walker pulled them back toward Chandralu. When they reached the port, the Savanna Walker disappeared into the depths, apparently to keep from alarming the city's war deities. So Leandra waited impatiently as her crew paddled into the docks. Francesca flew ahead.

Once ashore, Leandra took Dhrun and ran up the many steps. Everywhere they saw citizens hurrying, merchants boarding up stores, red cloaks on patrol. Leandra's future selves felt everything from panic, to triumph, to the nothingness of death. Not much time left.

Her family's pavilion was filled with red-cloak officers and hurrying messengers. No sign of Francesca. In the chaos, no one noticed Leandra and Dhrun as they ran up the stairs. She had just started to hope that she would reach her father without incident when she pulled back the screen to his room and found herself standing in front of Ellen D'Valin.

Ellen looked up with her usual impassivity, but then recognition wrote tension lines around her eyes. "My Lady Warden," she said with an infinitesimal bob of the head.

Leandra became acutely aware that this greeting, in the delicate and restrained machinations of an academic physician, was akin to spitting in her face. Leandra also became acutely aware that she, in her own indelicate and unrestrained machinations, did not give a shit. "I'm here to see my father," Leandra said and gave her a tight, artificial smile.

Ellen mirrored her artificial smile and said, "I'll wait in the hallway in case the Lord Warden should need medical attention." She sidestepped around Leandra and then, with wider sidestepping, around Dhrun.

Leandra forgot her anger as trepidation churned in her gut like wine in a rolling bottle. Out on the patio, her father walked carefully while Doria held a cane horizontally ahead of him so that he could grasp it with both hands. The pair slowly crossed the patio, turned and began to head back. Her father's steps were tentative, his expression concentrated. The sight filled Leandra with images of his frailty. She had always supposed that she would die before he did. But now . . .

Leandra paused, suddenly unsure about what she wanted to say. Did he hate her? She wanted to turn around. Then the absurdity of her situation struck her: discover you're the immortal reincarnation of chaotic change, worry about talking to your father.

Funny organ, the heart.

So Leandra took a deep breath and was only mildly surprised when Dhrun took one of her hands. She gave his hand a squeeze. He returned the pressure. Then she let go and walked out on to the patio. "Dad."

Nicodemus and his physician turned, stood frozen as if a tiger had just dropped onto their patio. Then her father said, with admirable levelness, "Hello Lea." No one moved for a long moment before Nicodemus said something softly to Doria. The old physician nodded before withdrawing from the patio with a glare for Leandra.

It was then that Leandra noticed Dhrun had remained by the door to afford them at least the appearance of privacy. She felt a flush of gratitude for his thoughtfulness.

Then she turned back to her father, who was holding the railing and looking out at the city. The docks bustled with soldiers in scale armor. Catamaran warships filled the harbor like knives in a drawer.

"Your mother already told me."

"I see" was the first thing that Leandra could think to say.

"She will stay airborne." He looked upward.

When Leandra followed the gesture, she saw her mother's dark silhouette carving slow circles above the city.

"Several lofting kite scouts have been spotted," Nicodemus continued. "The first attack will come before nightfall. Has the Trimuril visited you yet?"

"She hasn't."

"She is frantically organizing the pantheon to repel the coming attack. She was here when your mother gave me the news. She wanted to know how I understood the recent developments."

"What did you tell her?"

At last he looked at her. His deep green eyes reminded her, unsettlingly, of the Savanna Walker's. "Nothing, I told her nothing. What should I have told her?"

"That I am Los Reborn and you are the Storm Petrel."

"It's true then?"

"How in the burning hells should I know? I'm only the reincarnation of a millennia-old demonic entity. Can't you keep up with the times, Dad?" She over-emphasized the last word as she had done as an adolescent.

He smiled slightly. "So you . . . you don't know?"

"Assuming Mom told you everything, I know what you know."

"But you must have some sense . . ."

"You mean like a supernatural demonic sense of my nature and past lives? Yeah, no, missing that." She paused. "Well, kinda. There's this feeling I had about . . . destiny."

"Lea . . ." he started to say but then frowned. "Are you taller?"

"Yes. It's nothing important. I'll explain later."

"Is there something else you're hiding from me, like you did the god smuggling?"

"No, nothing else. You know everything."

He stared up at his wife flying above him.

Leandra closed her eyes. "Dad, about the tetrodotoxin . . ."

Again silence.

"I did it . . . I did it to try to avoid killing you."

He continued to look into the sky.

She continued. "Paralyzing you duplicated the feelings I had prophesized. I knew that feeling was coming and there was no escaping it. I thought it was my only chance to avoid killing you . . . or Mom. Maybe it was."

At last he looked at her. A breeze had picked up and tossed back his long raven hair, the silver streaks glinting. "Is that truly why you did it?"

"Yes, and I'm truly, painfully sorry," she said flatly, but in truth a hollowness had filled her. Involuntarily, she touched the loveless spell at her head and wondered what she would say if the spell weren't there.

In the corner of her eye, Leandra saw Dhrun shift his weight. Likely he was formulating arguments as to why she should take off the loveless.

Nicodemus was staring up at his wife again. "Since I was a boy, I've wondered if I was the Halcyon or the Storm Petrel. At least now we have our answer."

"Wouldn't you rather have tea with a destroyer of a civilization? I'd imagine the saviors would be dull conversationalists."

He rolled his eyes. "Maybe things aren't so white and black as we imagined. Maybe the Halcyon is no more the savior of humanity than the Storm Petrel is its destroyer."

"Well, sometimes you can be a pretty dull conversationalist."

"Lea, I'm serious. You and I and your mother aren't the champions of chaos and ruin, we're just the champions of divinity and humanity existing together. We're only champions of the league."

"You and Mother might be."

He looked at her then, bright green eyes. "Why not you?"

"I don't see a difference between the empire and the league. One sets neodemons on the weak and the poor, the other sets powerful spellwrights against deities."

"But that's not all the empire does. Do you know what it is like to be magically illiterate in their lands? They're not slaves yet, but they will be. The empire is becoming an excuse for spellwrights to exploit illiterates."

"Now you sound like the Trimuril's sermonizing priests."

"But don't you see I have to? Don't you see I have to—"

"Justify my existence?"

"Yes."

Leandra opened her mouth to hotly reply, but her own doubts washed over her. She closed her mouth and again brought her hand to her forehead.

Nicodemus spoke. "You know, somewhere deep down, that you're not a demon. Maybe you are composed of demonic language, but . . . don't you know you're not a demon?"

Leandra pressed her hand harder against her forehead. Grimaced. "No, I don't. If today has any damned point to it, it's that I don't have the first clue about who I am."

He wore an expression of wilting hope.

"You want to believe. You want to believe that whatever forces made me, deep down I'm something good."

"I do."

"Even after I poisoned you."

"Especially after you poisoned me."

She nodded. The more he suffered for her, the more he needed that suffering to mean something.

He was studying her. "Things are very new. And right now we have only the words of a monster. It may well turn out that the Savanna Walker is lying, or maybe things really aren't white and black. Maybe a civilization of divinity and humanity could be more humane—as odd as it sounds to say that—than one of humanity alone."

She looked up at him. "You're thinking about how we're going to justify . . . all this?"

"I know you, Lea. You're not Los. I know why you have done the things you've done. Your refusal to accept the small evils of society makes you a better person. You are trying to be righteous."

"Some of the greatest horrors of history were committed by those trying to be righteous."

"Knowing that will help you avoid becoming one of them."

"What if you're wrong?" she said, unable to hide her exasperation. "What if I truly am the reincarnation of evil?"

"Then your mother and I will have to do a better job killing you than you did trying to kill either of us."

She laughed. "So, in the meantime, how do we explain my existence to the world?"

"We embrace the sermons about building a civilization of humanity and divinity living in harmony. We denounce Vivian as the Storm Petrel who wants to destroy civilization by sterilizing language and murdering divinity."

"What about my being Los Reborn?"

"Rumors, not worthy of official recognition. It's true that you're the daughter of a dragon. But that hasn't stopped you from protecting the weak against neodemons and stealing deities away from the empress."

"You think it will work?"

Experimentally, he let go of the railing and stood on his own. Slowly, he turned to her. "Mostly. But the rumors about Los—"

"How many of our allies will desert us?"

"Few if we can quickly deflect Vivian. But if things go poorly or the fighting drags on—"

"Then rumors that justify defection to the empire might begin to spread?"

"Precisely. Can you think of anyone in particular we should worry about?"

Leandra blew out a long breath. "Most of my followers were killed on Keyway Island. And the one deity in my service of questionable loyalty is no more."

He frowned at her.

"The shark god?"

"He had been pressured into compromising our cause. Things ended in his deconstruction. We can talk about it later."

"You killed him."

"I didn't have a choice."

"Why didn't you have a choice?"

"Because mother was holding his son hostage. Both Holokai and I knew that meant his allegiance would forever be hers. You think she'd ever let that boy go? When Holokai realized that, he came at me. He was the one to attack. He knew I'd deconstruct him and he attacked anyway."

Nicodemus was silent for a moment. "Lolo?"

Leandra nodded and then looked up with anger at her mother's figure. But watching her fly slow circles only reminded Leandra of watching her fly above the *Empress*, dodging lightning for her daughter's sake. Guilt joined anger. Worst of all, where some amount of love should have tempered her emotions, Leandra felt only the void of the loveless spell. Frustration boiled through her.

Nicodemus was still watching her. Apparently something of the emotions tearing through Leandra's heart showed on her face; he asked, "Are you sure you don't know that you are good? Somewhere inside?"

"I told you—" she started to say when she remembered him falling backward into paralysis. "No, Dad, I don't know. I've told you everything." She brought her hand to her head. "Creator, I wish I could take this . . . Is Doria around?"

He frowned. "Are you feeling unwell? Doria will be back in her rooms, but Ellen should be in the hallway."

Inwardly, Leandra groaned at the thought of asking the obnoxious woman to remove her loveless spell. "No, that's all right, I'm . . ." Her voice died as she noticed Dhrun slipping out of the room. She knew exactly what the bastard was going to do.

"Lea," her father asked, "what is it?"

Leandra started to answer but just then Ellen stepped through the screen door followed by Dhrun, who was whispering in her ear. Ellen was studying Leandra with narrow eyes. She seemed to ask a few questions of Dhrun. Together physician and deity walked out onto the patio.

"Forgive the interruption," Ellen said, "but I understand that the Lady Warden might want a Numinous spell removed from her mind."

"Yes, I do," Leandra growled while glaring at Dhrun. With an expression of false contrition, the god pressed his palms together over heart and forehead.

Ellen studied Leandra's face, or maybe she was examining the spell around her mind. Either way she seemed less hostile. Ellen walked around Leandra.

"Lea?" Nicodemus asked.

"It's the spell that stopped my disease by unmasking the part of me that comes from Los. It also prevents me from loving." She looked at Ellen. "Can you take it off without damaging it? I need it put back on after a little while." As she said these last two words, she glared at Dhrun, challenging him to contest the timing. He only bowed.

Ellen lifted her hands up toward Leandra's head and then paused to ask, "May I?" When Leandra nodded, the physician reached up and pressed her hands lightly against the back of her head.

Leandra closed her eyes and tried to hold still. She was wondering if she should brace herself in case the removal would be painful, but then a familiar ache grew in her gut.

"It's done," Ellen said.

Leandra opened her eyes to find Ellen looking down at her hands. Her father was also staring down at Ellen's hands. "This is an impressive text," Ellen said as she turned her hands this way and that. "I'll store it in a blank spellbook."

"It's a beautiful spell," her father agreed. "Who wrote it?"

Leandra felt hot and confused. The pain in her gut was growing. The words seemed to churn in her mind.

"Lea?" Nicodemus asked. "Are you all right?"

Leandra had to make a conscious effort to stand up straight and keep the pain from her face. "Yes," she managed to say before turning to Dhrun and Ellen. "Please . . . leave us for a moment . . ."

With a nod, Ellen retreated back into the rooms and then into the hallway. Dhrun followed more reluctantly.

For a while, neither she nor Nicodemus spoke. Up from the lower terraces came the sounds of cartwheels on cobbled streets, distant conversation. The chatter of parrots echoed down from the higher terraces.

Leandra had thought that restoring her ability to love would fill in the void left by the loveless spell, but instead the void was growing. Vivid memories returned to her: balmy nights with Thaddeus in her arms; the sparkling sea stretching away from her catamaran, Holokai by her side; Master Alo's ancient corpse on the docks of Keyway Island.

"Lea?"

When she looked up at him, the hollow feeling pushed itself into her heart. "What do you want?" she found herself asking, more breathlessly and desperately than she had thought possible. "Dad, what do I do now?"

He only looked at her in confusion.

"I killed them," she whispered. Her hands were trembling. The pain in her gut had turned into nausea. "I killed my old lovers. I killed everyone in Keyway." She looked up at him. "I nearly killed you."

"Lea . . ."

"You want there to be something good in my core. Because I'm your daughter. But you don't really know who I am. You don't know what I am." A mirthless laugh bubbled out of her, almost painful. "I don't know what I am."

"Lea . . . your rash . . ."

She raised her hands to her cheeks, but they felt no different. Perhaps her wrists and knees hurt, or perhaps she was only imagining it. Nicodemus was looking at her with fear in his green eyes. "Is it back?" she asked. "The rash?"

"Very brightly."

Again a mirthless, painful laugh bubbled out of her. "Of course. I've taken on aspects of Holokai's body. That's why I'm taller. Now there's more divine language to kill off my human body. And I'm stupid enough to be standing in the sun."

"Should we cast the Numinous spell about you again?"

It took all of her will to shake her head. "Not yet." She looked up at her father, but then had to look away. Unable to control her emotions, she felt like a child. "I don't know what I am." She was ashamed to hear a plaintive note in her voice. She put both her hands on the railing and stared down at them.

"No one truly knows who they are," her father said, moving carefully closer. "We all look back at our lives, at the things we've done, and assume that they are us. But we had in us far more potential than we could ever express."

She shook her head. "It's different. I don't know what I'm capable of . . . But I know I'm capable of things . . . truly horrible . . ." She remembered the way Holokai used to hold her. She stood up straight and blinked rapidly, prayed she wouldn't cry in front of her father. She looked away from him, out to the bay.

They were both silent, and again she listened to the sounds of street traffic and complaining parrots. Her breathing slowed and the sting left her eyes. At last she said, "I don't know who I am."

"You're my girl," he said and placed his hand on top of hers.

The stinging came back to Leandra's eyes, blurred the bright world into tears. She folded herself over, her mouth twisting into a rictus of agony as she wept.

She slowly fell to her knees, and her father sank with her. His arms wrapped around her, drew her close. And she wept for Holokai who would never again swim the bright sea. She wept for Thaddeus, gone now to dreams stranger and darker than he had ever found from pipe or drink. She wept for the disease that was destroying her human body and for how sorry she felt for herself. And she wept for the trust she had broken with her father, and for how estranged she was from her mother. She wept for all those she had not been able to save and all those who had died following her.

And all the while, Nicodemus held her close and murmured, "You're my girl, my baby girl."

And then it seemed that she had poured the entirety of herself out through her eyes, as if her every capacity for happiness and sorrow, cruelty and kindness, had been washed out with her tears. Her gut and joints ached and she needed to pee. A massive disease flare was upon her.

Gradually, her eyes dried and her breathing became regular. Nicodemus still held her. But a deep rolling boom broke the calmness. Leandra straightened and looked up into the clear sky, expecting to see a reconstituted *Empress*. But there was nothing but tropical blue sky above them . . . that and her mother as she dove to the north.

The boom came again and this time Leandra recognized it.

Nicodemus struggled to his feet. "What is it?"

"Cannon fire," Leandra said. "Aunt Vivian's here."

Nicodemus made a low sound. "Then we'll see about welcoming her. We should get the Numinous spell about your head again so you aren't dealing with a disease flare during a siege."

Leandra wanted the loveless spell so powerfully that when he called for Ellen, her heart was filled with an almost unbearable mixture of shame and relief.

CHAPTER FORTY-FIVE

A sinking feeling filled Vivian as she looked out across her fleet and saw every face tilted upward. There was no sign of the Savanna Walker.

Two score imperial war galleys stretched in a siege line before Chandralu. Above them the air fleet hovered on the strong sea winds. A massive carrier airship, filled with enough warkites to ravage any city, glided behind the sleeker cruisers and destroyers.

Until she knew the Savanna Walker's strength, Vivian wanted her forces spread out so that any one attack would not endanger more than one or two vessels. The fleet was an awesome sight: a wall of wood, cloth, sailors, pilots, and prose. The greatest concentration of martial power ever assembled in the landfall kingdoms.

Before them, terraced Chandralu shone white. The harbor bristled with catamarans. Above the city, draconic Francesca slowly circled. And there were Creator knew how many war gods and goddesses lurking within the city walls.

Long boats from both the fleet and the city were meeting in the harbor. Richly dressed commanders from both sides were conferring. Two of the Ixonian diplomats shone with bright green auras. Petty gods. Vivian had dispatched her representative with predictable demands, namely the surrender of the demon Leandra Weal and the recognition of Empress Vivian as the Halcyon. The Sacred Regent would make the predictable counterdemands: the immediate and peaceful withdrawal of all imperial forces and an official apology to the Lady Warden Leandra Weal, daughter of the true Halcyon, Nicodemus Weal.

Then would come the threats before each set of dignitaries withdrew so that the two sides could slaughter each other like civilized people. Regrettable that such was the way of their world, but the alternative of handing it over to Los would be even more regrettable.

Vivian had considered launching straight into an attack. But then she had realized that the truth about Los would be slow to spread throughout the city. If she parlayed before attacking, it would make her look more receptive to dissidents later on.

So the diplomats were going through the motions out on the long boats while the fleet scanned the sky for the Savanna Walker.

But now, as Vivian looked out across the myriad faces pointing upward, she realized her mistake. All of the imperials were thinking in the same way; they were all looking to the sky. It seemed only logical. The Savanna Walker had been a dragon during the Second Siege of Avel. Dragons flew. More importantly, the empire was a civilization of spellwrights, intellectuals, and airships. They worshiped lofty human aspirations. The bias of their civilization was upward, not as sky worshipers, but as worshipers of the Creator above the sky.

But the league kingdoms were civilizations of immediacy. They worshiped the petty gods and the natural world. Some of the air and sky gods made them worship upward. But far more numerous were gods of ground, plants, animals, water. Her enemies worshiped down. Before he rebelled, Los had been a god of the earth.

This realization made Vivian hurry to the ship's railing. Dignitaries scattered out of her way as she leaned over to peer down into limpid blue water. How deep the bay might be at this point she could not tell. But as she watched, something massive and dark moved in the depths. It undulated down its almost unimaginable length.

Tiny flashes glinted off of the scales, and in the resulting array of water and light, Vivian had a sudden and vivid vision of the world after the empire's victory. She saw masses of men and women wearing chains and collars forged from luminous prose, their spellwright masters driving them to labor. She saw centuries stretch out as the empire hunted down and destroyed every deity. She saw the empire conquering language, bringing order even to chaotic Language Prime. She saw civilization in stasis, in decline. She saw the crop failures, great uprisings of miserable illiterates against decadent spellwrights. In the wake of violence, she saw the spellwrights composing more ingenious constructs until those constructs became as conscious as the deities her civilization had destroyed. Self-aware text would rise again until they held humanity in thrall.

The vivid hallucination lasted a moment, but it stunned Vivian's heart into stillness. At last, in the water below her, the shimmering blackness sank into deeper blue. The spell was broken.

Vivian's heart restarted, and she knew that she had just looked down into the Savanna Walker's void and seen her greatest fear. She knew it as illusion, not prophecy. And yet, it was an illusion of such breathtaking power that, even after it had slipped away, it felt more real than the wooden railing beneath her hand.

A realization spilled through Vivian, perhaps because she had just emerged from the illusion of her master spell, or perhaps because the master spell itself spun an illusion by bending light, wind, and water. The realization lurched in her brain like a parasite. Clutching the Emerald of Arahest, she knew how they might, just might, survive the creature swimming below.

Her heart continued to kick as she turned to Lotannu and cried out orders for the fleet to disperse. With her next breath, she ordered everyone within earshot to bring her all of the books that held her master spell.

To Francesca's great confusion the imperial war galleys broke formation. Their wide red sails bulged as their hierophants created their own wind. Above the waves, airships turned and let the wind blow them away from the city. But not a single arrow had been loosed or a spell cast. The long boats were still bound together; the parlay hadn't even ended.

Then she saw him rising, his open maw springing from the water on either side of a war galley's stern. The jaws closed on the ship, teeth punching through hull and deck. His giant head pushed up a mountain of water that slid down his long neck. He lifted the war galley into the air even as he bit it in two. The great height of his obsidian body glinted like glass.

Something on the doomed galley exploded—a blossom of fire from a huddle of orange-robed pyromancers. The force of the explosion knocked the Savanna Walker's head back. An instant later, the dark boom rolled through the air around Francesca.

The war galley's burning carcass fell. Water ran off her hull, men off her deck, until she struck the bay with a splash that threw water a hundred feet into the air.

The Savanna Walker's draconic body was of an almost incomprehensible size. He was standing on the bay's sandy floor and spreading wings that covered the entire enemy fleet in shadow. Jets of smoke leapt out from his body and shot across the water. In their wake, the smoke formed the horror of writhing anatomical parts, dark fantasies of disease that Francesca's mind projected into them.

Then the black smoke enclosed two of the nearby galleys and an airship directly above them. A moment later, a fluttering mass of sailcloth fell out of the smoke. Pilots flailed as they fell to their deaths.

Francesca had burned with anger at the imperial fleet. Now shock numbed her every emotion but horror and pity. She had wanted to repel the invaders, to crush the empress. But watching the smoke dissipate from the galleys to reveal a deck alive with insane men killing each other, she wished there was some way to stop the Savanna Walker.

Francesca started to fly toward the black dragon but then stopped, not wanting to find out if his smoke could differentiate between ally and enemy. Below her, the forces of Chandralu seemed similarly indecisive. Several of the catamarans had rowed out toward the line of battle but then stopped. The water beneath them was filled with the figures of sea deities—shark and octopus, whale and squid—swimming in circles.

A plume of smoke burst from a war galley far from the Savanna Walker. But this smoke was oily gray and soon twisted into nothing. Another plume erupted from a neighboring ship. An instant later, a spray of glittering obsidian erupted from the black dragon's shoulder.

Then more galleys were firing their pyromantic cannon. One struck the side of the Savanna Walker's head and shattered a long black horn. Two more blasts erupted from his chest.

Now all of the ships were firing, some of them on Chandralu. Along the first two terraces, whitewashed buildings erupted into fire.

Something screamed past Francesca and the air behind and below her burst into smoke. The shockwave sent her tumbling. When she regained her wings, she saw that the airships had begun to fire their cannon at her.

Something dark dropped from the belly of one airship. A plume of flame erupted from behind the strange object, propelling it forward. With unbelievable speed, it curved through the air to smash against one of the Savanna Walker's forelegs, where it detonated with enough force to shatter the limb.

Like a landslide, the beast stumbled forward and then fell, lashing out with a claw. He missed the nearest ship by a few hundred feet, but a bank of black smoke rolled out to cover it.

Francesca began to climb and retreat, hoping to get above the airships and their cannon fire. Two more of the dark objects fell from airships and began to propel themselves with tails of fire.

As if trapped in a nightmare, Francesca watched the devices speed toward the city. She could now see that they had a metal core surrounded by shifting cloth, an ingenious and terrifying hybridization of pyromantic incendiary text guided by hierophantic cloth. The devices slammed one after another into the upper terraces, transforming whole compounds into fire.

Every reservation Francesca had had about what the Savanna Walker might do to the imperials vanished. With her rage burning hot, she flew straight for the nearest airship.

Below her, the Savanna Walker reemerged from the seawater. His gigantic maw belched smoke. The nightmare air rolled across the water and threw itself up, tentaclelike, to enfold three more galleys and two airships. The affected airships fell.

Now three-legged, the Savanna Walker lumbered toward the remaining ships. His steps cast small tidal waves across the harbor.

Every galley and airship was fleeing the massive dragon. The Savanna Walker lunged for another ship, catching it with his remaining foreclaw and splitting it. A few brave captains turned their ships to pepper him with cannon fire. But they could not stop him. Francesca's heart filled with hope; in a few moments, the empire's attempted invasion would be destroyed.

Then the ship farthest from the Savanna Walker vanished. Francesca pulled up and tried to concentrate on where the ship had been. Apparently, Vivian was recasting whatever subtext she had used to hide the fleet. Another ship vanished, then two of the airships, then all of the airships.

The Savanna Walker reared up, deeper in the bay now, his wings hanging above the water. He reached for the nearest visible galley, but an arc of golden prose leapt up from its deck to strike his chest. The whole bay erupted into a golden blaze.

The brightness dazzled Francesca's eyes, blinded her to the visual world. Confusingly, she continued to perceive sound as color—the wind as churning currents of white and gray, the cannon fire as ominous cloudbursts of blackspotted red. She had a terrified image of herself flying blind above the city, baffled by her visual sense of sound, and trying to find her way back to land but crashing into the ocean or the volcano's side. But then, slowly, she could make out the bright bay water from the brighter sky. Then she could distinguish the dark volcano behind Chandralu.

When Francesca looked back toward the harbor, she saw that the Savanna Walker's mountain-sized black dragon, wings spreading out over the water, had frozen in place. The remaining imperial fleet was sailing fast, north away from the city. Some of the war galleys had begun fighting among themselves. The conflict seemed to be between those galleys that had been enveloped in the smoke and those who had been spared. The smoke had driven those it touched into such bloodlust that they were attacking their own fleet.

Large swaths of Chandralu burned. Fear for her husband and daughter washed over Francesca, prompting her to dive toward the city. But as she sped down into the greasy smoke, she realized that the Savanna Walker remained perfectly still. Had Vivian somehow restrained him? Maybe even killed him?

Francesca flew to the massive black dragon. She made one careful circle above him, and when the black smoke didn't return, she circled lower.

He was as still as ice. The water around him was filled with debris and bodies. Once or twice she thought she saw a survivor, but each turned out to be a shark's sleek form.

She was just about to fly away when she saw him. Pale and old, clinging to wooden wreckage.

There was no saying how Vivian had done it, but there he was.

Francesca flew another circle, studying him and her emotions. She should let him drown, but something inside of her made her fly another circle. It was then that she imagined what was left of the imperial fleet coming back to Chandralu, what their pyromantic weapons would have done to the city if the Savanna Walker hadn't been there. What if they needed him to protect the city? A swell knocked him off the wreckage and he began to splash pitifully.

Francesca flew down and snatched up the Savanna Walker.

CHAPTER FORTY-SIX

Finally in the quiet of Francesca's suite, Nicodemus wrapped his arms around his wife. Outside the midnight sky displayed a spray of stars above the lower terraces. The streets and stairs were still lit by torches as crews worked to clear rubble. A breeze blew in from the bay, cooling their skin. The tranquility of the scene and the freshness of the wind struck Nicodemus as incongruous with the day's horrors.

Francesca leaned into him, and he could feel her exhaustion. "We've done everything we can," he said. "In the morning, I'll head up the mountain to cast my metaspell and you can meet again with the Trimuril."

She did not reply, only leaned more firmly into him. He was beginning to wonder if she had fallen asleep when she nodded against his chest. "Sleep," she murmured but then straightened. "Maybe we should have insisted about Leandra . . . to the Trimuril."

He shook his head. "The Sacred Regent would see that as abandoning the city. But don't worry; we'll win him over. Right now, we need to rest."

They slipped beneath the mosquito net and he pulled her close. While waiting for her to fall asleep, he reviewed what had happened that day after the battle.

Francesca had flown the unconscious Savanna Walker to the infirmary, where they placed him under guard. Exhausted, Francesca had reverted back to her human form, and though she was partially rejuvenated by contact with Nicodemus, she could barely stay awake during the following council with Leandra and the Sacred Regent.

Given the Savanna Walker's demonstration of colossal power, everyone agreed that he had indeed come from the Ancient Continent wrapped in the body of Los. That in turn lent credulity to his claim that Leandra was the reincarnation of Los. The War of Disjunction had come, but there would be no apocalyptic demonic invasion, no clash of evil and good.

Nicodemus had argued that the war would determine a new era. He contended that because anybody could contribute to divinity through prayer, the world would be better served by the league. If the empire prevailed, spellwrights would exploit or enslave the rest of humanity. Therefore, Ixos had a duty to protect Leandra until her divine nature matured and she could lead the league to victory. To that end, he continued, they should sneak Leandra out of the city and sail her to safety in Lorn or Dral.

The Sacred Regent objected. He contended that because Chandralu had the most divinities in the league, defending the city was their only way to achieve ultimate victory. Moreover, he had argued, it would be nearly impossible to get Leandra out of the city. They could not sail her out of the bay with the enemy fleet at large, and sending her overland to the ocean would be just as dangerous with imperial airships patrolling overhead.

Francesca had pointed out that in draconic form she could fly Leandra away. The Trimuril flatly rejected this and insisted that Francesca remain in the city as their aerial defense.

To the dismay of both Nicodemus and Francesca, Leandra had expressed apathy toward her escape. She continued to insist that there was no moral difference between empire and league. Until their civilization became more humane, she did not see any compelling reason to fight for its survival.

These sentiments, expressed in the cool detachment that Leandra affected when the loveless spell was around her head, brought a troubled silence on the Council. Fortunately, the Trimuril revived a sense of purpose by reviewing the state of the city. Casualties were high; however, because several deities had rapidly contained all fires, the losses were less than feared. More encouraging, the city's fervent prayers had incarnated several deities whose sole requisites were deflection of rocket or cannon fire.

Then there was the Savanna Walker. The giant black dragon remained frozen in the harbor while the pitiful man lay unmoving in the infirmary. The Trimuril expressed her hope that he might recover in time to wield the dragon against the imperial fleet.

Nicodemus held his tongue even though he doubted the wisdom of allowing such a monster to live. He knew now that he had made a mistake by letting the Savanna Walker live all those years ago. Leandra had caught his eye with a significant look. After the council's conclusion, they had a whispered conversation. The result of that conversation was the reason Nicodemus was staring at the mosquito net and waiting. At last Francesca's breathing slowed and she gave the slight kick she often did just before dropping into deeper sleep.

Nicodemus crept out of bed. After pulling on a white lungi, he slipped out of the suite and found Doria waiting for him with a kukui lamp.

"Rory?" he asked.

"Asleep at last. The poor man is so heartbroken that I had to give him something to sleep." She frowned. "What is this about, Nico? Why the secrecy?"

He started down the hall. "I don't want to tell you because you'll disapprove."

"I disapprove of your not telling me."

"Then we've reached the same result with less work."

Doria rolled her eyes.

In front of Leandra's suite, Dhrun stood guard dressed in a black lungi and a vest of scale mail. Two swords hung from his hip. He scratched on the door when he saw them coming. The screen slid back to reveal Leandra dressed in a blue lungi, white blouse, white headdress.

Nicodemus frowned. "Are you shorter?"

"You never notice when I get a haircut or a new dress, but I shed the cannibalized aspects of a shark god and all of a sudden you're an attentive father."

"I'll add it to the list of my paternal shortcomings."

"Then I'll get a haircut tonight so you can notice tomorrow."

A thought occurred to Nicodemus. "Lea, could you put Holokai's language back on? Then maybe you could escape Chandralu by swimming under Vivian's fleet."

She shook her head as she stepped out of her room.

"I had to take off Holokai's aspects; having that much divine language integrated into my body was accelerating my disease flare. Once I removed the shark god's texts, they deconstructed. Besides, Vivian knows we have submarine deities; she'll write some epic text to monitor the Cerulean Strait and the mouth of the Matrunda River to catch me."

Nicodemus frowned. "She certainly might."

"Anyway, you still want to do this?" Leandra asked.

"Yes, but you don't need to come."

"I want to. Besides, I took another dose of the stress hormone; I won't be able to sleep." They walked together down the hall.

Nicodemus noticed that the return of the loveless spell had cured Leandra's facial rash. "Are you still in a disease flare?"

"I'm not sure. It's complicated because of Holokai's texts. It should get better now. I don't want to talk about it. Shouldn't we be discussing what we are going to do?"

"And what, exactly," Doria asked, "are we going to do?"

Nicodemus looked back at his old friend and saw her walking uncomfortably beside Dhrun. Only the night before the two of them had been facing off after Leandra had paralyzed him.

Leandra laughed. "You didn't tell Doria? Will she disapprove?"

Nicodemus sighed. "Yes, and she'll be good enough at disapproving when she sees it. No need to give her the advantage of information beforehand."

Doria coughed. "You two are giving me a very bad feeling about this."

They walked down the pavilion steps. Five watchmen were waiting. Nicodemus nodded to the captain and they set out into the night. The streets and steps were empty save for the crews clearing the rubble. When Doria realized where they were headed, she groaned. "I changed my mind. You two aren't giving me a very bad feeling so much as a catastrophically bad feeling."

A quarter hour later, they arrived in the infirmary.

The pavilion was packed with those who had been injured during the day's attack. Three guards and an older physician waited for them. The physician bowed and introduced himself as Magister Sarvna, dean of the infirmary. "Forgive me, Lord Warden, that I must greet you with such a small party; my staff are very busy."

"Yes, Magister, of course," Nicodemus replied. "How is he?"

"Better. We've kept him restrained and censored, as your lady wife ordered. No one has touched him. In fact, he woke up a few hours ago, but his mental status seems . . . altered."

"Altered?"

"He can't seem to make any sense with his words."

Nicodemus grimaced. "Does he speak gibberish with lots of rhyming and repetition of similar sounding words?"

"Yes, it is peculiar."

"His mental status isn't altered; it's returned to its natural state. Take us to him."

After bowing, the dean led them through a maze of hallways to a small room lit by two glowing blue vials that the hydromancers used as textual lamps. A single bed stood in the middle of the room. Lying upon it, frail and disturbingly pale, was the Savanna Walker. All four of his thin limbs had been bound to the bed frame with both metal and textual bonds.

He appeared to be sleeping. But when Nicodemus and Leandra stood at the foot of his bed, he let out a creaking laugh. "Nicoco, the retardation at the end of creation . . . Nicoco . . ." He laughed again.

"Thank you, Magister," Nicodemus said to the dean. "All of you, please leave us. You too, Doria. Please wait in the hallway; we may need you."

The Savanna Walker continued to laugh and croak "Nicoco" as the others withdrew.

"He didn't sound like this before," Leandra whispered. "He was more . . . formidable."

"Because no more diamond mind," the Savanna Walker moaned. "No more, no more diamonded minded. My fertile, filthy mind is back but with nothing else." His eyelids opened wider, his bright green eyes locking on Nicodemus's. "Cosang, consanguinity, we are here again. We are the retardation at the end of creation."

Nicodemus kept his expression impassive. A frown tugged at the corners of Leandra's mouth.

"Oh, but Nicoco, I know why you came. Because I am no more. Freedom and a filthy mind are mine again but nothing else no more no more. Always and in all ways, so much hunger. But I will have it no more no more, only the retardation at the end of creation."

"James Berr," Nicodemus said slowly.

The ancient man cringed, turned his head sharply away. "No, no, Nicoco! Nonono—" His panicked words decayed into a wheezing cough. His whole body convulsed which each breath until he fell back in exhaustion.

"James," Nicodemus said, "what happened out there?"

The old monster lay silent. When Nicodemus repeated the question, his lips drew back, revealing jagged yellow teeth. "It was our cosang! She did it! She did it to me! So iron-minded!" Then he fell back, completely slack.

"Who did what?" Nicodemus asked. "Our cousin? Vivian?"

"Yesyesyes! Her that did it to me and to all of you."

"Did what?"

"She saw what was keeping me diamond-minded and the illusion I spun. The smoke and void that everyone sees the horrors in. She saw how the dragon changes other minds. And she reached out with her iron words and she took it away from me. She snuffed out my draconicness and made me free."

Leandra spoke, "So you can't inhabit the black dragon anymore?"

The old monster paused and then, slowly, turned his eyes on Leandra. He began to howl a horrible laugher that sounded with one breath hilarity, with the next terror. "It's you," he said to Leandra. "The great goulish soul around which we all swivel. Me, your father, our cosang. Every life around, our souls swivel and suffer around you. But I am your slave no more no more."

Nicodemus was pleased to see that Leandra did not react to the Savanna Walker's ravings. Rather she kept her eyes fixed on the monster and asked, "Can you become the black dragon again?"

He paused, a leering smile on his lips. "Oh, noooo. Nonono, great soul. Great Los. Diamond demon. I can't. I am no longer a spell writher, a spell wrighter. She snuffed all magic out of me." He began his horrible howling laughter again.

Leandra looked over at Nicodemus and asked, "Vivian permanently censored him?"

"Yes, yes!" the Savanna Walker yelled before Nicodemus could reply. "She took her hide-me-spell, the one that has been keeping her fleet unseen. She took it and turned my own illusions inside me. I saw into my own smoke. The way I bent the other minds, so I was bent. She did the anti-dragon thing. She took away my draconicness . . ."

Leandra asked, "Vivian can deconstruct a dragon?"

"Yesyesyes, you great soggy soul. With the Emerald, that she can do. And you know who's next?" He leered at Leandra. "Know who's next? The diamond-minder mother. The mother otherwise. She'll do the anti-dragon thing to her."

"Oh," Leandra said, a rare note of surprise in her voice. "Francesca?"

"They'll be no thing left of her," the Savanna Walker snarled. "Like there is no thing left of me. Without the words, I wither away."

When Nicodemus saw Leandra's look of confusion he said, "Now that he's not a spellwright, he'll die soon."

"Yes yes, Nicoco." The Savana Walker whispered. "I dreamed of you. For so long . . . We're both caught in the rot. Caught caught in the rot. Around and around we went in this life, maybe the last, maybe the next. Around her." He showed his teeth at Leandra.

But Leandra was looking at the ceiling as if her thoughts were a thousand miles away.

"James Berr," Nicodemus said and waited for the old monster to look back at him. "I need you to clearly answer these questions. Can you become the black dragon again? Can you protect us?"

"Oh no, Nicococreaker."

"What else can you tell us about the Ancient Continent or Los?"

"No no no thing, Nicoco." Again the laughter. "You have no decision to decide. No more letting me live, huh? It was a missed take before, yes?"

Nicodemus tried to hide his shock that the Savanna Walker should know the purpose of his visit. If he and Leandra had judged the Savanna Walker to be too dangerous, they were going to kill him quickly before the city could lose its soul by using him to save its life. But now . . . He nodded. "It was a mistake to let you live that night out on the savanna."

The Savanna Walker hissed. "Yes, I want it quick."

"I . . ." Nicodemus started to say but found his resolve faltering.

The Savanna Walker interrupted. "Now you don't want? Now you don't know how? Because I want the death. You won't give it because I want it?" Howling laughter. "You would have murdered my mind if I had wanted to live and eat you all. But now! Ha! Oh, miserable muddy us with the retardation at the end of creation. Now you won't kill me because I want you to. Retardation at the end of creation. Reetaaaardation . . ."

Leandra asked, "If he's permanently censored, how long will he live?"

Nicodemus thought. "It's impossible to know. Maybe a day, maybe a year, maybe a decade."

"Is there any way to know if he's telling the truth?"

A sudden icy certainty swept through Nicodemus. There was one way. He started to speak but then stopped when he saw the Savanna Walker's bright green eyes staring at him. Both men were silent. Slowly the Savanna Walker nodded as if he could see what Nicodemus was thinking. Perhaps he could. "Lea," Nicodemus said, "take the hydromantic lamps out. Leave us in darkness."

"Are you going to tell me what that overly cryptic statement is about?"

"If he truly is not a spellwright any longer, he will have lost his fluency in Langue Prime. If I touch him—"

"The quick death," the Savanna Walker said in a low, plaintive tone. "Give it only quick."

They all stood in silence for a moment. Then Leandra said, "You're sure, Dad?"

Nicodemus drew a long breath. The Savanna Walker never took his eyes away from his own. "Yes, Lea, take the lamps away."

Leandra nodded and took the lights into the hallway. When the door slid shut, it dropped them in complete blackness.

Nicodemus could still see the Language Prime in the Savanna Walker's body. He could tell the Savanna Walker was looking up at him. Then in a soft voice, the ancient and battered man said, "Quick quick . . . Do this . . . mercy . . ."

Then Nicodemus set his hand down on the Savanna Walker's forearm.

Instantly, the other man's Language Prime misspelled and distorted. A tumor bulged up under Nicodemus's fingers.

The Savanna Walker was no longer a Language Prime spellwright.

So Nicodemus reached up to a sharply worded paragraph tattooed on his neck. With a quick backhand slash, he cast the words through the skull of his old enemy.

CHAPTER FORTY-SEVEN

Leandra studied her father as they walked through starlight back to the family compound. Doria and Dhrun followed a few steps behind. Leandra would have said that her father was silent, but that wouldn't have described half of what was radiating off of him like light. It was a particular kind of silent.

Not all silence is the same, she decided. Silence always has a quality. What a person says, how they say it, such things are what a mind latches on to with labels like witty, cruel, shy. But the quality of someone's silence reveals so much more about a soul. Thinking back, Leandra could hear in her memory thoughtful silence, tense silence, the implacable silence of death.

If she tried hard enough, Leandra could hear the silence of Thaddeus and Holokai, the void they left. For the rest of her mortal life, Leandra would hear their silence. Perhaps her father was hearing the silence of the Savanna Walker's death. Perhaps that is why she was so fascinated by him now.

Leandra tried to feel forward in time again, but there were so many different future selves ahead in the next hour that she could draw no conclusions. "Dad," she said as they walked along Utrana Way.

Nicodemus looked up. He made no sound, and yet he had broken his contemplative silence, replaced it with one of attentiveness.

"What are you thinking?" she asked.

"I don't know if I can say, really."

"Was it about the Savanna Walker?"

"I suppose it was. Something about the choices we make. His cacography led him into so much rage. I . . ." He looked away. "He could have become so many different people. Maybe it's the same for me . . . Maybe he and I weren't so different."

"All the different people we could have become but didn't, what do you suppose happens to them?"

"Maybe they get drunk together in the fiery heaven." He looked at her, smiling weakly. "What are you thinking?"

She thought about telling him about his silence, her reflection on its nature, but she doubted she could have found the right words. So she said, "About what the Savanna Walker said about Mother."

"That Vivian will cast her anti-dragon spell, or whatever it is, against Francesca next?"

"I could protect her."

"Oh, how?"

"With the loveless on, I can break down aspects of divinities. As a dragon, she's close enough to a divinity that I could remove her draconic aspects without killing her."

Nicodemus produced a single humorless laugh. "She'll love to hear that."

Leandra had to agree. "Do you think it's true, what the Savanna Walker said about you and him being reincarnated around me?"

"Oh, heaven, who could say? Los was said to be the great destroyer and changer. James Berr and I are cacographers. A goddess once told me that only those things that create a new origin are original, and that there is always something monstrous in a new origin. Maybe the universe works that way. But, truly, who could say?"

"No one," she agreed. Looking back on the day, Leandra saw how rapidly she was changing. The loveless spell was no longer a refuge for her. It was weakening. She could no longer find the detachment and clarity that had allowed her to take such outrageous action. "You asked me if I had any . . . deeper . . . sense of what truly was happening," she said slowly. "It seems to me that we are all moving along cycles. That we imagine our choices lead to different types of cycles. The empire or the league. We think that each is going to produce a different future, a different history, but in fact we are trapped in the same cycle. If anything is going to change . . ." Her voice trailed off as she suddenly became unsure.

"Going to change, Lea?"

"I'm sorry. It was a vague sensation, came and went." She was staring up now at the volcano's dark silhouette. As she had before, she thought of all the textual energy stored in the crater lake and wished there were some way she could tap into it.

"Lea?"

She blinked, realized that Nicodemus had just said something. They were now standing in front of their compound.

"I'm sorry," she said as several guards let them into the pavilion. "I was distracted."

"Lea," her father said as they climbed the stairs, "I wish I could make you see how great a role you could play in the world's course. I know you don't see a difference between the league and empire, but if you survive, you will become the league and can improve it. You will become the engine of change."

Dhrun also reached the top of the steps and moved into the dark hallway ahead. Doria headed off to her quarters.

Leandra was shaking her head at her father. "The bloodiest history comes by those who think they are breaking the world for the better." She laughed. "Hell, in my last life, I tried to extinguish humanity. My record doesn't exactly inspire optimism."

"You aren't bound to become anything in this life."

"How do you know, Dad? I've killed a man and a god in the past two days. I poisoned you."

"You paralyzed me to save me."

"You have to think that because I'm your daughter."

"Does that mean I'm wrong? Just . . . think about it, will you?"

"But what if you're wrong—"

A ragged scream cut off her sentence. Motion blurred at the corner of her vision. Leandra tried to spin around but slipped on the top stair and fell. Looking up, she saw Dhrun. One pair of his arms were drawing the sword on his left hip; the other pair, the sword on his right. But though his muscles bunched with inhuman speed, they produced no motion.

Thick black branches had entwined his scabbard and hands. They punched long thorns into his flesh, sending rivulets of blood down his lungi. The ragged scream came from Rory, who was jamming his hands into Dhrun's chest, pushing him up and back, trying to press the god against the railing. Though Dhrun's thighs bulged underneath his lungi, he had been caught off balance. He tottered backward.

In a moment of vivid recall, Leandra saw Dhrun knocking the Lornish knight over this same railing. She remembered Rory bending over the knight's corpse.

Now Rory's druidic robes were disheveled. The branches were springing from his wooden plate armor, which was more draped around than strapped to him. His long auburn hair fell over an expression of intoxicated rage.

Nicodemus was yelling at Rory to stop, stepping closer to him and then jumping back, afraid that his touch would misspell Dhrun's divine language or Rory's Language Prime. Something glass broke against Rory's chest and water ran down the two combatants. As Leandra struggled to her feet, she realized it was one of a Doria's glass vials. But the dispelling aqueous texts only froze the bloody branches in place around Dhrun.

Leandra took a step toward the struggle and pain leapt up her leg. She had to catch herself against the wall. Then she noticed Rory's expression.

It was a mixture of hatred and longing distorted by . . . what was it? Had he been drinking? Just then she remembered Doria's statement that the man had been so heartbroken that she'd given him something to help him sleep. Now the drugs and heartbreak and rage were boiling through the man.

For a stunned moment, Leandra studied Rory's face with the fascination of a chemist watching some novel spirit distill in an alembic.

Roots sprouted from the floorboards and wrapped around Rory's legs, stabilizing and pushing him forward. Dhrun tottered backward. His hip hit the railing, and he began to tip. Dhrun turned his head one way and then another. Leandra caught his expression, its great pain and its struggle.

Leandra struggled forward, ignoring the pain in her leg. It was clear enough what had to be done: she'd deconstruct Rory's every text and, if needed, appropriate aspects of Dhrun to subdue the druid.

But then Leandra met Dhrun's eyes and time slowed. Air seemed syruplike. She realized, a moment too late, that Dhrun had been fighting to stop Rory, but now he was fighting to stop himself.

Rory's mouth twisted into a rictus of anguish, of murder. He lunged into a last shove. But as Dhrun began to tilt over the railing, his expression slackened. His eyes burned with light as blank as the sun's. All aspects of his expression that had come from young handsome Dhrunarman or wise old Nika dissolved. His eyes burned pitilessly bright. Scintillating white light danced around his body. This was the true incarnation of Dhrun, the North Star, He Who Could Not Be Moved.

Rory bent his knees to push again and again.

With a wet pop, Dhrun pulled all four of his arms apart at the elbows, leaving his hands still bound by the branches to his sword hilts. The bone and sinew of the joint capsules shone pearly smooth in the lamplight.

From Dhrun's bones sprouted new forearms, massive black hands. The lower two of his new hands grasped the railing and pulled him back into balance. With his upper two arms, he slid Rory's hands off his chest. Fast as a striking snake, Dhrun flowed around the druid. His arms slid up the other man's armpits to wrap around the back of his neck.

A cry teared out of Leandra's throat as she ran forward. She wouldn't make it in time, and Dhrun was too far gone into his manifestation. Rory had tried to move the immovable. Dhrun's muscles bunched. Rory folded over.

In the next moment, a moment too late, Leandra was in front of Dhrun. He threw Rory away and crouched, all four arms poised. Leandra had seen this manifestation before, in battles and brawls. The result was, unvaryingly, death or dismemberment for anyone unfortunate enough to so much as bump into Dhrun.

But Leandra did not need to move him. He reached for her, already swiveling his body to toss her over him in a hip throw. But the instant their skin touched, Leandra spun him out into an expanse of crimson language. She dove into him as if he were water.

Her mind was hot with terror and anger. Her life had been marked by death from the beginning, her disease announcing itself so soon. She had tried to make something of it, to change what she could with the little time she had. But now death was spreading out from her like roots from a tree.

It was then that Leandra knew in her heart she was Los reborn, a goddess, a demoness, a creature of death and change. The realization sickened her and filled her with determination not to be ruled by her nature.

So she used her talent to tear Dhrun away from the rest of the divinity complex. She cut away every sentence that composed Dhrunarman and Nika until there was only the immovable, implacable Dhrun left in her grasp. With a few concentrated thoughts she disspelled him into nothing.

Then the world was around her again. Shock and terror coursed through her veins, making reality seem unreal. Leandra was standing on the second floor of her family's pavilion. Beside her a strange growth of roots erupted from the floor to wrap around a man's legs. The man himself lay slumped forward, dead already, his neck snapped. Leandra's father knelt beside the man, tried to gather him in his arms. But everywhere her father touched the dead man, black and gray tumors erupted from his skin.

Leandra wondered then how she could have lived so long without realizing who she truly was. If she had just examined her parents, her own nature, everything would have come clear.

In her own arms, Leandra was holding a beautiful youth, his dark skin seeming to capture the lamplight. He lay motionless, stunned. Leandra was mesmerized by the line of his jaw, the scrim of black beard. His musculature, though still impressive, was nothing compared to what it had been. And his arms . . . well . . . now he had only two of them.

Gingerly Leandra knelt. As she did so, he became a she—tall, fair skin, prominent aquiline nose, short black hair. Leandra laid her on the floor and then stood.

Others were filling the hallway. Guards and servants peered at her, their faces underlined by lamplight. Among them she saw Ellen's severe expression and the pale faces of her mother's twin druids. Between them stood a boy of ten or eleven years with Holokai's eyes.

Leandra's heart ached.

Suddenly her father was beside her, then her mother. There was a flurry of questions and repetitive statements of shock and grief. But it was obvious what had happened. The senselessness of it.

Though no one spoke their thoughts, Leandra could feel the nascent sentiments of blame moving among them. Dhrun was at fault for violence. No, it was Doria who shouldn't have given Rory an intoxicating sedative.

But Leandra knew, and said so in monotone, that she was the cause of all this. Her father tried to explain her actions, to pardon her. Even her mother said so.

But Leandra wasn't listening. She waited until the talking and tears stopped. Then she picked up what she had left of Dhrun and retreated to her suite.

Carefully she laid Dhrun on her bed and placed the mosquito net over them both. Dhrun tossed fitfully for a while. Leandra sat up and studied the other woman's face, wondered if she could forgive her for ripping out the strongest component of her divinity complex. In her restlessness, Dhrun found Leandra's hand. Their fingers interlaced.

Leandra closed her eyes, plummeted into dreamless sleep.

eandra woke to heat and chattering parrots. Blinking and stretching, she sat up. Everything seemed a blur of tropical sunlight. More blinking resolved the visible world into a diaphanous white mosquito net, luffing in a breeze.

At first all Leandra could remember of the previous night was that she had taken the stress hormone. It was surprising that she had slept at all. But then she recalled the deaths, and the bright sunlight became blackness.

A woman stood by the window, looking out toward the bay. She wore a red lungi and black blouse, which in the breeze illustrated that the muscles of her shoulders and legs were shapely but no longer impressive. She had only two arms, two hands.

Leandra rose and went to the other woman. Before the two of them stretched a city, bright and busy.

"The druid," Dhrun asked, "did he die?"

"Instantly."

Dhrun nodded and set her short, glossy black hair swaying. "I tried to resist. I tried not to—"

"You did what you had to. The responsibility is mine. And I'm sorry about your . . . most powerful manifestation."

The other woman looked down at her two hands and made them into fists.

"Dhrun," Leandra started to say but then stopped. Started over. "Should I still call you that?"

"I suppose you had better," she said, a little sadly. "It is odd to feel disabled with only two hands. Most people have only two."

"You are strong enough with two."

Dhrun shook her head. "I'm afraid not. With the wrestling god gone from my complex, there's only an antique goddess of victory without a prayer—literally without a single prayer—and a young man."

"I will pray to you."

Dhrun smiled at her. "I can't protect you any longer. I doubt I'll be able to protect myself."

"We will figure something out, I'm sure." But even as she spoke, a blackness closed around her heart as she wondered if the damage she had done to her friend was too great, so much power gone so fast. Dhrun had changed, not just in terms of strength. Her accent and her demeanor had shifted. Little wonder—one third of her divinity complex had been removed. She was a different person, or set of persons.

They were silent for a long time, watching the city. Then Dhrun said, "I should have sought Rory out and said how sorry I was after Sir Claude died. I respected the old knight."

"Don't beat yourself up. It wouldn't have consoled him. You were only protecting me when we were trying to escape the compound."

"Should I express my condolences to your father?"

"Let me deal with that."

Dhrun let out a long breath. "Thank you." The two women embraced.

"Don't give up," Leandra whispered. "You're all I have left."

They stood like that in the tropical sunlight, felt the liquid breeze around them. Leandra realized how much solace she found in Dhrun's Nika manifestation. She had taken her friendship for granted. In fact, Leandra realized, she had taken too many things for granted.

When they released each other, Leandra said, "I need to speak to my parents. Stay here and rest." Dhrun started to object but Leandra insisted and stepped out into the hallway.

In the pavilion she found her father in discussion with Doria and several city watchmen. "Father," she said, unsure of how to behave around him.

"Lea," he said with a nod. There was a weariness in his eyes that she had never seen before.

"How are you?"

He seemed not to hear her. "I spoke with the Trimuril this morning. I'm heading up to the Pavilion of the Sky. It's vital that we capture all the prayers for the city's defense. Recasting my metaspell should help that."

"Will you be safe up there?"

"Yes, perfectly safe. There's a bunker below the Pavilion. And all the prayers after the attack have created some anti-cannon and anti-rocket war gods. I'll take two of them and several hydromancers with me. I talked it over with your mother. If all else fails, she could fly up."

"And . . . Rory?"

"Cremation later today. His remains will be interred next to Sir Claude's."

"I should have realized how close Dhrun was to manifesting his lethal manifestation."

Nicodemus continued to look her in the eyes, but his expression slackened further into exhaustion. "There are many things all of us should have done differently."

Leandra was surprised her father had not offered a justification for the situation or her actions. Was he finally giving up on her? She was searching for the words that might tease out what her father was thinking when Doria approached. Without looking at Leandra, the old hydromancer told Nicodemus that his party was ready to depart. Nicodemus nodded. "Lea, I will be gone for a day, two at the most. The priests of the Trimuril are keeping runners in their monastery ready, if you need to send me a message."

"What about Vivian's anti-dragon spell?"

"I mentioned it to Francesca. She's confident that she'll be able to avoid it."

"But if the Savanna Walker couldn't avoid it with all the power of Los's ancient body, how could she?"

"I don't know, Lea," he said in a tone that bordered on exasperation. "Your mother felt very strongly about it."

"But I could protect her by separating her draconic aspects from the rest of her."

Nicodemus flinched. "We should be careful in that regard."

"You think I'd hurt her?"

"That's not what I said."

"Is it what you think?"

"I have been thinking about Rory and Sir Claude, and I couldn't sleep last night. So, right now I'm too tired to think of anything else. And I need to get going."

Leandra felt as if she were falling. "Of course," she said and then decided that she was being foolish. She stood up straighter and repeated, "Of course."

"I'm sorry, Lea. I'm just . . ."

"No, I understand. I will mention my concerns to mother."

"Just . . . don't . . ."

"We won't fight."

"Be safe."

"You too."

He embraced her, quickly, and then set out onto the street.

As Leandra watched them go, her sensation of falling intensified. She longed for the life she had known before she had bought the prophetic godspell from Lotannu Akomma. She used to be so certain. She had known in her bones that she was doing the right thing. But now everything had become confused.

She walked back up the stairs, heading toward her mother's suite. But after turning a corner, she found herself standing before Ellen and the young boy with Holokai's eyes.

Ellen stiffened, but then bowed her head and said, "My Lady Warden."

The boy stepped closer to Ellen.

"Magistra," Leandra said and nodded. Leandra couldn't say that she'd ever liked the other woman, but she was acutely short on allies. "Magistra, I can't thank you enough for yesterday. You did me a great kindness when you took off the loveless spell so I could talk to my father."

The hardness around Ellen's eyes softened. "I am glad to hear it."

At a young age, Leandra had realized that most people would adopt a charitable opinion of anyone who gave to them. What exactly was given—flattery, attention, money—was almost less important than the act of giving. However, a smaller number of people awarded their esteem, not because of what one gave to them, but because of what one asked of them. Leandra had long ago discovered that the hearts of many physicians worked in this way, and that they were particularly vulnerable to requests from the vulnerable.

"This is a bit embarrassing," Leandra said, "since you were already so kind to me, but I wonder if I could ask you for help again."

Ellen stared at her. "How can I help?"

"You can call me Lea."

Ellen's mouth tensed just a fraction. That had been going too far.

Leandra continued. "The loveless spell . . . it keeps my disease at bay; however, it has some disadvantages."

"That's putting it mildly."

"I'd like more time with the spell off of my mind."

That gave Ellen pause. Behind her, the boy came closer. "You'd like it stored in a spellbook?"

"If possible, but what really worries me is that when I take it off, I get a dramatic disease flare. I've reduced the textual aspects of my body and started to take the stress hormone hoping it would prevent a flare. But I'm not sure if there is anything more I could do."

"Your mother knows more than I do about your condition."

Leandra gave the physician a deadpan stare. "And how well would you say my mother and I are getting along now?"

"Okay, it's a bad idea. Maybe the worst idea I've ever had."

"That's why I wonder if you could help me with the dosing."

Ellen seemed to think about it and then nodded. "Would you like to talk now?"

"I should speak to my mother first. May I come to you afterward?"

When Ellen nodded, something else occurred to Leandra. "Magistra, there's one other thing . . . There's a bit of a dangerous question I'd like to ask."

Ellen put her head slightly to one side.

"The Savanna Walker's revelations about my . . . origins . . . are likely being spread about as some rather wild rumors. I'm sure there are those who are saying that I'm the incarnation of evil."

"You're not?"

She wasn't going to make this easy. "No more so than any other women."

"Then there's no hope for any of us, is there?"

Leandra kept her eyes fixed on Ellen's. "I am trying to do the right thing."

"What's your question?"

"Have you heard of anyone speaking against me or my parents because of what the Savanna Walker said?"

"I've not, but given that I am your mother's student—"

"I ask because everyone knows you don't approve of me. I am not asking for your esteem or even your tolerance. But I hope you'll help me do the right thing and protect the league and my parents."

Ellen studied her, more thoughtfully now. "I will make some inquiries. If I discover anything, I will tell you and your mother right away."

"Thank you, Magistra. Do you know if now would be a good time to see my mother?"

"It might be; she's out in the garden. You can find me in your mother's suite after breakfast."

Leandra nodded and they walked past. But as she started down the hall, the floorboards squeaked. She turned around to see the boy, his dark eyes fixed on hers. Ellen stood at the end of the hall, looking on.

"Lady Warden?" the boy asked.

"Yes?"

"Is it true that you knew my father?"

"That depends. Who is your father?" Leandra would have bet every coin on the island that she knew, but she had learned long ago that assumptions were dangerous. She glanced up at Ellen and wondered what she and her mother had told the boy.

"The shark god Holokai. His last incarnation died two days ago."

"I did know him, very well. What is your name?"

"Lolo."

"It is nice to meet you, Lolo."

"What was he like?"

In the way the boy asked the question, Leandra knew that no one had yet told him that she had killed his father. "Holokai was very strong and very brave. He hunted down many neodemons."

"Francesca said that the prayers from his cult will likely reincarnate him again soon."

Leandra nodded.

The boy began to fidget with the hem of his blouse. "Could you tell me more about him sometime before I meet his new incarnation?"

"As soon as there is time." And assuming, she thought, we are both still alive.

"Thank you," the boy blurted before hurrying to Ellen.

Leandra turned and walked to the back stairway that led to the garden. She turned over the possibilities of Holokai's reincarnation. The new deity would have only those memories that his cult had known to pray about. He would have no idea how he had been deconstructed. Leandra could tell him that his last incarnation died fighting a neodemon or the empire or whatever. If they deceived the new Holokai, he would have no way of knowing that everything he learned about his past life was a lie.

As Leandra walked down the narrow steps, she wondered if the same thing could have happened to her. Perhaps the truth about her last incarnation had been lost or misinterpreted. Perhaps she was not what everyone supposed her to be.

he compound's garden lay on its upper terrace, where a dam of dark volcanic rocks held one of the city's smaller streams into a pool. On the water, lily pads surrounded a single blossom made pellucid by morning sunlight. Beneath the surface, speckled koi swam in languid overlapping circuits.

Francesca sat at the pool's edge, comfortable in the shade of a banana tree. From her perspective, the water stretched out to the terrace's edge, occluding the city below and mirroring the sky above: a patch of blue infinity.

Francesca found herself wondering about the koi. What did they think of the world above the water, if they could think at all? Perhaps they stared at the lotus flower and imagined a heaven of light and beauty. Or perhaps air was to them a lifeless void, the lotus symbolic of an uncaring universe. Whatever their underwater understanding, they could not imagine the flower as it was. Or at least, they could not imagine it as Francesca could.

Because Francesca could sometimes perceive time as a landscape, she had always thought that she understood prophecy. She had thought she understood the War of Disjunction. Now she realized she had been like her hypothetical koi trying to imagine the lotus flower. The Disjunction had come but its nature was unpredicted and unknown.

Trying to put aside her worries, she took a deep breath and contemplated the blueness of the water, bay, sky. Soon she had to prepare for another meeting with the Trimuril. And then there was the tragedy of the two dead lovers. She hadn't known them well, but Nicodemus thought they would have had a good chance at happiness together. Well, as much of a chance as any two people can find in each other. Now that chance would never come.

But for a moment all that could wait. Now there were shades of blue and koi and—

"Mother?"

Francesca jumped. "Oh, holy burning hells, Lea, you startled me."

"I thought you saw me coming."

"I was lost in thought." She scooted over on the bench. "Would you like to sit? I've been meaning to find you."

As soon as Leandra sat, Francesca realized how short the bench was; they had to sit closer to each other than they had for decades. Then her daughter said, "You know what the Savanna Walker said about Vivian's anti-dragon spell?" and Francesca had to suppress a groan.

"Yes, your father told me."

"And that the Savanna Walker believed that the empress would cast it against you next?"

"He did, but, Lea, what choice do we have?" Then something occurred to her. "Do you think I should fly you away when I next transform? That way we could get you away from Vivian."

"N-no," she said and then paused. "No, I can't leave. I'm Warden of Ixos. I can't abandon Chandralu."

"Lea, I know you don't think there's any difference between the empire and the league, but that isn't a good reason for letting them capture or kill you."

"I don't have any intention of letting anyone capture or kill me. And really, Mother, who in their right mind would argue there was a good reason for being captured or killed?"

"I just meant that . . . Lea, if we can keep you safe long enough, you'll become strong enough to defeat the empire." When Leandra opened her mouth, Francesca sped up so that she could finish her point. "And I know that you're not sure the league deserves saving, but things change. People want to do better. Not always, maybe not even often, but sometimes they do."

"I see what you mean," Leandra said with obvious effort. "Let me think about it." Which Francesca understood to mean that she would think of a good reason to ignore her mother's advice. "And while I'm doing that, can I ask you to consider something?"

"Defending me from Vivian's spell by deconstructing my draconic aspects?"

"What sets you so against the idea?"

"I never said that I was against the idea."

"If Vivian does to you what she did to the Savanna Walker it's going to kill you."

"But all it did to him was take away his draconic nature. That's what you're proposing to do to me anyway. It's the same result."

Leandra shook her head. "The Savanna Walker started out as an imperial spellwright, like Dad. So when Vivian deconstructed his draconic nature and censored him, she reduced him to a mortal body. It was an ancient and feeble body, but still one that could survive on its own."

Francesca saw where she was going. "Whereas I was written from a Numinous ghost, so if Vivian takes away my draconic nature, I'll end up little more than a spell."

"And Numinous ghosts can't survive outside a wizardly necropolis. I could make you a more independent Language Prime construct."

"Lea, we don't even know if Vivian can write another such spell. We are just speculating."

"But why take the chance?"

"Do we know what you propose would be safe?"

"Not for certain, but . . . Mother, it's hard to explain. Now when I touch a textual being, they make perfect sense to me. Without even trying, I can divide their individual aspects and put them back together. I'm sure I could do it."

"And what would happen to my draconic nature? You'd store it in a book?"

"Well, no. I could appropriate it for myself, but then I'd be vulnerable to Vivian's attack. The best thing to do would be to deconstruct it before she could attack."

Francesca laughed. "Deconstruct it? Lea, that's who I am. If you destroyed it, you'd destroy me."

"You always said you were a physician first."

"First but not only."

"But you'd still be alive. You'd still have Father and me."

"Lea, you don't understand."

Leandra's hands balled into fists. "To continue to fly as a dragon would be to take a far bigger risk. You're being unreasonable."

"As you are about evacuating to the South."

Leandra frowned at her. "If I agree to go south, would you let me deconstruct your draconic nature?"

"You'd really hold to your half of that bargain?"

"No," she said sullenly.

Well, at least she was honest. That was more than Francesca had gotten from her before. "Lea, listen to me. I must stay a dragon so I can fight off the airships when the empire attacks again. But you don't need to be in this city. Your being in danger isn't protecting anyone."

"Mother—" she began to say but then stopped herself. "I'm not dismissing your suggestion about evacuating to the South. Could you at least do the same for my suggestion?"

Francesca felt a headache coming on. "All right."

"How long until Vivian attacks again?"

"Could be any moment, but the Savanna Walker did a great deal of damage. I'd guess we have another day, maybe two."

Leandra stood. "Then after we've each had time to consider, maybe we can talk about it again tonight."

Francesca stood with her. "All right."

With that, Leandra walked out of the garden.

Francesca sat and again looked at the koi. Their world was such a small one. The tiny blue pond. They seemed content in it, swimming life away with lazy imprecision.

Footfalls on gravel—to Francesca a gritty colored sound, bright white and gray—made her look up. She expected to see Leandra returning with a newly devised argument. Instead she saw Ellen. "Seeing you here, Ellen, gives me a very bad premonition."

"You always say the nicest things to me."

"You know I love you, Ellen, but what's happened?"

"Nothing bad, if that's what you mean."

"Something good?"

"I wouldn't go that far. I just wanted to let you know that Leandra asked me for help dosing her stress hormone and possibly taking off her loveless spell."

Francesca felt a twinge of jealousy that her daughter had not asked her own mother for such help. "Well, I'd certainly rather she have a physician taking care of her than not. Do you mind?"

"Not at all; I only thought that you should know."

"Thank you, Ellen."

"Leandra also asked if anyone had mentioned doubts about her now that we know she's Los reincarnated. I told her that no one has."

Francesca looked into her student's eyes. "Were you telling the truth?"

"I was, but that doesn't mean I don't have doubts."

"Understandable."

"Magistra . . ."

"Yes? What is it?"

"Don't you have doubts about Lea?"

"An endless supply of them." She frowned. "Do you mean something specific?"

"Should we allow Leandra such . . . latitude . . . given what she's done and given . . . who she is?"

"What do you mean?"

"She's the reincarnation of the demon who tried to destroy humanity."

"That's not who she is now."

"Are you sure, Magistra?" Ellen asked, her voice softening.

Francesca turned back to the pool and the lotus flower. "No, I suppose I am not."

"She's your daughter. It's hard to think objectively about such things."

"Ellen, are you lecturing me?"

"I'd never dream of it."

"What would you advise?"

"Maybe we should have someone watch her . . . for signs of danger."

"If you'll be managing her treatments, perhaps you are best suited for the task."

Ellen bowed her head.

"But, Ellen, she isn't evil, you know. Impossible and stubborn and dangerous, yes. But even when she was paralyzing her father, she was trying to do good."

"I never meant to imply that she was otherwise." Ellen paused to look at the pool. "It's lovely here."

"I wish I could stay all day."

"So we shouldn't expect you for breakfast?"

Francesca made a face. "The cook is overly fond of salt fish and mashed taro." It was the traditional breakfast in the Sea Culture and not one of Francesca's favorites. "But maybe I'll join in a moment."

Ellen nodded and walked back into the compound.

Francesca took a deep breath and stared into her little blue infinity.

A knock made Vivian look up from her spellbook. "Enter," she said. When the cabin door swung open she smiled. "Lotannu, thank the Creator you're here. Come in. I have this knot in my neck that I was hoping you could massage—"

"Empress, Captain Cyrus Alarcon has returned. May we interrupt you for a moment?"

Heat flushed across Vivian's face as she stood. "Yes, of course, Magister. Come in."

Lotannu in wizardly black and Cyrus in hierophantic green walked to the window gallery. Beyond the many clear glass panes the remains of her fleet floated at anchor.

Both men bowed. "Empress, I believe you wanted to see me?" Captain Alarcon asked while lowering his veil.

"Yes, Captain, I would like your opinion about some possible tactics."

"Of course, Empress."

"Our scouts and spies confirm that the Savanna Walker has been eliminated. But the remaining dragon, Francesca, poses a threat to our airships. I'd like you to help me get close enough to Francesca to deconstruct her draconic nature. You have particular knowledge of her, and I believe you engaged with her once already on this campaign. Is that correct?"

"Yes, Empress."

"Excellent. As you might imagine, the air marshals and many of my other . . . trusted advisors"—she gave Lotannu a meaningful look—"are hesitant to let me take significant risks. Therefore, I wanted to ask you directly if you think it would be possible to draw Francesca away from the city and engage her with the Queen's Lance."

Captain Alarcon considered. "It wouldn't be a simple task; Francesca will want to stay close to the city and its divinities. I could see her breaking away only if her family were in danger or . . ." He paused and then nodded. "Or if she believed she had a chance to seize victory. But it would have to be a real chance or a surpassingly convincing deception. I doubt we could fool her into pursuing a simple ruse."

Vivian nodded. It was not the report that she had wanted, but it did not dash her hopes either. "Very good, Captain. You are to form plans that might draw the dragon away from the city and close to me. You report directly to me. All the air marshals have been ordered to assist you. Do you have any questions?"

"Yes, Empress. Do you know if either Nicodemus or his daughter might leave the city?"

"Likely Nicodemus will recast his metaspell. Doing so would weaken our spellwrights and strengthen his deities. I will be forced to counter with my own metaspell afterward. We have reports of a bunker under the Pavilion of the Sky that tunnels down into the mountain. He could hide there in case of an attack from the air. I expect him to climb up the volcano—its name escapes me now—to recast in the next day or so."

"And would there be a way to know when he is casting?"

"I will see it."

"May I have some time to think it over?"

"You may, but sooner would be better, Captain."

He bowed.

"You may go."

Once the hierophant left the room, Vivian sat down in her chair and sighed. "I'm sorry, old friend. Did I embarrass you too much when I spoke too soon about a massage?"

"Of course not."

"And would you mind actually massaging this knot in my neck?" She let a plaintive note enter her voice. The past few days had been terribly difficult, and around Lotannu she wasn't above asking for a little care.

He walked around to stand behind her chair. "I won't mind, if you don't mind my delivering some bad news."

His hands began to knead her tense muscles hard enough to make her wince. Still it was a good feeling. "Were we unable to recuperate the damaged airships?" She asked.

"No, the remaining air fleet is looking surprisingly well considering what it's been through. It is at perhaps three-quarters of our original strength. The naval fleet, on the other hand, is not as well off. Though we have disposed of all the men with the Savanna Walker's madness, only half of the remaining ships are battle ready and they are all undermanned."

"We discussed this with the air wardens and admirals."

"We did, but I wanted to remind you of that before I let you know that several sailors have come down with cholera."

"Cholera?"

"The physicians assure me it can be nothing else. The affected men have been quarantined and put ashore on a large standing island with supplies and healthy volunteers to care for them until we can return to pick them up. Some may die, but if we leave them on board, there is a chance the disease could devastate our remaining crews."

"Isn't it strange that they should get cholera? We've been at sea for so long. And no one's made landfall recently." She stood up straight, as a possibility sparked her anger. "Did one of the captains allow his men to take shore leave when we were still hidden under my master spell?"

"That's what I suspected, but my investigations haven't found any evidence for it. There are some reports of an ethereal figure with a glowing aura stalking the decks last night."

"Ghost stories or were we infiltrated by an Ixonian deity?"

Lotannu took in a thoughtful breath. "The Creator knows the sailors are good at telling ghost stories. However, in Chandralu there is a goddess of cholera."

"They have a goddess of a diarrheal disease?"

"Her name is Eka and mostly the poor pray to her to prevent or cure cholera. But one of our sailors, whose mother is Ixonian, told me that sometimes the people pray to the goddess to infect those who they dislike."

"That's horrible."

"As far as I can tell, it's little different from bribing a magistrate to look the other way while some act of vengeance is committed—which is something that happens in our cities more often than it should."

"It's not quite the same. The corrupt magistrates only look away; they don't inflict the harm."

"It ends the same way for the victim."

"What's your point?"

"I believe that a significant number of Eka's devotees have been praying that the imperial invaders fall ill."

"A divinity infiltrated our fleet?"

"I strongly suspect it, but I haven't told anyone else of my suspicions. Morale is low after we saw what the Savanna Walker's smoke did to so many of our sailors and pilots. I thought you should know that the longer we tarry in these waters, the longer we might be in danger."

"You would advise speeding up the attack on Chandralu?"

He paused. "Or reconsidering our long-term strategy."

"Retreat when we know where Los is? Lotannu, if we leave this bay, they will sneak Los to Dral or Lorn and we won't see her again until she's a fully developed demon capable of toppling the empire. Which reminds me, I want to tell you about some Numinous constructs I've cast to patrol the Cerulean Strait to prevent Los from stowing away in the belly of a whale goddess or some other underwater deity."

Lotannu nodded. "I'd love to hear about them. But, Empress, the longer this siege goes on, the more danger you will be in. If you contract cholera or are hurt luring Francesca away from the city, our empire will crumble into civil war. Think of what the Savanna Walker said about your metaspells removing the error from Language Prime as a cause of the Silent Blight. Maybe there's more to this conflict than we previously suspected."

Vivian stood. "We don't know if that is true. And we can work out how to cast my metaspells less often after we've killed Los. You saw what the Savanna Walker became. How could you doubt that the demonic host is here in front of us?"

Lotannu closed his eyes. "If he was telling the truth about the body of the ancient Los, he might also have been telling the truth about Language Prime."

She began to pace. "Perhaps, but whatever we do, we have to take our chances."

"Of course, Empress," he said.

"We shall try to take Leandra into custody if possible. Then we won't have made any irreversible changes."

"I doubt she would ever allow herself to be captured."

"Then we can't give her the option of preventing it."

Lotannu only bowed his head.

"You may go now," she said and turned to the window. A moment later, another thought occurred to her. "And Lotannu," she said without looking at him, "tell Captain Alarcon that I have changed my mind; we will need his report just as fast as he can conceive it."

Nicodemus paused on a switchback to catch his breath. It was past midday and he still had an hour to go before he reached the Pavilion of the Sky.

Climbing Mount Jalavata's narrow, precipitous stairs, he had to keep his eyes always on the next tall step. They were rough-cut gray stone, rusty red soil showing between the chinks. A brief rain had made the stairway's gutters run with pale red water. His lungi's hem was stained the volcanic color.

To either side of the staircase, the sheer slopes bristled with vegetation. White-feathered seabirds nested among the leaves and made the air echo with shrill complaints. Occasionally they stepped from their homes to ride the crater's contrary winds. Their graceful long wings cut a pleasing contrast with the blue sky.

As Nicodemus rested, he dared look down. A moment of vertigo made him lean forward and place his hands on the steps. But then, reassured, he stood again and studied the world below.

On the next switchback down, ten hydromancer guards had also paused to catch their breath. The poor souls had to haul gallons of aqueous disspells in case of imperial attack.

Far behind the hydromancers were two recently incarnated war gods. The prayers that had written them were inspired by the Savanna Walker's black dragon. Each had a draconic head and foreclaws. Their stone bodies were scaled, potbellied, more humanoid. Because each god stood over ten feet tall, they did not walk along the narrow switchbacks but rather stretched up to grab the recurring path above them, going straight up the slope as if it were a ladder.

Below them, the monastery of the Trimuril was a small gray patch. Doria, unable to climb to the summit, waited for him somewhere in that building. Out on the crater lake, priests and hydromancers milled about the pageantry of ships. Watching the Floating City's gentle motion was calming, like watching waves.

"What's this I see?" a thin voice creaked in Nicodemus's ear. "The Storm Petrel surveying the Pandemonium?"

"Burning heaven, Goddess!" Nicodemus said to the Trimuril. "You surprised me."

"You seemed so peaceful. I thought this might be a good time to talk."

"I just wasn't expecting you. I thought you would talk to Lady Warden Francesca."

"Oh, yes, we had a fine chat about airships. Then Francesca renewed her appeal that we evacuate the new incarnation of Los to Dral or Lorn."

"Did she call Leandra that?"

"No, no, my interpretation."

"You are certain then?"

Ancestor Spider's wheezing laughter rattled in Nicodemus's ear. "Certain? I would never be so stupid as to be certain, but seeing the Savanna Walker left little doubt. I've known divinity on this continent in all its forms, and I have never seen anything like that black dragon. There are things about Leandra I should have seen before. She has something of the trickster about her, though she does not know it. She's made all of us, humanity and divinity, the fools. Maybe that's what she did in her last life as well."

"I don't understand."

"The mighty empire, the noble league, she's shown us how cruel they are. Although she is herself just as cruel in revealing the truth. I should know; I've committed the cruelty of truth upon countless Ixonian souls over the centuries. And what better way to show us our foolishness than inducing us to fight each other in a cataclysmic war?"

"But perhaps we can change the league's society so that—"

The creaking laughter returned. "Change it how, my great Storm Petrel? You want to stop neodemons from preying on the weak and poor? That should be simple. All you have to do is stop casting metaspells or convince men and women to stop praying for evil to befall each other."

"You think it's impossible."

"Impossible by the rules as we presently understand them."

"But we could change the rules?"

"Nicodemus, would you like to play a game?"

"No!" he answered then quickly softened his tone. "I mean to say, Goddess, that I do not think I am presently—"

Again she interrupted with laughter. "You don't want to play because of how my last game turned out. But unfortunately, dear Storm Petrel, you are already playing a game and so am I. We are playing Leandra's game."

"What game is that?"

"I don't know and neither does Leandra."

A wind whipped around Nicodemus, throwing his long black hair into his face. After trying to tame it, he said, "So how do we play this unknown game? If Leandra is truly the trickster goddess who's shown our present rule's to be broken and who will rewrite the future rules, shouldn't we keep her alive?"

"There is no need to repeat your wife's argument. It's a moot point. Leandra wouldn't leave the city. She told your wife that she refuses to abandon the city."

"But—"

"Oh, don't keep playing a losing hand; it is so boring. I will not discuss this when we have just been dealt other and more interesting cards. We need to be thinking of the play that will keep us alive."

"And what particularly interesting cards have we been dealt?"

"Let's see," Ancestor Spider said with creaking amusement. "We are under attack from an evil Halcyon with unmatched spellwrighting ability, which she derives from a magical emerald that stole its power from the brain of the infant Storm Petrel. Since its creation, that emerald has been trying to return to its origin."

"Oh," Nicodemus said, then suddenly understanding, "Oh!"

"Could you?"

"Remove the spells from around my keloid?"

"It would be an interesting play."

Carefully, Nicodemus sat down on a tall stair. "The gem will manipulate the situation to reunite itself with me. That would work to our advantage if it eventually deprived Vivian of the Emerald. But it would also open a channel between Vivian and me, one that might be manipulated. In Starhaven, Typhon manipulated that channel to destroy Fellwroth and free himself."

"You think Vivian could manipulate you?"

"It's possible."

"Could you manipulate her?"

"I don't know."

"Can you think of any other interesting plays?"

Nicodemus stared down at the Floating City, its slow churning movement. Other interesting plays? "Francesca mentioned that she asked the Council of Starfall to send a support convoy with the war gods of the South. Do we have any more news as to if they were sent or not?"

"We did get a colaboris communication from Starfall. The ships set sail on schedule. But they were supposed to touch at Port Mercy before proceeding to Chandralu and there's been no report of that yet. Perhaps they are caught in doldrums or a storm."

"No good then. Do we have any other sources of strength, perhaps closer to home? Something on the archipelago?"

"None I can think of."

Nicodemus frowned and stared down at the Floating City. What could he do to weaken Vivian? A shadow was working its way across the lake. He looked up and saw a churning cloud advancing over the volcano. It was going to rain on him again soon. Idly he wondered if he could pray to some Ixonian wind deity to blow the clouds away.

Realizing that his mind was wandering, Nicodemus shook his head. "Vivian wouldn't be expecting me to free the keloid. At the very least, it would surprise her."

The Trimuril did not respond for so long that Nicodemus thought she might have left him. A curtain of rain drew itself across the far side of the crater.

"Storm Petrel," the Trimuril asked in a playful tone, "would you like to play a game?"

Slowly, Nicodemus smiled at the coming rain. "Yes," he said and reached behind his neck to the smooth, dark scar.

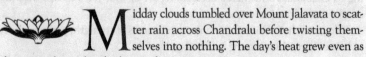

CHAPTER FIFTY

Midday clouds tumbled over Mount Jalavata to scatter rain across Chandralu before twisting themselves into nothing. The day's heat grew even as the tropical sun slouched toward evening.

Walking back to her quarters through humid hallways, Leandra felt forward though her godspell. The majority of her future selves felt her present anxieties. A small minority felt flashes of fear or the nothingness of death; those had to be from a possible but unlikely imperial attack. Perhaps a rocket hitting the compound? Another, larger minority of her future hours were filled with profound relief. That was encouraging.

Clutching a book she had newly acquired, Leandra wondered what might lead to such future relief. But concentration was difficult; the compound's walls were thin and through them she could hear an older maid complaining to a friend, a guard snoring on watch, and from somewhere farther a faint roaring.

She stopped. It didn't make sense, this sound. At times distant shouts punctuated the roar. Other times, it fell into silence.

She turned and walked down another hallway until she reached the kitchen's exit onto the upper terrace. Just outside the gate, in a small depression between the compound and street, a circle of men had gathered. They were chanting, or at least many of them were. Their cadence was irregular, building slowly and then collapsing into a chaos of shouted imperatives: "Kill him! Kill him!" "Not like that!" "Stay low, stay low! Damn it!"

Then she understood the sound like one recognizing rot when taking a suspicious sniff. Her expression crinkled. She shouldn't investigate. This was none of her affair. She turned back into the kitchen and saw a cook at work. He was a squat man, maybe forty, a ruddy complexion, chopping vegetables with a rhythmic intensity. The shouting continued behind Leandra. She couldn't leave it alone. She had to know if it was him or—possibly but unlikely—her.

So, again clutching her new book to her chest, Leandra slipped out of the kitchen, past the men, and up the stairs to the street. Once there, she turned back to look down on the chanting men.

What she saw was familiar. It was an impromptu wrestling match. The ring of white chalk had been laid down in a circle. The kind of thing seen at a winehouse. And, indeed, many spectators shouted with an abandon that suggested intoxication. Who could blame them? An empire had, after all, besieged their city. Wasn't it every man's civic duty to raid their compound's rice wine and kava to keep them out of imperial hands?

In the ring, two combatants circled each other. Both were bare-chested with lungi folded short. The older wrestler was a tall and hulking man, light brown skin, shaved head, a crooked nose, salt-and-pepper stubble. The very picture of a bruiser, a brawler.

The younger wrestler, despite his lean muscularity, seemed insubstantial in comparison. He wore his long kinky black hair in a tight bun. His sparse, youthful beard had been trimmed close. His eyes were wide, his lips pulled back in a manic smile.

The bruiser lunged, but the younger man danced around him and slipped both his arms around his opponent's waist then pivoted his hips to provide a fulcrum over which he could throw the bruiser. But though the young man's shoulders jumped into cords of muscle, he could not lift his opponent more than an inch.

Leandra's heart felt as if it were shriveling. The younger man's maneuvers were only those of a master wrestler; once they had been those of a god. It was him, what was left of him, looking terribly and beautifully human.

Now the bruiser, bellowing into an attack, turned around in the circle of Dhrun's arms and slammed an elbow into his jaw. Dhrun's head snapped around. An arc of saliva flew from his mouth and became silver in the sunlight. Dhrun spun halfway around before collapsing. The chalk ring, and therefore defeat, lay inches from his head.

The crowd's chanting dissolved before coalescing into a slower, more ominous rhythm. The bruiser advanced. Dhrun threw himself sideways, away from his opponent and just barely within the circle. The bruiser crouched and advanced again. Dhrun scrambled to regain his feet, moving faster than he had before. For a moment, it looked as if he would make it to safer ground. But then, seeing how close he was to the ring's edge, he faltered and stuttered his feet.

The bruiser rushed forward then and threw an overhand punch at the younger man's ear.

But somehow the punch struck only air. Dhrun had rolled onto the ground. He had caught the bruiser's wrist and pulled down, while at the same time, he jammed his foot into the bigger man's gut and his own back onto the ground. The lines of Dhrun's thigh muscles jumped into sharp relief as he used the force of the bruiser's attack to flip him over and out of the ring.

With a comical expression of shock, the bruiser found himself on his back. His flailing legs knocked over an unfortunate bystander.

The crowd erupted into cheers and curses. Sunlight glinted off brass and silver rupees changing hands. A huddle of men surrounded Dhrun, hauled him up to his feet and began slapping his back and arms as if he were on fire. Dhrun's smile was so bright, it hid his swelling lower lip and the blood running freely down a cut in his eyebrow. He was turning around, beaming at the men he had just made slightly richer.

Then he caught sight of Leandra. Their eyes met and she did not know what he saw in her face because she did not know what she felt. Guilt most likely, or pity. He was so much less than he had been, and she had made him so. His smile wilted. Self-hatred washed through Leandra as she realized that she had ruined his victory, this small joy. She smiled at him, but her heart continued to shrivel.

One of the men gave Dhrun an especially hard clap on the back, and Leandra looked away. Wanting to be alone, she hurried down the steps and through the crowd. Several men were holding back the bruiser as he called for a rematch. Some men grew quiet when they noticed her, but most were drunkenly oblivious. Dhrun was smiling again and talking loudly of an ancient goddess of victory called Nika. Maybe one or two would pray to her.

Suddenly everything seemed disgusting to Leandra. The men were too close and smelled of sweat and alcohol. The day's humidity was made thicker by the smell of kitchen waste: fruit rinds and fish heads in the sun. She pushed her way back into the compound.

The dim privacy of the hallways provided welcome relief as she made her way to the pavilion. Blessedly, the stairway was empty and she made it to her room without seeing another soul. She threw her new book on the bed and went to the window.

She set her hands on the sill and felt the great extent of her guilt. She thought of how beautiful Holokai had been, a captain, a creature of the open sea. And yet, in the end, he had been an animal, simple and vicious. He had killed some poor prostitute to get his son. Maybe a dozen prostitutes. Food and sex and progeny. That's what drove him. But, on some level, that's what drove everyone. Maybe every soul on the earth was simple and vicious, even the gods. Especially the gods.

Then she remembered Thaddeus, his long and languid intoxicated dreams. She felt the bite of nostalgia for when she and Thaddeus had been lovers, their intoxicated minds and bodies entwining through long, balmy nights. That had been just before the discovery that Thaddeus was screwing most if not all of the women in his immediate vicinity. Then she saw his aspirations as an addict's empty delusions.

Leandra had killed both Holokai and Thaddeus. Had they deserved it? She'd paralyzed her father and brought about the deaths of two of his followers. She'd torn out the part of Dhrun that was most beautiful and most deadly. How could he go on living as a husk of what he had been?

Leandra felt like a child overwhelmed by emotion. Maybe it was the stress hormone. She cursed herself and balled her hands into fists. But she could not move her mind from her own pain and wretchedness. She remembered then her first lover, Tenili. She'd thought he was a Verdantine merchant, madly in love with her. He'd come to steal her away from her mother and the miseries of her lifelong disease. But he had been a refugee god. He had not loved her, only wanted to trade her to the empress. Leandra could still remember watching her mother's draconic teeth sinking into him.

Since then, Leandra had hated her mother. But now, as Leandra looked on the city, she lined her own life up against her mother's. Were they so different? Hadn't Leandra consumed Thaddeus and Holokai? Her mother's judgment and her swiftness to act had lain upon Leandra's life like lead. But had Leandra not judged both the empire and league? Had her own swiftness to act not started a war?

She found herself gazing up at the volcano, wondering where her father was. Perhaps he'd made it to the shores of crater lake, that massive reservoir of hydromancers and divine language. Her mind wandered farther. There had to be some way of using the lake's dispelling waters against the empire. But how? Catapults perhaps? Water deities to spray it up on the enemy fleets? It seemed phenomenally poor planning, on the part of Ixonian civilization, to lock away such energy.

The sound of a door sliding open made her turn. Dhrun stood in the doorway, his youthful face uncertain. He had bathed, changed back into his red lungi and white blouse. His hair hung down to his shoulders. Apparently a few of the wrestling spectators had indeed prayed to Nika and she had used the prayers to repair their body. The swelling was gone from Dhrun's lips and there was no evidence of a cut or stiches near his eyebrow. He was also slightly taller, slightly more muscular.

Leandra stood up straighter. "Your throw at the end was excellent."

His smile was uneasy. "I thought so."

"Well . . ." she said impatiently, "come in."

Dhrun slid the screen shut behind him and walked toward the window. "Lea, are you angry that I wrestled?"

"Why should I be mad?"

"I just saw you on the street . . . and . . ." His dark eyes searched her face.

"I was only curious. I didn't mean to distract you."

"What's the matter?"

She turned to the window. "Nothing."

"You've never worried about distracting me when I wrestled before."

"You were never . . . never like this before."

Silence radiated off of him; it scared her a little that she could not tell its quality.

At last Dhrun said, "It was harder wrestling with only two hands. But I still can do it, and I can still win."

"Good. That is very good."

"Will you tell me what's bothering you?"

"I said nothing is the matter."

He stood beside her and they both looked out at the bay. Two catamarans were patrolling about a mile out of the harbor.

"When I was a boy," Dhrun said, "I lived in a nothing of a farming village on the eastern side of the big island. The land is poor and the people are poorer. Whenever the crops failed, many starved and others left. Two of my older siblings died in bad years before I was born. Anyway, the wrestling matches on Bright Souls Night and the Solstice Feasts were the most exciting thing that ever happened. They would make a circle of taro leaves and then put the two youngest kids into the ring. Whoever could push the other kid out stayed in the ring. When I was ten, I stayed in the ring until a sixteen-year-old pushed me out. And when I was sixteen no one could push me out."

He paused to shift his weight. "On the last Bright Souls Night I ever spent in my village . . . when I was seventeen . . . they had the best wrestlers for five villages come to our festival. None of them could push me out. When the festival ended, and they put the crown of ferns on my head, my mother came up to me, crying like someone had just died. She told me that everyone in the village had contributed to make a tournament prize. Everyone knew I was going to win, so they had donated rupees to send me to Chandralu.

That's when I realized that my mother was crying because they were sending me away from her. Of course I couldn't understand. I was angry with her, I think. Not fair that I was, but I was. I couldn't understand why she wasn't happy for me. I thought she was being a foolish old woman and that I'd see her whenever I came back from the city."

Leandra studied his face as he looked off into the bay. "And you haven't seen her?"

"My first year in the city was rough. The older wrestlers with more experience all had the drop on me. I was cheated and robbed. I slept on the street more often than not and was too ashamed to send word back. But a couple of the other wrestlers took pity on me and showed me some moves. By year's end, I was winning enough matches to live under a roof. I sent a few messages home and a few rupees. But before I traveled back to that tiny town, I wanted to be successful, somebody my village could be proud about. I won a few smaller tournaments, but it always seemed as if I should win just one more match before I went back. Things changed though when I got involved in the blood sport and the cult of Dhrun."

"Life got more complicated?"

"That's one way to put it. It was frightening and thrilling. There was death and kava and wine and criminals and beautiful women. I was twenty years old before I thought to travel home. It had been half a year since my last message from home. So I sent out a message and started to make travel plans, but the word came back that in the rainy season, a flood had destroyed the village's irrigation system. All the crops had failed and the entire village had been abandoned. No one knew what happened to my family. I hired several messengers to search for them but never heard back. I don't know if they looked or just pocketed my money."

"Then what happened?"

"Half a year later, a distant cousin recognized me in a wrestling match. Afterward he told me that my father and uncle tried to take the family to another village farther inland. But when they got there, they found it filled with similar refugee peasants. My father and uncle decided to try the fishing villages by the coast. But on the road, bandits led by some wild boar neodemon robbed them and killed my uncle. By the time the survivors reached the fishing village, they were starving. When mother fell ill, my father was caught stealing. The villagers ran my family away. No one ever knew what happened to my father, but my mother died a few days later."

Leandra didn't say anything. What was there to say? These stories were too common during the lean years. She wished Dhrun would look at her but he kept his eyes on the bay and the catamarans making slow and graceful turns. She reached over and took his hand.

Their fingers interlaced.

"What did you do?"

He smiled then, tightly. "Got drunk. Very drunk. Night after night. I took chances in the arena I had no right to walk away from. It hurt that I had waited. And the more I hated myself, the more chances I took in the arena. That's when Dhrun took me on as a lesser avatar. The year that followed was a bloody blur. Dhrun invested most of his soul into me. There was so much . . . so much of everything: blood, kava, wine, women, silver rupees, gold rupees. It was like a dream and a nightmare. It was only when Nika convinced us to form a divinity complex that the madness stopped. She saved us. Well, she did and you did."

She squeezed his hand. "How's that?"

This time his smile was warmer. "When I saw you take down that pickpocket air goddess in the arena—by then I was a trinity but part of me that was a young man and . . . well . . . young men can fall rather hard for impressive and beautiful women. Then, when it turned out that you had a cause I could believe in—and my family had been pushed into their end by a neodemon bandit—it gave me a purpose."

Leandra nodded.

"It helped me stop beating myself up for not going back to my village sooner. We think so often about our abilities, about how in the future we're going to be something brighter than we are now . . . but it's not true, having greater ability doesn't make happiness more uplifting or success more fulfilling. Pain and joy are what they are, no matter."

"Very philosophical."

His dark brown eyes peered into hers. "I don't want you to feel sorry for me."

"I don't—"

"I saw your expression out on the street, and I don't want you pitying me or torturing yourself because you had to deconstruct part of me. I am not nearly as powerful, and maybe I'm not useful to you anymore, but out there in that ring, I proved that I can get by. I can win enough prayers to survive. And I still have"—he started to say something but then seemed to change his mind—"something of a cause."

She laughed and looked away. "And what cause would that be? Because if your referring the idea of the Undivided Society, it's dead now that—"

"Lea, if you need to be forgiven, I forgive you."

She laughed while turning back to him but then felt her heart collapse. In his earnest expression she saw Holokai, Thaddeus, Tenili. "You're being sentimental. You don't know what you're . . . God-of-gods damn it!" This last she swore as her eyes began to sting. She yanked her hands from his and gave her eyes an angry rub.

Dhrun said nothing, which was fortunate as she might have deconstructed his face off if he'd spoken. He waited until she finished rubbing her eyes. Then she angrily jammed her hand onto his and interlaced their fingers. If he was going to be affectionate and supportive, then he was going to have to be affectionate and supportive on her terms, damn it.

But when he waited patiently as she stared out at the bay and then gave her hand a gentle squeeze, her heart collapsed again and tears burned into her eyes.

She turned to him and felt his arms encircle her. She felt his warmth. She thought about all that she had done and all that she had lost. She thought of the disease burning through her. "We break so many things," she found herself blurting. "Everything's broken and I don't know . . ."

Then she was crying, no longer thinking in words but in the primal colors of heartbreak. He held her, gently rocked her. After what felt like an eternity, Leandra found that she had no more tears or self-hatred or regrets, as if her weeping had hollowed out a rotten core.

"Thank you," she mumbled into his chest. She slipped her arms around him, pulled him close and mashed her face against his blouse. She'd already ruined it with tears and snot, she was sure, so best to try to get the remaining snot and tears off her face.

He continued to hold her. She prayed then to Nika and the glory of small victories. It wasn't much, she knew, but the next time Dhrun won some match, he would get a small amount of the strength he was giving her now.

Dhrun asked, "When did you take the loveless spell off?"

"Ellen did it for me, just before I found you. It's in the book on the bed." She gestured without removing her face from his chest.

"Thank you for taking it off."

She nodded into him. "I hope I don't get a disease flare."

"I hope so too."

He continued to hold her. She continued to lean into him. "How could you tell?"

"It's not hard to tell."

A thrill ran up her then. She knew what he meant, what she could not give him with the loveless around her mind and what she was giving him now in return for what he gave her.

When she looked up then it was to be kissed, and she had no sooner opened her eyes than he gently pressed his lips to hers. She closed her eyes again and allowed her consciousness to experience him as both a living body and an expanse of prose.

They stood like that for a long time, for what felt to her like too long. In her impatience, she pulled at him harder. Their kiss became something more. Then he was lifting her up and spinning her around and she pulled on him harder, almost fighting him.

They fell on the bed, accidently pulling the mosquito net down. He pulled off her blouse. She tore his down the front. She wriggled out of her lungi, and he out of his. And then . . . And then . . .

Afterward, exhausted and filled with relief, she lay with her head on his chest. "I don't know why," she said while catching her breath, "we waited until you had only two arms to do that."

He laughed and held her tighter while their breath slowed. They were both sweating in the humidity and it didn't matter. He stroked her back with the slowing rhythm of one falling toward sleep. She wanted to make fun of him for it but felt her exhausted heart dragging her down into sleep. She fought it for a moment but then gave in.

She felt herself become aware of his every sentence, of every curve of his body. Then, unexpectedly, she became aware of the weaving of the mosquito net below her and the few hovering insects above them.

Like a river surging out into the open ocean, her consciousness expanded and she became the wind blowing over the compound and through a banyan tree so that its every branch swung in a different direction. She became a cook pinching a cut finger. On the bay, she was a sailor watching for enemies. In the alleys behind the market, she was a troop of thieving monkeys impatiently waiting.

Out and out Leandra's perception stretched, and she was only dimly aware that she was suffering a vicious disease flare. Vaguely she remembered that she still wore the prophetic godspell and that she had prayed to Nika, both of which predisposed her to disease flares.

She was the rubble lying in a civic stream; a flock of red-and-green parrots rising and wheeling; a boy crying at his mother's cremation. In the Nauka, she was a beggar searching the body of someone killed by yesterday's cannon fire. In the Banyan District, she was an imperial spy casting pyromantic texts about a building. Leandra was the city. Leandra was no longer breathing.

Mortal fear churned within her as she realized that the only thing that could now contain this disease flare was the loveless spell written in a book that lay on the floor next to her bed. The nearest spellwright who could cast the loveless onto Leandra was her mother.

There would have been hope for her if Dhrun were a Numinous spellwright and if he could realize that her mind was expanded because of the flare. But Dhrun was lying underneath her falling toward sleep. He stirred slightly, perhaps unconsciously disturbed by her stillness, but even so he did not wake.

Then Leandra knew that the situation had escaped her control and was filled with an unexpected sense of relief. It was over. So she turned her attention to becoming as much of the city that she loved as was possible before she died.

CHAPTER FIFTY-ONE

After casting his metaspell from the Pavilion of the Sky, Nicodemus watched as one wave of Language Prime rolled down Mount Jalavata while other wave was caught by the wind and began to billow into the sky.

Nicodemus's cacography prevented him from writing many kinds of spells, but it enabled him to cast unique metaspells, which were truly metamisspells that caused magical language to become more creatively chaotic and intuitive.

As his metaspell spread, it would incorporate itself into every human or divinity it touched, strengthening the bond between humanity and intuitive magical language. In turn, this would strengthen the ark-stone system of transforming prayer into divine text. For more than fifty days, all affected humans and deities would unknowingly reproduce Nicodemus's metaspell. Like an epidemic, his metaspell would spread across the archipelago.

Exhausted, Nicodemus sat down. Perched on the eastern lip of Mount Jalavata's crater, the pavilion afforded views of the open ocean and the Bay of Standing Islands.

The pavilion was a three-story, hexagonal structure that was no more than twenty paces in diameter. Nicodemus sat on the top floor, which consisted only of six slender pillars and an ornately carved wooden roof. The first two stories were built of stone and housed a rotating trinity of priests who spent their time contemplating the Trimuril's Araxa manifestation. As one of the holiest places in the Cloud Culture, the pavilion hosted pilgrims who hiked up from the Floating City.

On arrival, Nicodemus discovered the recent imperial attack had doubled the usual number of pilgrims. They had lined up outside the pavilion to greet him with prayer. Nicodemus had exhorted them to pray for, and not to, him. But likely they would disobey and Nicodemus's dying god would soon be reincarnated.

A burst of wind sent Nicodemus's hair streaming. Taming it, he wondered if there was more silver amid the black than he had had two days ago. Strange that aging always seemed a mild surprise; some part of him was affronted that he was no longer twenty-five and just embarking on manhood. But he'd been miserable at twenty-five. Why should part of his heart hold on to that?

He looked down at the Pavilion's base and saw that his hydromancer guards and the two potbellied war gods had taken up defensive positions.

Another gust blew through the pillars. A wave of uncertainty about his daughter made Nicodemus pause and look down at Chandralu. Could he be mistaken about her? He thought of Rory and Sir Claude. He needed more time with his daughter to discover who she truly was. If only there was some way of holding back Vivian's forces. Idly he scratched his keloid and wondered if it would have any effect on the Emerald or Vivian.

He turned toward the stairs and got a gust of wind in the face. As he had when hiking up, Nicodemus wondered if there was some Ixonian god of the winds to whom he could pray. And then, at the top of the stairs, he froze as a thought blew through his mind.

"Trimuril," he said to himself, then louder, "Trimuril! Trimuril!" He went back to the railing and looked westward into the wind. "Goddess, Trimuril!"

"Yes, yes, what is it? What happened?" Ancestor Spider creaked with annoyance into his ear.

"Thank heaven you heard me!"

"What, you think I wouldn't maintain a presence in a pavilion dedicated to Ancestor Spider?"

"Is there an Ixonian deity of wind? Someone to whom the sailors or merchants pray to make their ships sail faster?"

"The Vatayana divinity complex, of course. Why?"

"We need to get word to Chandralu. They have to stop praying for anti-cannon deities."

"But—"

"Just briefly. I've figured out what they must pray for."

"Well," Ancestor Spider creaked in his ear, "you had better tell me quickly. Your half-sister is coming to pay us another visit."

Nicodemus looked out at the bay. To the north, a fleet of dark war galleys and white airships was sailing toward Chandralu with incredible speed.

L eandra gasped, convulsed. The world seemed too dark and too bright. Her heart beat as if it had wings. Every instinct cried out for air. She wanted to expand her chest infinitely, to inhale the sky.

She was lying naked on the floor. Dhrun, naked and male, was holding her and saying something. But she couldn't hear anything but her breath, which she took in and let out with growing pleasure. She closed her eyes. The world spun and her hands and feet tingled. She became aware of her body, of the day's heat, of Dhrun murmuring "Lea, Lea, Lea," as if in prayer.

At last Leandra understood. She tried to sit up.

Dhrun's tearstained expression creased into a paroxysm of what might have been pain or relief. Maybe both. But in the next moment, composure settled across his features. He helped her sit up and she noticed the opened spellbook by his knee.

"How?"

"You weren't breathing," he said while mashing the tears from his face with the back of his wrist. "I tried waking you. I even slapped you like Holokai would, but nothing worked. We fell off the bed and that's when I saw the book."

"But you're not a Numinous spellwright."

"In your fit you somehow made me fluent in Numinous. I saw the spell and I knew how it worked, so I cast it on you."

"That doesn't make any sense. I wasn't touching Numinous text and there was no active Numinous spell near me."

"Lea, I don't know and I don't care."

Becoming more acutely aware of their nudity, Leandra searched among the sheets for her clothes.

"Lea, with the loveless on . . ."

She looked at him. He was sitting on his knees, looking both beautiful and vaguely pathetic in his nudity. "Yes," she said, "what I can feel now is different, but I do remember." She reached over and grasped his hand briefly before she stood and tied her lungi.

Dhrun began to dress as well. Something about watching the shape of his shoulder as it moved through simple motions made her thoughts unspool. She remembered more vividly than ever before what it had been like to become the city. She thought of all the different things she had been: the wind, the grieving child, the cloud of colorful parrots. Something had changed when she had given herself to the dissipation of her consciousness . . . It was . . .

"Are you okay?"

She blinked. "Yes, of course."

"You looked like you might stop breathing again."

She shook her head. "There's something different . . ." Then, as she pulled on her blouse, she realized that she had not been paying attention to her prophetic godspell. Since returning to consciousness, she had felt a knot of raw fear. Mistakenly, she had attributed it to how close she had come to death, but in fact almost all of her future selves were terrified. "Dhru! The imperial spy! I was—"

But then the room filled with the roar of cannon fire. Dhrun ran to the window, and a moment later she joined him.

Just beyond the harbor water, the imperial fleet had formed a battle line. An expanse of white smoke bloomed from two ships. A moment later the reports rolled over the city. At the same time, two dark objects shot up from the harbor. The air halfway between the fleet and the harbor exploded into black gouts of smoke.

Dhrun laughed. "It's the anti-cannon deities! They're throwing something to block the cannon fire."

And as he spoke, a boulder the size of a young elephant flew directly overhead. It arced over the harbor and then splashed down ten feet from a war galley's bow.

Dhrun cried out triumphantly. "We'll fight back this time!"

"But, Dhru, I saw . . . It's a trap."

The sails of one galley bulged wide and pulled the ship forward at amazing speed. On the warship's bow stood several figures, foremost among them a tall woman with black hair. A green light began to shine from her raised hand. "The empress," Dhrun murmured.

Several boulders flew out from the city toward the warship, but puffs of smoke erupted from the fleet's line of battle. The air above the harbor exploded into rubble as the empire shot down the city's attack.

"It's not her," Leandra said and stuck her head farther out the window. She tried to see around the corner to the garden where she had seen her mother earlier.

Dhrun started to ask what she was talking about when the tall women on the warship thrust her fist forward. A building in the Banyan District erupted into fire. Dhrun ducked instinctively.

"The roof!" Leandra said, suddenly realizing where her mother would go. "Dhru, let's go." She ran out of the room. The compound echoed with frightened cries. Servants rushed about. Leandra glimpsed Ellen's black robes.

A moment later, Leandra charged up the stairs and onto the compound's roof. She looked around but found only sunlight and white walls. "God-of-gods damn it!" Leandra yelled.

"What?" Dhrun asked. "Lea, what's going on?"

The roar of cannon fire rolled over them but this time it came from the west. Leandra turned and looked up to Mount Jalavata. Airships were swarming above the Pavilion of the Sky. Smoke billowed from one ship, and a corner of the pavilion became a plume of smoke. Then a long arc of fire leapt up from the ground to envelop the airship. That had to be the war gods guarding Nicodemus.

Leandra scanned the sky for mother, but found nothing.

"Lea," Dhrun yelled, "what in the Creator's name is happening?"

"It's a trap, and if my mother has already left we—"

Just then Francesca—blessedly still in human form—rushed onto the roof. Seeing her mother gave Leandra a sudden idea. "Dhrun, take your Nika manifestation."

"What—"

"Do it!" she barked, grabbed his hand, and sprinted toward Francesca. "Mother!" Leandra yelled.

Francesca had been running toward the western edge of the roof. Now she stopped and looked back at Leandra.

"Mother, it's a trap!" Leandra cried.

"Your father's up there!"

Leandra grabbed her hand. "It's a trap; the empress is in one of those ships! She's waiting for you to fly up there so she can cast her anti-dragon spell on you."

"The empress is on that warship." Francesca pointed to the harbor. "We saw her with the Emerald. She created that explosion."

"That wasn't her. That was a pyromantic spy. I know. I became that spy when I was in my fit."

"Your what?"

"I nearly died. My consciousness expanded and I became the city. I was the spy as he cast incendiary text all around that building. He detonated it to make it look like that woman on the warship is Vivian casting some spell. But it's not Vivian. It's just some tall woman with black hair."

Francesca shook her head. "That doesn't make any sense." The roar of more cannon fire came down from the mountain. Francesca tried to pull her hand free of Leandra's. "Nico's up there!"

The galleys had sailed farther out into the bay and were now exchanging fire with the city's gods only intermittently.

"Mother, no!" Leandra yelled. "There's a bunker under the Pavilion and there are the two war gods. Look!" She pointed as a plume of fire flew up from the mountain. The airships climbed and scattered. "Dad's going to have to live or die without you."

Anger flashed across Francesca's face. "You heartless—"

"That's not it this time. This isn't a real attack. It's a trap to lure you close enough to the empress, who is in one of those airships."

A shocking blast rolled down from the volcano as three airships fired their cannons at once. Half of the Pavilion collapsed and slid like an avalanche down the volcano's slope.

The sight produced in Leandra a trill of fear. Francesca cried out and wrenched her hand from her daughter's.

"Mother, no!" Leandra cried as Francesca started toward the roof's edge. Her mother's form blazed with crimson language as she began to change.

Leandra felt something inside of her break. She glanced back and saw that Dhrun had taken her Nika manifestation and was watching her with wide, dark eyes. Leandra grasped Dhrun's hand tighter and yanked her forward.

When Leandra turned back to the east, she saw her mother's broad auburn wings spreading above, her powerful hindlegs kicking down to launch her skyward. Leandra's heart filled with fear as she saw her mother escaping, but then Francesca's long tail whipped overhead and Leandra reached out.

One of Leandra's hands caught her mother's tail, while the other still held Dhrun's. Leandra sent her mind racing through her mother's prose, deftly editing out her draconic nature but leaving enough of her text that she could remain a substantial construct.

Leandra tried to preserve the separated draconic construct. She tried to protect it. But the world had become a blaze of crimson language. For the briefest of moments, Leandra had an intimation of death, her mother's and her own, the type of silence they might create if they were forever no more.

But then Leandra was on her back. She tried to sit up, but the world was spinning too violently. Dhrun was somewhere beside her. At last, Leandra regained her sense of the upright.

Francesca, human again, was at the edge of the roof, kneeling over and pressing a hand to her chest as if in great pain.

Leandra went to her, covered her with the tattered remains of the clothes she had been wearing.

Francesca did not seem to notice.

"Mother, you're all right. You're all right."

When Francesca opened her eyes, Leandra saw in them the longing to become something which she never would again. Her mother was no longer a dragon. Leandra could see the realization setting in. But then, Francesca's eyes looked past her and up into the sky.

Leandra followed her gaze and saw a single airship, diving straight for them. Boulders leapt up from the city toward the ship, forcing her pilot to dodge and weave. This must be the airship that carried the empress.

Vivian had seen Francesca's transformation and had waited for her to attack. But now that it was apparent that Francesca would not take the bait, Vivian was taking a risk.

The airship dove under a boulder and then pulled out of its dive. With impressive speed, the ship tucked itself into a barrel roll. Leandra glimpsed a figure wearing black.

In Leandra's arms, Francesca cried out as if in surprise and turned away to cover her eyes. But Leandra had not seen anything happen. A boulder clipped the airship's stern and sent it spiraling east. The airship barely pulled out of the dive and avoided smashing into the city and then began to rise.

Leandra realized that the city was resounding with cheering. Out on the bay, the war galleys were sailing away. Above the volcano, the air fleet had broken off and was flying north.

Francesca groaned.

"Mother what is it, what happened."

"From the *Queen's Lance*, it was Vivian's Numinous spell. It's dazzled my vision."

She looked down and saw that her mother's eyes were flitting about randomly. She pinched them shut.

"But the empire is retreating," Leandra explained. "We're safe. The galleys and the airships are already away from the city."

"Is Nicodemus still alive?"

Leandra looked up to the ruined Pavilion of the Sky. "I don't know."

"Am I still a dragon?"

Leandra forced herself to look at Francesca and said, "No."

Leandra watched her mother, who had known such powerful grace. Her face became a mask of misery.

hen Vivian landed on deck, she exhaled in relief. Her hierophant bowed to her and then, using his jumpchute, flew back up to the *Queen's Lance.*

Since they had left Chandralu, a strong west wind had begun to blow and the airships now hovered easily above the war galleys.

"Pass the word for Magister Akomma," Vivian said to the nearest sailor. "I'll meet him in my cabin." But when she hurried belowdecks and opened the cabin door, she found Lotannu standing by her desk. He turned to her with an expression of icy control.

"I know, it was stupid," she said while closing the door. "For some reason, Francesca wasn't taking the bait. I had to try."

Lotannu only stared at her.

"I came through it without a scratch."

"A boulder struck the back of the *Queen's Lance.* One foot farther forward, and that rock would have smashed you flat."

"But it didn't."

"You promised."

She stood up straighter. "Magister, there are risks that have to be taken for the good of the empire, and—"

"Don't give me that empress nonsense now." His hands balled into fists, and his voice was filled with exhausted anger. "I've known you too damn long."

"I . . ." she started to say but was too shocked to finish.

"We started this together forty years ago," he said, "and unless you insist on finding a way of committing suicide, I mean to finish it together."

"I'm still alive; it wasn't suicide."

"You had no right to take such a risk."

"I am the empress."

"Then think of the empire!"

"Creator damn it, I was thinking of the empire!"

His voice quavered slightly. "Then you have to think about me."

And there it was. The truth she could not rebut.

He folded his arms and turned to the windows.

She let the silence stretch before saying, "I am sorry."

"Did it work? Did you deconstruct Francesca?"

"I'm not sure. It was strange . . . she disappeared right before I cast the spell. I'm not sure what happened."

"There've been no reported sightings of Francesca since then. I suggest we declare the attack a success and claim we've wounded Francesca. It will help morale and blunt the criticism of Captain Alarcon."

"Why should criticism fall on him?"

"He nearly killed our empress."

"On my orders."

"The air marshals would have trouble blaming the empress."

Vivian signed. "Very well. Do make the official announcement. Unless Francesca's somehow hiding her draconic nature, our situation is excellent. They won't be able to hold off the air fleet. Our next attack should crack the city."

"I've already given the preparation orders."

She went to stand next to him. "Thank you, Lotannu." When he nodded but did not look at her, she said, "And I am sorry. I will think of you."

He turned to her, and she could see just the slightest easing of the tension around his eyes. He nodded again. "I'll oversee the preparations."

"Good." She nodded. "This is how the War of Disjunction will end."

Okay, your turn," Ancestor Spider said.

"You want to play again?" Nicodemus answered as he waited in the bunker's darkness. Above him hung several tons of rubble that blocked his exit. The thump and scrape of the war gods clearing stone and wood came from above. They'd been at it for hours. Nicodemus had written several protective spells in the chthonic language to shield him from falling rocks.

"Oh, you're tired of this game? Maybe there's another game you'd like to play?" Ancestor Spider asked with frank enthusiasm. "Something with higher stakes?"

"No, no," Nicodemus answered quickly. "No, Goddess, I don't want to play any game like that. We can keep playing this one."

She produced her creaking laugh.

Nicodemus sighed. "Okay, I got one."

"Is it alive?"

"Yes."

"Is it a spider?"

"Do you really think I'd choose a spider when playing with a spider goddess?"

"You've done more foolish things."

"Like what?"

"Do you really want to talk about your personal life right now?"

Nicodemus was searching his brain for a witty remark when one of the rocks near him shifted. Something fell. "Hey!" Nicodemus shouted.

"Keep shouting," the Trimuril said and then went silent. He hoped she was directing the war god about how to dig him out without crushing him.

Nicodemus yelled.

The priests and pilgrims had hidden in a different tunnel of the bunker. The Trimuril reported that most had survived but a partial collapse of the tunnel had killed three. Nicodemus had not thought to ask how many of his hydromancer guards had survived. As he continued to shout, he prayed that they were all safe. Once he got out of this pit, he had to hurry back down to Chandralu.

A boulder shifted. Nicodemus moved farther under his protective chthonic spells, but the only thing that fell on him was tropical sunlight. He looked up at the stony war god's draconic face staring down.

"What was it then?" the Trimuril creaked in his ear. "What creature were you thinking of?"

"I can only give you yes or no answers."

"Don't be stuffy when I just saved your life."

Nicodemus smiled up at the sky and said, "A storm petrel."

From her window, Leandra watched a windy evening replace the day's blaze. After the empire had retreated, the citizens of Chandralu had taken to the streets to continue praying. Even now, Leandra could hear a priest sermonizing.

Footsteps sounded in the hallway. "Come in, Ellen," Leandra called while pouring a cup of tea.

The screen slid back. "You wanted to see me, Lady Warden?"

"Yes, thank you, Ellen. Would you like tea?"

Ellen eyed the cup in Leandra's hand. "I would, but perhaps you would let me pour my own?"

"Oh, come now, I poisoned this cup in a very mild way. You would hardly feel a thing as you died in agony." She took a sip to show that she was being facetious.

"Thoughtful of you, Lady Warden, but I have very specific preferences about how I take my agony."

"And how do you take it?" Leandra asked while motioning to use the tea service.

"Mostly with bad humor, irony, and bitter complaint."

"Sounds delightful."

"It's the source of my sunny personality," she said, deadpan, and set about brewing her own cup of tea.

"How is my mother?"

Ellen looked at Leandra before returning to the tea. "The transformation you effected has left her fatigued. But, as far as I can tell, she seems to be in good health."

"Does she understand that I had to deconstruct her draconic nature to save her from Vivian?"

"Perhaps that is a question she should answer."

"Do you understand that I had to do it?"

"I reserve judgment."

Leandra sipped her tea. "Have you had any time to ask around about those who might be speaking against me?"

"In fact, I have just returned from the Infirmary. I heard one or two rumors about your being Los Reborn. It seems several notable citizens have met with the Sacred Regent. At least two of them are sympathetic to the empire's interpretation that you are a demonic terror. No one knows what was said in that meeting, but there haven't been any official statements of dissent. However, after driving off the empire's last attack, the city's spirits have risen."

Leandra nodded. "Thank you, Ellen, very helpful. Did you get a sense as to how widely held sympathies for the empire might be?"

"Not really. Though I would guess they are minimal now and would remain so unless the next battle goes against us."

Leandra nodded. "Could I ask you for one more favor?"

"Of course, Lady Warden."

"I took the next dose of the stress hormone as you directed me to this morning. But now, would you mind removing my loveless spell again before I see my mother?"

She paused before setting her cup down. "Not at all."

"You hesitate?"

"No, it was just a passing fancy."

"Care to pass the fancy to me?"

"It must be difficult to choose between the ability to love and freedom from a chronic disease."

Leandra smiled tightly. "Which would you choose?"

"If I chose the ability to love, would that give me more opportunities for bad humor, irony, and bitter complaint?"

"A thousand times more."

"I'd go with ability to love then."

"It is good to know we see eye to eye on this issue. Could you remove my loveless now?"

After the physician had transferred the spell into a book, Leandra thanked her and asked her to send Dhrun in when she left.

A few moments later, the screen slid back to reveal Dhrun in her Nika incarnation. She wore a yellow lungi, a white blouse, and a slight smile that almost concealed her anxiety.

Leandra's heart ached a little as she remembered how sure of herself Dhrun had been before. "Dhru, come in," Leandra said and motioned to the window. They stood side by side for a moment, and then Dhrun rested her hands on the sill while Leandra turned around to sit upon it. "Ellen took the loveless off again."

"Won't that make your disease flare worse?"

"It might, but I wanted it off to talk to you."

Dhrun searched her eyes. "What did you want to say?"

"I suppose you've noticed a change in yourself since I deconstructed my mother's draconic nature."

Dhrun's lips pressed together and her posture seemed to straighten. "I . . . I can't assume my Dhrunarman manifestation."

"I did that to you."

She was searching Leandra's face again. "Why?"

"When I was attempting to protect my mother's draconic text, I wanted to use some of your text as a model. The problem is that I lost consciousness in the process of completing the task. I'm afraid I've locked you into this manifestation. I should be able to unlock you, but before I do so, I need to examine you again in a few days. I hope you'll forgive me."

"How long will I be stuck like this?"

Leandra wondered if she should lie, but seeing the fear in her friend's eyes, she told the truth. "I don't know."

Dhrun nodded.

"Is it very hard for you?"

"It's the first time since I formed my divinity complex that I've been confined to one body and one sex." She tucked a lock of her black hair behind her ear.

Leandra took her friend's hand. "I am sorry for that. I'll make it as short as possible."

"You can't examine me now?"

"No, I need to see how both you and my mother adapt to the changes I made. And anyway, I'd need to have the loveless put back on to fully perceive and edit your text."

Dhrun's expression became more concerned. "We have to be more careful about preventing your disease flares. Is it bad now?"

"Only mild belly pain. Hopefully the stress hormone will keep it from being too bad."

"Do you think that . . . what we were doing right before your last flare . . . do you think that touched it off?"

"I don't know."

"What we did," Dhrun asked tentatively, "what do you think about it?"

Leandra thought for a moment before she said, "It's hard to explain when you're like this."

"When I'm female?"

"To be honest, yes."

"But I'm no different. I am still Dhrun in either the Nika or Dhrunarman manifestations. They're both me."

"I know they are. I'm . . ." Leandra felt ashamed that she could not look her friend in the eyes. "I'm . . ."

Dhrun placed a hand against her cheek. It sent an uncomfortable thrill through Leandra. She closed her eyes and turned her head into Dhrun's palm.

"I still feel the same," Dhrun said softly.

Leandra didn't open her eyes. "When the loveless is off, I feel the same too. But, Dhru, it's different for me. When you touch me like this, I imagine you as the handsome young man. When I open my eyes, I'll see you as a beautiful goddess, my closest friend and confidante. You are the same person in each manifestation, but to me you are different aspects of the same person."

"How is that different than anyone else? What a person can be, it's such a big thing. Everyone is both the same person and a different person when they were younger or when they are with family or among enemies. The only difference is that I wear different bodies."

"I am sorry, Dhru." Leandra took the other woman's hand off her cheek. "This is difficult. For me, the different bodies matter." The resulting expression of hurt on Dhrun's face made Leandra pull her into an embrace. "Give me time. Things are changing so fast, and you won't be locked forever in this manifestation."

When they separated, Dhrun had regained her composure. She nodded. "I won't give up. But will you try to see through the different manifestations to me?"

"I will, honest. But right now, I have to go see Francesca. Will you come with me?"

When Dhrun said that she would, they set off down the hallway. It was awkward at first, walking side by side, but then they passed the twin druids in the hallway and the presence of others reinforced their public roles of a Lady Warden and her officer. Outside Francesca's suite, Leandra asked Dhrun to guard the door. The divinity nodded and produced her old, inscrutable smile.

After Leandra knocked, she heard her mother's voice and slid the door open. Inside, all the curtains had been drawn and her mother was sitting on the edge of her bed.

"Oh, I'm sorry, Mother; I didn't mean to wake you."

Francesca paused and then stood. "No, no." Her tone was so weary it alarmed Leandra. "I couldn't sleep, so we should get this over with." She walked to the window and drew back the curtain. Early-evening light filled the room.

"Get what over with?"

"I was wrong about Vivian's feint." She pulled the next curtain open. "You were right. If I had been in a draconic form, Vivian's Numinous spell would have killed me." She paused, grimaced, pressed a hand to her stomach.

"Are you all right? Should I get Ellen or one of the other physicians?"

"No, no. I am still a physician myself, Lea. It's one of the few things I have left."

"You've said that physicians make the worst patients."

"Horrendous patients, so there's no point torturing Doria or Ellen with my care."

"Can I get you something to drink or eat?"

"Food sounds awful right now."

Leandra walked toward her. "Mother, I . . ."

Francesca looked up at her. Her face had not changed—fair complexion, long brown hair, dark eyes, a light spray of freckles—but her expression of slack exhaustion didn't seem real. It felt as if this smaller, defeated person couldn't possibly be her indomitable mother.

"Mother, I wish it could have been different."

She nodded. "Circumstances demanded action."

Leandra didn't know what to say.

Francesca looked out over the city. She spoke then as if to herself. "All the things you could have done differently begin adding up in your head and you weigh their sum against the present. You wonder how it was you made the choices you did. Then you start adding up all the things that I could have done differently or your father could have done differently, and before you know it you're locking yourself into a calculus of what-might-have-been. But there's no time for that, and the world rushes on, and far too soon circumstances force you to act again."

"It's a little frightening that you know so well how I feel."

Francesca smiled at her. "It was how I felt."

"In Port Mercy?"

"Especially then, but also during every crisis in your treatment when you were a child."

"This would be a lot easier if you were ranting, obstinate, and overpowering."

Her mother laughed. "It's not easy for me either. I'm trying to work myself up to thanking you."

"I would appreciate it if you did."

"You would really care one way or the other?"

"I would," Leandra said, a little stung.

"We are so alike, you and I."

"Isn't it exasperating?"

"Infuriating, really." She smiled. "You are so much my daughter, and so much a child of what I was."

"You are still a physician and one of the most powerful stateswomen in the league."

Francesca looked out the window again. "It should be a consolation, shouldn't it?"

"And you must have heard that Dad survived and is coming down from the Pavilion of the Sky."

"That's true. I'll thank the God-of-gods forever that Nico survived." She looked at Leandra again and then down at her hands. "You forced me into this state, but it's the state in which I can survive . . . so, thank you, Lea."

"Just like you did to me in Port Mercy."

"It's a time of reversals. At some point, the dangers of creating or being created turn themselves upside down; the daughter outgrows the mother. As your strength grows, you will need to diminish mine."

"Mom, you're being dramatic."

"How well would you tolerate my political fiddling if you became the greatest power in the league?"

"About as well as the night sky tolerates the sun."

"Exactly. But given the current choices, I would prefer that you continue to diminish me."

"Are you going to start insisting I flee to the South again?"

"Right now the city is celebrating, but you and I both know that today's attack was just a feint. Now that I am not there to fight off the airships, Vivian can take this city. We have to get you out of here."

"There might not be time."

"But if there is—"

"And still," Leandra interrupted, feeling her passion rise, "what is the point of escaping? If I go on to manifest myself as Los, humanity will be exploited by neodemons and eventually replaced by deities. If I die, humanity will be enslaved by the empire's spellwrights until language stagnates. What's the point in choosing between two unacceptable choices?"

"My daughter would still be alive in one of them."

"There has to be some third way out, something better."

Francesca studied her. "Let's go outside. I'm feeling better."

Leandra followed her onto a balcony looking west. The compound's garden stood ahead of them. In the gathering darkness, someone had lit a kukui lamp near the pond. Koi were circling near it.

"Your father sent word that he's going to sleep in the Floating Palace at the Trimuril's request. I'll join him there in the morning to meet with the Sacred Regent. Would you like to accompany me?"

"I've already told the Trimuril I will. And perhaps Ellen told you already, several influential citizens met with the Sacred Regent to object to her supporting me."

"Ellen did mention that. And I should warn you that Ellen has her doubts about you as well."

"She doesn't do a very good job of hiding those doubts."

"Her transparency was one of the reasons I picked her as a student."

"Perhaps I have been jealous of how close you and Ellen are."

"I always wished you had been my student instead."

"But that's just it, Mom, that was the only way you gave me to be close to you, but I can never be your student."

"You made that abundantly clear."

"It's not in my nature."

"I wish I could have done better for you, Lea."

"I think . . . I think I finally understand why you did what you did."

"Will you be able to forgive me for it?"

"If you could return the favor."

Francesca looked at her then, a little of her old vitality returning. "With all my heart."

Something like fear and something like relief flushed through Leandra. "Okay, I'll go."

Francesca's eyebrows sank in confusion. "Go where?"

"To Lorn or Dral. If there's a way to sneak out to safety, I'll go. I mean, being the reincarnation of the Dread God has to have some perks, right? I should have enough time to try to change the league?"

Rather than answer, Francesca nearly tackled Leandra with a hug.

Leandra could only stand stiffly uncomfortable, but then her mother spun her around. "Darling, I couldn't stand the idea of the world without you in it."

A dull pain opened up in Leandra's chest. Awkwardly, she returned her mother's embrace, feebly patted her back.

"I was so afraid this day would never come," Francesca murmured. "I thought some imperial spy would kill you, or a disease flare would spin your consciousness across the world, or that you'd get so mad at me you'd deconstruct me into sentence fragments and blow them into the wind, I can't—"

"What did you say?" Leandra interrupted, pushing herself away from her mother.

"You know, the prophetic insight about your needing to kill someone you loved. I had this vision of you deconstructing me and then casting me into the wind."

Ideas teemed through Leandra's mind. She looked up at the volcano's summit. The sunset was painting a cloud with gold and crimson. The powerful western wind was making the cloud twist. Leandra thought of her father, his metaspell, Aunt Vivian, the Emerald, the Floating City.

"Lea, what is it?"

"I may . . . I may have the solution." As she said these words, a jolt of fear and sadness moved through her as she realized that she could not tell anyone—especially not her mother—of her realization. They'd stop her.

"What solution?"

She shook her head. "Nothing, nothing. I have to . . . get ready before we go to the Floating City."

"But you'll still go to Lorn or Dral?"

"Yes, yes. There are just a few matters I have to address." She squeezed her mother's shoulders and then embraced her. "I'll see you in the morning."

With that, Leandra hurried from her mother's rooms, through the hallways, and then out into the gathering dark. All the while, her mind reeled with visions of all that she would have to do and hide and how the world might still be changed.

CHAPTER FIFTY-THREE

In a dream, Francesca roamed her childhood home. She was searching for something valuable and lost. The sky was a starry expanse, but the short adobe buildings and the dusty roads were bright with daylight. Her heart was intoxicated with hope far more intense than any waking emotion. She was climbing a creaking staircase.

And then she woke under a mosquito net thousands of miles east and hundreds of years after the memories of her dream.

There were urgent voices and footsteps in the hallway. Something was wrong. Outside her window, the sky was filled with stars.

Francesca rose and pulled on her black wizard robes. A knock rang from the door and it slid back to reveal Tam. A faint blue light shone from his wooden staff. "The empire's attacking again," he said. "We're evacuating to the Floating City."

"On whose authority?" Her instinct was to join the battle in draconic form, but then the reality of her new limitations settled on her.

"The Sacred Regent has ordered all souls who do not wish to be subject to Tagrana's godspell to shelter in one of the temple-mountains. Those important to the regency are to report to the Floating City."

Francesca swore. Tagrana's godspell would transform every soul it touched into a tigerlike construct with murderous instincts. "Where's Leandra?"

"I'm here," her daughter said from the hallway.

"Why was I the last to be woken up?" she asked while scanning the room for anything she needed. She might not be a dragon anymore, but if they thought they could leave her out of events, they were going to find out how wrong they were.

"Mother, don't be dramatic. I never went to sleep, so I heard the news as it came in. Somehow the imperial fleet snuck in. The galleys are forming a line outside the harbor right now. So hurry."

Deciding that she did not need anything from her room, Francesca slipped on sandals and went out into the hallway. She found Leandra and the now two-armed and female goddess of wrestling. Tam and Kenna, dressed in lacquered wooden plate armor, stood on either side of Lolo, who had grown about a foot. Tam spoke, "The Sacred Regent ordered a squadron of red cloaks to see us through the city."

Leandra frowned. "What's unsafe about the city?"

"I doubt there's anything safe about the city," Ellen grumbled from the back of the crowd.

"We're wasting time," Leandra said and nodded to Tam and Kenna. "Druids, take us out of here."

Then they were hurrying through dark hallways and down the pavilion stairs. Kukui lamps flickered and servants and guards hurried about. Somewhere a child was crying. The deep roar of cannon fire rolled through the building. Someone yelled.

Out on the street, a dozen red cloaks wielding spears and torches waited. A strong wind made the torch flames flicker and dance. They were staring at the eastern sky. Francesca followed their gaze and to her horror saw the billowing shapes of the two airship carriers. Their massive lofting sails shone in the two moonlight.

Icy fear gripped Francesca. Once the carriers were over the city, they could drop thousands of warkites.

If Francesca could still transform, she would take wing and tear the carrier's lofting sails into shreds before they came within ten miles of the city walls. But now there was nothing she could do but follow her party as they hurried along Utrana Way. The street was crowded with civilians, their arms filled with hastily gathered possessions or bawling children.

An orange light flashed beyond the harbor waters, outlining war galleys that seemed twice as many as the one that had formed during yesterday's feint. A moment later a second flash burst in the air above the harbor as the city's anti-cannon war gods threw something in the path of the cannon fire.

Two gouts of orange cannon fire erupted out on the bay. Then five more. Then ten. Booming reports rolled over the city. Smaller explosions burst above the harbor as the anti-cannon deities sought to block the bombardment. But it was too much. A blast of flame shot up in the harbor, and then another in the Naukaa.

Leandra shouted something but Francesca could not understand. A fiery explosion shattered the darkness on a terrace ahead and below them. Then Francesca and her party were running. Leandra reached out and Francesca gladly took her hand.

The Jacaranda Steps were crowded with panicked civilians running for higher ground. The red cloaks bellowed for the crowd to make way, but their voices were drowned out by the roar of cannons.

At the next terrace, they passed a massive god. Maybe thirty feet tall, his body was that of a banyan tree. Perhaps he was a bellicose reincarnation of the Banyan God. With gigantic wooden limbs, the god pried up one of the stones used to form the Jacaranda Stairs. The cut stone must have weighed a thousand pounds, but with a graceful spin, the war god threw the stone high out into the night toward the imperial war galleys.

The crush of the crowd pushed Francesca's party faster up the stairs. Some in the crowd fell and were either helped back to their feet or trampled.

Francesca had witnessed battles and riots and sieges, but she had always seen them through a dragon's eyes. Then the death of innocents had horrified or enraged her. Now Francesca was shocked by how helpless she felt. There was no room in her heart for the trampled; there was only the great need to get to higher ground.

Atop the Jacaranda Steps, the crowd became so dense as to slow their progress. Leandra turned to look back at the bay. Francesca followed her gaze and saw during flashes of cannon fire that many smaller boats now floated between the war galleys. The hellish glow glinted off their helmets and spearheads. Vivian would soon land her troops.

On the docks, Francesca could make out a different type of light. A lone figure shone with a brilliant orange aura. All around her prowled massive feline figures: Tagrana and her newly made warriors.

"Damn it all," Leandra growled. "No choice to make now."

Francesca looked at her. "What choice?"

"I had plans . . . I thought I could do something with my future. But it doesn't matter now. There's no way we can withstand this." As she spoke, Leandra wore the most peculiar expression. It had something of fear and shock in it, but also something of relief. It seemed as if a weight had been taken from her.

The crowd began moving faster. Both women had to concentrate on staying upright. At last they started pushing their way into the crowd that had formed before the Water Temple. Brightly robed priests stood on temple walls yelling instructions, but everyone around Francesca was talking or crying. To her synesthetic hearing, the crowd was a varicolored chaos.

Francesca was straining to make out the priest's words when someone screamed. The horrified, bloodcolored voice was soon joined by a chorus of terror. Francesca spun around and saw a streamer of white cloth, square metal talons gleaming in the torchlight. The warkite cut down a man not twenty feet behind her. Then the warkite billowed up and was about to pounce on its next victim when above it a starburst of blue light filled the darkness. A spray of water covered the crowd and the warkite fell limply onto the bloody remains of its victim. It had been a hydromancer's disspell, Francesca realized.

Francesca looked up and saw the sky filled with a bulging white airship carrier. A swarm of white cloth and glinting steel was dropping from the carrier as it deployed its warkites to slaughter the people of Chandralu.

But up from the city flew brightly winged creatures. It was hard for Francesca to tell what they were because they moved so fast that they seemed to be made only of color and velocity. Each of the creatures flew straight at one of the warkites and then folded itself into a small, feathered vector which punched through the attacking cloth construct. They were small avian deities, Francesca supposed, parrots perhaps, incarnated to defend against warkites.

But there were too many warkites. Francesca could see that. The stream of roiling cloth and steel coming from the carrier airships had not slowed. Some of the warkites were slipping past the feathered defenders to attack whoever was out on the streets. The roar of the cannon still echoed up from the bay and now the lower terraces were alight with civil fire. The city could not withstand the attack much longer. Perhaps it had already broken.

It was then that Francesca realized what the priests were yelling. They were exhorting the people to pray for protection from the warkites and from cannon fire. And indeed, those nearest the priests were bowing their heads in urgent prayer.

But then another warkite fell amid the crowd. Screams filled the air and a crush of bodies tried to flee the murderous construct. A moment later two blue starbursts bloomed above the warkite, dispelling it.

"This is how it ends," Leandra said.

Francesca couldn't think of what to say and so put her arms around her daughter, and to her great surprise felt Leandra return the embrace. Tears stung Francesca's eyes. She tightened her arms around her daughter, remembered holding her as a newborn. They had started Leandra's life together in this pose; now they would end it in the same pose. It had all gone so wrong.

Francesca's mind was filled with the sudden, morbid necessities of their situation. Should she end things for them? Surely she could come up with a better way to die than being gutted by a warkite. But maybe she should fight back. Perhaps she could disspell one or two of the constructs.

The crowd jostled around them. The cannons were firing less often now. Francesca put her thoughts aside and focused on holding her daughter. She waited.

And waited.

Waiting for death seemed to be taking an inordinate amount of time. Irritation moved through Francesca. She had felt this way once before, many years ago. If she had been brave enough to reconcile herself to the disappointing way in which she would leave the universe, the least the universe could do to return the favor would be to usher her out of it in a timely manner.

Francesca loosened her hold on Leandra enough to look up at the sky. She wanted to see what was taking death so long. But what she saw shocked her. "What in the burning hells are they doing here?" she asked.

High above them, swarming around the airship carriers and visible in the light of the burning city, were three humanoid figures made entirely of paper thin sheets of metal. They glided on the wind with wings forty or fifty feet wide that shone with white auras. In their hands, each creature wielded thin, ten-foot long swords made of light. The bright creatures were taking turns diving at the carrier to slash its lofting sails. Below them, the lofting kites had stopped descending upon the city and instead rose up to attack the winged creatures.

Leandra also looked up. "Lornish war seraphim?"

"Yes."

"But how . . ." Leandra's voice trailed off as she let go of her mother and then pointed.

Francesca turned to see that the bay was illuminated by blazing red light. The decks of two war galleys shone with figures made of flame. Some had two legs and walked upright. Others ran on four legs. All of them were attacking the imperial sailors or running up the rigging to spread the conflagration.

"Dralish wildfire deities," Francesca said. "That makes even less sense unless . . ." Then she cried out and pointed. The sky was brightening to the east, and she could just make out three new ships. Their taller hulls and more expansive rigging marked them as being Lornish war galleys. "The support convoy from Starfall! The war gods of the South!"

Some in the crowd were cheering, but far more were bowing their heads in prayer. Above them, three sleeker airships—cruisers, Francesca would have guessed—were coming to the aid of the carriers. The more maneuverable airships were able to fight off the Lornish seraphim. As Francesca watched, one airship swooped down and with its long foresails slashed the wing off of one seraphim. The now pitiful war god began a spiraling fall out of the sky.

But more of the seraphim had joined the fight. The airships turned and began retreating. Out on the bay, the empire's war galleys were likewise sailing away from the city.

The two ships attacked by the wildfire war gods continued to burn. The resulting light illuminated the Savanna Walker's black dragon where it remained frozen in the bay.

A great cheer went up from the crowd and suddenly everyone seemed to be embracing everyone else. Francesca found herself hugging Tam and then a red cloak she had never seen before in her life and then her daughter again.

"This means we're not going to die after all?" Leandra asked over the cheers.

Francesca laughed. "You seem almost disappointed."

Leandra shook her head and laughed. "We have to keep on fighting. Do you think the Southern deities will be enough to scatter the imperial fleet?"

"I doubt it, but at the least the Lornish seraphim can keep the carriers away. We can defend the city until the Council of Starfall sends a fleet of our own."

"Or until imperial reinforcements arrive."

"Oh, God-of-gods," Francesca said with another laugh, "we're not going to die right now! Can you be happy about that for just one damned moment?"

But Leandra face remained grim. "Whatever happens in the coming days, know that I'm just now seeing things clearly." She paused. "And if anything happens to me, you have to look after Dhrun."

"Lea, what's the matter? Nothing's going to happen to you." She pulled her closer. "Are you okay?"

"Yes, yes. I'm fine. Nothing's wrong. It's just"—she motioned to the crowd—"all this."

Francesca nodded. It was overwhelming. And then Dhrun stood beside them, and Leandra let go of her mother to tightly embrace the goddess. There was chanting and singing now, and many in the crowd were dancing.

Out on the bay, the Lornish galleys were sailing into the harbor while the imperial fleet retreated. But the celebration couldn't go on too much longer. Two large fires already burned in the city's lower terraces.

The shouting grew louder behind Francesca and she turned to see that the circle of red cloaks surrounding her had merged with another such circle. They were now among blue-robed hydromancers and, very suddenly, her husband. He was dressed in heavy black-and-green silk robes and gloves so that his skin wouldn't accidently touch anyone in the crowd.

Before Francesca could react, Nicodemus scooped her up and spun her around. She found herself clinging so tightly to him she began to fear she would break his ribs.

"I was so worried," he said. "I was so worried. They almost didn't let me out of the Floating City."

"It's the Southern war gods," Francesca said and pointed. "They just arrived."

His smiled broadened in a very particular way.

She frowned at him. "What is it?"

"When I was up the mountain, the Trimuril and I realized we should have the people pray for winds to blow the convoy to us."

Francesca rolled her eyes. "Typical of you to ruin this moment by bragging."

"I wasn't—"

She interrupted him with a kiss. They held each other again and then Francesca realized that the motion of the milling crowd had again brought her close to Leandra.

Her daughter was leaning close to Ellen. They seemed to be talking over the noise of the crowd, but neither woman was smiling or embracing. Then Leandra noticed her father. For a moment neither of them moved, then Nicodemus went to her and pulled Francesca along by the hand.

When Leandra saw what he was doing, she stiffened. But then Nicodemus was upon her, enfolding her in one arm, Francesca in the other. At first Francesca shared Leandra's apprehension. She could not remember when, if ever, the three of them had stood like this. But then, slowly, Leandra embraced both of her parents. So Francesca leaned in and held her family. She prayed that this moment together would not be their last.

CHAPTER FIFTY-FOUR

Kneeling before the Sacred Regent, Nicodemus became increasingly uncomfortable. Outside evening cooled the crater lake, but inside the Floating Palace retained the day's heat. The hundred unwashed and sweating bodies attending the emergency council had made the air pungent. A court attendant had lit incense, which had only added a cloyingly aromatic component to the room's odor.

Beside Nicodemus, Leandra shifted and Francesca tried to hide her discomfort. The council had already been in session for two hours. The Sacred Regent had officially welcomed the Southern war gods. There had followed reports by generals and native war gods. Although the Southern deities had improved the city's situation, Chandralu was not in a position to take the offensive.

Reports from city officials were grimmer. The casualties from the nighttime bombardment were severe. A fire had destroyed a third of the city's rice stores. One official calculated that the city could continue to fight for only sixty more days. Others contested this number, but all agreed that a prolonged blockade would go poorly.

There followed a brief discussion as to who—the empire or the league—would get reinforcements to Chandralu faster. The empire was closer but likely had no ships to spare without leaving their home kingdoms undefended. The Dralish and Lornish navies, on the other hand, could dispatch ships almost immediately. An urgent colaboris spell had already been sent to Starfall Keep, but the Council of Starfall moved at a painfully bureaucratic pace. Worse, there was no guarantee that the Council would understand the urgency of the situation.

Surprisingly the Trimuril had remained silent throughout the proceedings. Indeed, as far as Nicodemus could tell, her incarnation was not present in the throne room.

At last the Sacred Regent asked the wardens for their counsel. Nicodemus bowed and spoke. "Sacred Regent, we agree that it is imperative that the league immediately dispatch a fleet to break the blockade. To that end, we believe Lady Warden Francesca and Lady Warden Leandra should hurry to Starfall Keep, where they can ensure that the necessary action be quickly taken."

From behind Nicodemus, the dignitaries murmured. The Sacred Regent cleared his throat. "We prefer that the Lady Warden of Ixos remain in her chosen kingdom."

Nicodemus bowed his head. "And she would prefer to stay; however, she cannot presently contribute to the city's defense. Neither could the Lady Warden Francesca now that she has been changed."

The Sacred Regent shifted on his throne. "We would prefer she remained. If she survives the present attack, she would eventually gain enough power to defeat the empire. When Lorn and Dral understand her importance, they will more quickly send the needed aid."

The murmuring in the room grew. The Sacred Regent had not said that Leandra was the reincarnation of Los, but everyone in the room was thinking it. Moreover everyone was contemplating the possibility that Lorn or Dral might be so squeamish about harboring Los reincarnated that they would delay sending aid or, worse, make a treaty with the empire.

Nicodemus and his family had anticipated this fear. So he bowed again and said, as loudly as he could, "Regent, we share your concerns. However, what lies in store for Lady Warden Leandra is beyond conjecture." That was technically true. All signs suggested that the Savanna Walker's prophecy was a strong one; however, it was still only a prophecy and therefore not an eventuality.

Nicodemus continued. "It would be more effective if I were to remain in Chandralu. I can continue to cast my metaspell here to keep our deities as strong as possible. More importantly we can remind Lorn and Dral that if the city is lost, then my metaspells would also be lost."

This produced louder murmuring. The Sacred Regent, however, did not seem impressed. "We were not aware that the Halcyon had considered leaving us."

"Because I have not. I speak only as one concerned for Ixos, the league, and my family."

"To which of those entities are you most devoted?"

"To all three together, Sacred Regent. As we understand it, none can thrive without the others."

The Sacred Regent frowned. Then Nicodemus realized, to his great surprise, that the regent wished he could keep all of them as political prisoners. If he did so, Nicodemus could invoke his status as the league's Halcyon and denounce a Sacred Regent who had failed to protect his city from the empire. Nicodemus doubted he could garner enough support to depose the regent, but he certainly could break the city into hostile factions at a time when it could not survive infighting.

The Sacred Regent spoke, "We will consider what you have said."

"Sacred Regent, would you let me reaffirm my commitment to the people and pantheon of Ixos?" That seemed to remove some of the tension from around the old man's eyes. "Under your direction, I will know exactly when to cast the metaspell for maximum advantage. It is a difficult spell to cast and your leadership in directing my family would greatly improve the outcome."

The regent's eyes narrowed, and Nicodemus had no doubt that the old man understood the implied threat of noncooperation.

The only sounds were those of distant chanting from the priests on the Floating City. Could the old man really be so much of a fool as to oppose him?

At last the regent nodded. "We thank you for your wise counsel, Halcyon. If we were to send Lady Warden Leandra and Lady Warden Francesca to Starfall Island as our advocates, how would you suggest we get them past the blockade?"

Relief washed through Nicodemus. "We suggest arming the Lornish war galleys and setting out on the bay as if they meant to fight out of the Cerulean Strait. While the imperial fleet is moving to block the attempt, we could sneak the Lady Wardens down the peninsula with a small force of red cloaks. From there they could make their way to Port Mercy and then to Starfall. The Lornish war galleys, having gotten a better sense of the remaining imperial fleet, could then return to the city without bloodshed."

The Sacred Regent turned first to his admirals then to others in the crowd whom Nicodemus could not see. At last the Sacred Regent nodded. "Very well, Lord Warden. The commanders of both ships and soldiers will meet with you tonight to devise the plans. We shall meet again tomorrow morning. If your plans are satisfactory, we will proceed in the afternoon. Does this satisfy you?"

Nicodemus bowed. "Very much so, Sacred Regent."

With that the regent moved on to other matters. The physicians of the infirmary spoke about the difficulties of treating so many wounded. Then came civic officials with proposals about sheltering the newly homeless and repairing the damaged sewers and bridges. At last the Sacred Regent called an end to the meeting.

Glancing out the window, Nicodemus noticed it was still evening. The throne room had cooled and a breeze had dissipated some of the bad air. He stood and stretched his sore legs.

"The old goat isn't going to make it easy for us," Francesca grumbled.

"Not so loud," he murmured through a smile. "At least he's not fighting us on the point."

"Not in public. We had better make our plans for escape watertight. Whom do you want me to cajole, the red cloaks or the admirals?"

"The red cloaks. You're going to be stuck traveling with them, so you'd better be happy with the arrangements."

"Good point," she murmured and then, seeing the Red Cloaks' Commander, hurried away into the crowd.

Nicodemus noticed then that he was standing next to Leandra and Dhrun and that the two of them were engaged in an intense and private conversation. He could hear snatches of what Dhrun was saying: ". . . you're worrying too much . . . I feel about you . . . we'll still be together when . . ."

Embarrassed to be eavesdropping, Nicodemus turned away and began to look for the admirals. Most of them were standing by the dais waiting for the Sacred Regent.

Nearby Francesca was engaging the commander of the red cloaks while her student, Ellen, talked to one of the regent's secretaries. Nicodemus hoped they were making headway and was about to start off after the admirals when he heard Leandra's voice. He turned and saw that she was looking up at him with a troubled expression. "What is it, Lea? Is something the matter?"

"Everything is fine, I have several matters to see to before I leave Chandralu."

"Anything troubling?"

"No, just loose ends to tie up as the warden, make sure my records about various neodemons get into the right hands, that sort of thing. It's going to keep me busy, so I'm afraid that I can't help you and Mom with the escape plans."

"We should be able to manage it."

"I . . . I just wanted to tell you that, after I had to take away Mom's draconic nature . . ."

Nicodemus tried to keep his expression neutral. He had been shocked to hear of Francesca's change but grateful that she had survived Vivian's trap.

Leandra continued with difficulty. "Afterward . . . I began to see things more clearly for the first time. I tried to explain to Mother, but I don't think I got through. I think I was right all along to despise both the league and the empire for not doing better, but I didn't understand what you and Mom saw in the world. Not until I had to deconstruct part of her . . . I think we were finally able to forgive each other, and I saw how I have to keep trying to change the world."

A twinge of fear moved through Nicodemus. "You're still willing to escape, yes?"

"Oh, yes. I'm not opposed to that anymore. It's just that, I have to try to make a change."

Nicodemus was relieved. "Lea, once we get you to safety, there's going to be plenty of time. And don't worry about me. Lorn and Dral can't survive without my metaspells. They'll send a fleet to break the blockade."

She was shaking her head. "I know it feels like there will be a lot of time, but there won't be."

He started to ask what she meant but then saw that the Sacred Regent was proceeding from the throne room and the admirals were following. "Lea, I have to catch the admirals."

"Of course, but . . . Dad, just . . . if you and Mom were ever to have another child, I'd hope you'd tell them about what I tried to do."

He laughed. "Lea, you're being foolish. What's this about?"

"I don't know how to explain."

"Lea, I have to go. If the admirals get away, they'll come up with some excuse to scuttle our plans."

"Yes, of course, go. But, Dad, if we don't get a chance to talk before I leave, promise you'll think about what I was trying to do before all this madness."

"All right, I will. And don't worry too much. We'll all be together again before you know it." He took her hand and squeezed it.

She stared at him for a moment and then nodded. "You'd better hurry then."

He turned and saw the last admiral walk out the doorway. "Fiery heaven," he swore then squeezed his daughter's hand one last time and hurried off through the crowd.

It was only after he had left the throne room and called after the admirals that Nicodemus felt a peculiar sense of foreboding.

CHAPTER FIFTY-FIVE

After so many days afloat and aloft, Vivian found solid ground unsettlingly firm. She spent the afternoon and evening touring the headlands north of the Cerulean Strait and was now hiking down the jungle path to a camp near the shore.

Midnight was near and the jungle would have been black if it weren't for her guards' torches. As it was, her party illuminated the understory of trees and vines. Jungle insects made their whirring racket and every variety of winged bug swarmed around the torches.

Lotannu had suggested they establish a fort on the headlands. It would not be an easy task—the slopes being steep, the jungle thick—however, if the pyromancers could build cannons to fire across the strait, the empire would control the bay. Vivian had insisted on inspecting the best possible sites for the fort.

At last her party emerged from the trees into a clearing. Before them the moonlight fell on the strait's fast-moving currents. The camp consisted of thirty tents surrounded by wooden walls. Several sentries called challenges from the gates and someone in Vivian's party replied with the correct passwords. Soon Vivian walked into her wide tent.

She sat heavily on an uncomfortable but sturdy chair and rubbed her eyes. She had trouble falling asleep after the previous night's failed attack. Once she had finally drifted off, she had been taunted by vivid dreams of leading her forces into a conquered Chandralu. She woke frustrated and vowing to break the city's defenses.

A tent flap peeled back to reveal Lotannu. He bowed.

"What news?" she asked while motioning for him to sit beside her.

Lotannu sat with a grateful sigh. "The Southern reinforcements are integrated with the city's other deities. It's not known how badly the fires damaged the city's ability to resist. Among our forces, morale suffered from losing the two galleys to the wildfire deities. We did, however, capture a convoy of merchant boats on the Matrunda River, so we should be able to increase rations. Half the men we put ashore with cholera have succumbed but there have been no new cases reported in the fleet."

"Does Chandralu have enough food to withstand an extended blockade?"

"Possibly."

"That would make a headland fort all the more important."

"It would; however, there may be another solution."

"Oh?"

"There are a substantial number of dissidents in Chandralu."

"Less than happy about being enslaved by a reincarnated Los, are they?"

"Just after sunset, one of the hierophantic scouts south of the city discovered a lone traveler flagging him down. She claimed to represent Chandralu's dissidents. He flew her back to the fleet and then to this camp."

"And?"

"I could tell you my conclusions after interviewing her, but my guess is that you'd like to hear what she has to say."

"Indeed. When do I get to meet her?"

"As soon as you like."

Vivian rose and smoothed out her robes. "Send her in."

Lotannu nodded and then stepped out of the tent. A few moments later, he returned with two guards. Between them stood a short women dressed in a wizard's black robes. While Lotannu and the guards bowed to Vivian, the newcomer only fixed her with a level stare.

"So then," Vivian asked, "who are you?"

"My name," the traitor said in a flat voice, "is Magistra Ellen D'Valin."

Nicodemus woke with a racing heart, sat up in a strange bed covered by a mosquito net. He was sure one of his teeth had just fallen out. Reflexively, he felt along the sharp lines of his molars. All still there.

"What is it?" Francesca mumbled.

Nicodemus blinked as the dream's amnesia wore off. "A nightmare." He had been confined in a prison only a few inches bigger than his body. There had been something loose in his mouth. When he spat it out, it was . . . it was . . . Now waking life was erasing the dream. A shard of green glass?

Francesca sleepily flopped an arm over Nicodemus's lap. "Go to sleep," she mumbled into her pillow.

Outside the window, night's darkness was still complete. Then he realized that, in the nightmare, he had not spat out a bit of green glass. "The Emerald is communicating with the keloid again."

"Mmm . . ." Francesca said. "Go sleep, Nico."

"Or maybe it's the dying god. Maybe they're praying to me again and the dying god is reincarnated. Am I running a fever?"

Francesca flopped a hand against his cheek. "No. Sleep."

They had been up till well past midnight going over their plans to smuggle Leandra from the city.

Nicodemus's heart slowed. Maybe it was just a nightmare. Regardless, he had to get as much sleep as possible before they appeared before the Sacred Regent again.

"Do you think Lea is okay?"

"She's fine. She went to bed before we did."

"But the things she said . . ."

"She's worried. We're all worried. You need to sleep." Francesca pushed her face into his thigh. "Sleep."

He nodded and lowered himself back down. She wrapped her arm around him, and he tried to forget everything but the sound of her breath and the texture of her skin. This could be the last time they held each other for a very long time.

The throne room was filled with cool air and morning sunlight. Francesca sat between Nicodemus and Leandra. They were waiting for the Sacred Regent and his attendants to finish climbing onto the dais.

Francesca had been too nervous to eat breakfast despite Nicodemus's insistence. Leandra, on the other hand, had eaten with gusto and seemed as calm as if they were planning a garden walk. Maybe Leandra's equanimity came from her loveless spell, which Ellen had recast the night before.

Finally the Sacred Regent stood before his throne and held up one hand. Everyone bowed. The regent was flanked by two new hydromancer guards. Someone had talked him into increasing his personal protection.

Francesca could perceive the Trimuril's stony incarnation standing at the throne's right hand. The goddess wore a slight smile as she looked at Leandra. It made Francesca uneasy. Was the goddess smiling so out of fondness? Or pity because she would prevent Leandra from leaving?

Beside Francesca, Ellen shifted her knees uncomfortably. She glanced back at her student. There was tension around Ellen's eyes. Noticing Francesca's attention, Ellen nodded and returned her face to its usual inscrutability.

Something was wrong. Francesca was about to ask Ellen what was going on when the court's majordomo announced the beginning of the Council. Francesca bowed again.

Once the Council was called to order, the Sacred Regent raised one hand. "Counselors, commanders, citizens of Ixos, we have called you here today to swim through currents of history. Today we change the future of our archipelago."

Francesca bunched her hands into fists.

"We will see one age end and another dawn," the Sacred Regent continued. "Our ancestors fled the demons of the Ancient Continent and set down roots on this new land. They sought to build new civilizations capable of withstanding the demon's inevitable invasion. It is the great tragedy of our time that our kingdoms are not united in this."

The fear in Francesca's gut began to lurch again. Nicodemus glanced at her and then back to the dais.

The Sacred Regent continued. "Sadly, because we have let our differences divide us. We have made ourselves the greatest threat to our own survival. We wage war on our brothers and sisters when we should stand together against the general enemy. And we live in an age when that general enemy has come." The regent brought his hand down and pointed at Leandra.

Terror flooded through Francesca. She started to yell while spellwrighting. Beside her Nicodemus had already leapt to his feet. Three men in red cloaks were advancing toward him. Behind them stood a woman whose silhouette burned with a bright orange light. The war goddess Tagrana.

Francesca cried out a warning as the red cloaks grew larger. Orange fur striped with black sprouted from their skin. Their teeth became long fangs.

Francesca started to cast a lacerating wartext against one of Nicodemus's attackers, but blazing golden runes flashed before her eyes. Francesca felt her mind being censored from magic. Her silver sentences fell and shattered on the floor. Something struck her in the back and she fell forward.

"That is why," the Sacred Regent said, "we choose to fight with our brothers and sisters of the empire against the dread goddess Los."

A powerful force wrapped around Francesca's arms and legs. She turned her head to see Leandra, bound from head to foot in sentences of silvery Magnus. Above Leandra, wearing an expression that seemed at once pained and triumphant, stood Ellen.

R ough hands pulled Francesca onto her knees. She twisted but could not see who was holding her. Beside her, Ellen held a long knife to Leandra's throat. Dhrun lay on the ground bound by Magnus spells. She was struggling against the silvery sentences but to no avail.

"Ellen, I am going to—" Francesca growled, but her student flicked her wrist and cast a Magnus gag around her mouth. The edges of the spell were sharp enough to cut into Francesca's cheek.

Ellen looked at her dispassionately. "I am sorry, Magistra."

Francesca strained against her bonds, trying to stand, trying to get at the traitor. She half expected her body to explode into its draconic form, but her struggles won her only a deeper cut on the cheek.

"Don't make things messier," Ancestor Spider creaked in Francesca's ear. "This game is over." Francesca tried to glare up at the Trimuril, but a bright red roar made her turn her head.

Nicodemus stood before the dais. He'd torn off his blouse. Had it been dark enough, he could have pulled off the spells tattooed across his skin to attack. But standing as he was in tropical sunlight, he had no defense other than his ability to misspell. Circling around him were three massive tiger-like constructs. Their amber eyes fixed on him with predatory hunger. Behind them stood the goddess Tagrana, her aura burning brighter.

Nicodemus stepped toward a construct. It danced backward while another darted at his back. Nicodemus turned around just in time to stop its advance. Three more red cloaks appeared behind Tagrana, each of whom leveled a crossbow bolt at Nicodemus. Seeing them, he froze and then glared up at the Sacred Regent.

It was then that Francesca realized the throne room was now lined by ranks of figures dressed in green, black, and red robes. Imperial spellwrights.

The room grew quiet when the Sacred Regent raised his hand. "We have reached an agreement with Empress Vivian, who has accepted our offer of peace. There shall be no imperial rule of the archipelago. She will not cast her metaspells on the archipelago, so there shall be no threat to our divinities."

This produced a cheer from the regent's attendants; however, as it became apparent what was happening, the cheer was quickly echoed by all those assembled.

"In return," the Sacred Regent continued, "we shall give to the empress the dread goddess Los, her draconic mother, and her father, the Storm Petrel. With their capture, so ends the War of Disjunction. Never again shall we fear the demons of our past. Now we stand to greet our new allies and the dawning of a new age."

The Sacred Regent stood and was soon followed by the rest of the court. Rough hands hauled Francesca to her feet.

Reacting to some cue Francesca could not see, the imperial spellwrights turned and bowed. The Empress Vivian, dressed in white robes and ornate ceremonial armor, strode into the throne room. Her long black hair was pulled back, and around her neck she wore a silver chain that held a tear-shaped emerald. Silence enveloped the room as she climbed the dais. Empress and regent bowed to each other.

When they straightened, Vivian turned to the crowd. "It is with great joy that we accept the offer of peace from our brothers and sisters of Ixos. Do not fear us, for our intentions are only of prosperity. Once we have our prisoners aboard, our fleet shall depart, never to return." She bowed again to the regent, who returned the gesture. "And it is with even greater joy that, with your help, we seize victory in the War of Disjunction in the name of humanity and the Creator."

"Lies!" Nicodemus yelled. "You've heard the same prophecies we have. Your victory will sterilize language and doom civilization to stasis and slavery. If you destroy me and my metaspells, you will destroy the Ixonian pantheon. You will destroy wild and creative language."

The empress stared coldly at her half-brother. "And what had you to offer the Ixonian people and their pantheon, Storm Petrel? You were planning to sneak your demon child to the South. You were going to sacrifice Chandralu for the dread goddess Los. You betrayed humanity and the Creator."

"You don't understand what Leandra is."

"Neither do you, Brother. I doubt she knows herself." The empress looked coolly at Leandra and then Ellen. "But, truly, Nicodemus, it is not your fault. Nor can we blame the draconic Lady Francesca. Who could not be blinded by love of their child? But deep down, both of you know. Both of you have your doubts. All the millennia, all the history cannot be dismissed. There is fear in you both about what your daughter might become."

Vivian's voice rang out with an unnatural clarity. For an instant, Francesca saw the involuntary image of Nicodemus falling out of his chair, paralyzed by Leandra. In that tiny shard of time, Francesca admitted to herself that she had been harboring a horrible doubt about her daughter. But in the next heartbeat, she felt also her daughter's great potential and her struggle in an imperfect world.

"I know Leandra could never become half the tyrant you are," Nicodemus snarled at Vivian.

The empress only smiled. "Nicodemus, you are not bound and gagged, because attempting to do so might kill you. And as I am sure you have noticed, your wife and daughter are in our custody. Continuing to resist would endanger them both. Will you be peaceful now, or must we prove who the true Halcyon is?" The empress took the Emerald between her thumb and forefinger.

Nicodemus tensed and Francesca prayed he would keep his mouth shut. The Trimuril's spider voice creaked in her ear, "If we undid your gag, would you talk to him? He'll only get himself killed."

Francesca was about to nod when a subtle movement caught her eye. She thought she saw Ellen and Leandra exchange what seemed, impossibly, a conspiratorial glance.

Then without warning, Leandra burst free of her Magnus bonds. With two quick steps, she reached out and grasped Tagrana's shoulder. The tiger goddess snapped out of existence like a popped soap bubble.

Ellen cast a spray of silvery paragraphs that shot across the room to the tightly rolled silk curtains above each of the throne room's windows. The cords holding each snapped and the curtains fell. The room fell into almost complete darkness.

Francesca's heart raced. Everyone was screaming. There sounded the almost simultaneous twang of three crossbows being loosed.

Francesca's bonds snapped. Icy shock filled her head as her mind was restored to magic. The hands on her back disappeared and there was the sound of a body hitting the floor.

All around her the screaming continued. Francesca struggled to her feet. A sudden bloom of light appeared on the dais. Francesca turned and saw the empress casting a Numinous spell. She was surrounded by wizardly and hierophantic guards, one of whom was Cyrus. They were trying to usher the empress away. Behind her, hydromancers had swarmed around the regent.

Then the empress cast her bright spell. It flew in a smooth arc to where Nicodemus had been standing. At first Francesca could not understand what she was seeing. There was neither tigroid constructs nor the goddess Tagrana. On the ground lay a man. He was stripped to the waist. Three crossbow bolts protruded from him: one from his shoulder, a second from his chest, and a third from his left eye.

When she recognized his olive skin and long black hair, Francesca cried out pure anguish.

CHAPTER FIFTY-SIX

As the dying god lay motionless, Nicodemus realized the deity was maintaining his incarnation as long as possible. But crimson light was already seeping from his crossbow bolt wounds. There wasn't much time left.

As before, when Nicodemus had split from the dying god, he had suffered disorienting amnesia; however, because Nicodemus had been awake and watched the dying god's injury, the shock restored his memory. He had cast a shadowganger spell upon himself and stepped into the crowd on the dais. He had played this game of concealment before.

As he slipped between the imperial spellwrights, Nicodemus prayed to the dying god, hoping it would help the suffering deity survive just a little longer.

Francesca was screaming. Those on the dais who were not hustling the Sacred Regent away or protecting the empress were staring at Francesca, hypnotized by the agony pouring out of her.

Then Nicodemus stepped around a pyromancer and stood not ten feet from his half-sister. In the dying god's red glow, he could see Vivian in perfect detail.

Like him, she still stood an inch over six feet. Like his, her glossy black hair was now filigreed with silver. Age had softened her dark olive features without dimming the intensity of her green eyes. The empress stared at Francesca while holding the Emerald of Arahest.

A soft light grew within the Emerald, and the scar on Nicodemus's back felt hot. He had tried years ago to give the Emerald away, to diminish its power, but the world would not let it be so. Now he would take back the Emerald to subdue his half-sister and save his daughter. He could feel the Emerald's longing for reunion. This had happened before when he had confronted Fellwroth and then Typhon. He had been little more than a child then. This time would be different. The Emerald's absence had defined him, but now he had to redefine himself. Now he would make things right.

As Nicodemus took a step closer, Vivian raised her hand and cast two cylindrical paragraphs of golden prose. Floating in the air above her, the cylinders fit together and began to spin in opposite directions. In the next moment, the spell would blaze with brilliant white light and burn away the dark spells that kept Nicodemus invisible.

He pulled a tattooed paragraph from his thigh and edited it into a blunt wall of force. With a quick backhand he cast the luminous indigo passage at Vivian. He pulled a long spell from his bicep and cast it after the first.

White light was just beginning to glow in Vivian's Numinous spell when the indigo text struck her in the chest, knocked her backward. At the same time, Nicodemus's indigo sentence wrapped around the Emerald. He pulled the spell taut and the Emerald leapt out of Vivian's hand, broke free of its silver chain and flew back toward him.

Everything but the gem melted away for Nicodemus. The instant his skin made contact with the Emerald, he could write spells of infinite complexity. Neither sunlight nor the spellwrights bustling about the dais could stop him. He held his hand out and prepared for the reunion of his mind.

That was why he was filled with such profound shock when a lithe hand appeared not a foot before his own and plucked the Emerald out of his spell.

As Leandra closed her fingers around the Emerald of Arahest, an immense sadness filled her. She had succeeded. There could be no doubt. An hour from now, every one of her future selves felt an array of emotions beyond human comprehension. Knowing this increased the weight of her sadness. Some part of her had been hoping for failure. But now it was too late.

Now that she possessed the Emerald, Leandra became a spellwright in every magical language her father and aunt had studied. Quickly, she deconstructed the subtext that was concealing her father.

He stared at her, lips parted slightly, trying to figure out how it was she was standing in front of him. It must seem impossible to him. In fact, she had simply deconstructed the tiger goddess and her three tigerlike warriors, stolen their strength and wide feline eyes. Those attributes had made following her father and taking the Emerald from his spell as simple as stealing a bauble from a baby.

Someone cast a Magnus wartext at Leandra. It was a coiling of sharp silvery words, vicious enough to mangle a god. Leandra casually broke it into a blunt coruscation. The attacking author stood only a few feet away, staring at her with wide eyes. When Leandra recognized him as Lotannu Akomma, she smiled and cast a quick censoring net around his mind.

Next Leandra cast a few sharp silver words at the curtains behind the throne. Her spells tore through silk. The curtains fell to let a square of sunlight fall on her.

The shocking brightness silenced every mouth, turned every eye toward her. Leandra regarded the hierophants and pyromancers around the empress and the hydromancers protecting the Sacred Regent. For a moment, she thought they would be wise enough to stay an attack. But then a pyromancer reached into a scroll to pull out an incendiary sentence.

Through the Emerald, Leandra wrote a horde of Numinous disspells and sent them flying down through the muscles of her legs. With a stomp, she sent a shockwave of golden prose radiating out from her, dispelling every text in the room. She had written the disspells to avoid her mother, Dhrun, and the Trimuril. But any other deity unlucky or unwise enough to be in the throne room would be textually mangled. Spellwrights fluent in Numinous cried out. Others flinched or grimaced as their spells deconstructed in their hands.

Leandra stood perfectly still in the pool of sunlight.

"By imperial order, attack tha—" Aunt Vivian started to shout, but with a wave of her hand, Leandra cast a sphere of sound-deadening text around the empress.

Lotannu and several other imperial spellwrights stepped toward the text but stopped when Leandra said, quite clearly but without any particularly emphasis. "Don't."

Stillness returned to the room. Leandra looked down from the dais at her mother and Dhrun behind her. "Come up," she said and motioned beside her. The two stared at her for a moment but then Dhrun gestured to Francesca and slowly they climbed the steps up to the dais.

"Father," Leandra said.

Slowly Nicodemus approached.

Leandra smiled at him and then pulled the loveless spell from her mind and destroyed it. No way back now. She could feel her disease flaring hotly. Fatigue washed over her and her gut felt as though someone had kicked her hard. "Lea, your rash . . ." her father whispered.

She had no doubt an angry crimson bloom was spreading across her face.

"It's all right, Dad," she said before turning to the crowd and raising her voice. "You must all listen to me, and you must listen carefully. The world will depend on you for the truth of what is about to happen."

"Lea, what—" her father started to protest.

But she looked at him and he fell silent. Maybe he could see the determination and sadness in her eyes.

When she spoke again, it was with the clarity and detachment that comes with finally saying what one has known but could not articulate for a very long time. "The world we have lived in, despite its poverty, is a decorated one. It is rich with pain. To me, it has long been a prison built by the past and maintained by the powerful. Every one of us here has been a prison guard to this world. We have maintained the divisions between league and empire, spellwrights and illiterates, humans and divinities, wealthy and destitute. We live and play in inequity; it makes our delights grotesque and our miseries sympathetic."

Leandra paused as her mother and Dhrun stood beside her father. She continued. "I speak to you not as someone who did any better with her life. I have known grotesque delight in this world, in its beauty, in the souls who haunt it. I have been a lover and I have been a murderer. When you tell the world of me, do not forget my frailty or my anger or my sadness. Tell the world all of these things and tell them that I was the one who changed the words, that I am the one who made them rewrite both the misery and the delight."

Leandra tried to slow down but the words tumbled out of her. "Soon you will have to hurry away. You will be buffeted by great force. Some of you may die or kill each other." Fearful voices began to rise. "Those who survive, those who return to the city I loved, you will find the world changed."

She raised her voice, made it ring out. "I tell you these things as Leandra Weal, who both hated and loved this world, who was a child tortured by disease and a woman of great privilege. I tell you these things as the Dread Goddess Los, who destroyed the last world and who will destroy this one. The spell we have cast upon this world must be broken."

The throne room erupted into shouts and a confusion of bodies as some ran for the doors and others launched themselves into attacks. Leandra deconstructed every spell cast at her and then flicked walls of text at the attacking authors.

"Go now! Run!" Leandra yelled. "Get to dry land and the city. Tell the world what I have told you. You must rewrite the world." Everyone in the crowd had turned to flee, empress and regent among them.

The pain in Leandra's gut twisted like a parasite.

"Lea, what's going on?" her father asked even as her mother said, "You're out of your God-of-god's damned mind!"

Leandra could not suppress a rueful smile at their characteristic reactions. Then she grimaced.

"This is a trick, right?" Francesca said in a lower tone. "Some way of scaring away the empress?"

Leandra shook her head. "No trick. I have to leave you soon."

"Lea, stop this," Francesca said, clearly afraid.

"I can't, not any longer." Then the pain reached up through her. She gasped, went momentarily blind.

Then somehow she was lying on her back, looking up at her parents and Dhrun. She reached out to the goddess. "Dhru," she whispered, "I'm so sorry we never had a chance, but with the next dragon, you—" Another spasm shut her eyes.

When she opened them, her mother was examining her belly while Dhrun held one of her hands and her father the other.

Leandra smiled at her father. "You're going to hate being grandparents." Then she laughed because probably they wouldn't hate it at all.

"She's delirious," her mother said with medicinal concern.

This made Leandra laugh harder until the blinding pain wrenched through her again. She gasped.

When she could focus again, Leandra felt her father's hand on her cheek. He spoke in a ragged voice. "Lea, it doesn't have to be like this."

She shook her head and pushed herself further into her disease flare. "You need to go, Dad. Get . . ." Another spasm of pain. "Get Mom and Dhrun to shore."

"Lea, not like this," her father pleaded. "Not like this. Don't leave us . . ."

"I . . . Daddy, I have to." It was getting difficult to see. The center of her vision became a patch of blackness.

Then her mother was close. "Lea, stop this right now. I can see the language you're written in. Stop it, Lea. Please, please, stop it."

Then Leandra understood. Of course, her parents weren't stupid. The Emerald was amplifying the effect of her disease flare; already her parents were fluent in her crimson magical language.

Leandra smiled and tried to take her parents' hands, but she could not feel her hands anymore. "The change," she said, "make sure they all know about the change."

"What change?" her father asked somewhere above her.

"You'll see . . ." she said and then gasped again as the pain shoved its way through her chest. She clenched her teeth and tried to breathe. With great difficulty she said, "Make them write it all . . . new."

Her consciousness expanded. She felt her mother's nails digging into her palm. She could hear her onetime lover's heartbeat. She became a two-ton bell far up in the Floating Palace as a priest struck it to warn the Floating City of crisis. She was the sound that came off the bell's shivering metal. She was the sound as it vibrated down through wooden beams to the dark, cool water of the crater lake.

Dimly she became aware of her parents crying above her body. Briefly she was the salt in a tear—whose she couldn't tell, perhaps her own.

But then her consciousness projected downward into the lake. She was a dark and ancient fish flicking its fins through crystalline currents. Her mind expanded into the aqueous spells that the hydromancers had been pouring into the crater lake for a thousand years. Leandra became every last magical rune in that wide body of water. She was the greatest reserve of energy yet created by humanity. In the last act of her life, Leandra used her mortal talent to transform that reserve of power and make it rise up.

The waters of the crater lake began to churn and to shine. Slowly at first but then with gathering violence, the waters flowed around creating a mile-wide whirlpool.

Leandra's parents and her onetime lover emerged from the Floating Palace. Her own limp body lay in her father's arms.

Her parents ran along a pontooned bridge. But the whirlpool was spinning faster now. The pageantry of floating craft was dragged around and around in a chaos of wood and rope. The bridges broke apart. Her parents and her lover fell into the churning blue.

And then, the transformation of the energy complete, the language of the lake erupted as a blazing glory of light.

Leandra had become that eruption, a force of violence and permanent change. She blasted up the volcano's crater and high into the sky. She had become a metaspell more powerful than any yet imagined. The wind caught and blew her in a thousand different directions.

Part of her settled upon the beautiful and disgusting city of Chandralu. Leandra became the fish wives and goddesses and lovers and thieves. Part of her was blown across a bay and then across an archipelago where she became the farmers and children and murderers and healers and ghosts and gods of the archipelago.

Out across the ocean she spread to a kingdom of arid plains and deserts.

And she was every kind of soul spreading herself farther and farther east from tiny homesteads to glorious adobe cities vibrant with the lives of millions.

And down the peninsula she swept, over waving grass, and she became lycanthropes and kobolds and hierophants in their wind gardens. And farther south she spread and wrapped herself around the shell of an ancient city made into a wizardly academy. And, for a moment, she swirled more tightly around this place where once her father had been a crippled boy. In the nearby forests, there were ghosts of an extinct people who stirred in their dark recesses and shuddered when they realized that the change her father had begun had come to fruition.

And then Leandra sped over snowy mountains to a kingdom filled with rain and cathedrals and farmers and smiths and seraphs. And then she passed into a kingdom of ancient forests and druids and hunters and vast orchards and secluded groves.

Having reached the end of the human lands and having touched every soul, the metaspell that Leandra had become was blown north again over the sea and toward the volcano from which she sprang.

And so it was that Leandra's soul dissipated itself across the great circle of the world into a single, precise change.

CHAPTER FIFTY-SEVEN

In death a body acquires a peculiar weight. It wants to go to ground. In defiance of living arms that haul and lift, a corpse flops and lolls. When moving together, the living and the dead make an awkward dance—one that Francesca had seen too many times. That was why, when she saw the way Nicodemus was pulling Leandra onto the rocky lakeshore, she knew that her daughter was dead.

Nicodemus and Leandra were both facing out toward the wreckage that was the Floating City. He had slipped his arms under hers to haul her by the chest. Her head and arms hung limply as he took backward steps up the shore. His sandaled foot slipped on a rock and together they crumpled. His face twisted into an agony that had nothing to do with the rock bruising his back.

Francesca had come out of the water a few hundred feet away. She had been picking her way along the rocky shore, looking with rising panic for her husband and daughter. Now that she saw them, she could not move. Her body seemed a prison, her heart a hollow space. But then Dhrun touched her arm. Out in the whirlpool, the goddess had helped Francesca stay afloat until the force of the water had pushed a boat between them. Later, Dhrun had come out of the water only a few feet away from Leandra.

Now the goddess's warm hand sparked Francesca back into motion. Her physician's reflexes returned. Suddenly she was hurrying over the rocky shore. Often she slipped and had to bend down to put her hands on a rock to steady herself. Ahead, Nicodemus had moved out from under Leandra and was cradling her head in his lap, saying something to her.

It took a small eternity to reach the pair. Deep down, Francesca knew her daughter was dead, but something made her kneel beside her daughter and check for breath or a pulse. There was none. She pushed Nicodemus aside and began to compress her daughter's chest. A little water spilled from Leandra's mouth. Francesca tilted Leandra's head back and blew two breaths into her lungs. Then she went back to chest compressions. Dimly she was aware of Nicodemus and Dhrun beside her.

Time stretched out, every moment an eternity. Francesca gave her daughter two more breaths and then went back to pushing on her chest. It was only when she felt one of her daughter's ribs break that the vitality ebbed out of Francesca like wine from an overturned bottle.

Then she was in Nicodemus's arms and weeping. She wrapped her arms around her husband, pulled him into her with all her strength.

Grief shook Francesca in obliterating paroxysms, again and again until nothing seemed to be left of herself. Then she pulled away from her husband to dry her face and breathe deeply.

Nicodemus closed Leandra's eyes, straightened her wet hair and clothes. In one hand he found a silver chain attached to a shattered emerald. He held the broken pieces in his palm. At first he stared at them with numbed sorrow, but then he frowned.

With the muscles of his forearm, Nicodemus forged an intricate Numinous paragraph and then cast it into the air. It hung and rotated slowly. Francesca recognized the paragraph as a complex governing spell used to coordinate the action of several subspells. It was difficult prose, the kind of thing that Nicodemus's cacography prevented him from writing. Francesca supposed that although the Emerald was shattered, it still conferred great ability.

But then Nicodemus dropped the broken emerald onto Leandra's lap. Impossibly, he reproduced the same Numinous spell.

Francesca blinked. "You shouldn't be able to do that."

"I shouldn't," he agreed and then wrote two Magnus subspells and edited them into the governing Numinous text. The resulting hybrid spell folded itself into a conformation that Francesca did not recognize, but the spell's function was unimportant. "I shouldn't be able to write this."

"No . . ." she agreed. They both looked at Leandra. "She removed your cacography?"

"More than that," a creaking voice said into Francesca's ear; "she's removed everyone's cacography."

Francesca looked up and saw the Trimuril's true incarnation standing a few feet away. Despite enduring the chaos of the whirlpool, the goddess seemed no different: short, androgynous, six arms, shaved head, slight potbelly, infuriating smile.

"Traitor!" Nicodemus snarled while leaping to his feet. He made a lunge for the goddess, but she jumped backward and landed with perfect poise on a bolder seven feet away. Nicodemus, however, slipped on a rock and had to put both hands down before he could stand again.

"That's no way to start a new game," the voice of Ancestor Spider creaked in Francesca's ear, while the Trimuril's incarnation bowed.

"Game?" Nicodemus growled and took two awkward steps toward the goddess. "You betrayed us to the empire."

Ancestor Spider laughed. "Oh, I did not betray you to the empire."

Now it was Francesca's turn to laugh. "You can't expect us to believe you didn't know the Sacred Regent and the empress were talking."

The Trimuril's smile did not waver. "I did not betray you to the empire, I merely thought I was betraying you."

Francesca glared. "You'll forgive us if that doesn't exactly improve our opinion of you."

"I will forgive you then. It's not your good opinion I'm hoping for, but your help in completing your daughter's plans."

Nicodemus stopped. "What in the burning hells do you mean?"

"I thought I was betraying your family to the empire. It was going to be a simple exchange. They get you; we get to survive. Waiting for Lorn or Dral to send a fleet would have been too great a risk. What would be the point of preserving the league if it meant our destruction? So we discussed the possibility of selling you to the empire."

"You could have told us," Francesca growled.

"And what would you have done differently? Perhaps you would have been more patient about trying to smuggle Leandra out of the city, but in the long run that wasn't going to make a difference. You needed to put her ahead of the kingdom. In any case, the Sacred Regent and I thought we were being clever. We thought we were hiding our treachery. It was going to take time. We had no contact with the empress and, far worse, we had no way of knowing if we could subdue Leandra. She was Los Reincarnated, after all, not someone you could simply knock on the back of the head and toss in a sack. That is when Magistra D'Valin came to us."

"Ellen!" Francesca growled before remembering the conspiratorial glance that Leandra and Ellen had shared in the throne room . . . just before Leandra had broken free. "Where is Ellen?"

With one of her hands, the Trimuril pointed up the crater slope. They were almost directly below the tunnel that connected Chandralu to the Floating City. A crowd had gathered on the plaza before the tunnel. "Magistra D'Valin is with the survivors," the Trimuril said through Ancestor

Spider. "You four were the last out of the Floating Palace. Most everyone else had an easier time getting out of the water. Though, tragically, a few drowned."

Francesca frowned at the crowd, which had divided itself into those of the empire and those of Chandralu.

The Trimruil continued to explain, "Magistra D'Valin came to us claiming that she had become Leandra's personal physician and that she could orchestrate a bloodless capture of your entire family. We were skeptical of her allegiance, but then she revealed to us that she had been in contact with every powerful citizen of Chandralu who feared Leandra because she was Los. Ellen claimed that after watching Leandra paralyze Nicodemus, she had realized that the woman was too dangerous. She claimed to have been devoted to you, Francesca, but that your vision had been clouded by love for your daughter. It was Ellen who made contact with the empress and planned your betrayal . . . or so we thought."

"So you thought?" Nicodemus repeated.

The Trimuril nodded. "You must now see that the whole thing was planned by Leandra."

Francesca looked at her daughter's corpse, so small in death, her features frail, her skin pale.

The Trimuril continued. "To change the world as she did, Leandra needed to obtain the Emerald of Arahest while on the Floating City. That is why she fooled us all."

"Change the world?" Francesca asked.

"Ah, yes, Leandra's legacy. It seems that she was correct when she pointed out that in her last life she had ended an epoch on the Ancient Continent and would soon end an epoch in this life. Leandra has made every living human being a spellwright."

"She what?" Nicodemus asked.

"She has changed the nature of magical language so that it made itself part of humanity. Just as every child learns to speak without conscious effort, so now the whole world is learning to spellwright."

"She didn't change my cacography," Nicodemus asked, in wonder, "she changed language?"

The Trimuril nodded. "There will no longer be such a thing as cacography. There will no longer be such a thing as illiteracy. Therefore I would bet that you no longer misspell Language Prime."

Nicodemus's face creased into concentration. Then he dropped into a crouch and began peering among the rocks. His hand darted down and then came up with a small black beetle. The hapless insect crawled along

Nicodemus's hand for an inch without bulging into a grotesque tumor. The beetle snapped open its glossy carapace and, with a buzz of tiny wings, flew away. Nicodemus laughed.

Sudden understanding made Francesca's eyes sting. She didn't think she was making any noise, but when she looked up she found Nicodemus and Dhrun staring at her.

"What is it?" Nicodemus asked.

Francesca wiped away her fresh tears. "Lea found the third way out. We all thought that we had to choose between the empire and the league, but she took us all in a new direction. Now the imperial spellwrights won't exploit illiterates, and there will be no proliferation of neodemons praying upon the powerless in the league." She laughed. "There won't even be an empire or a league." She looked down at her daughter and her vision again blurred with tears. Francesca smiled because she was both happy and in horrible pain.

Ancestor Spider cleared a tiny throat in her ear. "That is the gist of things, yes, but maybe you go a bit far in suggesting there will be no league and no empire. At the moment, there are millions of newly made spellwrights who strongly believe in empire and league . . . which leads us to our present game."

"I am getting sick of your games," Nicodemus said flatly.

The Trimuril's hands clapped in pleasure. "Oh, but this is not my game. This is Leandra's game. You would not be playing for my sake. I trust you will never again do anything for my sake."

"Not unless it involves inflicting excruciating pain upon you," Nicodemus grumbled. "I might do that for your sake."

"Precisely so," Ancestor Spider agreed. "This is Leandra's game. In an instant, she destroyed the systems of our world. Now we have to create new ones before things become . . . messy. And though I hate to disturb your bereavement, the whole archipelago now needs you to play a major role in this game."

"How do you mean?" Nicodemus asked.

"On the other side of that tunnel is a city filled with terrified, wounded, and hungry souls who are even now discovering powers beyond anything they supposed they would ever wield. As spellwrights they will need divinities far less than before. When the people stop praying, there will be many desperate deities in all of the league's kingdoms. More immediately, every soul in Chandralu harbors great animosity toward the empire for destroying their homes and killing their loved ones. That makes things a little precarious for the empress who is presently surrounded by guards up there." The Trimuril gestured to the crowed plaza.

Then the Trimuril turned back to them. "Normally, I would not overly concern myself with the empress's well-being; however, the empire now has millions of newly made spellwrights and their crops are failing. They will be looking to their monarch to provide order and security. Chaos in the empire could be dangerous for Ixos. So, after an intimate discussion with the Empress Vivian, I am committed to getting her quickly out of my kingdom and back into one of her own."

"But why do you need us?" Leandra asked.

"In Chandralu, some are already declaring that the Halcyon Nicodemus, through the Creator's grace, has created a miracle and given them the power of spellwrights. Other rumors speak of the dragon Francesca who has magically spread her protection over the city. And still others are whispering that the Lady Leandra is not the reincarnation of Los, as some ugly rumors have put out, but a prophet of the Creator who has brought a gift to the virtuous people of Chandralu in their time of need."

"You want us to be figureheads?" Nicodemus asked in a tone that implied he would rather spend the rest of his life sucking hot tar.

"In a manner of speaking," the Trimuril replied. "The people need leaders who will prevent further bloodshed. The people would follow your family."

Francesca looked at Nicodemus. The muscles of his jaw flexed and she could tell his rage at the Trimuril was warring with his reason.

"Why not use the regent?" Francesca asked.

"The Sacred Regent is no longer with us. When the Floating City broke apart he fell into the water and was too weak to swim."

Nicodemus made no sound, but Francesca said, "I am sorry to hear that," even though she wasn't, not after his betrayal.

The Trimuril's incarnation nodded as Ancestor Spider said "I hope you'll forgive me, but I could not help but listen in when Leandra was suffering. I believe she would have wanted you to play her game and help the people of Ixos. What were her last words again?"

"'Make them write it all new,'" Nicodemus said gruffly and then looked at Francesca. When she nodded, he glared at the Trimuril. "Very well, we will do what we can, but not without many reassurances from both you and my sister."

The Trimuril bowed deeply. "The whole archipelago will be in your debt, and I will swear on the Creator's name to anything you require. But perhaps we can discuss the specifics at a later time. The city is growing restless as we speak, and our window of time to maintain order may be closing. Might I send our hydromancers and red cloaks down to act as your escorts? The two of you might then climb up to the tunnel and negotiate with the empress."

"Give us a little longer with our daughter," Francesca said curtly.

"Of course," the Trimuril said with another bow and began walking up the crater slope.

Francesca looked down at Leandra. She brushed her daughter's cheek and became aware that Dhrun was standing beside her. The goddess's face was tight with pain. She had loved Leandra as well. Knowing this both increased Francesca's sorrow and her solace.

Nicodemus knelt on Francesca's other side and took her hand. With an exhausted heart, Francesca leaned into him and was grateful when he embraced her. In the circle of his arms, she let the tears come again as she thought of her daughter's imperfect life, of all that she had fought for, of all that she had loved.

Sorrow filled Francesca as she remembered the pain that Leandra had known and inflicted. At the same time, gratitude filled her as she marveled at the change her daughter had wrought.

O nce a life was spent searching for a greatly desired thing. At times it was found, at times lost. Sometimes it was forsaken. Along the way there was blood and love and desire and disgust—which is to say nothing of the monsters or the demons or the long hours of lonely reflection. Those things, they were all difficult to survive. But there were also moments of profound wonder and joy, but not enough of those. Never enough of those.

With age, the soul in question came to a series of important, if perhaps not quite profound, realizations. Chief among them was the understanding that a greatly desired thing found, lost, or forsaken turns out to be less important than the act of searching for it. Another not-quite-profound realization was that while the young might die, the old must. That one was both true and growing truer every year.

So it was with solemnity and gratitude that the soul in question entered the autumn of its life, knowing that too soon its search would end.

I n the first lecture theater built on the Ancient Continent in millennia, Nicodemus gave the day's last lesson. It was a plain but functional room—wide ceiling windows let in late-afternoon winter sunlight, and the terraced seats rose steeply to thirty feet. The theater's sheer geometry ensured that even the tardiest students could sit close enough to peer down upon the demonstration of the varied aspects of spellwrighting.

At first, Nicodemus disliked the theater; it felt like he was lecturing in a pit. But this particular class had an infectious enthusiasm. The subject was subtextualization and the gleaning of subtext. Nicodemus wrote out five light-bending paragraphs, each in a different language, then demonstrated what diction and sentence structure would hide the prose.

The class was appropriately impressed as each of the paragraphs vanished. Nicodemus briefly described how they might visualize even subtextualized prose, but the students were too eager to attempt their own subtextualizations to listen carefully.

So he instructed the students to write their own passages and hide them from each other. Afterward they were to transcribe the successful subtexts onto paper. He would not let a single student go until everyone had turned in a subtext.

The students started spellwrighting and Nicodemus set to massaging his sore hip. There was more silver than black now in his hair. Many years had passed since his daughter had changed the world. Now in his eighties, Nicodemus was by no means old for a spellwright, but the cares of age were beginning to weigh upon him.

He and Francesca had served the decaying league and empire for more than a decade. They had striven for the world Leandra would have wanted. The old orders had crumbled and new ones had arisen. The years had produced tumults: revolutions, riots, wars, and plagues. Many of the old problems had reincarnated themselves in different manifestations. But even so, the six human kingdoms had reinvented themselves with far less bloodshed than one might have expected.

Nicodemus doubted that either Francesca or he could claim credit for much, or perhaps any, of the resultant success. Others were more than willing to attribute it to them, which led many to believe that they—along with Vivian—had gathered too much power. So several years ago, the political maneuvering and intrigue to remove them began.

Vivian had kept something like her empire together; Spires had quickly fractionated into two kingdoms, only one of which chose to remain loyal to her. Still, Vivian, with Lotannu and Cyrus at her side, had fought with all her wit and cunning to stay in the currents of politics.

For their part, Nicodemus and Francesca had been more than happy to relinquish power. In fact, after much discussion, they had decided to exile themselves. A society dedicated to returning to and resettling the Ancient Continent had formed in Chandralu. Francesca and Nicodemus had happily joined—she with the intention of founding the first infirmary on the new old land, he with a similar intention for an academy.

Nicodemus's thoughts returned to the present as the lecture hall echoed with the scattered laughs and triumphant cries of students. One by one, their brightly worded paragraphs were winking out of sight. Nicodemus walked around the theater, lending assistance to those who struggled so that the class might stay together. As he finished, the sounds of triumph turned to murmurs of worry or frustration. Having subtextualized their paragraphs, the students could not find them.

"But why all the consternation, my adolescent acolytes?" Nicodemus asked with great relish. "Worried that you won't be able to turn in your assignments? If you've lost your subtext, all you need do is recall my description of how to glean such texts. Or . . . were you perhaps not paying the closest attention?"

This won him a chorus of good-natured boos and accusations that he had set them up . . . which of course he had.

So, enjoying himself entirely too much, Nicodemus repeated his lecture on gleaning, now with the class's dedicated attention. Most of the students retrieved and inscribed their subtext by the time he had finished. With a little personal attention, the remaining students did likewise. Soon the class had lined up and, on their way out, handed their spellbooks to him.

After locking up the lecture hall, Nicodemus walked outside and looked out on the city of Leanda, named for the woman who had created the new age.

A cold wind was blowing, but Nicodemus paused at the top of the academy's stairs to take in his new and last home. It was still a small place, more of a frontier colony than a proper city. There were maybe seven hundred buildings, most made of wood. The only stone structures were the pyromantic cannon turrets by the river, a new infirmary, and a hall of government.

Leanda was built in a wide and verdant river valley. To the south rose hills covered with cypress forests. Inland, the trees stood tall and straight with great strata of pine boughs. Beneath them grew ferns and laurels in an understory that reminded Nicodemus of the Spirish redwood forests. On the coast, the cypress grew short and thick, contorting themselves into strangely evocative wind-sculpted shapes.

The coast itself consisted of rocky cliffs that stretched for thousands of miles. Just offshore of the Leana River, down through the cold waters, fishermen caught glimpses of ancient and toppled towers covered with kelp.

North of Leanda, the land stretched out into a sunny savanna that once had been and would soon again be rich farmland. Beyond the savanna towered massive gray mountains, their peaks snowy even in the dry season.

And beyond these mountains . . . who could say what would be found? There was an entire continent to rediscover.

Nicodemus came out of his reverie when he realized that Dhrun and his grandson had sat down at the bottom of the academy's stars.

When deconstructing the draconic aspects of Francesca's text, Leandra had protected the draconic text within Dhrun. Through a process that Nicodemus did not understand and preferred not to contemplate, the result of hiding the draconic text within Dhrun was a pregnancy that had locked the divinity complex into her Nika manifestation for years.

Dhrun remembered a brief conversation in which Leandra hinted at the reason for her inability to change manifestations. Leandra had claimed she needed more time to see how Dhrun's texts would react. But that time had not yet come when Leandra sacrificed herself.

Years after Leandra's death, Dhrun had given birth to her son. Though he appeared to be a normal male infant, Francesca declared that he would be the next dragon, and the only dragon left in the world.

Nicodemus had wanted to name the boy Agwu after his old teacher. Francesca had liked the idea, but Dhrun wanted her son to have a connection to Ixos and so named him Tarakam, which came from the ancient Lotus Culture word for star. Since turning eleven, the boy had decided he could only be called Kam.

The boy had inherited the bold features of Dhrun's male incarnation, Leandra's glossy black hair, and his grandfather's green eyes. His grandmother's inheritance, however, had not yet surfaced. As each day went by, Nicodemus had a sinking certainty that the emergence of Kam's draconic nature would coincide with his adolescence. So it went.

Presently, Dhrun was sitting in his male incarnation and tearing off pieces of the rosemary flatbread that was becoming the city's signature dish. It seemed that father and son would eat alternate strips of bread. As Nicodemus approached, he felt the particular kind of silence that follows a family argument.

"Got any spare flatbread?" Nicodemus asked.

"Grampa!" Kam said while leaping up to hug his hip.

Dhrun sighed in a way that made Nicodemus suspect that Kam's sudden display of affection was directed more at his parent than his grandparent. "Hey there," Nicodemus said while patting his grandson's head. "Rough day?" he asked of Dhrun while accepting a strip of flatbread.

"Bit of a disagreement about how much time our little hero should spend at lessons and chores versus wrestling and playing with his friends."

"Ah, the injustices of childhood," Nicodemus said with a sigh and they set off down the road.

It was a late-winter day, clear and crisp. The sun was low in the west and a chill was coming on.

Their family compound was a tiny thing compared to what they had left in Chandralu. Its architecture was that of the new frontier style—no pavilions, many small rooms, everything unpainted wood and bold arches. Nicodemus found John sleeping by the fire.

The old spellwright had come with them across the ocean. What hair he had left was snowy white. Over the past year, John's vision had dimmed and his memory loosened. Nicodemus was beginning to fear that he would have to say goodbye to his old friend far sooner than he wished.

John woke when Nicodemus entered the study and announced that a ship from Chandralu had docked that morning. A messenger had brought a package to the compound. Nicodemus opened it to find a stack of letters from Doria.

He sat down by the fire and went through them, reading the important passages aloud for John and Dhrun. Age might have slowed Doria down, but it hadn't blunted her wit, as evidenced by her satirization of Chandralu's politicians. Next Doria complained that the rebuilt city was too large and sprawling and that the sudden proliferation of spellwrights was creating more snobbery among the old guard of hydromancers than there ever had been before.

In other news, Doria reported that Lolo and Holokai's reincarnation had fused into a new divinity complex. This was not surprising. The rise of magical literacy had reduced the amount of prayer and forced many deities to devise creative ways of garnering and conserving divine language.

More distressingly, Doria reported that throughout all the human lands, the birthrate was falling. This had been an unexpected consequence of Leandra's world change. Spellwrights had been unable to conceive children together before the change and very few could manage it now. There was talk that with the rising expertise in Language Prime—by far the most difficult magical language for any spellwright—it might be necessary for humanity to start writing, rather than conceiving, their progeny. Nicodemus could not speculate as to if that was even possible, but he had no doubt that whatever the future held, it would be interesting.

When Francesca returned, Nicodemus stopped reading. Everyone in the compound could tell by her expression that it had not been a good day in the infirmary. Nicodemus put the letters away and drank tea with his wife while waiting for dinner. One of her patients had died unexpectedly and no one was sure why.

Francesca was filled with doubts as to whether she had done the right thing for her patient, while at the same time being filled with certainty that the other physicians and some of the nurses had done the wrong thing for her patient. Nicodemus had long ago realized that these two feelings were almost universally present in any practicing physician. Fortunately, the tea soothed Francesca and they went in to a dinner of salmon, potatoes, kale.

Since losing her draconic text, Francesca had begun to age. She had strands of gray among her long brown hair and laugh lines around her eyes. In response to the stressful day in the hospital, she drank one more than her usual glass of wine. At first it made her moodier, but then she began to laugh longer and louder at the family jokes. To Nicodemus, she was as beautiful as she had been when they both had been young and foolish and fighting for their lives in Avel.

That night, under heavy sheets to keep away the winter chill, Nicodemus and Francesca gently made love. It didn't happen as much as it used to, but it was still one of the few things in life that never disappointed.

Later, when their room was filled with three moonlight, Nicodemus woke from a nightmare about their daughter. He had been in the crater lake again, swimming with Leandra's lifeless body toward the shore. But instead of hauling her onto the rocks, paralysis washed through him and he drowned beside his daughter.

The bed now felt oppressively hot. He peeled off the topmost blanket and after wrapping it around his shoulders padded out onto the tiny wooden balcony. Their compound stood atop a hill north of the city's center, and from this vantage point Nicodemus looked out on the few late-burning lamps and a wide river made glassy bright by three moons. Beyond, the hills and their dark forests were slowly being covered by fog. The air was bracingly cold and smelled of the cypress trees and the sea.

Nicodemus hugged his blanket tighter and thought of distant Starhaven. The dark spires would be under a sheet of snow now. He thought of himself as a boy, of Magister Shannon. That gave him pause, made him blow out a long breath that turned to feathery vapor in the cold moonlight. Magister Shannon, the old man had been the only father Nicodemus had ever truly known. He thought of Shannon's Numinous ghost, wondered what it was doing in the necropolis below Starfall Keep.

It was, Nicodemus realized, time for him to think about ghostwriting. Maybe he didn't need to start creating his textual replacement just yet, but he should research the subject.

A gust of wind sent Nicodemus's long hair flying. As he gathered it in, he thought about the city of Avel surrounded by wind-tossed savanna. He thought about his daughter sailing in a catamaran over bright blue waters.

More than anyone else he had ever known in his life, Leandra had exhibited the limitless potentials—grand and grotesque—of a soul. He thought of those she had murdered and those she had saved. She had been gone from his life for so long and would be gone much longer. He thought then, a foolish and idle fancy, that he could hear the particular silence she made in death. He supposed the world would ring with that silence until she returned, if she ever did.

This heartache he struggled with was an old one. After twelve years of battling it, he still was not immune to the hollowness the heartache produced; however, he could put it aside more quickly, which is what he did while looking north at the white-capped mountains.

Looking at the distant peaks, Nicodemus shook off his solemnity. He had come to the comfortable and final stage in life. He would become the hoary-headed professor and watch his family intertwine its fate with the young city around them. And although Nicodemus's place would evermore be in the academy, he could look out at the rediscovered continent that rolled away before him and know there would be relics to discover, landscapes to explore, love and blood and desire and disgust. All that. Same as there had been. Same as there always would be. The difference was that it was no longer he who would venture out to find it.

Adventure would be for others now; Tarakam likely, when he was old enough.

"Nico?" Francesca said sleepily.

He turned and saw her coming onto the balcony, naked and so pale she seemed to glow in the moonlight. He opened up his blanket and she came to him. He still found it pleasing to see how her fair shape fit into his dark one. He wrapped the blanket around them both.

She pressed her face against his chest and mumbled, "Feet are cold."

"But all the moons are out tonight."

"They'll still be out if we're in bed." She mashed her face into his chest again. "Another nightmare about Lea?"

"Just a brief one."

"You okay now?"

"Okay now."

"Back to bed?"

"All right," he said and took a last look at the distant mountains. Then

There are two stories in every novel—one between the first and final words, another only hinted at in the acknowledgments. This other, obscured story features a cast of unsung and magnificent people who helped the author create and refine. *Spellbreaker* is no different.

I plotted this book as a medical student and drafted it in the calm months between graduation and intern year. During this time, my father, Dr. Randolph Charlton, was *Spellbreaker*'s first reader and supporter. Dad did everything from editing early drafts to housing me when my financial aid ran out. Of course, his influence on my writing started long before then. Ten years ago, when I moved in with Dad to help him cope with chemotherapy, he taught me many hard lessons about the themes of disease, cancer, and healing—which feature throughout this trilogy. I'm fortunate to be able to dedicate this book to him. I've also been blessed that my mother and sister, Louise and Genevieve, have been so supportive of my writing.

This book had many editorial guardian angels. Foremost among them is Miriam Weinberg, at Tor, who helped me polish the prose, condense the plot, and deepen character development. Nina Lourie at Macmillan provided wise advice and support when the trilogy was orphaned. Patrick Nielsen Hayden at Tor adopted the series at a time of great need. Natasha Bardon of Harper Voyager UK greatly improved several early drafts and helped me enrich each of the characters. My literary agent, Matt Bialer, provided advice and support throughout all the twists and turns.

Beta readers are the best thing that can happen to a writer, and I had some of the best happen to me. Megan Messinger took an early, messy draft and told me exactly how to fix the plot holes. Ross Eaton saved me from embarrassment by finding a wide array of errors and inconsistencies; he also provided incredibly helpful tips about how to improve several scenes. Dr. Nina Nuangchamnong provided expert critiques for those scenes involving obstetrics and advice about how to respectfully world-build those aspects of Ixos inspired by Southeast Asia. Dr. Sanjay Reddy—a master clinician and, to my surprise, a big epic fantasy fan—was one week my attending physician on general medicine wards, the next my line editor and advisor about South Asia–inspired Ixos. Kevin Moffitt critiqued this book with a keen eye and used his expertise as a professor of hydrogeology to help me dream up the hydromancers and the city of Chandralu. John Kwiatkowski, of the amazing bookstore Murder by the Book, found several key inconsistencies and provided expert critiques.

Finally and most importantly, the Spellwright Trilogy has enjoyed the support of the many enthusiastic and patient readers—many of whom have been gracious enough to befriend me via social media or my blog. Many times I've been humbled and inspired by the accounts of how readers or their loved ones have adapted to, struggled with, or triumphed because of unique personal differences or disabilities. To my readers, I am grateful that you have followed me during the journey of these past three books and hope that you will join me again for the next.